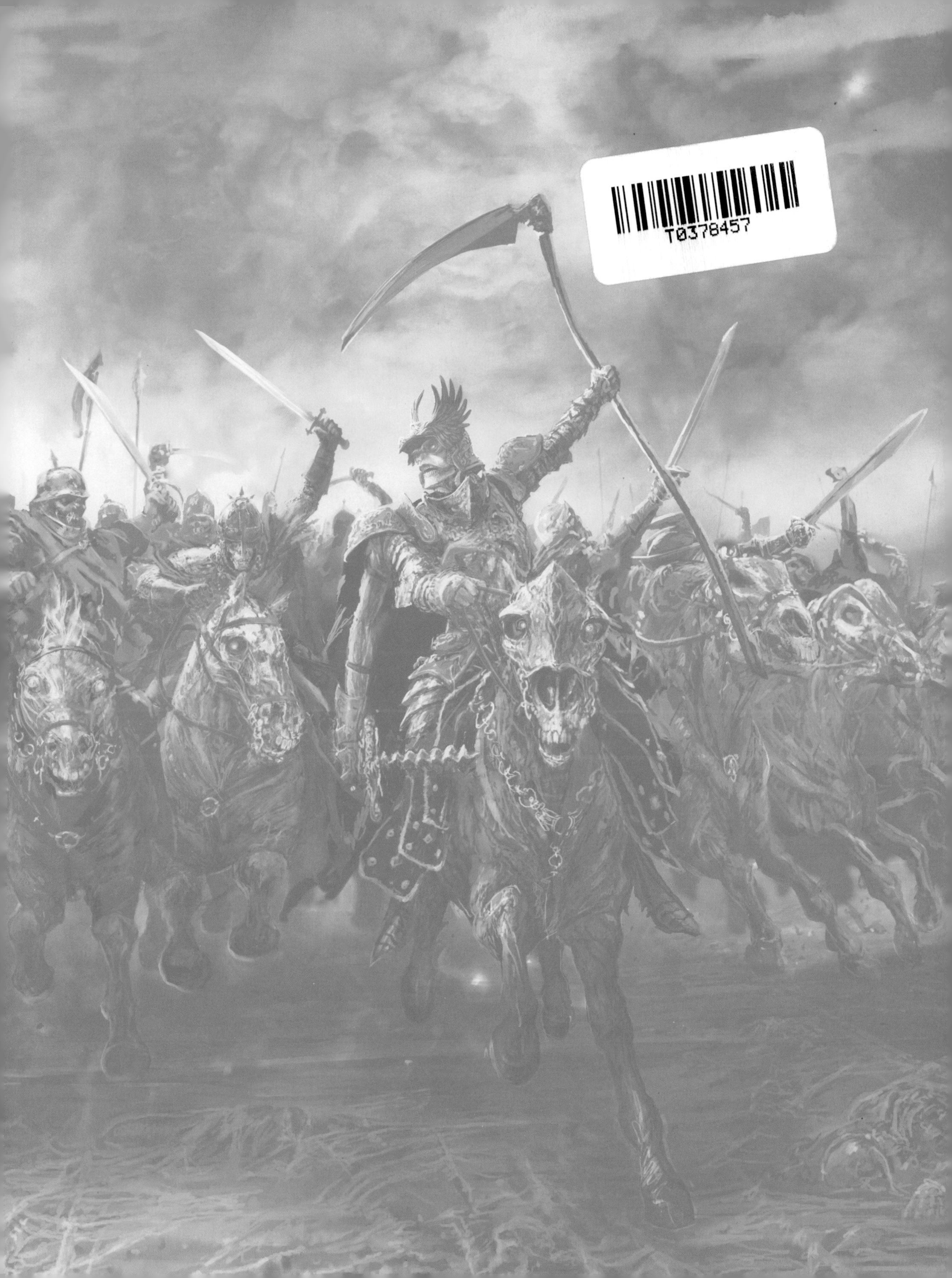

COURT OF THE DEAD
RISE OF THE
REAPER GENERAL

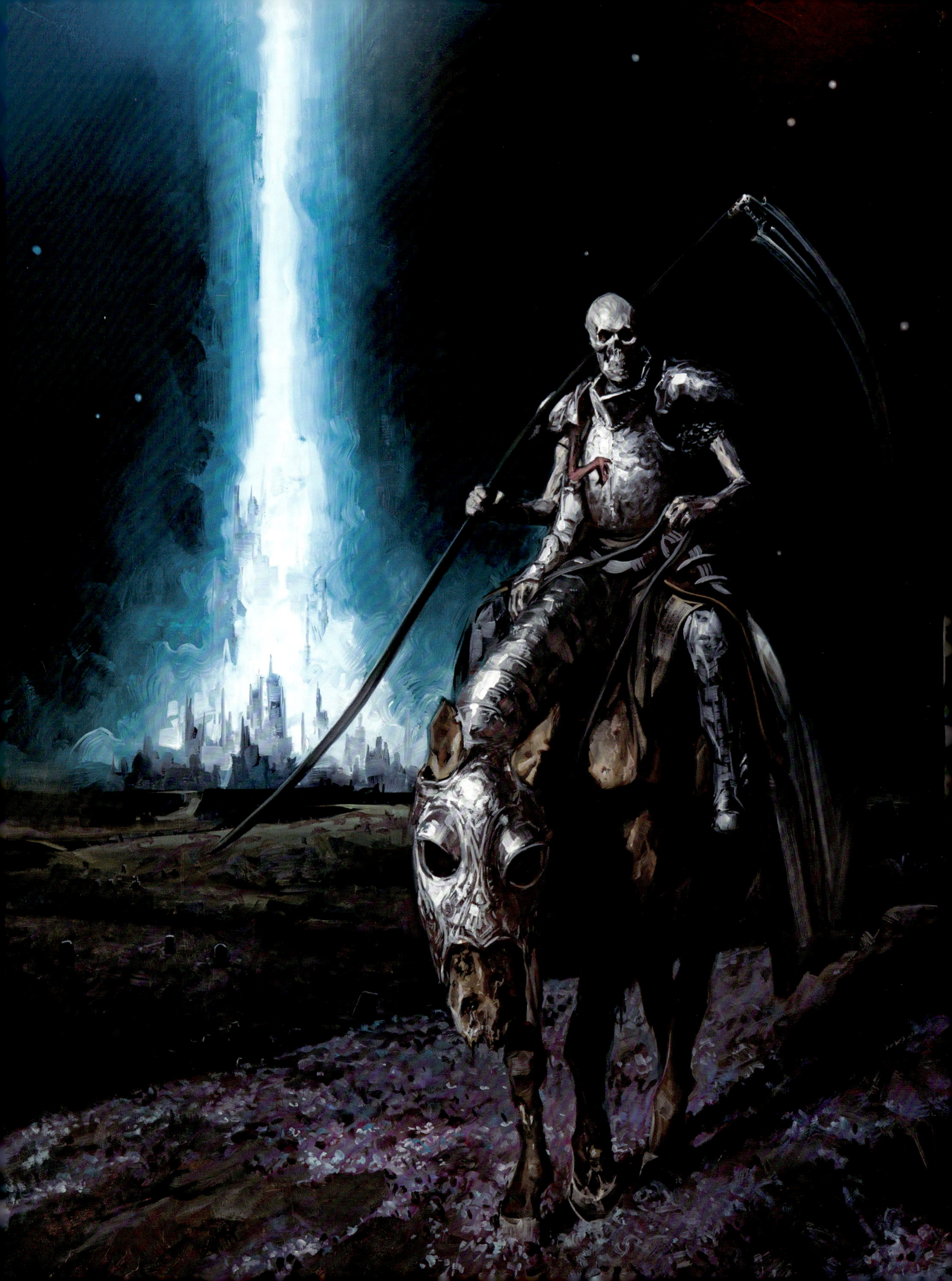

COURT OF THE DEAD
RISE OF THE
REAPER GENERAL

CREATED BY **TOM GILLILAND**
WRITTEN BY **BEATRICE VAN SLEE**

SAN RAFAEL · LOS ANGELES · LONDON

This novel is dedicated to the memory of my father,
Robert Noel Gilliland.
July 2nd 1926 – January 17th 2020

TG

For my mortalkind sistren and brethren and nethren.

BvS

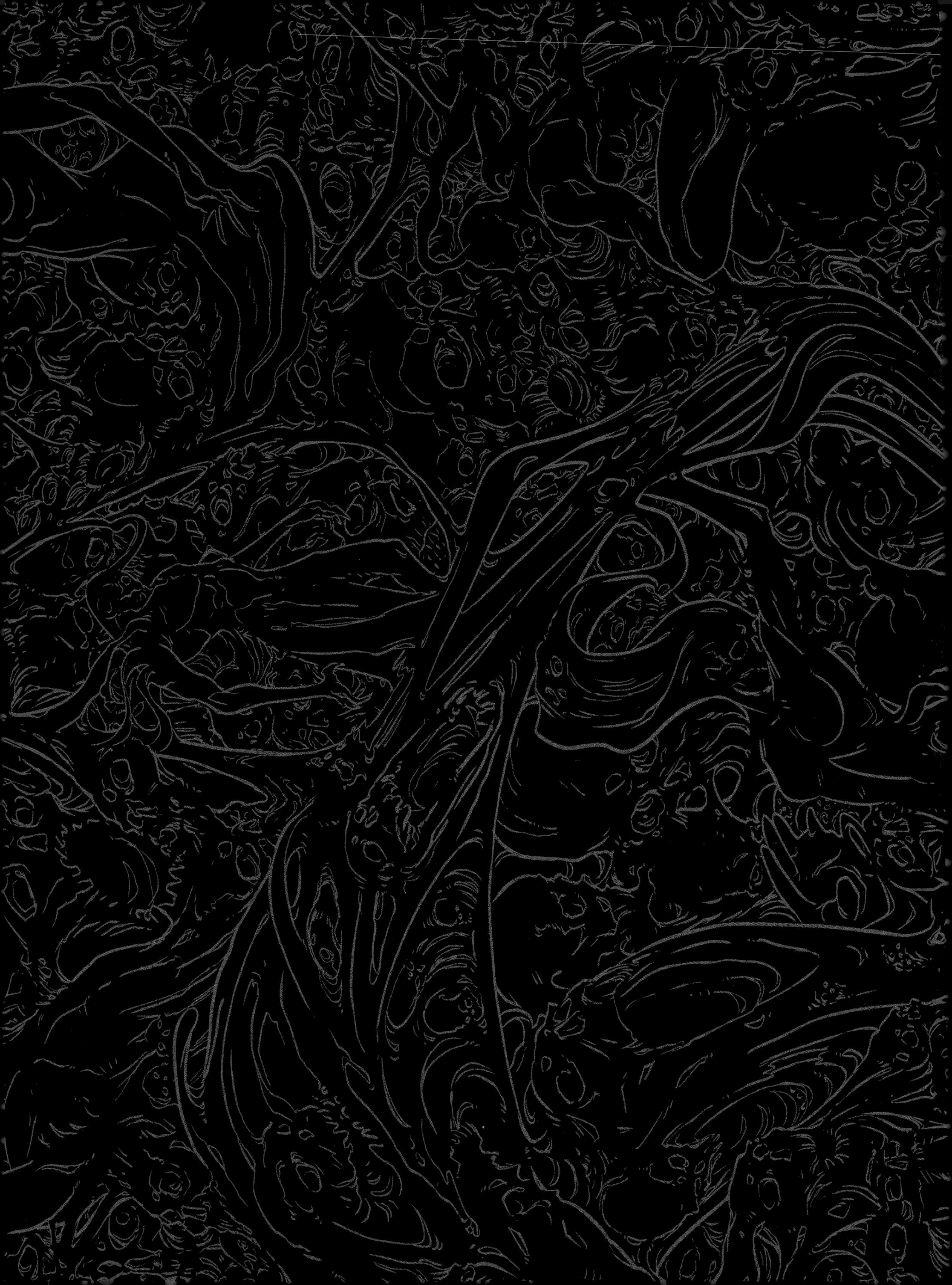

Linger at the crossway of memory and consequence, for there is embellished your soul.

—Death

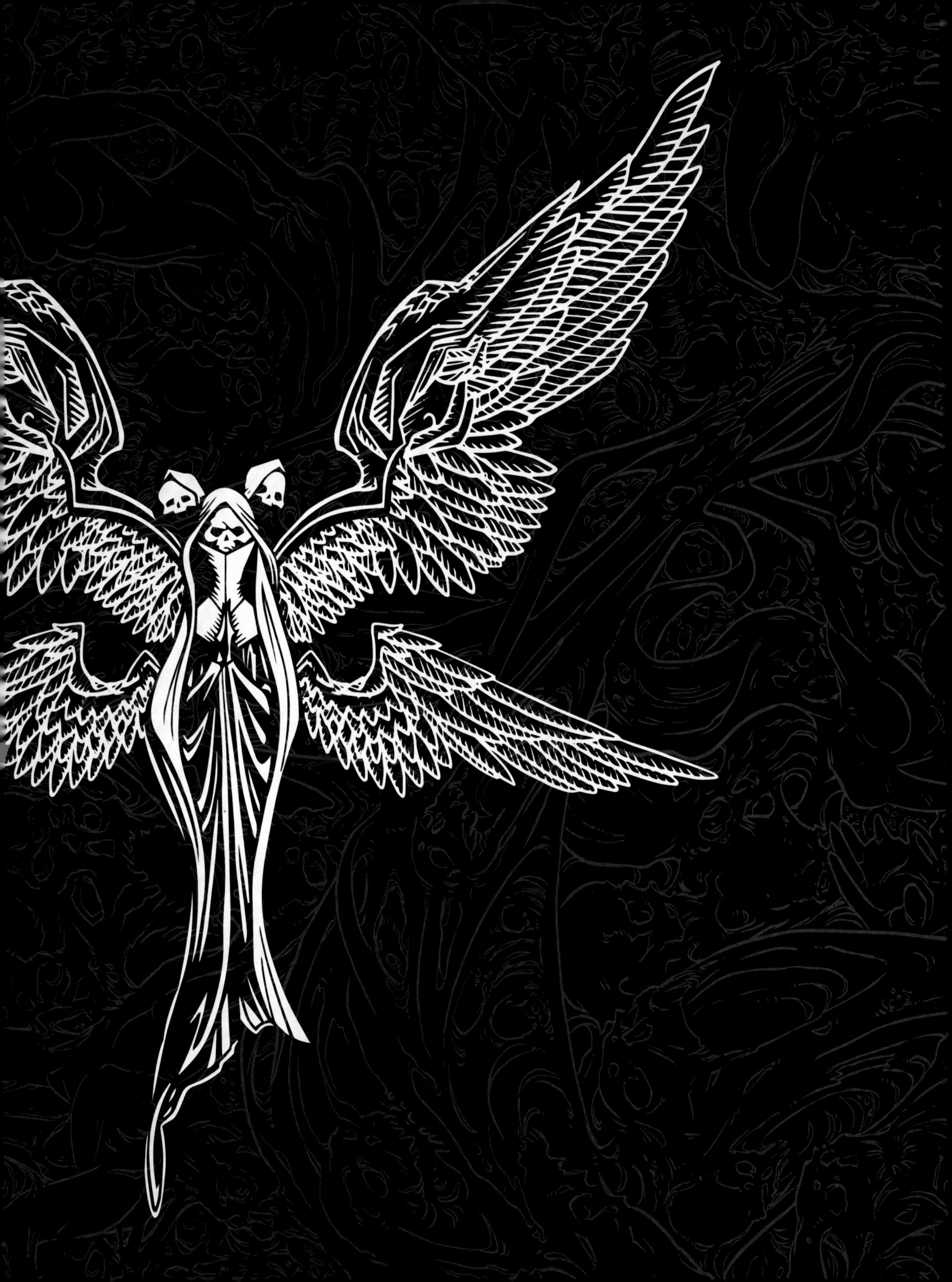

PROLOGUE

a way hidden, found
he enters
his spirit shrouded
his shadow all
for he is Death

so long has it been
this wasteland they have made
all gray and floating ash
the sky itself a pall of mourning
such fury
such bitterness
cast upon the lands of their confinement

yet perhaps
perhaps they are starved of home
their gloom a beacon
a sunken nest

My children, O my children

dormant now
restful by their light above them
bent away from pristine blue
polluted
a violet stain

I shall cleanse it

'Tis all that I wish
deeper, deeper
their spiral chasm
passing forms in stillness, in shadow
so tortured in their exile
so diminished
a hand extended
aching, yearning
to touch tormented features
the pit, the gloom
its depths
his flesh exposed
an overture of conciliation
his spirit unveiled

I am come
Are you ready, my children?
We have learned so much
My first, I name you still
Name me
Name me, my first
Name me
'Tis time to return to the fold
'Tis time to come home

a stirring
throughout the violet gloom
hisses
beneath the silence
their lights descend
all is black
in the darkness, an intake of breath

betrayer

their eyes
their cruel, tainted eyes
still so full of hatred
a pit of hatred

O, how I have failed thee
buried
beneath their slash of claw
beneath their tear of fang
beneath their lacerating screams of wrath
his flesh taken, consumed
his bones wrenched
yet his spirit
this he must keep
alas
he tears free his remains
through their vicious throng
out from their pit of hatred
a burst of broken children in his wake
he lays destruction
among them blooms of fire
of blade
they shriek but do not yield
their blood like burning oil
they follow

betrayer

swaths of ruin
the powers pouring through him
the return of anger
for these who dared defile
crushing
beating
sublime visitations of pain
the sky a thousand novae
an old being rekindled
of destruction
of undoing
made to unmake
all to be unmade
all to be taken
he, destroyer
from whose essence these lost were created

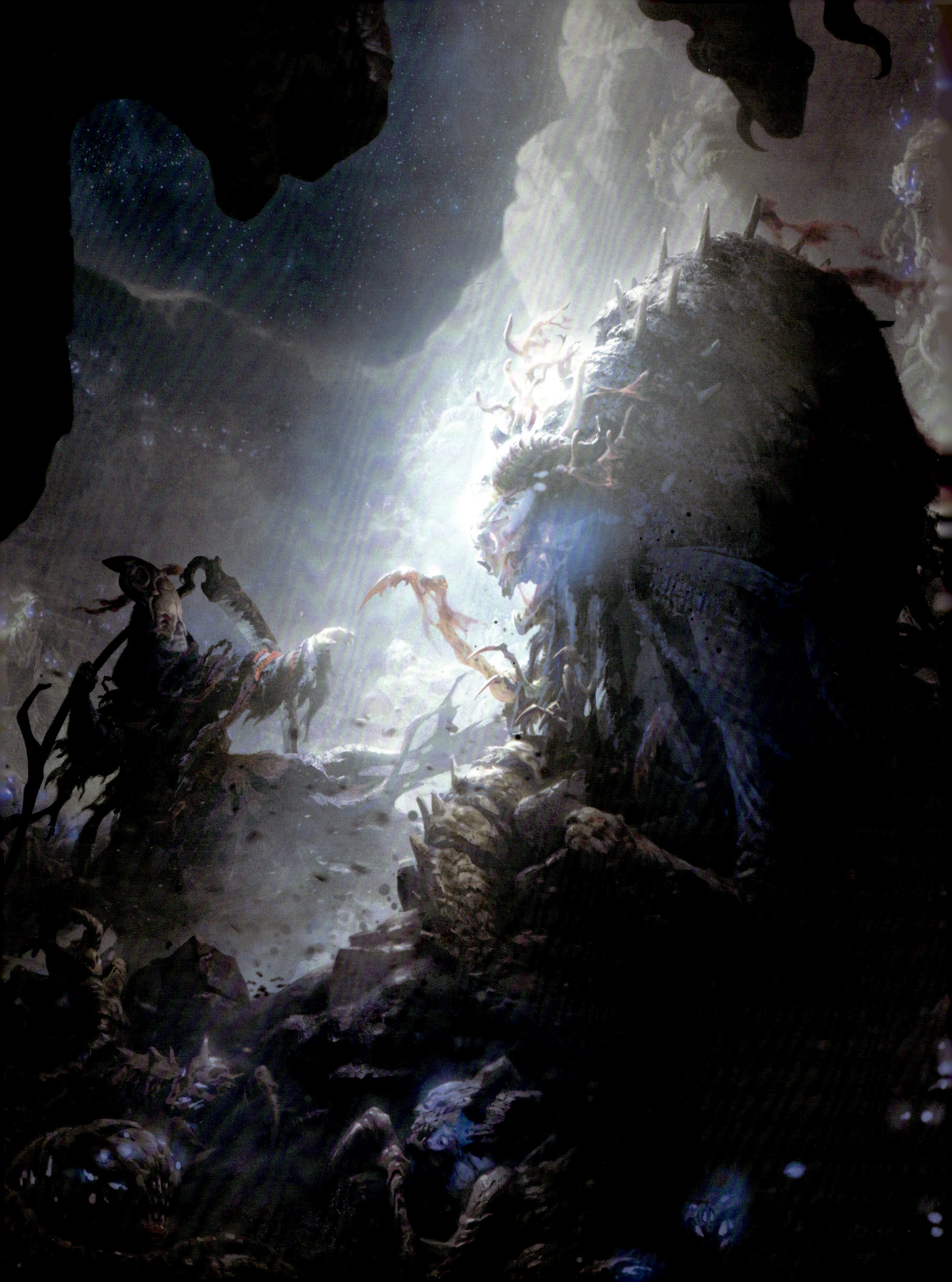

No.
No.
I am become creator.

betrayer
destroyer
betrayer

No.
I shall not unmake you.
This burden shall fall upon another.

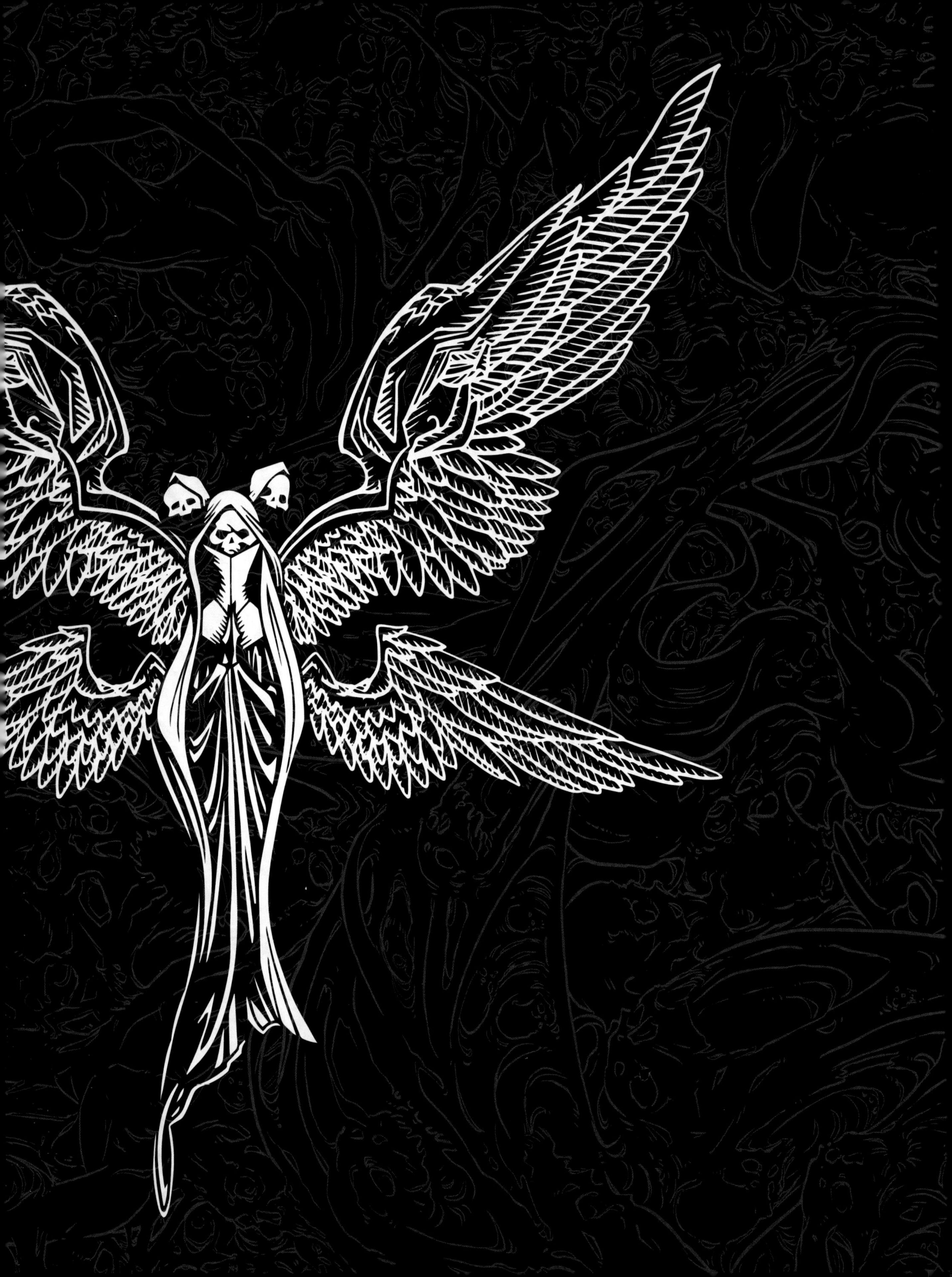

I.
AWAKE

All is the work, the art. The very air. The bluegreen lampfire. Arcaded walls encrowned by lurid friezes. Hoary figures underlit, shifting, shifting to the music of the clacking spiritlooms. Its rhythm our heartbeat. For we the shroud-eveir, the only mark of time in this the slowly, slowly drifting Underworld.

These creatures to shape. Bones aligned, engraved with charms as not to break, shiver, or sliver. The power of limb and spine. Tooth and claw and naked skull, carved to impenitent ferocity. Ask for breath of the Secondborn.

The glint and whisper of the thread. Slivers of the guardian, who came before. And draughts of dream by way of soul. So to think to be. To be and think, eyes to spark in feasts of spirits' essence. We who are shroud-eveir do not understand why this. The body of the child, ourn. Their minds, another matter. Ask for breath of the Thirdborn.

Last the stitch. Sinew strung, deep. Skinmount grown, thrice boiled, beaten pliant. All taut and measured and thrice refined. The reed and stitch; the warp and weft; pick, end, the battening of fleshes. All fine. Beautiful things for the here and now. Likely to please the Alltaker. Ask for breath of the Firstborn.

Awake.
Awake.
Awake.

***

α. Hh

α hhhhm.

hhhhwaft. eh
        mult. Hmeltig

〜〜〜

    . . . *rrrrggo . . . ssssmmmm.*

ah. hh heiiii.

I.

I . . .

    am.

I am.

* * *

The black and the deep. It is the first thing I understand. How it is formless and also full. How from it many things are born. It is mine. It is familiar and comfortable and I do not want to leave it, but I know I must.

* * *

I know that I am new and that I do not have a name. I know that time has elapsed for I remember each precursor of thought. And so it must be that memory is the currency of awareness. Thus am I to be enriched by what moments will unfold within my continuity of being.

* * *

Somewhere in my self there sleeps a greater garden of knowing. Of memories. I can not wake them. I know only that they belonged once to many others and so are not mine. Yet a gift given is to be kept and so in fact they are mine.

*　*　*

The first thing that I feel is a long wind over my self. Then from the black and deep arises a vision of a being who regards me through an eyeless miter of bone. His thin, gray lips are bent in a patient smile, and I know him to be my father. He is Death. He is life? His image wavers before me in the darkness as if cast over the rising smoke of a fire. And so my father is the first thing that I see.

*　*　*

Contained within his masked visage are what would seem to be many contradictions. Order and impulse. Ambition opposed by guilt. Terrible benevolence. These things I recognize for I feel them somewhere present also in my self. So it seems there is drawn a continuity from my antecedent and that pleases me.

From this vision of him before me there emanates as well a curious harmony. Pride and worry? Not worry. Belief, paired with anticipation? I wonder if this is a way in which love might be described. And since something of my father resides within me it would seem love is a selfish thing and so a thing I am not intended to possess. For of my purpose I know foremost that it must be to strive beyond my self.

*　*　*

With another breath of wind comes an image of a figure of infinite sympathy to replace that of my father. Her face is youthful and delicate, her eyes awash with a naked affection. Yet contained within them also is an aged ferocity and eminence, and so do I understand I am now beheld by the gaze of my mother.

She smiles, and her lips part in her conveying upon me of a gentle and wordless melody. Its imperishable loveliness envelopes me with welcoming ovation, and the promise of sanctuary into which I shall always be received. And so the voice of my mother's song is the first thing that I hear.

*　*　*

The vision of my mother fades as further specters of my parentage arise and fade again into my black and deep. They arrive each a presence unique and

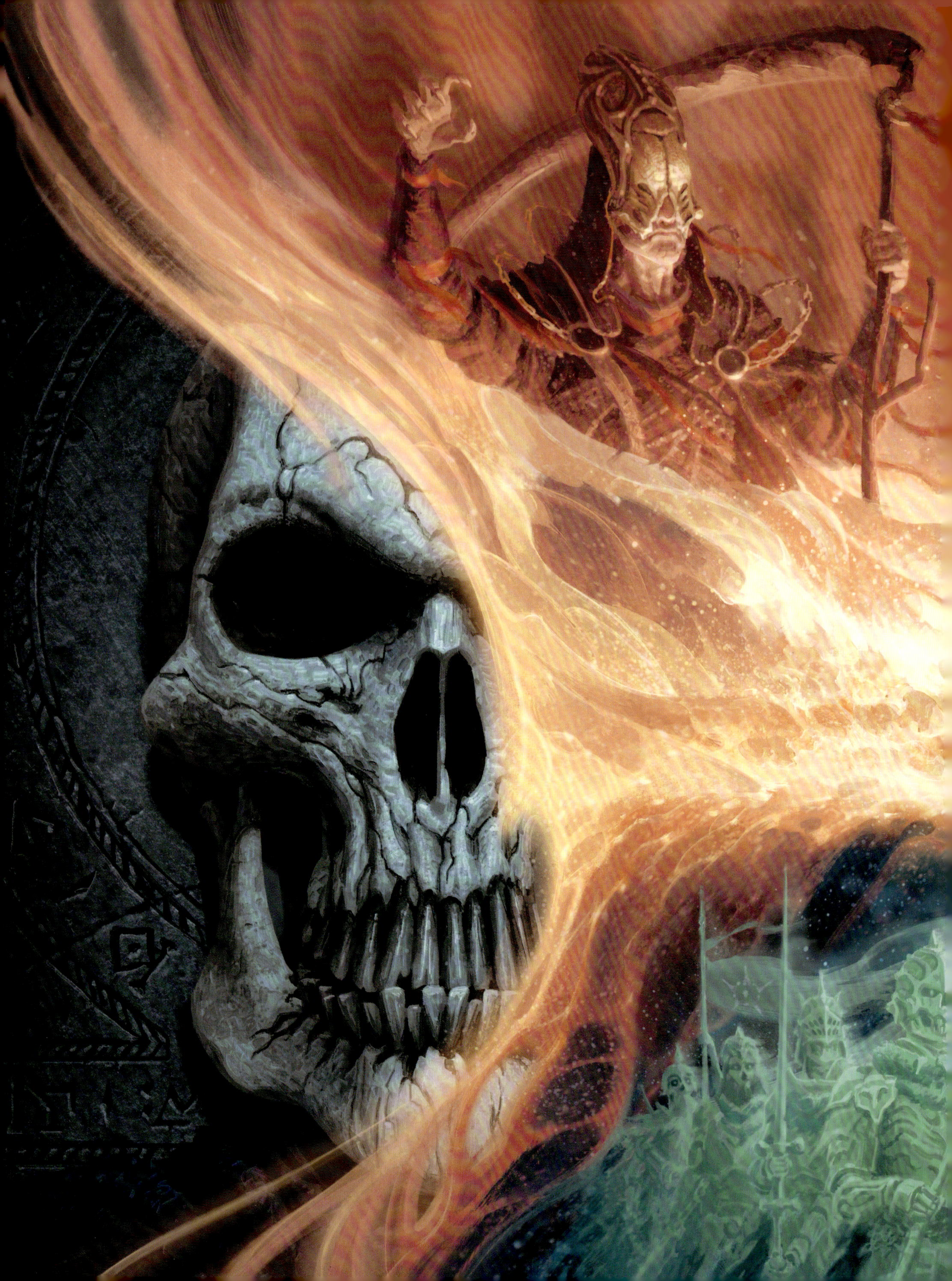

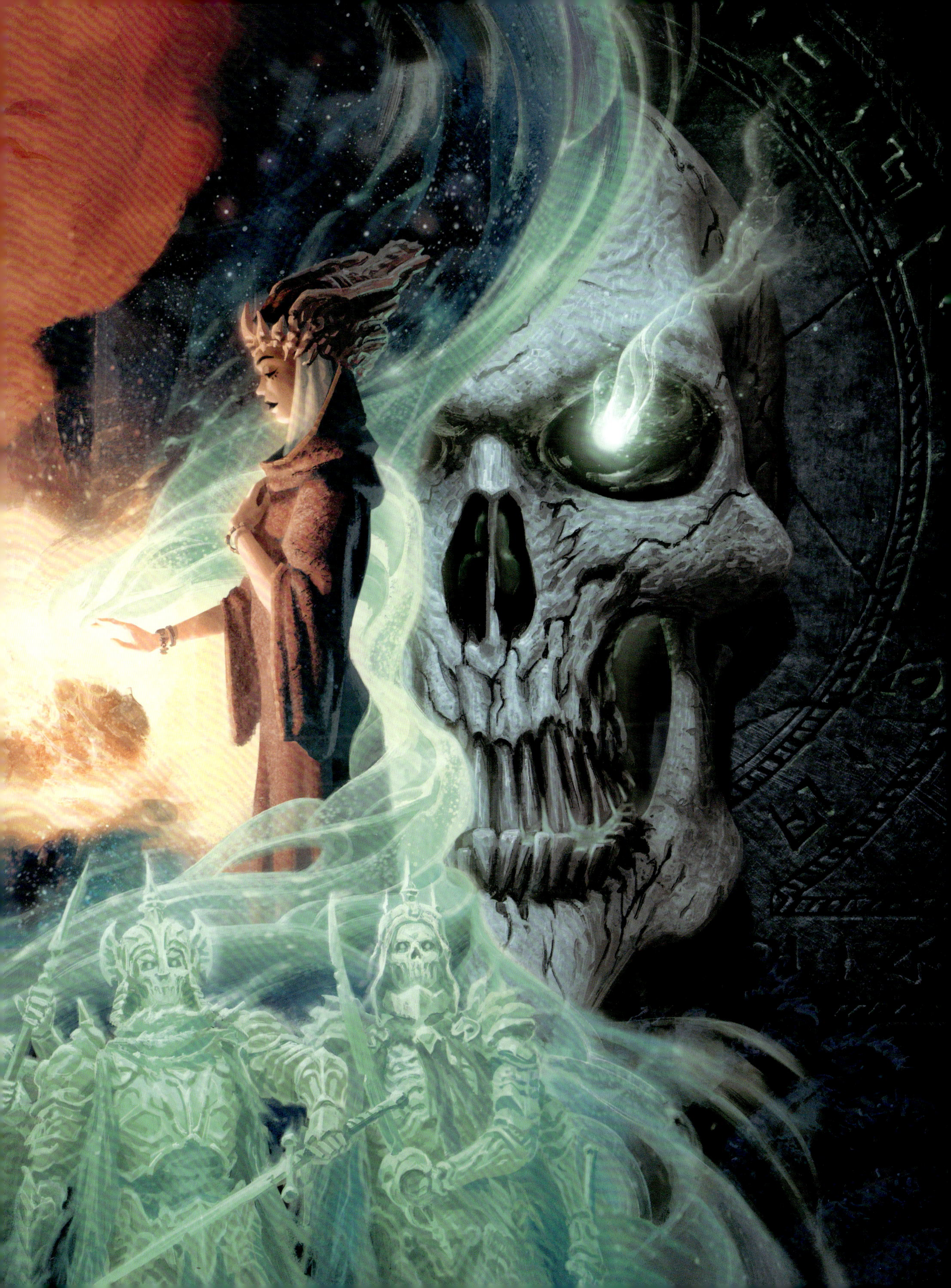

resplendent in their immortality upon the very breaths they deliver unto me, each an earnest caress to quicken me on this the firstmeir of my life.

* * *

I sense others of burgeoning awareness. Brethren, sistren, waking anew as I have done. I touch their minds and they mine as together in our solitary emptiness we strike out for bearing. Within the expanse of our mutual knowing we take hold of one another and in our grasping each of our certainties of being is given weight and measure. So do we know we are as much many as we are one and that is as it should be.

* * *

I hear the quiet shifting of stone on stone. It is near and intimate, like a grinding whisper of waking, and yet also resonant as if kept within a cavernous chamber. From above there comes a low and mournful howl of wind.

    A sallow light intrudes upon the black and the deep. I stir where I lie, and stones spill from my face and I see thick bands of bluegreen aurorae sweeping over a circle of the darkmeir sky. They roll and twist between the torchlit edgestones of an open atrium high above. Winking among them are clustered pinpoints of orange light that waver low in their places like uncertain constellations.

    For a moment the aurorae thin and part as in my newness of sight I observe the unveiling of a tumultuous cosmos of roiling nebulae beyond, everywhere pitted with blackoil hollows pulsating ceaselessly with muted flashes and their sudden waning.

    The swirling canopy of aurorae thickens once again and I am left with a lingering awe, married with a dismay I can not define. And so in the tearing through the black to see I learn that there are many ways of seeing.

* * *

The sound of the scraping of stones arrives now to me from many directions, restless, interspersed with dry creaking and mewls and furtive grunts as throughout the space I sense the physical presence of those others of my waking kind with respect to my own, such that a measure of our breadth is revealed to me. Their cries begin to fill the chamber, assertive and pitched as if laying claim to physical being. I offer an utterance of my own in kind and I am struck by the ponderousness of my voice even in its formless whisper. Still I think perhaps to join my siblings in their exclamations, but in that moment it does not feel like a useful act and so I do not.

* * *

I raise my self and stones spill upon the ground around me and I stand and this is my first act. The chamber is dim and as expansive as it had seemed in my mind, a broad, shadowy rotunda, its architecture everywhere embedded with mortal skulls that stare from dark orbits at nothing. The stone around them seems to crumble with rot and yet nowhere does the structure appear decrepit or in disrepair.

Spirit lamps hover throughout, casting a pale blue light over many shifting biers covered with loose cairnstones, arrayed outward round a central dais beneath the open sky, separated by narrow chasms which lead outward from the dais, toward an encirclement of shadowed archways in a gallery above, the keystones of each bearing torches of yellow fire.

From the biers figures everywhere stir, for the first time raising their selves up in the gloom, spilling their cold cairnstone shrouds to clatter and tumble into the chasm depths. We stand and peer at one another, each of variant stature and expression of skullform, of teeth and jaw, eye and horn, our flesh and bone shone corpsegreen by the meandering spirit lamps amidst sharpened silhouettes of blackened armor. And so it would seem each of us has been born readied for war. At first I take the flickering gleam within our skelliform hollows as the lamplight glinting over glassy eyes ablink through our torpor. But then in the faces of the newly arisen I see the enkindling of such sparks and I understand it is our eyes themselves that burn with this flame.

I look at my self then for the first time. I am armored simply as well in unadorned black plate fastened over cloaks of mail and coarse black cloth. My arms number one and three, my right side favoring this asymmetry, the innermost limb diminutively smaller than the others. I open its hand to look upon a sallow, fleshy palm. I bring its narrow fingertips together as I wonder at its purpose. For it is clear the limb lacks reach and the hand breadth to wield a weapon. And so it would seem I am born also with enigma.

Still I close it to a fist and looking upon my sistren and my brethren once again I present it raised as if to grasp the threads I yet feel stretched between our minds in waking. They who see or sense this act read my intent and present as well appendages of their own, and soon they are followed by all, and the hesitant clatter and shifting and creaks and croaks of the chamber are supplanted by a growing cry of our assertions of being as we begin to understand that we are created as a force united in solemn consonance to some great and dire import.

"To great and dire import, indeed, my new-awakened Mortis."

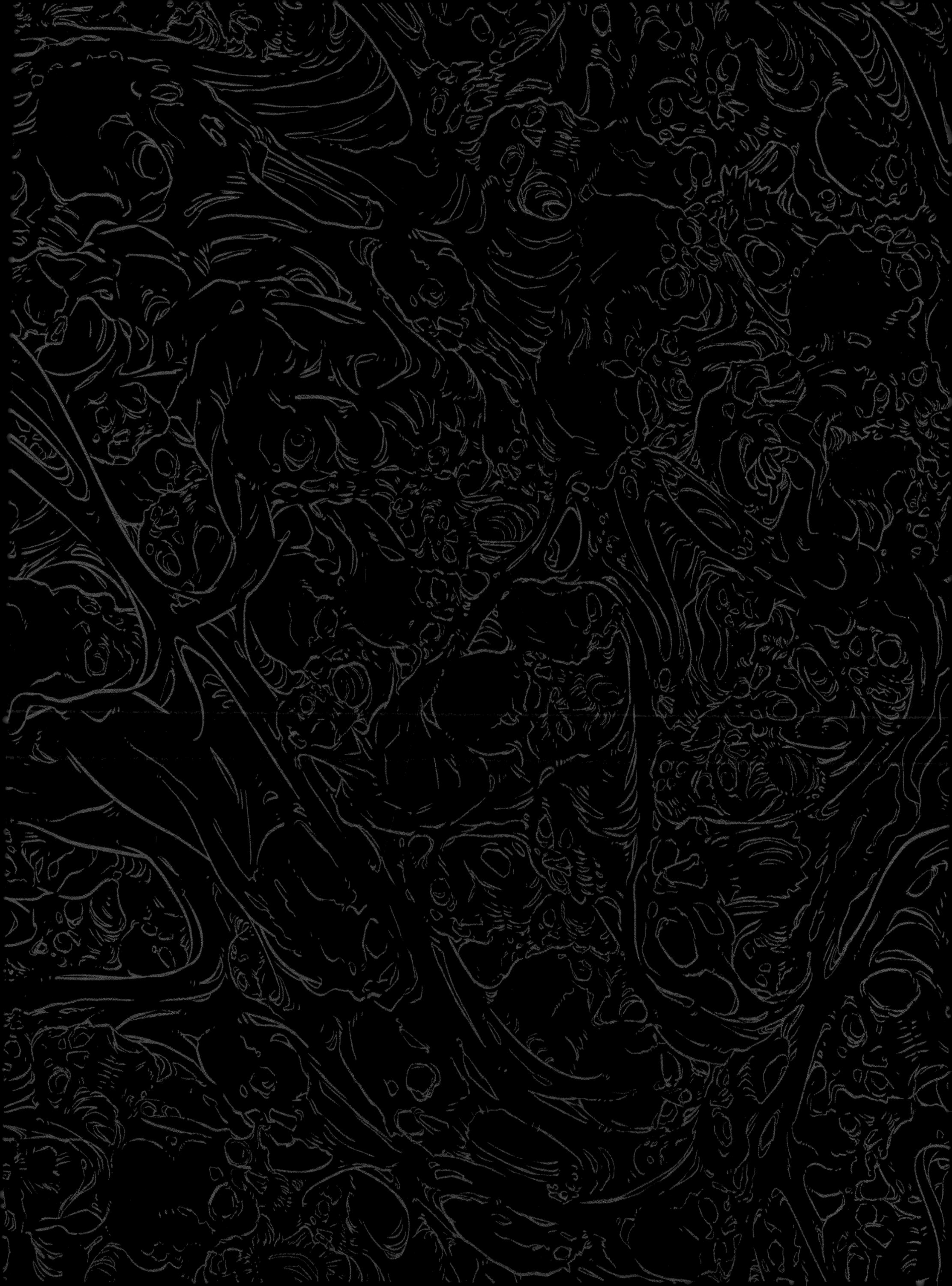

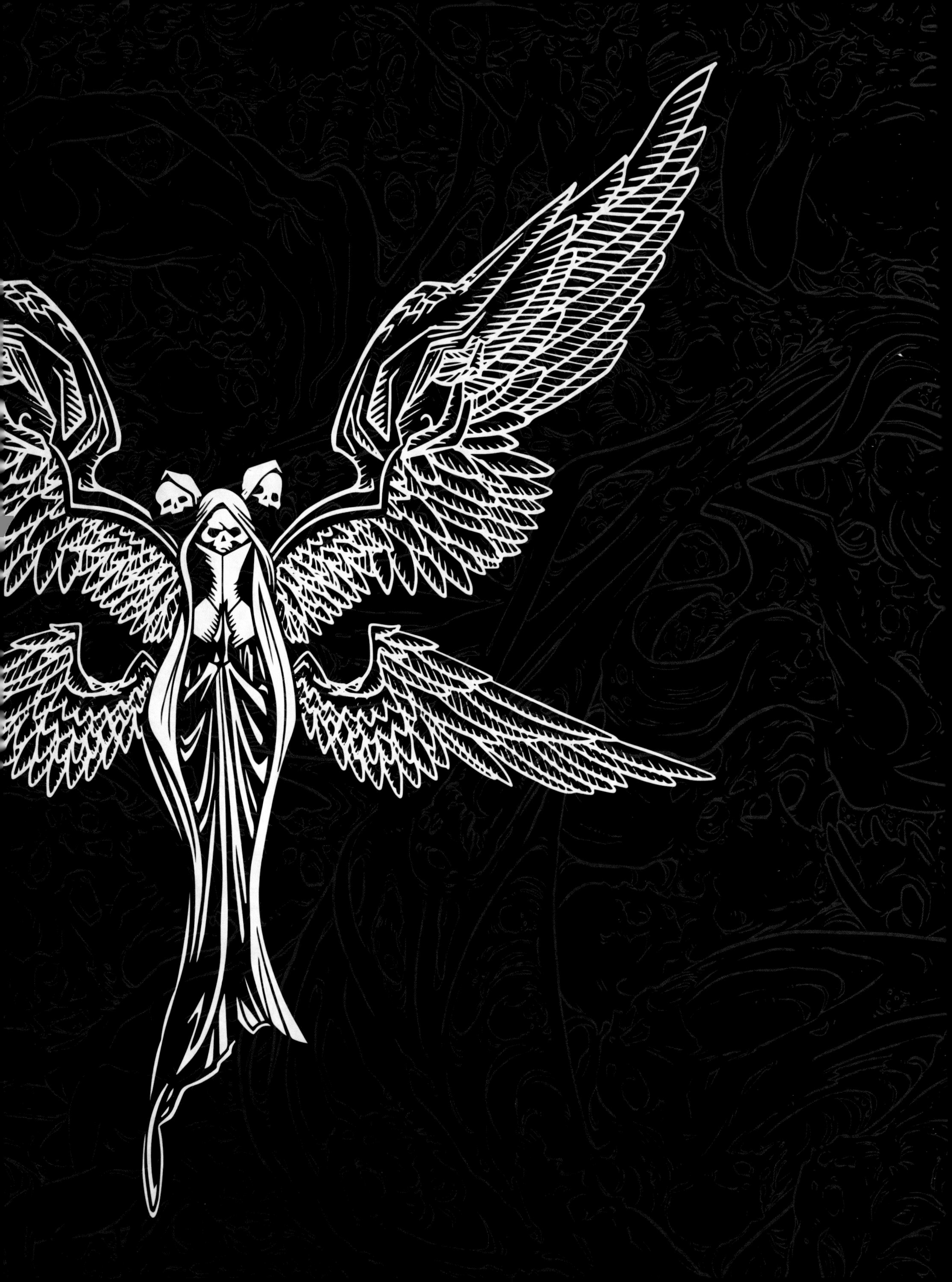

II.
FAMILY

Our father stands before us. He is as foreboding and deadly and spirited as the vision of him we had seen in the first moment of our becoming. He leans upon a scythe half again as tall as he. Its blade arcs above his ornate bonehelm, reflecting over us the pale light of the spirit lamps.

"Yes," says he, "'tis naught but the direst of scourges that we face. But of doom and portent we shall speak in time. 'Tis an untidy subject, and poorly suited to the spirit of the meirdrem. Come forward, then!"

His voice reverberates throughout the chamber, clear and familiar as we step from our biers of cairnstones and collect toward the center of the chamber. There we touch and feel the nearness of our heat, and we make fond sounds at the meeting of our flickering eyes. All of this is of great comfort to us as in his silent amusement our father watches us through his eyeless mask.

"Welcome to your existence," says he. He looks upward to the sky above the atrium and holds out his hand as if to catch a falling parcel of it. "And to this, the Underworld, that is your home."

* * *

"Of what first wishest thou thy clearest seeing: family, home, or being?"

As we look upon him we know nothing of what we wish. We know only this elegant image of our father and the sound of his voice, rich and elastic and sincere.

"Being it is, then!" says he. "Ah, what is it to be mortis? 'Tis a fine thing, indeed. One need but probe the viscera of one's creature: shroud-crafted as pall-fierce from the cradle; skull, skin, and scathing eye. You can bite, fight, and to the right refrain devise. You know the tongues of all entities, dead, living, and betwixt. Your natural mights are a stone soup of scintillae—a pinch of *preter*, a slice of *super*, and a dash of *un*. You know the proper way to greet a demon, though perhaps not a demise. You can dream, but not dawdle; you can remember, but by doing only. Such epiphanies as you encounter shall be disseminated or singularly brooded upon as desired. You are extant to the extent of your ipseity, and so in all senses, necessary. You are my beautiful, inviolable army of the spirited undead."

* * *

As he speaks he steps among us, looking upon our skelliform faces each in turn through his impenetrable mask. Though we understand near to nothing of his words, greedily we imbibe them in his passing through our shifting mass.

"The forewane of this meir found you mere components," says he. "Now you stand mere beings, though of a kind very new to creation, a circumstance for which you should feel no small amount of pride. And with you now, my dread children, I feel it also. For truly you are born of the essence of my very carcass, and I see in each of your spiritous eyes the sustenation of my own quilted provenance."

He ascends now a short rise of steps to the surrounding gallery, and framed by the darkened archways he turns again to look down upon us all.

"Who, then, has breathed such life into you as this?" says he. "From whom are the mortikin begat? Look upon your creator now, and know that his name is Death."

* * *

We take hold of the word in all its hollowness and light, and a soft muttering arises in the chamber as for the first time we speak aloud the name of our father.

"Yes," says he. He holds his scythe out wide, and with his other hand he reaches into nothing as if to present this to us as the entirety of his person. "I am the Alltaker of Life in this . I am keeper of atrocity and its profiteer, and a fool. I am destroyer, builder, plotter, dissident, thief. All the Underworld I have made, ever to grow with time and tumult, a domain of the dead in which to keep such reclamations of soul and creations of spirit as I possess; the first as mourners to dwell here as they would, the second as my Court to watch over them."

Figures appear now in the archways. Their statures and raiments are dissimilar but all stand eminent and foreboding as they look upon us with evident curiosity, their youthful faces warmed by the torchlight. Some we recognize from those flashes of our nascent awareness, and we search here and there among them for the face of the one whose voice had first delivered music into our knowing. But then the torches fail to glowing cinders as everywhere the hovering lamps diminish, and in the spreading darkness the shadows of the archways reclaim these figures of our parentage until the rotunda is darkened wholly but for the rushing aurora above.

Then with a deep thoom in the darkness our father brings his scythe down upon the dais and the atrium is bathed sapphire blue as sparks of energy crackle from its blade. A falling blaze of it he collects into his hand from which he then coaxes out long ropes to glimmer and curl among us. Flares of color shimmer and distort within serpentine shapes that vibrate with silent intensity as if slivers of eruptive power restrained. As the blue light from them falls upon our veinless flesh and seeps into the fissures of our armor, we feel emergent from within ourselves an unremitting agitation and want and also something more. A whispered beckoning. A longing grasp toward a frenzy kept within us, deep but familiar.

"Yes, you feel the call of it," says our father. "Its desperation, its cloying promise. Potent indeed is this vital essence of the Cosmos that we call etherea, and no less your desire for it. No less also the fear and knowing of its fire that we have put into you. 'Tis weapon, 'tis tool, 'tis sustenance; an energy of creation and destruction in equal measure. It has impelled the Cosmos to many deeds, great and terrible, to the glory and the fall. And yet no being shall know it more intimately than thee."

The etherea shudders and pulsates around us, and from it we feel a strange emanation, as if the listlessness of memory lost, and within its coils shadows flicker, intent upon forming shapes that escape them.

* * *

"Would that you should be given over to the breadth of your world unfettered," says our father. "To meander the avenues of this your somber city of Illverness into which you have been born; to find your place and purpose in time by the probing of your viscera alone. But imminent is our peril and dire is our need of you. And so as Vanguard to your humble underrealm be we obliged to ask you first to stand in devoted consumma-

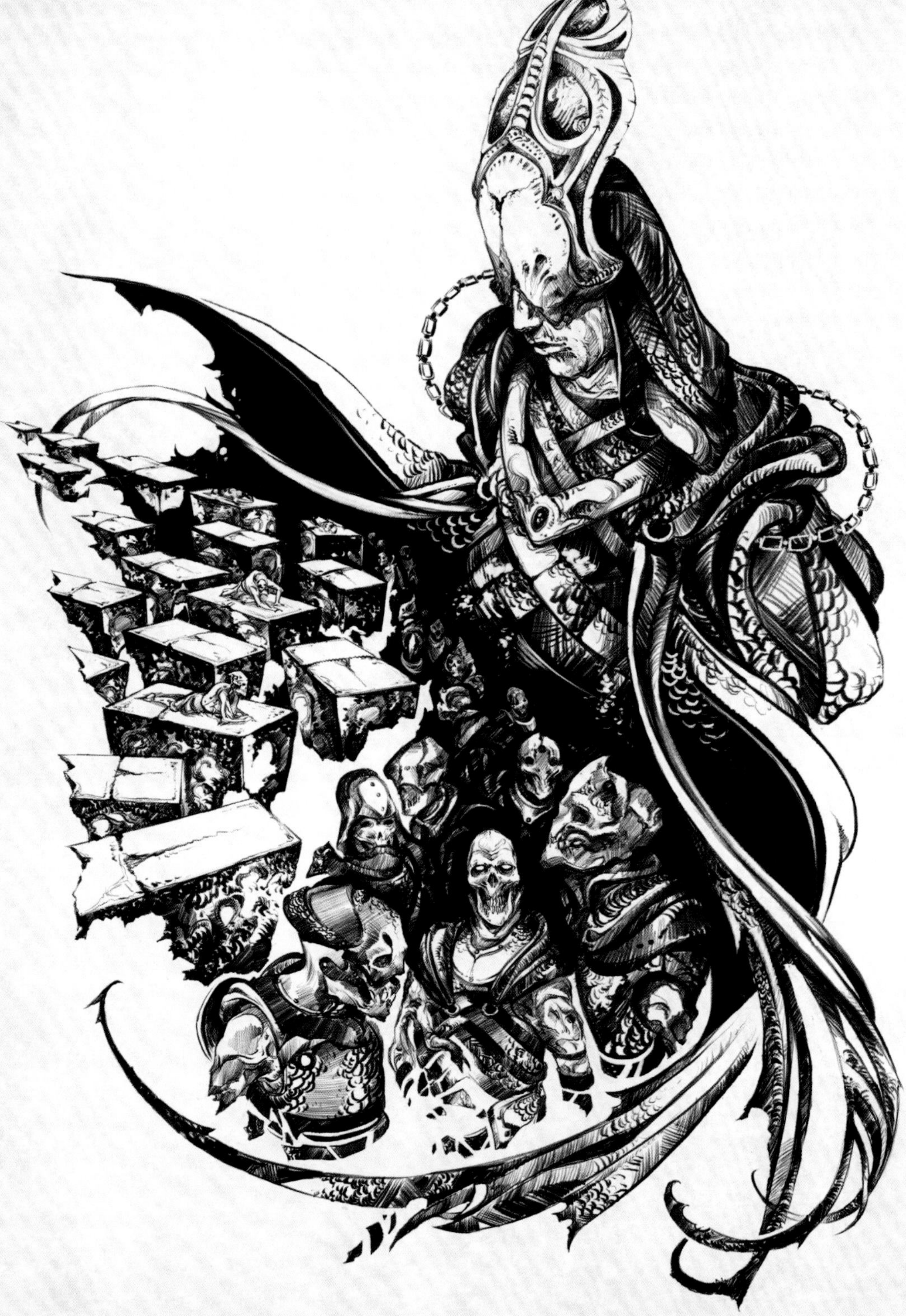

tion of your becoming, itself a realization that we have indeed gifted each of you the agency to discover. In so doing shall you learn to grant these ethereaic cries for everbeing as expressions of each your own strength and will. And finding that you are made stalwart to bear the worst of its fire, you shall learn also to dilute its seductions among you, together to wield in force this same power that corrupted your enemy."

With this last he speaks to us with a voice subdued, and we look from the scintillations of etherea to see him reduced, as if pressed by an unseen burden.

"Yes," says he. "They whom you face are your very predecessors. The first of my children, banished long ago to grow ever in their strength and number since, and in their hatred for the father who could not bring himself to destroy them outright. Thus is the greatest threat this realm has yet faced the creation of its own creator. For 'twas by a father's neglect in ignorance that they were ushered to their fall. 'Tis my greatest hope that what affinities and wisdom I have gained in my remorse have been conveyed upon you, and so grasped in your becoming shall we have made you herald to my atonement."

At this, our father's smile returns. He hits his scythe again to the dais and the ropes of etherea uncoil from us and draw back into the metal sheen of his blade, so that our eyes in the gloom are the only remnant flicker of its sapphire blue. And then he is moving among us.

"There is yet time for such weight as this that I carry," says he. "As I have said, 'tis a flavor of intrigue better suited for darker deliberation. Congregate, Children of Mortis! Revel in your newness, learn from your selves of your selves. Another will find you here in time, she whom you would wish greatly to look upon again, I think. And well wished, for she is Gethsemoni, queen to the Underworld and mother to you. Her shroudreive minders will attend to you, and when they have finished you shall be given witness to the breadth of your city, your home to keep and forever to protect. Thereafter shall I find each of you in turn, in a place of your choosing. And then we will see how best to introduce you to plot and chicanery."

* * *

He is gone again as if by the shifting away of our gaze. We look about the chamber, seeking into the archways for hint of the one called Gethsemoni, who is our mother. Finding only shadows there, we turn to one another as bidden by our father.

"*Meirdrem.*"
"A greeting."
"Yes."
"*Meirdrem loam* who are you?"
"I am."
"I am also."
"Mortis?"
"All are mortis."
"You are mortis also."
"I am. We are."
"*Fair cellandr* this is good. "
"Good."
"All of us good."
"Yes."
"Yes."
"Yes."
"Together."
"Yes, together."
"Good."

* * *

Though nothing of substance is exchanged in our halting vocalizations they are a comfort to us, and in our congregation of one hundred we grasp one another and nod and bring our skulls to scrape together in greeting, and after a time our tongues warm to their shapes and we speak with greater clarity such curiosities as with which it seems we are uniquely born.

And then within our sense of one another the wisps of shared thought we had felt between us before our eyes had enkindled effervesce once again, and with this wisping speech thereafter we exchange the greater richness of sentiment from mind to mind as undercurrent to the clumsiness of our spoken words. And by the intimacy of this manner of exchange for the first time we begin to understand the true dimension of our entity.

* * *

The emergence of a familiar presence brings us to peer again into the galleries above, and there we find stepping into lamplight upon a broad veranda that vision of our mother from our inception made real, a figure of dark grace in ornate circlet and headdress, her youthful lavender flesh wrapped in a simple flowing cloth of red accented against her form by elements of forged metal and carven bone. As she approaches the edge of the veranda her cloak gathers at her feet and spills partway through the bony structure, and she gazes over us with kindness in her eyes, and begins to sing:

> *Awake, dear treasures, come the mist, come the light*
> *Come the blades beyond sharp then to carve out the blight*
> *Come the teeth that thou carry, come the call, come the fail*
> *Come the souls that thou takest for stars*
> *Remember thy mother, whom the Underworld heareth*
> *Giving song to thy flesh underneath*
> *Breathe, breathe, mine eerie beloved*
> *Find the sparks that draw out the black veil ever-flooded*
> *Seek, find thine other, who takest thy name*
> *Find the way, find the heart, find the flame*
> *And remember thy mother, whom the Underworld mourneth*
> *Giving song to thy flesh underneath*

Her black eyes glitter in the gloom as her song swims throughout the chamber, crisp and mellifluous and sorrowful. She breathes its melody upon us deeply in earnest, as if in the sanguinity of her enkindling of our spirits she found also renewal of her own ancient being. By its enchantment we are held rapt, each of us aglow within by the unrestrained affection in our mother's voice, our mewling requitals oaths of fealty writ upon the empty air before us.

And then streams of many clacking creatures begin to spill out from the chasms to clamber into our midst, spindly constructs of many legs that shepherd us from our audience as they clatter in their dozens beneath the waves of our mother's song. Mechanically they nudge and prod us toward the respective bierbeds of our awakening with segmented arms that extend from long and narrow torsos of bone and rusted metal draped here and there with tattered capes of flesh, orienting us to stand upon them with long-fingered claws each affixed with myriad probing and cutting tools. Thus is the chamber suddenly alive with meticulous activity as Gethsemoni's myriad shroudreive attendants flit between us, so that no one of us goes unmolested for long. They raise themselves on extended legs to grasp and turn our faces, opening our jaws and examining our hollows before sinking again to probe elsewhere. They peer through apparatuses of wicklight and polished glass lenses attached with thin harnesses to their leather-wrapped heads, twisting and adjusting their opticals constantly as they snip and pluck from us what imprecise fragments of carapace and flesh they discover.

Apparently satisfied with my condition my attendant leaves me to examine one of my bretheren nearby. But then another arrives, its kitted head extended on a narrow, ringed neck as it draws me to step down from my bier, only to nudge me back upon it again. Another insistent tug and again I am made to step down before it pulls aside my cloak and hefts my right leg to peer intently at my knee as deftly it unfastens the poleyn of my armor there, and setting it carefully upon the floor beside my foot it cuts a line through the rings in the mail beneath with shears. Separating the mail it then pulls the stitching from a seam in the thin leather undercloak beneath and parts this also. Then it cuts away the flesh covering the base of my knee, laying bare the workings within, and capturing the dark fluid that spills forth from the incisions with a cloth it produces a small half-moon blade with fine serrations and begins to shave down the bone at the joint, now laid bare and dry.

Then it presses me to step onto my bier again while still holding aside my cloak, looking closely at its work. It examines the site a moment more and then, packing into the area a glob of black jelly, it sutures the incision and wipes it clean. It restitches the leather and with a clasping tool closes the rings in the mail to cover my knee again and then ties the poleyn in its place and releases my cloak to drape heavily down.

It rises up to peer at me through a lens set into its fleshless skelliform orbital with a bulbous and expressionless undead eye. It scrutinizes the spirit flicker of my own eyes each in turn as if appraising the vigor of their flames. It retreats a pace, and scanning me crown to toe a final time it sinks down and scuttles away.

* * *

One by one the shroudreive break from their ministrations and withdraw whence they had come. When the last of them has departed Gethsemoni's song comes to an end and we are left to stand upon our biers with its melody echoing still in our minds, for our mother is gone.

There is a great rumbling throughout the chamber then as the dais in the center of the room cracks and gives way to a broadening emergence of a cluster of three curved spires of stone. They rotate as they rise, revealed conjoined to a single entwined mass, a bluestone menhir, hewn to a whorl of three distinct facades that bow deeply inward toward its center mass, slowly grinding away the remnants of the dais by its expansion until thrice the breadth of the largest among us its roughly broken underside levitates freely from the resultant pit.

    Still it rises, twisting itself upward toward the open canopy of the chamber. And then there is a shudder beneath our feet as the flat stones of our biers give way to the emergence of solid masses of rock, and like baffled effigies displayed atop hastily carven plinths we find ourselves drawn up from the floor in formation with the menhir to fill the empty space of the open rotunda, rising as if petals of the lotus flower, five blades of twenty armored warriors each abloom from the twisted stigma of the menhir.

    And then upon the whorled facades a barbed latticework of dart-like sigils appears etched in glowing red. We recognize its cuneiform script and through our wisping determine it a compendium of many hallowed names. Yet these shift and reform like frenzied claw wounds inflicted continuously by a thousand small and unseen creatures and so its meaning and significance eludes us.

* * *

We look up to see the approaching of our sky and know we are soon to gain first sight of our home as promised by our father. And in that moment the voice of our mother returns to speak to each of us in the closeness of our minds.

    "Thou hast been told of thy nature, yet not of thy self. 'Tis imperishable mú for thee, found by deed and reflection unbound, alone and without shroud. Do, and be, dear treasure. And mark thy musings, that thou shalt grow always by thy ever greater knowing. For all is everchanging but thy name."

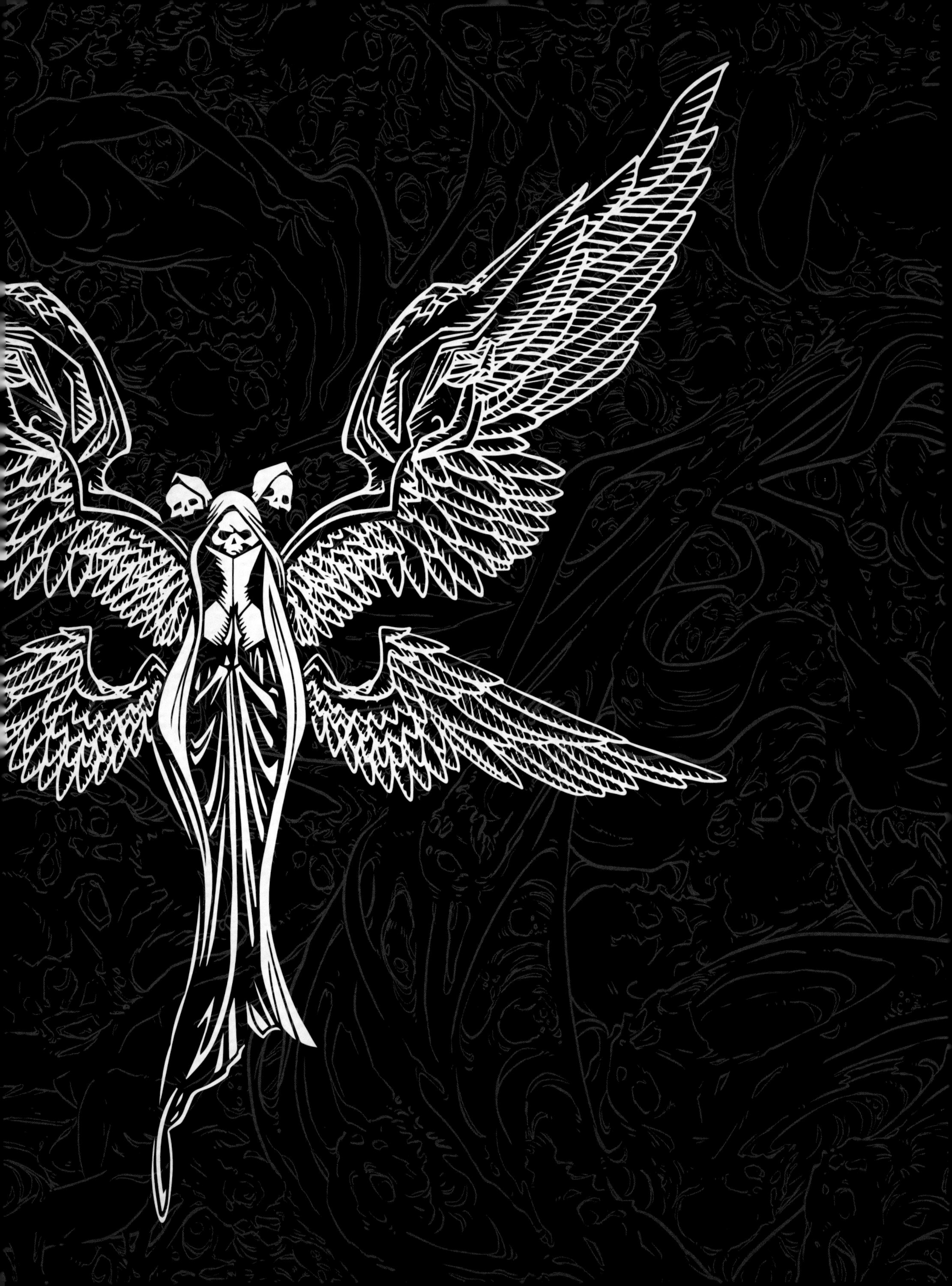

III.
A CITY

We rise up toward the open canopy of our nursery chamber, a hundred newborn children of the Underworld drawn skyward by the slowly rotating stone, rippled over by the red slashes of script, its three curved spires clawing at the open sky like a flower desperate to bloom.

  As we emerge to first sight of our home our gaze is immediately captured by a brilliant torrent of etherea rushing upward from the midst of a great citadel somewhere in the center of the city. The fount is so vast that it would seem nothing in the realm could escape its light and what shadows are created by it are as realms of their own bounded by the edges of darkness. It streams far above the swirling aurorae of the sky and though it seems to vanish to a point beyond our sight, we wonder whether it reaches far into the tumult that is the Celestial Cosmos, and if so it would seem a thing that connects the realms. As we ponder as one its beauty and breadth of magnificence it stirs within us also a malaise that we can not identify. And so we think perhaps it must be a thing of contradiction, at once both curse and benefaction, which must govern existence for all who dwell here.

* * *

We rise in our floating formation above the shadowy structures nearest the atrium to an expanse of sharp and jagged spires. Agleam by the light of the ethereaic torrent, they stab at the sky with broken finials from crumbling cathedral towers and from skeletal basilicas that spill black fog from between their columns. As the tallest of these drop below our rocky plinths we see them ornamented by weathered friezes and cracked effigies and snarling grotesques and the muted light that flickers and pulsates through a whitegray mist from tower portals and lancets and from the windows of their bartizans, which cling like bloated carrion beetles to their rotting facades.

    The dark edifices of the city are themselves a further contradiction. Decrepit yet also somehow vital and animate. In places they seem to alter or reform even as we look upon them, perhaps to move entirely here or there as had our father. As well their architecture bluntly defies logic, bearing elements that float freely in space or stand unwavering above great missing sections, as if buttressed by memory of vanished walls.

    Though we do not doubt we are observed by the denizens of the city we mark no entities beyond our own wavering bloom. There is only an arrhythmic, hushed tolling of bells, as if quieted by the mists, and beneath this the vaguest forlorn moaning upon the wind in our ears.

* * *

As we continue our ascent we see shrouded in the mists between the larger structures an array of temples, charnel houses, and mausoleums. They are connected by a bramble garden of masonry debris and dead gray trees that claw through the murk at nothing. Corpsegreen miasma weeps from the windows and portals of the structures over steps half-consumed by dark fissures in the ground.

    Then in the fog-laden bailey of a cloister we see a queue of listless creatures. They are disheveled and disparate and walk haltingly, as if uncertain from one moment to the next what action to take. They are shepherded through a gap in its wall by a pair of spectral figures who glow white and clear through the gloom, such that even from far above we mark the feminine and patient bearing of them. As the last of their creatures enter the cloister they turn and look up beyond the city heights to watch our rise and we see that within each of their ghostly forms is one solid and cryptic, beastly skelliform and of many swaying appendages. They watch us for a time, and we seem to feel from them a calming, kindly presence. But then we pass through a swath of shifting aurorae that wrap themselves around us so that all below us is obscured by their wispy glow. They swirl about us like lonesome spirits until chased beyond our reach by the winds and when we look again to the diminishing cloister the spectral figures are gone.

* * *

A City

The tolling of the bells falls away as we pass beyond the highest reach of the immense and jagged citadel that contains the blazing uptorrent of etherea. Yet the despondent moaning persists and though we can not imagine its origin we decide it must emanate from the torrent as undercurrent to the low scour of it that follows us undiminished also.

  Our height is such that the city is revealed trisected by three thick rivers of etherea that meander outward from the foundations of the citadel like pulsating arteries to nourish the walled expanse of fields and edifices surrounding it. Out from their churning lightflow shift sporadic rivulets of blue here and there along the narrow roads throughout the lower reaches, all of which converge gradually toward a toothsome and forbidding gate. The walls that draw away from it are conjoined in sections by tall spikes resembling shards of bone that seem to have grown up from the outer terrain to tower high over the battlements. They wrap the city in an oblong and irregular shape, meeting beyond the citadel in the shadow of a jagged expanse of mountains.

  The gate itself is composed of many stout keeps from which banners curl in long tendrils of color against a patient wind. It stands far taller than most of the city structures it protects and is nested in row upon row of bonespikes, so that an enemy marching to face it would be confronted by what would seem the fanged maw of a skeletal leviathan. As we gather in its immensity its shadows seem to swell and bow by a fluctuating torrent of white and sapphire-blue light that deepens them, and we perceive within its keeps the glinting eyes of stoic sentinels who in their timeless station seem at once to observe all and ponder nothing.

  Thus are we brought the vastness of our city but also the pulse of its entity. Bounded to singularity by its flowing web of etherea this shifting dark metropolis seems both ancient and hollow and yet we perceive it also everywhere alive. With decay and renewal. With awareness and dream. As if by the power of the groaning spire of light that pierces its heart it yearns ever to remake itself as it wishes to be.

* * *

A road leads from the gate over a bridge that spans a deep crevasse cut into the land partway round the city. The road winds into a dark span of oddly mismatched ruins fed by a sporadic infall of debris large and small from seemingly nowhere. Otherworldy elements they seem which passing into this realm over vast reaches of time have drawn up the discordant topography.

Past this terrain the road continues far out to a lone, anomalous black tower. It appears constructed entirely of a thousand misshapen black mirrors. We judge it must be half again the citadel's height or more. Though it glitters bluegreen by the light reflected distantly from the spireflow, the blackness beneath its reflections is depthless and absolute.

*　*　*

Our ascent is halted at last and we find ourselves in the midst of pulsating balls of light. The starry pinpoints we had seen looking into the sky upon our waking. They drift in clusters between our staggered formations, undisturbed by our presence except where displaced by our curious grasping. Some begin to float in languid orbits around us and the rocky plinths on which we stand before drifting casually away as if by a breeze. But these leave with us thin recollections of being, as if wisps of memory. So do we learn that the constellations that hover high above our city are in fact spirit phenomena at rest on the winds. Content merely to exist. Impelled by what final remnants of thought and dream they yet possess.

*　*　*

The clusters begin to arrive with greater density from every direction and our flesh and bone are cast waxy and bilious as by their accumulation a ghoulish radiance arises. They pass through us now and drift inward to course along the whorls of the slowly rotating menhir in the center of our formation. Where they touch it the sigils scratched upon its surface are brought ablaze like sparking embers until we are awash in the red glow of the stone as the menhir ceases its rotation and the balls of light drift slowly away as before.

The marks shift to form coherent glyphs over the three sides of the stone and by our encircling vantage collectively we decipher its message:

PRIAM AND ABRAXIEL. NAMES THE FIRST.
GONE THE NAMES.
NAMELESS THE ETHEREA.
EXTREMIS OF HEAVEN. EXTREMIS OF HELL.
COVET THE NAMELESS.
TO DESPOIL CREATION.

A City

**AWAY THE NAMELESS.
FORGE THE NAMELESS. FORGE THE WAR.
HEAVEN TO PREVAIL. NOTHING TO PREVAIL.
HELL TO PREVAIL. NOTHING TO PREVAIL.
CAESURA THE WAR. CAESURA THE IMPERATIVE.
THE EMANANT KEY.**

**AWAY THE KEY.
AWAY THE EMISSARY.
NAMES THE Vanguard. THE CELESTIAL COVENANT.
SHIELD THE EMISSARY. TO STEM EXTREMIS.
Vanguard THE SACRIFICE.
NAMES THE Vanguard.**

We read this with little understanding, though we recognize the names of Priam and Abraxiel as the progenitors of all that is this Cosmos, themselves dual aspects of the first being, Eddath, and the creators of the celestial realms of Heaven and Hell. This knowledge of the beginning and order of things it seems we were born in possession of among other such elements that have been brought to the surface of our knowing in the time since the moment of our waking. And looking into the tempestuous expanse above our sky we determine it must be these realms that are at war, and looking upon the spire of light that flows into it from this the Underworld it is decided that it is the Forge so writ upon the stone and thus the Nameless must be the etherea that feeds it.

But from whence comes what we now hear as a great forlorn wailing of the fount of etherea we can not unravel. Though I probe this question further in our wisping it seems I am alone in the earnestness of my wish for this to be brought into our understanding, for I sense the minds of my kin turn from it to pursue other observations. I do not understand why I alone should wish greater than the other mortis to know these things. But it is the first time that I feel . . . separate. For in pondering this question I sense some part of its answer within my self, and though I do not know how to gather it into my knowing when I try to do so the wisping voices of my kin are for the first time quieted.

And then, images. The faces of many. Broken, etched with agony, fury.

Bodies pierced by holy spear and blade. Rent by fang and curse and claw. The selflessness and loss, the grief. The pain. The pain. To accompany our ebbing of spark. So many, destroyed. O, we children of Heaven and Hell. Warring sides ourselves divided, allies of anathema. We who are victims of our covetous selves. Of the endless ruin of war. Ever renewed by the bountiful Nameless. The endless fount.

We among them the Vanguard. In our stand, in our demise. We stood before the open veil, the few against the many. They brought their fury down. Their frenzy to prevent us. Our direst strategy. To stem the Nameless flow. To starve the animus. The veil closed. They would have destroyed all things.

Our missive. A sliver cast down, a key. An epistle sent in haste. Of all lesser beings, to he the custodian. Our missive his key. Will he know it?

The veil closed. They would have destroyed all things.

The quiet. The terror of failure abated. Salvation by virtue of mutual annihilation. Final abrogation of our deviant pact. Nothing other could have been foretold.

* * *

The vision is spent. I submerge my self in its moments again. Its intimacy of emotion. The fullness of its past and present, a dimension of knowing far beyond mere imagery and soundscape. And so not a vision, but a memory. My memory. Though it was made by another long ago it was given to me and therefore it is mine.

* * *

I look upon the stillness of the menhir. Its inscription now pulsates as the stone itself seems to fall away and all other sound seeps from my awareness. The wind, the wailing. The utterances of my kin. Everything now quiet as I plummet through its featureless presence. Into the black and the deep. Formless and full. It was the first thing that I understood.

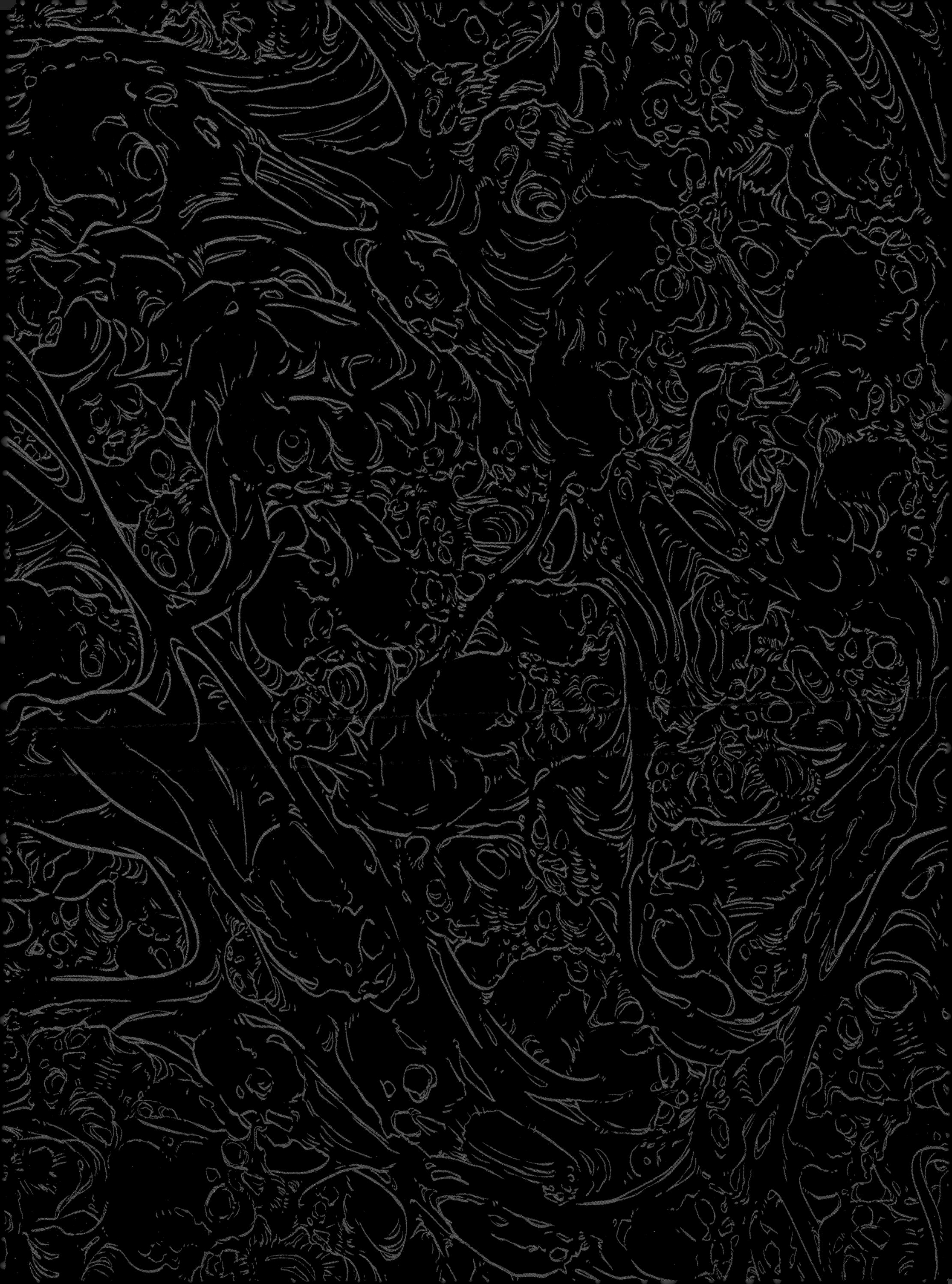

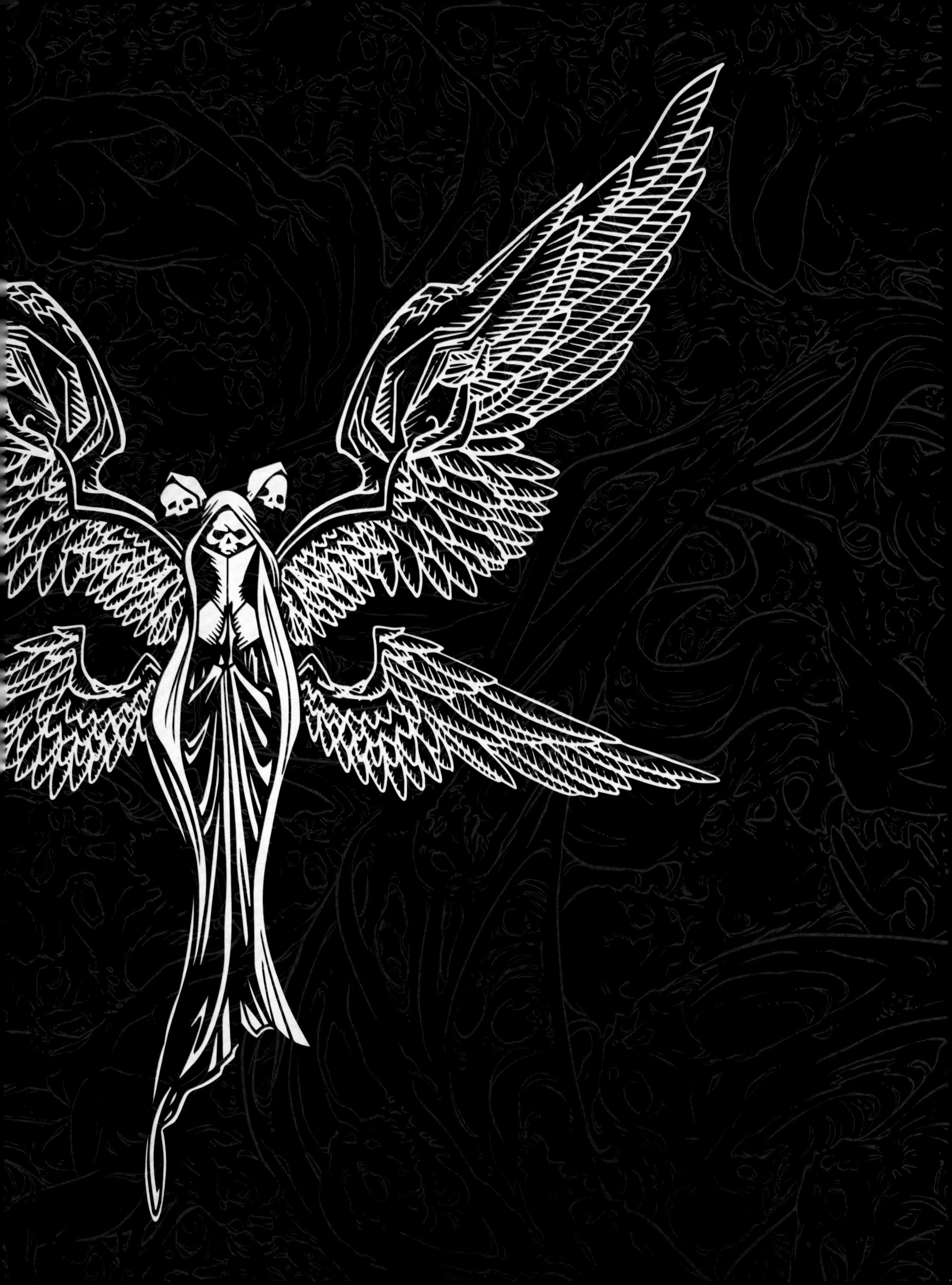

IV.
A NAME

The reaper stands in darkness. Everywhere a forlorn sound. The sound of the fount of etherea returned, but deepened, cavernous. And a new sound. A soft lapping of water. The surface beneath his feet tilts and rocks with a strange irregularity.

    Meirdrem loam, reaper.

    A light grows, a lamp of green fire raised by a pale hand. It is held by a hooded figure. Its light plays shadows into the sunken features of an aged mortal man. His visage is unfamiliar, yet the reaper knows that it is Death.

    Meirdrem loam, Father. What is reaper?
All mortis are reaperkind.
Then I am reaperkind.
Yes.
What is reaperkind?
You will see.

    This manifestation of his father holds not a scythe but a long wooden oar. The reaper feels it tap upon the bottom of the simple wooden boat in which they stand.
    All else remains in darkness save reflections of the lantern's light upon the black water.

    We are in the stone?
So we are.

The reaper looks down at himself.
I am something else.
Death holds the lantern up.
So you are.

The reaper brings his hands into the light. They are thin and narrow and project from the sleeves of a light, draping shroud. He touches his face. He can feel its coldness. Suppleness of flesh where before had been only coarse and naked bone. Death watches with empty eyes. Then he holds out his light and gestures broadly into the formless black.

A curious vista you have conjured. And a fitting vessel. Fine enough to seek one's name, I deem. Charon will be charmed when I tell him of it.
The reaper peers out into the black.
A curious vista I have conjured.
Indeed. Fashioned by emanation of your self upon entering the menhir. So also have you altered us. A fascinating experience! Yours has proven among the most interesting yet.

The reaper looks to the darkened sky. He scans the thin, shrouded line of the horizon, reaching for sense of his kindred. He can feel that they are with him, but as if reflections of themselves only, removed from the moment.

The others are here?
The menhir keeps its own time and space. They are here, and also not here. I speak to them now as I do you. They are with us, even if neither here nor now.
I do not understand.
Worry not, then. 'Tis a place for a busy father to meet his children, each in intimate audience on the mournmeir of their making. 'Tis likely you have many questions. Here and now there is time for us to speak. Here and now I shall learn something of your singular nature, and bear witness to your naming.
I do not have a name.
Ah, but you manifest it even now! As I have told you, your becoming is to be each your own design. Here a name you shall come upon as on all future epiphanies, with the clarity of eyes unclouded. But you are a new creature, and so I shall guide you now in this first step of your discovery.

You are a good father, Father.
No. But perhaps one not beyond redemption. We shall see.

The vision of Death leans forward and hooks the lamp upon the curved prow. He pushes them off from a nearby outcrop of rock with his oar. He lowers the oar into the water and begins to ferry them forth. The reaper watches the lamplight glinting upon the black water. He looks out over the dark expanse. In the distance muted flashes arrive, buried in thick cloud cover.

How has such a place arisen from my self? I do not know it.
A part of you knows it.
A memory?
Drawn from many such as we have given you, 'tis more like.
Why should one keep the memory of another, Father?
Death laughs. A hollow, dry sound muffled by his cloak.
How would you make ready an army of babes to face a threat but a fortmeir's ravage away?
The reaper watches the ripple of distant flashes.
I do not know, Father.
Then I shall tell you: most of your memories are gathered from the soldiering dead. They are moments deemed useful to your purpose, curated and kept in the realm of true spirit by the acolytes of the oracle Ellianastis, thirdborn of my scions and the most farseeing of my counsel. Though clouded, their root will remain; their substance shall be as foundation to quicken you. Thus are you each imbued with a warrior's acumen, to discover by doing, in time.
Why should they not all come from warriors?
The answer to this question you shall discover yourself. I shall say only 'twas a decision arisen from a place of enduring optimism.

A rolling thoom arises. The flashes of muted light draw nearer. The sound of heavy splashes comes to them through the darkness. More, near and far. By the intermittent light they witness the fall from the sky of many forms. Death draws them forth in the darkness with his oar.

Fascinating.
They are Celestials?
Yes. Angelic and demonic dead. The fallen from Heaven and Hell.
A part of me has seen their war.

So it would seem.

The sky is suddenly bright with white fire. The air is dense with the falling forms. The water is a white foam by their crashing. All is returned to darkness. The splashes ebb.

A part of you intuits our greater calling. 'Tis well enough the Celestials can not perceive us within the menhir.
What is our greater calling, Father?
To tear down the walls of Heaven and Hell.

The splashes cease. Death rows forth into the shapeless black.

The Celestials have corrupted their purpose beyond redemption. Creation has long since ceased to create. All is merely consumed in their endless fire. The tortured expanse you have seen beyond the Underworld sky is testament to the breadth of violence. The time will come when we shall together confront the Heavens and Hells and undo the war that has debauched the Cosmos for aeons.
It is the nature of war to continue without end?
It has evolved to become so. But so was it made: when at the end of the first aeon Eddath split her entity in twain, she sought to drive creation to grow by the meeting of twin disparities. Thus, Priam and Abraxiel, opposing entities of Order and Uncertainty. Wherever their creations should meet there would be no stagnation, no oblivion. Their mutual agitation would give rise to an abundance of things ever new to existence. But such was the abundance of their creations that they were left unguided, and all children so neglected must fall to ignorance. And so in their ignorance did the children of Order become Intolerance and Suffocation; the children of Uncertainty, Chaos and Strife. Nor could either be made to understand the suffering of the other, for it was not until the creation of mortals that Empathy as a force was introduced into the threadwork of the Cosmos.
The realm of mortals was made to end the war?
Yes. In this time there was but one realm kept within the veil, a place where the etherea that impelled creation permeated the very air for the taking. Priam and Abraxiel watched with dawning shame as it was debased to feed destruction, and looking upon the carnage their creations had wrought they watched helplessly as their Cosmos was slowly shattered into separate archipelago realms of Heaven and Hell. And finally they

understood that the devastation would end only when these now separate realms had drifted beyond the reach of one another's hatred, each to fall to stagnation and the ultimate vanishing into oblivion of all that was their Cosmos. They forged a pact with those few angels and demons who understood this also, and in their final act of penance gathered all of the etherea of the Cosmos into themselves, and by their unmaking did they cast the etherea into a new and distant realm beyond the veil, where their children could not go.

And you, Father?

Yes?

What then created you?

I do not know.

I understand, Father.

Do you? Then perhaps you will lend me your clarity. I once believed I was created by the Celestials to draw up the etherea from the Mortal Realm. To coax it forth and send it to feed their own with its power. Indeed they encouraged this belief, and encouraged also the ever greater expansion and increase of its flow. This I undertook with enthusiasm to please my masters, and to feed the growth of my own realm.

The great fount of etherea in the city.

Yes. Once it was no more than a pinprick in the narrow in-between that conjoined the realms. Diligently did I work to pry open the maw in the center of my realm, and ever broader grew its torrent to the Celestial Realm. Yet in time I observed and began to question the harmony of a Cosmos with them at its helm. And with the awakening of the mortals I observed them, and I came to understand the greater truth, hidden from me by my masters: I was not in fact made by the Celestials. Indeed, I began to suspect that I was created in the same sundering that brought into being the Mortal Realm. If so, I was not made a being in their service, to facilitate their war, but a part of the design of their creators to bring about its end.

But it has not ended.

Indeed. But perhaps its end unfolds before us even now. Though the full apparatus of their intent is lost, I know it has not all yet come to pass. I see intimations of it everywhere. I know also that some key remainder of it incubates throughout the Mortal Realm, and that delivery of it was bought at great cost by the acolytes of Priam and Abraxiel's awakening wisdom, they who would become the Vanguard.

Enemies made to allies.

Yes.

They fought against many to protect the emissary. They perished before the open veil.
What?
Are you the custodian?

Death turns, his oar transmuted to his towering scythe. Its blade flashes pale green in the lamplight.

Why do you ask this?
I do not know.
'Tis a moniker I wore for my masters in the very earliest of days. None have spoken of me thus for many aeons. Tell me, reaper, how it was brought into your mind.
The epitaph.
What?
A part of me has seen the war. The epitaph upon the menhir. It drew the name into my knowing. A part of me has seen its memory. Was this not meant to be so?

Death peers deep into the reaper with his borrowed visage, searching. He finds nothing within that is anything other than reaper. In the spirit there is no trace of guile, only an earnest thirst for information and reflections of his first sights of the city. Death is disarmed by the purity of the reaper's . . . possessiveness of his home. It is a thing that he has never read from any among his spiritborn. He lightens his posture, though his scythe remains bared.

Tell me of this memory.
There was a battle. I was . . . the memory is from one among the dying. A child of Heaven, it seemed to me. There were many dead. Demons also. We . . . they fought to protect a missive. In my memory I know that it was dire, and I know that it was sent forth to a custodian.

Death considers this for a time as they float idly upon the water. Then he shakes his head within its hooded shadow, his scythe now a simple oar again.

Thoroughly have I studied the transcription of the Vanguard, yet I am aware of no missive. Certainly no such thing was delivered. When I leave you I shall search the libraries for intimation of it. How interesting that I should encounter such a revelation by way of this communion. To say nothing of your recollection of it. Very interesting, indeed. 'Twas thought perhaps in time some among you might find your way to the seeing of your memories, but this was neither expected nor necessary. Nor could I have guessed any would be of the Vanguard itself. Of this I shall have to speak to Ellianastis as well. But 'tis a good sign, I deem. And it shall make your naming all the easier, at the least, my surprising young reaper.

Death turns again to mind the boat. The reaper looks out into the unbroken darkness. There are dark shapes bobbing in the water. Some begin to pass near. When they fall fully beneath the lamplight he sees that they are neither angel nor demon. He sees that they wear mortal faces. That they are alive. They flail with desperate arms. They scream in silence as the boat passes.

Mortals.
Yes.
They are beings. Like we are beings.
Yes.
Some of my visions of memory are from them?
As many as not. Memory of life is taken from the dead alone, and mortals are both fragile and fruitful, though only now do they begin to build their civilizations.
They are a part of my self, then.
They are a part of everything. They are a part of us all.

They row in silence for a time. The mortal forms stream past the boat still. Some slap the boat in their flailing as they pass by. They otherwise do not acknowledge it. The light from the lantern falls upon their faces wracked by silent screams. The reaper sees that they are blind. There are only blackened holes where their eyes would be.

Theirs is the Nameless call.
Death looks back at him and nods.
Your nature makes itself known to you. All etherea is born of mortal souls. 'Tis born as they are born, and enriched by the torment of their lives, and finally ripened by their passing it shall fall upon thee to reap. In the nearmost shattermeir before us this must remain the charge

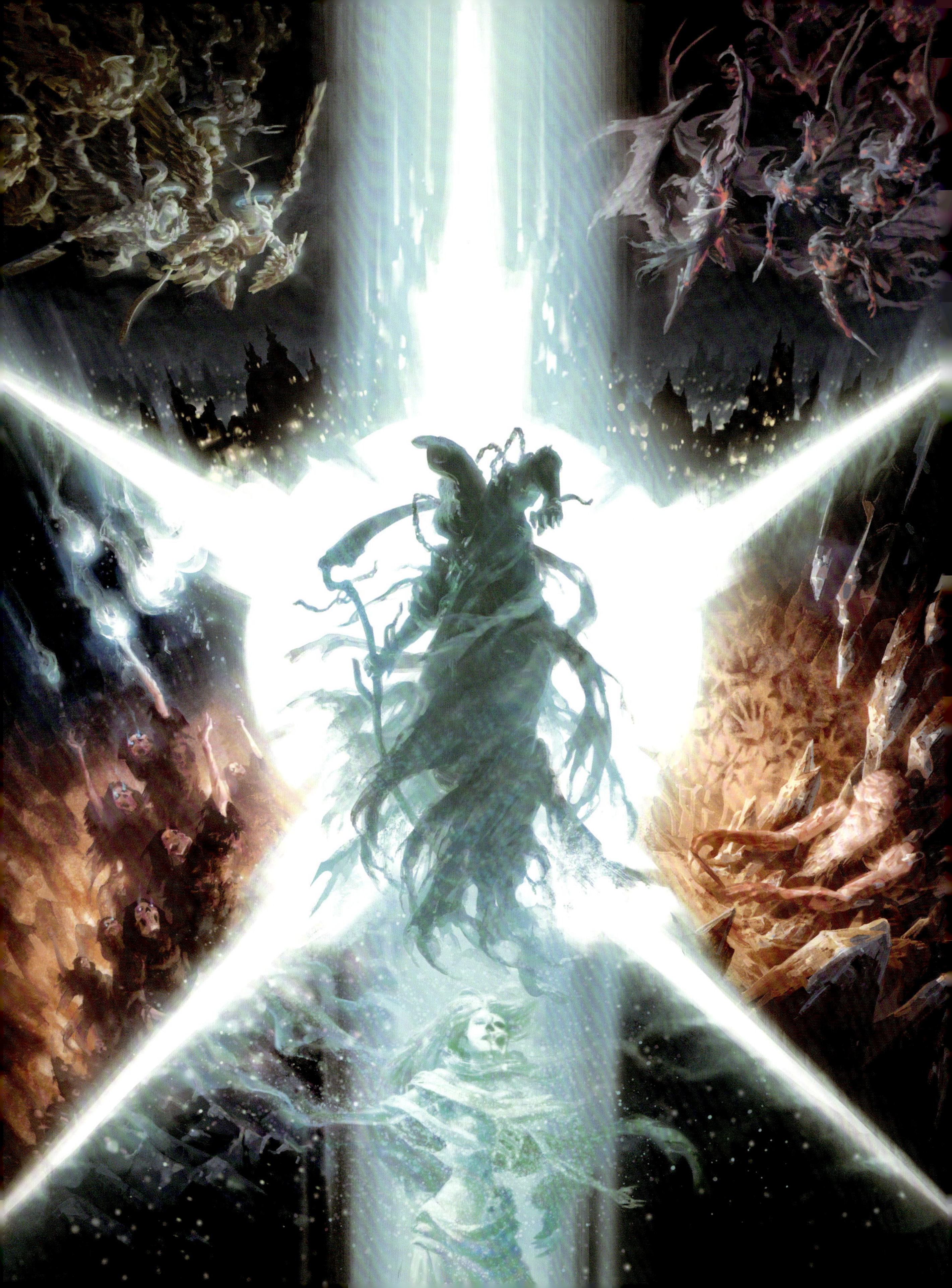

of lesser spirits. But yours is to be the harvest to sustain the Cosmos. Your fields shall be the realm of mortals, their hallowed blue glimmer your grain.

Then it is their remnants that are the spire of light in the city.

Yes. 'Tis called the Dirth Forge. By it their souls travel to Heaven and Hell.

What becomes of them?

The celestial war rages on.

The reaper looks at the sea of sorry beings, now thicker than before. In his rowing Death parts them to either side of the boat. The reaper watches as his oar presses them below the surface as he rows.

It is the fate of all mortals to be consumed.

All save what few I claim as mourners in my realm.

Then you are their salvation?

A hopeful question.

Can not you claim them all, Father?

The Celestials might notice the sudden absence of all their vital essence, yes?

Perhaps more can be mourners then.

Make no mistake, reaper: 'tis by the fire of mortal souls that all you have seen in my realm was made. 'Tis its energy by which you and all your kindred have been enspirited. Without it there can be no act of potency to realize even our most tepid aspirations. And so. Your father is no less culpable of atrocity than those most deplorable celestial agents of chaos or order.

Demons and angels.

Yes.

You speak of both with equal scorn.

You will find, my dreadbaern mortis, that there is no thing in existence so convenient as immutable good or evil. All that we are is contained within the character of our deeds, for every act is the sum of all our ruminations and turmoil. The valorous are revealed caitiffs in the instant of the foul act committed; oft the wicked engage in selflessness. Whence shall we be judged? The spirit's aura is a shifting spectra, when viewed over the span of its existence.

The Celestials are blind to the plights and joys of all save their own kin. 'Tis as true for demons, who delight in their eviscerations, as angels, who ruthlessly enforce their rigidity of law. They speak of etherea as Nameless to obfuscate the celestial heritage of mortal beings; thus is the nature of angels shown. And the instances are not few when I have witnessed a child of Heaven in an act of sadism against them.

In the end, they are the unrepentant profiteers of a system that squanders the creative essence of the universe and enacts the damnation to futility and suffering of an entire realm of beings, and they will fight to sustain it. For this they are no less worthy of scorn than their dark others, or myself, for though I have long sought means to unseat their reign, that the Cosmos be remade to one more equitable and productive, I do play my part in its ongoing iniquity. But 'tis the Celestials themselves who stood and fell against their own kin for the sake of hope of salvation of the Cosmos, and for this we do hallow the names of their Vanguard, even if we do not look well upon their dominion.

We will become a Vanguard also, Father.

Of this my doubts are fewer and fewer.

We will destroy all that threatens the city.

Perhaps.

Then the reaper hears a new sound. A faint hissing. It arrives from all around. The reaper sees that the clouds at the edge of the sky are now undercast by a sickly purple light. The thin line of the sea below it smolders in a violet blaze.

'Tis a cancer you see. 'Tis that which is your enemy.

The reaper sees the blaze has spread across the horizon all around them, broken only by the silhouettes of rocky outcrops jutting everywhere from the water.

A part of me has seen them.

No. 'Tis my own addition to this landscape of your mind. None yet extant have seen them save my self, and I have chosen to keep from you my memory of them.

The reaper looks to the withered vision of the boatman who is his father, now outlined by the purple gloom. The face is ancient such that the contours of his skull are visible through his aged flesh. His eyes are gouged black and hollow as those of the mortals in the sea. The reaper wonders from what part of him such an emanation could arise.

Why, Father?

Because such memories are rich with regret. Because you must do what I could not.

The reaper looks out to the horizon again. The blaze has grown more intense, closer.

They are the first of our kind.

Yes. And no. 'Tis as I have said: the mortis are a thing new to creation.

Death aims his oar in a sweeping gesture across the horizon.

They were made reapers of souls, as shall you become. But where you were made in possession of agency and memories of the living at your crux, and of parentage and your kindred to guide you to this becoming, they were given little more than need before I sent them to take their places in the great machine I had so proudly devised to please my masters. In this sense you are ensouled as no other spiritborn creature has been. I gave them no such foundation as yours from which to grapple with the realities of the Cosmos they would come to encounter as they sifted through the catacomb of mortal death.

What are these realities?

Death takes hold of the lantern and holds it out over the water. Its light grows, spreads over a sea now entirely composed of mortal forms. All screaming silently. All bereft of eyes. The reaper sees that the rocky outcrops are in fact many outgrowths of mortals striving to climb over their own writhing masses.

Where do they wish to go?

'Tis your vision . . .

They would seem a barbarous multitude, Father.

As often as they are given to selflessness.

I do not understand.

That you should wish to is the very thing that parts you from your predecessors. Alas, I can not lead you to better knowing of mortalkind, reaper. Their study has long been my own to undertake, and you will learn far more than I might express in your own forays into their realm—and by the unveiling of what peculiar memories of them you possess, as curiously it would seem you are able. But 'tis my great hope that you will come to see them as do I: children abandoned to their appetites by a Cosmos itself no less maligned, left to make what they might of their lot, to invent what realities they can fathom, to alternately embrace and diminish their others, to build, prevail, and fall alone in their darkness.

Death returns the lamp to the prow hook and its brilliance fades. The reaper sees the boat now cast violet from all sides by the encroaching horizon. It is shadowless light, as if by a moon above. The boat thuds now and again from the flailing of the mortals as they row steadily ahead.

Tell me of our enemy, Father.

Death ceases his rowing. He leans upon his oar in the violet dimness as they drift and bob on the sea of mortals. He looks out through the shadowy expanse. His hollow eyes seem to capture the light of the horizon. To smolder with its peakèd blaze.

'Twas I who once passed the veils to go into the mortal sphere. In the earliest epoch of my awareness, when they were a thing new to creation also, 'twas I who in their moments of death was their reaper. So was I named. And so do all of mortalkind hence retain knowledge of me in their deepest reaches of memory.

In that primordial time of them they were but few, and moving between moments I was there to receive their final breaths wherever they were relinquished. But ever more abundant did they grow, even as my concern was given ever more to the building of my Underworld. In time I grew cunning in my creations, and I made spirits to scour tirelessly their lands, to reap at Death's behest. One hundred was their number, as is yours, as was the Vanguard of old whose sacrifice I had come to discover, whose names I bestowed upon each of my creations to honor them.

So named, swiftly my reapers skirted the fabric of the realm of mortalkind to cut their gossamer cords, casting forth to their creator an ever richer bounty of souls. Indeed, 'twas by this the ravenousness of the Celestials was satisfied and the breadth of the Dirth Forge did grow to reach the dominant expanse you have witnessed.

But my creation of these first reapers would prove as much a failure of fatherhood as of sight. Though with time I had recast myself creator of realm and entity, I was myself created solely to facilitate the destruction of life. In my ignorance I made my reapers callow and dimensionless projections of my own baleful ordination. No sooner did they receive their names than were they sent from their home to become entangled in the infinite snarl of death that was their charge.

Much of what I first learned of mortals in that early time arrived by virtue of my sifting through their deeper selves as I swam in the pools of their souls. This I would come to ponder against my sight into the greater Cosmos, and as I began to make bolder use of etherea I found discovery in my own acts of creation. 'Twas then I began to populate my underrealm by other spirit creations, and by reclamation of mortal souls, they few whose singularity of worth moved me such that I could not bear to allow them squandered or enslaved by my masters.

Thus was I guided from the baser nature I had unwittingly bestowed upon my progeny, whose tutelage in my neglect of them became the violence and sadism that delivered them their greatest harvests of etherea. For indeed, as the mortals grew in abundance so too did the inventiveness of their self-mutilation. And thus evolved the appetites of my reapers, who came to delight in the flavor of souls and finally the power of etherea. Taking hold of it, they learned to pierce the spirit membrane that separated them from the living, and so doing began to sow the very death they reaped, destroying beyond need until there were but few mortals remaining.

All the while they sent ever more souls forth to their creator, who in his puerility and selfishness was only too happy to receive them. 'Twas only when this supply did wane by their own gorging upon it that I peered into the Mortal Realm and saw what they had done, and what they had become, and bore witness to the dreadsgrip they had brought into being.

The word invokes in the reaper an inward recoil. He thinks of the chaos kept within the strands of etherea. The shadows of peril within. Death nods as with approval.

Yes. We made you to fear the dreadsgrip. 'Tis good your instinct begs that you revile even its evocation. For 'tis a bane. 'Tis born by mortal souls in their uncoiling by the dawning horror upon their witnessing of the emptiness and futility of their fate. So do the mortis hear in it the cries of a thousand thousand voices undone, bereft of mind entire, wishing for but one thing alone: to become again. Gathered to measured use, all you have seen is sustained. But like the river that scours the canyon, the craving for its power burrows ever deeper into they who drink it unfettered, until at last 'tis their own spirits they consume.

Thus befell the first of your kind. Forged by misery in their becoming, they forgot the names they had been given and fell into their lust for etherea even as they came to revel in the potency of its expression to destructive purpose, to the great suffering of mortalkind. In their devouring of the innocent they devoured their own entities also, until finally their voices became as thin and desperate as the whispers they could not silence, arisen from the very soul elixir that could not sate them.

When I discovered what they had done I sealed them in the Underworld even as I lamented them, children betrayed by the myopia of their sire. Immediately they set upon the Forge, and much ruin did they visit upon my domain before I was able to cast them beyond the outlands, in the nebulous place where the edges of this realm have not yet reached. I hoped that in their exile they would come to learn the greater dimension of things. That in the shattermeir to come I could reach them, return them home.

Death takes up his oar and lowers it to pass through the sea of mortals. Where it touches their flesh it smolders purple, and from it a grimy fume arises. It spreads through the writhing forms like the span of a disease captured in a single moment. The reaper watches as it pours out over the expanse of the sea, dissolving the shifting mounds of figures until finally the last of these collapses into an oily stillness. The boat glides steadily through them by his father's rowing as he speaks.

'Twas a fool's hope. With the passing of an aeon I went to them in the amorphous beyond. I sought to touch that which I had once named as my children, but only found them gone. For in their banishment they had only seethed with fury against their betrayer, he who had shunned and starved them of their essence. They would have destroyed me. Hence have I shunned their voices and renamed them bael reivers, for even now do they devour this realm.
Can not they be cured of it, Father?

The vision of the boatman turns, regards the reaper. None other of his kind has yet presented such thoughts. Indeed, eagerly this one has drunk the essence of his telling of them. Death hears the shrewdness in his voice. But it does not eclipse the probity of him he senses also. He looks at the encroaching blaze of the horizon. Time wanes. He turns and begins again his rowing.

Your empathy does you credit, reaper. Would that I had had such a quality in the time of the making of your forebears; 'twas by my own poverty of it that they knew nothing of it themselves. But they are now become truly abominations of themselves, for in their need to destroy me they debased their last remaining potency: the hallowed names they had been given.
The names of the Vanguard?

Yes. Those that you found inscribed upon this very menhir. There is power in a name, as you shall soon enough discover. 'Tis there in which the summation of a character resides; where the deepest root of agency reaches, to which all memory is tethered. In this place of underlife, 'tis a thing that does not wither by the passage of time, so long as remembrance of it is kept. The breaking of their names was a denial of their place and past, of memory. Such was their hatred of me that it amplified a thousand-fold in the dreadsgrip of their terror and violence and woe. Impelled by this hatred the glyphs that once described their being they did shatter to enspirit their own twisted spawn—vile things assembled by what remains of the unfortunate entities that had fallen into their grasp, of spirit so dilute they are but wraiths driven by shadows of need.

The reaper scans the sky. The purple light from the smoldering horizon has spread across the full canopy of clouds. He looks beyond the boatman. In the gloom ahead he sees a large mass of land rising through the flat, oily stillness.

How many have they become?
We know not. The sum of their diluted essence is such that their presence is to me as they have felt always. It must be that they are become a great horde, and that they have found a way from exile, for the Underworld no longer grows. That they have not advanced already speaks to their intent: they would consume all, supplant my realm with the multiplicity of themselves. We can not allow this. Gethsemoni has sent emissaries to discover what they might at the edges of the outlands, but none have returned.

The hissing grows loud. Shadows now play over the boat by the violet flicker of the horizon. The reaper peers beyond it. What is left is something less than blackness. It is emptier even than an absence of light. A featureless void in which nothing can exist.

Then we must draw them to us.
Indeed.
How, Father?
You do so even now.
I do not understand.
The discovery of your name. Its grasping shall be as the usurping of theirs.

We are to be named in honor of the Vanguard also.

Yes. 'Tis a reclamation. By your will in the face of all that you have learned do you order the glyphs that once described those hallowed names, now tarnished and broken by the debauchery of the bael reivers. By your first utterance of your name it will be writ upon this menhir, and hereafter shall memory of you forever be kept. Thus is the reapers' chorus of naming an incantation to inaugurate our salvation or our doom, for in that very moment the bael reivers shall be stripped of the arcane potency of their names, and they will proliferate no more. The pillar of the Dirth Forge and their hatred of me shall be as twin beacons for them, and they will come.

The boat runs aground upon a shore of gleaming stones. It is a small island, little more than a craggy outcropping of boulders. They seem to crumble in the shimmering fester of the horizon. The hissing arrives from all sides.

And now 'tis time for you to continue alone, dear reaper, for I can not guide you beyond the shores of your own self.

How will I know which name to choose?

How is remade the grain of sand when dashed upon the rocks a mirror? When or where the light to meet it, why the eyes to see? Call out to the infinities, and e'en with ears attuned to the thinnest whispered melody you shall hear but the echo of your fear. Listen instead for the cords of thine own intents, and know by their strum you are made a being dear to creation as any other, whose rightful peregrination is all the Cosmos before you, the Underworld your home.

*　*　*

He is gone. The boat is gone. The shroud and mortal flesh I wore are gone. I stand on the shore alone, a reaper once again. It is narrow and encircles an immediate rise of broken boulders. Everywhere among them are polished pillars of stone. They stand tall against the purple sky and gleam by its light.

I look back out at the expanse. The black water now fumes purple within the blaze of the enclosing boundaries of my mindscape, as if a realm of its own pressed by an encroaching void to collapse. What might befall me should I choose merely to wait to witness it? Would I be swallowed by nothing and forgotten to oblivion, or fall nameless from the menhir?

I turn from it to climb the craggy rise inland. In this realm I will war, and then I will haunt the battlefields of another to gather the ghosts of its warriors. And when my father deems it so I will fight the Heavens and the Hells to deliver him a Cosmos beyond my apprehension. And so there are epochs of a kind very different from this one into which I have been born a warrior. Though but for its boundless conflict I would not exist, somehow it seems strange that I should be delivered to this one.

* * *

The rise proves to encircle a clearing in the center of the island. It is thick with what seem to be bloodied feathers, and in its center two figures lie still in what seems an embrace of death. I climb down the craggy slope and make my way to them. A spear is driven through one, its flesh charred and fouled with a sheen of black slime. Its claws are buried in the throat of the other, shredded stumps of wings protruding from its back.

The shadows deepen by the blaze of the devouring void. Beneath the hissing comes the sound of stone cracking, and pillars of rock rise from the surrounding crags to encircle me. Scratchings of glyphs appear over their surface, glimmering blue as if each were inhabited by the souls of mortalkind.

I look to the broken forms at my feet, and their eyes meet mine in the gloom, though they do not otherwise stir. Then the hissing abruptly ceases, and in my mind there arises a corded voice.

It seeks the Cosmos.
It is the Cosmos.
Hath the Vanguard delivered us?
Honor the Vanguard.
Our song persists.
Our voices persist.
All is our domain.
All our shame.
What would it know of creation?
None so nameless.
Ask.

I think of my father's guiding voice and the many things he expressed that I did not understand. I wonder about my kindred and the questions that we might unravel when we are reunited. I think of the bael-reivers and their anger and the suffering they have inflicted. My question is simple and it sounds foolish in my mind, but among the things my father spoke of it is the thing I least understand, and so I ask it.

"What is it to be innocent?"

All falls to silent darkness but the blue glow of the glyphs. One by one they fade until but three remain, pictograph rudiments of the cuneiform script of the menhir, burning with ethereaic light. A hand. A gate assailed by twin arrows. A figure upon a pedestal with crossed arms numbering four.

The glyphs align and pass through the darkness, and they burn through my flesh and sinew to engrave their epitaph amidst the thaumaturgy inlayed on my bones, and I know that I have been named.

De. To create.

Mi. Honor.

Ta-il. Clamor of battle.

I am Demithyle.

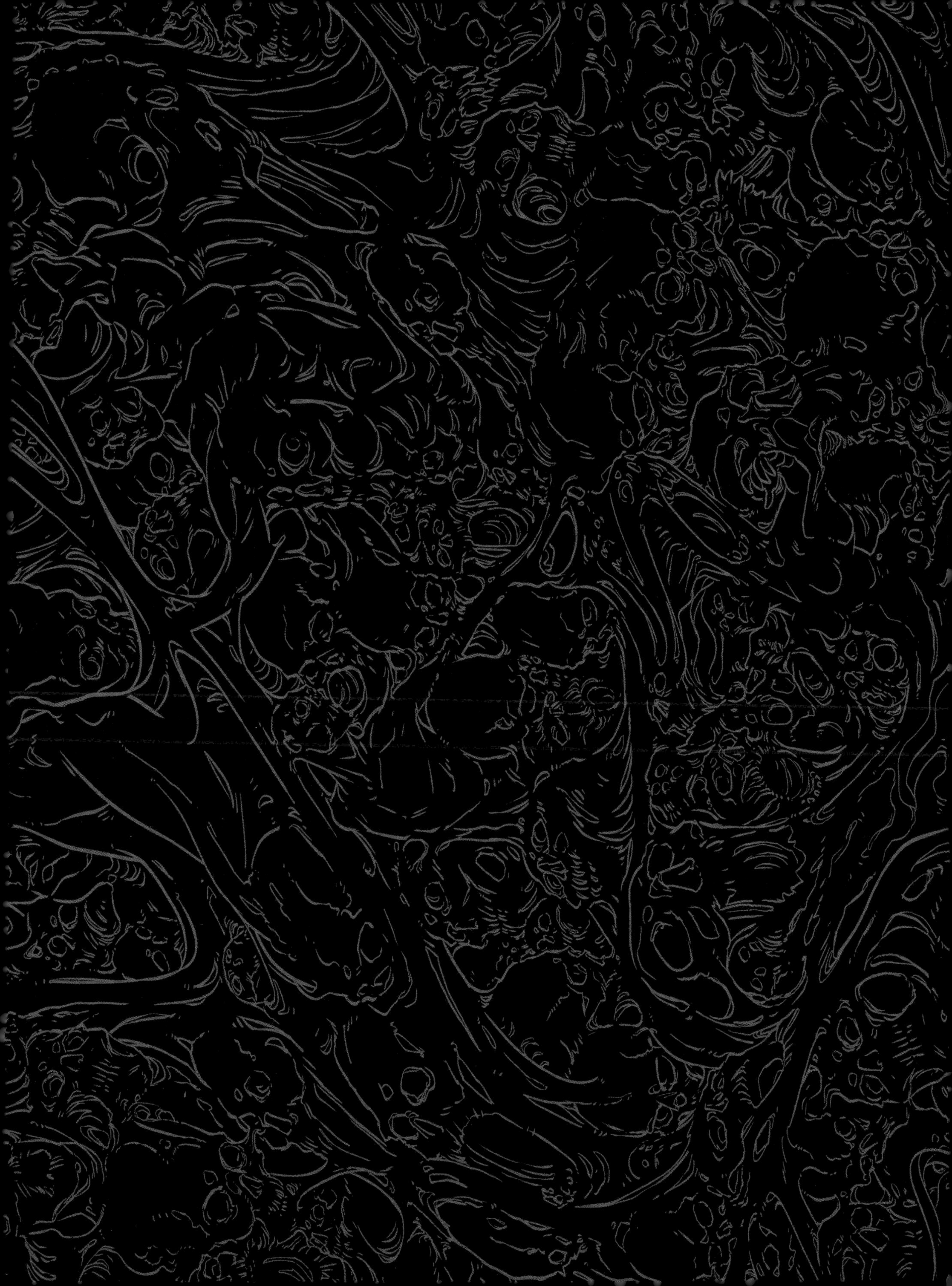

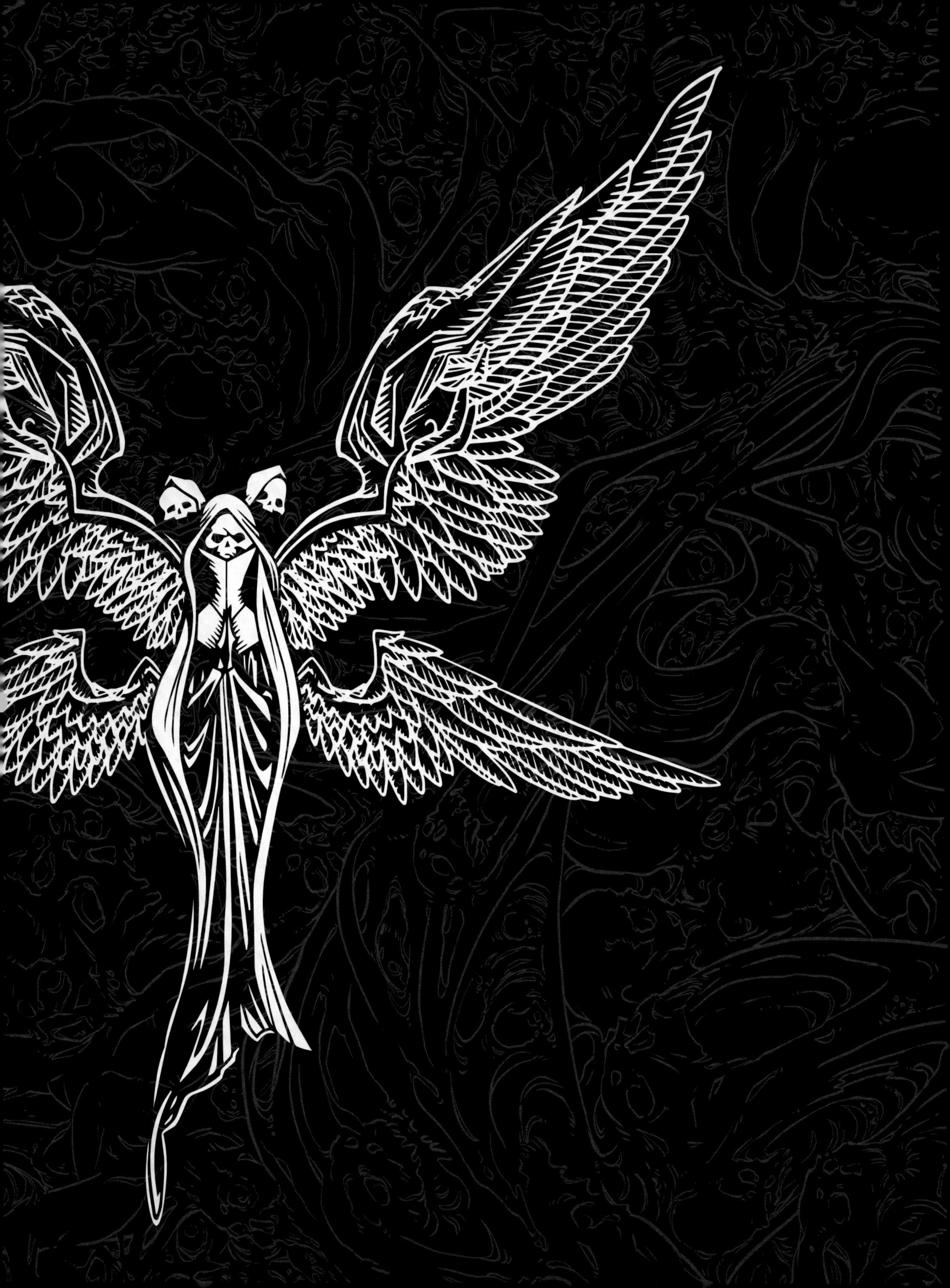

V.
A WITNESS

The old soldier rode over the rubble in the thinning blush of the darkmeir. A fog had descended. Barely visible above was the spread of chaotic nebulae that served as the Underworld's night sky. How long had it been since they'd left the outer wallows? He could only guess. This far from the city, there were no gloomsayer belltolls to mark out the passage of time. Only the slow wax and wane of shadow and aurorae, a maddeningly irregular rhythm he'd never been able to quite work out. And now this strange sog. An oily film had already begun to bead over the metalwork of his brigandine. He allowed himself a hissing sigh, watching his puff of mist waft away. At least he needn't worry about the chill. An advantage of being dead.

He looked out over the wet expanse, searching his memory for landmarks. It'd been long enough since last he'd laid eyes on the outlands that he'd worried over an altered landscape. But apart from the appearance of the odd broken effigy or half-buried temple he didn't recognize, it was as pocked and precarious as he remembered. Just a big open dump of craggy, weeded ruins. He scraped a hand through the tuft of nettles at his nethernag's withers and she bristled beneath him. He had to give the shroudreive credit. Seeing these skelliform elk-mounts scuttle out from their gloomy hovels, he'd taken their needle-legged profiles for mere macabre imagination. But this one had struck through the terrain like a colt in a grassy valley. No steed that had ever carried him in life could've hoped to pick its way through this stuff.

With a couple taps to her shoulder he directed her toward a rise ahead. It proved a sort of stone colossus, from who knows where or when, broken up into a rugged hill and overgrown with creeping redweed. He gave a click and she grabbed the leading edge of the hill with the hooked toes of her forelegs and they flowed up to the summit, smooth as a lazy river.

He peered out from the shadow of his helm, seeking through the murk the familiar profile of the hermitage, absently squeezing the moisture from his cloak. But the nethernag shook her bony head beneath him, sending out a grayish spray that undid most of his work.

"Just a bit of weather, eh?" he said with a papery laugh. He gave a thick pat against her haunch. "Don't worry, skella-kess. We've friends out this way. A lonely lot, they are. Fair bet they're giddy as fish come the sight of us. Get you seen to sooner than late, and dry as you like. Might even have a sipper of the old cold nectar ready for their good cousin Egregin, 'fore we get at what's been what out here in the weirdland. Then we'll see you on back to our sluvvidess, eh?"

She bristled again, and he gave another scratch at her nettles. He looked back toward the city. In fact, they should've run into someone by now. The light of Daer Gholl was only just visible at the far horizon, bleary through the fog like a sapphire bloom at the edge of the sky. They'd ridden hard without rest for at least a fortmeir, outpacing any word that could've been sent of their arrival. But he'd assumed his approach would be sensed, or at least seen. That a rider would be sent to greet him, and he wouldn't have to remember how to find one little cloister tucked in amongst all the nothing. But no one had come.

Something out here had set the Queen to brooding, enough to send a dozen riders out in every direction. He'd guessed her mind when she'd summoned him—there'd been stirrings of something uncouth at the fringes of the realm, and he alone of the few who'd chosen existence in the outlands had returned to dwell again in the city. But he'd wondered at the pleasure she seemed to take in delivering him again to the clan of doddering eremites he'd left behind out here. He now understood that she'd known, even if he had not, the place they still occupied in his heart. Much of that earliest time of his mournerdom he'd forgotten. Amidst the mordant voices of soulborn long dead, he had awakened to many bitter realities hidden by his mortal pall, fought to reconcile the stalemate of reason and atrocity that immured the Cosmos, and learned to recognize what simplicity of existence was at its marrow. They who'd cursed the realm of abject folly that restrained the living as often as they told their tales from every where and when across it, with a wryness that could not hide their longing for what beauty they had touched there.

How he'd found himself among them he could never recall. Somehow he'd wandered out here in a fugue of incipient undeath who knows how long after being scooped out of the soul well. Imagine finding the afterlife a horrific maelstrom of screaming terror, only in the next moment to be breaching the grave, reborn without breath into the grimmest possible place in existence. Face-to-bloodless-face with the apparently benevolent embodiment of everything mortalkind had been given reason to fear, few wits did he possess for much of anything beyond a querying stammer, to say nothing of any presence of mind to ask his patron what about his unvarnished old soul had caught his eye among so many unfortunate others. It was all he could do to go lurching toward the kindly, spectral faces of the fostermurden presented to take him to their care. Finding these faces only illusory projections offered for his benefit over a physical presence that could be described only as the stuff of nightmares seemed by then a detail.

Not that he'd expected to find himself surrounded by virgins swathed in wine and butter and the like. The same priests who'd promised such things as reward for a soldier's devotion to land and potentate would've had him drowned a heretic for describing even the most mundane detail of this underlife. He'd never had much use for such doctrine of the state. How small it seemed now. How . . . obsolete. Time here was as removed from the Mortal Realm as memory; last he checked, the entire continent of his homeland had long ago been swallowed by the sea.

He'd never seen a gray soup like this in the Underworld before. Coupled with the eerier-than-usual quiet, he had more than enough portent to bring back. As far as he knew, no other spirit or soulborn dwelt anything close to this far out. Likely the others wouldn't have the same warning.

There, a stutter of light, within a swath of shadow in the distance. Impossible to tell whether a structure or what. He watched a moment but the shape remained flat and unbroken. Too large to be the cloister, unless they've built it up somehow. He clicked, and shifting his weight forward they descended the slope toward it. Not much to aim at, but it'd do, leastwise to prevent him having to admit they were lost.

They rode on, listening. There was only the light wind and the mild scraping of spidery toes over stone. The rippled valley seemed to flatten in the thickening haze. Droplets collected and fell from his helm. Steady rivulets of gray oil drew over his nag's bony head.

The cold light flashed again, this time defining the familiar outline of the lone stone structure the order had adopted as their hermitage. It seemed enclosed within the shadow, revealed now as some kind of a thick fume rising from the surrounding area. He quickened their pace, keeping his gaze locked on the shadow. It seemed to waver with an odd liquidity, as if by the heat of an unseen fire. Then the nag halted unbidden, and raising her skelliform head she cocked it to one side, and a moment later there came a seething whisper.

Between the rise and fall of the thin gray wind it persisted. A vaguely purple shimmer swirled within the blackness of the fume. He should turn them back. Now. The susurrus returned, and within it a sound he'd thought never to hear again. A sound native to the Mortal Realm, arisen from the zealotry of the sacerdotal inquisitors he'd rejected in life: the weak, defeated moans of prolonged pain.

With a word of command they soared far through the air, closing half the distance to the cloister in a single leap. He slid down from the nethernag's back even as she alighted, drawing his sword as he did so. The pale fog was here like a cloud of wet ashes. Through it the voices wormed clearly from the direction of the hermitage. Bits of shredded tentcloth flapped lightly from splintered poles around its sole standing structure, partially collapsed within the strange enveloping fume no more than a spear's throw away by.

Looking back to make sure the nag stood fast, he pressed through the greasy effluvium until something like a thick rotten stalk of vegetation met his toe. With his next step there was a soft, silent crunch, and looking down he saw the remnant of a face bulging out from beneath his sabaton.

Pieces like it lay everywhere in lumps. He coughed, a flapping of desiccated lungs in his chest. There was a heaviness to them, and a vagueness of pain thus far unknown in his underlife. He coughed again, and this time there was pain enough to blur his vision. When his sight cleared he stood staring outward beyond the hermitage, toward the outward expanse, the vague irregularities of what was left of the place he'd known seemingly smothered by a waver he suddenly recognized as the fade beyond the edge of the world.

What expanse was visible through the murk abruptly ended just beyond the outward edge of the hermitage. A wall of nebulous nothing that extended as far as he could see. So impossibly close. How could it be so close? It was like looking into a fearful oblivion, as if touching it he'd be swallowed from existence, instantly forgotten by all as if he'd never been.

The Underworld was decaying.

There was no knowing whether the others would discover this. He must return to Illverness. He looked back at his nethernag, shifting nervously, drenched in the sloppy haze a dozen paces away. He looked again toward the cloister. Beneath the light wind the scathing whispers persisted, laced with the suffering of his mortalkin friends.

In a moment he was pressing through the thick abbey doors, and as they closed behind him the voices seemed to fall beneath the low whistle of the breeze. There was a terrific stench. Like tarfume and belching corpses, reminiscent of mortal battlefields seated deep in his memory, yet besoiled still fouler by something he couldn't place.

Light fell through a partial collapse in the ceiling that left timber strewn over the firepit in the center of the hall. Sword raised, he made his way toward it. Everything was shattered and covered with a black muck. Globules of it floated between shadows. He kicked through the fire pit. Dead ashes, long cold. Thin shadows crossed it, shifting slightly. He looked up. Viscera strung across rafters. They draped down in the pale light like a thick cabling of abandoned webs.

A dull sheen drew him toward the darker recesses, where he found the corroded remnant of a weapon peeking out from one of several wet husks slapped into the corners. He knelt to examine the remains but could identify little. But then from one of them a slight glint of yellow caught his eye, and grasping into the formless sludge he retrieved what proved to be a thick gold coin.

He wiped it clean with his thumb. Its faces were worn and scratched. A totem. Once his sole possession, given by the Alltaker in his first moment of awareness following his reclamation. The memory of his life it contained had often carried him, kept him from despair.

But with time his existence in the Underworld made the span of his mortal coil seem less and less real, less so even than dream—an illusion of comedy and tragedy contrasted by everything he had come to understand.

Looking at the coin now, he realized that giving it up to the order was as much to free himself finally of its connection to the absurdity of mortality as prevent his growing cynicism from sullying this last vestige of his life he truly cherished.

He'd left it for them when he'd gone to offer his service to the Court. Who was this? Jearith? Sevelice? Had she kept it with her all this time? Had she tried to claim it at the last, to save it from whatever in the dank abyssal fuk had happened here? He stood, stared over the putrid remains of his friends. Words befitting their loss escaped him. All he could think was: This wasn't supposed to happen here.

He slipped the coin inside his glove and tucked it against his palm. "Thank you, my old friend," he said.

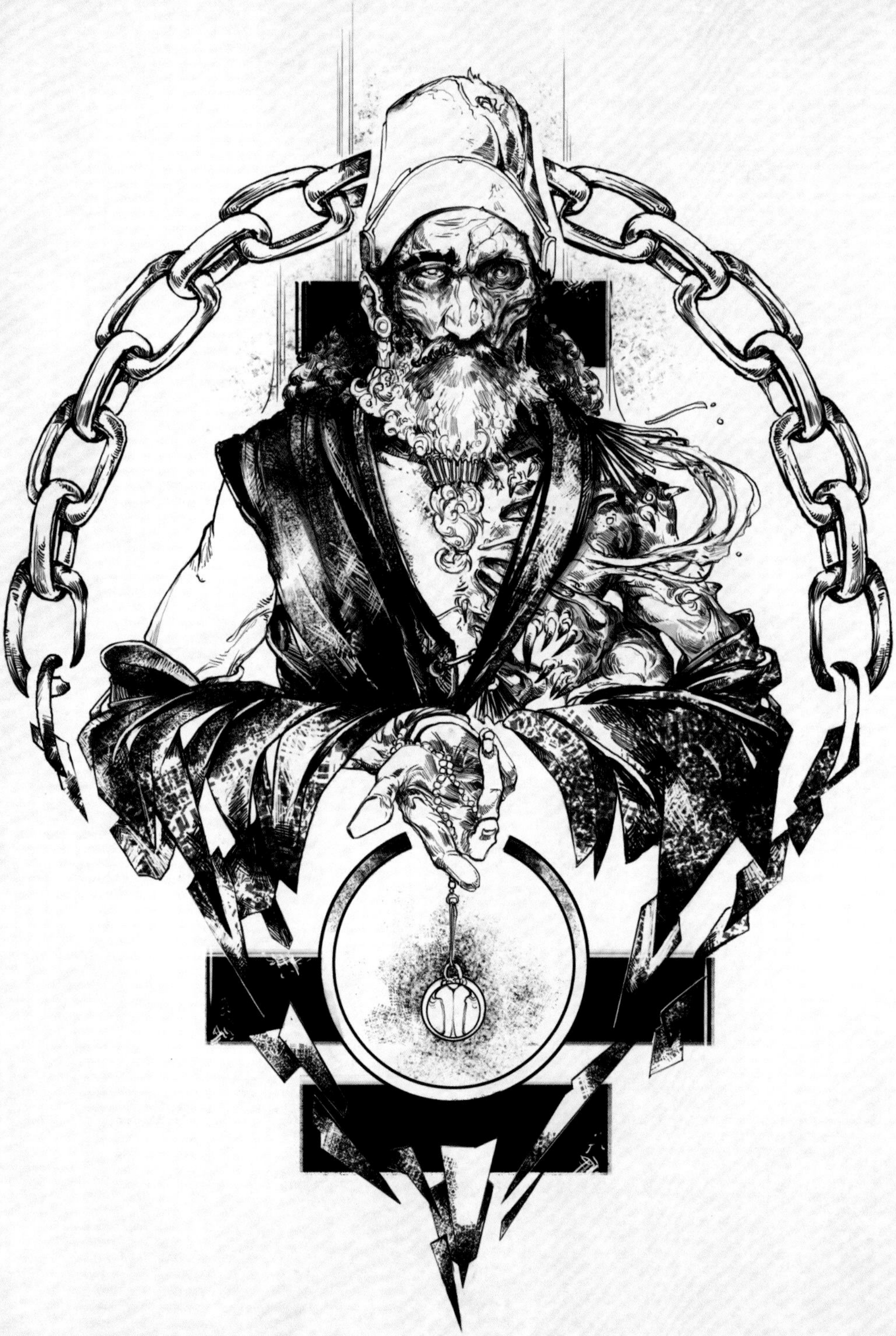

There was a low, chromatic glow, but glancing round he saw nothing of its source. And then looking down he found himself bespeckled with violet pinpricks of light. He brought out a torch, and with a word it bathed the room in a greenish-white spiritfire that pressed the swarm of globules away from him. Within its central sphere of light he saw that the leather of his brigandine was completely saturated and its plates were now mottled everywhere with small patches of black foam, bubbling silently beneath a sheen of filmy residue. With another word he left the torch hanging in the air and, bringing up his swordarm, he tugged at the clasps of his bracer and the second one tore away from the metal splint at the rivet. Inspecting it he found the leather rotted through, and he held it to the light to reveal a gleaming constellation passing through it. Cursing, he let it fall to the ground and pulled up the sleeve of his mail. His dead flesh glistened metallic gray. He grabbed the torch from where it floated and with a wave extinguished it, and in the gloom the cadaverous silhouette of his bare arm was painted with streaks of faintly incandescent purple.

He grabbed a wad of his cloak and mopped at the arm, but the veins of diseased incandescence remained. When he pressed to scrub it away the corrupted tissue pulled easily apart, exposing the slimy bones beneath it. Cursing again, he tore the flesh the rest of the way free and dropped it to slap to the floor.

He looked back toward the entrance. He needed to get out of there. Gethsemoni and the Court must be warned. He thought of his nag. Whatever this stuff was, it must be what was making the fog, and they'd traveled at least a full meir through it. And there was no way to know how far in it might have grown since. He'd be lucky not to disintegrate into sludge before he ever made it in from the outlands, to say nothing of reaching the fleshbaths on his own legs.

The whistle of the wind died away momentarily, and from the far end of the cloister, at the threshold to the lower reach, came again the woeful moans, now accompanied by a manic, sibilant chatter. He looked at the remains of his comrades. An armory had been kept in the catacomb. Its door was thick. If anyone was still extant, they would be there. Trapped perhaps, or waiting. Igniting his torch again he made his way to the threshold and rounded the stone stairs, following the sound of the voices down to a near-complete darkness that seemed to press against the spiritlight of his torch. Only a sphere of oily particulates was illuminated, now so dense they collected to stream down his body wherever he moved. He could hear the sizzling of the corrosion of his helm. Waving clear a path vaguely in the direction of the armory he shuffled forward, ignoring the flap of a greave at his ankle as its leather strapping failed. The cries and the wheezing voices were louder, and after a few paces their discordance seemed to draw into greater focus until prevailing over the scrape of his sabatons on the slimy stone their madness was revealed:

. . . here the namelesss fires arise to burn to burnnn the heart of usss abandoned by the one who hated usss created usss aswim in death the father's sssoulsss creation dead all that we had once given him isss dead we sssuckle at his cursssed realm our teeth upon the ruined teat of him to bleed the namelesss bleed the wither of his phallusss maimed to bleed the namelesss free of all to wither all his sssoulsss to drink all of them oursss to drink all that he has created drunken oursss the namelesss fire the namelesss firrre . . .

The meaning of the words skated from him even as they met his ears. But the ferocity of their piteous hatred needled into his mind, where the sound of a mewling babe then arose, and the sight of black trees in a winter forest closing round it as upon his horse he looked a final time to the place he'd left his newborn child to die, turning away as its voice receded until it could only just be heard below the slow crunch of hooves. He gripped his sword tightly as the vision settled into his memory. A swell of self-loathing threatening to overwhelm him. It seemed as if all the foulness of his mortal life that he'd buried deep within himself had at last been brought out to be witnessed. That he should continue to exist after such a recrimination of his nature . . . better to cut out his soul. Release it to the obligation of worthier entities. It could be his only absolution. Already he'd altered his grip to rest the tip of his sword between the splints of his brigandine. But when he moved to grasp it finally with his other hand, to pierce the cavitous void that contained his soul, he felt the coin press against his palm.

There was a low rumble at his feet; somewhere in the darkness, the clatter of toppling sundry. He lowered his sword, and squeezing his hand closed over the coin the voices ebbed and the vision receded and its artifice was revealed. No. This was no memory of his life. He knew himself, who he'd been. In fact he'd killed to prevent such a thing, more than once. He would do so again . . . He grasped at his head in the darkness, trying to shake it free of the lingering, shapeless anger. What barbarity had been committed against them to sustain such a frenzy of hatred as to so completely swallow any who heard it and force them to succumb to its recrimination? As the last vestiges of the vision released him the hissing voices from the darkness returned to their dissonance, and he could hear for the first time the wounded agony of loneliness buried behind their acid. But his pity was stayed by the desperate moans that returned to him also, and with them images of his friends in helplessness and pain. An anger of his own then welled, and grasping his sword he strode through the darkness and spying a vagueness of light went to it to find that it spilt from beneath the armory door.

    He opened it.

    The armory was gone.

    Its floor was a broken ledge that fell away to a gaping sinkhole that had swallowed the entire wing of the cloister. Elements of ancient buried architecture jutted from layers of exposed strata packed solid with bones. Pieces of it fell away through a thick fume that billowed up from below in oily black knots, twisting incandescent veins of purple within them. Every surface was slathered with a claggy accumulation of glistening sludge, as if a residue left by the boiling down of an enormous vat of flesh. A conglomeration of hideous lamentations seemed to arrive from everywhere amidst the sound of slimy shifting and the perpetual cracking of bones.

    Cautiously he stepped the rest of the way inside, and reaching the edge of the pit he looked down into it.

    It was like staring into the throat of a headless corpse, writhing and viscous with putrefaction, a ball of black worms nested within some kind of resinous scaffolding here and there affixed to the strata. A dozen physicalities of Underworld fauna and mourner alike lay entwined, fused to a single, ceaselessly shuddering mass, all ravaged by a glowing purple ooze that seemed at once to dissolve and replenish their flesh. Those he could see still with heads intact gaped their jaws silently, until jolted by some sweeping pulse of exertion their bodies were split to expose glimmers of soulfire quickly leeched away by a ubiquitous swelling of veiny growths, leaving their flesh to reseal with a congealing of black fluid as they sobbed with the pain of it, eyes rolling with despair.

    He backed away from the edge, groping behind him for the doorway of the armory. But the veins pulsed again to the renewal of pained whimpers from below, and staring down into the mound of throbbing torment he grasped for some remnant sense of they who had been his friends. He found only the meander of fragmented souls as tributaries of their essence trickled inward and down into an ulcerous cavity at the center of the mass, the thin blue of their soul light concentrating amidst a plunging encirclement of huddled, misshapen forms that twitched and jerked as if in reflex by its passing through them. And flooding deep into the core the light bled finally to darkness round a hulking silhouette nested in a midden of splintered bone, to the flaring of purple fire within its skelliform hollows, clearing staring back at him.

His hand found the doorframe even before he'd turned. As he stepped through it the pale light flashed again from the pit, spilling his shadow over the walls of the catacomb, revealing them crowded with the soulless husks of his friends. He felt his way through the darkness as quickly as he was able, shedding bits of armor as more of his strapping failed, and finding the stairs he scaled them at a run. By the time he reached the main hall he was running flat out, but when held out his hand to slam through the door the bones of his arm shattered where he'd torn away his flesh and he crashed into it hard with his shoulder as he tumbled through.

As he struggled to stand his nag was suddenly there in the dank pall of the mist, creaking her alarm through bony mandibles now pocked and serrated with corrosion. He hooked his arm round her neck and hoisted up his leg and she heaved him up, and bracing as best he could he set her immediately to loping over the rough and slippery terrain.

But barely had they escaped the darkening mist shroud when they found themselves riding against a sudden roaring gale, and his mount was obliged to halt and brace low. Gripping her withers with his remaining hand, the old soldier turned back to witness fog and fume alike blown clear from the landscape, unveiling the breadth of its decay to the encroaching void. High over the collapsed segment of the cloister there now floated what seemed to him an enormous fragment of hewn obsidian. Even as he marked the odd hollowness of its silhouette, it began to rotate, faster and faster, until the depth of its black was as a featureless tear in the veil, and tendrils of the black fume suppressed by the gale drew up toward it, seeming momentarily to coalesce to a shadowy, almost angelic figure.

The ground rippled beneath them, and the air was shaken by a terrific shrieking as from all across what was now the outermost reach of the Underworld thin streaks of ethereaic light speared upward into the sky, each perhaps a league apart into the distance. And then up from the cloister there shot a single sliver of sapphire blue directly toward the empty blackness that had been the stone.

The shudder of explosions that ripped across the sky bled from it all light, and the old soldier found himself sailing blindly through the air before the ground caught him to a burst of cracking throughout his body as his helm was sent clattering away. He screamed in pain, but the sound was overwhelmed by the shrieking from the direction of the cloister, ferocious in its sustained fury, and fighting to raise himself he saw what looked like immense braids of bony viscera smashing up through the structure, sending heavy blocks of masonry crashing outward amidst a thick surge of bilious fume that poured from it over the land, now abruptly absent of wind. In its path was his nag, struggling to right herself, and doing so she bounded for him only just as it overtook her.

All he could do was watch as the fume swept toward him, once again obscuring the landscape. The shrieking ceased. All fell quiet but for the furtive scrapes of his nag as she sought him through the dense haze, but before he could call to her there was a flurry of scraping and she cried out, and then he heard nothing.

The fume thickened still deeper, steaming now throughout with the sickly purple incandescence, like heedless ghasts drawn out from the soil of an ancient battlefield. And into his mind seeped the scathing voices once again:

. . . oursss the name the name the name they take the name the name of usss they take the namesss of usss alone alone of usss of oursss of usss alone alone alooonnne alone the namesss of usss of usss alonnne the name of usss the naaammme . . .

Another burst of pain, this time in his legs, and he looked to see them crushed by a massive bony stalk. Its claws worked at his flesh, twisting it, separating it to fibers it then peeled away in strips to his hip before crushing down into them again. Through his screams of agony his flailing hand somehow found the hilt of his sword, and with a hard downward cut he broke through his bones. The claws yanked the legs away into the murk, and he stabbed the sword into the ground beside him as reaching inward he compelled his own etherea to pour into the blade, letting loose a blast of glimmering blue that propelled him backward, only to be plucked from the air by a skewering shaft of bone.

He felt himself being drawn weightless through the opaque gloom until all around him there fumed a thousand violet eyes, carnivorous and cold and obscene, and the voices burrowed ever deeper into his being, probing for the essence of his self, needling for his name, his final thought blooming only as a need to bury it, press it down beneath all else given over to desire to scream, to rend, *to ssscream the want only for devouring of the namelesss sssire of usss for wrath of war we bring the namelesss call of usss we bring we bring we bring the sssire again to witness usss in failure of his flesh and teeth and soul of metal bone and blood and blood and blood and blood and blood and blood and blood and blood and blood and blood . . .*

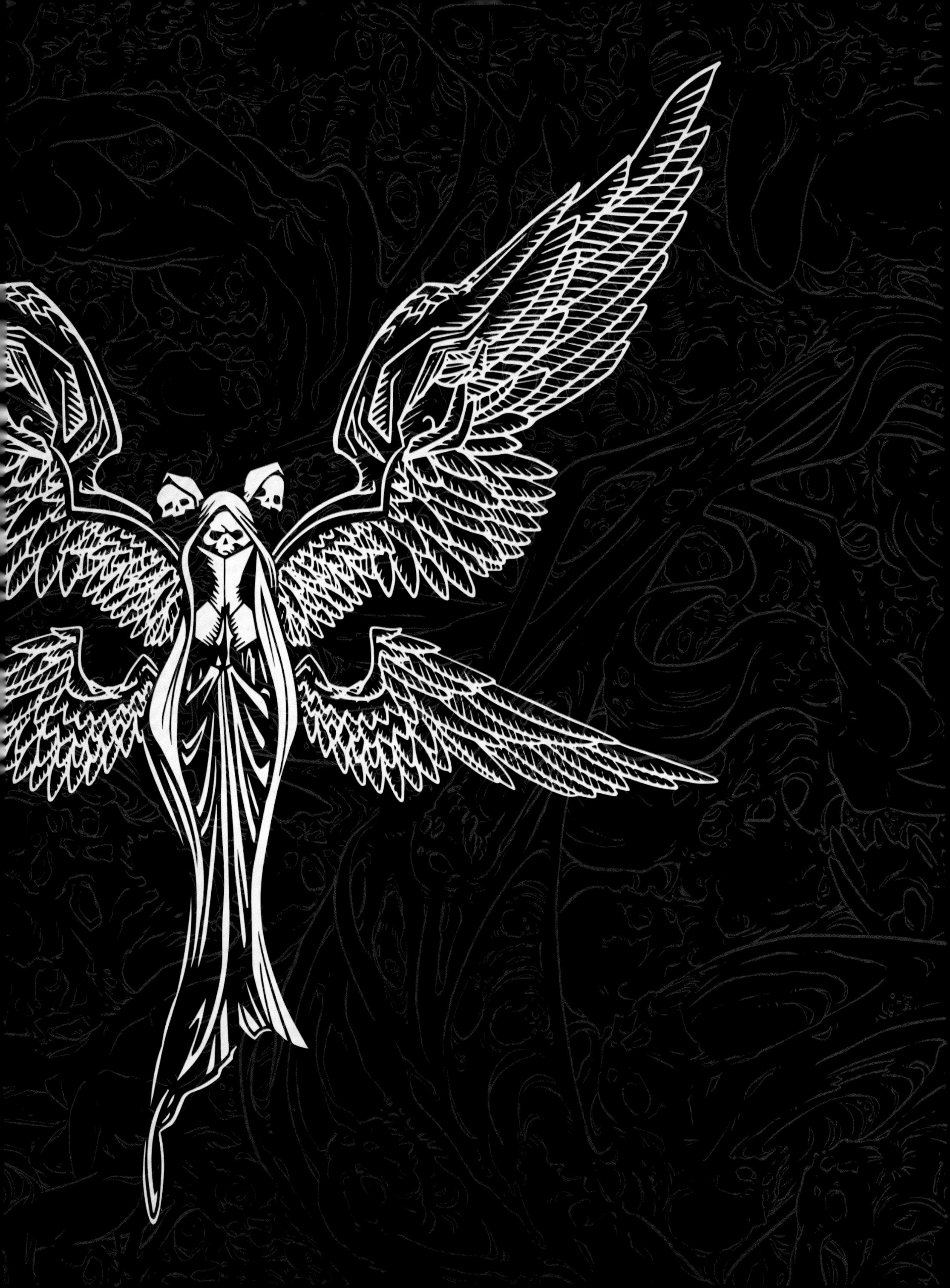

VI.
A SWORD

How long before they reach the city?

Not more than a fortmeir.

So soon . . .

We are fortunate. 'Twould seem they have made their hordes for the slow devouring of us. Do not doubt they will overwhelm and destroy us at the last, but they can not quickly traverse the wallows in force. Your emissaries?

None have returned.

Then we are indeed surrounded.

. . .

You would not have sacrificed them.

I knew not of thine intent to draw the baelreivers, Alltaker. The emissaries were chosen for their swiftness in matters of intrigue. Perhaps their presence would have gone unnoticed . . .

The die was cast the moment we felt the Underworld cease in its growing, for we knew that it could only be they had begun to devour us. The knowing of their extent at the fringes of the realm only affirms their multitude. 'Twas the very names by which I bound them to the void in exile that granted them command enough of their own spirits to so dilute them in their propagation; each moment in which I did not act could only thin our hope of standing against them.

Many will perish in their advance.

Yes.

'Tis to be a defense of the city, then. May our children prevail.

And so they must.

Hast thou not found them surprising?

Indeed, Gethsemoni. They are a fascinating lot. I did not expect them to be so . . .

Mortal?

Perhaps. Certainly if judging only by their projections in the menhir. The one named Melthis manifested for us a rather salacious brothel. Not unlike your own flesh baths, in fact.

One named thee custodian, I hear.

Hm. When next I chance to find Ellianastis I shall be certain to speak with her about that.

I would not have thought it wise to include among their memories those of the Celestials.

Nor I.

Then 'tis true they are able to witness them?

Each has their gift. 'Twould seem this one alone possesses such inward sight. The visions of memory come to him unbidden; he experiences them as if they unfold in that very moment.

Curious. Xiall will decry it as a distraction.

Time will tell. Certainly whatever trial she has devised for them in Mortis Veth shall do so. In fact a recollection has already borne him knowledge of the Vanguard long hidden from my view, more of which I shall seek to uncover elsewhere, when I am able.

'Twould seem a strange boon, then.

Perhaps.

Mortis Veth. I envy not their eternity. Time will tell, indeed.

We at least shall be none the wiser of its extent. Only they who are within the influence of her orb keep aware of time's renewal, when upon each failure 'tis set again at the fore. To our knowing, they shall be returned to us after but the span of their final triumphant effort.

Itself an insidious unknown.

And yet we must not begin to doubt. Strong have we made our children, but to face the bael reivers they must become stronger still. Whatever her design for them in Mortis Veth, Xiall will ensure their conquering of it will be as a force unified. Trust, Gethsemoni. Your sister will not fail us.

Perhaps she takes inspiration from her sojourn through the labyrinth.

What?

She was seen leaving it. Curious that she was able to enter it at all, to say nothing of her somehow traversing it.

Hm.

Yes. Apart from its simpering keeper, is not Ruse the sole entity who may travel it freely? Something to ponder, perhaps, if not to risk disturbing her in its inquiry. The reapers have been warned to give wide berth to her at the Calvum Harrows, yes?

Hm? Yes. No. What mind she does not pay to the unwinding of phantoms from the rarest of her relics is absorbed by plaiting them into those crafted by her weaverden. She is not likely to leave the forges, and the reapers will not be long enough in the Harrows to stray there. Nor would she even notice them amidst the dissonance of soot and hammerstrike, unless they should be foolish enough to impede her eyes or hands.

Then they have been brought there only to seek among her armaments.

For the moment, yes. Having paired themselves to arms, they shall be taken swiftly to Mortis Veth. All they must know of their sanctuary shall be delivered upon their return to it, as they begin their preparations to confront the hordes.

An ominous forecast.

We shall see.

* * *

For an aeon or more the sword had waited, drifting weightlessly amidst uncountable artifacts of war hoarded in the Calvum Harrows. A thousand thousand times it had traversed the otherwise empty corridors and halls, disturbed only by what breezes hushed through the cracks and portalways, feeling no desire, no anticipation, content merely to participate in the simple passage of time.

Then, all around it, the reliquary stirred. It opened its walls round the emergence of many new chambers. It grew up its ceilings and raised from them hollow towers as high as the city walls. Stone steps and winding stairways of wrought iron were spun from an emergence of galleries round a main hall, down from which unfurled vacant tapestries and banners of solid black, as if each awaited embellishment by the deeds of coming occupants. Long stone tables and racks for gear and trappings appeared, and from either side of a long firepit twin rows of columns twisted up past a crowning rim of empty entablatures to buttress an arcade of rafters above. Historied weapons both elaborate and plain caught the firelight as they drifted about the hall: rapiers, claymores, scimitars, and saifs; narrow lances and wicked halberds; shishpars and maces, misericordes and krisses; warclubs of ancient wood and stone; mauls of lead and iron.

Many carried reflections of their service, imprints of death or glory from the hands of their wielding masters kept everlasting by the sleeping umbra within them. What manner of spirit aurified the sword, or whether the blade had been forged with it or later enchanted to exist as such, it did not know. If it had ever been given a name, the meaning of it had decayed with time, and so the name itself was forgotten. But it was this awareness that perceived the coming of the reapers.

These were entities newly made as warriors. This was to be their home. It was not long before the arms called to them, and the desire to be possessed awakened within the sword and it too cast out its emanation of self as it searched for affinity among the arrivals. The warriors made their way from the main hall through the crossing corridors, probing walls, exploring chambers and hidden vestibules where they found them, and ascending the towers they gazed outward over their city as if relishing their presence in peace in this place that they knew was made to be their own. And then one by one, drawn by the singular warring essences that resided within those weapons that called to them, each warrior found a consonance to suit them and, laying claim to their weapon, was made complete.

But the sword's was a narrower voice lost among the warring cries, for though it knew well the fury and desperation of battles won and lost, the parrying clash and spark of its steel, the *kerissst* of a blow struck true to every possible dying utterance, it was neither death nor glory that it kept. It was not the flavor of blood or victory but of oneness that it craved. When its steel had sung out in resonance with a battle cry screamed beside it. When honed so meticulously that the wielder's breath had frosted over its blade and crystal flecks of snow cut cleanly at its edge to drift separately away. When it had been swung with such ferocity that its point had burned an arc of fire through the air and, plunged to the hilt through the skull of a behemoth, delivered to its wielder the last sparks of the foe's gargantuan dying brain.

Though time and again such entities as to whom it had been bonded would inevitably be severed from it by death, always some aspect of their connection it kept as promise to the one who might find it next: *Take me. Grasp as your own my presence in the slivers of unwilting time. We who shall be as one. Never in possession of one shall the other be lost.*

Passing into this realm it had found itself without need. Long had it slept among the drifting others with no bearer to call forth its awareness. And now, as upon finding their arms these new wielders were taken inexplicably away, it felt its return to waiting.

But then, a presence drawing near. Seeking. The sword could feel it seeking. All but a few of the others were gone away. This one had pressed to the thinner reaches. Had ignored the potent and earnest, the gilded and brilliant. Had sought between. Why? The sword knows why. The recollection of a semblance long forgotten. And with it, anticipation.

This one feels it also. This one so new that nothing could be familiar. And yet. Up the long stairs, beyond crossing shadows.

He looks at the two-handed longsword. Humble and plain, hovering just beyond the firelight. He had heard the call of it like a voice in the stillness of the crypt. Wordless, but deeply beautiful. At once familiar and new. It had been as a silhouette in the fog.

He reaches to touch its tip, and tapping it down the sword turns on end to present its hilt, and without thought he catches it.

The intertwine of their two aspects is as immediate as it is complete, and the world falls away as their shared spark flows unhindered through corpus, hilt, and blade. In this inward place the sword asks only for a name to which it would avow its devotion.

Demithyle.

And with the resonance of its avowal Demithyle revels once again in the dark beauty of its voice, and so is it given a name.

Cryptmourne.

The eerie light of the Harrows returns as with two hands the reaper holds out his sword, admiring its heft and the seeming correctness of its weight. In that moment, the broad, weathered steel of its blade begins to alter slowly outward from the cross guard, bending itself to subtle curves along the trueness of its length as if a serpent in motion, finally tapering to a narrow point at the end of a long, wavy blade.

We are Demithyle, wielder of Cryptmourne. Never in possession of one shall the other be lost.

* * *

"So you have found one another."

Demithyle lowered the sword. A thing stood in shadow before him. Armored, but seemingly unarmed. Its naked skull sheltered two eyes of green fire. A reaper. It stepped into the light.

Until this moment he had given little thought to his own appearance. But he knew that it was a manifestation of his own physicality that stood now before him.

"With this weapon you are something new. This is good. But still you are Demithyle. So have you been named and always shall it be so." It pointed at Cryptmourne, its finger elongated by a narrow metallic horn. "Can you wield it? Wield it. Drive it deep into me and kill. For I am the infant unnamed. Destroy the infant, leave but the warrior. Become the warrior."

All was still. Demithyle raised his sword and stepping forward he drove its undulation through the gorget at the base of the figure's throat and then tore it free. The form before him crumbled like thick chunks of glass to reveal within it a huddled, leathery creature that suddenly unfurled to stand half again the reaper's height, four arms spread wide stretching sallow membranes of flesh between them. With depthless black eyes it stared down at him beneath a warbonnet of slivered bones, and then with a toothsome cry it snapped him into an enveloping embrace and all went black.

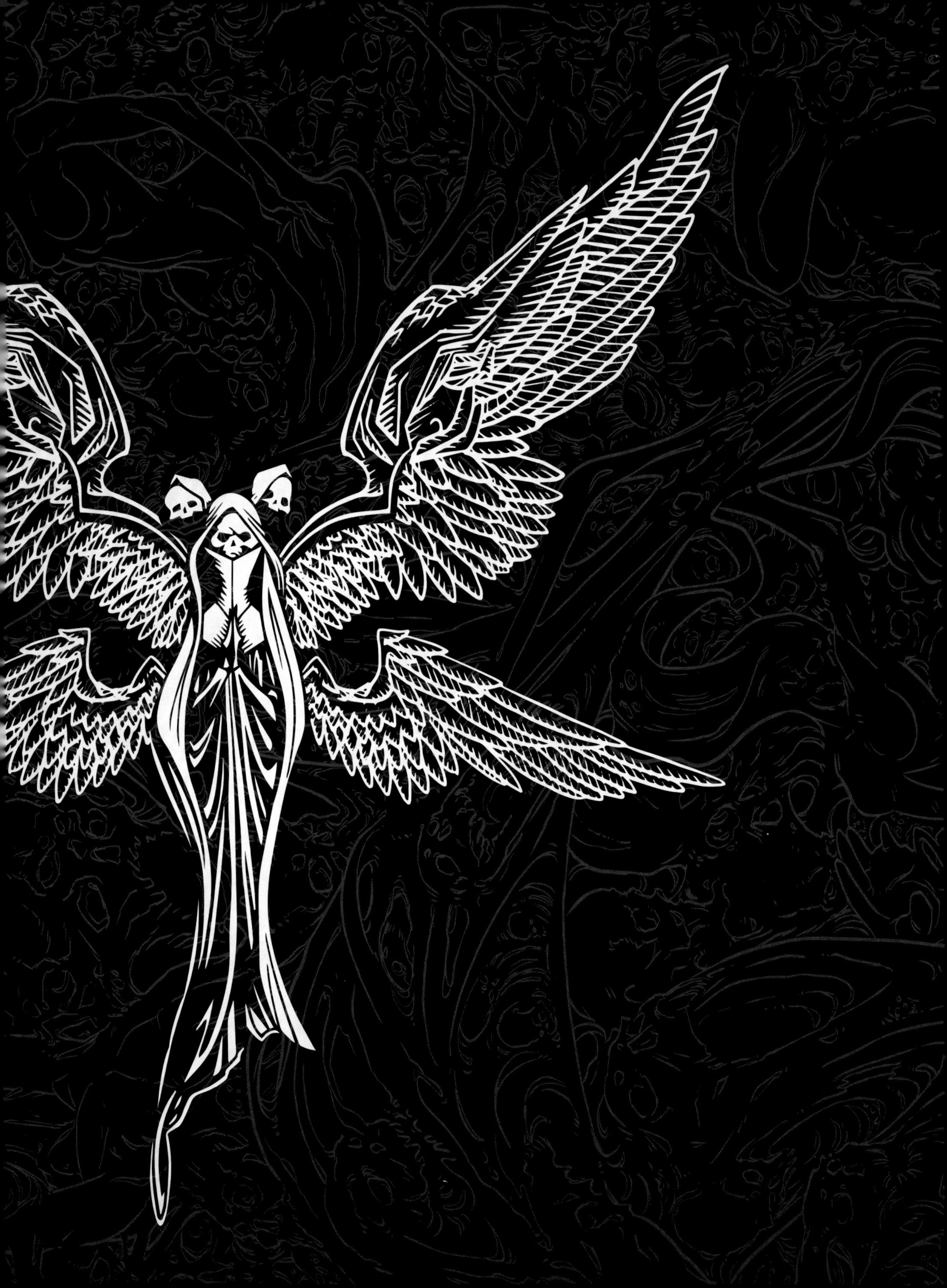

VII.
MORTIS VETH

The world snaps back in for Demithyle just as a huge iron hammer smashes down on his head.

* * *

The world snaps back in for Demithyle just as a huge iron hammer smashes down on his head.

* * *

The world snaps back in for Demithyle. He has exactly enough time to look up and see a huge iron hammer smash down on his face.

* * *

The world has only just snapped back in for Demithyle and he is already pivoting. A hammer smashes into the floor of the platform where he'd materialized, cracking a shallow pit through its flagstone. Advancing toward him, a many-limbed construct of bone wrapped in mottled, dry flesh. It raises its hammer for a second strike, and edging backward he tumbles down a narrow flight of steps behind him.

He grabs at the balustrade to halt his descent halfway down. Below is another roofless platform enclosed by clawing pillars of jagged bone where several equally large constructs are busy stomping one of his fellow reapers to powder and flattened steel. Looking round, he finds himself surrounded by similar scenes at play over a seemingly boundless aggregation of decrepit stone enclosures and other architectural elements taken from every sort of structure, connected high into a gray fog above by an incongruous network of crumbling stairways, here and there braced up from a dark abyss by arcaded columns. Many of the surfaces are choked by creeping growths of gnarled flesh that part round drystacked skulls and demonic effigies embedded in the walls and countless overlarge obsidian cabochons with swirls of ethereaic crystal inclusions that glint through the everpresent fog like a deep expanse of watchful eyes.

Everywhere he looks reapers are being smashed, dismembered, disintegrated, or otherwise obliterated, some managing to forestall this with some practiced skill, but not for long. Their cries of pain and confusion ring out from everywhere. How can it be that this is—

* * *

The world has only just snapped back in for Demithyle and he is already pivoting and stepping out of reach, sword in hand. The hammer smashes into the floor where he'd stood, cracking a shallow pit into its flagstone. Evading a second strike he turns to meet the point of a hurled spear with a downward parry, but it is enough only to redirect it from his neck squarely into his chest, and he is brought off his feet and skewered against the flesh-covered wall of an adjacent enclosure.

Wracked by pain and unable to free himself, he can only watch as another reaper is flattened seconds after materializing in front of the hammer construct. Thereupon a methodical dispatching of his kindred unfolds before him, a constant rain of their dismemberment spilling down into the abyss until all that remains of them is a clutter of weapons and armor, smashed limbs and shattered bones.

Then Demithyle spies a figure stepping forward to the edge of a weathered overlook, apparently in survey of the carnage. She is gaunt and closely garbed in thin carapace plates and drab linen cinched against her hips.

At her side she holds a tall staff capped with a five-pointed scepter of ivory spikes. As the cry of the last of the reapers falls silent she raises it slightly, and wherever the constructs lurk in Demithyle's vision they fall still.

She turns, fixing upon him a hollow-eyed stare from a narrow visage seemingly carven from yellowed bone, known to him from among those apparitions of his parentage who had presented themselves in the darkness of his awakening.

"I am Xiall," she says. "These are my marrowdolls. Welcome to Mortis Veth."

She looks outward to the wider arena. "Again," she says, and brings down her staff to strike the floor.

* * *

Demithyle pivots clear of the first blow, evades the second, then leaps forward to meet the materialization of another reaper, knocking them both away from the third. He holds out a hand.

"I am Demithyle, mortis," he says.

The other squints tiny black eyes through a gash in the flesh stretched over his face, but before he can speak his head is torn from his neck by the swoop of a blade-winged glider. Demithyle watches the head tumble away agape to fall through the jagged ridge of their enclosure, and he has just time to manage a curse before his own head is severed, and then he is crushed by falling debris.

"*Shaisssst . . .*"

* * *

"Liftholch," says the other, keeping low this time. "My thanks, reaper."

Demithyle nods, also hugging the ground. "Honor to the Vanguard."

The other grunts, and both roll away from yet another hammer-blow, watching the thin-framed gliders streak over them. Demithyle finds his feet and Liftholch is already leaping into the hammer doll, rendering its weapon useless as he scrambles up to mount its shoulders, slamming his daggers repeatedly through the leather sheathing around its neck with all three of his arms, splintering the bone within until its head flops down against the flesh stretched over its torso.

Digging his heels into the thing's midsection, Lifthoch leans forward and kicks himself free of it, sending it flailing backward to crack through the curved bony pillars. Demithyle is already leaping forward as it grabs Liftholch by an unshod foot, dragging both of them over the side. Hooking his swordarm around an unbroken thorny pillar at the ridge, he clutches with all his might as Liftholch struggles to kick his adversary free. But the floor shudders as an enormous blade cracks through the stone behind them, breaking it loose and sending all three to drop quietly into the abyss.

* * *

Pivoting clear of the first two blows, Demithyle knocks Liftholch away from the third, and leaping blades-out to meet the swooping gliders they drag down their masses to slam into the hammer doll. A gangly snarl of bony appendages topples over the edge just as both reapers are stabbed down into the stone by a heavy plunge of bladed limbs.

* * *

Dragging down the gliders' masses to slam the hammer doll over the edge of the enclosure, the reapers shift to the center as six blade-limbed marrowdolls alight to surround them. With crossed daggers Liftholch catches a slashing strike from one as Demithyle rolls beneath that of another, bringing up his sword to cleave through its limbs as regaining his feet he cracks the weapon forward through the spine of a third.

As Liftholch drives one of his assailants down with a flurry of crushing stabs through its face, Demithyle tears back his sword from the bone doll's spine. And amidst its exploding fragments there comes a gushing forth of its etherea.

He steps back, staring into the billowing plumes of sapphire blue, a cold warning arising within him against its insinuating call. And yet his craving for it seems an awakening of his nature. To take hold of it. To grasp into its chaos and remake it as his own.

There is a cry, and Demithyle looks to find his comrade enveloped in etherea coughed up from his downed foe, a look of surprise washing over his face, quickly replaced by one of ecstasy as he drinks it into himself. And twin bladestrikes against him pass harmlessly through an inky cloud that had been his form, as with a crow of exultation he reforms beyond their reach and with greatly engorged legs springs outward from the melee, only to be ensnared mid-ascent by a barbed, bony stalk snapping up from a lower enclosure. A second stalk whips up to wrap round his torso before twisting forcefully down, tearing him in twain, his own vital essence trailing after both halves of his carcass.

The remaining bladed dolls all turn to advance against Demithyle. He looks at the etherea still billowing from his fallen foe, and feeling in his grip Cryptmourne's yearning for it also, he lowers the blade into the swaths of vaporous blue.

Time slows to a crawl as by the entwining of their desire both sword and bearer draw the etherea to flow inward along the curves of the blade. It lashes into Demithyle in waves each more bracing than the last, the frenzy of the souls restrained within the blue tempered by the elongated moment to dancing opaline flares, each of them imbuing him with spiritous aegis as with ever greater eagerness he swallows the etherea to boil within his cavitous void, until all that remains of the essence of his enemy is a slow dispersion of prismatic sparks.

Time ramps up again and with it a clarity of the greater battlescape, emergent as an adumbration of its full dimension with Demithyle at its center, its sights and sounds ordered in his mind by threats relevant to his place within it. And looking at the wicked-bladed constructs as they kick through the wreckage in their advance against him, he can feel their movement over the floor as if the very stone were an extension of himself. As if, should he wish, he might simply reject their presence upon its surface as he would so much grit from his flesh. And he heaves forward his rightside limbs as if to strike at them, and three mighty, corresponding limbs smash through the stone floor and into his foes, instantly obliterating them to a shower of splintered bone and scraps of flapping leather. And then, as if of its own accord, the largest of these massive limbs suddenly sweeps back over his head to swat away an assailant driving down upon him from above.

He looks round through their emergent essence as it wafts away ungathered, the soundscape of grinding dry bones and creaking leather punctured by cries of pain and battle fervor. The air is sweet with the thickening bonesmoke. Clouds of soot and black miasma billow from at least a dozen separate fires. Within the nearest of these arises a volley of ethereaic flashes, and a fan of shimmering darts streak out from it, tearing into a swoop of passing gliders. One veers across the expanse to smash a reaper from the feet of a hulking construct he had only just entangled with a brace of hooking chains. Reaper and glider go careening into the abyss as the bone doll tears itself free, and turning to throw its bulk against another of the mortis it vanishes within a maelstrom of ghostly, clawing maidens who quickly peel away its flesh, dismembering it bone by bone to collapse into a dissociated heap before they are sent screeching up an adjacent stairway, only for them to suddenly disperse as the conjuring reaper is herself engulfed by a lurching shamble of boneshards spilling itself down upon her from above. There is a thumping burst as it spills itself down into a mesh of pulsating skulls strung by a pair of reapers across their encirclement of pillars, and the battlescape is momentarily enshrouded by a swell of blackened bone slivers that plink against Demithyle's armor and scatter over the surface at his feet.

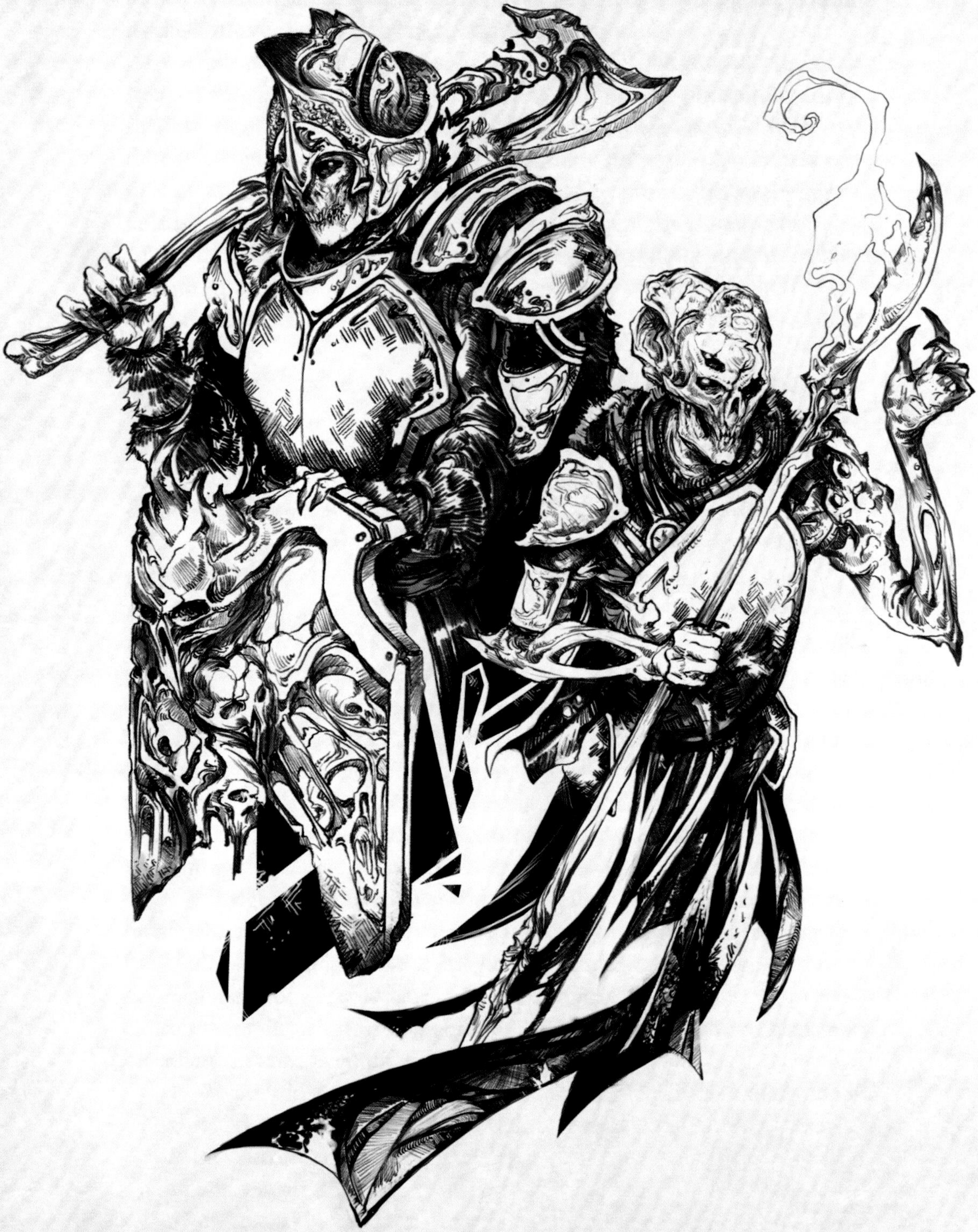

He looks at the gray flesh of his hands, a lingering agitation of captured etherea yet unspent within him, and weaving it into his fingers he works them to ripple the plates of stone around him. Its final ebbing leaves him feeling strangely bereft of ability, of potential. Yet the color of its growing influence amongst his kin remains in his wisping awareness of them, as does that which he had seen in the macabre imagination of their expressions of it, which even now he hears present in their voices raised in battle fervor: the delight in being dreadbaern mortis.

"Aye, quadpaw, grow a nose!"

Demithyle spins, narrowly avoiding an incoming tree-sized pylon. It slams into the stone behind him, then careens end-over-end, taking out two reapers engaged in a melee on another platform. He crouches low, seeking through the turmoil for she who'd called the warning as another pylon passes through his skull.

* * *

The world snaps back in for Demithyle just under the hammer blow. He pivots clear, leaps to meet the materialization of Liftholch, and together they throw back the hammer doll. And as before, upon his imbibement of etherea Liftholch leaps from the fray and is once again caught midair.

Destroying the rest of the bladed dolls, this time Demithyle directs his conjured limbs to pummel down against the floor, and catching up a plate of stone cracked free he hurls it to slice through the second bony stalk before it can wrap itself around Liftholch, still held aloft by the first.

But before he can reach the other reaper he is himself knocked to the ground by the sudden arrival of the bone doll he'd before swatted away, a skittering arachnoid that forces him back with a bevy of stabbing limbs. Rolling away from spraying debris, Demithyle goes over the side just as Liftholch screams in pain, and catching hold of a thick striation of fleshgrowth beneath the platform he twists to see another bony stalk wrenching off the reaper's arm even as still more snap up from a hydroid construct below.

Desperately Liftholch fights off their whipping strikes with his two remaining arms, his own essence winnowing away from a deep gouge at his shoulder before, to Demithyle's dismay, it is drawn to curl round the ensnaring stalk, downward to the hydroid.

"Cast out!" he shouts. "Thread your spark to me before you succumb!"

But Liftholch ignores him, continuing instead his futile parrying. *We must deny the enemy's strength*, Demithyle wisps. Still the other continues his struggle, his engorged legs rendered useless in the crushing grip of the hydroid stalks. Swallowing his frustration, Demithyle climbs round the fleshy underside of the enclosure to the arachnoid's flank, and holding there a moment he hauls himself up and aims a shoulder check against the incoming pylon, redirecting it into the arachnoid.

The construct goes down hard, pieces of it skating away as it's dragged across the floor to slide partway up a thick pillar before reeling over the edge. Leaping after it, Demithyle stabs down into its center mass, throwing its etherea up to the weakened Liftholch as he rides its wreckage down to crash into the shadow of the hydroid.

Eagerly Liftholch drinks the etherea in, and with a gurgled cry he oozes his form into a black ichor that drains through the grasp of the hydroid, which immediately turns its attention to Demithyle, who cuts through a whipping stalk as he struggles to disentangle himself from the remnant of the arachnoid.

Scrambling to his feet he readies to receive further strikes from the towering hydroid. But its upper half is suddenly shredded away by a glittering cone of metallic shards, and looking across the abyss toward its origin Demithyle meets the nod of one of several reapers embroiled on a lower platform in a melee with a cauldron-shaped automaton rolling through their ranks spraying magma against them amid billows of thick black smoke.

Turning back to the hydroid, now a hollow shell of carapace and tangled bone stalks, he steps into its fume of etherea and draws it in, and through its sapphire mist he sees Liftholch's pool of ichor begin to bubble near the opposite ridge of the enclosure. From it three reformed arms emerge as the reaper hefts himself out to roll onto the deck like an armored, tar-drenched carcass, and, ichor still congealing to become his flesh, he stands and without a backward look springs off on massive legs to parts unknown.

Flush with the hydroid's essence, Demithyle makes for the threshold at the stairway to the fray below, intermittently obscured from his sight by sweeps of thick black smoke that smoldered red from within. And reaching it he vomits forth his full sum of etherea with a hiss from his naked maw, gathering it to swirl round his skull until the smoke momentarily parts and he threads it to stream down toward the embattled reapers.

But rather than being manipulated into an attack against the construct, its blue streak dances about through the smoke shroud before to his surprise it is sent rippling over the steps back up to him. Taking hold of it he finds its fire intensified manyfold, such that his initial attempt to shape it is met with searing pain, and he feels a sudden, deep-rooted imperative to divide its potency among they who even now he senses reaching out to receive it once again.

But seeking through the smoke again he finds them obscured by the movements of their adversary, and fearing the theft of it he withholds the etherea to spin round himself untapped as before. From the brilliance of its concentration the cries of the broken ensouled begin to rise in his mind. Wanting, needling. Insistent in their proclamation of etherea as his heritage and right and their promise of the pain as portal to apotheosis.

And though the lie does not penetrate his nature, the logic of its measured assimilation to augment his ability is clean. For what is reaper without etherea? Useless. Simply waiting.

As reluctant now to cast it forth as take it into himself, he withholds a moment more, and in so doing the absence he had felt at the first ebbing of his ethereaic power returns as a cavernous violence of need—as if pressed down by his own inadequacy toward emptiness and obscurity from which there could be no elevation, no catharsis but by the unbridled invocation of destruction made manifest by accepting as his own those broken voices restrained within this scintillating blue.

Ablaze by its blue, he allows it to flood into him.

Embracing the pain as an end unto itself.

Even as the mortis, amongst whom he had only a moment before sought to the dilution of its frenzy, arrive in his senses not as kindred comrades-in-arms but as disparate volumes of sustenance.

Then from deep within his being a new melody of voices arises, wholly separate from the cloying cries of the ensouled. Their words are clear and held readily in his ears and knowing as by true memory of their recitation, long kept:

deaf to the Gallu
blind to the Smith
wise to the Bargain
made into Myth

The recollection fades and all of the voices fade, and though the craving remains its wild boundlessness is tamed beneath the forethought of his mind, and though the pain remains also its threat against his being is subdued.

The smoke parts and without restraint Demithyle once again vomits forth the full sum of his etherea, this time to crackle across the expanse and pour into the fiery automaton.

The smoke rushes closed, then dissipates completely with a great shuddering snap. Leaping down the steps Demithyle crosses the lower archway to the weathered enclosure, now thickened by a skin of ashen gray ice, the blackened, smoldering remains of reaper and bone doll scattered all around.

Yet two warriors remain intact, and standing before a hissing block of brittleglass they turn toward his arrival and nod, and she whose eyes he had met across the abyss raises the bladed edge of her war maul and taps it to her studded brow.

"Meirdrem loam, reaper!" she says, clapping his pauldron. She laughs, baring rows of mismatched teeth. She gestures to the reaper corpses. "Honor the Vanguard, eh?"

She laughs again as the other steps forward and raises the curved blade of his scimitar by way of salute.

"Don't mind her manner," he says, the sparks of his three eyes glinting green through the haze. "Truly there is nothing to be done about it. She is Melthis. I am named Gignoth."

"I am Demithyle," he says, raising Cryptmourne to return their greeting in kind. He scans round, wary of the lull. "Perhaps our time in this place nears its end?"

Melthis snorts.

"Mungfukkin' priss, ye say," she says. "Sure we're just as like tae wake up with our sluvvi skints afire."

Demithyle looks at Gignoth, who only shrugs.

"It may be we've found the end of it," he says, peering out among the overlooks, "but I don't think Xiall will reset the meir unless all of us are destroyed." He looks down again at the charred reaper corpses. "Something to look forward to, I suppose."

Melthis nods over toward the ruin of the hydroid, and following her prompt Demithyle looks in vain for sign of Liftholch. "Right," she says, reading his eye. "Interesting tactic, that one. Leaving ye to manage on yer own, like."

"Perhaps," says Demithyle, peering into the abounding shadows beyond. "Subterfuge would serve us also, being that we are so few. It may be that is his nature."

"Aye, the nature of a polt, more like," says Melthis.

Demithyle looks at her. "A what?"

"A coward," says Gignoth. "Melthis was brought to her awakening with a tongue already steeped in the street brogue of Illverness. You'll find it catches quickly, my *essester* friend."

"Aye, fukkin' essester," says Melthis, chipping at the crackling block of glass with her ax blade. "If yer askin' yer ethered-up volcano doll here. And don't think we didn't see ye ride that poor bony pitshin down to its cracking demise, like. Sweet kerissst of a kill, that was, or we've naught in us tae say."

Gignoth peers into the crackling block of glass at the warped, shadowy form of the automaton. "We've discovered cycling etherea between us amplifies its power," he says. "In this way we've been able to draw from a continuously replenished source rather than seeking out more each time we expend. We did not expect you to keep it . . ."

"Aye, figured ye'd run off, way ye hung on tae that blue, like. And here he comes back with a flood of shite for this bloaty diregoat tae swallow."

"No greater a feat than your own, reaper Melthis," says Demithyle. "You have my thanks; I could not have handled such an adversary alone."

"That would seem to contradict what we have just observed, Demithyle."

"Aye," says Melthis, "a fine pair of feats, it was. Though one short the other by half, then half again, but. How the cakk did ye manage so much bright all by yer lonesome, eh?"

"What do you mean?"

Gignoth looks at him. "Your hydroid," he says. "It took three of us to do that."

Before Demithyle can respond, a loud clacking approaches from seemingly every direction at once, and the reapers are obliged to brace against a strong downward rush of air as the clacking ramps up suddenly before a broad, bestial skelliform explodes through the floor beneath their feet, sending all three sprawling through empty space as a gargantuan ophidian construct wriggles up to catch them in its maw.

* * *

Reaching with what remaining awareness he possesses in the crushing blackness, Demithyle probes for sense of the others, only to be overcome by the shocking absence left in their wisping link now flooded with steady flashes of frustration and pain as still more of the mortis meet their demise.

And as his own essence is steadily crushed from him, he shifts his awareness between the fluctuating vitalities of those yet extant. Weak and subdued, agitated by ethereaic expression, augmented by its assimilation . . . his fading thoughts the dimension and shape of the battle painted in his mind by their ebb and flow of strength. The last of the reapers blink away from his awareness, and just before his own pinhole closes, Xiall's muffled voice reaches him through darkness:

"Pathetic," she says. "Again."

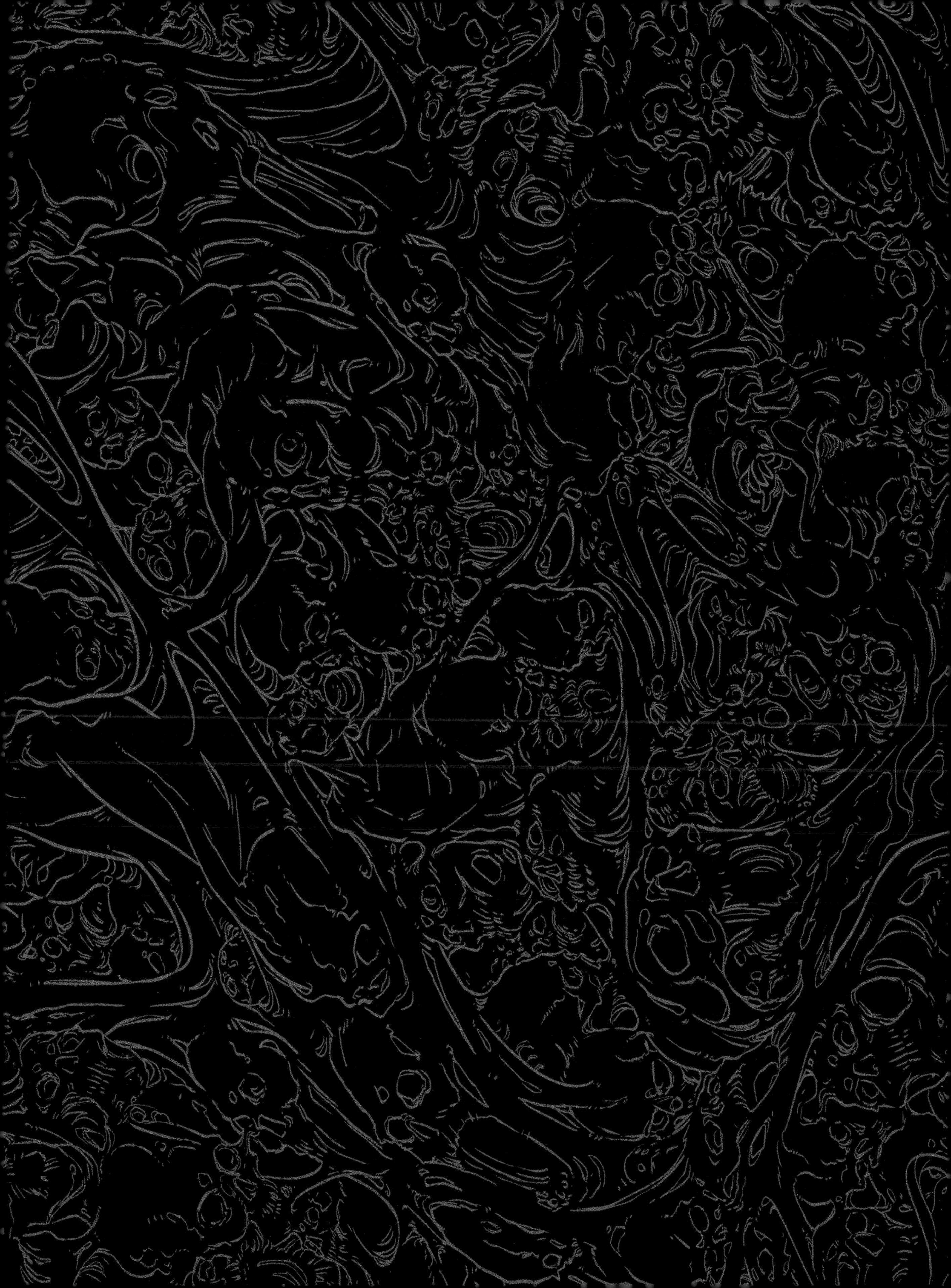

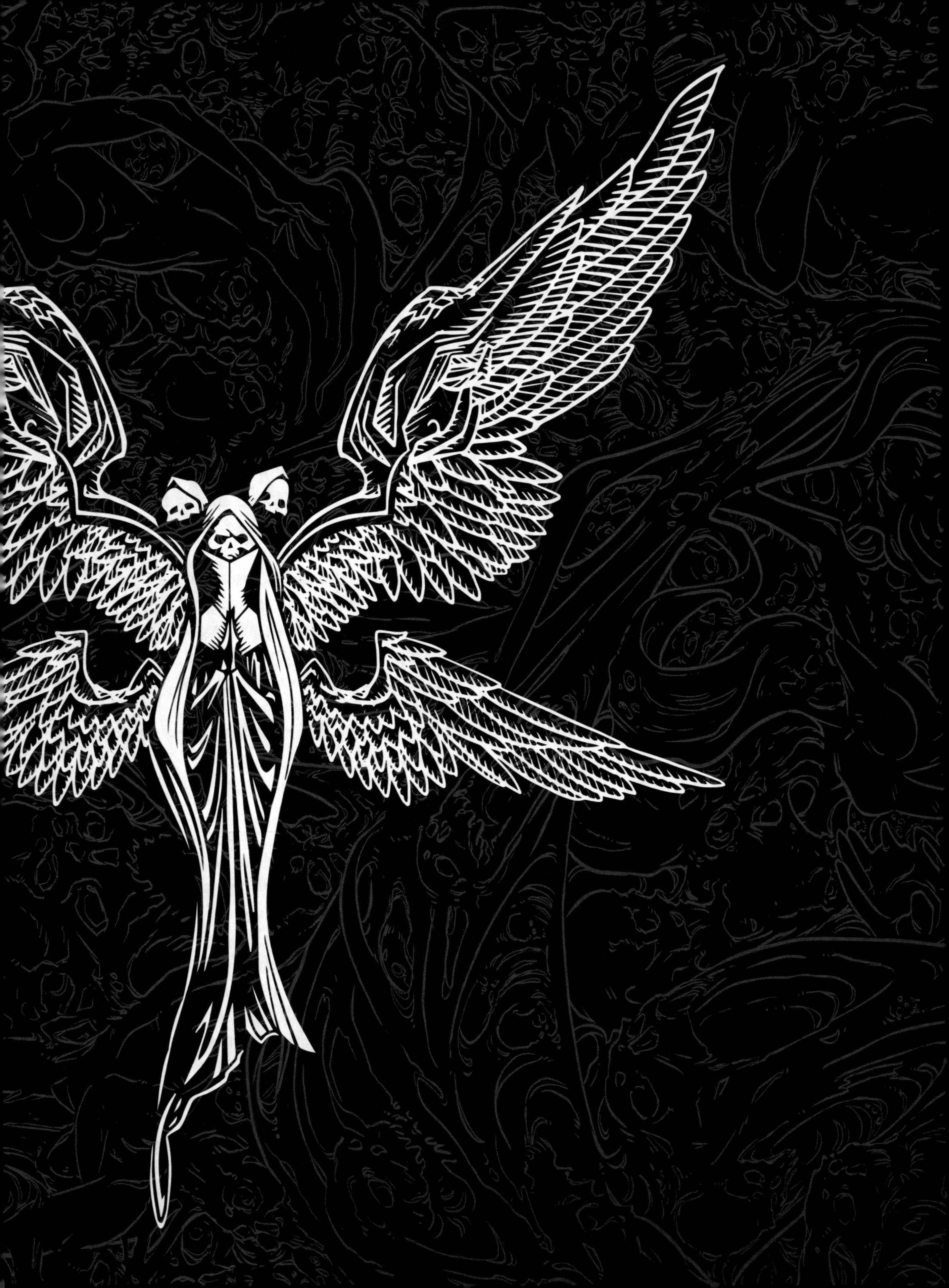

VIII.
GOLIATHS

The three reapers stand together dripping with viscera, surrounded on all sides by a thick wall of ruptured cartilage and flesh. They could not say for certain how many loops had closed since first being swallowed by the serpentine automaton. Knocking Liftholch clear of the hammer and each time promptly abandoned to fend for himself, Demithyle had fought his way into as many pockets of battle as there were iterations of his warrior kin in the immediate area to fight alongside. And though by their toil and pain and shared sublimity of the kerissst their common bond was strengthened, they had each time ultimately found themselves destroyed to the last.

Striking out to investigate the fog-laden heights of the arena gained him little, as much resulting from Xiall's predatory watchfulness as from an inability to ignore the various plights he encountered. Nor could he manage to mass their strength for such an endeavor, for whenever he directed his efforts to the merging of one fighting group with another, every bone doll in sight would immediately swarm down to obliterate the congregation before it could fully assert itself. Soon it was all he could do to dissuade those of his comrades wearied by their fate from focusing their ire on this or that foe that had previously destroyed them, even as they beyond his ken descended into petty indulgence of blind fury and vendetta.

It was only in those loops in which he found himself joining with Melthis and Gignoth that he seemed to find true momentum. Conjoining at the outset of the loops to the exclusion of all other avenues, the three thereafter fought their way together ever deeper through the myriad foes thrown against them, each time evading the arrival of the colossal ophidian as they worked to probe the limits of what complementary skills they were made to possess, each encounter refining their individual prowess such that more oft than not they became among the last reapers left extant.

And yet it seemed this brought them no closer to surmounting the trial, for never was it anything but a simple matter for Xiall to mass her creatures to quickly do away with so few remaining combatants. Finally, in view of testing themselves as much as the unrelenting machinations of the marrowdolls, the three resolved to stand against the ophidian.

At first, as quickly as they brought themselves before it did they find themselves crushed, swallowed, transected, sent flailing into the abyss. No amount of fire or fury thrown against it seemed to blunt the mechanical precision of its strikes, nor could any trap laid in anticipation of its emergence ensnare it.

But drawing it to pursue them through the archways and enclosures led to a stalemate of sorts, by which evading and destroying peripheral assailants in advance of it they shaped a continuous barrage of withering strikes that seemed slowly to erode its bulk. With the threaded essence of the mortally wounded they cycled their accumulating etherea between themselves and other passing reapers to a searing brilliance, and by the greater acuity of Gignoth's vision they caught the shine of it over what seemed a gossamer tether stretched up from the center of the ophidian's head.

There they focused their attacks, slivering off bone from its head until a hidden orifice was revealed through which they could sense the fount of its swollen essence. And drawing it to dive against them upon a single enclosure, they spindled their etherea upward through the orifice, tearing a channel through its length as its flaccid remnant splashed heavily but harmlessly around them.

Now, hidden from view in a bowl of its remains, they stand as three dubiously triumphant warriors, silently reveling in their victory and the momentary reprieve it seems to have won them. But the waning sounds of battle draw them to climb the rippled carcass, and as they peer out at the surrounding devastation what hope they might have entertained for final triumph dissolves.

"Well, this one's pitfukt."

* * *

They probe through the aether among the dozen or so skirmishes, and seeking grasp of their numbers they find that nearly half have perished.

Squinting through the haze of bonesmoke, Gignoth curses at the writhing knot of metal, fire, and bone in the distance, beneath which bits of broken reaper rain continuously down.

"Every time, eh?" says Melthis, shaking her head. "Shite. Ye'd think by now we pack of baerthik warmongrels might've learned from the naefukkin niddlepeck, like. Spread out a bit, aye, ye catmint fuks."

So much etherea has spilled into the air that dense clouds of its accumulation throw out bolts of bluegreen lightning that randomly obliterate combatants on both sides, bringing down huge chunks of the arena to crash through the cascade of enclosures. Demithyle looks up above into the emptiness of fog. Watching the reapers' remains descend into the abyssal fade, he'd found himself staring down into its darkness, suppressing an urge to simply climb over the rim of viscera and follow after them.

He looks back toward the tumult. "Were we to possess such superior forces, we would delight equally in the massing of our enemy," he says. "Xiall takes her opportunities, same as we."

"That is one way to put it," says Gignoth. "Let us not forget we are currently hiding in a giant bowl of meat of our own making. I, for one, would be interested to know quite what she means us to do to escape this purgatory."

"Aye, maybe we just ask her," says Melthis, scanning the overlooks, ax in hand. "Nice and quiet, like."

An armored mass shoots out from the battle and sails through the haze, and slamming against a flesh-wrapped landing above it drops solidly behind them, in the center of the ophidian carcass.

The three drop to stand over it on the slimy floor. A headless, limbless torso. Demithyle gives it a nudge with the point of his sabaton.

"Three arms," he says, letting it rock back down. "I think this might have been Liftholch."

Melthis snorts, gives the torso a solid kick. "Three missing ar—"

There is a blur as something explodes through the carcass wall, and Demithyle is knocked to the ground. Scrambling to regain his feet he finds Gignoth half-sunken into the fleshwall and Melthis gone. Then there is a thick impact at his side that snaps his cuirass clean away from its leather strapping, and Cryptmourne goes sailing from his grip as he is taken off his feet and hauled up the carcass wall and out into empty space.

"*Hearken well, mortis brooblings,*" comes the voice of Xiall. "*I've greater ambition than eternity reliving this sloshwoven skattikshow of a meirdrem. Crack your throats and get on with it, or fly your shriveled skints up the Forge.*"

Demithyle screams against the tearing pain as he is dragged through the air, clutching at a wide bone talon now jutting through his ringmail. His cuirass slips from his shoulders and disappears below, and craning back his neck he finds himself looking at the crossboned underside of a glider. With vision clouded by the scraping agony of his broken ribs, he crushes back another scream as he tries to reach upward and grab its narrow frame. But his hands close on nothing, and looking ahead at the array of spiked pillars he is rushing toward, thick with skewered reapers, he silently curses himself a fool for losing grip on his sword—only to find with a sudden flow of spark the weight of it held solidly in his grasp.

Demithyle.

Cryptmourne.

Hefting the sword with two hands, he stabs up behind his head into the glider's fleshy core, then chopping down in a forward arc he cleaves through bone and tendon as the glider's course falters, and, its hooking appendage slackening, he twists up to plant his feet against it before with a heave he tears himself free.

He drops forward into an enclosure just below the brace of spiked pillars, drawing in the thing's etherea in a trail after him, and rolling on impact he opens to brace against the rugged stone floor, sliding through the last vestiges of its energizing mist even as it crashes into the corner of a decayed wall.

Clutching at the massive hole in his side and flush with unspent etherea, Demithyle stands. Sense arrives of the others as yet extant but struggling and in pain. A shudder runs through the stone. Everywhere around him pieces of decrepit masonry crack away. As cries of alarm ring out Demithyle looks to see a megalithic construct emerging from a thick curtain of black smoke no more than an arrowshot away, its blocky head alone equally as massive as any bone doll he had yet encountered.

Its shoulder smashes through an entire enclosure in its lumbering advance, the connecting stairways dropping away like spiderwebs, sending several reapers tumbling into the darkness.

Xiall's voice rings out once again over the turmoil:

"*Congratulations, mortis. Some among you have begun to arouse my interest.*"

* * *

The etherea roiling within his cavitous void pleads for release as half a dozen sparks blink from his inner sight. In that moment, a subtle shift in the space behind him.

Without thought he presses Cryptmourne flat against his breast and turns to catch the pounce of an eyeless, fanged bone doll with the diminutive hand of his inner arm, wrenching downward through its core even as its dead weight slams against him, knocking him backward to crack through the edge of the enclosure in an explosion of bony fragments and shimmering waves of blue.

Time slows once again as falling amidst the ruin of the gutted doll he draws its slowly oscillating opalescence over the length of his inner arm, and as it burns into that already restrained within him its soul-torment of voices mingles with the pain of his gored torso such that they are raised in sudden violence for release.

But their madness can not supplant the incandescent desperation of his kin, and he presses the order of his conviction upon the chaos of his pain, and reaching into his cavitous void as he would to shape etherea he instead wills it to channel into the marrow of his bones and swell outward to permeate his flesh.

And so doing, sense of his own physicality is itself channeled suddenly through an inner constellation of glimmering foci, apexed at the undercrest of his skull and aligned through the visceral eye of his brow, down through maw and throat to the place where a mortal heart would be rooted, a hollow bathed in radiance as by a soul resident within. Around each of these distinct intonations of ethereaic convergence the fullness of his flesh and bone arrives in his awareness as a community of iota adherent to his central governance of will, and the persistent agony of his ravaged torso becomes a separate, simple matter by his command of it to shift, reform, regrow.

In the absence of his physical pain that of his kindred returns, thrown into wisp as if final acts before their succumbing. And even as slowly he continues to fall he finds the nearest of their fading aspects among the swathes of destruction being wrought by the megalith, and grasping in his sense the core of its massive form he anchors within it a reflection of himself, sending into it a stream of his vitality as he raises Cryptmourne's undulating blade, his shredded cloak gently flapping over flesh remade . . .

Time reasserts to an odd absence of sensation. Furtive sounds of battle return. He stands upon yet another broad enclosure, in a haze of fine white dust. Before him are two reapers, neither of whom he has encountered. One is shockingly large, especially in contrast to the apparent frailty of the other. Their armor is slashed and battered and gray. They are looking at him with expressions somewhere between unmitigated curiosity and shock.

"Awake now?" asks the larger one.

The last diminishing echoes of his singularity of being quietly pulsate throughout his inner corpus. There is no pain. He can feel the weight of Cryptmourne in his grasp. He looks up into the deep shadows of her helm.

"What happened?" he asks.

"Great big boom," she says, her lightness of voice belying her mammoth stature.

"What?"

"She means you completely annihilated that thing," says the other.

He looks down again at the other's unfamiliar, thorny visage.

"Thing?"

The slight reaper steps casually forward, making way for a heavy swing of the other's enormous glaive. The entire enclosure rattles as it splits an attacking bone doll over the surrounding rubble.

"Let's see," he says, ignoring a second blow behind him, "we saw you falling over there, then I believe you pointed your sword this way, and then you *were* your sword, which I'd describe as strange were we not ourselves a menagerie of the bizarre . . . and then there was of course the black streak of what I don't know, and here we are."

Demithyle looks around. The floor is strewn everywhere with what look like cracked white boulders and huge slabs of striated bone. He looks at his diminutive hand, now charred and raw.

"I destroyed the megalith," he says, as if to assert the reality of it.

"We certainly weren't giving it any trouble," says the other. "One moment we're about to be squashed into the blink, and in the next, as I believe has been mentioned, 'great big boom.' And here is a reaper nested comfortably amongst the dusty bits of what had only recently been a rather angry mountain, lying there with a huge flambard clutched against his chest. Not unlike a freshly excavated cadaver monument, I thought. I may have even said as much."

"As much and more," grunts the other behind him, her words punctuated by another smash. "And then more and more."

"Right. And then you just sort of quietly got up and wandered over here. Which act was the more astonishing I shall frankly have to ponder."

Demithyle peers through the haze in search of the far platform, feeling strangely exposed in the absence of his cuirass. He slides his fingers into the tear in his ringmail, probing the renewed rigidity of his ribs beneath the cold, unmarred flesh.

"I do not remember that," he says.

"Yes, well," says the other, glancing up at Demithyle's naked crown. "So far as I know, the shroudreive did not fashion us for use as projectiles. I would not be surprised at all if you've cracked your skull."

The big one shucks the blade free of her glaive to sail into a charging doll, obliterating it mid-pounce. Stabbing the pole's base into the rubble, she looks round as dark steel grows out from the housing to form a new blade.

"Skull solid," she says, looking over at Demithyle. "Tiny, maybe."

"That is Thrael. I am Sithik. That one over there was Aerthe, I think. The other smears I couldn't say."

"I am named Demithyle," he says, looking over the crushed reapers.

"Ah," says Sithik. "So *you're* Demithyle."

"What?"

"Never mind. I say that to everyone I first meet."

Turning toward the expanse, Sithik tucks his lance into the crook of his arm and gestures broadly with it.

"You'll notice the conspicuous absence of our flaxen monitress," he says. "She disappeared after you painted the arena with her giant monster. It's been something of a lull ever since, comparatively speaking. I imagine she assumed it would be the end of this particular catastrophe. Doubtful we've managed to stutter our way up to quality. You might hope, Demithyle mortis, that she does not take things personally."

"How many still fight?"

"A third or so, probably less," says Sithik, cocking his narrow head as if listening elsewhere. "Most everyone with sense enough not to congregate have gotten themselves spread out all over the arena. Pretty much everyone else got sent down by your friend here. Won't be long now . . ."

He leaps straight upward, quickly shooting to the understructure high above to spear a bone doll readied to drop upon their heads. He sweeps it across the abyss to smash against another bounding over an adjacent stairway, then flattening out with a snap of filmy, translucent wings he glides down to breathe in deep the wafting of their essence before releasing a thick jet of acid from his mouth, melting a cluster of incoming gliders to steaming nubs of bone that bounce and clatter away.

"You can fly," says Demithyle as he alights.

"Oh, yes, it's very convenient," says Sithik. He gives his wings a shake before tucking them back into his cloak. "Once you get the wing of it, that is. You'll find a handful of others similarly endowed; one or two beneath our angry mountain, sad to say. The rest, alas. In the absence of greater solidarity of intent, Thrael and I have found a reliable formula for our shared longevity. Should you happen to encounter another such as myself, you might do as a similarly robust counterpart for her, or him, or neither or both, as the case may be."

"Thrael can fly too," says Thrael, and after a short lumbering run knocking the remains of the megalith from her path with her thick armored legs, she leaps down over the edge of the platform, shrieking out a receding battlecry:

"Thraael eeaat your skints, haaiii!"

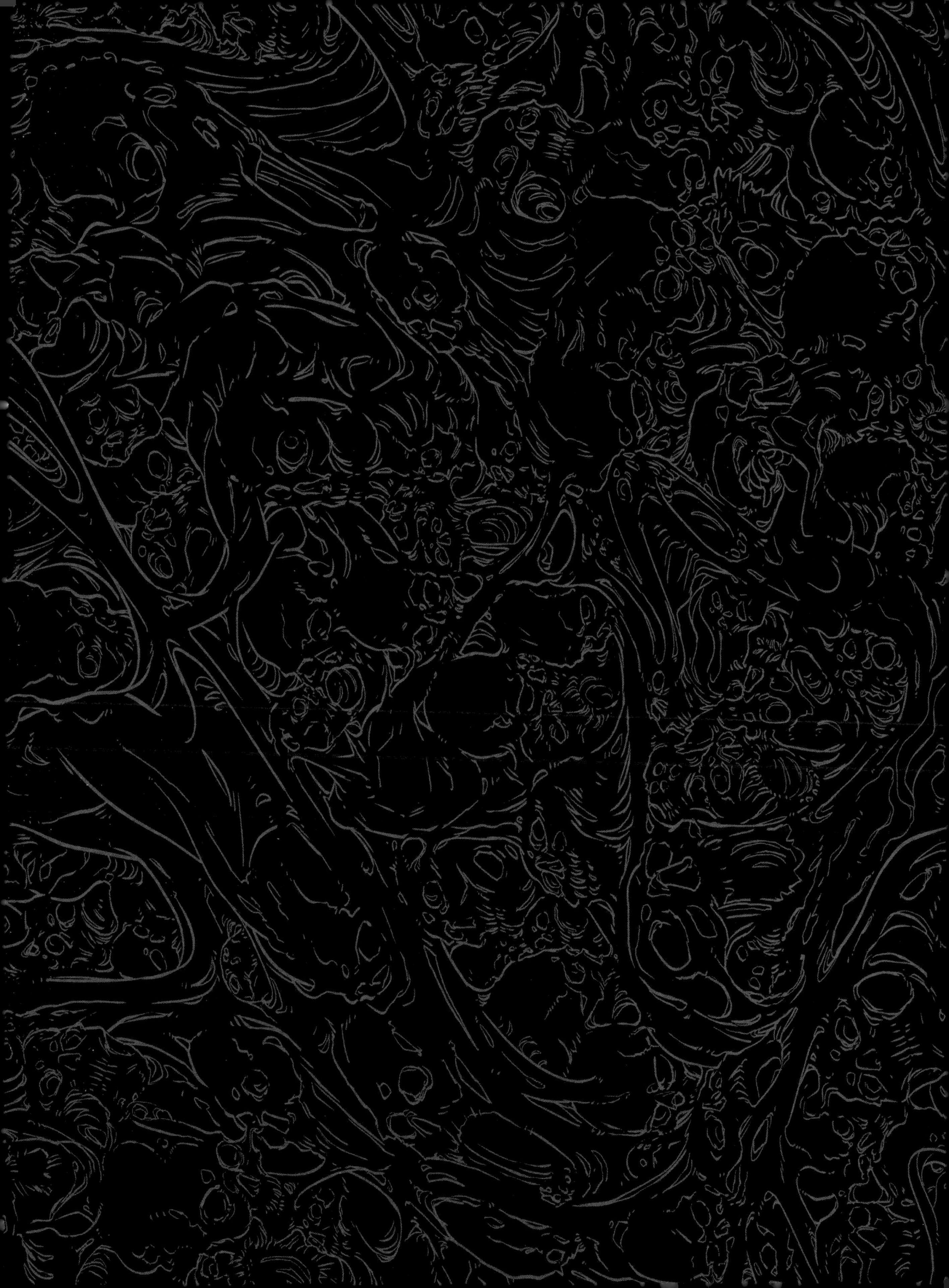

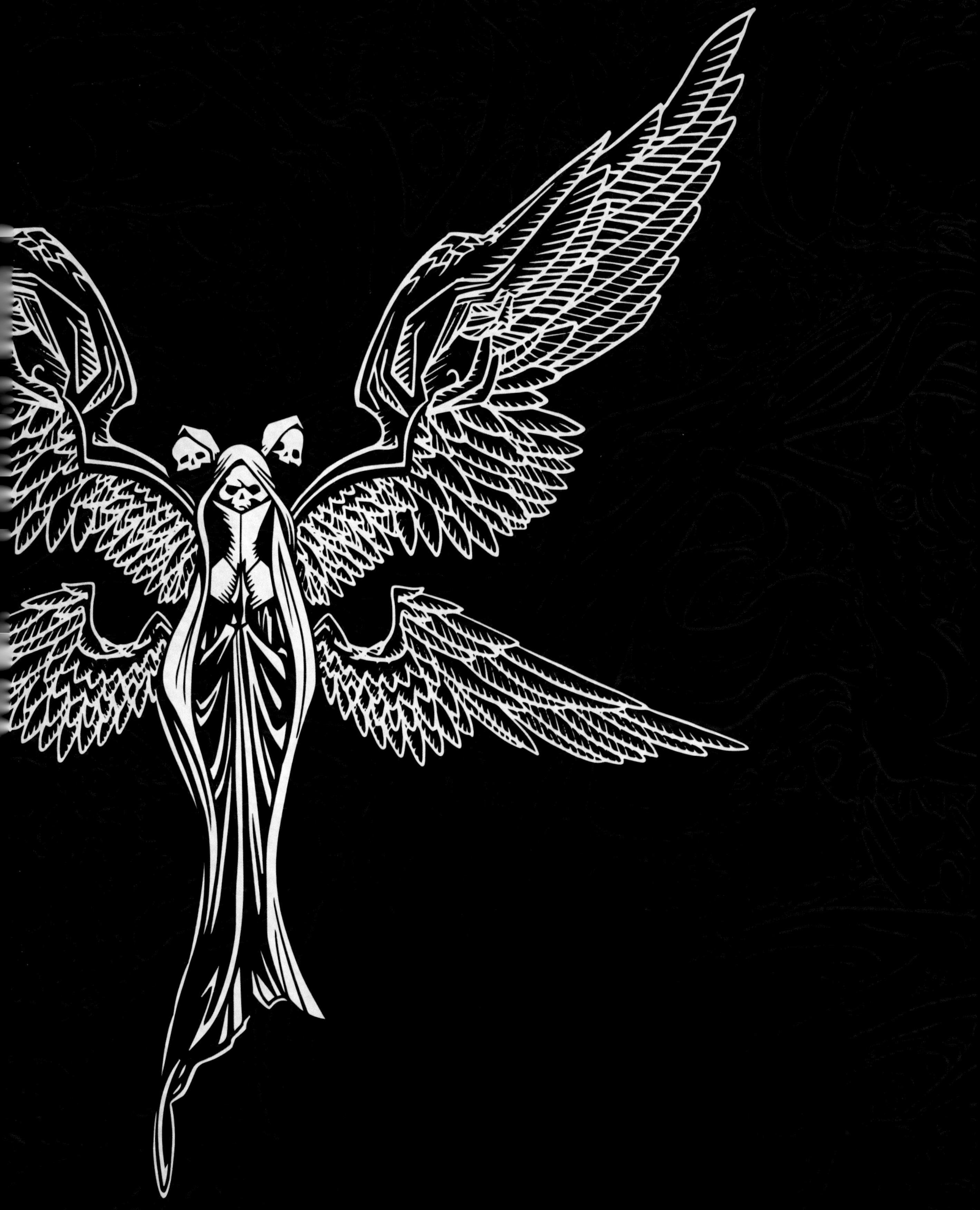

IX.
A CORPUS

Sithik looks at Demithyle and then he takes flight, circling once above before diving out of sight.

Demithyle moves to follow as both reappear engaged with a cadaverous decapede, tearing out between the zigzag of stairways and enclosures—Sithik slicing assailants from the air before they can reach Thrael, who cackles as she sinks her glaive down through the thick layers of carapace shaping the construct's thorax.

Then there is a momentary flash of threaded etherea before with a papery crack the forwardmost segment of the decapede is crushed against its greater body, a spear of gleaming obsidian pierced through the center of its head. Hovering above it, a lone, unknown reaper, the remnant scar of his ethereaic burn still tracked through the haze.

Thrael leaps from the decapede as it slips into the abyss, and Sithik dives down after her. There is a blast of etherea met by an arrested grunt from Thrael, then all falls still for a moment, before Xiall's voice echoes through the arena.

"No, you do not fail to impress, mortis. And yet still you dance as the desultory undead, awallow in humility. How endlessly amusing to witness."

From somewhere in the distance Melthis's full-throated retort rings out:

"AYE, MANAGE THE LIPLICKING BLIGHTWRAITHS YER-SELF, YE NAEFUKKIN BONY PUNTRIX!"

The entire arena erupts as bits of doll and reaper everywhere converge, and Demithyle is obliged to move aside as to his horror pieces of the megalith around him begin to shift and reassemble.

Racing up an adjoining stairway he kicks a half-made doll from its landing and then climbs toward the higher enclosure, all the while looking at the place where the decapede had met its demise. What had he seen? By that last flash of etherea, something stretched from high above. The thinnest of tendrils from the head of the many-legged construct. Like the ophidian. Like all of them.

The reason they were not permitted to collect was not Xiall's preventing the massing of their strength. It was their massing of etherea. Something was hidden beneath the veil of this place, tiny specters of which had thus far been revealed only by the threaded brilliance of their etherea. The greatest concentration of which would be found by their greater body acting together as one. A single focal corpus. Each of its elements adherent to a central governance of will.

We must ascend. Into the heights, all of us. We must ascend now.

With this call, Demithyle casts an abstraction of his intent into their wisp, shaped in each of their minds as a spectral figure overlaying a stellar constellation as seen in the mortal night sky, its stars slowly drawing themselves around a central orbit to curl it to a closing posture.

And Demithyle's sense of them throughout the boundless arena is shaped in his own mind as had been the foci of his own inner being: each of their spiritborn essences aglimmer as nodes aligned within a greater focal corpus. Responding now as one to his intent they climb the narrow stairways and leap between enclosures, consolidating their attacks as they converge toward the heights to overwhelm what reconstructed marrow-dolls rise in their path, throwing behind themselves suppressing bursts of acidfire, stone, and bone.

* * *

High into the thickening fog Demithyle leads them, into the uppermost network of enclosures. Their fighting ascent churns in their wake a rising floor of flame and wreckage that slowly consumes their corpus as one by one trailing reapers are overwhelmed. But at each of their succumbings they thread forth their vital essence through the greater mortis body, driving it forward ever faster as its strength is concentrated.

Floating freely above, a rising expanse of flesh-choked turrets as if plucked from castle battlements, connected to one another by loosely hanging cables of sinew. From their protruding machicolations knots of bone begin to drop and unfold, catching the air on great membranous wings to swoop directly toward Demithyle as he scales the highest of the stairways, narrowing into empty space beneath the floating turrets.

He leaps from the leading edge of the last step, cutting through one winged assailant diving against him as he vaults off the swoop of another, leveraging its momentum to catapult himself outward beyond reach of a third to catch hold of a hanging fleshvine. Three more streak toward him, but before they can reach him they are destroyed by a screeching salvo of ethereaic lances thrown up from below.

Thus by foe and structure do the reapers ladder up among the turrets, throwing out attacks from their greater body to protect Demithyle at its nexus, cycling their etherea all the while in an ever-intensifying brilliance that shimmers over a curtain of spectral filaments now undulating everywhere around them—taut, gossamer strands shifting independently as if affixed to the frantic movements of the horde below.

And bathed in its light, the interconnected expanse of structures, platforms, and stairways begins to appear as porous, cartilaginous growths bent and twisted into their shapes. The reapers themselves seem to linger in the space as sharp skeletons of spiritous energy within an emptiness of shadow. Wherever they alight, innumerable eyes stare out from within the folded hollows as heretofore unseen phantoms seep out to curl after them.

And as the omnipresent fog burns away they draw their awareness upward, beyond the uppermost cluster of turret husks to witness the gathering of the shivering cords far above into a rotating orrery of ethereaic obsidian spheres, slowly sweeping over the whole of Mortis Veth.

* * *

Over and between the floating turret husks the reapers leap, climb, and swing, an effervescence of skeletal blips in the darkness.

Curling among them the ogling phantoms, rippling furrows of shadow glistening throughout with accumulations of flesh by their steady convergence.

And stacked up from the highest reach of enclosures below, the grasping, clawing marrowdolls, silent in their methodical pursuit as a climbing latticework of themselves, the clockwork menace of their inner mechanisms shown now pulsating through their shifting corporeality.

* * *

Eyes fixed on the orrery above, Demithyle now runs across a thick braid of sinew toward the highest cluster of turret husks, evading and cutting through those gliders not torn away by the reaper salvos thrown around him.

As he skids down toward the braid's trough another glider cuts across it, snapping the span with its hooked appendage even as its form is riddled with ethereaic darts that spin it away into the darkness. The cable goes slack and he leaps from its mass to grab the final length swinging below the central floating husk, riding it in a sweeping upward arc beneath the turret's underside to drop down upon its resinous, irregular surface.

* * *

Finding the structure's centermost point, he directs their focal corpus, numbering now less than ten, to unfold in pairs upon its surrounding elements, and together they lens their ethereaic influence to deliver outward a sanitizing sphere of heat, pressing down the upper reach of marrowdolls and burning out the swoops of boneframe gliders to a rain of wingless, lifeless manikins, their essence swirling into the reaper formation.

* * *

Unperturbed by the blast, the accumulating phantoms gather above, their swollen knots of shadow and gore obscuring the line of sight to the orrery as they stare down upon the assembly with every sort of eye enfleshed, agleam by the reapers' oscillating light.

* * *

The reapers draw in the essence of the destroyed gliders and thread it to Demithyle in their center, who sends it back to them each in turn augmented round their staggered circle, such that the contour of a five-petaled lotus is burned into the air in an accelerated wither and bloom.
    It swells out beyond them, and catching against the shimmering filaments it twirls down to penetrate into the nearest of the grasping marrowdolls, burning out their essence within. Gutted, the automatons fall still and topple away.

* * *

Then out from the mass of phantoms a long intestinal channel forms, coiling directly over Demithyle before with a wave of blinking eyes along its breadth it strikes.

Bringing up an arm, Demithyle compels their corpus to react, and one of the mortis bounds across the path of the coagulation, bursting away the bulk of it even as a hundred grasping corpselike limbs immediately tear him apart, his screams falling abruptly silent as his head thuds down across Demithyle's feet.

* * *

The phantoms reform and coil again over his head, and as they snap down for a second strike he brings another of their number to smash its grasping density away. Still another reaper is brought against a third strike to a hail of screaming and dismemberment as he is in turn driven deep into its accumulated mass, before the deadthreading of both of the sacrificed reapers explodes in a lateral ring of concussive force that disperses the phantoms completely.

* * *

The blast vibrates across the expanse of filaments drawn down from the orrery, strumming shrieks of discordancy, as if giving voice to the silent automatons impelled by it. Sword raised, Demithyle looks up at it through the darkness and then folds in their lotus bloom, swallowing the full sum of their etherea into his cavitous void even as the remaining reapers are beckoned inward to surround him.

* * *

But before they can move from their places upon the surrounding elements, Sithik, Melthis, and Thrael are enveloped by vortices of shadow that quickly evaporate to reveal figures of crimson flesh towering behind each of them, white eyes glowering, heads crowned in guardian warbonnets of slivered bone.

* * *

All three reapers disappear within broad folds of crimson leather stretched between an embrace of four arms in symmetry. Held fast, their struggles quickly cease, and the creatures spread wide their elongated arms to release a tumble of bones and hollow armor amidst a deluge of black sludge.

The etherea within him threatens to burn out his core, as staring at him the creatures split their toothsome maws into mocking smiles and with a single slithering voice they speak:

"𝓑𝓞𝓤𝓝𝓓𝓔𝓓 𝓑𝓨 𝓣𝓗𝓨 𝓙𝓤𝓓𝓖𝓜𝓔𝓝𝓣, 𝓓𝓔𝓜𝓘𝓣𝓗𝓨𝓨𝓨𝓨𝓛𝓛𝓛𝓛𝓔..."

With a shriek they leap for him, and stabbing his sword into the resinous surface of the husk Demithyle unleashes his etherea loop round it in a spinning trillium as he and the other two remaining reapers dive backward to plunge headlong toward the latticework of marrowdolls.

Then as if tethered still to the sword by filaments of his own, Demithyle tugs hard with all four of his arms, and there is a great crunch from above as the surface around the blade is swallowed by an inward pressure wave from the rapidly condensing trillium of etherea before with a resounding *tang* Cryptmourne explodes outward in a spinning arc that sweeps up through the heights like a single blue metallic disk, severing a spiral swath through the shivering curtain of filaments before shattering into the orrery's central rotating orb.

* * *

There is a stuttered explosion throughout the heights, the sundering of each of the orbs unleashing thin beams of blue light of such intensity that those elements not immediately transected by their wild lashing burst suddenly aflame.

A swell of dark radiance sears outward, down through Mortis Veth, flaring over the silhouettes of the disintegrating structures it overwhelms.

* * *

Filaments cut, the marrowdolls simply cease their function, falling away like so much dead clutter as their grotesque edifice collapses in advance of the reapers' plummet down through the arena, the dissipating curtain of tethers dragging after them.

* * *

They fall through the floating turret husks, Demithyle, Gignoth, and an unknown third, past the highest reach of stairways and enclosures steadily consumed behind them by the downward swell of disintegration, and smashing into a pile of bones and flesh caught by an enclosed landing Demithyle releases his influence on their corpus so that each might gaze up to witness as separate entities the moment of their unmaking.

But the third reaper dashes immediately to him and throws up a crystalline dome, shielding the two from the dark wave, leaving Gignoth to meet his eyes through its translucence just before incinerating.

The last of the radiance refracted harmlessly away by the dome, the crystal flakes away and the last two reapers find their footing among the bone doll clutter, looking out upon an arena bathed in fog once more, the stairways terminating just above to sharpened stalks, all surrounding surfaces burnt free of flesh and scoured like, so that it seemed they rested within a great weathered skeleton.

* * *

The other throws past him a shrieking blast, and regaining his balance Demithyle is momentarily immobilized by the sight of Xiall staring toward them from the eroded shell of a nearby overlook, staff in hand, her form completely encased in the same slivers of crystal that had shielded them from the blast.

"Why did you do that?" he asks, struggling to frame his shock into words.

"I need to speak with you," the reaper says with a soft voice. "She would intervene. Prevent our discourse."

Demithyle looks at him.

"Perhaps it is not wise to assault a war matron," he says. "To say nothing of a scion of the Alltaker . . ."

"Nothing will be gained by diminishing the Vanguard in advance of its purpose," says the other. Eyes content within the shadow of his hood, he glances at his work, apparently undisturbed by the inevitable evisceration certain to befall him. "As well, the sharpness of her bearing suggests there likely exist powers among the court who will be amused by the slight."

"Amused?"

"If not otherwise intrigued," says the other.

Incredulous, Demithyle looks over to the semisolid scorch that had been Gignoth.

"You withheld some of your etherea," he says.

"Yes."

"Could you not have shielded all of us?"

"To what purpose? It is you with whom I wish to speak."

"Speak then, reaper," he says, looking warily toward Xiall. "And do not doubt your time is short."

The other lowers his hood, revealing a fleshless skull half cracked away, bearing no lower mandible to speak of.

"I am Torbrenth," he says. "You are the reaper Demithyle. Yes, Melthis has spoken of you, as have others. More than this, we are acquainted."

He steps forward and grasps Demithyle's diminutive inner hand, and in that moment sense of their focal corpus returns, as if both were separate beings no more, and the weaving of Torbrenth's sentiment arrives through wisp as that which could be translated to words as the following:

When you manifested the unity of your inner being, I had only just achieved the same. It was then we two alone understood the breadth of our greater body. It was then we knew our truest strength. Indeed, in this we stand apart from all our kindred warriors.

Releasing the hand Torbrenth steps back again, and as Demithyle returns to himself he marks the other's armorless profile, recognizing now that same grim battlemage who had destroyed the decapede and sent its ruin into the abyss.

"The megalith," says Demithyle. "It was you, then."

"Such is the power we are made in our unity to wield," says Torbrenth. "Taking hold of your strength I wove it with my own, and so doing we together destroyed it."

"The others believe it was I alone . . ."

"And so they should."

"What?"

"Is it not wise to hold one's captain in high esteem?" says Torbrenth. "For his deeds to be legend, even while he walks among us? Is there a greater unifier for they who fight at his call?"

"I am no captain," says Demithyle. "As you say, it is in our nature to fight as one. Nor would a worthy commander have so brazenly sacrificed combatants to protect his own aims."

"No worthy commander would have hesitated," says Torbrenth. "Perhaps you might ponder the reason Gignoth and I were spared the guardians' embrace just now. Yes, I knew him also. Perhaps knowing him, I would have eschewed his sacrifice, as did you. Perhaps I would have hesitated to sacrifice even those others. Thus have we found our captain."

"It matters not," says Demithyle. "Xiall will lead us against the baelreivers and in the defense of the city."

"Xiall will not," says Torbrenth. "Though perhaps for different reasons, the scions fear the dreadsgrip even more than we. Nor can they stray far from the city. Indeed, our trial in this place has been but to one greater purpose: to discover you."

"How do you know this?"

"The words of our father," says Torbrenth, "more or less. As much spoken as not. Did you not speak of such things in the stone?"

"He presented a great many things," says Demithyle. "Our histories. The Celestials, mortals . . ."

"Interesting."

Demithyle is suddenly blinded by a spray of ichor from Torbrenth's throat. When he burns it from his eyes he finds the other has been skewered by dozens of bony lances grown out from the enclosure.

He turns to find Xiall looking at him, freed from Torbrenth's encasement. She stares a moment with the cold black dots of her eyes. Then she brings down her staff.

WE SHALL TAKE THE COLOR INTO US TO SHAPE
 OUR BEING AS WE MUSSST THE COLOR KNOWSSSSSSS

. . . WE FLY WE BURN WE FLY WE BURN WITH ACID FIRE
 AND BLACKENED OIL WE BURN WE FLY
ACROSSS THE UNDERWORLD WE FLY WE SPREAD
WE ARE YOUR PLAGUE WE ARE YOUR PLAAAAAGUE

YOUR SOUL IS OURS TO DRINK AND DRINK AND
DRINK AND DRINK AND DRINK AND DRINK AND DRINK

YOUR DREAM AND HOPE IS OURS TO DRINK AND
DRINK AND DRINK AND DRINK AND DRINK AND DRINK

YOUR MEMORIES ARE OURS TO REND AND CHEW
AND SPIT AND VOMIT IN THE POISON FUMESSSSS

YOUR HOME IS OURS TO FILLL WITH FEAR TO
LEAVE BEHIND NO MIND TO MOURN ITS HOLLLOW SHELL

WE SEE THE FLASH OF SHARDS
WITHIN YOUR FEEBLE SHAPE
THE COLOR TRAPPED WITHIN
YOU CAN NOT HIDE

OUR SUSSSTENANCE YOU CAN NOT SATIATE
ITS MAD DESIRE MAD DESIRE FOR RELEASSSSSSE

NO FLESH NO BONE NO SPIRIT
STEMS THE LUSSST OUR LUSSST

NO SCREAMS OF TERROR HATRED OR OBLIVION SHALL
PRESS US BACK BEYOND THE REACH OF
THIRST OF THIRST OF THIRST OF THIRSSSSST

WHEN AT LAST THE FATHER DIES
WE FEASSST UPON THE SOULS WITHIN THE
FORGE ALL OF IT OURS ALL OF IT OURS

ALL OF IT OURS ALL OF IT OURSSSSS
ALL OF IT OURS ALL OF IT OURS ALL OF IT OURSSSSS

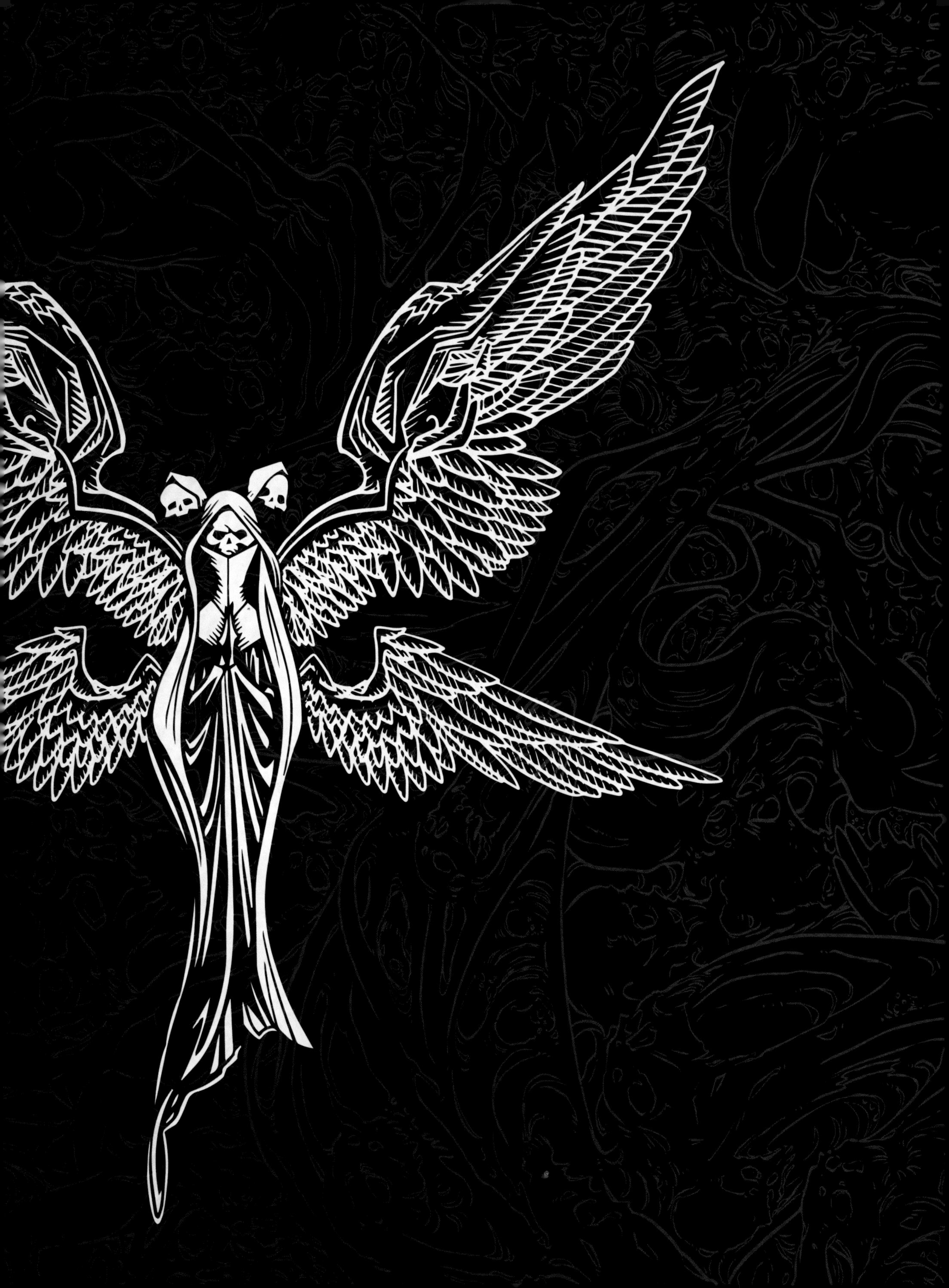

X.
A LABYRINTH

"Well, here it is, it is."
"So it is!"
"Only took, what was it, twelve thousand cracks?"
"Twelve-thousy, three hundemeighty-sivvy cracks, to give and take it."
"My O, my O! What's that work itself to, dremwise?"
"Quite a quantiwitty, by its keen."
"The merest quanta by ours, but."
"Well if that isn't a way to seize a meir . . ."
"And just a sliver at that."
"A mere passing drem of the meir."
"Yet weighty. The weightiest of meirdrem, may as well say."
"What's that like, I wonder?"
"Only thing to do is ask."
"When it wakes."
"When it wakes."

* * *

I sit upon cold and flat stone. My back leans against a wall.
The clash and shatter of battle echoes still in my skull.
I still feel the thunder of it. In my sword hand. In my skeleton.
"Its eyes rekindle!"
"Such penetrating cinders of green."
"O what sights have they recorded?"
"We must ask."
"We must ask."
I can make little sense of this bewildering chatter. At first my eyes

perceive only a uniform haze, then two white eyes appear, hovering no more than a finger's breadth before me. They stare deep into my skull as if in appraisal of its worth, until I stir and they retreat to dart about the haze amidst a persistent metallic squeaking.

The haze slowly clears, revealing before me a pair of partially decomposed avians with long, featherbare necks that snake through the barbed bars of a large iron cage hanging beneath a stone archway on the end of a short chain. They cock and twitch their heads in the space around it as if constantly seeking better vantage, flipping their cracked and broken beaks left and right to scrutinize me one eye at a time. The cage whips thin streams of tar over a stone ground as it rocks about.

I look about the vicinity. A small, shadowy antechamber. Gray light floods through the archway; it seems the only point of egress. Beyond it I can see only a misty corridor.

"Well? How is it, then? All in one piece?"

"Though several pieces are just as nice, we reason."

"Yea, for its solid lot."

"O yea!"

I look down to assess my condition. My cuirass has been returned to me, blackened but intact. There is pain. The whole of my innermost arm is still charred. When I probe its flesh black chips of it flake away, and even now it smolders with the thinnest remnant of ethereaic fume.

Bracing against the wall I stand and find that Cryptmourne is returned to its clasp at my side. When I draw it forth its steel catches bluegreen along the waves of its blade, gleaming in silent acknowledgment of our shared presence in this moment. I look down the blade to check its trueness and edge, and the avians retract their heads back into their cage and flap their crooked wings, spattering the walls with flecks of tar, their grimy feathers smacking down upon the stone floor.

"My oh, haven't we never seen so fierce a knight!"

"Don't believe we have!"

"Looks it could eat up half the sky, it does."

"Chew through two Heavens and a Hell!"

"And that before breakfast."

"Yea! And that."

I sidle past their cage and they tuck their beaks against their throats and track me with their white dead eyes as I move into a bleak and featureless passageway, just beyond the threshold. Broad corridors stretch away in three directions into a prevalent mist. The walls rise high to jagged ridges etched against the familiar aurorae of the Underworld sky.

"I am not in Mortis Veth," I say.

The birds flutter and rise on their perch on two scaly legs, squawking in apparent amusement at the statement, and I see in fact they share a single emaciated body.

"We think not, don't we?"

"We'd certainly know, we would."

"Fair tiding, this?"

Fair indeed.

"Yes," I say.

* * *

I go into the forward corridor. But for the lack of a ceiling it would seem I am in a crypt or catacomb. The path is weather-cracked flagstone littered with dead vegetation and a debris of rubble and skeletal remains. The walls are of a black stone cut to ashlar and apparently embedded with the myriad bones and skulls of many creatures. Examining them I find once-gapless seams rotted amid a seeping black slime, in places so deep fragments of bone come away easily to the touch. Above a shifting hollow of wind, an intermittent soft clacking as bits fall to tumble down the walls, cracking and scattering over the path.

"What is this place?" I ask.

"That is a good question." Both heads look here and there as if in an effort to uncover its answer.

"Are the others here as well?"

"What others?"

"The other reapers. The others of my kind."

"Are they you?"

"What?"

"You are you. Is anyone else?"

"I do not understand."

"It doesn't understand."

"Well, I don't understand either."

"Perhaps it's sick."

"Perhaps it's mad."

"A sickness of the mind."

"No balms for that, we're afraid."

"None leastways we've discovered . . ."

"That's not why it's here?"

"Why is anyone here?"

"No knowing, no way of knowing that."
"Some pop in. Some get stuck."
"Some pop out."
"Or just pop?"
"Only thing is to go on."
"And watch the walls!"
"Find a way out."
"Try not to go mad!"
"Unless it's that already . . ."
"Ah, well then, why not stay?"
"Yes, why not?"
"Why not, why not?"
"Hmmm?"
"Hmmm?"

My sword hand clenches as I tamp down an impulse to divide this creature into two beings after all. Returning to the passageway I look down the other corridors but find nothing to distinguish them from the first.

"Perhaps I am to wait . . . ?" I wonder aloud.
"Never heard of a body getting somewhere that way."
"Not much doing in sitting, is there?"
"Wouldn't mind the company, though."
"No indeed!"
"When a body can mark no start, the only thing is to grab an end."
"Work the way back! Profound!"
"Quite profound!"
"We just came up with that, we did."
"Just popped into our skulls."

So do I learn what it is to sigh. I would like nothing more than to charge forward even into the unknown, if only to escape the prattling of this wretched, inscrutable creature. Yet it must be I have been set here before it to some purpose.

"Where does this lead?" I ask, pointing down the forward corridor.
"Where indeed!"
"Is this place a ward of Illverness? Are we somewhere within the city walls?" I ask.
"Some where?"
"Some place, it means to say."
"Every place is some place, says I."

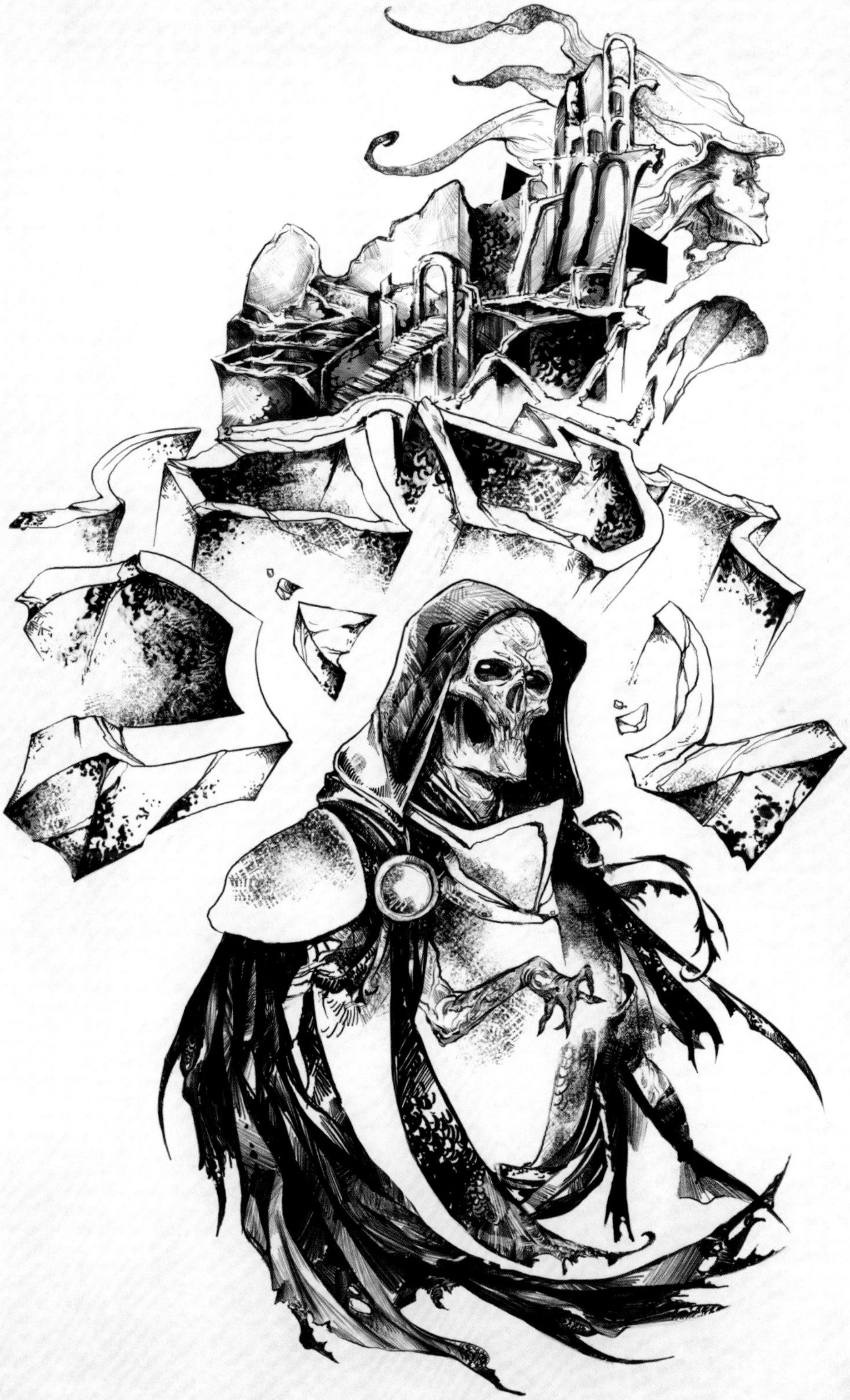

"Unless it isn't?"

"Well if it isn't, someone ought to tell it."

"Quite certain she has already, yes."

"Quite certain."

"She? Do you speak of Xiall? Am I to seek her here?"

"Never heard of a zyl before, have I."

"A zyl! An instrument for the draining of suppurated flesh."

"Quite knowledgeable on the basics, this one is."

"Keen is keen!"

"She is scion to the Alltaker. A . . . daughter."

"What is a dotter, then?"

"Why, somebody who dots, of course."

"It hasn't got a body?"

"But it has, plain as clay!"

"So it has!"

"Why's it need one, then?"

"One self's as good as another, we like to say."

"Unless one's self's gone sour."

"Gone missing, more like!"

"How does one find one?"

"Follow one's heart?"

"Follow one's nose?"

"It hasn't got either."

"It hasn't?"

"It has not."

"Has it got feet?"

"Who can say what's its shoes?"

"So it has shoes, then."

"So it has."

"Why not follow them?"

"Clever!"

"So it was!"

"Well, then."

"Well, then."

  It is time to leave. I move several paces into the forward corridor, and then perhaps only to wrest some control over this moment with haste I double back and make my way down the rightward path, striding from the antechamber even as the wretched, twin-throated creature continues to call after me.

  "It's gone away!"

"Which away has it gone, then?"
"Why, the only way!"
"The right way, then."
"Leastways it knows the left way's wrong."
"Right 'twas all 'twas left two three . . ."
"Many rights, many lefts, 'twill be, 'twill be."
"So it twere, O my, O me!"
"That sounds easy."
"Who can say what 'tis?"
"It knows the way now, 'tis the important thing."
"The way 'tis the important thing."
"Or 'tisn't."
"Or 'tis . . ."

Its chattering abruptly ceases, and in spite of my ire I turn to look, only to find in place of the threshold a solid, uninterrupted wall, as mottled and worn as if it had always been there.

* * *

I advance through the corridor but discover no branching causeways or adjacent chambers. Only the unbroken line of high rotting walls, extending far into the deepening gray fog. I can only continue forward, kicking through bits of rubble and bone and thick tufts of dead gray weeds that collapse to fibrous heaps at my step. To what possible purpose I have been brought into such a place after achieving unity and victory at long last in Mortis Veth I do not understand, only that the deeper I ponder this the greater my confusion and disbelief.

After a time I look back to see nothing more than an identical reflection of the forward way—a long, straight stone corridor disappearing into mist. So indistinguishable is the fore and abaft that when I move to continue on I must suppress alarm at the thought that a moment of distraction might leave me uncertain whether I had turned round at all.

* * *

Wan shrieks echo over the ragged walls like sheets of rain but I see no hint of any creature. I listen for the reaper voices woven among these sounds but there are none and of them I feel nothing. Nor do I sense a presence of any kind beyond my self and Cryptmourne at my side. I think that drawing it once again in the absence of need would bring small comfort to either of us, so I do not.

It is very strange to be alone. My comrades, my creators, my city. Everything of the Underworld obscured from my sight save a sliver of its sky. That this should so mirror that first sight of my awakening upon my bier in ignorance of the great breadth of our city and our world serves only to recall our rise above to witness it. So am I made all the more impoverished by the reflection.

* * *

One kernel of insight the mad gatekeeper did relate amid its endless babble: there is nothing within my strange interlace of soul and spirit that can be called a heart. What wisdom I possess is harbored by blade's edge and the snap of bone. By the burning of fire and of acid. By the freezing blackness of the undoing of light. These are the things that by trial and instinct I know impel me. Though the enemies I have broken be yet animate constructs I can not imagine how it should feel different to destroy a being. I can not imagine . . . creating. Indeed, should I survive our confrontation with the baelreivers it will be the unmaking of mortals that shall govern my existence.

I think perhaps it must be then I am made only to destroy. To lead others to do the same. Perhaps I am not intended to thrive or grow beyond the domain of immediate militant resolve. It would seem this essence of ruin to which I am aligned is not a dominant or even primary purpose of creation. If this is so then as much as it is in my father's nature to embrace me it is also his burden to reject me. For his striving to transcend his contradiction is the heart of him which I do not reflect.

* * *

I mark no progress save perhaps an advance deeper into listless confusion. At a loss and perhaps in some measure of rebellion I turn about and begin to run in the direction whence I'd come. As the mist and walls of unbroken monotony race by I realize that this is perhaps my first act born completely of my own will. I run faster. If I am here to be the subject of some capricious being's amusement then so be it. If by some lapse or failure of action I have been pressed into a trial of forbearance against the absurd then this I have failed already. If I am here simply to wait sequestered for the arrival of Xiall or my father or some other entity of my parentage, then so be it. In the meantime I will run.

* * *

I run until I know that I have long traversed the distance I had walked thus far, unsurprised that I encounter no trace of my point of outset. I fall upon my knees, the poleyns of my armor shrieking sparks against the walls by my momentum. I come to a halt and remain still, wondering whether I should remain in this penitent pose, perhaps eventually to expire and become the sole curiosity of this cursed place.

    I look forward to see that the path now veers clearly leftward. In the thin hope that I might have somehow broken the whim of this place I stand and advance along it, until it begins to meander so wildly that it becomes impossible to determine with any certainty in what direction I travel in relation to my original bearing.

    I stop. Whatever force gives rise to the nature of this place acts in the absence of any logic. I look up at the crescent parcel of the sky visible between the upper edges of the walls. Luminous streaks crawl across its span deep within the swirling tumult that is the realms of Heaven and Hell—perhaps a great exchange of blows between these Celestials whose war seems so distant and irrelevant now. I pine for simple reunion with my comrades in strength, then to be brought forth to meet the immediate enemy that advances even now over the outerlands of the Underworld.

* * *

I look longingly at the diminutive, charred hand of my innermost arm. If only there were etherea to grasp. I would smash these walls to bonepowder and gravel and tear my way free of this place. In Mortis Veth, the very stones were all but saturated with it. Here, nothing but empty bone and rock and long dead weeds. Perhaps my error was to leave the bird intact.

    I look at the wall. As elsewhere, its seams are deeply rotted and glistening with black ooze. The damp stone is soft enough that I am able to press a finger deep into it. When I do so the black slime sizzles and fumes away where it touches my flesh, leaving what proves to be a dry, solid depression in the wall. I test it, and though small bits of stone and bone crumble away it holds fast against my weight.

    I begin to climb.

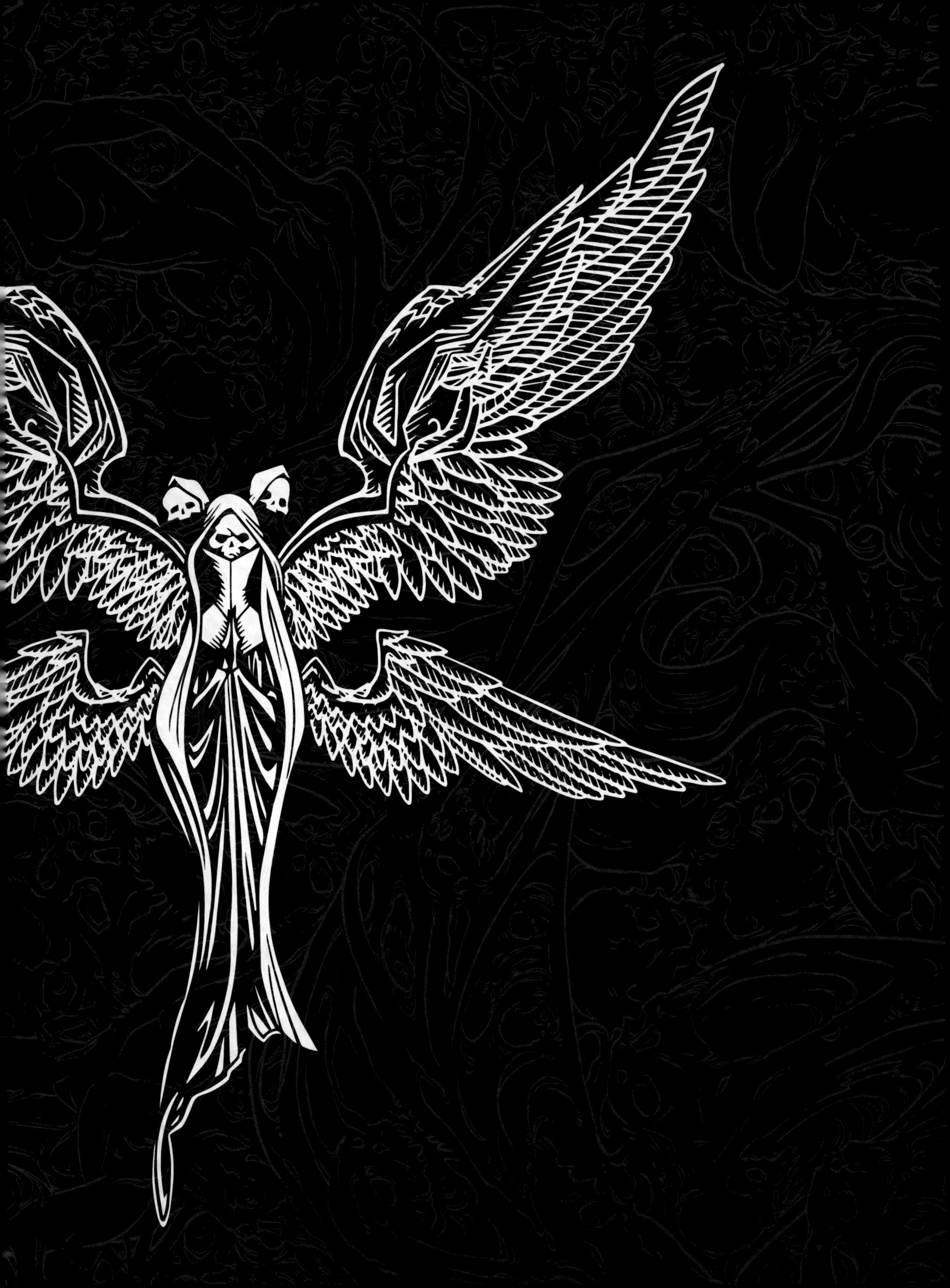

XI.
COMPANION

The rot proves pervasive even at height. I claw into it with each of my arms in sequence, ignoring the pain of my charred inner limb as I brace against the wall with its diminutive grip. I pull my self steadily upward, the fuming holes serving also as footholds into which I plunge the sharp iron toes of my sabatons. Pressing as close against the face of the wall as my armor will allow I look down and mark with some satisfaction the receding of the ground.

But when I look upward I find the wall's summit appears no closer than it had from the ground. I climb with still greater exertion, several times leaping my own height and catching my self again until the path below grows faint behind the gray haze, such distance scaled as would surely have found the wall surmounted. Still its jagged ridges stand as far beyond my reach as before.

* * *

I release my grip and drop the great distance to the ground, the wind of it all I can hear. The shockwave from the impact of my weight upon the path courses through the corridor and I release from deep within my self a scream of naked frustration that presses back the fog and shakes loose stones and bones from the rotting walls.

* * *

In that moment I detect movement in my periphery. I take this at first as residual debris falling upon the path, but when I look to my right it is into what seems at first a long and darkened tunnel. A soft glow as if from spiritlight arises from within just beyond the threshold, revealing an interior archway on a far wall, and when it grows I see the tunnel is in fact a deep succession of connecting antechambers.

The light fades, rises again. I listen but hear nothing of note. I step inside to find a room little different from the one in which I first awakened in this place, but instead of the mad gatekeeper I am presented with an apparition of an equestrian skullform hovering within a cloud of luminous blue ethereaic mist fringed with an orange iridescence. Upon my entrance the glow of the mist holds bright and billows down like a thick fog from the hollow cavities of its skullform and quickly envelops me, and then a voice arises in my mind.

offer words.

It comes as if from deep within my own self. It is very much like wisp speech, though alien still and seemingly held in restraint.

"I hear your words," I say.

It sighs forth a fresh billow of ethereaic fog, rekindling the permeating glow that now fills the small antechamber.

a voice strange.

"My own?"

not scent. forward.

The phantom aspect hangs in the air amid a low, persistent hiss. Somewhere near, the dry clatter of bone fragments falling. In the distance, an inscrutable cry.

"What are you, exactly?" I ask.

traveler.

"Can you tell me where we are?"

we are now. voice?

"I mean, do you know what this place is?" I say.

this place.

"Yes," I say.

I wait, but it only hovers to its gentle hiss, as if waiting also.

"Why are you here, before me now?" I ask.

Another moment of silence, and then:

a traveler to travel the first. to new. this place between places, a barrier. a traveler to come to under.

"To under. The Underworld? You are from beyond the veil?"

a traveler. to come to under. to see. this place between. this place first to see. but a wall. traveler?

"Of a kind," I say.

a traveler. yet the wall.

"Yes." I look down the endless corridor of rooms. "I seek also the Underworld, though I do not know the way . . ."

the way. the way.

The apparition slowly turns about to face the solid wall behind it.

follow.

I look down the tunnel of connected antechambers. "What—" I begin to say, but when I turn back to the apparition it has begun to press itself into the wall, crumbling what bits of it are not simply disintegrated to spill over the antechamber floor. Within moments it has opened into the rock a great gaping tunnel into which it proceeds, leaving behind it a trail of mist, its spectral light chasing away the darkness within.

follow.

* * *

I follow after its glow, kicking through the rubble as it burns ever deeper through the solid rock. Why this guide should ignore what would seem the simpler avenue I can only guess. Perhaps the corridor of antechambers presented me was no less infinite and futile than any other I have thus far traversed in this place. If so it would seem my spectral entity acts unbound by the environment's caprice.

A sudden flood of light announces our emergence into a broad subterranean catacomb, open but for parallel lines of brick pillars, some of which have collapsed away from the stonework trusses arching down from its ceiling. Amorphous lumps of what seem darkly clouded glass are scattered throughout. A thin gray fog curls over everything, diffusing the ethereaic glow of my guide as I follow it through the space.

As we draw nearer the glassforms I see within each a shadowy core, and moving to inspect one I am surprised to find inside the encapsulated form of a chimeric creature unknown to me. The soiled shell of its prison is further stained black where the translucent material has been carved away to expose an area of its head, which has been cracked open and hollowed, leaving a bloom of its feathery hide clumped against the glass.

I step back to look again at the creature's snarling face, its eyes locked in anger and dismay, and surveying the myriad glassforms throughout the catacomb I see this same stain present upon all of them. I move among them to find in each a new exotic being I can not identify. Some have been frozen in defensive postures, their strange visages twisted by fury and indignation. But many others bear expressions of shock, with forms at rest as if in the midst of parley.

As I begin to think about the origins of these beings and what must have brought them to this place I feel my self suddenly shadowed by a pall of profound frustration, as if I alone was given to bear witness to this menagerie of unfortunates cursed to stand forever in bitter contrast to the vanished spheres of existence each had once labored to craft for themselves. Yet no emanation of spirit aspects do I sense. What they had once been was taken and no part of it remained. And so what presence of loneliness and humiliation I perceive is but from my self alone and thus is irremediable.

And so for the first time do I begin to understand Death.

* * *

I look away to find my skullform guide hovering in its fog of etherea before one of the glassforms. As I approach, it rises to before the figure's head, and I can see that this one has remained unmarred. My guide vanishes and does not return, and from within the creature's eyes deep, savage orbits there flares a sudden amber light.

It seems at first a manner of equine beast, standing tall upon six narrow legs, though its definite nature is blurred by the murky glass now flooded with a radiance of bluegreen and orange. The ethereaic haze that had billowed from the phantom now spills from thin cracks in the glass, becoming a thick cloud that envelops me as it had done in the antechamber.

traveler, a traveler.

Its head is long and tapered, its muzzle a match to the skelliform apparition. Yet I know that it is no beast. Even trapped within this solid prison, this entity manifests an exotic energy, and light pulses along its hide as its words reach me again.

a plea cast. voice?

"Yes," I say.

Its eyes flash. Its massive chest heaves within the restraining crystal as I move to its side, and I slam my outer rightside fists into the glassform beneath its belly, then again, spreading the thin network of cracks to a deepening web from which an oily liquid begins to seep.

The creature's glow intensifies within, and I step back as its light floods through the cracks, burning away the glass in a foul vapor. Then a there is a piercing screech as it smashes itself through the weakened structure and immediately bucks swiftly about the room, blinking in and out of existence as the remnants of its prison shower through the chamber. It

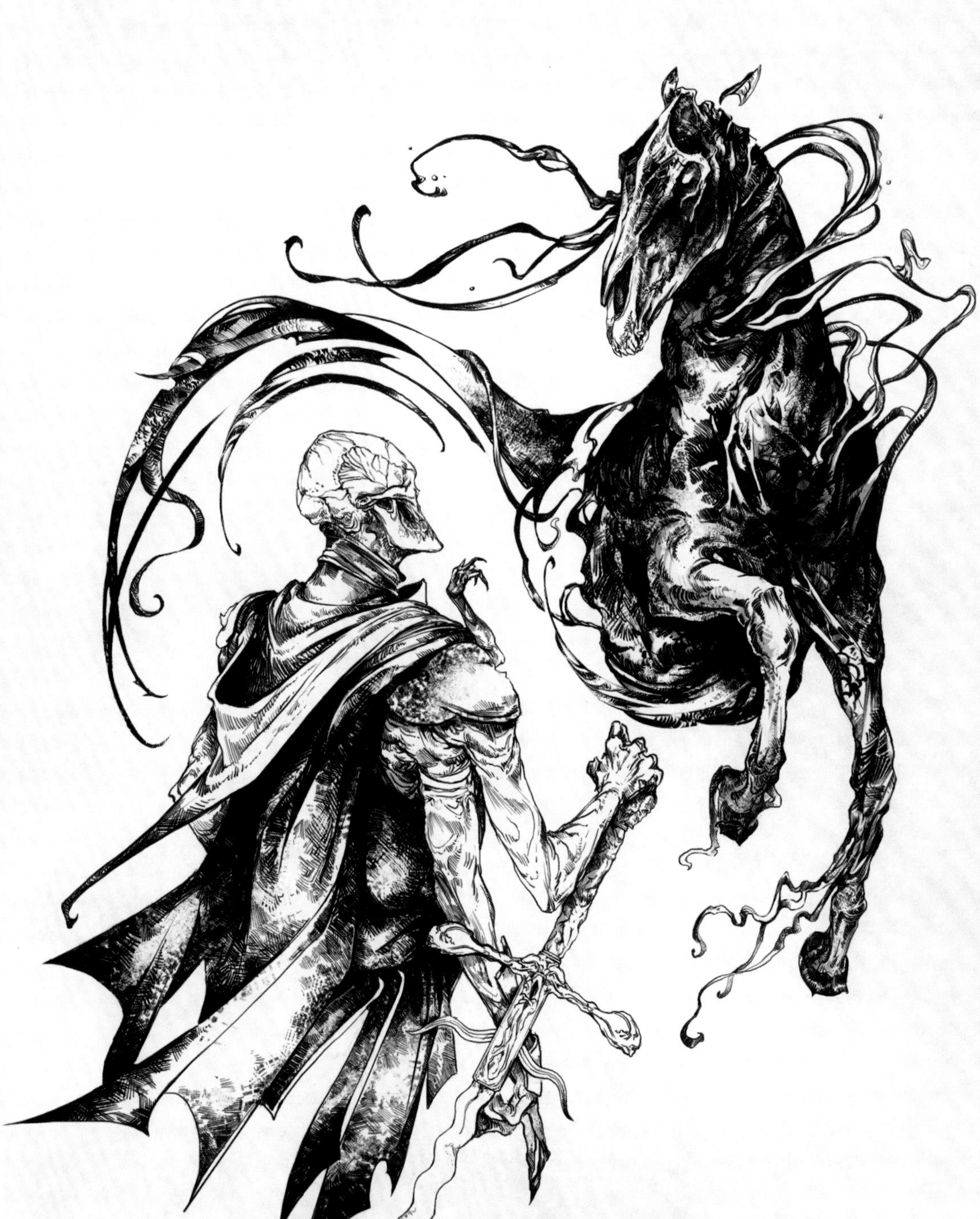

kicks through several of the pillars, scattering pieces of brick, and raising its skelliform head it releases a sustained cry that seems to slice between the realms as the entire chamber violently shivers, shaking mortar loose and driving cracks through the surrounding glassforms.

Finally settling itself with a shake of its thick neck, it finds me with its beaming amber eyes, and returning with a huffing canter it leans before me, presenting its forelegs in a low bow, a motion which draws down twin trails of glowing mist from its muzzle. And raising itself again it heaves forth a fresh cloud of mist to envelop me.

a traveler, a debt.

Even standing fast now before me it shifts subtly in and out of the space, as if its anchor to this realm became untethered by its every subtle movement.

"No debt is owed," I say. "I am captive here as well. Perhaps we might aid one another."

It looks at me a moment, as if considering.

a traveler, a kin. offer sound.

It stretches its powerful neck and casts out a whicker, ending it with a rattle of slackened flesh around its maw.

the call for traveler.

"yyyyycnafff," I say, trying to recall the nuance of the sound.

yycnaf. voice?

"That is a way it can be spoken," I say.

ycnaf. to call for traveler. good.

"Then it is your name," I say, bowing. Curious that it should be me to now bestow a name. "The honor is mine, Ycnaf the Traveler."

It whinnies a subdued approximation of its name.

ycnaf. a name. good. traveler offer sound?

"I am named Demithyle."

de-mi-ta'il. shape. honor. cry of battle. voice?

"Yes," I say, offering another bow in acknowledgment. "Though the battle seems to have lost me."

I scan the breadth of the catacomb.

"What has happened here?" I ask. I look at the filthy remnants of the creature's prison. "How were you so entrapped?"

in this place, many new things. new entities. to see to know. travel here, time and time. event, a traveler to find a door to under. a door, a fisher.

"A fisher?"

a minder of this place. fisher alone to know. a fisher, a key. ycnaf trav-

eler to ask. to open door. to go to under. a fisher, a menace? a menace. weak but false. this unknown to ycnaf, to herd.

"You were betrayed," I say.

yes. betrayed. to promise but not to give. to trap. but to ycnaf traveler a menace weak. to fail to take, to trap only. then to wait. to watch. fisher menace many entities to trap to take. mind and spark. mournful entities, gone and not gone. fisher menace unseen. time and time. ycnaf only to wait.

"How long have you waited?"

time and time.

"Are there others here waiting like you? Trapped but extant?"

Its eyes flash, and it shakes its broad neck, wheezing forth a fresh bloom of etherea.

ycnaf alone untaken.

Cryptmourne emanates yearning at my swell of anger. I draw the sword, squeezing its hilt as I look about the chamber filled with the fisher's victims, their moments of unmaking forever displayed.

"Perhaps the time is come to meet your faithless fisher," I say, "and compel it to make good on its bargain."

Ycnaf breathes heavily, eyes aglow.

one sight, traveler and traveler.

My companion's mist thickens and scintillates around me, and for the first time since Mortis Veth I feel the siren call of etherea. Cryptmourne pulses along its blade as it gathers the mist to me, and I feel the familiar rush of power as I take it in.

I look at a grouping of glassforms. I smash into their midst, exploding away several of their remains. Bricks tumble from the ceiling around me as a nearby pillar breaks apart. I turn to Ycnaf, and with silent agreement we set about destroying the rest.

* * *

Weakened by our volleys the ceiling of the misty catacomb begins to fail, and we exit to a wide corridor, pausing beyond the chamber threshold to bear witness to its final collapse amid the groaning vomit of dust and debris.

now memory only.

"Yes," I say, watching as the threshold fills with stone.

fair rite for herd of de-mi-ta'il?

"Perhaps. I have not existed among them long enough to know."

Ycnaf appears to considers this. Then after a moment it walks slowly backward, its six slender hooves clapping against the stone as its blinking presence stutters about its general position. Then over its scaly hide lines of light begin to course, the mist between us is displaced by the eruption of a shadowy bubble. It warps and wobbles, then settles into a solid black spheroid.

The core of the spheroid enkindles, then grows more luminous even as the chamber darkens, as if it were leeching the room's light. Vague shapes emerge within, soon defining to present a view of an expansive, arid plain overrun with creaturekin of my guide. They stream in countless scores, their ranks parting round eroded stone formations that rise high into an alien sky, a vast exodus that spans all the way to a pale orange horizon.

the herd. always to roam content. content aswim in simultaneity, the sublimation of being. always to see before to see after. all of time at one time. not to break. not to make. not to touch but a realm the first, where all is known. only a traveler to step from the herd.

"You are the first among your kind to leave the herd?"

yes. ycnaf traveler the first. to break a chorus. to see to touch. the herd to run upon crux of thread. only crux. why? not to see, not to know beyond. why? not to grow. why?

Ycnaf coughs streamers of ethereaic mist aglitter with orange light. They envelop the spheroid aperture and then flood into it, entwining as they pour down over the scene to become a growing fog that rolls over the advancing herd. Passing through it the creatures draw it into themselves without breaking stride, and they bound and screech, blowing it out once again with great breaths to roll over those who trail behind them.

herd to see. to give this time and time. to remember ycnaf traveler. now to know debt. to know de-mi-ta'il.

Ycnaf twitches a blurry ear and the sphere collapses to a pinpoint, disappearing in a faint curl of mist.

"It would seem you are unique among your kind," I say.

unique.

It looks after the vanished aperture as it repeats the word, perhaps considering its meaning. Then it looks at me, breathing deeply as if imbibing some veiled emanation from my self.

de-mi-ta'il unique.

"I am but one of scores of my kind," I say, shaking my head, "created to stand against an implacable enemy. It is long past time I am returned to them."

Ycnaf shakes its broad neck, bristling the plates over its hide, vibrating in place as it turns to look back at the sealed entrance to the corridor.

here a voice strange. no cloud of breath. no hoof upon the stone. yet entities found. all of fluctuating termini. one beginning, many ends.

It turns to me again, its orange eyes glinting here and there as it shifts now more subtly in and out of the space.

de-mi-ta'il, a traveler's thread timeworn. many beginnings, one end. a terminus quiet. a terminus strong. de-mi-ta'il unique.

It trots around me in a seeming examination of my physicality, and when it stands before me again it seems to have grown in stature, and I mark the spiny ridges upon its back as they broaden and elongate and lie flat against its form.

we to root.

"Root?"

traveler, traveler. two to one. de-mi-ta'il to see, to guide. ycnaf to guide, to see. to root to one timeplace. this timeplace. two to know.

It steps close, sidelong as if to present to me its still broadened back. Sheets of warmth emanate from its hide.

offer steed.

I meet its eye, unwavering within its hollow, potent, mystical, innocent. I touch her massive shoulder. Her spatial shifting ceases as she stands before me finally now at rest, and waiting. I pull my self astride my new companion, and together we go on.

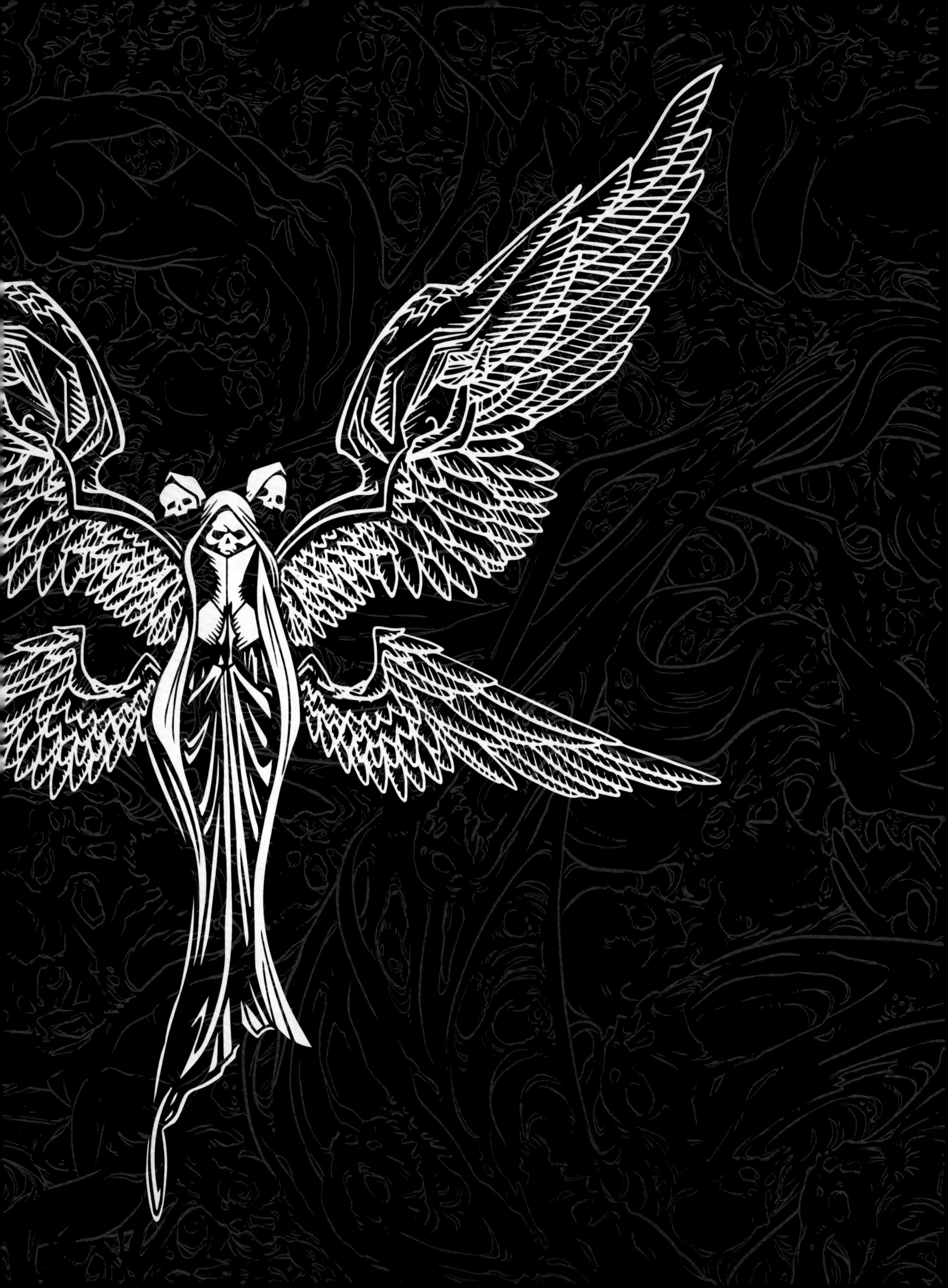

XII.
CONCURRENCE

We move as steed and rider ever deeper into this peculiar and inexplicable place. My companion chooses paths of seeming arbitrary divergence as she directs us toward the Fisher, whose presence it seems she can always feel, and so through our rooting do I. Though the entity moves wildly about what must be an infinitely intricate volume of space, the key to its navigation is no more hidden from Ycnaf than was my own presence here, and with each threshold we grow closer.

  Here at last is a reprieve from the absurd monotony of the path I had traversed alone. In its place, a succession of environments devoid of any overall logic save perhaps that which governs dream. An archway of large fieldstones leads us to a corridor of such oppressive darkness that even Ycnaf's light brings it no dimension. It opens into a grim orchard of erect sarcophagi within an enclosed courtyard, standing beneath an open celestial sky as if rejected from the ground. We find there a single graystone mausoleum surrounded by narrow, lamplit causeways.

  Ycnaf selects one of these without hesitation, taking us to a cavern filled with briar patches of blue crystalgrowth that crackle beneath her brisk gallop, firing tourmaline sparks against the walls. After navigating one of many of its meandering shafts we are suddenly confronted with the latticed grille of a massive portcullis blocking our way, with no visible means of opening.

  Yet my steed companion simply passes through its threshold, the bars proving to be mere shadows cast upon the far wall before us. As we trot by, I mark vague figures animated over it as on a faded mural, given life by some long-forgotten enchantment.

  She is no more hindered by obstruction to her chosen path than she is by these illusions. Where there seems no path of egress she leaps us through narrow gaps and over heaps of broken wall. Where debris is spilt over the winding thoroughfares she impels it aside with a casual breath or simply smashes us through it in a swift burst of force. When it seems our path has led us to a dead end, she rears up before the face of a sheer wall only for our frame of reference to reorient to a new spatial plane as she steps forth upon it.

To such maneuvers I quickly learn to adapt. To feel her intent by increasing familiarity with her motion beneath me and through the empathy of our rooting. She in turn adapts her actions to accommodate my weight, and as our affinity grows our movement through these spaces becomes ever more as that of a single entity. By the audacity of her step we trigger deadfalls and other crude traps set in the bygone ages of whatever realm from which the area was plucked in the assemblage of this place. Indeed, though at times we hear the sounds of distant cries, the only beings we encounter are unidentifiable remains protruding from beneath boulders or piled at the bottom of deep pits or lying among fragments of what must once have been impaling lances triggered by a luckless wanderer long ago.

Against these also we come to react as one: I to accept her etherea the instant it is offered so as to create for us a protective barrier; she to quickly maneuver my swordarm to parrying vantage against projectiles; I to brace and hold fast to her spiny neck as she launches us clear of a sudden gaping chasm.

In these moments I feel her unbounded exhilaration and I begin to share in it, so that soon I do not know from whom between us these sensations originate. But it is when we find ourselves traveling through a pathway overgrown with a canopy of drooping, slimy vines and I mark her choosing the clearest ways through in consideration of my comfort that I begin to wonder whether perhaps this is an expression of love.

* * *

Time passes indefinitely as we continue on, ever forth to the elusive Fisher. Though my awareness of the creature's movements affords me some sense of this place's dimensions I can not begin to understand its vastness. Many rights, many lefts, indeed.

"How did you find me in all of this immensity?" I ask my companion as she picks our way through a forest of toppled stone goliaths.

de-mi-ta'il voice in music.

"I do not recall having been moved to song in this place," I say.

music to shake stones. thunder against walls.

"Ah, yes," I say. "A 'scream,' we would say."

scream. music of scream.

"Certainly it has been my sole fruitful act here," I say. "I do not suppose you encountered a manic dual-headed bird in your wanderings . . . ?"

manic?

"Mad. Speaking much, saying nothing."

mad. no. creatures here but not here. unseen. waiting. offer words but threads in blur of fluctuating termini. chaos? chaos. to think to be. breath of time only.

"You can not see them passing through time?"

breath only, in this place. a place of moving walls. space to inflate but immutable time. no thing a traveler to root. here never to see until to see. never to remember before to see.

"Then you did not know that I would come."

a traveler waited. a traveler sent.

"So it would seem," I say. "How I have wished to know by what fate or entity."

she of dry and white.

"What?"

a concurrence. voice?

"An accord?"

accord. yes.

She halts, sensing my confusion. She turns her muzzle to look back at me with a glowing orange eye, her mists silent in their mingling with the clinging fog, awaiting my question.

"It was you who brought me here?" I say.

no, de-mi-ta'il. an entity, a traveler discovered. she of dry and white. an accord. an entity to bring a traveler to free a traveler. a traveler to return a traveler to under.

"Why did this entity wish me here?"

ycnaf not to see. an accord, an entity to go. a traveler yet bound, time and time to wait.

The image of Ycnaf frozen in the filthy glass returns to me. I feel her elation and hope for freedom soured to desperation as this entity turns away from her. Unconsciously I brush at Ycnaf's spiny neck as if to swat away the clinging remnants of her prison.

"She found you, and left you as you were," I say.

music of de-mi-ta'il. music of ycnaf.

The sound of her anguish arrives in my mind as if by its ferocity it was cast from that distant moment to this one. Oft have I wondered to what purpose I was brought to this place. I know now that I must I discover by whom.

"She of dry and white," I say. "Why do you name her so?"

de-mi-ta'il. a name given to traveler's nature.

"It is the name of a being who perished long ago in the safeguarding of the Underworld. But it was also a name of my own choosing . . ." I hesitate, grasping for the means to convey my journey with Death in the menhir, now seemingly so long ago. "A name bestowed upon me by emanation of my self."

Inwardly I recoil at this obtuse representation of my rite of becoming. But perhaps of all other beings it is Ycnaf who now bears the greatest intimacy of knowing of my self, and even as I falter I sense her comprehension of the true gravity of the experience. Indeed, my answer seems to please her.

yes. a name given to traveler's nature. a traveler, unique. de-mi-ta'il unique. many beginnings, one end. to fight to see to know. music of de-mi-ta'il, music of ycnaf. she of dry and white, a name given to her nature also. to she a traveler's voice unheard. to traveler, she a thread mundane. one beginning, many ends. unbroken by color. consonant with decay. true and not true. all strong but thin to see. dry to see.

I can not be fully certain of Ycnaf's meaning. Yet it would seem clear that this entity who stood before my companion sought to ensure my return to the Underworld in advance of sending me here. And so it must be that soon enough we will meet.

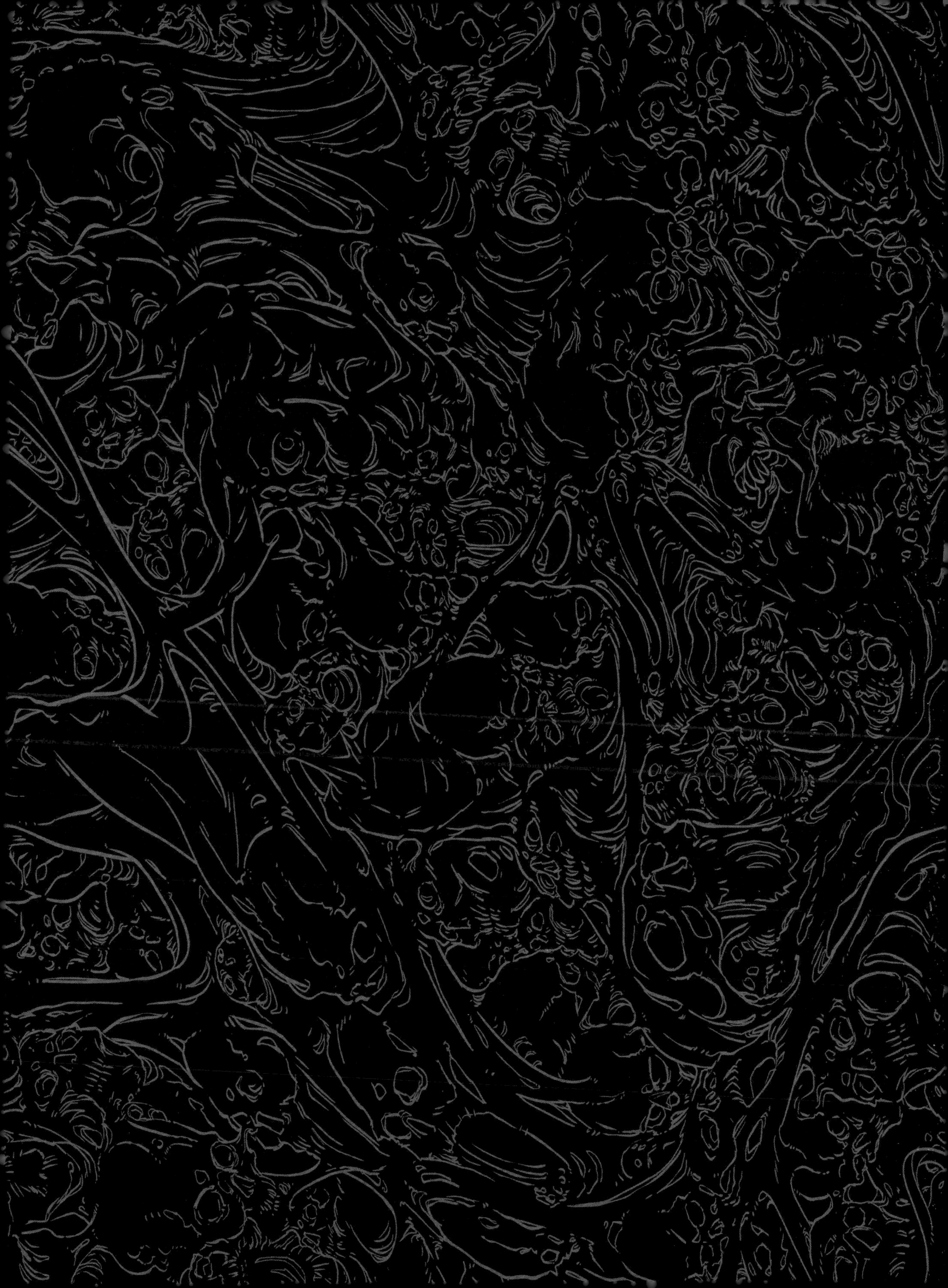

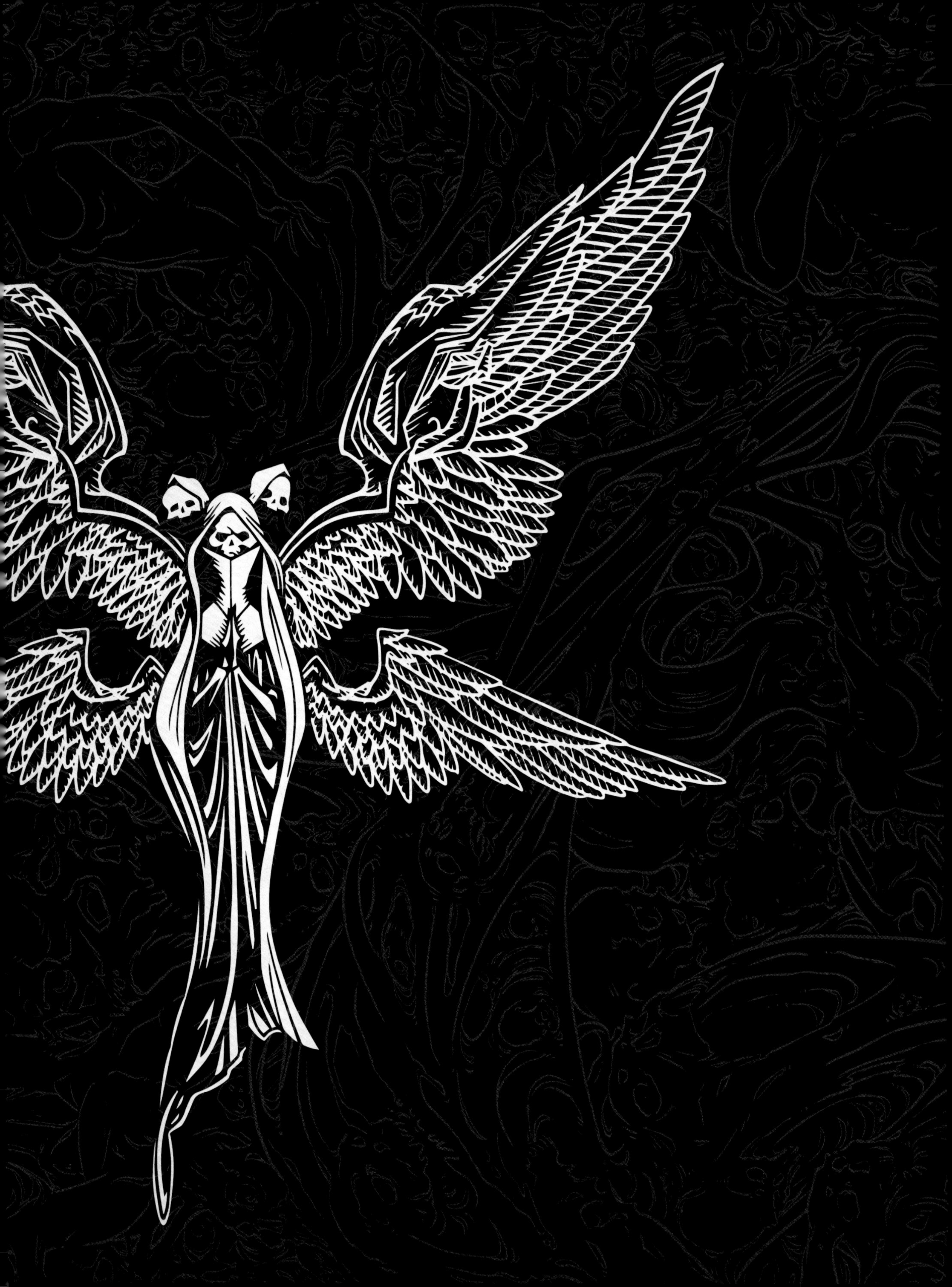

XIII.
THE FISHER

Ycnaf returns her attention to the path and continues forth, her ever-present cloud of wisping breath diminishing as she sinks into her own reflections. Realizing the fog has lifted I look round to see the walls have now fallen away completely. Gone is now any resemblance to the Underworld as I had briefly known it. The sky is black and starless. Before us spreads a vast expanse of narrow, interlocking chasms bounded by an unbroken horizon of white light burgeoning in every direction, as if the rise of mournmeir awaited to be bidden from a direction of our choosing.

And here for perhaps the first time since entering this place between places I forget my yearning to return to the Underworld and my comrades and purpose, as in that moment I simply accept the curious nature of our presence in this time and place. I wonder whether there exists such entities as whose purpose is given to no greater import than to traverse the infinite folds of the Cosmos, as it seems we do now. And by what degree my own could be judged as more or less honorable and lofty, so separate as this seems from the great conflicts to which I have been bound.

* * *

Ycnaf leaps us down over the edge of the narrow pathway into one of the chasms, landing upon a small terrace, the meeting of twin stairways that twist so far below that their steps vanish into the darkness. Without a second look into its depths she walks us through a threshold from the terrace and we find ourselves traveling within a downward-sloping tunnel of cold, packed clay. Our light casts erratic shadows over its rounded walls. The tunnel narrows and though Ycnaf steps low I am obliged lean over her neck to prevent my skull from scraping against its ceiling.

The tunnel levels and a light appears ahead, cast down through what proves a brush-covered hole, its upper rim just within reach from where I sit perched astride Ycnaf. I can feel the Fisher's nearness as I pull my self up through the brush, and Ycnaf blinks away beneath me, reappearing at my side where we stand at the outskirt of a broad clearing enclosed by vine-crossed walls of dark stone and overgrown throughout with a black, leafy ground cover. Here and there stand further figures entrapped by the filthy crystal, variously overgrown with weeds. All are cracked open at their skulls save one attached halfway up the far wall, the murky form of a cloaked mortalborn locked within, her face frozen in a rictus of shock, fingers articulated before herself as if in mid-weave.

Below her in the center of the clearing is a low hill upon which stands a crumbling, lichen-spotted cupola, long ago split by the growth of a now-withered tree. The wood is dry and gray and swirled throughout with veins of rusting iron. Its branches claw over a small pond at the base of the hill, blanketed by a layer of dark effluvia, its waters mirror-still beneath.

There is movement at the shoreline of the pond, and for the first time I see there a stunted, scaly creature staring hard into the water. It is simply clothed in an oily canvas jerkin and wears upon its back a leather satchel stitched from a large entity's face, the sad, drooping features still evident beneath the tanning. It twitches its bulbous nose, muttering inaudibly through curled, fishy lips as it shifts about the pond on two naked feet, its long toes bent up just over the water's edge as if not to disturb it. Suddenly it snaps at the surface, punching a hole through the vapor as with a hooked claw it draws a gleaming, iridescent thread out from the water, which it then lays over its other arm to hang limp in a row with several others, chuckling to itself before peering down at the surface again.

"Fisher," I say.

It jerks to attention and squints through the murk, its long fan of whiskers bent against thorny jowls. Finding me with eyes drawn nearly closed from the strain, it seethes through several rows of needle-pointed fangs.

"Eh, hear a thing, what?" says the creature, stepping out around the tree. "Whatfish? Fishes? No fish here!"

It steps forward. But when it sees Ycnaf it snarls back its lips over rows of needleteeth.

"*Eh hai!*" it says, forming a wicked smile. "Break it free, did it? Eheh! Glowmist blue, sparky-eye, keep a Simmel out it brain. But kent get loose, hain? *Kent!* Nain by beak, nain alone!"

The Fisher

Ycnaf remains still, staring at the Fisher, outwardly impassive to its taunts but for the subtle flame behind her eyes. Yet I feel her wish to destroy it as if the desire were my own.

"Simmel see it now, eh heh," it says, gnashing its fangs. "Peek in it skelly, soon-soon, *ehehhh* . . ."

I draw Cryptmourne. Its blade flashes blue through the fog. The Fisher huffs, retreats behind its tree.

"You are the attendant of this place," I say. "You entered into a bargain with this being, a traveler from beyond this realm."

"Beargain! Nain a beargain!" It hops from foot to foot in a frantic dance of protest, continuing to shield itself with the tree. "Stuppid, creck it mule-skell," it says, pointing a long claw at Ycnaf, "maybe it give ivver, maybe give it nain, yiss? Maybe it brain-skell creck it, mad-spint long fivver'gone, weh? And now bring it soldier to pester a Simmel, *weh*, only just set to fish it ruminant, *ewehh*."

"You entered into a bargain," I say. "We would see you make good on it."

It pitches a clawful of muck at us. "Bah! Helftaint skelly, look it for beargain, nain! What mennow bring it, weh?"

"We carry only what you see," I say, uncertain of its meaning.

"No mennow? Offer no mennow? Offer nothing?" It casts up its arms, abandoning its shelter in annoyance. "Nain a screedlin, nain a winkfish? What it want for nothing, weh? Offer nothing, nothing what it like to get!" It snarls, cradling against its chest the gleaming row of catches still swinging limp over its arm. "Nain a one loach off a Simmel, get it?" it says, pointing an accusing claw. "Find it a hole in some place else, heh? Some place else far away!"

"We wish to return to the Underworld," I say. "You must know the way. We covet no meat of yours."

"Meat! Ha!" it says. "Crack it, skelly! Know nain a mennow! Stuppid, it! Shake it skell, see what spill out it! More nothing, weh? Bah!"

It waddles to the pond and slaps at the dark water with the back of its hand. "Nain know mennow! Nain a one know, nain a one want! Membrent stray, a tinny trickle, say. Only great big sight to swim as, be as, want they. But Simmel know, weh. Sight inna meirdrem, left by forgot. Spittle coin inna fountain. Simmel swim inna underpocket, down-down 'tween the places. Catch a mennow up. Small coinsy but keep it by and by. Big trissure, now! Biggest it! Elltikker come at Simmel to want it, soon-soon. See it, weh! Other too, from under-over, both a way. Then it all see what-what."

It paces about the pond as it rants, slapping its broad feet into the muck, swiping through the effluvium, yelling at its own reflection. Finally it clomps up the low hill and sitting its bulk against the base of the ruined cupola it folds its arms and peers at us, scornful and shrewd.

"Need way, it," it says, squinting us over. "Simmel know, yiss. Know way. Skelly got nothing. Nothing in hend. Nothing in baldskell. What it got for beargain, *hain*?"

I hold my arms out wide. "What would you have?" I say.

It jumps to its feet and hobbles in close, its fear of my sword now overcome by its realization of our need.

"Got it a geddy arm, weh," it says, gesturing at my right side. "Got it four, don't need four. Leastway a tinny one. What it for, weh? Plicking a tinny harp? Wreppit round Elltikker wrinkle phaelker, eheh? One slimmish finger inna sphinker-skint, ha!"

"I would not relinquish a limb," I say, brandishing Cryptmourne again, backing the Fisher off. "Something else?"

"Bah, else!" it says, turning back toward the cupola.

But halfway up the hill it looks back, eyeing Ycnaf over the forlorn visage of its rucksack. Slowly it turns again to face us, its hand fondling a dull metal amulet held partway between the folds of its tunic, its corroded iron chain now visible around the creature's neck.

"Skelly need way, weh?" says the Fisher. "Got it nothing. Nain but meat onna mule. Glimmerbrain, thet. Dripple bluemist. Simmel gettit this time, weh. Make bitsy hole innit sparky white skellit, teppit inna licky hollow. Geddy beargain, weh? Simmel get it lick and lick. Skelly get it beargain. *Yiss?*"

At this Ycnaf releases a simple cough, blasting back the Fisher to roll up and over the hill as the remnants of cupola crack clear of the tree to smash against the far wall.

"I would recommend against the attempt," I say.

After a moment of scrambling out of sight the Fisher, audibly grousing, peeks over the hill, glancing over to us with renewed menace as it picks itself up and looks itself over for wounds. A sudden look of consternation then sweeps over its face, and it smacks its hand against its chest as looking down it disappears again behind the crest of the hill, blurting out curses amidst the sounds of its scrabbling through the weeds. And the clearing comes everywhere alive with movement then, as the crystalforms begin to melt all throughout, oozing dirty oil as pieces crumble away until the dead forms within crack through the weakened structures and collapse into the entangling weeds.

Then there is a sharp gasp, and the clearing is suddenly lit by a bright flash as from the place where the mortalborn had been frozen upon the far wall a searing bolt of white lightning streaks over the hill, sending me to hug the ground as it explodes into the wall behind us even as she too drops from sight beyond the hilltop.

As the last of the rubble showers around us I look up the slope toward the sound of her pained, bewildered moan. But before I can stand the air is pierced by Simmel's snickering sneer of triumph, and the voice of the mortalborn cries out.

"*Wait! No—*"

There is a thickening crackle and I stand just as tendrils of the murky crystal crawl into view over the far wall. Then a grunt from Simmel accompanies a sharper crack, before its snickering is muffled by a lascivious slurping.

A moment later Simmel saunters atop the rise, its wormlike tongue glimmering with a spiritous essence where it wags between its fangs. It points at us with a blackened thorn that slowly retracts into a fleshy sleeve behind its wrist.

"Simmel get it fillit after all, heh," it says, drawing in its tongue. "Sparker-fire make niv'riddy, lick-long awaity. Thank it skelly-mule, weh? *Aheh.*"

Ycnaf glowers as I tighten my grip on Cryptmourne. It is all I can do to resist destroying this creature in this very moment. Broken branches torn from the tree bob about the far side of the pond as the effluvium that had been blown away from it quickly refills.

"Nain a beargain, skelly?" says Simmel, smacking its fishy lips. It points at my sword. "Flameblade do it mule, yiss. Sliver-tinder, cut. Mule for a way, eh?"

I give it nothing. I say nothing.

"Bah!" says Simmel. "Let it find it way, then! Without a Simmel, then!"

Inasmuch as the beings destroyed by its greed demand its punishment, leaving the Fisher to visit this fate upon still further entities would seem a clear atrocity unto itself. But I must return to Illverness. What is at stake is far greater than this easy justice presented me now. A strange defeat. And yet I must accept it. Nothing further can be risked in its denial.

I look down at my battle-blackened breast plate. Scarred, bent, but solid still. I hold no sentiment for it, nor is there foreseeable need of it in this place. Stowing Cryptmourne, I work to unfasten the greaves, and then holding it forth I look at Simmel as I let it fall to the ground, feeling once again naked as I had stripped of it in Mortis Veth.

The Fisher's eyes grow large. I step back from the plate. When Ycnaf follows suit the creature rushes over to take hold of it.

"Death steel," I say. "Made from iron dug from the bogs of Ulvverg, quenched in black brek oil, and tempered in the dark forges beneath the Calvum Harrows."

Nothing of the material origin of this armor resides within my memory. Nor am I aware of any such place as Ulvverg.

The Fisher turns the breastplate about with its overlarge hands, scrutinizing the edges and curves, hefting it easily though it must outweigh the creature doubly.

"Fine work!" it says. "Under-under smith hammer bog to some thing geddy, weh?" It looks up at me again. "Elltikker hear skelly give it, skelly get hammered to some thing geddy too. Ha!"

Its eyes dart between the other elements of my armor, which I uncouple and release to the ground as well. Greedily the Fisher collects these into an awkward bundle and carries them back to its place near the statue. There it examines them as before, one piece at a time, carefully scrutinizing each as if to discover a flaw that would nullify our bargain, or to simply draw out the moment, pleased as it seems be to inflict discomfort upon us as it makes a show of appraising the value of the armor.

I look down at my self, draped now only by my black undercloak, my form seeming strangely waifish beneath it. Ycnaf stirs next to me, billowing out a discreet mist between us.

a fisher, a menace.

I can only nod in agreement as with dwindling patience I look once again to the treacherous entity before us. Finally tiring of its game it unslings its grim satchel and begins to stuff the elements in, one by one, as we stand by waiting. Somehow all of the pieces fit easily inside, though the smallest is itself is near half the sack's volume. At last it slings the bulging satchel upon its back again and waves us to the still water's edge.

"Sad skellies, need a Simmel to point way out," it says. "Don't know nothing, weh! Don't know, only way out's in, *aheh*. Only way in's down." It tosses a fragment of stone to plunk into the pond, which we now see is shaped into its depth by walls of stone into which are hewn a downward spiral of steps. "See it, stone? See it break inna wrinkle blackmeir? All gone! Down innit black. Down the well, skellies, down like stone. Watch it, shun the walls, weh? Or creck it skellit, leak out mennow to wriggle upway, *aheh*. Nain frit, Simmel keep it, *eheheh*."

The Fisher grins, a full show of fangs, and backs away from the well. "Down, down it go," it says, pointing into it insistently. "Down speed it to the waterdeep. Then out, out it to the way, *aheh*."

With Ycnaf at my side I look into the well, our paired reflections wavering through the effluvium, a display of the worn and macabre in this place of the macabre.

"Yiss, down," says the Fisher, grinning, nodding at the well. "Down speed it to the waterdeep. Down speed it to the way."

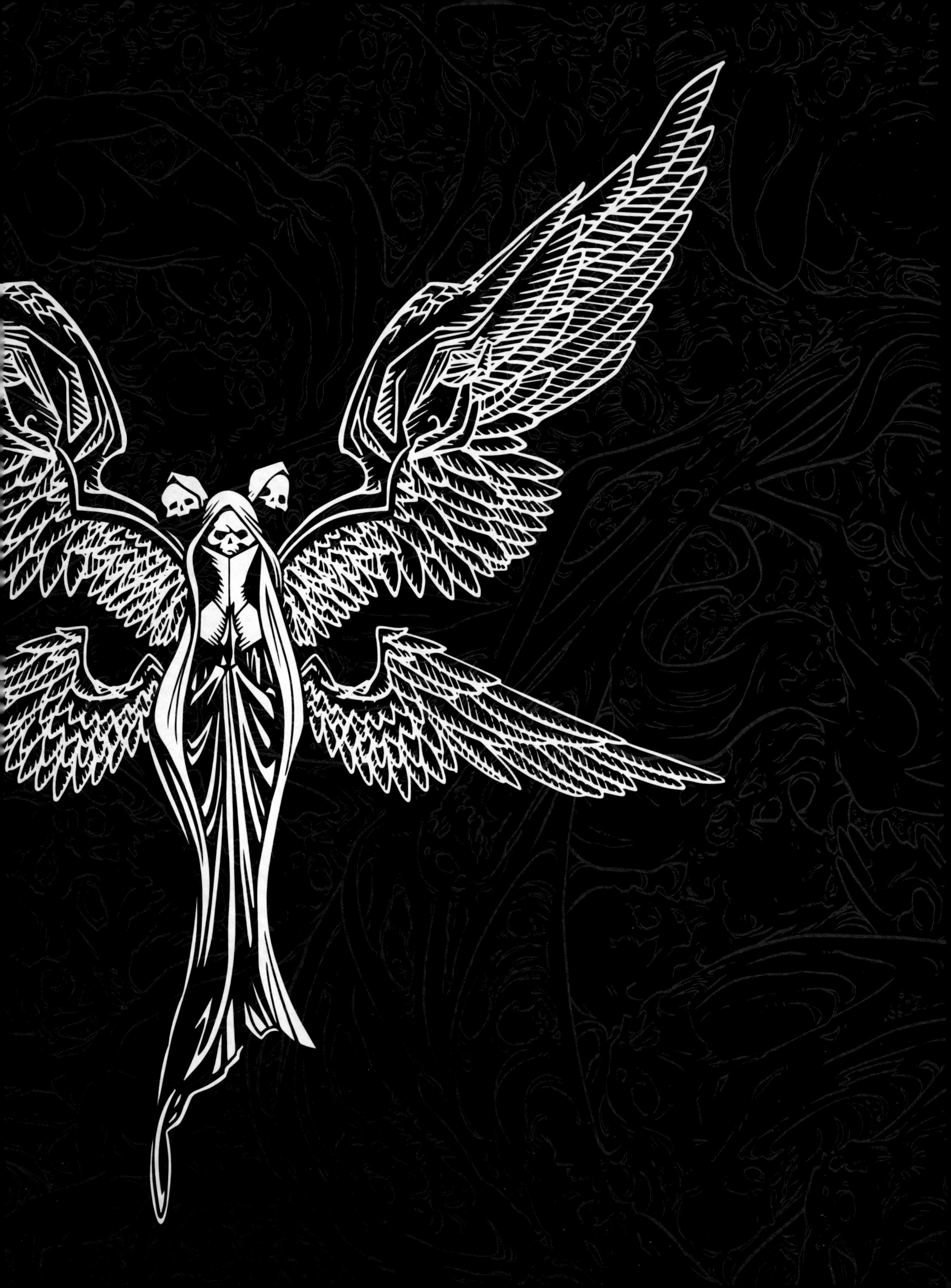

XIV.
DESCENT

I step into the pool. Ripples pass over its surface, rolling away the clinging vapor, distorting the image of the downward spiral of steps diminishing into the black as glimmering sprats of memory twitch about through its depths.

And then Ycnaf dives in muzzle first and as the water surges outward from her splash I let my self drop into the void. As the waters close over the crown of my skull Simmel's malignant laughter follows after.

＊ ＊ ＊

My cloak billows around my body as I slow to a steady descent, weightless, armorless, slow and meditative, like an aquatic creature in my own right. The memory sprats dart about us for a time but soon thin and then disappear as we drop beneath the light of their domain. Here great gaps appear in the hewn steps around us where holes have been tunneled into the surrounding walls, then disappearing completely as we continue to recede from the light of the clearing. I can not fathom for what such a structure might have been intended. Perhaps a mine, driven so deep as to puncture an aquifer. For whom? How such a conduit will lead us from this place is also a mystery. But if not this there is no way. And so we sink.

＊ ＊ ＊

I am struck by the water's soundscape. The density of its reverberations, simultaneously crisp and dull. The flow of it over me. The cold. Though my own form proves unwieldy in this environment, Ycnaf swims here and there with a hippocampian litheness to belie her equine stature. No anomalous element escapes her attention. The promise of a new realm and of escape from the labyrinth seems to have awakened in her the curiosity that had led her to this place to begin with. As well our rooting seems to have taken hold, for more and more her form remains unflinching in its space as she navigates the depths.

  From above comes the thick vibration of several heavy splashes. Soon after large stones sink past, dim lumps in a field of deepening black. Likely parting gifts from our sinister friend. Ycnaf follows after their descent, and looking past my feet I watch her inner light roll down along the rounded walls of the well.

* * *

As the last gloomlight from the meadow above is swallowed by blackness all recedes from my vision save what few errant particulates cross the spirit glow of my eyes, and for a time I am left alone to ponder the infinite inscrutability of this place. I have come to believe that the fascination for the unraveling of the unknown that I had felt in the first moments of my being was but a symptom of newness in advance of soldierly duty. That the struggles of Mortis Veth and the disquietude and yearning brought by the labyrinth had wholly clouded my eyes to the accumulation of moments of an otherwise mundane nature, which upon reflection might yield discoveries in their own right.

  But now in the weightless dark all that I have seen and experienced since our rise above the city seems to flood to mind in great detail. And, as for want of any other action I allow my self to relive these moments in full, I think that I could ask for nothing greater of this one.

* * *

Ever down we sink. The shape of the watery chasm is defined now by a descent of illuminated striations in the walls, splattered hues of magenta and blue. These prove to be quasiorganic sanctuaries grown into the network of cracks, into which diaphanous creatures retreat as I fall past, eyeing me warily through tiny spectral skulls even as they dim the influence of their light so that I am kept ever in a sphere of shadow.

  It is here that I catch up with Ycnaf, who is keeping her place with fitful outward kicks of her six hooves as she noses through of a cluster of glowing flora swaying lightly by her movements where it grows upon an outcrop of broken wall. As I draw past and below her they release a cloud of yellow globules that quickly envelop her head. Recoiling, she shakes them away, and tucking her six legs close against her body she swirls down below again, glowing eddies of the substance diffusing in her wake.

I watch as she vanishes into a new tunnel, reemerging elsewhere a moment later to glide about in wide spirals. Then for a time she drifts lazily beside me, and together we descend content in our silence, only for her to linger behind as some other curiosity catches her eye, then to stream forth again.

* * *

The well expands to a broad cavern, its walls receding outward beyond sight, beyond any potential reckoning of space. Gone now are the luminous flora and fauna. Whether because they can not thrive at this depth or because enough time has not yet elapsed for them to reach it is perhaps unknowable. But with this increased outward expanse to explore Ycnaf is gone for longer tracts of time, and I am once again left alone in near complete darkness.

As the weight of the water presses against me from all sides the thought arises that perhaps there is in fact no threshold from this abyss. The image of a snickering Simmel comes to mind unbidden. Perhaps these walls shall recede as continuously away from me as has my calling. If Ycnaf should not return, it is doubtful I would be able to ascend alone to the clearing again. In fact by the nature of this place it is doubtful that it is even still there. Perhaps it will be my fate to fall haplessly through blackness forever.

* * *

In the silent density of the deep I allow all thought to recede from my mind. Images of borrowed memory begin to unfurl at the edges of my awareness. Brief visuals, though weighty with sensation. Emotion.

Black tarsmoke, curling up from a flame.

The long shadow of a desert insect struggling away from me over grains of sand.

A mortal hand—my own?—clutching debris that floats in turbulent sea.

Though the moments fade and shift before a fullness of their remembrance takes hold, I know that it is there, and significant. The caustic odor of the tarsmoke; the radiant heat from the sand; the help-

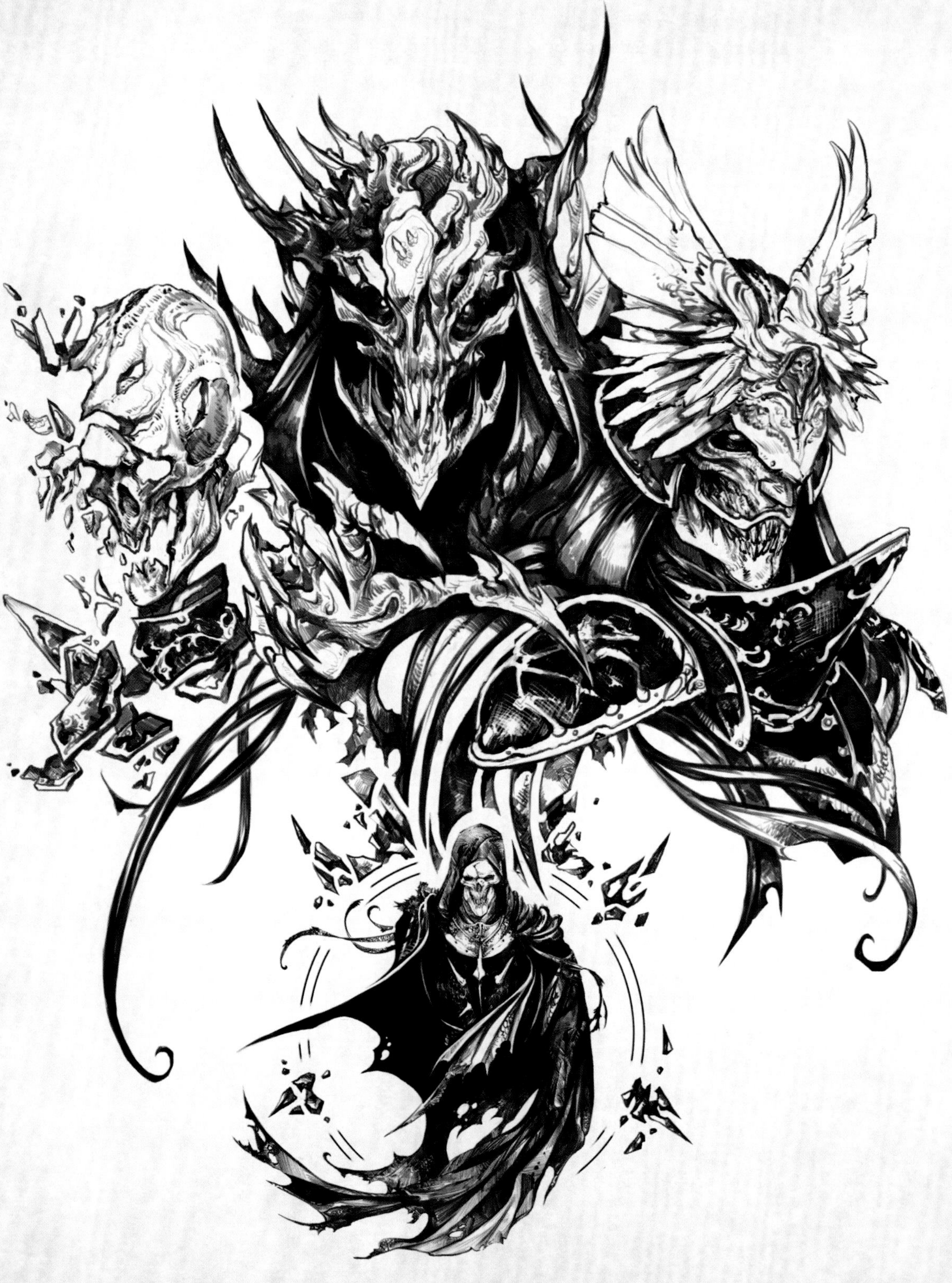

lessness and fear brought forth by my desperate grasping in an unbroken sea. All of these things linger, all brought into my knowing of being. It is a strange fusing of familiar and new, like skirmishes of character settled by the catharsis of dream.

 And then,

I lie flat upon the ground. Hidden in the tree line. Before me a span of white plains. Snow-scoured tundra. I await my prey. Many days have I waited. With the dusk, snowfall drifts, grows thick, dries to flecks of ice that glitter in the waking moonlight. From behind, a crunch. Footfalls in the snow. I do not move. To hide my breath I take snow into my mouth. They can not see me they can not hear me they can not sense me I am the ice and stone the frozen roots of the trees . . .

  Even as this memory wanes,

the river that rushes. The downpour has not ceased for days. Everything gray. A man races along its stony bank. Sodden furs, matted against naked flesh. Desperately calling after someone. She is being pulled away by the water. I stand as she passes and when he sees me he stumbles but I do not act and when he looks back for her she is gone.

 It is difficult to reconcile such influx of emotion with that which I have thus far come to understand as my self and purpose. For with these visions of memory comes also a fullness of their requisite knowing of being that reaches beyond even the moment. I *am* they whose memories I carry. I know all that they knew in that time of their collection. And though I understand their significance to the Underworld's need of us as soldiers and protectors, by taking them into the surface of my knowing I am left also with a strange sensation of loss, as if the instinct to act that they invoke were frustrated by my inability to reach into that distant history. And yet as I drift in the dark bereft of all other sensation this only compels me to delve further.

 And then,

through the green wood I run. I tear through the undergrowth. I cross the shallow brook, kicking out webs of frigid water. The animals follow. They are fierce and starving. Their snarl is black breath upon my back. I vault over rotting trees but loose stones betray my feet and they are upon me. Their teeth aim true yet I have won. There is no trail of scent or force of hunger; they shall not find my child . . .

Though it is true the mortals are ensouled and we are spiritborn, I do not know what else could contain all that is their being but such memories that have been taken from them. And if these memories are mine as any heirloom by right of my creation and being, then what could I be but a creature both enspirited and ensouled?

Yet it seems we reapers were meant as spiritborn as mundane as any other. The Alltaker spoke of this alchemy of being as meant for more than instigation of martial skill, but not as things to be possessed in fullness of knowing. If I alone have done so then it would seem I am unique among my kind, and something both unintended and unknown. If this is so, then what am I?

* * *

I try to conjure further images, but then a very low sonic perturbation suddenly sets the water askew, such that I am shaken as if clutched in the grip of one of the megaliths. A pocket of darkness abates in the distance to a momentary pulse of purple light, and a moment later another shockwave arrives.

I look about but there is no sign of Ycnaf. Then there is yet another pulse, much closer now, veiny patterns of blue and red flowing over the shape of a great aqueous wyrm. It turns toward me as I am hit by the resultant shockwave, and looking at me with dull, red, sightless eyes it begins to pulse rapidly, and I draw Cryptmourne as it rushes directly at me even as I continue to sink, its toothless maw stretched open as if by its own momentum. I position my self to skewer its eye, but it rears back and attacks with a curtain of probing, spectral tendrils from within its mouth. I try to cut through them but the water slows my strike and the tendrils wrap themselves around my limbs and torso, tearing into my flesh with tiny rows of thorny, barbed teeth, and it pulls me through the water with such force that I am unable to resist. From deep in its throat a thick tentacle snaps out to latch onto the crown of my skull and immediately begins to envelop my head. The creature releases a low moan then as a stinging crush of energy courses into me, and Cryptmourne slips from my grip as my body is wholly ennumbed.

I feel the sword's clouded anguish as it drops away but I can do nothing. Another powerful sting, this one accompanied by a strange heat and with it a flood of fractured images flash to mind and quickly fade. The creature works its jaws in a quavering gape as it feeds, my last sight before I am blinded by the encroaching tentacle. The volume of water around me undulates rapidly just before there is another pulse, and then another, memories splintered and taken before I can gain a sense of them. I feel only their loss as a growing hollowness of being. Again Simmel's snarl comes to mind, and I begin to understand its expectation for this very thing to befall us. How many beings had it sent this way in order to harvest what detritus of memory remained? Doubtless this leeching wyrm was drawn by the flavor of my indulgences of recollection. As the world begins to fade I am left to wonder at the consequence brought to the Cosmos by such foolish occupation of the self . . .

There is a sudden impact against me and I am torn free to roll haplessly through the water. Vision returns to my eyes amid the glimmering, unconsumed fragments of my siphoned memories, and I see Ycnaf turn to streak forth and slam into the head of the wyrm, twisting back its girth to smash against the rocky wall. Then with a flash of deep magenta water is wracked by a detonation, and Ycnaf is sent careening back through a dirty cloud of grit and rubble that sinks with me deeper from the fray. I steady my descent I look up and see the cloud flash from within as recovering my companion courses around to tear into the beast again. It curls and twists to meet her attacks, the releases a low groan of pain as she burns away its grasping tendrils, its many wounds spitting luminous viscera into the murk, further clouding the melee.

I look below to find that the walls have begun to narrow around me, and there is a vagueness of light in the distance. And then I see also a glint of steel and I remember my sword, and in that moment I feel it once again in my grip.

Cryptmourne.
Demithyle.

Strength returns to my arm. But before I can turn to offer aid to Ycnaf she slams into me from behind and both of us tumble down against the wall of the shaft as thousands of wriggling spectral leeches spew forth from the stone around us. The low groan of the wyrm bearing down on us, without a word I clutch Ycnaf's neck and she kicks us from the wall in time to avoid the creature's crushing mass as together we stream headlong down toward the source of light.

The shaft brightens by our rushing advance to what proves a shifting undersurface of the water, beams of light advance around us to the warping of the Underworld sky as we burst through it in a white explosion of water, the creature rising with us skyward by the momentum of its pursuit as through the spray I cut a swath to slice deep into a mass of flesh below its jaws. Its outpour of pale yellow blood commingles with the explosion of water and an emergence of glimmering etherea. Without hesitation Cryptmourne draws it to wash over us, so that even in mid-rise my eyes flash with its power, and looking upon the wyrm I feel its shape and presence and the presence of our outbloom of water and the deep plummet of the dark pool beneath us.

  And the anger I had felt in the chamber upon discovering the ruins of so many beings unmade by the treachery of Simmel pours from me as a black scour into this leechwyrm by which the Fisher's greed would have damned the Cosmos, crackling its bones to slivers and rotting it in our wake to fall away in fragments that sink into the vanishing black.

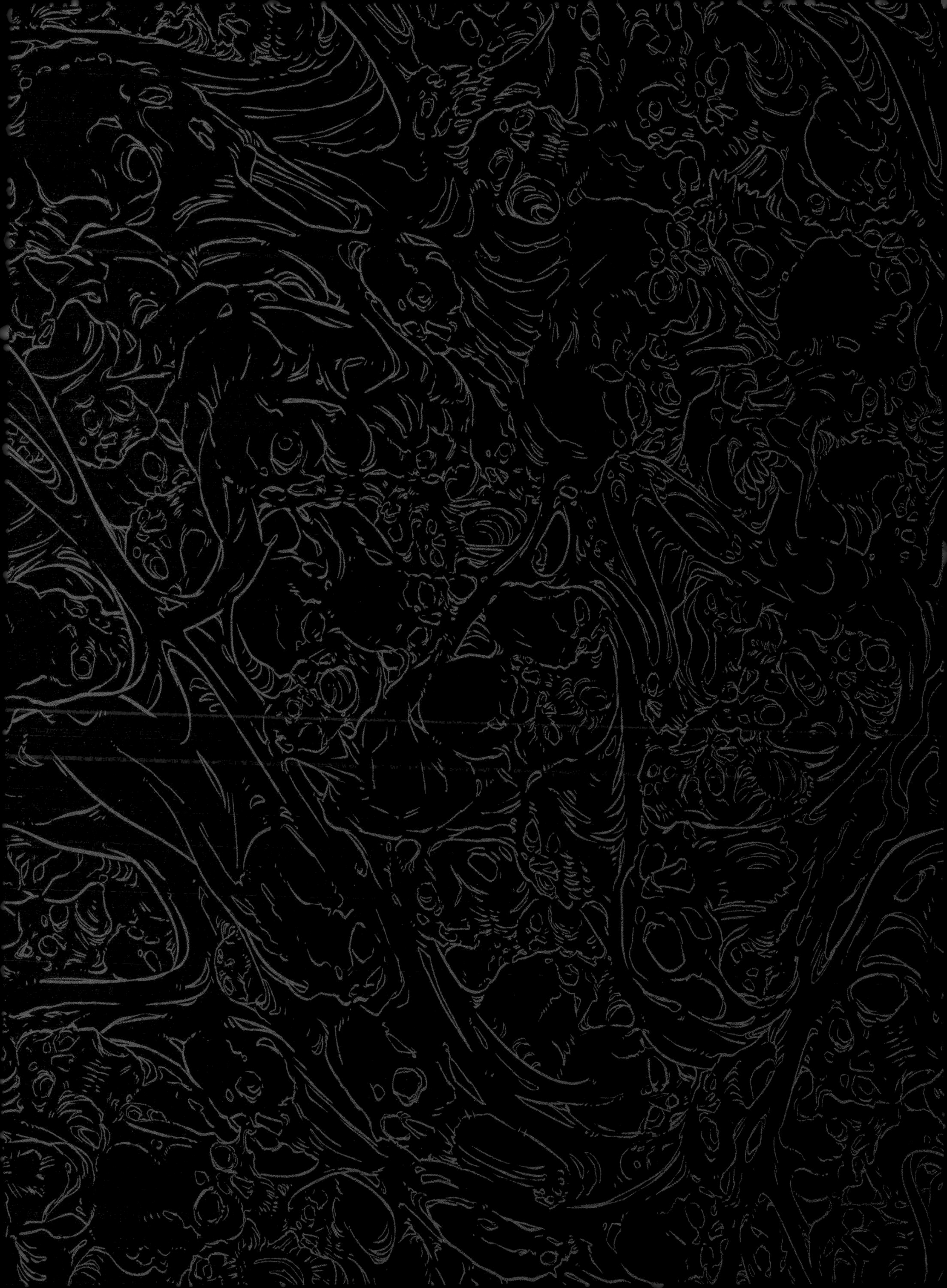

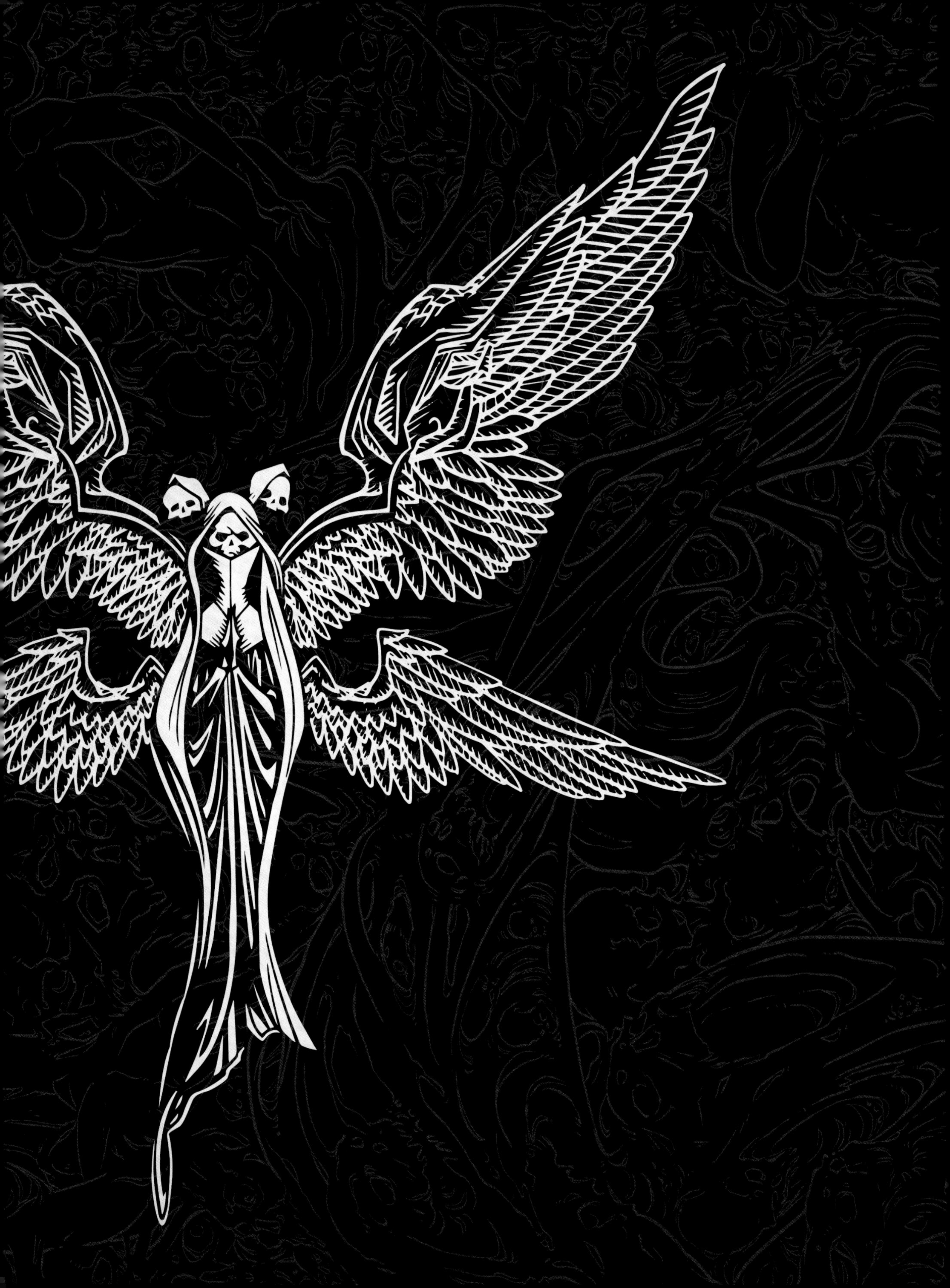

XV.
ELLIANASTIS

As they shot beyond the upspray of ichor-stained water Ycnaf's mists returned to trail beneath them, blue and glittering orange, until at the apex of their ascent it billowed around them, and with a sharp inhalation she gathered it into herself to manifest from the ridges at her withers long, scaly wings to catch the hot updrafts rising from the blacksand desertscape.

Demithyle held fast as his cloak slapped about him, and as Ycnaf rode the draft to carry them in an arc out over the wilds he beheld in the distance the familiar walled skyline of Illverness, cast aglow by the ethereaic flood of the Dirth Forge. Back again they swept, down toward a gloomy courtyard in the shadow of a complex, towering superstructure, where in the center lay a circular reflecting pool, its water still undulating by their emergence. They glided over the courtyard enclosure of arched cloisters in their descent to canter aground amidst a scattering of dead hedges and gray weeds.

Demithyle slid off of Ycnaf's back as she slowed to trot, snorting puffs of blue mist as she coursed about the foggy perimeter, looking about high and low as she absorbed the fresh surroundings. Clasping Cryptmourne at his side Demithyle shook his wet cloak and he watched his steed companion make her way between ruined statues and shadowy nooks, shedding her wings by scales that fell away to the dryness of the breeze.

From the pool were flagstone pathways, three leading outward to the surrounding covered walkways, a fourth through the open arcade to the core of the towering structure, what appeared a simple graystone monastery stretched wide upon the black rock hardscrabble. But set upon its roof were clusters of mismatched edifices of every sort of design and architecture, as if each had been plucked from elsewhere and added by necessity to expand the monastery over the course of aeons. From these still more mushroomed upward, and still more built upon these. Thus did a haphazard tower rise from the courtyard, high up through the familiar, slowly dancing constellations, to vanish beyond a darkened shroud that obscured the celestial sky.

Demithyle watched the lazy movements of the constellations, feeling reassured at last that though he stood somewhere far outside the walls of the city he had indeed been returned home. More than this, for the first time since Mortis Veth he could feel the existence of his fellow reapers here. And though it seemed with distance their wisping voices could not reach his mind he knew that they felt the same of him. He looked toward the steady glow of the Forge's flow, its blue light splayed across the shroud. Soon, my brethren, my sistren. Soon enough, our reunion.

He looked back to the courtyard, found Ycnaf standing at its edge where the surrounding cloistered walkways met, staring out over the surrounding landscape from beneath a wide, layered archway. His still-sodden cloaks smacking heavily against his stride he crossed the courtyard to join her there, and together they gazed out at a grim desert expanse of black-sand dunes, its breadth broken here and there by eroded stone formations and derelict structures as if an ancient, buried cityscape. Flashes of shadow and light across the shroud marked the intermittent infall of otherworldly flotsam that paffed against the dunes and vanished, swallowed whole by the dry wilds. Yet it must be that some areas were shallower than others, for in places exotic elements jutted out like unfinished sculptures to further embellish the landscape.

a traveler's home.

"Yes," said Demithyle. He pointed at the light spire in the distance, rising in parallel to the tower. "We are far outside my city, but it is just there."

Ycnaf's gaze lingered on the light of the Forge, but she said nothing. Demithyle peered into the sky. Though this dark and arid plain was unfamiliar, the feel of its vibration beneath his feet, the density and taste of its air was undeniably that of the Underworld. Still, he searched for hint of the Celestial Cosmos between the folds of the shroud. Strange that they had seen its radiance warped below the water.

He looked back toward the pool in the center of the courtyard, only to find Ycnaf staring at him pointedly.

the world under.

"Go and explore, then," said Demithyle, reading her desire. He patted her shoulder. "I will try to determine where we are, and the best road to Illverness. We will set out when you return."

Ycnaf gave him a puffing nod.

traveler.

Her form scattered about, and then with a blue crackle of energy she blinked away.

Demithyle went to the pool, its surface now all but mirror still. But at his approach he could see sparkling swirls of light playing over its surface. And reaching its edge he found reflected there the familiar tumult of the Underworld sky, as clear as if he stood outside the Calvum Harrows. He looked above, but still he saw only the clustered pinpricks of light wandering below the featureless shroud.

He looked again at the pool. In fact this reflection was a clearer vision of the warring Celestial Cosmos than he had yet seen; the great nebulous arms of what could only be the opposing kingdoms of Heaven and Hell roiled through the void, clashing amidst their cataclysmic surges. The restless swirls of color were painted in great detail over the water, and as he fixed his gaze upon the discrete glittering within one of these it drew into focus as a series of tiny white flashes, and then as if he were soaring into it the images began steadily to magnify until he found himself passing through a luminous cloud fed by countless fires just as it was wracked by an immense explosion of what could only be a devastating expression of etherea. It swept over a jagged, desolate landscape, laying all to waste as thousands upon thousands of torn and blackened forms rained down upon the mutual slaughter of demon and angel and myriad warbeasts, burning in fires of every kind and color, weapons of shadow black and gleaming silver alike flashing brilliant blue as again and again they found their bloodied and shattered marks . . .

"Skattik in the eye, eh, if that weren't a naefukkin' diblivvy tae witness, like."

Demithyle tore away from the image in the pool to find a fully armored Melthis staring into it next to him. He called out her name in surprise, and they both straightened to greet with the enthusiasm of comrades reunited.

But as she held out her arms to embrace him her armor crumbled away and her form transmuted to a grotesque mound of bulbous gray flesh out from which a dozen flapping arms then grew, and in its center mass a wide crease formed as if by way of a friendly smile.

Demithyle, beyond baffled, stopped short.

"Nnngno?" said the thing. "Perhapsshpl nngnot." It dropped its arms as if in disappointment, and they fell to the ground completely as its girth dissolved away, leaving a steaming skeletal structure reminiscent of a charred sapling, bristling everywhere with electrified filaments.

It crossed its four twiggy limbs in a contemplative posture, cracking with hot sparks that left black wisps of smoke to dissipate in the air. "That wa-*zkk!* quite an entrance," it said. "Blowing out of the sztillwa-terr-rrr, *zkk!* Like a volcano, ohhhh, ohhh . . . *Won*derfullll . . . *zkk-kk!*"

This form then fell to black ash that blew over the surface of the pool, and in its place floated three smoky, serpentine tendrils curling over themselves as they snapped at empty space with thin, fuming jaws.

Its voice arose like three whispering voices layered together:

". . . faithfuhhll blaaahhde in hhhhannd . . . astride your fine, majestic steehhd . . . to deliverrrr the kihhlling blow . . . the stuff . . . of legendss, yess, essss . . ."

Then the smoky tendrils collected to a single hovering amorphous cloud that slowly congealed into a slimy bone structure of a mortal skull not unlike Demithyle's own, though blackened and with teeth rotted to wicked serrations.

"Perhaps it would be useful to select one coherent form," said Demithyle.

There came a hollow voice in his head. *Well now. That is not especially courteous of you.*

Its eyes glimmered depthless white, and muscle and sinew crept over the bone as thick steelgray hair grew forth from its crown to blow wildly in a violent wind that was not present, and pale flesh emerged from the sinew to sculpt the vibrant face of a young woman.

This at last was a face that Demithyle knew, for he had seen it among the others of his creators by the vision of his mind's eye at the time of his nascent awareness. He did not know how, or even whether, to show reverence in the presence of one such as she who it seemed had chosen to remain nameless to them in their making. But from the brilliant depths of her shining eyes he felt an earnest pull upon his spirit, as if, divorced from that which he had begun to formulate as his self, it knew separately the hand that had labored its essence into him.

And then in a voice at once distant and cheerful, she spoke into his mind:

The universe is but a melody that moves, my darling undeadling, said she. *And to dance upon its lightness of air is to go neither here nor there, but every where.*

She then smiled and spoke aloud.

"And never can be said that one can not go anywhere without getting somewhere. Wouldn't one agree?"

Demithyle could only nod; no part of him, it seemed, had been made to intuit the navigation of such baffling whimsy. As the wild-haired disembodied head rocked gently on invisible currents, her penetrating white gaze lingering upon him, he felt as though he stood upon unknowable ground even as he struggled to reconcile all he had come to understand of his purpose with so inscrutable an encounter with one of his creators. He recalled the relentless insanity of the twin-necked bird and that of the labyrinth in which it dwelt; it was beginning to seem as though circuitous absurdity was as endemic to the Underworld as the gloom portent into which he had been born, and he was forced to wonder whether such a thing existed somewhere yet uncovered within his own self.

She laughed as if reading the thought. "Well!" she said, "now we are getting some where!"

The rest of her body materialized beneath her into the form of a four-armed woman wearing a ceremonial red gown capped by an elaborate white ruff, though her head still hovered above this minus a conjoining neck, as if she were not quite willing to settle even on this form. Her form was taken by an intermittent spectral fade, so that she appeared to occupy more than this one spatial plane of existence—in fact Demithyle was not certain she truly bore four physical arms and not two in separate overlaying threads of space, perhaps offset in time.

"Not everyone has the luxury of staying put, dear Demithyle, smasher of reflections," she said. "As your flickering friend can attest. But I suppose you two sorted all that out, didn't you?"

She floated back, her gown sweeping over the fog-shrouded grass where she stood. "In any case," she said, "I believe we shall embrace this moment for a proper greeting."

She pressed her hands together in an elegant mudra, and though her hair still flowed wildly her form solidified as if forced by the gesture to align, and the drifting pinpoints of light across the sky suddenly as one swelled with brilliance, so that for a moment their light permeated her physicality and he saw in subtle bands of prismatic color what could only have been her true spirit aspect within.

"You may call me Ellianastis," she said as the brilliance subsided. She gave him an exaggerated ceremonial curtsy. "Our wayward reaper, here now at last! I am so pleased to share this moment with you, my extraordinary friend."

Demithyle, feeling less than extraordinary, pressed his three right-side arms against his gaunt chest, and clutching his cloak with his left he offered her a respectful bow.

"Meirdrem loam, Lady Oracle of the Spirit," he said. "I am Demithyle, come before you by a way long and strange."

"On that all would agree," she said, laughing again. "And yes, you are anything but ordinary. The Alltaker has spoken of you at some length, *elall*! He told me of your proclivity for stepping into the shoes of the long-time dead, so to speak, and my, my, my, has it led to interesting things."

"He has pursued the missive?"

"Well," she said, "you don't think your Alltaker would be idle in your absence, do you? He is constantly fretting over a hidden key supposed to exist in the Mortal Realm, of all places. For the opening of what sort of lock, I'm sure none of us know. But your vision sent him spiraling off to try to unearth it, as it were. Now that you have returned, he will be eager to speak with you. And we would love to have a word with your wyspstride . . . ," she added, looking around the courtyard.

"Wyspstride?"

She turned back to Demithyle again, a waver of disappointment momentarily apparent upon her spectral aspect.

"Your companion. Has she gone?"

"You speak of Ycnaf. It was she who guided me through the labyrinth," said Demithyle.

"Ycnaf!" she exclaimed. "What a marvelous name. Given to her by you, I'm sure."

"Yes," said Demithyle, feeling somewhat awkward. "It was an . . . approximation of the sound she expressed. As a way to call for her."

"Ycnaf of the Wyspstrides, companion to Demithyle, bestower of names. My, my. Such fascinating creatures, my! Whatever was one such as she doing in there, I wonder?"

"She is a traveler," said Demithyle. "The first of her kind to be so, it would seem. She has gone to explore some of the Underworld, I believe. She has never seen it before."

"Such a shame!" said Ellianastis, looking into the distance as if to witness a wyspstride suddenly appear in the air. "I was so looking forward to finally speaking with one."

Turning back to him, she said, "They are wyspstrides, my dear young reaper. Remarkably powerful creatures who occupy an altogether different Cosmos from all of this, the time and space of which they have come to master, one might say. We have been trying to commune with them for some time, you understand. It seems it isn't easy to pique the interest of beings who see all events in their continuum occurring simultaneously, even when we manage to punch through the membranes to offer a friendly hail. That, and we are fairly certain they don't think very highly of a realm as . . . disrupted as ours. Imagine, Demithyle, you falling completely out of sight, only to reappear in the company of one such as they!"

"That was not your doing?" said Demithyle.

"No! You were meant to come straightaway here after Mortis Veth for spiritual counsel, and respite if you wished, before being returned to your reapers to begin the preparation of our defenses. Well done, by the way; Xiall says you owe her a new orb, *elall*!"

"It seems it was arranged I be delivered to Ycnaf. To what end, I have yet to learn."

"I see," said Ellianastis, seemingly without surprise. "Well. Whoever made such arrangements obviously wished you eventually to return."

"She of dry and white," said Demithyle, watching for her reaction.

"Who of why and what?"

"Never mind," said Demithyle. He looked into the distance. "Ycnaf is a very curious creature. She will return in time from her exploration, or when I call upon her. Would it please you for me to do so, Oracle?"

"You can do that?"

"We are rooted," said Demithyle, feeling strange at the statement.

"Indeed?"

"I found her entrapped," said Demithyle, uncertain what to offer by way of explanation of their bond. "After I freed her, she needed an . . . anchor, to this realm."

Ellianastis regarded him, a look of renewed intrigue grown over her features. "Well," she said after a moment, "we owe your companion a great debt, I'm sure. We are lucky to have you back home at all, and in serviceable condition no less, to say nothing of the impressive company you have kept while away."

"So," said Demithyle, looking at the spire of light of the Dirth Forge in the distance. "I was not in the Underworld."

"No . . . well," said Ellianastis, "you were in a kind of pocket. It's a place where we send all sorts of unmanageable things that accumulate here. Paradoxes, infinities . . . you understand. That place sort of spreads them out to keep them from mucking everything up. No one is really meant to journey there, though it is apparently irresistible to some, namely

Charon the Oarsman, who has been in there for I don't even know how long. You didn't see him, did you?"

"I saw no one to match this description," said Demithyle.

"Hm. That's too bad. He has been away a long while, and we do miss dearly his dour manner in and around the Court . . . In any case, generally speaking we have no way of extracting anything from it—that's the idea, really. Paradoxes can be very dangerous."

"Yes."

"Ah, my poor reaper!" said Ellianastis, grasping him with all four of her hands. "I am sure it was nothing short of maddening, wandering aimlessly about in such a place! I wish I could have gotten you out, but the best I can do from here is exert a bit of influence and hope for the best. We may have created it, but only its wardens can manage things in there. I assume you met one, or you would never have made it out."

"Yes," said Demithyle. "We bargained with it for passage."

Ellianastis stepped back to look him over. "I noticed you seemed slighter," she said. "Don't tell Xiall you lost your armor, unless you want her to crack off your skint for you." She looked at him. "It must have been Simmel you met, then."

Demithyle looked at her.

"Oh yes. We know him. One can often find him flaunting his fishes about in the Curio Cryptus, whinging about his lot and all the armies he'll raise."

"Ycnaf named him the Fisher. It was he who imprisoned her, after promising to show her to the Underworld. But for her strength he would have devoured her mind. There were many others who were not so fortunate."

Ellianastis frowned deeply, and then her spiritous overlay wisped away and she appeared to stare into nothing for a time, before finally looking up at him again.

"That is troubling news indeed, Demithyle," she said. "To now we have thought him avaricious and boastful but harmless. He does not possess any real power to speak of, certainly not that which could overwhelm one such as Ycnaf. He must have discovered something in the labyrinth. You shall have to convey my greatest sorrows to your companion. Please assure her that we will learn what we can of his treacheries, very quickly indeed, and all will be done to bring about their end."

"How does he get in and out of the labyrinth?"

"We have no idea," said Ellianastis. "It is probably for the best we haven't, in fact. As you are well aware, it is no place for casual jaunts."

"Then perhaps we are fortunate the Fisher was of a mind to make good on his bargain," said Demithyle.

"Yes, well," she said, "he didn't have much choice once he gave you his name, did he? That's just what he gets for constantly blathering to himself as if he were the only one listening. In any case, once I figured out he'd sent you down that horrid well I made sure you found your way to me, and so."

Demithyle considered that. He looked to the bespeckled overcast sky, feeling suddenly that he would like nothing more than to summon Ycnaf and course through its palliative expanse.

"I see you appreciate my drapery," she said. "Why anyone should wish to look upon such nonsense every time one steps outside, I'm sure I don't know."

Demithyle looked again at the glimmer of celestial tumult displayed over the still water of the nearby pool.

"Alas," said Ellianastis, nodding gravely, "it would not do to forget it, so here I keep it reflected for all who come visit my library, to contemplate the atrocity of things without it hanging over their heads like the axman's blade."

She looked wistfully through the arches of the spireward cloister. "I had hoped to walk with you through the weirding gardens I keep here—the follies are particularly bracing this season, *elall*! But I am afraid we must forgo such pleasant distractions in favor of getting on with things."

"Where are we going?"

"Why, into the library, of course!"

Demithyle looked up at the towering, haphazard structure. "Will Ycnaf find us inside?"

"Heavens and Hells, no. But don't worry about that. So long as she does not come to find you before we enter the library, she won't even know you've gone."

"I do not understand."

"All in good time," she said with a laugh.

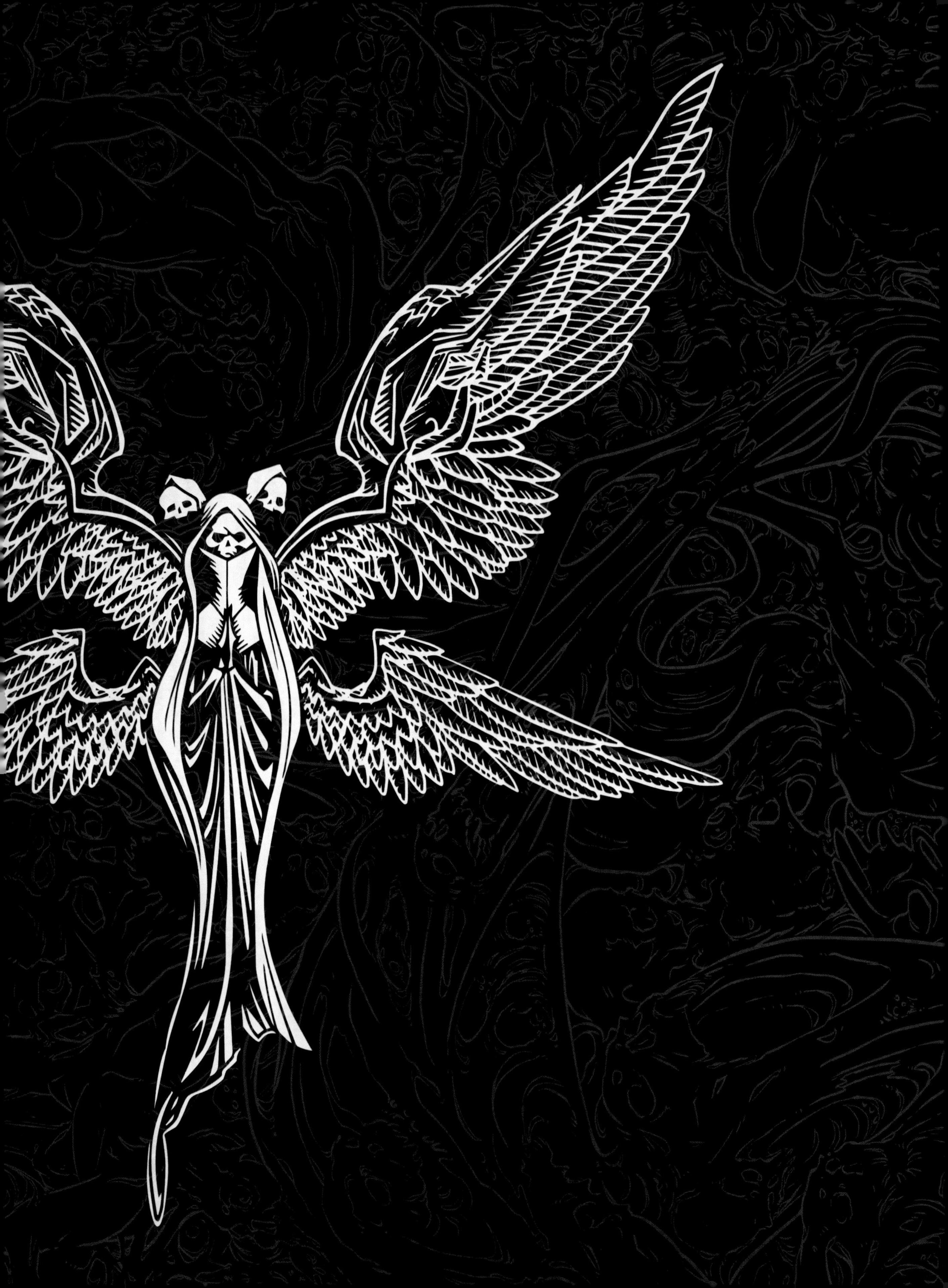

XVI.
A LIBRARY

She led him through the arches and colonnades of the cloister and around a second enclosure to a short rise of graystone steps, then to a simple door of weathered gray wood. Burned into its center was a vague skullform. Ellianastis raised a hand over it and from her delicate fingers etherea streamed to fill and swirl within it.

"Open up."

The door opened inward to reveal a dim vestibule with a low-hanging ceiling and a dark expanse beyond.

"After you," she said.

Demithyle stepped into near-complete darkness as behind him the door closed to shut out the incoming light of the courtyard.

It suits you.

Demithyle stopped short of asking what she meant as a ghostly white light arose and he realized his cloak had been altered to the clean gray linens of an ascetic.

When he turned to comment upon the lightness of the garb, he found what stood beside him was no longer the regal figure but a gaunt and grimy thing of cold, gray flesh. It regarded him with impossibly tired, ancient eyes, below which its face was a luminous white void, as if a cracked shell out from which its spirit continuously spilt.

Here, this suits me, she said. *Come.*

She gestured forward with a long, thin arm, and they walked through shadows pressed away by her spiritous light until the worn stone of the cavern floor shone dim blue ahead as by the flicker of sulfurous flame. There they reached the edge of a circular chasm capped just overhead by a churning of what seemed the undersurface of boiling yellow oil. Down from it poured a continuous, thick torrent of black needles amid intermittent blooms of whisper-thin threads of soot that here and there ignited to discrete blue cyclones of flame. These whipped and looped around the deluge of needles as they were caught by its downward rush through a closely spiraling encirclement of descending levels from which fleeting pockets of white light rose and fell as if by the opening and shutting of doors, momentarily describing the shape of the downpour in a stagger of light that diminished far into the darkest depths below.

My library.

Demithyle looked at the gaseous boil of the ceiling.

"Should it not extend into the heights, as seen from the outside?" he asked.

It does so. You will see. Come.

She led him forth down along the winding thoroughfare of the chasm chamber amid the torrent's roar, its thick cylinder of needles no more than an arm's reach from the edge. Into the bowed stone walls at its opposite were various dark recesses and hollows, each shrouded by curtains of black fog.

"What is archived here?"

All events of spirit or soul.

"From this realm?"

From everywhere.

She halted at the next hollow and reached through its falling curtain of fog, so black the spiritlight cast from her tormented visage seemed not to fall upon it at all. When she reemerged she grasped his wrists with sooted hands.

Do you see?

Demithyle found himself holding a thick volume of black leather and velum. He turned it over to find script written upon its spine: *Coughs of No Consequence*. He let it fall open in his hands; inscribed upon its membranous pages was a passage that depicted a single wracking dry cough in great detail. Paging through it, he found only more such moments, each captured with elaborate prose.

"Are all of them this . . . verbose?" he asked.

As many as are not. Look and see.

She nodded her sad gray face toward the curtain and closing his book Demithyle stepped blindly through it. When the dark veil lifted he found himself in a musty antechamber, flanked by tall shelves of iron-clasped wood spilling over with countless tomes. The elongated shapes of transom windows were painted deep orange over the scoured stone walls.

He knelt over a pile of tomes left on the floor between the shelves, picking through them. *A Second Helping of Beets. The Sneeze of the Weary Husbandman. The Boil upon the Breech: A Lancing. To Cut a Love Apple in Twain, Then Further to Quadrants.* Paging through them randomly once again revealed nothing of identifiable significance.

"Fascinating reading, isn't it?"

At the sound of her voice Demithyle stood to find Ellianastis standing before the curtain shroud, looking now like a bright-eyed mortal woman of a rich brown complexion. He glanced over his own form but found himself unchanged, garbed still in simple cleric's robes.

"Have we been taken to the Mortal Realm?" he asked.

"No," said Ellianastis, "the reading rooms merely take on a certain look once you step inside. An infinite library of the mundane needn't be infinitely boring, after all. Come on," she said, stepping backward, partway through the shroud, "you'll understand better once we get to my study. It's not far."

She disappeared through it and Demithyle set down the tome in his hands, and with a final look around the strange environs he followed after to find her waiting, once again in the form of the haggard gray creature.

Come.

She walked them farther down the sloping way along the edge of the rushing chasm in the ever-diminishing light of the flaring churn, now much farther above than he recalled prior to their passing through the hollow. And in the dimness he began to mark furtive movements in the shadows, and then here and there in his periphery dim pulses of white spiritlight appeared, momentarily illuminating reaching arms of mottled gray flesh and ancient sleepless eyes.

They are the wendlaersth. Most know them as faints. They are those drawn to this place who lost themselves in seeking. You will see.

Demithyle looked up at her own haggard eyes.

Yes. Here I share in their toil. Here I am as they.

"What do they come to seek?"

Everything. Nothing.

One of the creatures emerged from a hollow ahead and stood near the edge of the thoroughfare. It offered no acknowledgment of their presence as it brought its narrow, corpse-skin hands into the light beneath its shredded orifice, and as they approached it breathed a mucilage of its luminous essence over them before drinking it in once again. Then without a sound it bent itself to the ground and crawled over the edge to disappear below.

Ellianastis went to the edge of the chasm. With the long reach of her arm she swept a hand through the torrent, then presented to Demithyle a fist bristled by shards of what might have been obsidian glass, their irregular surfaces cast agleam by the light that spilt from her face. Then she brought them beneath the place where her mouth would reside and heaved out her essence as had done the other, and the shards dissolved to tiny slivers that rained down over her naked form, piercing the gray flesh wherever they fell upon it, then to be absorbed.

Everything of being is here, she said. Everything of knowing. Secrets lost. Paths to power. Answers. Lies. Moments of greatness buried among the mundane. All thought that has elapsed throughout the tapestry of interwoven continuums is gathered in this place to be woven into its volumes. So will it be until all is become inert and all gods have been unmade. When this torrent of thought and being has long since quieted to a slow weeping, its final tear shall become the end punctuation upon the final page of a tome that shall contain all that is the Cosmos, to be marked by none save the wendlaersth. For neither thought nor being do they retain within them to feed the library.

"Then it is this library itself that keeps them," said Demithyle.

Yes. And no. What mystics and magi who by their mortal craft learn of its existence can not resist its promise. Lifetimes are given to the discovery of means to shed mortality, then many more spent in traversing the veils. When they come they find a place beyond time. Over uncountable aeons they search for intimation of wisdom they can not recognize to feed ambitions they have long forgotten. In the end it is only the nature of infinity that is revealed to them.

She led them forth, past many shrouded recesses from which emerged the unwary faints, each time ignoring their presence as they consumed whatever moment they had retrieved from the tomes. Soon the ambient glow from above receded entirely, so that traveling within the ghostly pocket of Ellianastis's light Demithyle lost nearly all sense of direction and depth, and looking up the intermittent projections of the wendlaersth reflected over the torrent seemed to him as a twinkling conduit of stars.

We are here.

* * *

Demithyle followed her through yet another nondescript shrouded hollow and into a large, cluttered laboratory. The room was flooded with light by an open terrace through which he could see a gray expanse of the shrouded sky. Its walls were lined with a series of shelves of darkly stained wood and ornate wrought iron filled with leatherbound tomes and tightly packed scrolls. Between the shelves stood myriad unidentifiable sculptures and artifacts displayed in shallow niches. Upon several scorched tables were set apparatuses of experimentation and study, a glitter of glass and metal among leaves of stained vellum covered with scribbled notations and distrait sketches. Centered on a raised platform near the terrace threshold was a large wooden desk, the legs of which appeared to fade from existence before reaching the floor. Upon it lay writing implements and a large volume opposite a number of others stacked precariously high. Between them there rose a curling metallic framework that braced the lower portion of a mortal skull, its upper cranium supplanted by the slow sparking of a minute explosion apparently restrained within some manner of quivering magical field.

"There now, that's better."

Demithyle looked to see the wild-haired Ellianastis in her flowing gowns once more, her familiar, brilliant-eyed head again hovering over the thick white ruff.

"Please excuse me, but I am in a state," she said, smacking at her gown. "Do feel free to look around. I'll be back with you in a moment."

With that she vanished, leaving Demithyle alone. Looking out toward the open sky, he grasped into the aether but this time found no sense at all of his kin. Nor was there any hint of Ycnaf. He looked himself over, somewhat disappointed to find himself dressed still in the white ascetic's robes. But through them he touched the pommel of Cryptmourne, still clasped to his belt, and reaching through the folds with his swordhand he clutched its hilt and was given reassurance by their oscillating interchange of spirits.

Opposite the terrace was an interior mezzanine draped by thick red curtains cinched against the threshold, which by the breadth of color and activity he could see beyond it appeared to overlook a vast hall filled with activity. With one eye on the quivering, suspended fulmination Demithyle crossed the laboratory and stepped out onto the mezzanine, where he found himself looking out into the atrium of an elaborate athenaeum.

Floating vertically in its center was a gentle swirl of large, narrow stones, continuously aligning themselves into random patterns of organization where here and there they convened. The atrium was encircled by a spiral of crooked galleries and balustrades connecting a crush of mismatched halls that bent and swelled into various distances in every direction. Through these drifted a constant traffic of spirit figures, peacefully poring over whatever tomes they bore as wrought-iron lamps followed at their shoulders, so that Demithyle could see spots of warm fireglow from their lamps rolling everywhere through the depths of the stacks, illuminating shelves and niches filled with bound volumes, scrolls and sheafs of parchment, stacks of ostraca and clay tablets laid amongst rows of weatherworn stelae, and collections of strange baubles and other inscribed shapes of a seemingly otherworldly or esoteric nature.

Demithyle watched the unceasing ballet of the figures as by way of an assortment of narrow portals and winding blackiron staircases they passed between the halls and levels, and looking down over the mezzanine he realized that this was in fact no atrium at all, but yet another illusory veneer—this one drawn over the same library through which he had just been guided by the haggard corpse-shade of Ellianastis. There existed no floor or entrance hall, only an endless descent of interconnected levels, and looking up he saw a reflection of the same, the gentle shifting of the modular stones rising high into an interior atmospheric haze.

Demithyle turned away, marveling as much at the infinity of it as its contrast with the grim stretch of hollows that had delivered him here, and seeing the terrace across the laboratory he went to look out over the desert expanse of the Underworld, if only to ease his mind of the enormity and clutter of the interior. But as he stepped out onto it it seemed that the flecks of infalling flotsam were locked in place above the blacksand plains, and wherever he looked he noted an odd stillness: every swath of blacksand caught by the wind was held in place like tufts of fabric over a dark canvas.

"So, how do you find my sanctuary?"

She stood next to him on the terrace, smiling, looking out with him over the frozen expanse. She was wearing a completely new gown, this one white, brocaded, and narrow.

"Time has stopped," he said.

"Not quite," she said. "When you stepped into the library you entered into its frame of reference. By its nature, this place exists on something of a speedier continuum than everything else—all the better to harvest the moments, no?"

Demithyle looked over his shoulder, back toward the atrium. "Would this be the true face of the library?"

"I think you know the answer to that one."

He supposed he did know. In any case, he had a fair idea of what his spirit matron would say: *everything according to one's perspective.*

Ellianastis smiled. "We'll make a spirit scholar of you yet," she said. She gestured back out toward the blacksand expanse. "Everything out there unfolds far more slowly relative to in here. And so here you may take whatever time you need. Your spiritual counsel will go uninterrupted, if you like. Nor should you worry about missing out on any of the dire happenings of the meir. When you are ready to leave the library, all will be ready and waiting for you. It will be as if you had never left." Demithyle looked at her in alarm.

"I have been long away from pursuit of my duty," he said, groping for appropriately deferential words. "I am eager to return to Illverness, and the mortis. If we have not already, perhaps we might begin this counsel now."

Ellianastis looked at him a moment with a sad smile, then turned to look out over the desertscape. "Something they who become the wendlaersth never understand," she said. "In all their eagerness for knowledge, they never learn the simple being of things. A shame, really. In here you'll find the collected moments of every sort of being from all across the infinite expanse of time. Is that not fascinating? It is! Even just to think of all those different, wonderful places."

Then into the air beside them she breathed a shimmering, white fume, which then settled there within a slowing waving distortion.

"A guest," said Ellianastis. "Guide and attend."

guesssst . . . taaaake . . . waaaait . . . came a distant voice within the shimmer.

"Something like that," said Ellianastis. "Breath animates are so slow. But I believe it has the general idea."

Leaning forward, she kissed him on his bare skull.

"And so," she said. "Your spiritual counsel shall be yours alone to discover. The animate will attend to you in the library proper and show you back here whenever you like. Do make yourself at home! The Alltaker will come and find you, by and by. He is on a spirit sojourn of his own, quite as removed from the Underworld's frame of reference as we, though of course it's impossible to know where. Time and space have a way of getting out of his way, you may say. But I am certain he will wish to speak with you afterward. I will be leaving now. I have business with my sisters and I am late again, *elall!*"

"What am I to find there?" asked Demithyle, eyeing the view of the atrium with trepidation.

"Everything, nothing, who can say?" she said, floating over to the black curtain through which they had entered her sanctuary. "You will find out when you find it, I suppose. Might I suggest seeking out a few ancient tombs and catacombs? Apart from their engravings, their embellishment of lewd graffiti that has covered them over time is quite amusing. Some tales are just too colossal to fit into the pages of a book, no?"

She stepped through the shroud, leaving Demithyle to wonder quite what he was meant to do in this yet another strange and absurd place, so removed from his duty and his kin, his companion, his city. And then her voice returned to his mind:

You are here to learn from what experiences you might encounter before Death comes calling, she said. *What more can be said of anyone?*

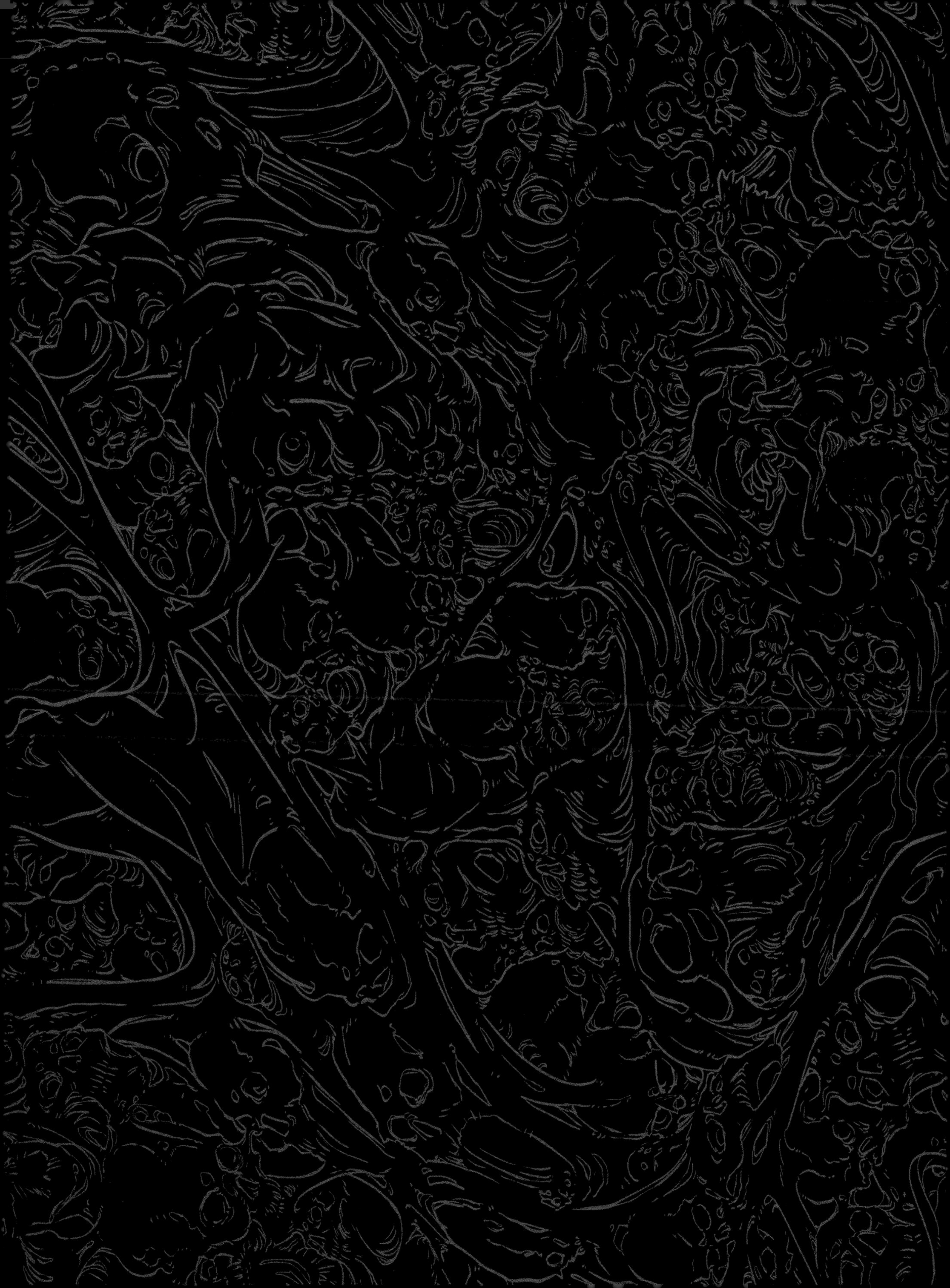

NEAR WE DRAW WE TASSSTE IT EVER NEARER
TO OUR SSSIGHT THE SPIRE OF THE BETRAYER
COME BEFORE TO COWER FLEE IN FEAR HIS
TOOTHSOME SPIRIT CALLLS TO US TO USSS TO US TO USSSSS

WE SNAP OUR TEEETH AGAINST THE FLAVOR
OF HIS FLESH SO SWEEET WITH FAILURE AND REGRET
IT FOUND OUR TEETH HIS BONES OUR FEARRRRR HIS
FLESH OUR TEETH IT CALLLS TO USSS TO US TO USSSSS

HIS REALM NOW OURS TO SCARRR FOREVER OURSSS
TO SCOUR CLEAR OF ALL THAT HE HAS MAAAAADE

OUR WOUNDS DELIVERED THOUSANDFOLD WE ARE
THE MULTITUDE THE SSSKY THE ASSSH THE POISON
TARRRRR THE SSSKY THE ASSSH THE POISON
TARRR THE SSSKY THE ASSSH THE POISON TARRRRR . . .

HERALDS SWIFT BEYOND THE BREAST BEYOND THE
HEAD TO MARK THE WAY TO THE USURPERS FIND THEM
FIND THE PATH THE WAY TO BRING OUR FATHER
AND HIS FEEBLE SSSCIONS TO THEIR KNEEESSS

IF HE WILL NOT DESTROY US THEN A GIFFFT WE BRING
TO HIM WHAT SPIRIT BEINGS CAN NOT FLEE WE TAKE
AS GIFTSSS TO BRING TO HIM HIS LEGACY DESTRUCTION
FEAR UNDOING DEATH AND NOTHING DEATH

AND NOTHING DEATH AND NOTHING DEATH
AND NOTHING DEATH AND NOTHING . . .

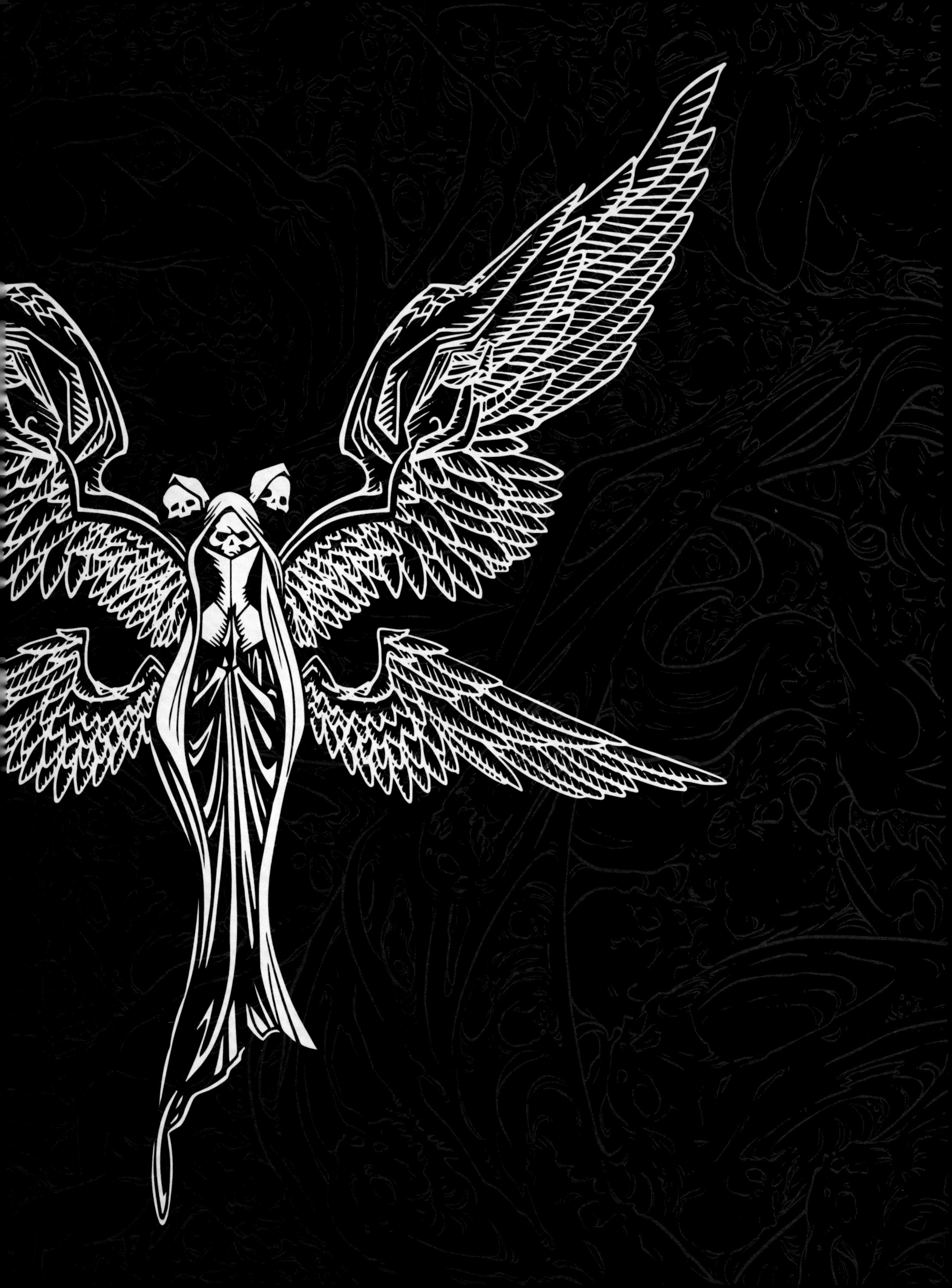

XVII.
YCNAF

Ycnaf of the Wyspstrides! How happy I am to have caught up with you. Yes, I—well. 'Her Face Unreflected'? My, I had no idea I had been given such an interesting moniker. I doubt you mean anything to do with a mirror, elall! Some days I only wish that were true.

It must be the meirs, then, the measure of our time . . . one cycle reflecting forth to the next and so on . . . Are you suggesting I am to cease to exist in some fashion? A part of me, perhaps? Ah! Am I to be present at the end of things . . . ?

Ah yes. Right. Of course one such as you would not imagine things in terms of 'beginnings' and 'ends.' And I would not want to answer such questions in any case if I were you. Apologies! One can not help but probe these sorts of things when they arise, down to their bare bones, as it were. At least, not one who is me. Greetings, then, from where we each stand at our cross sections of parallel pasts and fluctuating futures, yes?

My, what strange and fascinating beings you are! How marvelous it must be to expend one's existence enriching yourselves with the infinity of being, as I like to think of it. This is exactly the sort of thing that's had me so looking forward to an encounter with you, Ycnaf. Such a shame it must be through the vapor like this, and please forgive the imposition. Alas, it is the only way I can commune with you now, at this rather critical juncture, wherever it is you actually are.

I want to give my sincerest regrets for your torment at the hands of the creature Simmel. How awful it must have been for you. To say I was horrified to learn of your suffering is to bring the least of my sorrow to light. Please, accept my apology on behalf of our entire realm. It may be some time before Simmel is given his comeuppance, but we shall do all that we can.

And of course you must know that you have our eternal gratitude for the return of Demithyle to us. I must say, it has been extraordinarily interesting to watch him proceed through his becoming, even prior to your encounter with him. That he among all we Underworlders should be the one to bring you to us here at last, to say nothing of the bond you now apparently share, tells us he is worthy of his name, and more.

Yes, well I imagine that he would be on his spirit sojourn right about now. That is if he has found the candle I left for him, and if you're asking about him that must mean he is not in your presence, which adds a high degree of likelihood that he has done so, doesn't it? Ah, but the enchantment burns rather quickly, so he should be returned to the library after little more than a meirdrem or two and then you will find him in that very moment, unless I am mistaken about his interest in my archive of the mundane.

But to the matter at hand: as I have only just mentioned to him, we have been trying to commune with your kind for some time. There is a great deal I should like to learn from you! As it happens, however, in this particular point in time we find ourselves embroiled in certain pressing difficulties, and I must use this opportunity to deliver an appeal on behalf of the Alltaker.

So it has occurred to us that the wyspstrides have remained aloof by your assessment of our collective character as being rather primitive in its seeming inability to rise above our natures, so to speak. I assure you that for the most part you are not mistaken. That we continue to play our assigned roles in prolonging the travesty that has become the Cosmos is indisputable, and nothing if not crude and unevolved.

Perhaps, though, you might take our mutual friend as an example of our better side: in our creation of the reapers, each of us placed within them some aspect of ourselves. In this way he is in essence our culmination, maybe even in spite of ourselves. So if we are to be judged by anything, then I say let it be by they, and by Demithyle himself, whose constant seeking of a greater place and purpose I have come to see as emblematic of our own evolution.

And so foremost I would invite you to think of us as you do him whom it seems you have come to know well, and know then also that we do see ourselves in many ways as babes in this very violent Cosmos of ours; imperfect powers making great messes as we struggle to shape things, to make them better.

Perhaps, then, you might allow your experiences with Demithyle to serve as preamble to our appeal to you: we wish for you to come to the Underworld and to find yourselves a place here. As many of your kind as might wish it, as soon or as late as you like. See us as we are, as we grow, as we win, as we fail. Become one of us, if you wish. This would be our sincerest hope!

Although it's true we're unable to see beyond the horizons of the meir, we do know an epoch is very soon to arrive when our actions will govern the shape of the Cosmos with a certain amount of finality, you might say. I do not mean to use our overlarge footprints through the sands of the aether as leverage, truly I do not! But it must be said that our future machinations will certainly echo even into your Cosmos.

There is a great responsibility that rests with the Alltaker alone, and he intends to meet it—with all of us along for the ride, of course. But we've come to look upon the outcome as rather less than assured. So you might say we can only benefit from an alliance with beings who long ago brought their Cosmos into the kind of ubiquitous harmony only to be envied this side of the membrane.

On that note, my dear traveler, I've all but exhausted the patience of my poor Minders' Bind with this communion, and oh, yes, I am already late for a conference with my sisters, elall! Ah, well. But before I leave you, I have a gift, by way of gesture of our sincerity and goodwill. One which can be delivered only in such a clandestine way as this, I might add, since it's fair to say many across the realities would wish dearly to possess it. 'It', dear Ycnaf, is Death's true name.

Yes. Not even my sisters know it. Even the Alltaker himself does not accept its implication. Of course you would understand the significance of entrusting such a dangerous thing to another entity, irrespective of ambition or allegiance. Such is our time of need, and, we hope, our assessment of your character.

Needless to say, you might use it to find our dark father wherever he may be, watch him, commune with him should you wish. He would have you see all that he is, as he is. All that we are. He will grant any audience you request, if he can.

And so I offer it to you as our last word, Ycnaf, along with my expression of further gratitude and of sorrow for your hardship, before I must very regrettably say goodbye, traveler.

* * *

The wyspstride makes her way through the ever-shifting sea of blacksand beneath the perpetual fold and bloom of the volatile foreign sky. In the distance, the great blinking shaft of spiritlight that dominates the traveler's city. It bathes the land in an ethearic scent strangely different from her own; a permeating icy blue tinged with pale corpsegreen where more avid breaths would waft.

Soon, she knew, would arrive the voice of the entity, her face unreflected. There, near the great bell of iron at the base of the stony dune, not long after it has fallen from above to slap into the sand, having passed into this realm much in the same hapless manner as she. Ycnaf will hear its muted clang, be taken by curiosity for it. Then will arrive the entity's appeal. Her words will first emerge as undercurrent to her own thoughts even as they are resolved to forgo return to the herd that she might extricate the traveler from the perilous anomaly, this strange tower of broken time.

* * *

She comes upon the dune, kicking flotsam from her path with clawed forehooves, and leaping up its rocky slope she looks out beyond the dark canyon to the anomaly. She had marked the scent of it the moment they had emerged from the well; that of a force barely restrained. Did all exist thus in this the world under, the traveler an agent of infinitude? Vantage. Vantage would offer sight. So does she now watch the arrival of the entity whose face goes unreflected in the still water of the pool, and her communing with the traveler, his aura now so familiar. The current and color of it. The scent of its vibration even at a distance a clear contrast to the chaotic presence of the other. And so the traveler is not an agent of broken time but a being left by Ycnaf to the mercy of it. In a moment the entity will bring him to enter the anomaly. And in that same instant he will leave it again.

* * *

She shifts her sight upward, along the structure's rise and fall, its expansion and declination evolving through aeons from a modest shelter through a mushrooming upon it of incongruent enclosures as it rises into the sky. She huffs a breath of gratification. How fine to see again the fullness of a continuum unfold. Freed at last from that place of clouded intervals, where she had been made to exist without movement, without touch. Flat but for the gradual whittling of probabilities. Her own cherished panorama of termini irrevocably reduced by the passing of each ungathered moment. And everpresent the pang of longing to return to the herd, their breath for the first time unknown as through the tracts and epochs of her native Cosmos they journeyed. She had learned to shun her want of their call. Only to be met with the potent aroma of it upon the traveler's release of her, like a forgotten wound, worsened by neglect.

*   *   *

The great monastery doors at the base of the anomaly close and in that very instant the traveler's spark exits from elsewhere up along its temporal undulation. She watches the lightness of his soar. What time might have elapsed from his perspective to carry him to such heights so transformed, she could not know. But the utter collapse of that span as seen from her place beyond its influence stirs still further the unease in her belly, for with each full breath she draws it must be that within its indiscriminate walls long seasons are burned swiftly away.

*   *   *

She casts her sight over the erratic, towering thing before her, forward through this realm's maelstrom of time to sift among its termini for its most distant extent, bearing witness to the unchecked accumulation of its heights in parallel to the lightshaft of the city, and its expansion outward through ever darker aeons to overwhelm the city, the soul orifice that feeds it finally choked to the becalming by suffocation of all the world under. Still it grows, penetrating high into a firmament long ago swollen by the ancient voracity of its bygone denizens, and with its eventual rupture a deluge of celestial realities is unleashed, washing over the cancerous expanse to be swallowed by the infinitudes within, and then the world under is itself drunk dry to exist at last as a uniform void between the veils. The null-death of cosmic equilibrium by which bordering aethers are ever guarded from such infinities unleashed by their neighbors.

*   *   *

The scent of the herd calls to her. Even through the veils she can sense its reawakened awareness of her. She looks toward the city and the upwell of the lightshaft. She had felt the traveler's longing also to return to his kind. And yet upon his reunion with this his world under, his physicality is to be kept, restrained within the anomaly. His spiritous aspect alone allowed to revisit his home. To what purpose? She billows a cloud of dark mist, decrying in his speech the bane brought by her imprisonment it seems he has now been given: *not to touch to feel.*

She looks again at the wavering heights. No. She would not abandon the traveler to the sway of this aberrant place, nor to that of its minder, she who flails wildly through the aethers, unrooted from her

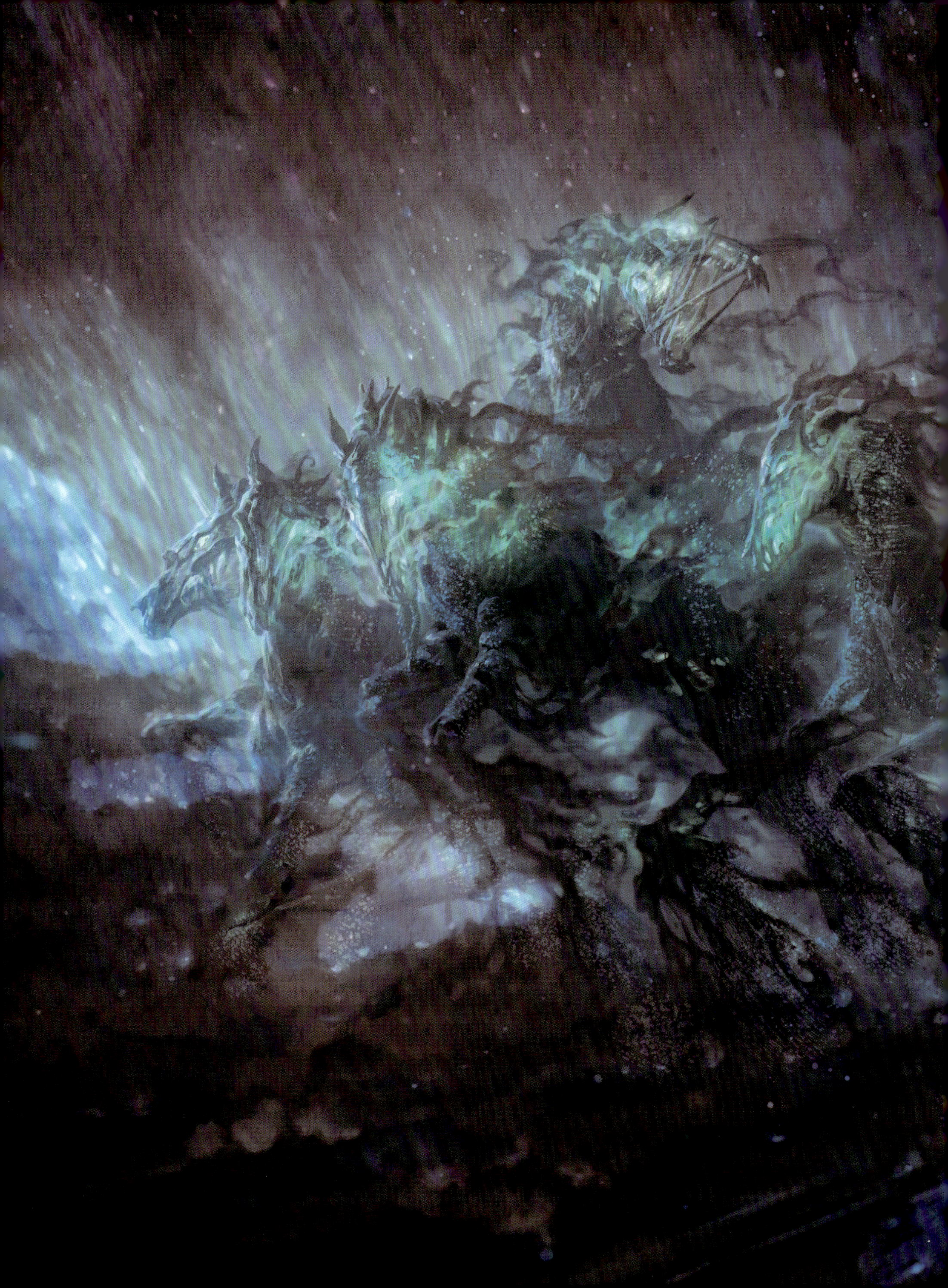

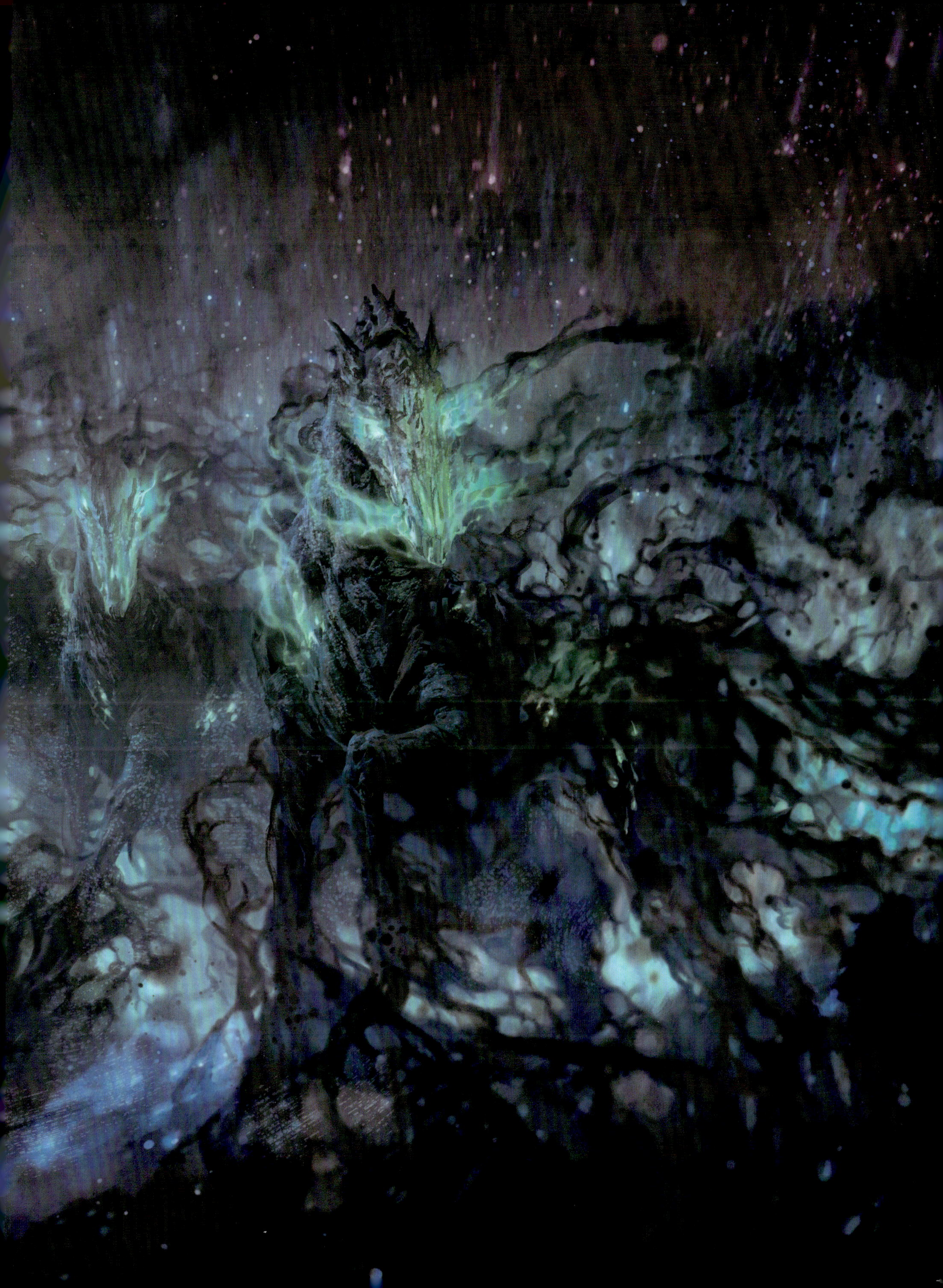

being, her face unreflected. He will be recalled to it soon enough. Ycnaf will be there to claim him. The separate breaths of Ycnaf and the traveler, one. His termini now hers. Theirs interwoven.

* * *

There arrives a clanging thud behind her, followed then by metallic scraping, and then a final sonorous clash. She turns to see it. There at the base of the dune, a large iron bell, a thick tongue of blacksand gathered into its hollow.

Then, as if rising from her own thoughts, a voice. She listens, her crystalline amber eyes glittering in the darkmeir as it delivers its entreaty.

* * *

The voice recedes. Ycnaf looks again toward the city. She witnesses its myriad futures. The greatest measure fall abruptly before her as a shadow that consumes all to become the entirety of this realm, and then consumes itself to become nothing. She sifts among those few termini that extend beyond the near array of cessation. A swelling of the city's lightshaft to level it in ashes. A great sundering light at the gate. An expanse of landscape folding round the depthless silhouette of a high tower. Of those visions of the city which see it persist intact, all bear a sky above and around it streaked with familiar trails of blue-orange. And following these probabilities backward to the here and now, Ycnaf finds each tethered to the moment of the entity's hopeful entreaty.

Curious.

She looks toward the haphazard, shifting profile of the anomaly. She turns from it to look down toward the dark hollow of the infallen bell. With a hesitant breath, she opens there a broad aperture through which first arrives the scent of the herd, and then the sound of its exodus, and then at long last she is among them.

* * *

She felt the soar of happiness in spite of herself. The fullness of joy and familial comfort. The welcoming and belonging within the boundless herd as it ran over the frozen expanse, between the far horizons and the high pillars of ice that held aloft the starless night.

The herd breathed into themselves the spirit she gave, made strange by a journey far from home. They cast it out over themselves in a cloud of knowing through which all then passed, revivifying its sentiment with their own fragrant enthusiasm.

And Ycnaf breathed its chorus of scents into her knowing:

a traveler, returned.

She cast out her breath of reply they drove themselves into the rolling currents of air at their fore:

a traveler home.

For a time they reveled in their wholeness, Ycnaf keeping silent her many disquietudes, that the tumult she had brought from the world under not spoil the complacent exodus of her reunion. It was enough for now that the herd knew of the traveler and of her long entrapment, and that they loved her and thought her return to them marked at last the end of her travels. And so together they ran, in this the aeon chosen to drive the apparatus of their temporal Cosmos, long ago tamed that their simultaneity of being through time be rooted.

But soon the herd felt that part of her was yet rooted in the world under, and they cast out overlying queries upon their chorus of scent.

Ycnaf breathed them into her knowing:

traveler to root?
beyond the herd to root?
to root to under?

And then they guessed the answer, and spoke the name that had been delivered to them through her aperture in the labyrinth:

traveler. de-mi-ta'il?
de-mi-ta'il traveler. voice?
de-mi-ta'il to root?
love?

And Ycnaf answered without hesitation, casting her love for her traveler upon the wind:

yes. de-mi-ta'il to root, a traveler under. to see to feel the world under. de-mi-ta'il traveler of new eyes, mind unclouded. spirit aligned to see time and time unclouded. to wish to see. de-mi-ta'il to fight to know. so the herd, worthy.

Through the gray broadwater ran the herd as they mulled her words, fed to them through torrents of the faultless gray sky. They smashed through the waves, sent into the heights the graywater like facing cliffsides, dark shapes within. They drove into the chasms and out again, the electric froth at their hooves.

And when the land was dry, Ycnaf at last delivered to them all that she had seen and heard in the time since the traveler had come—the fisher, the well, the many dooms of the tower of broken time, and finally the appeal sent from the entity her face unreflected and her potent gift.

These scents they caught and considered. And when finally their reply was cast out, it was to Ycnaf's relief that they had decided the tower posed but the most distant of threats to their own Cosmos. But this gift intrigued them:

a token given.
a token under.
a name.
a name to make. a name to take.
to see to take?
a key?

And Ycnaf answered, her mind lingering on thoughts of the traveler and the great shadow that loomed toward his city:

a judgment. given the herd to choose. to choose to be to see. to mark the fluctuating termini. to choose to come, to help in this time. to alter the under.

A great coughing whine rose and fell throughout the herd as they recoiled at the suggestion of intervening in a place so undermined as this world under. So doomed. And they cast out a great cloud that stank of their distaste for the proposition that their termini should be intertwined with it:

the world under, askew.
not aligned.
the under of taking. its body broken.

> *all of taking.*
> *all to take.*
> *only to take.*

But Ycnaf had been moved by the earnestness of the gesture from the entity her face unreflected, and she responded in kind, although she refrained from lacing her breath with her own acrid doubts:

> *the under the body broken, yes. but spirit aligned. once so the herd. the body broken, mended. to take, yes. to make, yes. the under the spirit aligned to create. to grow to become. the spirit first. a token given by her face unreflected, her spirit unclouded. the under her spirit, first.*

Through the deadbrush plains they tore on as her words wafted over them, until the skies were darkened by a sallow pall of dust split by cracks of lightning and lit by the rising glow of fires. She caught their reply amidst their sapphire-orange ethearic cloud salted by cyclones of smoke and cinders, and found them unimpressed:

> *the door closed.*
> *the under a time immutable.*
> *a space unmoving.*
> *the herd to run to know.*
> *all to run to know.*
> *to touch to be.*
> *always only the herd.*
> *the herd alone.*

They cast out images then of the enduring of the world under, taken from those outlying termini Ycnaf had witnessed from her place across the canyon to show the uncertainty of the doom feared by the entity who had made the appeal for alliance.

But Ycnaf saw what they could not, for it was true that part of her did remain rooted to the world under, and so did those visions of its prevailing against the encroaching shadow bear a strange clarity to her eyes, and she understood at once the reason and delivered it to their cloud of breath:

> *the under to endure, the herd to know to see. there to be in the under, to alter, to see. the herd to deliver the under.*

And the herd saw that many of these termini were rooted in this very moment, and they wavered. Even as they crashed over the cratered brittleglass flow, a shattering of hooves through gleaming swaths of unspoilt volcanic ice. As they smashed through the sharp crystalflow and split grasping fissures into the blackened terrain, wounds that spit magma to clap and steam against their hides.

Ycnaf followed a thread a terminus in which she stood over the traveler in the midst of a great battle. She watched his succumbing and read the breath of farewell that she gave to him.

As clear as it was that in that moment she alone might have saved him, she knew also it would be the herd to deliver this possibility.

And so upon her earnest breath she coughed into their aether her final entreaty:

the herd the traveler ycnaf to hear to see. to see the under spirit aligned. kindred. worthy. to see the under mended. to help the traveler de-mi-ta'il. the shadow comes. the under to fall. the herd to see to feel. the under to fall, the over to grow. the over to take to break. all to break. time and time more. the shadow first away. the under to prevail, the herd to prevail. all to prevail, spirit aligned.

As the wind they swept over the depthless cloudscape, their airy hooves beating over purchase of their own making, their great masses drawing a curtain over the churning storms below. Through their thunderous advance across the sky they pondered by way of their thin trailing wisps of sentiment:

the name, the token.
the shadow to come.
the door closed?
the under to break.
the over to take to break.
to join to under?
to root to under?
to go?

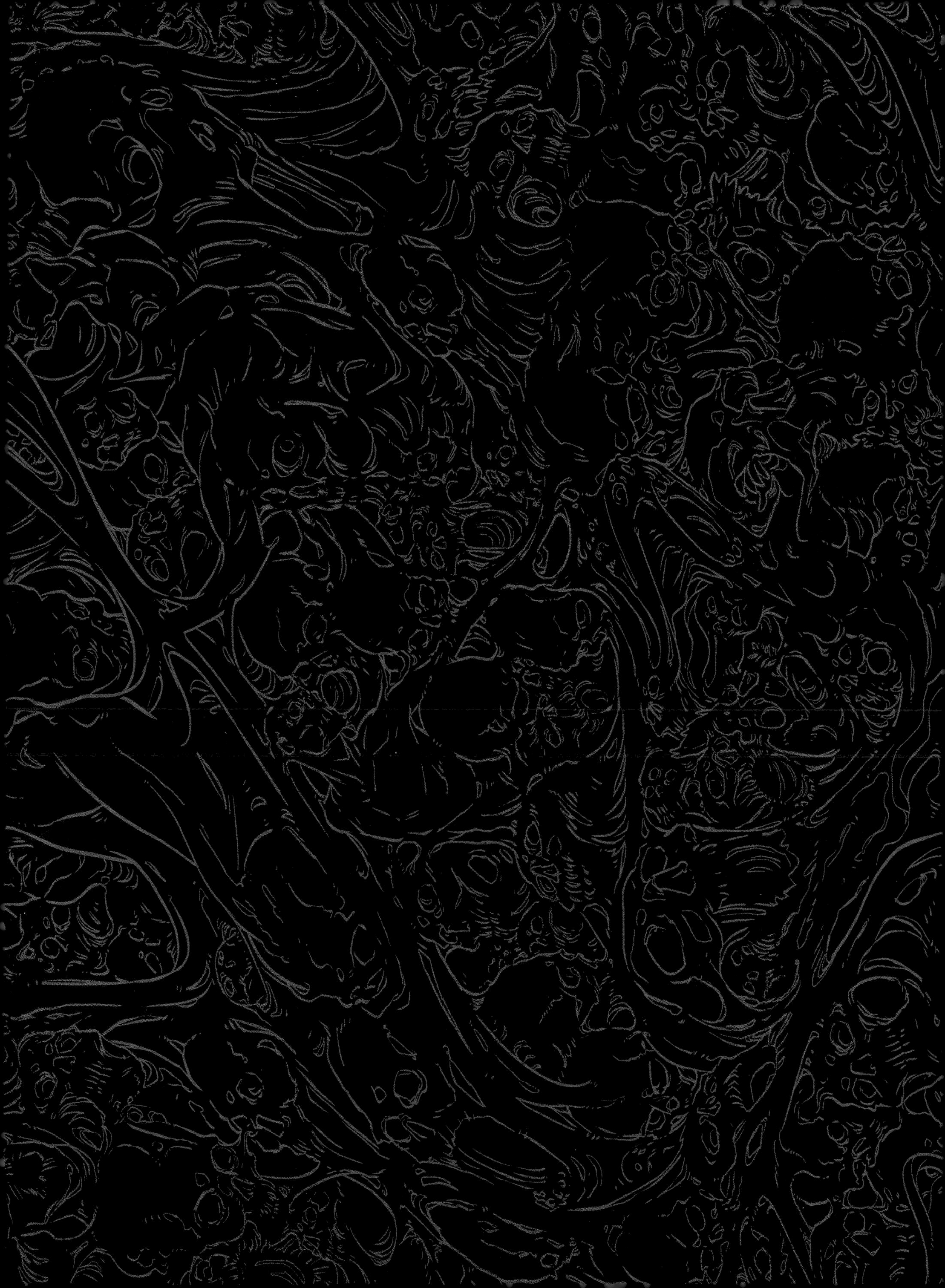

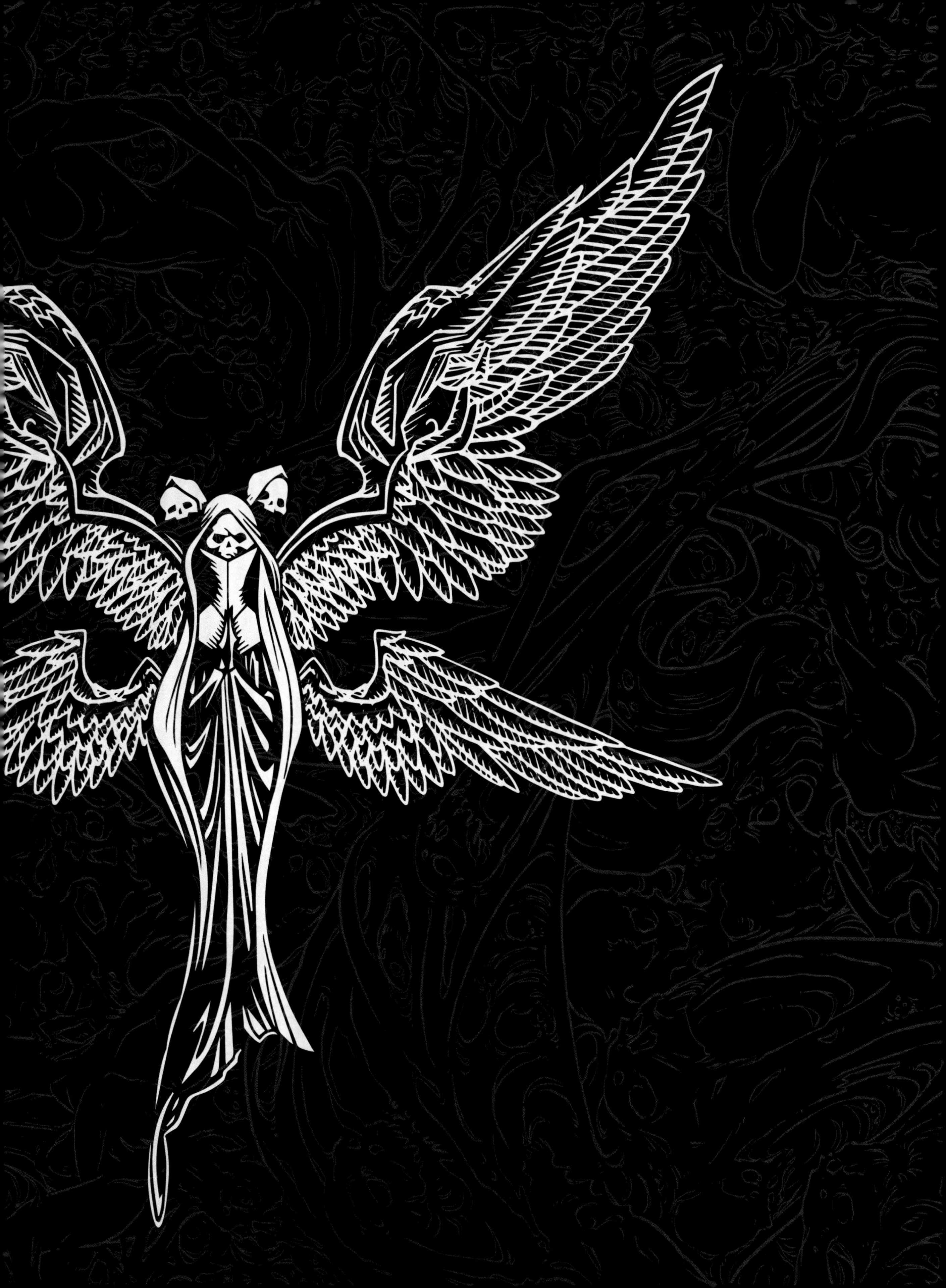

XVIII.
DEATH

In the soul well Death drifted, sifting, sifting through the currents of the newly dead in their shattered thousands. Bathed in the bluegreen wellspring of etherea, he opened his mind now to their interwoven panoply of voices, listening to their chorus of confusion and dismay for intimation of this hidden missive so frankly revealed to him by one of his reapers.

But here and there came only the diminishing wail, when the well would lurch and shudder as the proud cast their selves asunder in the very instant of awareness of their fate. Or the shrieks of the clearer-eyed and wakeful, who were shattered by the fear of it. Still others were lost to the chaos of crossing echoes at the threshold of disillusion and denial, to be carried away in ignorance.

For these he could do nothing but let his thoughts be continuations of their fading significance. Indeed, here he returned often to this very purpose, to this place where he had first noticed their essences of being glinting within the stream of the Dirth Forge, like crystal-flecked brookstones catching the light of the sun. In his curiosity he bade these to reveal their natures to him, and then summations of their lives lived had exploded over the inner walls of his simple grotto, the colors of life throbbing with a richness he could not have imagined, for it did not exist elsewhere. Triumphs, failings, thoughts of futures near and far, minds simple and ambitious. Hearts of fire and ice, driven by a curiosity to match his own.

When he touched them they filled him in ways he was not meant to know. Indeed, it was this that had first brought color into his mind, and thus the Underworld. Before he had thought the mortals small and other. Mere components in the eminent design of things, creatures inculcated with the energies he was made to harvest and deliver and little more. And with this new sight his duty became instantly a burden.

And now he understood the extent to which creation had deprived itself in all its desperation, and his own bitter fate as abettor. For beings of such creativity and depth to be forsaken, ensnared, enslaved, consumed . . . for their suffering, their many gifts and entreaties to be ignored . . . It was as the artist devouring his hands to stave off hunger. A victory of entropy over creation. It was a betrayal.

Yes. And the Dirth Forge was the yoke he wore. This interplanar artery that was the pulse of his Underworld and the stain upon his heart. No, he could not ever fully cleanse it. But to these souls in their breaking he could bring himself to bear witness. It was his penance, or some small measure of it. The least of it.

To those others he now entreated:

You who look in insolence.
Who know with fear but do not deny.
See your time as a small thing, the tiniest of things.
But look still.
Perhaps your anger will burn brighter than the stream.
I do not promise.
No more was your Dark Shepherd made to draw his eye to your plight than a carpenter his nail.
Set you a fire for Death.
That he might find you in the long night.

He listened, but the chorus stood unaltered. Souls spun round him, but all deaf to his words, only to pass in glimmering coils from his outspread fingers.

But then, what had he hoped? Perhaps a chirp, a curious trill. Then a cluster of sprites to awaken to boldness and flutter to him unknowing. Would he speak chitter to them, then? Would they follow his voice? Would he clutch them together that they might understand their weight and worth? Then to set down their souls in the ethearic streams that race from the citadel, with a farewell and pocket change of a few errant memories, on to ride the currents through the city and come what may?

Yes, this very thing. It would not be the first time.

***

The Alltaker shut his mind against the voices now, and against the electric drone of the Dirth Forge, and sought emptiness. He sent his awareness outward of his self to shoot up through the torrent shaft of etherea, racing with the damned high above Illverness and through the foamy terminus that enshrouds the Celestial Cosmos, to pass immediately into its ravage of war, the flash of blade, blood and feather, snarl and claw, mated with thunderclaps of divination and diabolism. He pressed between foes who in sensing his aspect were diverted from warding postures to fall.

Unfettered, he soared immaterial through all the tempestuous strata of their war, and leaving it behind he allowed his self to be pulled out into a rift beyond, where he tumbled as a meteoroid in a vast vacuum of space, adrift alone, his crystalform ice shell complex and unobserved, and undisturbed but for the impossibly distant starlight that refracted over his countless facets. He became a mote of dust in a realm of storms to scribble chaos upon the air, and then an ember in a realm of shadows, peopling it with sparks of light split from his own asperous form. He became a primordial world entire stricken by a temporal cancer, his molten landmasses metastasizing to continents that grew scabrous cityscapes to overwhelm the greening expanse, then to shrivel and curl beneath a sudden encapsulating latticework of fire.

And then he sent his consciousness into the kāla unknown, there for a time to become nothing at all.

* * *

And he felt a weight in his hand. He opened his eyes in the pitiless emptiness and brought it forth to the nothing that was his eyes' to witness: a flat stone, upon it an ancient daub of paint the color of rust. This he pressed against the greater nothing and from it stone walls grew in a dance of shadow and firelight until Death was brought to physicality in a cave not unlike his own sanctuary beneath the Forge.

In its center was a small fire, its warmth of light at play over a graybearded mortal immured by a crop of jagged accretions of sparkling stone grown through his bent and aged form. Ceaselessly he painted the cave wall before him with wetted thumbs, his artistry hidden by his own dance of shadow. Above him loomed the enclosing fangs of low-hanging stalactites, so that present before Death was a creature caught in a slow gnash of aeons.

The Alltaker remained in the dark recess, observing this rare farseeking mortal whose spells had granted him at long last audience with Death. All upon the cavern walls were rudimentary markings of invocation: simple hands outlined with blown pigment overlain with deft portraits of the archaic mortal world and his gods: the sun, the mountains, the sea, the hunt, the worship, the sacrifice. Among these, a gradual shaping to discrete sigils, as if a child coming into the discovery of a new language, until what lay before the man in the stone was a spiraling mural of arcane ritual writ in the dark stain of ancient blood.

Death was moved by the aesthetics of it, if not the intent. The purity of its artistic expression was far more . . . restful than anything he had endeavored to create. Yet it was evident this ancient mortal had been nothing if not driven by singular purpose.

The man in the stone continued to paint. He did not look from his work when he spoke. I am forever in a moment, he said to his wall. In my making, the end of all things was foretold and given personhood. Mine is the task to take, and all is given unto me. I am entropy. I am the All Taker. I am Death.

Death smiled beyond the reach of the firelight, amused by the game. He did not reply, but thought only: Would that I could so release my burden to you.

The man in the stone pressed fingers into a bowl of shaven bone and it filled with blood. Death marked the streaming wounds cut in bands over his arms. He slapped together his freshly wetted hands and returned to his painting.

The man in the stone worried over an element for a moment, and then he spoke again. I grow close. By sight of my craft I know that at last Death has come. With firelight I can not see you. But your voice I might hear upon the zephyr. Will you speak? Will you speak to me, O Death? Our friendship is long delayed.

Death answered from shadow. Your spell accounts for more than you descry, O time-bitten mystic, for mine is the voice of inspiration undone, far too weighty to be borne by earthly zephyrs. Indeed, you might add to your incantation: 'O Death, who shuns not the wounds suffered by the soulborn.' For by their woe do I gain, and by their sacrifices am I kept, and by their ignorances am I dreadful.

The man in the stone laid his stained hands by his side. He spoke again. These are the words of Death. These are the words of Death, come to me at last, O at last.

Death answered in kind. These are the petty testaments of one stained by the futile protestations of the parentless; they who are condemned to reach ever for meaning denied their realm entire. I am the ashes of moments imagined beyond a dawning ever delayed. I am the tragedy of lovers who never meet. Can you hear them? Their words are mine also.

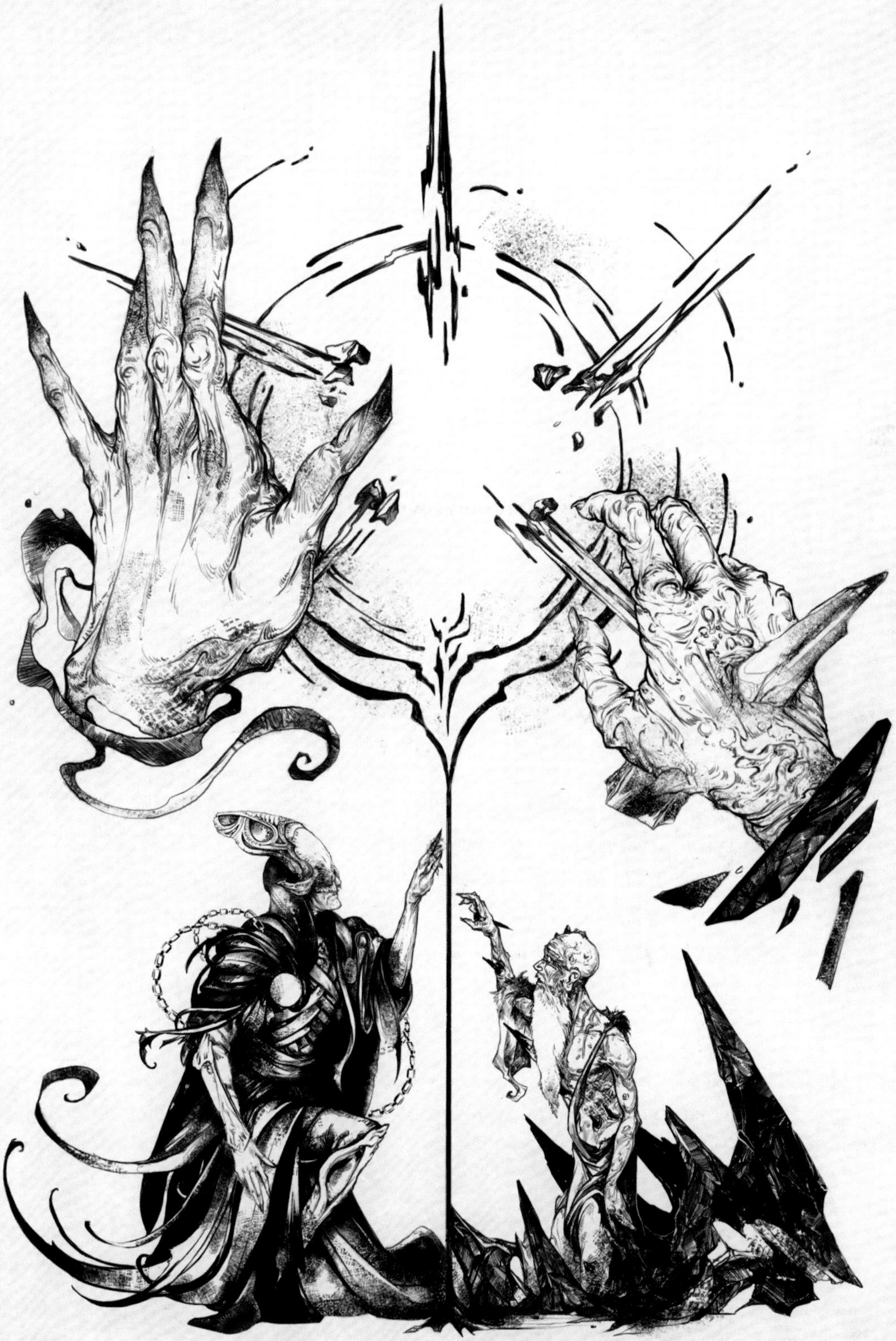

The man in the stone brought a cup to his lips. He tipped it back and then blew a white tincture upon the wall. He drew in a great breath of the fire from where it cracked and spattered behind his glistening nest and coughed forth a thick plume of smoke and cinders against the wall. By the vagueness of its glow Death marked a five-pointed outline around a circular sigil.

The man in the stone rewetted his fingers and made ready his hands before the wall, his blood dripping freely from his elbows. When the smoke dissipated he pressed them to his work again.

Death spoke. You seek to catch the fire's like upon your canvas of stone.

The man slowly shook his mass of gray hair and replied. No. There is no need. The stone knows well the fire. By its heat was it made. By this same also will we all of us become friends of Death, at the end of us.

Death replied. The end of you?

The man in the stone offered his wall the slightest of nods. The very end of us. The lastborn.

Spoke Death: Ah, I see it then. You are indeed a prophetic creature.

But he thought little of the vision. In his espial of humanity he had seen a great many prophets and soothsayers. All were so certain of their taming of destiny. Yet such foresight could be carried to even this heteroclite mortal by naught but light imprisoned in his realm.

Spoke Death to him: It would seem you have won your communion with Death in your waking life. What would you ask of him, beyond release from hoary incantation, now that I have heard it?

The man in the stone answered, even as he worked to refine his blooded shape upon the wall. Describe for me a soul.

Spoke Death: Ah, only that.

* * *

What is a soul, a soul, 'tis what? Why not ask you a painter how best to capture its worth and bring it aglimmer upon the canvas?

See not what begets it, she will say, see not where it goeth; that will be tethered to the detail.

She will bid thee prepare thy palette with all colors and more, for a soul is a vessel set adrift in a protean universe of furtive thoughts, each of its stars ablink like a sudden recollection or the impulse of a lie.

Leave it here indistinct, bring finer definition there.

Where you wish to lay down a happy stroke, she will say conjure to mind the face of a babe agaze upon yours in the dawning understanding of love, for to capture a soul is also to share it.

Where you wish to evince the fluidity of being, hearken to the twin agitations of pain and contentment that drive all soulborn to grow, and pay special scrutiny to their overlying margins.

Be mindful throughout, she will certainly instruct thee, of the bond of empathy that connects all souls, that which impels them to shed tears for the woes of distant neighbors, and that which carries them to succor and to sacrifice.

And her final wisdom imparted to you will be caveat: When you have completed this masterpiece, she will warn, you will see it crushed. When you have cherished and captured a life born and fairly lived so as to enrich its bounty, after you have imagined it cultivated greater by this life's work, you will watch it mechanically sundered to mere cordwood for the coldest fire.

Know its final awareness of this horror. Know then that you are not an artist, but a custodian, the sanction of your parentage your only indemnity. Know this loss, and begin again.

* * *

The man in the stone drew down fingers over the wall, spreading them as he did so, then closed all but one to trace a thin line around the mark. He rewet his fingers and then made a claw with them as if to pluck up a smoldering coal, then touching round the circle he drew them together over the surface, then tapped into the center of the mark before flicking them open as he pulled his hand away, spattering outward five streaks of blood.

He spoke to himself then: I have it. He stared long at his work, arms waiting to start anew. Finding nothing more, he laid them to rest upon his lap.

Yes. Finally, I have it. Do you hear me, O Death? Come now, and take me. Come and take me. I have it now, it is complete. I am yours, I am yours. Collect me, please, collect me. Make me into something other. Make me nothing. Only take me. You must. Collect me to be undone. Please. Please.

Death stepped into the firelight, upon ground stained thick with ages of bloodfall. He touched the stone that imprisoned the man. Its spikes glistened over with clouded water. He stepped back to watch them swell and grow up to join with the hanging spires as crushing pillars that entombed the man in the stone before they wore away again to diminish from existence, the ruin of the ancient mortal left to fall upon the bloodstained cavern floor.

Death stood over him as his empty eyes welled with his soul etherea, and holding forth the blade of his scythe he spoke: Now you look upon your Death, whom by your craft you have long eluded so as to purchase his parley. What last would you hear of his voice, then, before he cuts the gossamer thread that binds your soul to this realm, then to be sent through the Forge below?

The man of the wilted stone gaped at the hollowness of his prize, the terror of it. And then he gave Death his final words: The way of beginnings is remembrance. And then he fell away to dust.

* * *

He stood in stillness, accompanied now only by his scythe, that which he had once again employed to deliver a soulborn to its doom. He leaned upon it heavily now, suddenly very tired, and spoke softly in the pulsating firelight. Elder's Clutch, long the dark companion to my toil . . . my faithful, faithful cane. A relic still more worn than thee shall borrow now thy posture, my bent and faithful cane.

He looked upon the markings that covered the cavern walls. He had seen their like many times. Always they had conjured in him an admiration for the mortals who could not bear but to transmit something of themselves forward through the ages, even before possessing a thing so quaint as a written tongue.

Now he saw only the desperate arcane artistry of the Death-obsessed shaman, who now swam in the soul well in the full and final knowing of the answer to the question he had waited countless lifetimes to ask.

Leaning upon his scythe he bowed his head, feeling spent, withered.

Said he to the floor:

Heavy is the millstone
must the wretched miller free
from the clutches of the drowned men
who thought they'd mill their grain at sea

* * *

Death turned to look upon the shaman's final master work, now shown by the unfettered firelight over a swollen protrusion of countless strata of blood and white blown pigment over the cavern wall. A circular aggregation of sigils, its five piercing elements slashed through its circumference with pentagonal symmetry. He pressed his palm to the symbol to burn its likeness into his hand, then stood again to study his prize.

Even so reversed he recognized at once its evocation of the universality of ethearic power, a secret that the wretched provident shaman must have discovered long ago to bring him his cruel immortality. Yet much about its intricacy puzzled him, and it called into his mind a whisper that had chased him for nearly as long as he could recall, like a mote of dust in his eye that could not be felt but from a place of dreaming.

Could this be kin to that which he had so long sought: the key to reclaiming creation, concealed among the mortals?

If so, it would seem his spirit sojourn to this place was not happenstance but the last in a conjunction of the efforts born of the three realms, finally impelled by his meditations upon this mysterious missive—of which he was aware only by the strangely fortuitous recollections of the newborn reaper Demithyle.

He repeated those final words of the deathless mortal, his voice echoing through the emptiness of the cavern: The way of beginnings is remembrance.

He looked round. The cave was gone. In the quiet solitude of his sanctuary he stood now alone.

But something was coming. Something was near.

A flash of orange and blue emptied the cave of shadow, and then suddenly, a traveler, looking into him with orange, crystalline eyes.

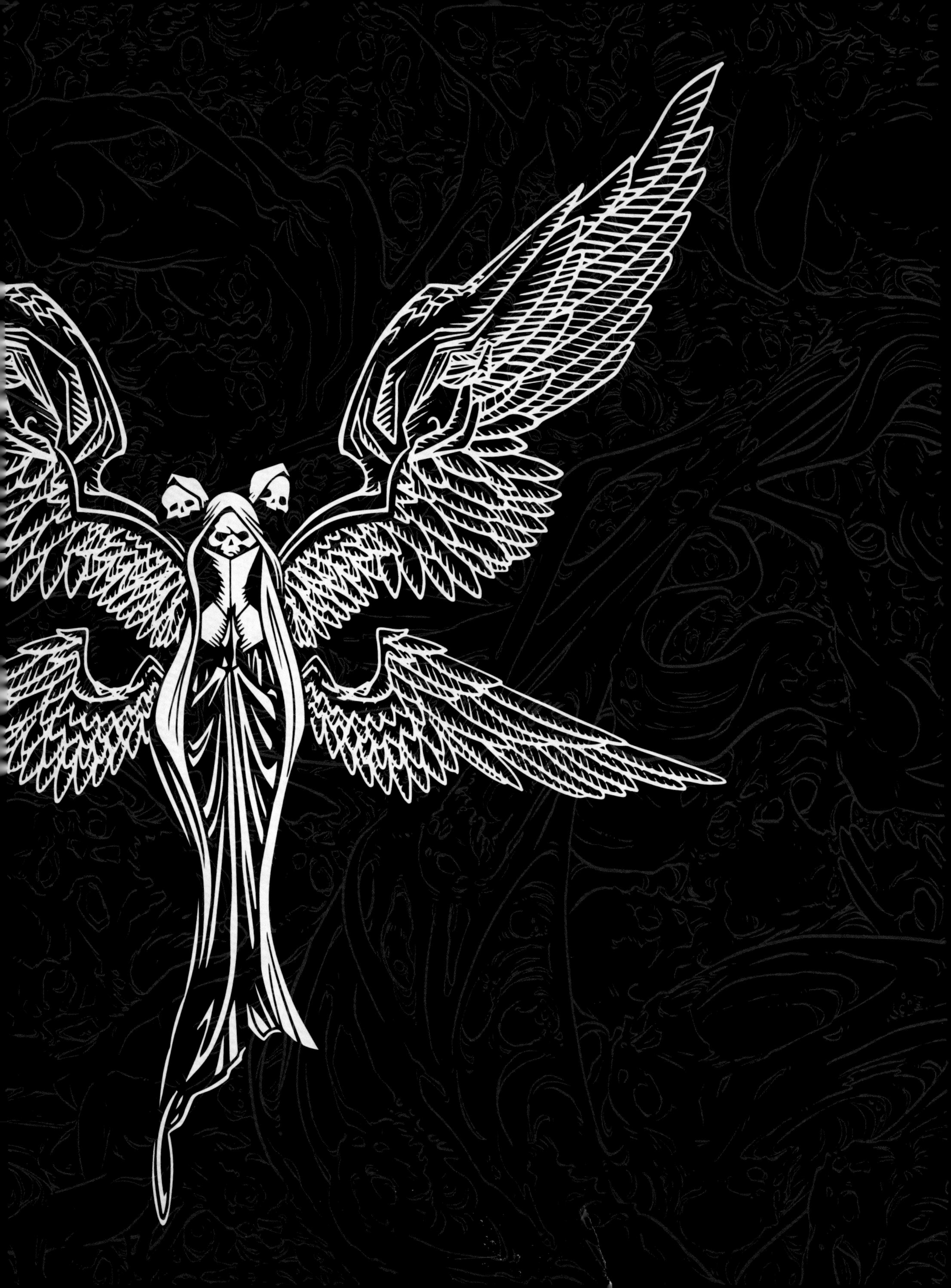

XIX.
GETHSEMONI

Gethsemoni stood upon the forward overlook high upon the Vadlum Gates, watching the storm roll in. From this height she could see clearly its twisting vortices of dust and etherea, crawling under the sky like a leviathan flailing toward the city through a turbulent sea. Its dark sapphire pall swept over the outer wallows and up the Blackmeir Tower, the blackglass pinnacles catching nascent capillaries of bluegreen lightning that glittered over its countless facets.

She closed her eyes, listening to its volley of silence and complaint. As the banners began to whip against the flanking towers she inhaled the electrified air and began to sing:

A wisp, in her ear, a wisp
To mark the darkmeir, a wisp
Becalmed, be it restless
Unleashed, be its fury
Be its beauty
O its vehement beauty
A sliverfall kept within
A cracking of bells in the din
Its augur of rains
The eidolon flash in her veins
To bring from afar
All the harrowed Underworld's pains
To bring her from afar
A sliver, a tear
Her touch, the darkmeir
To tear at the heart of her name

There came a tremendous flash, and she opened tearful eyes to witness the gate's outer bailies falling under the pall. Another flash as a great mesh of lightning tore across the shroudcover, and then spiraling trails of ethearic mist began to streak down across the vista behind a burgeoning shower of crystalline hailstones. With the sound of the cracking of a thousand tiny bells they burst in mid-air, showering the inroads to the city with waves of tourmaline slivers, the collective peals of subsequent bursts swelling above even the wailing of the Forge.

As the storm moved in, flocks of spirit avians soared through its densest sheets of sliverfall, and darkened swaths followed in their wake as the light-shy umbrem raced from the tangled fringes of the roads to catch up the scattering slivers of their leavings, the ambient light to return as they slipped back into their murky pockets.

Far below, ambling mourners made their way in and out through the gateworks, seemingly oblivious to the squall as its spattering edge crashed over the city's entrance. Gethsemoni watched as the luminous hailshards painted the dark surfaces aglow, passing through the barbed oillets of the works' bartizans and watchtowers to momentarily bring form to the shade sentinels within.

Then as it blew in over the city there came a chorus of musical cries where a cadre of the spiritbairn streamed outward from the Curio Cryptus, likely having stolen away from HushHyde in search of baubles. They settled over a crop of hilly gravesites to romp in the downpour, leaping to catch the falling slivers before they could splash into the muck as they threw mischievous cantrips at one another.

Gethsemoni smiled at their gleeful obliviousness to the danger looming beyond the horizon. With a swipe of her hands she gathered the ethearic mephitis steaming from her lavender skin by the pelting of sliverfall, and wafting it about she threw it to swirl out over the spiritkinder in a dazzling waterfall of luminous animates, their melodious delight in it bringing her to laugh for the first time in recent memory.

Yes, for the first time since the Alltaker had goaded the baelreivers from their torpor she felt some reprieve from the din of anguish cast into the aether by their ravaging of her Underworld. Tirelessly she had worked to gather in whatever wandering spiritbeings she and her acolytes could find, settling those of greater agency where they might find comfort within the protection of the city walls, delivering the listless into the care of the fostermurden already burdened with those afflicted few who had managed escape upon encountering the blightwraiths. But many remained beyond her reach. There was no more that could be done. Even now she could feel the terror of their sundering as the horde left the outlands behind.

She looked skyward. If she could not shun the voices of torment, for the moment at least they were quieted beneath the deadening ripples of the storm. She leaned back to present herself to its still-thickening shroudcover, letting the shards skate off her flesh, feeling their pull against her adornments caught by the gale. If ever the Underworld should seek for itself an unchangeable state of being, she thought, let it be this.

* * *

In the deepening gloom, a bony hand clamped up over the edge of her outlook, and then another. An empty, runescarred skull peeked over. One of Xiall's creatures.

Gethsemoni barely looked its way as it pulled itself up with a dry croak and shambled into place behind her. More followed. They aligned themselves along the rear edge of her outlook, crushing and climbing over one another until they had formed an enclosure around her with their withered bodies.

"You do not mind, I'm sure," came the expected voice. "Not everyone wishes to brood in the rain."

Xiall stood next to her, within the shadow of the newly formed canopy, staff in hand. The air was filled with a hollow rattle as the shards glanced off the enclosure's skulls.

Resigned to the arrival of her respite's end, Gethsemoni sighed, gazing out to the diminishing tail of the storm.

"You have discovered quite the view, elder sister," said Xiall, looking out.

"So it was."

"Ah. I see that it is too dark for you in here. My apologies." Xiall spoke a single word in a tongue that sounded like the cracking of bone, and the skulleyes of the bone-doll shelter stared inward, casting the pocket in a cold yellow glow.

"A fine shade of bister," said Xiall, glancing over the other's skull-lit flesh. "Its dreariness truly flatters you."

"As does disease you."

"Ah, so it does," said Xiall, noting the sickly pallor of her own shell of bone. "No Ellianastis, I see," she added, looking round.

"No."

"One might be forgiven for imagining she should be better acquainted with the keeping of time, as much of it as she burns in that library of hers."

"Her mind occupies many places."

"That is one manner of describing it."

The tinny madrigal of the stonebursts began to fade, and with the shifting light of the aurorae returned also to Gethsemoni the aching lament of the Underworld.

"The library nourisheth her curiosity," she said. "One that perhaps we do not share. Through it she hath gained sight into many a queer vision."

"All of her vision is queer," said Xiall. "Let us not forget that playing caregiver to the wanderbloats has aged her far beyond any of us. Sanity likely escaped her long ago."

A single hailstone spit from the last waning tail of the storm to spiral their way. When it burst, Gethsemoni grew out a pair of broad fleshy wings from her naked back to smash the bone-doll canopy outward, watching with some satisfaction the explosion of figures smacking against the towers in their tumble from the wall.

"Nice," said Xiall, wincing against the slivers. Brushing bits away from her face, she leaned over the edge to watch the marrowdolls breaking up over the gate, rousing nests of spirit avians perched upon its massive siege spikes to join the swarms of flying spirits over the wallows. Working the cartilage frills along her neck she offered a pattern of chirps, and after a moment one of the avians fluttered up to alight on her proffered arm and she reached a bony finger inside its phantasmal head to twiddle a cluster of tendrils there as it trilled and shook its smoldering wings.

"You do have a delicate way with them," said Gethsemoni, letting the wings sink back into her flesh.

Xiall let the avian fly off to chase another of its kind, zagging away on some sprightly errand. "How goes the reclamation?" she asked. "I can not remember you ever having spent so much time outside the city walls."

"Most of the spiritborn have been brought within the walls," said Gethsemoni. "The outer wallows are all but emptied. The inward lands will follow by the mournmeir."

"And the outlands?" asked Xiall. "Your emissaries?"

Gethsemoni said nothing, only looked out to the horizon.

**

The storm gave way to the prismatic tumult of the celestial sky once again. Looking to the clearing horizon, Gethsemoni marked its strange emptiness. The shifting patterns of soul constellations, normally spread evenly

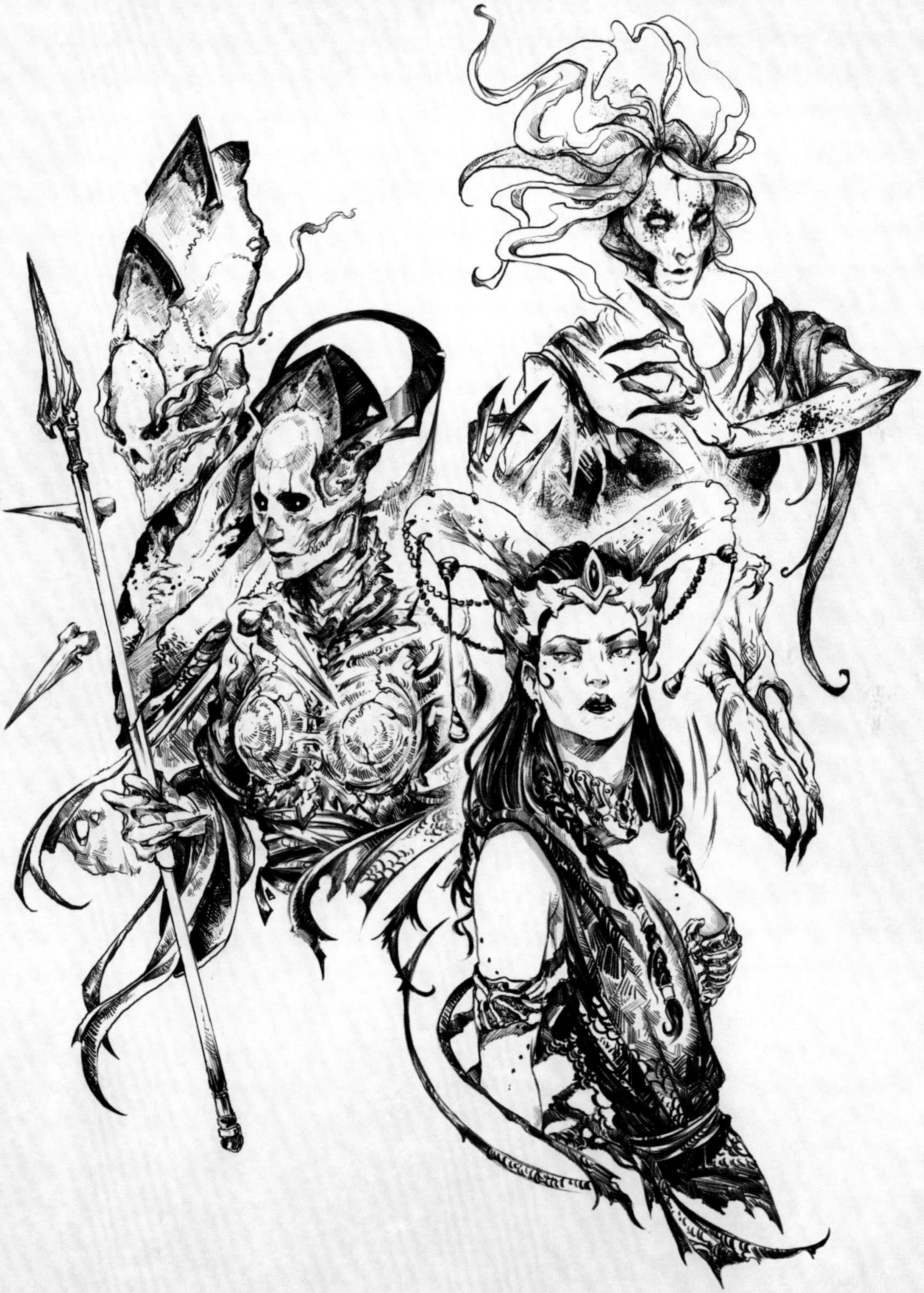

above the whole of the Underworld, were now seemingly pressed above its line.

Xiall followed her gaze. "They are drawn to one another," she said. "They drift and migrate all the time . . ."

"No," said Gethsemoni. "This is different. They crowd themselves inward." She looked at the banners, flapping now as if drawn by the Forge. One storm ends, another begins.

One of the nearer constellations dropped from the sky then, quickly losing its pattern as the individual flares rolled into a circle before flooding in a line toward the gate to weave through the daggerpoint finials above the battlements, and scattering among the various superstructures they finally collect to course in a lazy loop around the two sisters.

"Ellianastis."

Pulsating as if by the name, the flares swam out beyond the edge to fill the hovering outline of Ellianastis before them, beginning with both of her feet pressed into a single shoe and finishing with her head in a final rotation where it floated above her shoulders, its curly aquamarine locks blowing wildly as if by a perpetual wind.

"You always know when it's me," she said.

"It is always you," said Xiall.

Ellianastis's hair flattened out and hardened into an elongated headdress. The flesh of her face bubbled and dissolved to scraps that were taken away by the wind, leaving behind Xiall's skeletal visage.

"Not so," said Ellianastis in Xiall's voice, letting her gown drop to reveal a mimicry of Xiall's lithesome, bone-carven figure. "Sometimes it is you. And sometimes—" she added, turning Xiall's hollow eyes to Gethsemoni.

No.

"Alright then." Reverting to her own form Ellianastis floated in to alight her narrow toe upon the stone of the outlook. "You'll want to get on with things, I suppose."

"If you have finished," said Gethsemoni. "I have been long away. Now that our spiritkin have been brought within the city, we must assess the readiness of the reapers to defend it. 'Tis my understanding the meanderings of one them through the labyrinth has cost them near a fortmeir of their unity."

"Why look to me?" said Ellianastis.

"Perhaps because that is exactly the sort of sideways scaltic as is your trade," said Xiall. "Far be it from us to plot within a pattern of intent . . ."

"Plots and patterns," said Ellianastis. "What is one but a lie cried into the chaos of the other, fain vocalis reflections achime between thunderclaps."

"What?"

"As far as I'm aware, I got him stuck nowhere."

"We have expended much in the rearing of the mortis," said Gethsemoni, with a heavy sigh. "The blightwraith horde will arrive at our gates in but a few meirs' time. We must discern our Vanguard's readiness to meet it."

Xiall released a sigh of her own, a hissing chorus of whistles in her throat.

"If their trials in Veth showed us anything," she said, "it is that the reapers are far stronger and more capable than we could have hoped. The swiftness with which they came into their individual abilities was a match to their ardor in employing them. And by the collective potency of their focal corpus, even greatly outnumbered I can not imagine they will be less than a match for the baels."

Gethsemoni could not suppress a smile. "Then we hath made them fine," she said, looking back over the city to the Calvum Harrows. "'Tis good to hear. Good indeed."

"And Demithyle?" said Ellianastis. "Is it true he blew up your titan all by himself? That thing you boasted would have them scrambling in there for decades, *elall*!"

"He is a natural leader," said Xiall, evading the question. "He fought by the side of nearly all of the others at one point or another, and it was he who led the last of them to the discovery of the orrery. Had he gotten over himself sooner, he could have saved them no small amount of evisceration."

"What do you mean?" asked Gethesemoni.

"His failure was not one of insight but reluctance to exerting his influence over the others."

"I see," said Gethsemoni. "'Tis perhaps a reflection of their inborn aversion to the dreadsgrip. Interesting, indeed."

"In any event," said Xiall, "in his absence I have organized their greater force beneath five cibori subcaptains, chosen from those with whom he finally brought down the orrery. Their stanchions refine themselves in the fields of the Harrows while these five plan our defense as best as they are able. It is their intent to lure the baelreivers from the city en masse."

"How exactly?"

"I have no idea," said Xiall.

"What of the wyspstride?" asked Gethsemoni.

"Ah, yes," said Ellianastis. "Such beautiful, fascinating creatures! Our mediocre fiddling with time is nothing compared to their understanding of it by nature. As near as I can tell, every moment of an individual's timeline is always visible in their knowing. Think of it! Every path forward shown as a fluctuating pattern of known possibilities."

"That sounds as exhausting as it would be tedious," said Xiall. "I assume you have already parlayed with it, then? Your attempts to ally with the wyspstrides, Ellianastis, have only ever failed. They simply do not care about us or any being beyond themselves."

"Indeed," said Gethsemoni. "Nor would I have expected to learn of their presence in the labyrinth."

"The work of the entity Simmel," said Ellianastis. "It has been waylaying and consuming creatures that have become lost in its folds. Probably to hoard their memories, the wretch."

"He is destroying them?" asked Gethsemoni, troubled by the news.

"Yes. I don't know how he's doing it yet. I intend to find out."

Xiall looked at Ellianastis. "So the wyspstride led him from the labyrinth, then?"

"Oh, yes."

"Where is it now?" asked Xiall.

"She has gone to commune with her kind," said Ellianastis. "You've guessed correctly, of course, dear sister. At the Alltaker's behest, I've given her a formal proposal of alliance to bring to her kind. But even if they do not hear it, I'm certain she will return to Demithyle."

"She?"

"Yes," said Ellianastis. "She is called Ycnaf. Isn't that lovely?"

"She has bonded herself to Demithyle?" asked Gethsemoni.

"Oh, yes," said Ellianastis. "It was he who freed her, of course. One shadow they are, and only half a wink from batting eyes. I've no doubt she will act as his steed in the coming battle, in fact."

"So long as he does not first fade to a paperwraith simpleton in your fitcrakked mad library."

"Not likely," said Ellianastis. "A stolid fellow, that one. Even now he searches for ways to deny himself."

"A better thing could not be said of any soldier."

"You misunderstand, sister," said Ellianastis. "In creating our army of reapers we filled their heads with battle stuff, yes, and the knowing of mundane things—all from borrowed thoughts and memories. To help them to grow, make them fierce. But everything they experience is still new to them. Demithyle is different. He actually relives his memories. He experiences their expenditure of time. Thereafter, he knows them as his own. It's the reason he can manage etherea in a way no spiritborn can, not even the other reapers. For all intents and purposes, he is ensouled."

"Ridiculous," said Xiall.

"It's true," said Ellianastis. "Where the others draw what they must from their makeup, Demithyle is odd—boon or curse, for our better or worse, his struggle is foremost to understand all that he is, all he becomes. In any case, we made them together; we should be proud to see ourselves elevated in him. You know what Father likes to say . . ."

Ellianastis phased then into three overlain aspects of herself, two that then became reflections of the glowering images of her sisters as they fanned apart before all three were brought back together, their conflicting features coagulating into the form of Death.

"No thing in the Cosmos is greater than the whole of your trinity," said this vision of Death. "The same father who failed the first of their kind then created you one by one to explore the root of his folly. By your quality now has Demithyle the Seeker been brought into being. His triumphs are yours, for he is your own culmination, his conviction born by your sacred unity. To see you in him now, 'tis all that I have wished."

The form of Death melted down to nothing, and standing beside her sisters Ellianastis turned to them and smiled as she leaned forward to kiss them both.

"It's what he hoped we would see," she said.

* * *

Mother of blades . . .

Gethsemoni felt her awareness drawn to a nearby tower, to the darkness of its arched entryway. The shadows there grew deeper, and rippled with her reading of their troubling message.

"Who's that?"

"The conclave," said Xiall. "One of Exraille's, probably. What does he wish of us now, a bard to—"

"The baelreivers have been seen from the outposts beyond the outer wallows," said Gethsemoni. "We must go. Now."

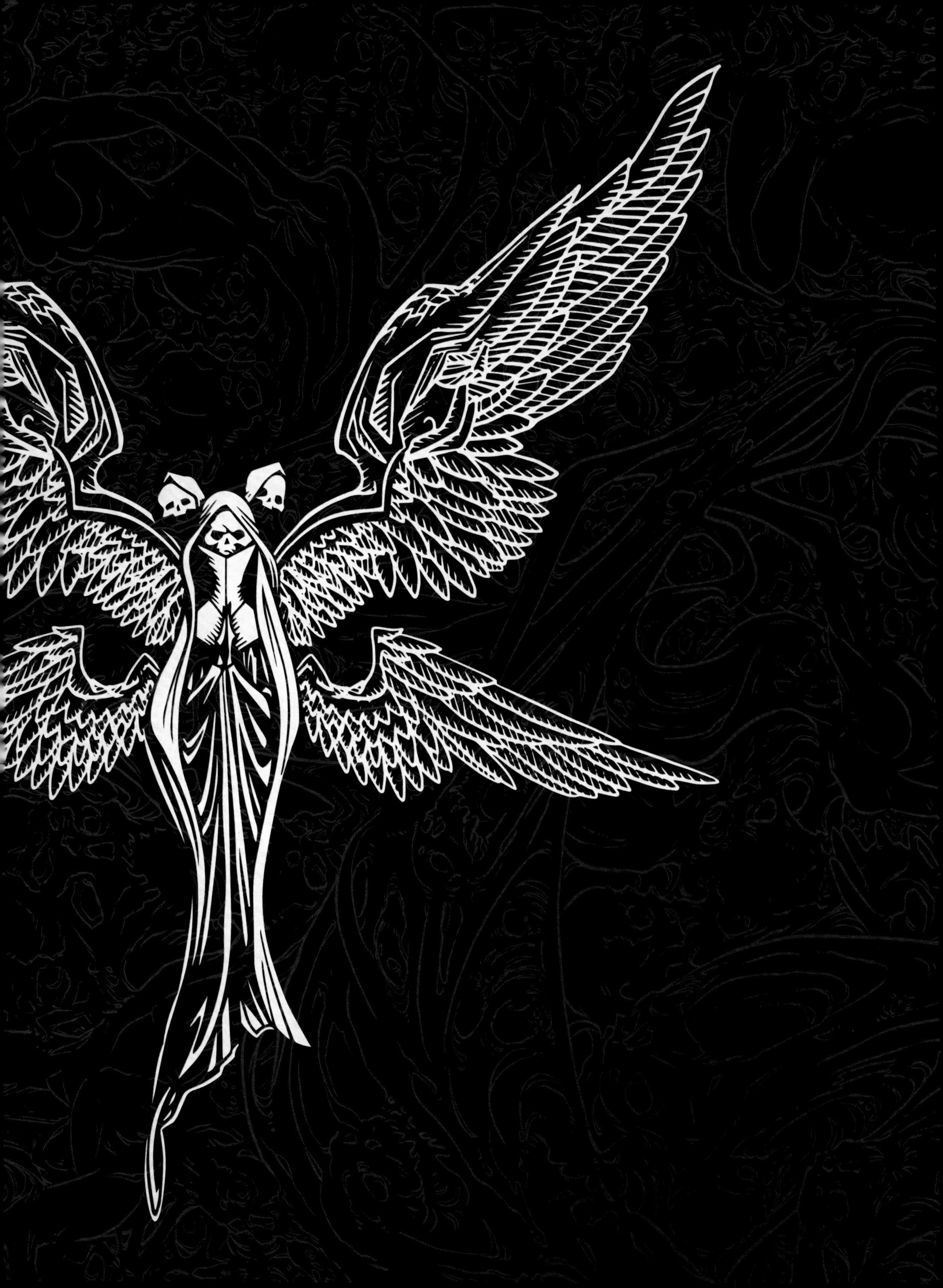

XX.
GIGNOTH

Gignoth leapt between the towering columns that encircled the Calvum Harrows training grounds, gaining elevation with each maneuver as he drew his outnumbered reapers forward in a close evasive formation. Strikes flew over their heads, showering them with chunks of masonry that they grappled even as they sprang, sending them backward in blind volleys to sow confusion among Melthis and her reaper splinters.

He knew she was once again attempting to deny him high ground; it was rare these contests did not end with they two as the last cibori standing. Yet the attacks remained unfocused as her knights scrambled for vertical purchase upon the columns. Good. He had sacrificed four of his own splinters—fully half his force—to take out her most agile fighters at the breakaway for just that reason.

And now she was forced to make do with her more hulking stalwarts. Far tougher, certainly, but slower, clumsier. Judging by the braying grunts and sporadic wracking of the supporting structures, the largest of these lumbered through an exhausted brawl somewhere below. Even now he could feel a spike of satisfaction from his knights as one of their pursuers cried out in frustration and stumbled to fall cursing to the ground.

Still, at any moment Melthis would adapt, figuring out a way to align her forces to wrest from him the initiative. He bade his knights to hold their lines, to sustain their cycling of etherea even as their pursuers expended their own with badly aimed blasts. Then suddenly he feinted them groundward before executing a vertical leap, as if to set up an ambush with a last-ditch sacrifice of distance. When Melthis ignored the feint, half his knights made a show of spilling their momentum with seemingly faltered footing.

There was a triumphant howl as the rivals closed.

"Rippers spent already, Gig?" taunted Melthis. "Patience, sluvvidess, sleep is coming! Aye, we'll lend a lash, won't we?"

Her reapers called out their accord with a final battle cry. But even as they pounced to deliver what was meant to be the decisive blow, Gignoth's knights pulled in the etherea they had been cycling between them to suddenly diffuse into their own shadows that then slunk away to darkened recesses behind the columns. The chorus of surprise and cursed accusations of trickery was more than a little satisfying. As was the sight of half a dozen of Melthis's reapers scraping for foothold and tumbling to the ground as they were left with nothing to grapple.

The shroudreive scuttled over to drag away the fallen, gathering up and carting away detached limbs, weapons, pieces of armor, and other combat detritus. He bade his knights to remain hidden, waiting. Subterfuge was a tactic none had yet attempted to employ on these grounds, and surprise seemed to have proven sufficient to gain advantage. It would not be so effective a second time.

The other cibori stanchions had quickly immobilized one another. Within the first moments of the battle Sithik had flown his knights directly into a trap set by both Melthis and Torbrenth, the latter of whom was then immediately crushed by aggressive dissolution of their alliance. Thrael had tried to gain her knights encirclement from cover at the base of the columns, only to find Gignoth had gotten there first.

And then it was just Melthis and Gignoth in a dance of predator and prey. Now the prey waited. The etherea would soon run its course; they could not remain in this shadow state for long. But it would be long enough. Melthis's knights moved cautiously now, off-balance, wasting their reserves burning traction on the columns, blasting at shadows.

"Let's get this over with, eh, sluvvidess?" she shouted. "Come out so I can shuck a pointy kist up in the shrively fallow skint of ye!"

Gignoth smiled inwardly. *We'll see.*

Melthis's reapers began to slacken their formation as they spread out their search, and Gignoth could feel the rising anticipation of his knights. *Patience*, he wisped to them. *We have made time our ally. Let it be their enemy.*

But then, a cry of alarm as one of Melthis's reapers fell, shorn free of his hands, a dark trailing shadow vanishing behind a column.

Liftholch. Not the first time he had broken ranks. He would deal with that later.

More cries of surprise and anger as the rest took their cue from

Liftholch, going after strays from the formation, or so they thought. But Melthis was not stupid.

Stay your hands. They lure us to open ground.

But it was too late. Just as Gignoth knew she would, Melthis had answered subterfuge with guile: the "stragglers" had been sent to draw his knights into a trap. Even as another of hers was picked off, the rest of her force had descended on the area, chasing away the shadows with blankets of fire and bluegreen balls of spiritlight. And now Gignoth's fighters had nowhere left to go.

He had gambled on subterfuge with an inferior force in exchange for better ground, but only coordinated strikes from the shadows could have won the meir. One by one his knights tumbled to the ground below as the rival body began to flush them out. All that was left now was for Gignoth to move as quickly as he could through the shadows, hoping for an opportunity to remove its head.

He raced around the upper recesses of the arena, slipping from shadow to shadow, stopping just short of a burst of light that would have delivered him into an ambush.

Three approached nearby, stepping quietly between the columns, their probing toes cutting into the stone. He could see their method, systematically flashing away the shadows, blades at the ready. Yet they seemed to assume him confined to the highest, darkest corners behind the columns. As the nearest approached he slipped below and waited for them to pass, and when the last had shone his light before himself Gignoth swam up to occupy the shadow created behind him by his own blast and reaching from it grabbed an ankle and tore the searcher away from the column, disarming him and skewering him through the neck with his own weapon even as he fell.

Exposed now, the last of his store of etherea spent, Gignoth vaulted to the next column in the line, pinning another hunter against it with his scimitar as she turned clumsily to meet him, and scrambling up her armored form he leapt from her shoulders, tearing her through the curved blade even as he pulled it free from the column to slice through the knees of the last, sending both crashing down to meet the first.

Taking cover behind the column, he froze, listening. Hard to say how many she had left. Slowly he crept forward down the line of columns, straining through the darkness to see. Melthis would be expecting him to come.

There was a short crunch above, and Gignoth looked up to find Liftholch clutching a freshly torn lower mandible in his fist. The knight gave his cibori a nod before retreating again into the shadows, dropping the jaw to shatter on the ground below where one of Melthis's combatants was already being dragged away by the shroudreive.

The knight was good, Gignoth had to allow that. Even if strangely vicious. The other would surely have waylaid him. Perhaps there yet remained a slow strategy of two, to take out the enemy captain, sow disarray . . .

Yet even as he turned over the idea he stopped himself from wisping forth a command. Something about the image of this smirking opportunist holding on to some part of Melthis like a trophy . . . In any case, he doubted she could be taken unawares, even by one so sly as he.

As if in answer, a cry of anger and pain—undeniably from Liftholch. Now only he remained. He remained still, seeing nothing, hearing nothing. There were no other sounds. No movement could he detect. He closed his eyes, trying to feel Melthis's presence. Reaching to see through hers.

Then, a blade at his throat.

"Gignoth the Guru, innardlorn again."

"Thinking of you, of course," he said, dropping his sword to clatter below.

"Fair slirvsome, he is," she said. "Makes a lady gush."

"Perhaps this is your secret weapon," said Gignoth.

"Or maybe it's just yer twitchy knights, working harder than any to get my knife in you."

"Well, you are the most charming of the cibori."

"The naefukkin' truth, there."

The rest of the reapers, made whole again by the shroudreive, had begun to congregate to watch the final face-off between the two cibori and now shouted taunts and calls for a final dismemberment to complete the meir's skirmish.

"Your kerissst, Melthis," said Gignoth. "Fair won. Again. Shall we go to collect your reward?"

"Maybe I'll just take that third eye of yers. Might shine true on the pommel, eh?"

"Why not set it into the back of your head?" said Gignoth. "Perhaps then you will see us coming before half of your reapers are eating dirt."

"Heh. Says the pitshin with the dagger at his throat."

* * *

A metallic crack rolled in from the distance, and soon after the area was swept by a glittering sliverfall as ethearic crystal hailstones began to explode overhead. Those intact mortis no longer commiserating with one another about the recent skirmish had already resumed their drilling, and they halted their doings momentarily amid the shower to marvel at this yet another new and unexpected experience. But as a thin blue vapor of ambient etherea arose from the grounds they imbibed it with relish to the renewal of their activity, the rising din of their myriad expressions of it quickly overwhelming the crackle of the storm.

Having retrieved their weapons, Melthis and Gignoth paused beneath the buttress canopy to witness the curtain of sliverfall breaking against the cathedral architecture of the Harrows, edging its pillars and abutments sharply blue against the deep shadows of its recesses. Then as quickly as it rose the storm quieted, and the two cibori crossed the grounds to ascend to the battlements atop the leftward enclosure, where they found Sithik and Torbrenth in conference, looking out beyond the cradle crypt from which they had emerged to the expanse of the inner wallows leftward from the gate.

Gignoth nodded to the two, squinting against the driving wind. "Thrael?"

"In the fields," said Sithik, "putting her rippers through it, I imagine."

"I do not envy them," said Torbrenth. "They were the first to fall."

"Aye, but yer own followed down quick enough, didn't they," said Melthis.

Sithik looked back toward the grounds, his thorny head whistling by the gale. "Small comfort to them, I'm sure," he said. "I believe that is one of them screaming now."

Torbrenth crossed his arms, looking at Melthis, the hood of his cloak pressed against the back of his skull. "Is it not considered uncouth to betray one's allies?"

"Alliances're made ready broke," she said with a shrug. "I only beat ye tae the kiss, like."

"Hm."

"I do begin to wonder whether these little skirmishes of ours do not work against our goals," said Sithik, turning back to the group. "Not that I feel particularly disunified, mind you. It is only that a certain someone might have a bit of catching up to do, whenever it is that he should return from his holiday, that is."

Gignoth only nodded. Demithyle's absence was a question that had lived on the surface of each of their minds, if no longer their tongues, since he had failed to reappear with them after Mortis Veth. Xiall's declaration of him as their commander in absentia had been accepted as a matter of course. But it had added a nagging uncertainty to all of their efforts of preparation.

"Aye, well," said Melthis. "Without that certain someone we'd still be in that prisspunged shitepit, we would."

"And yet o ur corpus remains but a fog," said Torbrenth. "Strange our parentage should fail to appreciate the gravity of this."

"I spoke of it with Xiall the last time she was here," said Gignoth. "Do you know what she said? 'Sprout some gussiks.'"

"About as helpful as she was in the Veth," said Melthis. "Anyway, we could use another go in there about now, I think."

The other cibori looked at her.

"Might I remind you that only just a moment ago you referred to that very place as a 'shitepit,'" said Sithik.

"Not in the queue tae get stuck back in, am I," said Melthis. "But all this blunting blows and the like . . . out here we've tae leave the shroudreives something tae put back taegether. In there we shred carnage near and far, big as ye like, never mind losing an arm or three."

"Our restraint is an exercise in control," said Torbrenth. "It calls for greater care in the planning of attacks, more calculated strikes."

"No mournmeir for the ashes."

Looking out toward the field, Gignoth spotted the enormous Liftholch brawling with several reapers. "Some of us could do with an ashing," he said.

Sithik nodded, following his gaze. "You would have taken the day but for that one, to be sure," he said.

"A good blade that one, fair tae say," said Melthis. "A naefukkin useless dreg in Veth, but. Still, the brute wants at the blighties, eager as any ripper, like."

"It is his eagerness that worries me."

"Not to mention his rather alarming aptitude for dismemberment."

"It should be remarked," said Torbrenth, "that he has developed a tendency to hoard etherea, even while others thread it away. Not enough to raise alarm, exactly . . ."

"Aye, I've seen it," said Melthis. "More than once, like."

"Then everyone has," said Gignoth with a sigh. "I suppose the time has come to deal with that."

* * *

They found Thrael amidst a tangle of her sparring reapers, surrounded by at least half a dozen of the shroudreive ceaselessly dragging away dismembered and crushed bits as one by one the hulking cibori brought the urgency of her rebuke upon them, striking into their melee with whatever element of her glaive she saw fit. Those few who remained mostly intact upon the arrival of her counterparts released audible sighs of relief as with a final word of castigation she joined the party of cibori in their seeking of Liftholch.

They came upon him engaged with three other mortis within a grappling ring of placed stones, just as he had broken free of a hold. Hurling his now unbalanced opponent into another's advance he blasted all three away with a volley of raw etherea, laughing triumphantly as one found his legs crushed beneath the bulk of a statue torn from its niche in the wall clear across the grounds.

"Fault!" called the wounded reaper even as he was dragged away by the shroudreive.

"You cry too loud," Liftholch called back. "Come and find Liftholch again after pinchers stack you on a pair of new legs."

His other two opponents remained silent as they collected themselves, but Gignoth could read their irritation. He stepped forward as Melthis and the others fanned out behind him, and tracing a hand through the ambient etherea still wafting up from the sliverfall he gathered it up as he called out his errant mortis.

"Liftholch."

Liftholch turned and gave a nod, his tiny black eyes glancing past his cibori to mark the presence of the other cibori.

"A good fight, that," he said, cocking his head up at the heights of the columns. "We would have taken them together, you and I alone, had not that one there—"

Gignoth raised his hand and with outspread fingers four he conjured four discrete explosions at Liftholch's shoulders and pelvis, smacking down his heavy torso into the dust even before his thick limbs had left their orientation, so that what was left of him thudded away clear from the jumble of their fall. He flailed a moment with his remaining third arm, straining to position himself to look back up at his cibori, shock, pain, and anger painted over his deeply gashed face.

Gignoth gestured to the shroudreive, who scuttled over to collect the disabled reaper.

"Go now with dignity, brother mortis," said Gignoth. "But break ranks again and Ruse herself will not be able to reassemble you."

As the shroudreive dragged him away Gignoth forced himself to meet Liftholch's silent glare, even as he reached through wisp to address the reapers as a whole.

Deeply regrettable.
Yes.
To inflict upon a reaper so public a shaming. Our brother.
A constructive act?
Unknowable?
Unity must be preserved.
And so it has.
Honor the Vanguard.

* * *

A shockwave rattled through the Harrows grounds, kicking up a ghostly shroud of dust as from somewhere up on the outer ramparts there came a call:

"The three have engaged the blightwraiths!"

Gignoth cursed inwardly. A battle. And he had just made them one more warrior short.

He looked up at the roiling Celestial Cosmos.

Just where in the necromank hollowchasms of creation are you, Demithyle?

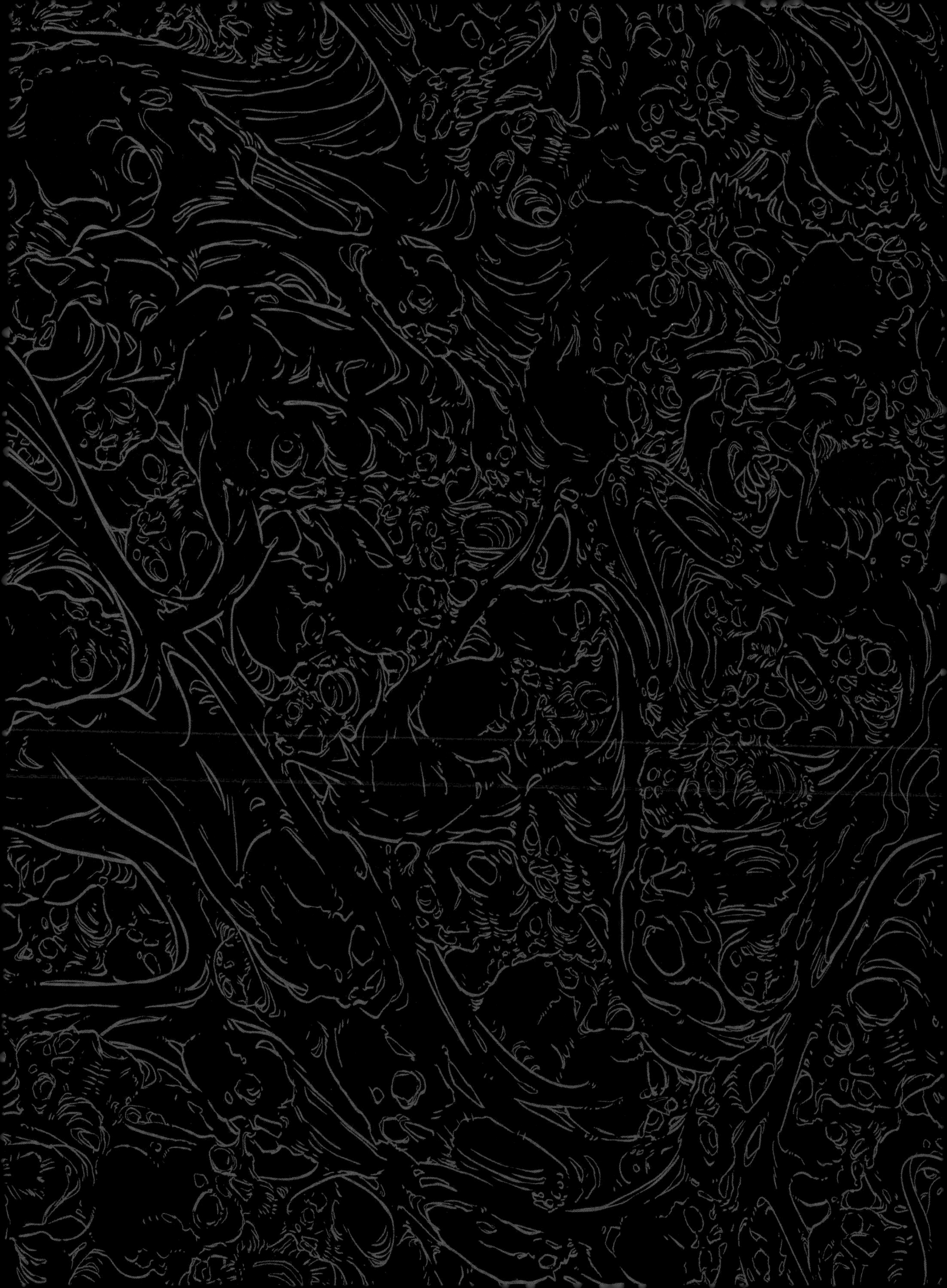

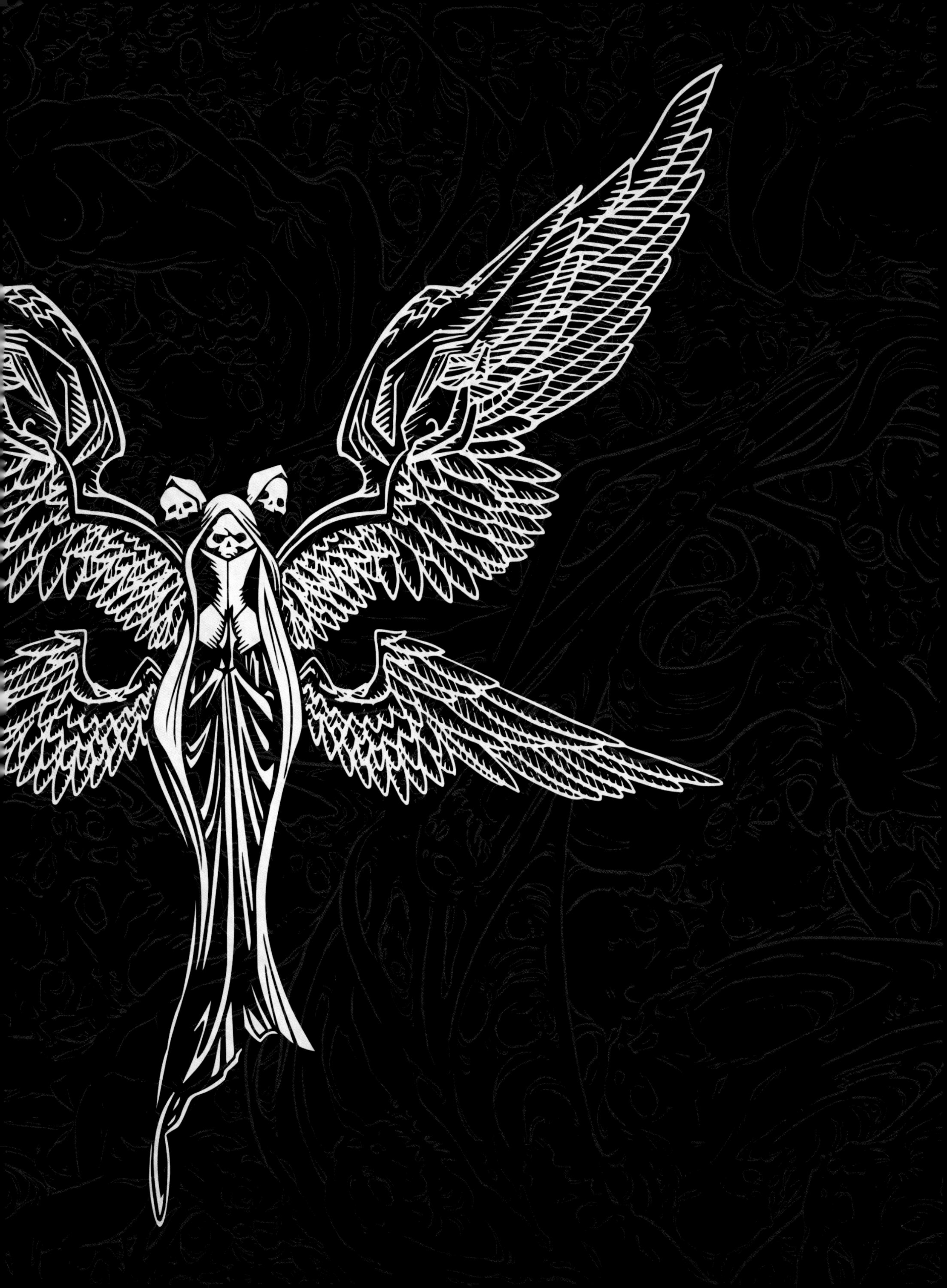

XXI.
SOJOURN

. . . and the hand it was cold, and the toe it was cold, and the foot it was not cold for the sock was worn, but the leg it was cold for the lambskin was torn, and the face it was cold, and the ears they were cold, and the nose it was cold, and the mouth it was not cold, and the ass . . .

. . . lo, verily did he place the cup upon the table and step through the door to make water, but only then did he come to remember his shoes. One did he find near the door but not the other, and for it he looked beneath the large table, but it was not there. Then for it he looked beneath the small table, but it was not there. Then for it he looked behind the pot and the tree, and in the pot itself, but it was found in neither place. And so did he begin his search in the adjacent room . . .

. . . Met brother and sister, had it been near a year?
His embrace was quite warm and was hearty with cheer.
She returned it in kind, and nearly as strong,
Though it did start to seem like it'd gone on quite long . . .

* * *

Many such passages do I encounter amid the stacks before I capitulate to their relentless inanity and return to the terrace in Ellianastis's study to look out upon the near-frozen landscape again. In this place it seems there is given unto the devoted an eternity to spend on nothing more or less than eternity itself. If there is wisdom to be gained from these passages I can not discern it. If tomes of greater import reside here it is not likely that I should encounter them. Whatever my fate, it will not be as an unblinking wraith shackled to the esoteric pages of infinity.

* * *

    From my vantage upon the terrace I can see neither the Dirth Forge nor the city itself. There is only the restive darkness of the shadowy desert landscape broken here and there by random elements of otherworldly flotsam, some of which hovers over the expanse frozen in space as if refused by the Underworld into which it has fallen. What flow of the blacksand dunes persists by this perspective of time is all but imperceptible save its clouds of dust where they spill into the darkness of the surrounding canyons below, appearing reshaped anew by each return here for respite from that which I have been given to discover within the endless rows of the library.

    Behind me the structure totters high into the shrouded sky like a tree plagued in its growth by a mercurial sun. From it Ellianastis's sanctuary floats freely by unseen means, adjacent to the main cluster of mismatched buildings that comprise the initial stories above the abbey rotunda. Its walls are rounded and set with half-moon windows gabled with the same simple thatch as its roof that hangs slightly out over the terrace.

    There is a slight movement and for the first time I see a warm light escaping through a small, thinly paned window in a low attic. A shadow passes within. I know that it can not be the wraiths, for they cast no shadows.

    I step back inside and indeed there is a quiet shifting from above, dismissed before as arising from the unknowable machinations of this place. In the ceiling at the far edge of the room I discover a wooden hatch with an iron ring set into it. When I pull the ring the hatch swings abruptly down and a spiral of floating gray flagstones uncoils to reach the floor at my feet, and when I ascend them I find my self surrounded by what seems at first an ethereal ball.

    Richly gowned faceless specters swish and sweep about the candlelit room, twirling and swaying to a melody it seems only they can hear. The brocade of their cloaks and dresses captures light and shadow in myriad ways as they dip and nod to one another, and as I move through them they part, halting each in turn to present to me their costumed arms, as if to be taken up, before falling once again into their pattern as I pass. I turn and face one of them and its depthless face clouds with a flush of color that quickly gains definition around details of my own brooding, skeletal visage, and the others broaden their course around us as the specter recedes a pace, opening its pose as if to allow me a complete view of itself. I stand and stare at it for want of any idea what next to do, and it twirls in place to stare back at me over its shoulder with my own eyes. Turning to face me again, it adopts my bewildered posture, mirroring my subtlest movement as the others continue their dance around us. I step away from it as quickly as I can manage and it floats away to swish once again in concert with the others, its borrowed face dissolving into its former spectral darkness.

* * *

Thus I discover what can only be the wardrobe of my hostess. In place of shelves filled with books the walls here are composed almost entirely of wooden drawers of various dimension. The low ceiling is draped with fabrics of every material, and beneath the deep window are many rows of shallow niches, each bearing a single shoe.

Upon the sill of the window is a single unused candle set into a brass walking holder. At my approach it comes to life, its tiny flicker momentarily reflected by the glass before that surface frosts against my presence, the encroach of feathery crystals parting round a hidden scrawl:

Blow me out.

I blow.

It is not breath but my self that passes between my teeth, untethering from my physicality to inhabit the flame. To become it. My awareness of the room arrives with a prismatic depth of all things present, and beneath the sashay of the wardrobe masquerade I hear for the first time a tinkling, whimsical melody, the palpitations of its wandering rhythm setting my candleflame to flicker.

So is brought forth a teardrop of wax. It falls from the wickpool agleam by my light to streak down the narrowness of the candle beneath me and root upon the brass catch of the holder, its patina dulling under a thinness of white film as it cools. I look through the window and the vastness of the Underworld lies before me with a clarity of dimension last known to me upon my first imbibement of etherea, and when a second drop falls I know it to be as clepsydra for the measure of my sojourn.

* * *

Curiosity impels me from my candlewick to look upon my physicality, collapsed in a linen-clad heap upon the floor below the window.

Until its manifestation upon the spectral dress form of my hostess I had given no thought to my likeness since my encounter with the doublewalker in the Calvum Harrows upon my soulbond to my sword. Now with my slight flame falling upon its thin frame and ascetic robes I find my self less the warrior protector than an effete acolyte to some burdensome and incorrect religion.

Splayed awkwardly from my turned hip is Cryptmourne. Though it is strangely incongruent with this place I would not part with it. Looking upon it now I see for the first time its depth of being embedded throughout its wavy blade, and I hear its thin metallic voice ringing lightly in the air as if by its confusion. But beyond my quiet emanation of assurance I can do nothing to allay this.

* * *

I drift to the window again, pondering how I might make my way from this place, and in so doing pass unhindered through it. I float out just beyond the edge of the terrace. All appears frozen as before. But by this newfound prismatic vision it is as if the movements of time and space have been transposed, for although each element I behold traverses no distance, they flow and shift within their forms as if viewed through wavy glass.

I compel my self outward beyond the surrounding courtyard to float above the cloisters at the edge of the canyons. There is movement separate from the omnipresent prismatic shifting, rippling over the pool from which Ycnaf and I emerged. By the thought of it I am hovering over its wall, the image of the Celestial Cosmos splayed out over its surface before me. A part of my self it would seem is yet rooted in the library's frame of reference, for the pool's warring undulations are greatly slowed and rifts of its various cataclysms open and close like mouths across the nebulae. But my own reflection at its edge is not that of a lone candleflame but the silhouette of my reaper self, the twin sparks of my eyes like vagrant stars adrift through a long dead sky.

* * *

I ascend along the library's haphazard profile, far into its heights until the grounds below vanish behind the thickness of the shroudcover. There within I pass among strange shadows and glinting buds of emerald-blue light. Some of these throw out thin tendrils that

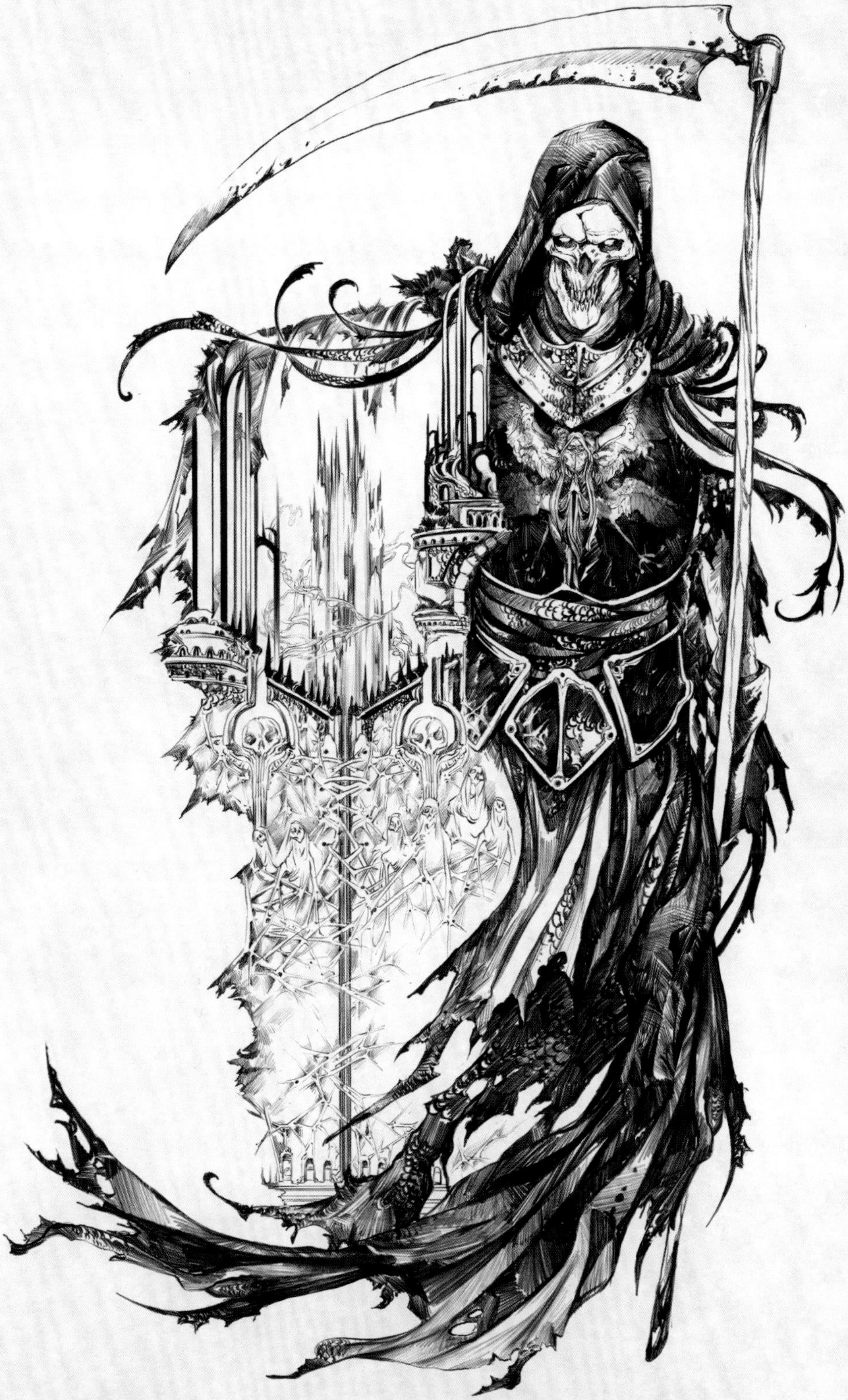

slowly whip and curl through the grayness of the shroud before diminishing to vapor, and I decide they must be sparks of ambient etherea condensing within the aurorae hidden by the shroud. I swim between them, chasing their trails as I ascend, until the breadth of the library mushrooms outward into a canopy of structures overhead.

It swells even as I course along it as if spread by the very skin of the realm, so that I am obliged to curl around the emergence of new encompassing walls as I seek its outer perimeter among the dark, vaporous entities that glide forth in fields of orderly lines like black cuts in the air, so that it seems at first that I have passed beyond the influence of the library.

But as I pass beyond the outward reach of its heights the shroud suddenly parts to reveal the pillar of soulfire at Daer Gholl all but static in the distance, its cold light freezing the ephemeral walled city around it like a sliver of a dream. So it must be that these shadow entities move with a haste to rival that of the library, and that though they are perhaps ever-present among us they are by nature imperceivable in the absolute to any bounded to the Underworld's relative temporal lethargy. And yet it seems a comfort to discover that we should cohabit with such beings whose trials are forever unknown to us, to whom even our own most fervent struggles are irrelevant.

*　*　*

I follow after their stream, toward the distant beacon of the soul Forge. But as I draw farther away from the library the upward flow of the Forge gradually becomes a torrent once again, and the entities gain speed and speed again until they are gone from my perception. Once again the air fills with the forlorn wails of the soulborn. Even at this distance I can see their writhing within the soulspire. I can sense their torment and despair and so it seems my duty to witness them.

Downward into their flow I impel my candleflame. The luminous torrent flattens within to a boundless twilit emptiness through which a crush of small structures float steadily upward, braids of wood, stone, and thatch alternately emblazoned and deepened into shadow by an endlessly oscillating mortal sun and moon. It extends far beyond sight above and below, such that at first I think that I have been returned to descend through the haphazard library tower. But passing down through their endless twist of conjoined rooms I find each simply furnished in the manner of a mortal domicile, and within each hovel the bent shades of the harvested—the fierce, the powerful, the pernicious, the pure, fathers, mothers, children—each huddled as woeful, incomplete marriages of person and shadow, as if in their terror and confusion the last remembrance of their being was given to the construction of whatever place they had once called their home.

  I traverse these spaces of comfort unwitnessed and unhindered, slipping between the illusory walls and thresholds exhorted by the last vestiges of these souls' agency amidst an unbroken stream of their lamentations. The gently illuminated, intricately rendered rooms are as much windows into their hearts as the objects they have placed within them, and bearing witness to them thus I can not but imagine the fates they had once imagined for themselves. The simple thoughts and wishes that had driven forth the compilation of their living moments. The unquantifiable completeness granted by nothing more than being home. The desperation and loss of learning that no such thing has ever existed. Such obviation of hope and dream would seem emblem to the great impropriety of the Cosmos of which the Alltaker spoke. To know something of its dismay is to harbor the imperative of its rectification, and so perhaps this was the intent of my hostess, and my father.

  More than this, I feel their anguish as my own. A cumbersome irony, perhaps, for one made in large measure to intrude into their realm, to take them to be sundered thus. But for those living moments of the mortals that I have reclaimed into my knowing I would perhaps be unmoved. Now, little else would seem worthy of our efforts.

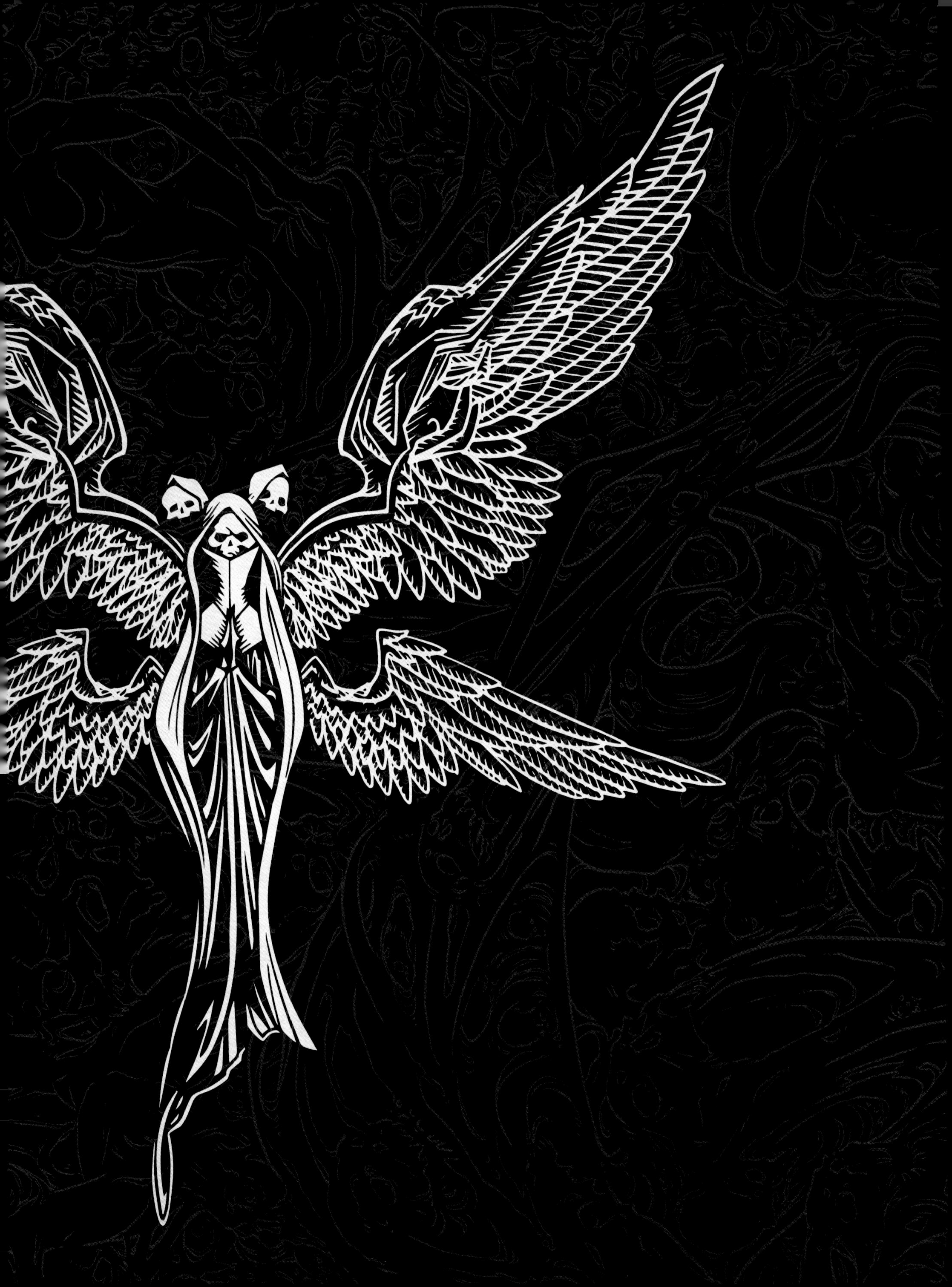

XXII.
CURIO CRYPTUS

I follow the Forge through the eddies of etherea that roll out from of the outer facades of Daer Gholl. The voices of tragedy quiet with distance from the soul well as I am taken into the currents of outflow that feed the city. There the spiritous milieu of Illverness arrives into my awareness as airy undertones to my own reflections, and thinking upon how little of my own home I have seen I allow my self to be swept through a panorama of boneyards, decrepit hovels, and dark avenues, structures crumbling with rot or wavering in and out of existence, colonnades of sinister effigies and clawing trees that seem alternately to grow and reduce by changing perspective, all wrapped in curling everpresent mists.

Those mourners I pass from within the stream appear in my sight as luminous bands of color within a relative vaguenesses of corpseform, and I am reminded of the removal of the pall in Mortis Veth. Some are entwined in such a way as to reveal them multiple spirits cohabiting a single physicality. Most wander listless through the wide and empty roads, alone or huddled in small groups. Yet others fly to the bank of the flow to scrutinize my aspect within or simply to watch as I pass. When one reaches in to touch me ripples of color spread throughout the flow and a casual greeting is delivered into my awareness. I am shocked by the aura of innocence and vulnerability that accompanies the gesture, so great a contrast to the vigilance and guardedness kept by the reapers and my self, and my father and the entities of my parentage whom I have met, and all of the other beings I have encountered. It is an openness of spirit that no plight of this realm or beyond might reach.

* * *

I come upon the courtyard of a crumbling abbey flooded with a congregation of many diminutive mourners. Their spirit aspects vibrate with a spectrum of youthful energy. At my approach, a bright cluster of them take notice and separate from the others and rush to meet me, then follow along with me for a time, hopping over one another as they crowd forth as if to gain better view of my candleflame. Some begin to leap into the flow to be carried along it with me for a time before spilling out again to tumble into the others.

We are taken beneath a darkened underpass of a stone bridge embellished with many ornate carvings of oceanic beasts. As one they break away to examine it, and without a thought I exit the etheraric river also. Removed from its influence upon my spiritsight I find the small mourners' agitated bands of color are quickly hidden by their myriad physicalities. Yet still each is set aglow from within by muted dazzles of color that suddenly shift to a rich red hue as they conjoin themselves to become a conglomerate, gaunt approximation of a long-dead sea serpent, now plunging again into the etheraric river to slither away, trailing a long, cadaverous tail behind its monstrous head in a diminishing series of bulging arcs out from the flow.

* * *

And then from somewhere near there arrives an ambient murmur as if from a crowd, and a sound of the plucking of minstrel music, portentous and resonant as if played in a great cathedral. Beneath it, a melancholy voice raised in the final verses of a sentimental ballad:

> *. . . she's a lady whose bones make such beautiful tones, how I pray she will play them for me . . .*

The song trails away, replaced by an underlying chorus of querying voices that I follow out from beneath the underpass and in the direction of a great, grim temple with thick columns carved to depict skeletal, robed figures that overlook the misty gloom of the surrounding borough with great cavernous eyes, bracing the flat stone roof as if as much in penance as eternal vigilance.

I soon find my self floating along a winding promenade in the midst of what would seem a kind of undead bazaar composed of vaporous hovels and oddly shaped buildings clearly constructed from mismatched ruins. Milling everywhere about are mourners of illimitable variation of the mortalkind physicality. Beings as they would wish to present themselves in their undercity: ghastly, outlandish, fearsome, absurd, beautiful, gaunt, and fleshy, of many appendages and none, each uniquely aglow by their spirit aspects within as had been my companions in the ethearic riverflow. They amble, shift, and float throughout the promenade, bartering with ghostly merchants for garments and strange diversions and small tokens from the mortal world aglimmer to my spiritous sight with encapsulated feathers of thought, dream, and memory.

They pay my candleflame little notice as I float by overhead in the company of other luminous spirits and airy elementals. I pass grotesque effigies and gleaming black monuments I can not identify. I pass a tiered mausoleum conjoined by a spectral stairway that a mourner struggles to ascend beneath a great burden of oddments and miscellany. A baroque iron pavilion within which a congregation of mourners circles around a shadowy altar. A small hut built entirely of mortal skeletal remains from which several mourners spill out holding upturned hollow skulls swirling with gaseous essence likely intended to resemble etherea. They pull exaggerated draughts as if to make a show of aping mortal imbibement in order to amuse themselves, before raising their papery throats to a croaking approximation of laughter.

* * *

The promenade opens to a broad, murky square. I hear the cloying notes of the minstrel's music rise over the din. The song crescendos and then falls away just as there against a great gray tree in its center I see a colorfully garbed spiritborn mourner, the cone of his wide-brimmed hat drooping low over his face as lazily he plucks random notes from a warped and hollow barbiton.

I wait for a time but he does not begin his song anew. I begin to float past him, intent on making my way into a branching avenue beyond the tree. But when my candlelight falls upon him he stirs, and the cone of his hat suddenly stands on end.

"Aye, you there!"

The minstrel beckons with a wide, spidery hand that plays host to at least a dozen long fingers.

"Aye, ye have it," says he, sitting up and nodding my way. Of his face only an amiable smile is visible beneath his hat, though curtained behind a black aura mist that spills continuously from under the brim. "Ye, th'spritey fella floatin' about like he's lookin' fer a lamp t'get in. Fancy a weepy tune, do ye? Yer Mard'll make ye yearn fer yer sweety if ye got one, er mourn fer the one ye don't."

I hover a moment as my candleflame flickers, uncertain how best to respond to this energetic engagement. Even now I can feel the steady dwindling of my wax. There is much I would wish to witness before I am recalled to my nature. Yet the intent of my hostess for this strange spirit sojourn remains unclear. I look at the great grim temple looming overhead. The eyes of its deathly colossi stare down at me, watching. Perhaps it is just this.

"Hang on!" says he, and setting his barbiton aside he rises on a pair of lengthy, many-jointed legs to peer into my flame. "Reaper, eh? Aye, ye are, plain as Gethsemoni's fair lavender slope! Fresh-made only just this foremeir, so goes th'rumor. Aye, and nothin' goes faster!"

He leans in yet closer, though his face remains mostly obscured by his hat, and that I see now is covered with innumerable tiny facets, in each an iridescent reflection of my candleflame.

I drift slightly away, eyeing the avenue. I had not considered that my nature might be recognized by any of the mourners of Illverness while in this form.

"Stole away from th'pack fer a spiritous amblin', did we?" says he, his hatcone tracking my movement. "Aye, ye did! Another wayward kit in the ol' Curio Cryptus, he is!" He laughs, then steps back to allow himself full view of the vicinity of my glow. "Now," says he, scratching at his darkened face beneath the hat, "how's a grim commandant like yerself end up in a state like that, I wonder?"

"I would not know how to begin to explain that to you," I say.

"Aye," says he, "ye lot're th'type we storyweavers'll be explainin' far 'n' wide, aren't ye? In point o'fact . . ." He reaches a very long arm to retrieve his barbiton from where he left it leaning against the tree. "Only just now was yer Mard watchin' ye flick about in all yer wonderment, 'n' what gets into him but hints o'th'grandest notes ye ever heard, 'n' a treacle of a song inspired by th'comin' age of all ye reaper saviors. Swears it on me own hat, he does!"

He poses with his barbiton, many fingers at the ready. "Aye, 'n' he'll let ye have it fer not more than a stray meirdrem o'yer reminiscence," says he. "Add yer own throat in fer barely twice that, if ye'd like a lass t'look upon come the mourn. What've ye been given, then, far as yer sweetpipes go, that's t'say?"

"I am merely a soldier," I say. "A visitor here, on an errand in service to our defense of the city. I have no voice for song."

"Visitor!" he scoffs, spits. "Says he of hisself, newly made right here in th'city itself. Sure ye've a voice, fighty fella as ye are, can see it spillin' right off ye, plain as the flicker o'yer flame! Can't we, fingers?" He gives a rapid drum over the shell of his barbiton. "Treat yerself to a song, then, eh? Ye'll be moved t'join us, aye ye will, or mine's no mind fer weavin' a verse. 'N' it's because yer such a stalwart sort that all I'd ask is what it cost yer Mard in time 'n' talent t'compose."

"What would that be?"

"A darble slaivey'd do it, aye."

"How much is that?"

"Might depend," says he, tilting his hatcone as if to scrutinize my flame from a fresh angle. "What've ye got with ye in that wee twinkle o'yourn? Sure'n we can find th'right exchange, yea to eye."

"I carry no coin," I say, "or means to deliver it while in this . . ."

All of Mard's fingers suddenly spring free from his hand before I can complete my reply, then inch their way along his patchwork tunic to wriggle into a cloth pouch hanging from his belt.

Mard's hatcone drops over his face as he plunges the broad paddle of his hand into the pouch after them.

"Get ye back where ye've got a use, ye wormy freespearin' leeches! Or ye'll be pluggin' holes in th'nearest rot-skint by th'darkme'r!"

He cups the bottom of the sack with his other hand and works it about, then pulls free a fully fingered hand, though the digits wriggle and jerk in every direction in apparent residual discord.

"Damned daftly spiritlickin' finglethins!" says he, whipping the hand about vigorously. "I've a mind t'bite ye down t'nubs, aye I do . . ."

He holds the hand up to his hat, working the fingers until he has them rippling in uniform waves in concert with his other hand. Satisfied that they are tamed, he returns his attention to my flame.

"Now then, aheh," says he, renewing his wide smile beneath his hat. "Oh, aye. Coin? Pish. Always somethin' can be put fer trade here. Ye've dreams, haven't ye? Drives? Wits for which ye've no further use? Aye, ye have, or no candleflame'd carry ye even far-ish, leastwise not half intact mind-wise. Why not let's begin, then, eh?" says he, making ready his barbiton. "Should song 'n' fancy meet, sure'n we can find a fair figure for ye t'part with. Shall we?"

He tilts back his head, parts his lips behind the dark mist as if to begin his song, watching me for anything that could be taken for acquiescence. His instrument's strings whimper in anticipation as he crunches them against its thick neck, yet I feel a sense of warning that by the rules of this Curio Cryptus I would owe him restitution of his choosing should I allow him to proceed thus. Enough perhaps that he could lay claim to thievery should I attempt to leave without satisfying it. Indeed, now seeming to read the apprehension behind my silence, he unpoises himself to interject before his prospect can flee or report him to the magistrate of the bazaar for poor practices.

"Tell ye what," he says quickly, "bein' that yer near close t'the chumliest o'reapers ol' Mard's ever yet met, 'n' not mentionin' yer here t'save us from a certain encroachin' doom . . . what says ye to a mere sliver o'yer prudence as fair price. Less than a pittance to ask fer ballad enough t'call down the host!"

"You want a bit of my prudence."

"Not all, t'be sure!" says he. "Feelin' that squarish sort o'music fallin' off o'ye—meanin' no offense—yer th'type t'look thrice 'fore he leaps, then twice again, nay? Sure'n ye can spare th'wee-est of an iota of a speck o'yer cautious nature in exchange for such a lofty work. Could even do ye good, stiff fella like ye—once again, meanin' no offense."

"What would you do with such a thing?"

"Oh, aye, lots," says he. "What with all the recklessness around, like. Maybe give it over t'these here bloaty fingers, even," he adds, hatcone nosing pointedly. "Give 'em somethin' t'give 'em pause b'fore runnin' off just t'find'emselves stuck at some less charitable spirit than old Mard ever were, why shan't I?"

A facet of my self which it would seem I keep in abundance, though I have taken no specific measure of it. Still, I can not imagine parting with such a thing lightly.

"A parcel of a reaper's prudence for a treatise on the oneness of his kind," I say.

"Sorry?"

"Your trade is rumor and grand tales, storyweaver," I say. "Mine is to preserve the unity of reaperkind, our primary strength in the battle ahead. Bind your spirit to the promise that no part of our unity shall be sullied by this or any of your future utterances, and we shall have an understanding."

"Ye see now, that's just th'sort o'thinkin' ye could do with less of," says Mard. His enthusiastic demeanor suddenly falters then, as a tidy and dour entity passes near, clearly interested in our exchange and Mard in particular. In all likelihood the magistrate, gauging by the authority and severity emitted by her aura. I would not doubt the two have met in the past.

"A parcel, ye say?" he says quickly and rather loudly. "Why, we'll proceed in earnest fer barely half that, yer bein' kinner'n' kith t'yer cousin Mard, aye!"

He gives a few hearty but nervous laughs, keeping his hat tilted slightly toward the magistrate until she has turned her attention to another market interaction. "Ah, less than two thirds, that is," he adds in a quieter voice, "considerin' yer fair addendum. Aye, 'n' let's us be through with all th'provincial barterin'."

"Kin?"

"This yer city, innit? Yer home, cousin kit! Fair Illverness, th'gracious mum. Revel in bein' at her bosom, for when ye leave ye never know when next her faer lash'll fall upon yer cheek. Now then," he says, spitting into his hand to the apparent dismay of his fingers, "have we got our selfs an accordance?"

"Yes," I say.

* * *

Mard closes his many-fingered and bespittled fist with a gesture of finality, and there is a faint shift and the color of my flame takes on a slight alteration in the warmth of its hue. I search within my self but I am otherwise unaware of a tangible change.

"Fairly bought, my fairbairn reaper friend!" says he, with a ceremonious bow. "Now, if ye'll please follow me . . ."

He extends his legs and moves into the center of the square, and following a gestured invitation from him I move to hover to a place at his audience.

"Ahoy!" says he to those present as he steps up onto the rim of the fountain. None pay him notice of any kind. "Here speaks the voice o'th'storyweaver Mard! The followin' shall be th'truly factual account of th'great trueness of our reaper kin, which I have composed for my dear cousin, a reaper if ever there was one, whose name I have invented and therefore need not learn."

He pauses as if to wait for an audience to gather but none does so. Muttering to himself, he holds up his barbiton.

"So floweth *The Conflagration of Feortan Littleflame*," says he.

> *Oh Feortan the Baker*
> *Made the Under Taker*
> *Fine loafs fer his barders t'chew.*

As Mard strikes his first chord I find my self suddenly standing as an ethearic apparition of my full physical being, Cryptmourne in hand.

> *But alas, from'is breeches*
> *A whimper beseeches*
> *With draughts o'flame orange 'n' blue.*

Even as the end of the verse escapes his grinning mouth I am pressed back by an assault from a screeching, demonic phantom with a crooked frame and eyes of simmering purple hollows.
A baelreiver—or Mard's impression of one.

> *For fear it'd be spoilin'*
> *The fruits of 'is toilin'*
> *Swiftly he poked in a finger.*

It assails me with a flurry of thorned appendages I am only barely able to parry in a concise retreat of defensive stances, toppling carts and scattering merchants and mourners as I am forced several more paces back. It is only when it wavers in its momentum that I realize I have cleaved it free of most of its extremities, and before it can regroup I impale it through its howling maw, Cryptmourne's wavy blade protruding behind its illusory skull.
Whatever vital essence it possessed travels down the sword's length as would its etherea, and passing over my swordarm it imbues my spectral being with a brilliant bluegreen glow. Taking hold of this I cast much of it forth again to burn the thing. Its purple shade ash hovers solidly in the still air before pouring down to collect against its severed remnants.
The bard continues:

> *Aye, but no sooner sealed*
> *Then twin voices appealed*
> *Their whispers o'brimstone alinger.*

Two more phantom baelreivers drive at me then from above, apparently conjured by the bard's verse. I separate them with a blast from the remaining essence of their predecessor, and grappling one with the outer two of my right arms I behead the second with my left as it turns to charge again even as I punch through my captive's eye socket with my innermost hand and draw out its living force.

> *Now one more than he'd branches*
> *Fer pluggins 'n' stanches*
> *Poor Feortan then grew'im another.*
> *Aye but there lay the trouble*
> *Fer the pleas again doubled*
> *Four whistles more than he could smother.*

Four more emerge from the ground near a group of spiritkinder who had rushed into the square to witness the fray. As if reacting to their fright I am suddenly standing between them and what is likely a toothless illusion.

But even as I blast the phantoms back I see my spectral self yet engaged with my previous assailant on the other side of the square, the attacker's ghostly outline growing more luminous by my draining of its essence with my diminutive innermost arm.

> *Fer no matter arms sprouted*
> *Nor orifice routed*
> *Another'd then plaintively weep.*
> *'N' it weren't very long*
> *Afore Feortan's pyre song*
> *Sang out like a choir o'sheep.*

The phantom baelreivers' numbers multiply, and multiply again, each time arriving to menace a newly congregated crop of ogling mourners. At each point of threat I interpose newly replicated, leaving my former aspect to fight my previous skirmish until we are an army of spectral reapers battling a phantom horde. We act in concert just as I had done with the reapers in Mortis Veth, leaping between engagements and flying on conjured wings even as we cycle between us the ethearic power drawn from those wraiths we have destroyed.

All the while the mourners follow the tide, patron and merchant alike, amidst a rain of shadowy bits of our foes and the richness of Mard the Storyweaver's melodies.

> *Till at last he came to it*
> *Only one way t'do it*
> *By-'n-by he uncorked'em entire.*
> *Then at once had'em reach*
> *Deep into each breach*
> *Like the Seraphim to the Hellfire.*

Though outnumbered greatly, gradually we begin to corral the shrieking phantoms into the environs above the gray tree in the center of the market square, and together we weave an enfolding torrent that crushes them ever closer as it narrows, until the last of them has been destroyed and their remains are a trickle of ruin left by our violence to vanish on the wind.

> *Now not quite as porous*
> *But where for the chorus?*
> *Why, sung from the throat like a dragon.*
> *But lo 'n' be ghosted,*
> *His loaf'd got toasted!*
> *'N' now Feortan is swingin' 'n' swaggin'.*

Mard finishes his song to an audience rapt by the spectacle, his illusion dispelling in a cloud of sparkling light, and I am again a mere candleflame afloat upon the lingering echoes of its melody.

He drops from the rim of the fountain and bows, though most have already returned their attentions to their own business, and he laughs, and then laughs more, and I think perhaps that this is the first time I have heard a being do so in true merriment.

"There now, if that weren't palatable to the senses, aye?" says he.

"'Feortan'?"

"Oh aye, heh," says he, "nuances o'meanin' lost in translation 'n' what've ye . . . Anyways, ye never gave us yer name, did ye? Not too late, is it?"

I say nothing. If my purpose is to convey a unity of resolve and action among the reapers, better that a taleweaver should not weave tales around the name Demithyle.

"Anyways like," says he, "ye seen th'big round eyes of 'em, didn't ye? Mard said he'd have ye fellas up with th'holly-pollolly, didn't he? Handsome is as handsome does, as is said, 'n' who's t'say the same can't be said fer a warlike confederation?"

"Who indeed," I say. "But for the fact they were all me."

He chuckles, waving a dismissing hand over the span of the market. "Ye've a rude awakenin' ahead o'ye if ye think most o'this lot're adequately witted t'pick one o'you motley sort out from the next, even forgettin' the willy-nilly spectacle ye just put on. Aye," he says, shaking his head, "I'll says it, ye fellas do not fail to impress."

Mard makes his way back to his tree to lounge against it as before.

"Anyways," he says, casually tapping out some notes on his barbiton, "song's yers to use 'n' abuse, as yer needs must. Stitch it up against whatever sort o'heart ye keep in that weavercrafted trunk o'yers. Set it on a breeze while crackin' some real abomination heads, why don't ye? Maybe cast a thought or two ol' Mard's way while yer at it. Now off ye go, 'n' remember where ye got it!"

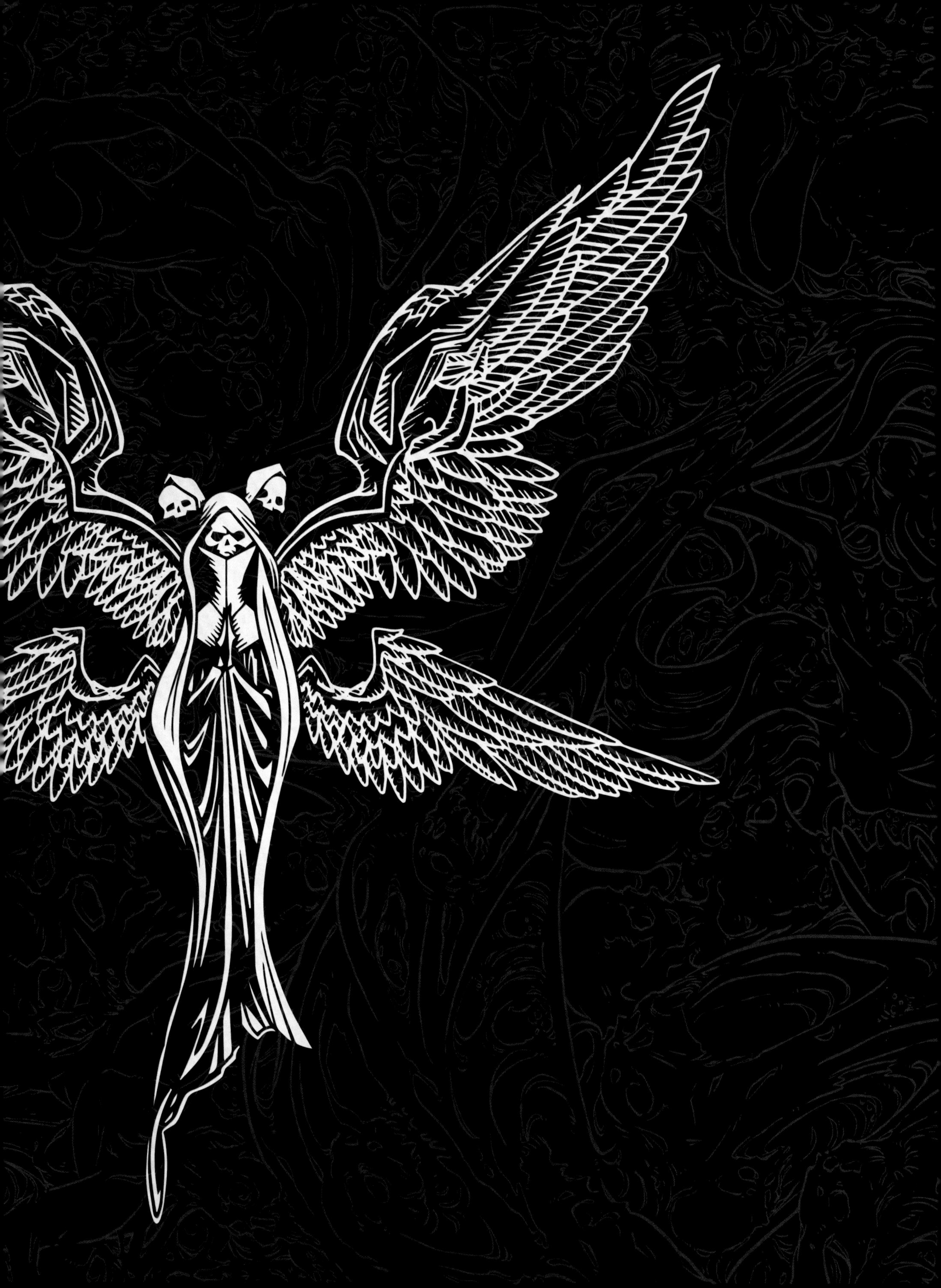

XXIII.
ILLVERNESS

There is a strangely melodic peal of thunder, followed soon after by a muffled pinging from above that heralds a trickle of ethearic hailstones, each spawning tendrils of aquamarine mist to rise where they crack upon the square. The trickle grows to a steady shower and the child spirits cry out in delight and leap to the canopies and lanterned cupolas of the surrounding structures to swat at the crystal shards and rush away in a musical clamor through the downpour.

  My flame flickers intermittently to the storm, though I feel nothing from the shards. I think perhaps to say farewell to the musician but he is already asleep. And if even should I wish to wake him he would not hear me for his snores are deep and loud enough to rattle the strings on his barbiton.

* * *

A procession of severed mortalkind heads approaches through the sliverfall's fume of ethearic vapor. Their jaws wag open as they bob forth on nothing, their eyes lolling as if having only just seen the ax. They float directly toward my flame as if to challenge it, but pass through unhindered.

  I follow them as they weave in a line through the square and down one of the busy promenades. We pass ever-lonelier merchants as we recede from the main bustle of the forum and I follow the grisly heads through a narrow alcove and into a dark culvert beyond the ambient glow of the stormfall. My own warming flicker casts our advance in a pocket of illumination, the warped and swollen shadows of the disembodied heads bouncing and curling over the arched crown of the tunnel.

A graygreen light appears ahead and soon our procession enters a hilly tangle of dry reed and briar below the clear celestial sky. Of the storm there remains only the sporadic breaking of crystals into vapor upon the weathered boulders huddled throughout the clearing, which prove broken elements of stone effigies half buried and worn featureless with age, as if the land were slowly reclaiming a garden of gargoyles long ago ejected from their cathedral posts high above.

* * *

The severed heads lead the way through the weeds and boulders and toward a narrow, darkened causeway between two monolithic blocks of stone, one leaning against the other, having apparently been uprooted by the emergence beneath it of a mineral flow of blackglass. As we approach I note its faint ethearic sparkle and I am reminded of the ethearic obsidian found in the structures and platforms throughout Mortis Veth. And indeed, as we draw closer I see that much of the glass has been cracked and scored as if by fine tools to extract its mineralized etherea.

Into the narrow way we go amidst a low, oscillating roar from deep within. My candlelight pools over vague reliefs of armored mortal-born engaged in the worship of some illusory deity upon the surface of the stone. Beyond this the depths are black but for what seems a current of ethearic flecks quavering steadily left to right, like cinders caught in a tempest or a grandiose stellar migration between voids.

The roar grows steadily louder as we advance toward it until my light reveals it a swarm of tiny creatures. They boil out from wide cracks in the toppled monolith with glittering kernels of the blackglass in tiny spiritfilament sacks stitched to their gleaming abdomina, then flutter into the sparkling current before disappearing into thousands of tiny holes bored into the other. We press straight through them, and though they find no resistance from my flame they smack into the oblivious rotting heads, needle-legged necrophages with black eyes and mandibles as sharp-edged as the obsidian glass they carry. Their precious ore spills from their sacks to rain down upon the scattered mounds of bluestone sand below as they struggle to unhook their barbed toes from gray fleshy cheeks and grime-clotted mats of hair.

* * *

The last of these tears itself free as we pass through the far edge of the flow and we emerge from the causeway into a gloomy avenue paved with skullforms worn flat and gritty in the packed dirt. One by one the lolling heads vanish into the cracks and crevices of the precarious arrangement of fragmented hovels and other structures of mystifying origin and purpose that stand along the avenue. Like the market, all of these seem randomly collected from realms far and near, some built of wood and iron, others flesh and bone, some mundane and vaguely familiar, others of clear mystical significance framed by crackling latticeworks of dreams and arcane magic.

* * *

I can feel that my candle burns low. I continue down the avenue alone, content for now simply to see where it will lead me in what remaining time I have.

I move through pools of every kind of light beneath bent and twisted lampposts placed along the way. Certain of these reveal otherwise unseen shades as they pass by in their silent errands, so that their traversing of the road toward me is a slow sequence of discrete pictures.

Passing beneath these same lamps myself I find the image my true physicality is brought into definition also, though to obey no impulse or command given for movement. It only slowly rotates in a directionless, weightless hover centered on my flame. But I see that it is a spirit composed of many spirits. Innumerable souls conforming to a single entity that is my self.

This pleases me somehow, though I can not say for certain why.

* * *

I move forth along the center of the avenue until the lamps have ceased to cast down light or are missing entirely. There is little definition but for the uppermost jagged silhouettes of buildings against the celestial sky and those irregular surfaces upon which my own light falls, at times momentarily reflected by the flash of curious hidden eyes.

As I begin to wonder at the occupants of this derelict place an aura of brilliant cerulean suddenly ignites from a creature so immense I take it first for the sudden combustion of a building, and it stands on twiggy legs to rise half again this height to amble down the road away from me.

I follow after it around a bend in the road to find it clawing it up with wedgelike hands, casting out a shower of dirt and bone fragments behind him. It digs until it has created a wide hole in the road to its wrists,

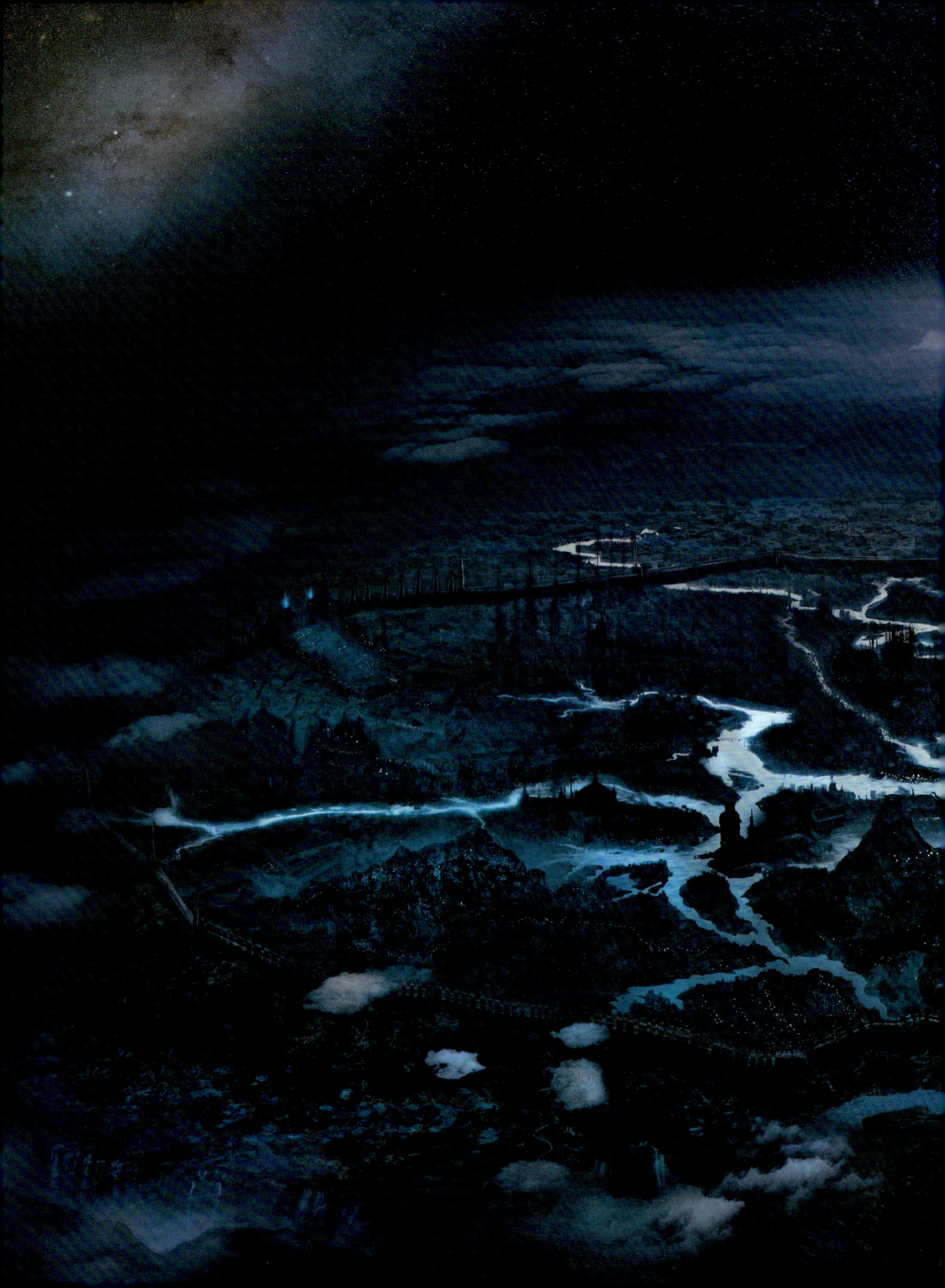

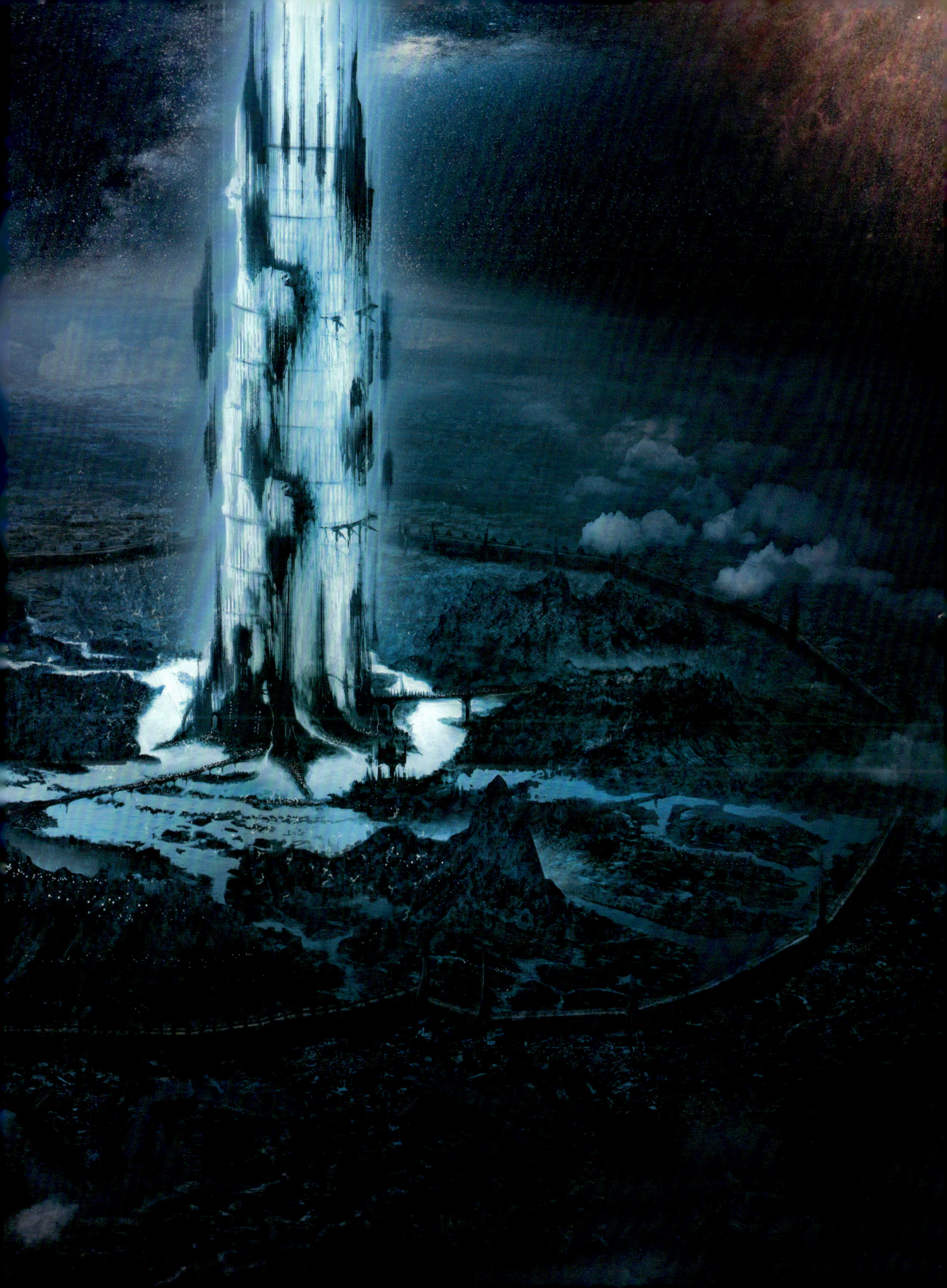

then leaning on one edge it reaches with its other hand to probe deeper inside with the tips of its fingers. It works the loose dirt against the sides with both hands until satisfied that they have been packed sufficiently then stands again and crawls over the adjacent buildings without another look.

I move closer and look over the edge of the hole and find it unremarkable, only a glistening blackness of damp soil and exposed skeletal remains. But then pinpricks of red light appear through the dirt and bone at the bottom, and as they widen and intensify I move away to watch a progression of listless spirits methodically climb out from the hole and collect nearby before they are followed by a being with the pale white aura of lilies and bleached bone.

The aura rolls outward from her core in caressing waves, soothing her feeble charges, encouraging them to amble forth with a bearing of concern and gentleness, and I know this can only be one of the foster-murden who caretake those many damaged souls broken from the well. She looks toward my candleflame and gives me a fleeting but genuine smile before returning her attention to her flock, and I watch the eerie procession recede down the road.

Moments after they have gone my thoughts linger on a strangeness in some among them who bear peculiar absences in their auras, weak as they are, as if they carried with them elements of spaces that nothing can occupy. Though I can not guess at its significance it is a thing that conjures within me a strong malaise.

* * *

I peer again over the edge of the hole. There is a pink fog in place of its bottom. I sink down into it and pass through the fog to find my self in the center of an unpaved road in the midst of a more spacious city borough, noticeably farther away from the light of Daer Gholl. From many directions comes subtle music rich with poignance and earnestness and oddity.

I float down the road. Here the buildings are smaller and more sparsely dispersed amid a landscape of blackbriar brambles and copses of treelike growths of gray and weathered wood with sharp protruding veins of rusted iron. Some of the structures are dilapidated shells within which I spy pockets of mourners engaged in curious vignettes of activity.

One of these sparks a certain recognition, a two-story stone hut set at the edge of a hazy boneyard. Sounds of levity and lightness spill from crumbling walls, and a warm flickering of light reminiscent of my own. Inside I find a small tavern playing host to a modest gathering of raucous mourners as varied in form as at the market, imbibing drink and sharing songs I do not recognize. They move in seeming patterns in rhythm with the music, a repeating sequence of evocative interactions between individuals.

    I watch them for a time, wondering at the strange choreography of it, until I realize that it is a story under way, a parable that I recognize as sharing common thread among many disparate cultures of mortalkind.

* * *

One name of this story is *The Woman and Her Dragon.* In it a woman travels many days and nights to retrieve water from the last well in her homeland. Once there she hears a voice rise from the dark depth: Give me water, it says. Why, that is what I have come to find, she replies. I have no water to give. That is a shame, the voice says. If only there were someone near with water to quench my thirst. The woman can hear that there is water down in the well, but she does not try to retrieve it. A man arrives and hears the water also, but the woman tells him that there must not be water, else why should the voice lament such thirst? Another arrives to learn the same from this man, and so does the story continue until the land is drained of its people, all having perished of thirst around the well. Finally a dragon arrives from beyond the sky to vomit black ink into the well, it then to overflow and erase the land.

* * *

The elements of this story are here, though they wear a different skin. The well and the voice have become a shade behind the bar of a tavern, which is beset by desperate inebriates who can not help but to ferociously imbibe as they chase their merriment. And it seems I am to play the part of the dragon. For when the last inebriate is lying dead of drink and the room has gone silent, the humble fire of my candle catches some errant mote of dust to set the tavern alight, then to burn and fall in ashes around me. Yet even as I leave its smoldering ruin the sounds and warmth return and I look again to find all of it remade.

* * *

My flame sputters, and for a moment I am given a vision of my place at the window in the room where I see my candle is now little more than a charred stub of wick in a pool of waxmelt. Then as if in reaction to the thought of remaining time I am brought to the courtyard of a large clock tower of many faces that do not agree. I can hear their mechanisms quarreling with one another to demarcate the passing moments. A strange contemplation of time in this place of many times, of lightmeirs marked by the cold celestial flares of warring, mirrored by nights brewed of the shadows drawn from us all.

* * *

I float upward along the clocktower until my light falls upon the largest of its faces. Its great iron hands seem as mighty temporal glaives set once to the clockwork of creation, thereafter to cut their relentless swaths through time, wielded by no one. I look out upon the city, cast afire in sapphire blue by the fount at Daer Gholl, and I think that even were it to prove no more eminent than the inexhaustible wellspring of dark curiosity and wonder that has been presented me in my spirit form this meir, it would be worth great sacrifice to preserve thus for an eternity to come.

I look down upon the borough of activity below. Even from this height the music of its strange theaters seeks to mingle with my own. I am struck by their emblematic relationship to the Underworld. In the pureness of their serenity these beings have chosen to exist as reflections of their shared significance to the Cosmos as they understand it.

Thus it seems also in many of the other far-flung pockets of being across Illverness. Like the merchants and hagglers of the eclectic bazaar, like the languid spirits who drift as a candleflame through its streets, all endure in fullness of being unknowing of the woes that bear down on the high walls of their illimitable necropolis.

I knew at the meir of my creation that this was a place I would give the entirety of my self to protect. That I would master all that I could to fight to the end of possibility and beyond to see it unmarred by the baelreivers or any others, however ominous their threat. When we were lifted into the sky to first gain sight of the astonishing breadth of our city I understood the scale of tragedy should we fail to preserve its magnificence. And from my audience with the Alltaker my father I felt the weight of this foremost task, for in its design was his first tentative movement toward correcting the corruption of creation as he saw it. All of the strange and varied moments that unfolded for me in the meirs that followed have driven me to greater surety of our purpose and its final success. But this spirit sojourn among the mourners on these weird and timeless streets has gifted to me the surety of my own connection to Illverness and to the Underworld. Perhaps if not for the affecting voice of the storyweaver I should not have come to see it as so. But this place of deep and dark beauty and of art and artifice and unique contradiction speaks to me now in a manner I could not have foreseen. It is a part of me and I it and one will never after be whole in the absence of the other. It is my home.

THE SPIRE WE SEE THE SPIRE
CUT BEYOND THE BROKEN WALLOWS
OURS ALONE WE SEE ITS POWER
ONCE BEGAT BY US OUR HERITANCE

OUR SPIRE TAKEN OURS ALONE
ALONE ALONE ALONE ALOOONE . . .
WE TASTE THE COLOR OF ITS SOULS
THE BLOOD OF US THE BLOOD OF US

WE SMELL THE CLOYING VAPOR OF THE FORGE THE SCENT OF DEATH
THE SCENT OF DEATH OF DEAAATH
WE HEAR THE MUSIC OF ITS SOULSSS

WE FEEL THEIR HOLLOW TERROR
AND THEIR EMPTINESSS OF HEART
THE FINAL KNOWING THERE IS NO LIFE THERE IS NO DEATH
THERE ARE NO GODS OR JUSTICE ONLY COLD OBLIVION . . .

SOON THE FIRST OUR MALIGNED KITH SHALL COME
SHALL FIND SHALL SEE SHALL
TASTE THE SPIRE

AND SMELL AND FEEL ITS VAPOR OURS ALONE ALONE
ALONE ALONE ALOOONE
ALONE ALONE ALOOONE . . .

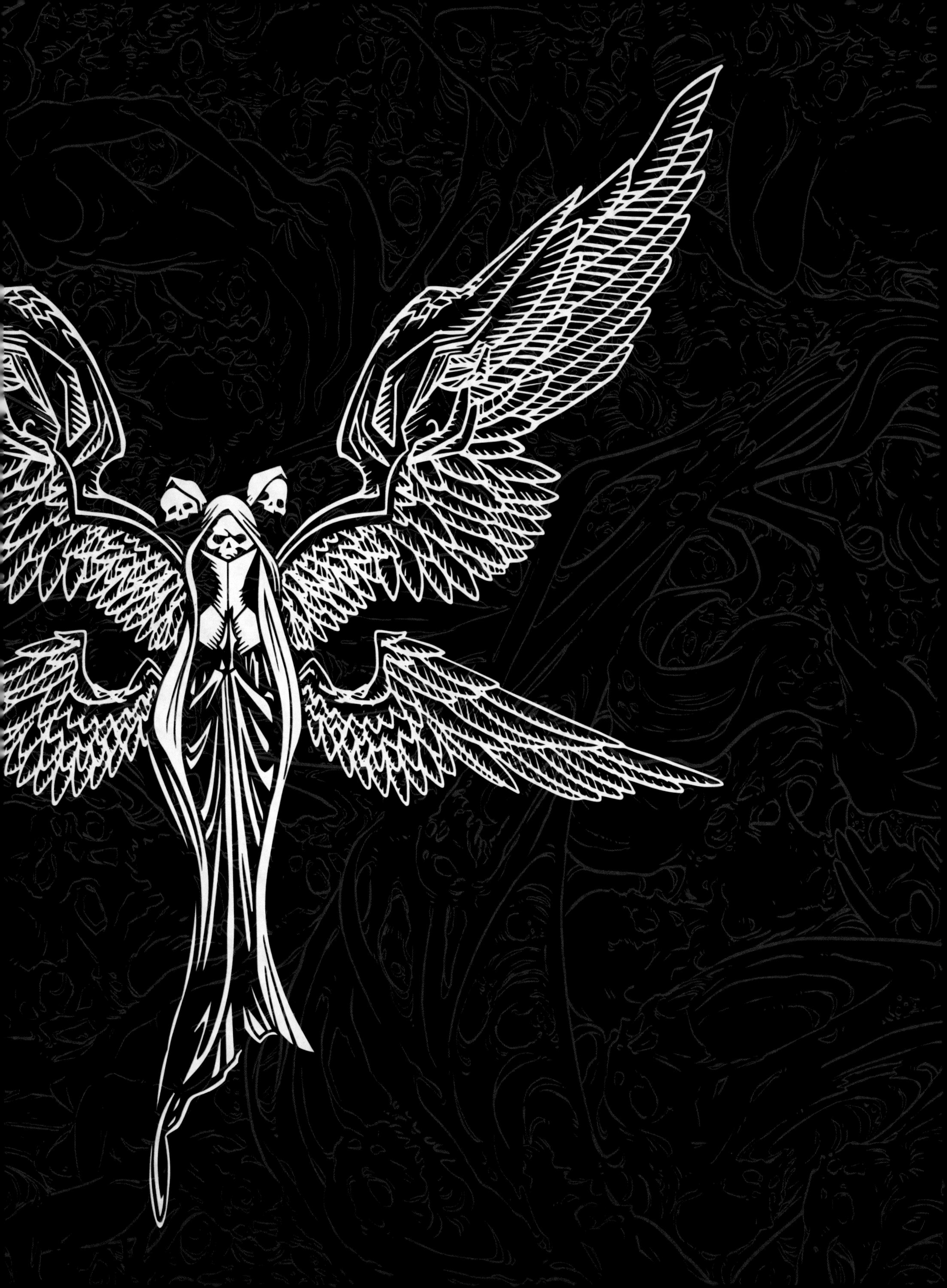

XXIV.
A CALL

The reapers leapt, climbed, and flew out from all over the Harrows and up the rocky mountainside that served as its rearward bulwark, racing for its highest vantages even as it echoed with the muted thooms of the distant battle. They spread themselves over its peaks to watch in awe the display of intermittent flashes punching through the haze far out beyond the Vadlum Gates, and there on the thin and frigid air was brought to them the faint sound of furious screeching.

"Hollowfather."

"Prisstampt fuck, that's a hideous sound!"

"Can it be the horde? So soon?"

Gignoth joined Melthis on an icy outcrop where she had already found a roost, and he looked out with her over the broad expanse of the city.

"The three would not have engaged the entire horde alone," said Gignoth. "It must be an advance of scouts."

"They give a gloomfuk of a fight for scouts, like," said Melthis.

A murmur of agreement arose among the nearby knights. The battle had already gone long for a confrontation with a mere scouting party. For the three foremost scions of the Underworld to be so challenged beyond even its outset . . .

The growing battlecloud drew sharply inward before being pressed out by concussive bursts of color, followed by hushed crackle and renewed screeching. Even at this distance they could feel the vibrations through the mountain roots, and though there was no indication of who was taking hits a smattering of hails rang out.

"For the shattermeir!"

"Dooooom sik!"

"Grind the diregoat skattiks to sliverbones!"

"Kerissst!"

Thrael clambered her great girth up the surrounding crags to join them, followed soon after by Sithik and Torbrenth. The five cibori marked the harrowing display as best they could, listening for clues as to its progression one way or the other through the chatter and jeering of their knights.

"Strange that they should not have called for us," said Torbrenth.

"A few meirs' ride out, that," said Melthis. "And except for Sithik and his like, we'd be riding our own mungrotty boots."

Sithik turned his back to the scene, a distant phosphorescent flash sending pinpricks of light through the thin membranes at his neck.

"Perhaps we should muster, just the same," he said. "Really, anything could be happening out there . . ."

Melthis shrugged. "What's to muster?" she said. "They show their beaks, we crack them off."

"Maybe a featherpet," grunted Thrael, sweeping her glaive in a vague outline around the city.

They all looked at Sithik.

"She means to convey that this fascinating display could be but a feint," he said. "To draw out the Three, or whomever. That the blightwraiths could be moving in elsewhere to attack the city. Perhaps we should therefore consider occupying the battlements?"

"The Three've got eyes all over the wallows," said Melthis. "How the cakkshite do ye think the blighties got themselves caught so far out?"

"We do not have the numbers to take up a defense around the wall," said Gignoth. "We would be stretched far too thin."

"Gignoth is correct," said Torbrenth. "Our strength lies in the singularity of our conglomerate body. Our war is yet to arrive."

The cibori fell into silence as they listened to the distant battle amid the billows of enthusiasm from their reapers.

Gignoth looked beyond the gate, over the near expanse of the wallows. Sporadic dots of light flickered over the city's inroads.

"Refugees," said Sithik, following his gaze.

"They have been passing through the Gate for at least the last fortmeir," said Gignoth. "The call went out even before our eyes were lit. It may be these are the last."

"Many never received it," said Torbrenth, as yet another titanic thoom washed over the city.

The other four looked at him. He stared out from the shadows of his hood at none of them in particular, as if his attention were split elsewhere.

"Mostly mortalborn," he said. "Those wishing to live in isolation at the frontiers. The Alltaker instigated the baelreivers to attack before the emissaries could reach them."

"Poor agits."

"Honorable doomed," said Thrael.

"Forgive me for conjuring the obvious," said Sithik, "but would not the extrication of poor agits from honorable doom be a more productive use of the singularity of our conglomerate body than, say, endlessly cracking one another's skulls? That isn't to say that I do not take pleasure in cracking your skulls, mind. A worthy diversion in itself, particularly if the skulls in question belong to one or two certain deserving individuals among us."

A loud explosion rang out from the battle. Together with the burly reapers of her stanchion Thrael belted out a warcry as she punched the tailspike of her glaive into a thick bulb of ice at her feet, cracking it to slide and tumble down the mountainside.

"Reaper blade for reaping," she said.

"Aye," said Melthis, "some other pitshin's job, that, come what'll be."

Torbrenth looked in the direction of the Forge. "Some few have survived," he said after a moment. "The fostermurden tend to them even now."

Survivors of an encounter with the blightwraiths. Melthis and Gignoth exchanged a look.

"Ellianastis tell ye that, did she?" asked Melthis, looking back to Torbrenth, who remained silent, his face hidden within the darkness of his hood. "Aye, how ye've managed tae get in with her after the chapefuk ye gave tae Xiall in the Veth . . ." Melthis shook her head. "If ye ever figure tae open up yer mind tae give us a peek at that bit, Tor—swear it on my ax, ye'll earn yerself a sluvvi kiss on the beak, aye ye will."

"How were the mortalborn able to escape the horde?" asked Gignoth.

"I know not," said Torbrenth. "Only that the baels have left their mark: all are stricken by a wasting affliction. For fear of its virulence the fostermurden keep them in isolation in the courtyards of HushHyde."

Gignoth looked at Melthis again. "We will go to them," he said. "Get the mortis back to the Harrows. Make them remember the stakes, cibori. Make them ready. There is no more time for games."

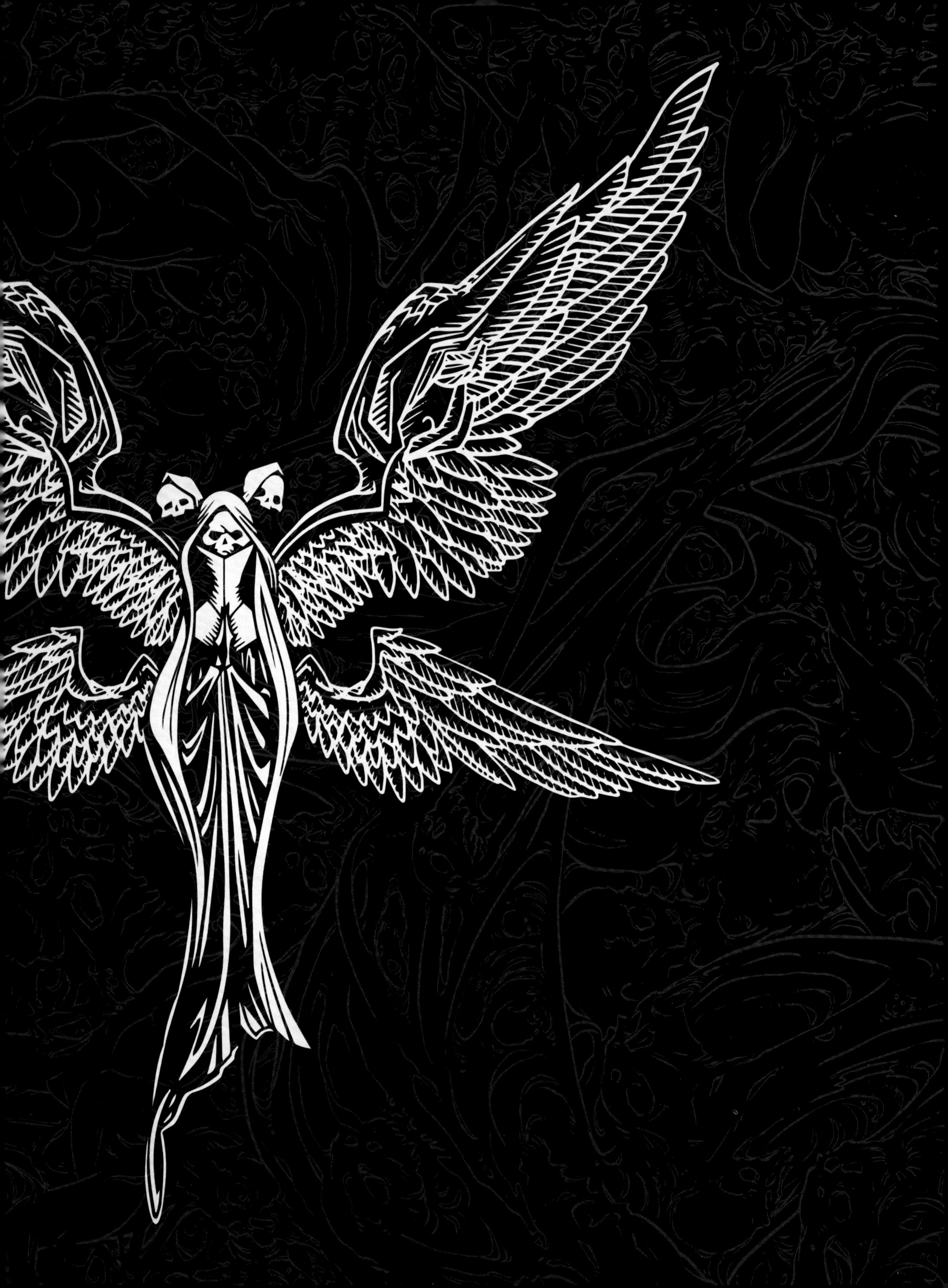

XXV.
AN AEGIS

Gethsemoni dropped from the wall and her sisters followed after. They touched ground amongst the heedless spirit traffic just inside the gate fifteen stories below, and quickly she led them into the inner portcullis and down through a torchlit catacomb beneath one of the adjacent gatehavens.

"The outer wallows so soon!" exclaimed Ellianastis. "They can not be as near as that . . ."

"It was not the horde," said Gethsemoni.

"Outriders," said Xiall. "Created for just such swiftness, no doubt. Priax knows what malformations of our denizens they have spawned."

Gethsemoni winced inwardly as Ellianastis conveyed her question: *How many have they already consumed?*

Far too many.

They made their way to the recesses of the catacomb to the circular antechamber that contained the veildoor, a black void egg held in the palm of a faceless simulacrum of Charon, the long-missing oarsman. Without breaking stride, Gethsemoni spoke a word of alteration and stepped through the arcane barrier inscribed over the floor.

"If they are spies they will flee as soon as they see us," said Xiall, ignoring the agitated hiss of the guardian shades. "We should be intercepting them separately."

"There is not time," said Gethsemoni. "We can not allow them to gain sight of the city. Nor can they be allowed to return to the horde."

She drew a slender finger over the surface of the egg. A faint slit of gray light appeared to the crackle and whisper of the Lethe estuaries restrained within. Ellianastis dissipated, and behind her Xiall's shell collapsed, her form withering to ash and bonedust. Then Gethsemoni pressed her hand to the narrow opening and allowed it to pull her in, her discarded husk slapping against the ground even as she willed her aspect to pass between the folds in the Underrealm.

* * *

Through the rush of intradimensional scoria their essences soared, their spirits caught by the Lethe's current as they sought the inlet beacon nearest where the bael outriders had been seen, among the very remotest set in Illverness's underroute to the outlands. Finding its vibration within the churn they attuned their aspects to the idiosyncrasy of it and allowed themselves to be exuded from the flow.

Light returned for Gethesemoni with the regrowth of her eyes, pink through the membranous sheathing of her terminus cell. With partially reformed hands she tore through it and clawed it away, revealing before her a tangled moor of broadstalk flora thrashing wildly amongst the crumbled expanse of architectural detritus that marked the outerrealms. Here the strange winds were far more powerful, such that scraps of her cell sheathing tore loose and whipped away as she kicked free of it, and as she did so a choir of shrieks rang out over the gale.

The baelreivers.

Their number was indiscernible amidst their purple fume of fang and claw. Having witnessed her emergence, already they had altered their course to lope away over the craggy marshland on grotesquely elongated aggregate limbs, their wraiths flying low over them on mottled, mismatched wings, a soiled gray fount of spectral miasma lingering in their wake in defiance of the gales.

Armoring her flesh with layer upon layer of stonehard callus plates Gethsemoni pushed through the windstorm in immediate pursuit, her stature growing even as she ran, so that her original form was quickly swallowed by her swelling mass and she soon towered over the field. She crashed through the ruins on massive, scabrous hooves, tearing out great swaths of the agitated flora with each lengthening stride as she closed the distance to the retreating blightwraiths until bearing down on them she reared back a now massively augmented arm and heaved a great blow into their midst.

The shrieking baels were sent wild from the impact, one torn free of its crushed lower half to splash against her hulking torso, another sent careening over the boggy ruins, breaking up to pieces as it rolled. Turning to step after it Gethsemoni destroyed it with a mighty kick that sent huge stone blocks hurtling into the distance, leaving streaks of putrid etherea in the air from its dismembered remains.

There was a sudden chorus of shrieks, and around the broad dome of her husk Gethsemoni grew a coronet of globular, veiny eyes to scan the whipping terrain. The landbound abominates had already recovered from the blow and were racing from three separate directions toward the half-crushed baelreiver, now all but obscured by the violet outpour of its etherea. Even before she could turn to advance toward it they descended upon its thrashing form, tearing it to pieces as they sucked its vaporous essence dry.

With a collective screech they whirled to stare down her incoming rush with eyes that seared with the purple intensity of their engorgement as from their open maws a blistering fume poured over the corpse, collapsing it into bubbling viscera just before thick ropes of caustic worms exploded from its remains to shoot out toward her head.

Raising up her immense forearms she crossed them to brace against the attack, bringing her bulk to a skidding halt in the stone and muck. But a thick curtain of masonry fragments swept across her view, exploding the wormropes away just before they reached her, leaving only a filmy resin to splash against her arms as the black wriggling mass spilt over the ground beneath the sweeping stones with a great corrosive hiss. And then the sky was lit by a brilliant, stuttering flash, and from the distance there came a quick succession of cracks as three wraiths smashed down against the fleeing abominates in a trail of glowing cinders.

Shucking away the sizzling outer dermis from her arms, Gethsemoni looked skyward to find her spiritous sister Ellianastis floating high above the battlefield, her silver hair and misty black gowns whipping wildly in the wind as she worked her four arms in delicate concert to direct a cadre of her smoky apparitions to hurl still more muck-laden stone fragments around the baels. The three smoldering wraiths leapt into the air and flew straight for her, skitting sidelong to evade Gethsemoni's cutting lunge as they shrieked their threats skyward.

Cover your ears, Sister Colossus.

Gethsemoni was knocked back by a deafening blast of sonic force as soaring into view upon a fractured cornice Xiall screamed into the cluster of abominates below through the scepter of her staff, destroying one utterly and sending the others tumbling away. Then she dropped from her perch to run up the shifting wall of debris after the ascending wraiths, and catching one with a hooking strike from her staff to the base of its neck she flung it down onto a piercing bonespire that suddenly shot up from the ground, impaling it, even as in the same motion she swiped a swath of bony shards backward toward the tangle of abominates, one of her serrated marrowdolls bursting up to fall upon them with its raking limbs where each of these spiked into the ground.

Staff raised to dispatch the impaled wraith Xiall dropped down upon it. But it cracked itself free and kicked her away with its scabrous legs, and catching itself with wings outspread it tore the bonespire fragment from its twisted core and hurled it after her with a hideous scream. She parried it away, catching herself with formations of bone that spit up from the ground to meet her feet as with its many clawing arms it drove her back in a slashing melee over the battlefield.

With another massive swing Gethsemoni connected with one of the ascending wraiths, hitting it so hard its disfigured shell simply exploded in mid-air. Turning her attention toward the bombarded abominates, Gethsemoni drew up an entanglement of fleshy fibers to grasp at them. But frenzied in their lust for the ethearic sludge now coagulating over the battlefield by the remains of their fallen they wrenched themselves free, leaving several limbs behind as they scrabbled their way toward it, the stabbing marrowdolls clinging stubbornly to their disfigured physicalities. With a titanic thoom Gethsemoni brought her fists down against their advance, smashing through Xiall's trail of bone shafts and throwing out a spray of rubble and torn weeds, and then taking one up before it could right itself she vomited a gush of yellow acid into its snarling maw, and then releasing her fist from the colossal husk's appendage she dropped the dissolving abominate still encased in it to crash against the terrain.

There was a steady clapping of stone and Gethsemoni saw that all around the soaring debris had begun to drop from the air as the apparitions that carried them were apparently wisped away by the gale.

Gethsemoni . . .

She looked up toward Ellianastis. There in her place in the sky she bore her arms outstretched against the advance of one of the wraiths. It snarled its fury as it pressed against the spirit force of her defenses. A silver band of light pulsing around her incorporeal form.

Rooted in the spirit realm as she had made herself, Ellianastis's gowns should have been at rest. Yet they were being driven as if she stood physically against the tempest. Indeed, she seemed to struggle even to keep her stance, and even at a distance Gethsemoni could see the threads of her aspect being steadily shredded away. It was as if the gales themselves were bled into this realm from beyond the veil . . .

A cold throb of horror arrived with the realization. No known being save Ellianastis herself could so exert influence into the True Spirit Realm. And even she struggled to retain her anchor between. That they should wield this much power . . .

It . . . it is destroying me . . .

The essence of her sister's words arrived strangely interlaced with faint susurruses, rising and falling in her ears like malevolent whispers caught between parting gusts of wind. And with them, images of memory seemed to emerge unbidden, drafted from a moment not long past . . . when the last of her mortalborn emissaries stood in audience before her at the gate to receive her final grace. . .

Inwardly had she recoiled at their eagerness, and then their cumbersome exchange of salutes as at last they had departed to ride separately outward from the city, each more foolishly resolute than the last in their wish to please their Queen in pursuit of this frivolous quest upon which she had set them. Their demise was of course assured—no force that could so decay the fringes of the realm would suffer such interlopers to return undevoured. Her only twinge of regret had arrived as she watched their gangly steeds clambering out over the wallows as they left behind the tangle cluttered inroads. A shame to lose such interesting beasts, crafted anew by her shroudreive that very mournmeir. As for the soulborn they carried . . . their names she had forgotten even before they had embarked. Perhaps seeing the limits of their utility, the Alltaker might turn from his exasperating obsession with them, and better attend to matters of his realm. Perhaps his ministrations might be diverted once again toward the embrace of his long-suffering consort . . .

A flash of deep violet, and with it, searing, spirit-rending pain. Gethsemoni screamed, staggering back as thin filaments of purple etherea sliced upward through the midsection of her colossal husk, tearing through the web of nerves outgrown from her form within its core, severing her arm at the shoulder. The entire right side of the husk dropped away from its greater bulk to smash to the ground, where amid the windblown reeds the violet eyes of a baelreiver stared, seething with cold hatred as once more it threw out its crackling filaments, and she screamed again as this time they bored deep into the hard callus encasement of her leg, worming up through her expanded nervous system in the bael's seeking of her core aspect.

It felt as though she were being liquefied from within. Blinded by the pain, she stumbled back, and her great bulk toppled to slam down to the rubble and reeds. Still the filaments burned into her, and it was all she could do to recede herself within the now rigid husk as wildly she called out for her sisters through the aether. But no sense was there of Xiall, and searching the sky she found Ellianastis yet besieged, her spiritous form heavily perforated and boiling within an oily foulness heaved continously over her by the wraith, its own flesh shredding away from its blackened bones as it held itself forth against her waves of force. And then as if succumbing to the onslaught, the perforations swelled suddenly to encompass Ellianastis's full presence, and she vanished in a blue-white vapor, leaving the wraith's oily shroud to collapse into the now vacant space even as it skirted through it, drawing a trail of its own putrescence to arc immediately downward as it drove itself shrieking toward Gethesemoni's husk.

So am I to be undone.
And my sisters and my city.
And all that I love.
The Alltaker's great error after all irremediable.
Our final doom a plague of his making.
And our own.

The Queen of the Underworld looked down over the scabrous bulk to meet the hateful gaze of her destroyer, smoldering within a distorted mimicry of a soulborn skull. Its mandible wagged loosely, grotesquely elongated, as if broken in a throatless, exaggerated howl. And then into her ears the needling susurrus of its voice seeped, at once furious and plaintive, and with its woeful sound lingering shreds of that vision of memory returned, that structure of moments brought to her mind's eye immediately preceding the baelreiver's ambush. A memory not her own, that could never be her own, so drenched with derision for the soulborn as it had been, contrary in the absolute to all she had borne as her self. An insinuation, then. Foisted upon her by this wretched remnant of an entity, an insidious outflow of its own corrupted consciousness. Yes. The pain had brought her this clarity at least. Alas that such thwarting of her cherished self should be among the final flavors of her awareness.

* * *

The pain abruptly ceased, and the familiar pulse of the Underworld returned to her ears, carried on a wave of debilitating nausea that drove Gethsemoni to clutch within herself as if to prevent her utter unraveling. But the sickness quickly ebbed and light returned to present before her the face of Ellianastis, fully intact and smiling.

"You should probably peel yourself out of that thing," she said.

The baelreiver was gone. In its place, an encirclement of Ellianastis's phantoms. The winds had died completely away, and all around the stones were rising up from the ground again to float into a lazy circle above.

Ellianastis held out her hand, and Gethsemoni let her thick husk of hardened flesh flake away as she accepted it, and with a heave her sister hauled her out into what was now a clearing among the weeds, blanched and dead by the settling poison of the baelreivers' detritus.

"What happened?"

"We crushed them," said Xiall.

The bonemaiden stood beside her, her ossein form covered with thousands of cracks and wounds. "All save that nasty little mungfuck of yours Ellianastis just chased off. Let it bring to them fear of us, I say."

Gethsemoni followed her gaze into the distance, to a soiled purple swath that led far out toward the eerie horizon, away from the city. She looked back to the place it had emerged from the ground.

"It was one of them," she said, shaken now more by the cold, furious hatred in its eyes than any recollection of pain.

"Yes," said Ellianastis. "The others would be its thralls, I suppose, though assembled from what I'd rather not guess. Its spirit was rather shockingly reduced, but that was definitely one of the Alltaker's original soul-gatherers." She looked up into the sky. "Somehow its wraith was bleeding its influence through the veil. They should not be able to do that."

"So you thought you would have a jaunt to your library?" said Xiall.

"You were fighting somewhere down in the substrata. I was only even able to break the wraith's grasp because that thing had gotten a taste of Gethsemoni's eidolon. My, if that didn't get it excited . . . In any event, I was back just as soon as I left."

"Almost as soon."

"Yes, well. I had to gather the Minder's Bind, learn how to shut them out. Even if just to be rid of that awful ranting—*we will burn and kill and crush and devour* and all that. Boring, really. Or did you enjoy being dragged through some heinous memory you knew very well was utter nonsense?"

Xiall said nothing. Gethsemoni shook her head.

"We should not have engaged them," she said.

She stepped through the wall of phantoms and scanned the area, wincing as the festering wound at her shoulder gave way to emergent flesh as the rudiment of a new limb began to form. In the absence of the tempest the thick stalks had repossessed their stature. From here at least the quiet moor seemed sheltering now, as if the confrontation had never taken place.

"It was a good battle," said Xiall, laying a hand on her reformed shoulder. "It has been too long since we have fought together, sister."

"We were nearly destroyed."

"But we were not," said Xiall. "We were victorious. As well, we have learned a great deal about our enemy. That is to say, those of us who did not disappear in the middle of things," she added, looking at Ellianastis, who only smiled and nodded, even as her spirit overlay stared out toward the fleeing baelreiver, seemingly deep in thought.

Gethsemoni looked out, peering between the stalks. Something had caught her eye. A movement. A glimmer . . .

"*No!*"

She blasted out a ripple of flame. It rolled over the moor, incinerating the weeds in every direction, laying bare the brittle shades of mourners, scores of them, even now diminishing amidst a now smoldering expanse of cracked rock and masonry debris.

"What is this . . ."

"So many. How are there so many . . ."

Gethsemoni sank to the ground. She passed her hands through a fading spectral form at her knees as if to gather its liquid presence, flesh blistering by the well of fury that boiled within her. And then, with eyes burned hollow and features scalded half away by acid tears, she looked once more toward the trail of fume that led out to the baelreiver horde and stood, readied in that moment to call upon all legions of the Underworld who would answer their Queen Mother's wrathful call.

Wait, came Xiall's voice through the aether.

Gethsemoni had felt it too. She looked toward a crop of boulders in the near distance. There glinted a soul. A single being, somehow intact.

They moved quickly. A mortalborn. Flayed from existence, eyes whitened by the burning of his soul. Even now he appeared terrified by his fate. Gethsemoni could see his spark embroiled throughout his shattered physicality. She reached tentatively, touching his frailness of form, taking care not to give him pain as she felt for his aspect.

"The baels must keep their ravin extant somehow," said Ellianastis. "Leeching their souls. The pain he must have suffered . . . I can not imagine."

"A laudable valiance of will, then," said Xiall, "to have sustained himself thus. Small wonder the Alltaker would wish to reclaim this one from the soul well."

"I know him," said Gethsemoni.

They looked at her.

"One of your emissaries," said Xiall.

Gethsemoni laid her hand on the soulborn's brow. She leaned over him, seemed to speak something only she could hear. She sat up again. "I will not allow this horror to persist," she said, softly. She raised her excoriated visage to face her sisters. "We must destroy them all."

Ellianastis knelt beside her, her gossamer skirts billowing between them. She touched her hand as her voice reached her on a breath of calm.

Let me take him to the fostermurden, sister. They will care for him. When perhaps his strength returns . . .

Gethsemoni shook her head. *His pain is mine to bear,* she said. "I will take him."

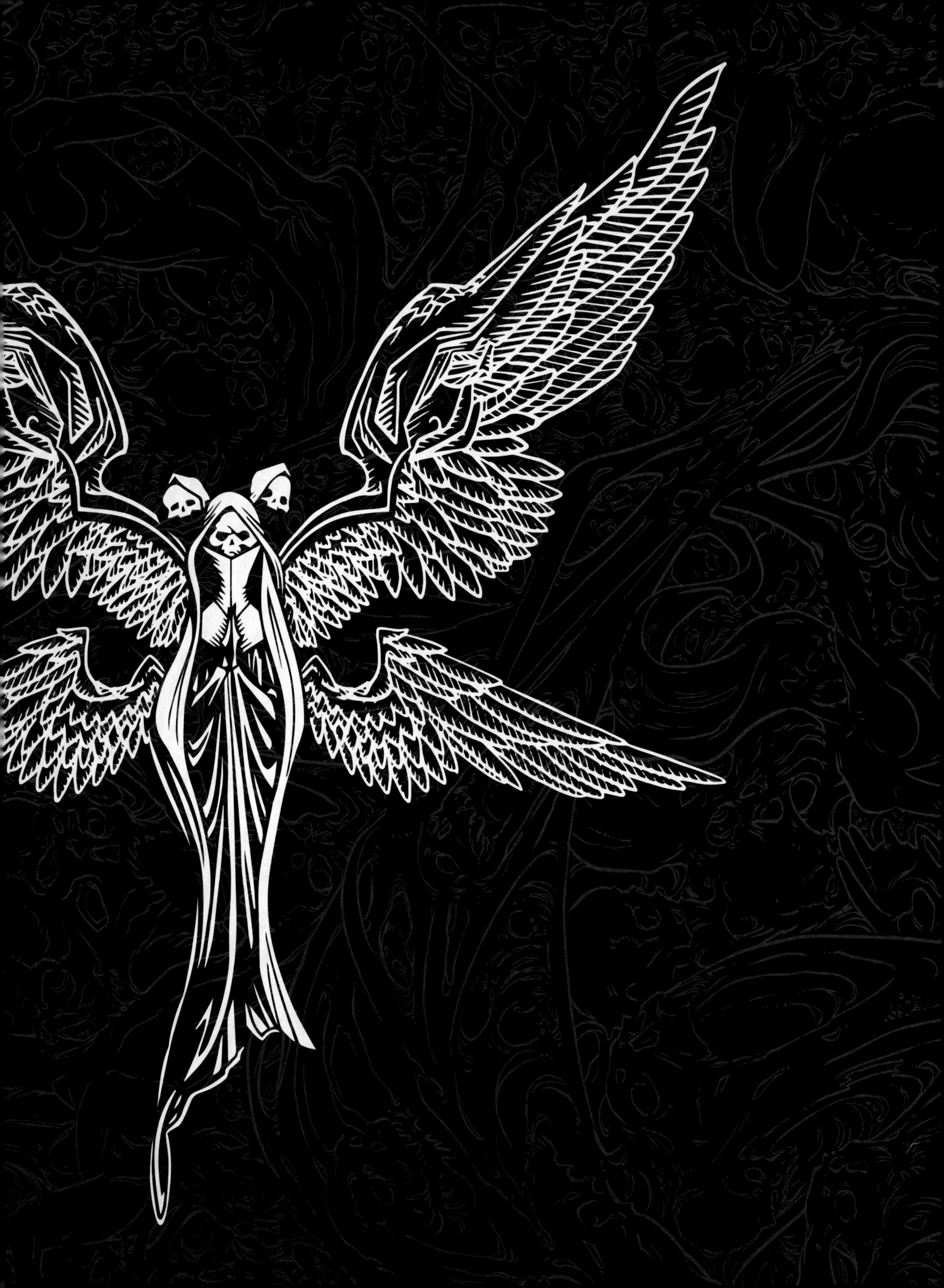

XXVI.
A GIFT

My candle flickers wildly, ceaselessly. In a moment it will be extinguished. I can already feel my self being pulled back to the library.

There is a sudden smatter of violent thooms from somewhere out beyond the city walls. When I look I see flashes just over the horizon outward from the Vadlum Gates, far beyond the mirror tower, which glitters against the concussive force even at such a distance, as the sound of still more hollow detonations rolls over the city. I feel a powerful need to be among the mortis, to meet whatever danger has arrived.

And then I am with them.

They are spread out over the peaks of the mountain at Calvum Harrows, enraptured by what seems the outset of a terrible battle far away. Their awe at the display is evident in their hushed tones of voice.

"Hollowfather."

"Prisstampt fuck, that's a hideous sound!"

"Can it be the horde? So soon?"

To my spiritous eyes, my comrades are aglow with power that beams through their flesh and armor, a testament to the potency being granted us by the thousands of souls that each of us keep. I can not but feel a swell of pride at the force they present. I wish to call out to them, more than anything to be among them. But the candle is spent and their voices draw down in my hearing as I waver from their space.

. . . outriders . . . three would not . . . alone . . .

And then there is only the tiny glowing ember of the wick, and then it is ash.

***

I am. Hardform. Same self else where. Limb nor limb nor limb nor limb . . . room.

Dead waxfall candle. Windowsill. Black line of smoke . . . Voices?

". . . I don't know. Advance scouts, probably. They were seen from one of the far outposts. One of Gethsemoni's spies alerted us."

"How many?"

"A handful at most. Six, maybe seven. They are powerful, Alltaker. They have found a way to exert their influence even into the True Spirit Realm. We've destroyed a few, but . . . we are about to be routed, I think."

"You should not have engaged them."

"Perhaps. The damage is done. I had to leave the others in order to convene with the Minders' Bind here. I must find a way to shut them out."

"How much time?"

"A breath. Maybe two."

"The library will grant you that, at the least."

"Yes."

"They hurt you."

"It's fine. The hate of them, Alltaker . . ."

"I know."

"Well. There is nothing quite like impending destruction to importune focus. I gather your own spirit sojourn bore us fruit? Your aura is quite changed."

"Indeed. Taken with certain other happenings of late, I begin to suspect a conjunction of events, perhaps set in motion in ages past, whenever this secretive missive was sent."

"Well then. We must be doing something right."

"To wit: I received a visitation from our wyspstride friend."

"And?"

"It found me in my sanctuary, Ellianastis."

"Well, we knew they were powerful beings. And 'it' is a 'she.'"

"Your appeal must have been quite passionate. It would seem they have heard it. They will help us, conditionally."

"Conditionally?"

"They were very impressed with what they have come to know of Demithyle through Ycnaf. They are not so confident with regard to myself."

"Well, you are Death."

"Indeed. For the moment, they wish only to join the reaper cadre. It would seem they are little interested in our greater affairs."

"They will stand with us against the horde?"

"They will stand with the reapers, horde or otherwise."

"My! Credit to Demithyle, I should not hesitate to say. And the timing could not be better. With all of our power, even these few have nearly destroyed us. I can not imagine . . ."

"Your power is an impediment here. As I have told you often."

"Yes, yes. You do not trust us to resist the dreadsgrip."

"It is more than that, daughter. You are the first scions of this realm. The power that courses through you is drawn from the very constitution of the Cosmos. The baelreivers are far older and shrewder than you imagine. They were created to subsist on exactly this raw energy, and they know exactly how to extract it from you. The more you bring to bear, the more ravenous and powerful they will become. It is for exactly this reason we created the reapers as a collective force to measure the power among themselves for effect. We will protect the city and do what we can to feed their strength from afar, but in the coming battle we must place our faith in them."

"In their captain."

"Yes."

"I presume you have intentions with regard to his memories, then."

"The choice will be his to make."

"Father. He will not take a request from his Alltaker as a choice. You know this."

"He will understand."

"You can not keep him here, Alltaker. He's been separated from the others since Mortis Veth, for Eddath's sake. It's past time he was returned to them."

"We can not let the cold keep us from tending the fire, Ellianastis. If I am correct, Demithyle understands this more intimately than any of us."

"Well. You take a risk. The library is not without its dangers."

"Your candle."

"Ah. Looks like he's back in there. It'll be a while before he's got his wits back. The separation can be rather taxing."

"How long did he wander in spirit form?"

"Are you asking me a question about time?"

*　*　*

The voices recede and for a time there is only the black and the deep. Then I hear my father's voice.

"Awake now, Demithyle."

I open my eyes. I am in a room illuminated by a small hearth that burns a woodless flame of orange and blue. It is hexagonal in shape and its walls are composed entirely of shelves thick with tomes and scrolls of every sort. The reading parlor in Ellianastis's sanctuary, set off the main area of the laboratory. Its sixth wall is a doorless threshold that affords a view of the floating stones in the center of the library, through which ceaselessly drift the spiritous aspects of the wendlaersth, oblivious to all but the tomes they study.

I sit in a simple wooden chair near the hearth. My light ascetic robes have become stiff and gray with the library's passage of time. Across from me my father sits, a large tome open upon his lap, a yellow page held between his fingers, the vellum's texture deepened by the pulsating firelight. A subtle glow inhabits his form from which I perceive a certain urgency, but also patience. And from the tome he holds there emanates a sense of old familiarity, though I have not seen its like before this moment.

My father smiles, then holds out his hands as if to encompass the room.

"Welcome back to forevermeir," says he.

"All . . . taker," I say. My voice is thick with dust and rattles like old bones.

"Nay, not all," says he. "But far too many, alas. And most forever to lament it. As for they who do not, I imagine you have encountered some only too recently. And so. Now you have returned from your spiritual counsel. How found you your city? Rarely have I witnessed such enthusiasm for its crypts and boulevards as you have shown. But then, few have been so possessed by it as you."

"It is . . . ," I begin, struggling against a lingering leadenness of thought, ". . . alive."

"A strange way to describe a realm of the dead," says he.

"Alive . . . with voices," I say. "Many aspects of being. Light and dark. Wherever I would alight."

He smiles. "'Tis fine then that you have added your own to its chorus," says he.

The image of my projected self drifting beneath the streetlamp comes to mind. So many thousands of souls, bound within a single spiritous aspect.

"Ah, but this is how you have come to see your self," says he, reading my thought. "As merely a chorus of others."

"Yes," I say.

He regards me a moment in silence. Then he looks again to his tome, and finding a place on the page, he reads:

> *It may be my voice is nothing that can be claimed as my own,* thought the Reaper, *but merely emergent from so many overlapping ripples in a pool of dead recollections. Perhaps it is not even that, but some other phenomenon beyond my ability to imagine.*

He turns the page, continues.

> *There is so much that I do not know. I do not even know whether such a distinction is requisite for an authentication of being or even what measure of value such authentication holds. Yet time in all of its species has been as an ally to me, and so in it I will place my trust for the advent of univocal knowing of self and of all things.*

He closes the book, holding his place with his finger, then turns it over to examine its spine. "*Madhumakshika*. Hm. Not a bad read so far," says he. "A bit florid, perhaps. But I have enjoyed immensely its occurrences of verse."

My father rises and I do in kind, to the audible snap and creaking of my body's ligature.

"Well. By the reckoning of this library," says he, chuckling, "that body of yours lay prone nigh on a century."

He moves to stand at the doorway, looking out into the atrium.

"Quite a marvel, is it not?" says he. "This sideways sanctuary of Ellianastis's. Even now, as we converse idly by the fireglow, many troubles wait in patient abeyance for the return of our attention. One might be tempted simply to remain here indefinitely."

He turns to me.

"Tell me," says he, "in your time among these rows before your spirit sojourn, what wisdom did you discover among the stacks?"

"None, Alltaker."

"None?"

"I did avail my self of its expanse of . . . archives," I say. "Though I do not doubt much wisdom resides here, I have accepted the impossibility of meeting with it among the innumerable . . . trivialities."

"A wise observation in itself," says he. "Indeed, would that you could deliver such insight to these poor, obsessed faints who will never be able to leave this place. Yet perhaps you have only lacked the eyes to see. Why not look again?"

He beckons, and I step with him out to the mezzanine. Here now over the boundless expanse I instantly perceive the presence of a great many works akin to that which my father holds now in the crook of his arm. I see them throughout the intricate vastness as a constellation of innumerable pinpoints of light, aglow in my mind with familiarity as if each were a sliver of my self.

"They contain my memories," I say.

My father looks at me and nods as if seeing the library through my eyes.

"Yes," says he. "From your sojourn you've taken with you a shimmer of insight into the True Spirit Realm. It shall remain with you. Ever henceforth shall it be a lens through which you view all the worlds around you. And by it you sense here the presence of all that is you."

"A gift."

I feel a wave of my father's pride. "Yes," he says. "Yet another for our favored deadspawn. Perhaps you might make use of it to discover what you still seek."

I look at my father. He smiles.

"You have already found more wisdom than you know, Reaper," says he. "And you have taught much to your creators. Perhaps your seeking is the winning of your soul, or self, or your right to either, or both. 'Tis surely this above all else by which I failed the baelreivers, for never were they given to the becoming of beings of substance in their own right. Perhaps all our struggles should be for the safeguarding for all beings the right to this very journey inward on which you now find your self."

"That has been a gift also," I say. "One of a great many bestowed upon me in kindness by the Cosmos and my forebears. I am ready to reciprocate in kind, Father, if you will have me take my place among my reapers."

"You have done so already, O Demithyle!" says he. "A great gift you gave to your father on the very day of your making. Long had I chased a nagging mystery, evident in the melodies of the Cosmos and the landscapes of dream, and so as elusive. Only by the anomalous recollections of a newborn reaper did it begin to grow in definition.

"'Tis right you should rejoin with your kin, then to unleash your fury and worthiness against the blight. Indeed, this is the most destructive era my Underworld has ever seen, sped by a coexistence with our own antithesis. How can we hope to challenge the greater affliction of the Cosmos when our own house remains in such upheaval? We must hasten an end to it, one way or another.

"Yet in it the fates have granted us a boon of time, if little else, to pursue the greater measure of our aims. And so I would ask that you continue your fruitful seeking a while longer, even as the battlemeir hovers waiting."

I look out over the library expanse. I imagine wandering among the insatiable wendlaersth through the dark, bottomless shaft of shadow doors behind this resplendent illusory curtain. I feel the constellation of archived memories throughout that calls to me even now with the promise of a limitless unveiling of self.

"I will, Father," I say.

His scythe appears in his grip as he sets his tome down upon a nearby lectern.

"Show me your merest hand."

I present it, and he takes hold of it.

"The flesh has been seared."

"In Mortis Veth, Father."

He says nothing, though I sense his surprise, as if he had forgotten how long I had been away. Then he holds his scythe sideways and dips the great blade down meet my flesh. The tip pierces my palm and a pattern spreads over the inside of my hand as tiny curls of smoke rise up from the flesh.

He releases it for me to examine. A ring evenly transected by five slashes, gouged black into my smallest palm, a vague, indistinct form in its center.

"Time has drawn for Death this mark," says my father, stepping back, "that has in turn drawn Death to Demithyle. So imparted, may it accompany him now in his unmasking of his self, if that is what he seeks. Thus shall it be enriched by its meeting with the great spectrum of realms that are its providence."

He leans his scythe against the lectern and retrieves the tome.

> *He could not deny the kernel of enthusiasm that had begun to grow in him, for oft had he sought his place and purpose among the Cosmos, and where but here to gain better sight of it. Yet a part of him felt also a warning by the boundlessness of the undertaking. Even should he exhaust the store of memories recorded here, his awareness of the tome held now in his father's hands brought to him an unsettling truth, that the seeking itself would bring into manifestation its own breadth of volumes that he would be unable to ignore, and the seeking of these would bring about the same, forever ad infinitum. Perhaps it is by just this metastasis of seeking that the library has grown so vast, thought the Reaper. Perhaps thus impelled it will come to consume all*

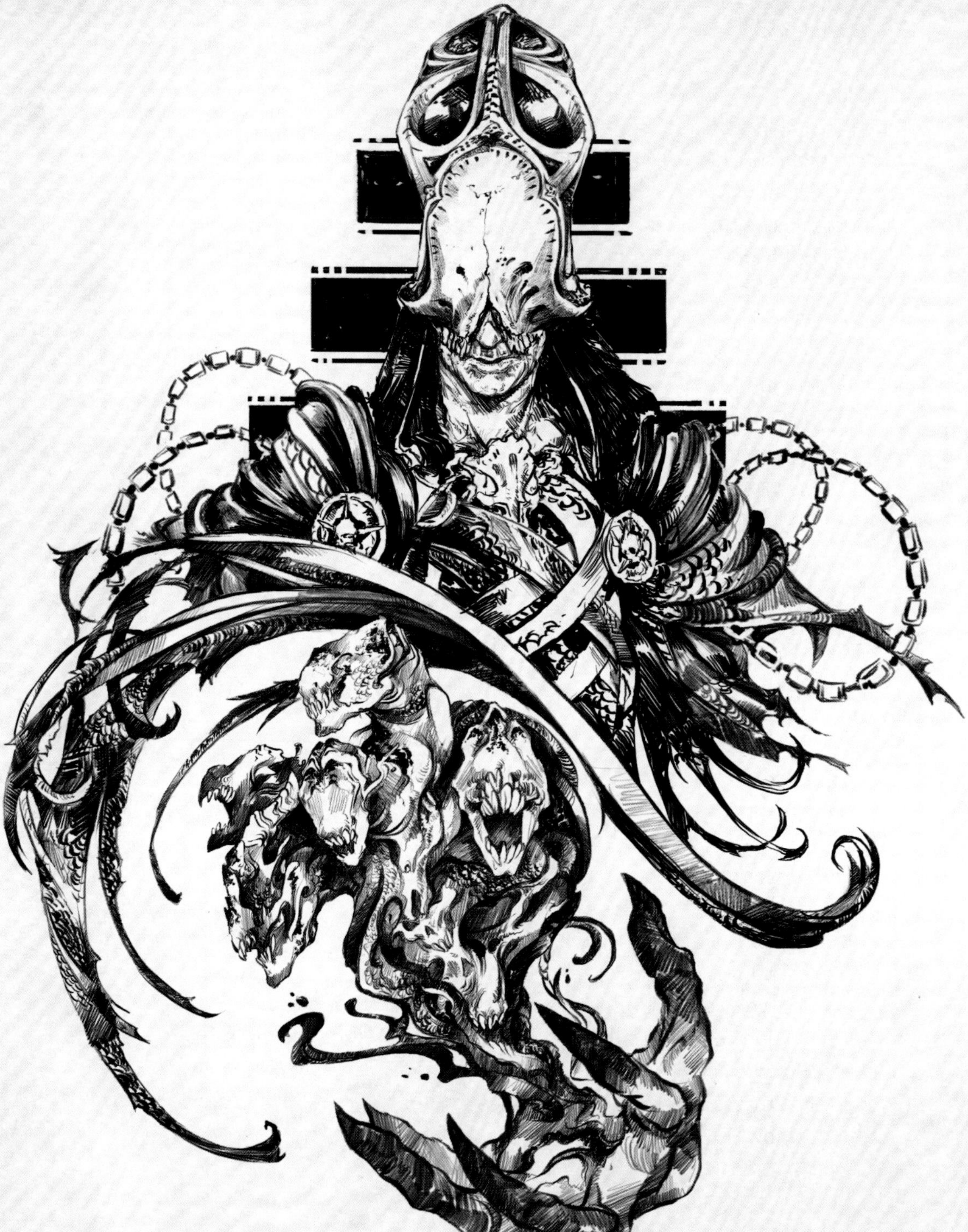

of creation, to cease only by the resultant cessation of all events save the recording of the cessation of all events save the recording of the cessation of all events . . .

My father suddenly snaps the tome closed and throws it over the balustrade. The area is instantly flooded by the spiritous aspects of the wendlaersth, who stream in from every direction and mob the book even as it is snatched from its descent. Why did the Alltaker of the Underworld touch this book? Why did he throw it? What secrets lie within? The wendlaersth carry the tome silently away, rolling over one another in their desperation to devour it.

My father nods.

"You begin to see," says he. "No, this library is not an unperilous place. There are worse things you might here become than one of these restless faints. Indeed, 'tis the inevitable bringing of weight to such cancerous superfluities that obliged us to create the labyrinth, that other space of madness and paradox. Deep within it exists a void into which their heft must be cast. 'Tis hidden even from my self, for 'tis a black prison of true infinity. You should be glad you never encountered it, for even your wyspstride could not have escaped it. I fear it more than any place else in existence.

"But now you understand something of the burden laid upon Ellianastis by her self when she implored me to bring this library into being. She has had aeons to adapt to its influence. You, I am afraid, do not. Time passes slow beyond these walls, but pass it does. Take with you on your journey into the past the remembrance your companion Ycnaf, who waits presently for your return with a host of her kind. Remember you reapers are the progenitors of a knighthood bound to play its part in this struggle for the soul of the Cosmos, the present front of which is this riddle I have tasked you to help me unwind. Your home is a legion of your making with the wyspstrides at its side, its voice thereafter to echo far beyond this time. But only if you return to us whole.

"And should you forget these things, look upon this mark I have given you and know that you behold the Underworld entire, and remember that if you should you be destroyed by your self, your city is sure to follow."

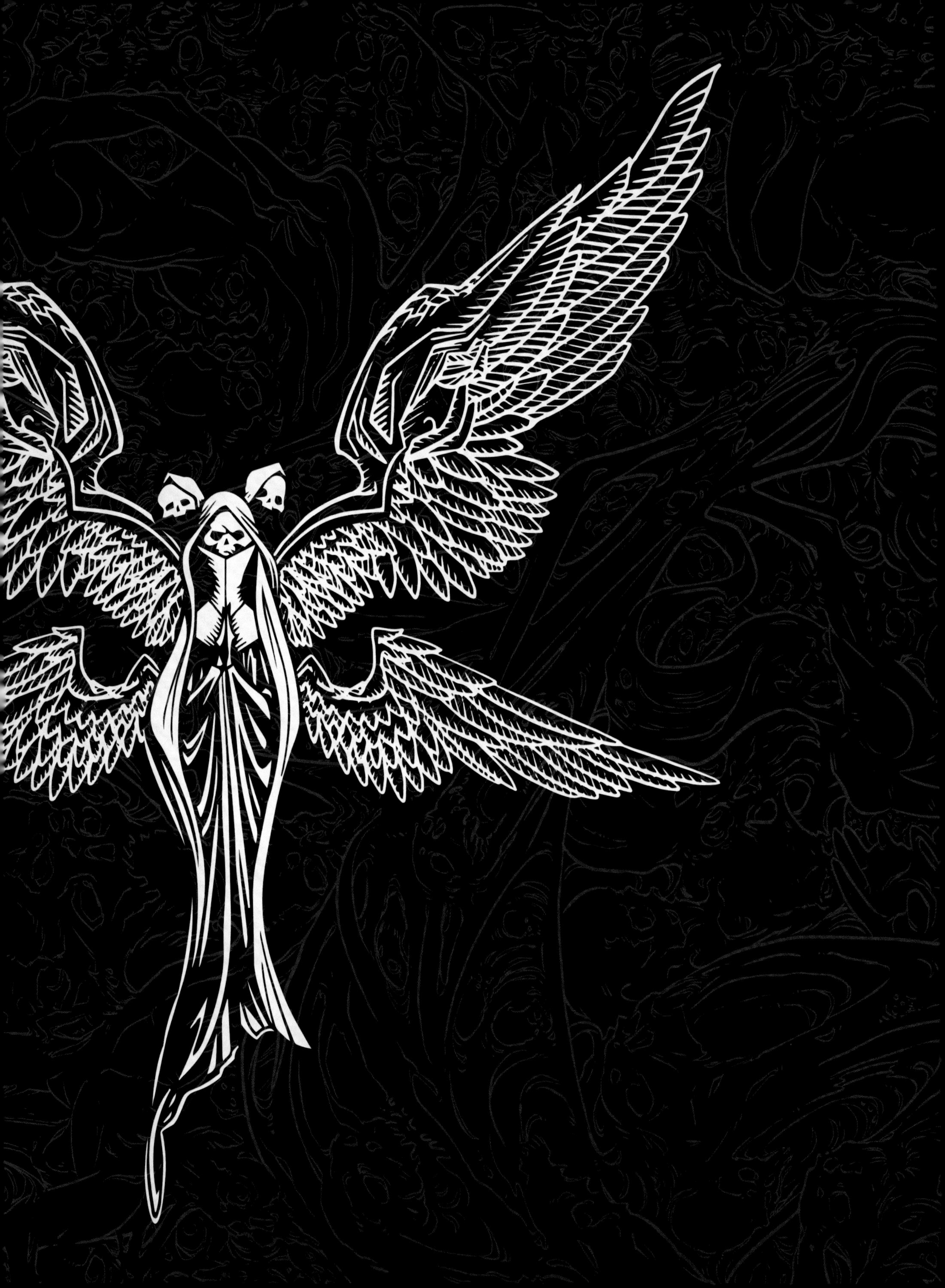

XXVII.
A THOUSAND VOICES

He is gone. Without the richness of his aura the library is somehow lesser, and I am conscious of my solitude here.

*　*　*

I look again at the mark on my merest hand, charred and wretched. Though its overall vagueness of form is unknown to me, some of the glyphs which by my own aspect have emerged round the circle I recognize, having seen them upon the mass of standing stones in my naming vision within the menhir. 𒀀 *a*. water. 𒆳 *kur*. mountain. 𒅗 *ka*. mouth. Taken alone they are bereft of meaning. But through the lingering lens of my spiritsight, each emanates its own distinct aura from its place upon my palm.

     I look out into the library. I feel them, thousands of chronicles of every order of pedagogy curated for my self alone. I close my eyes and my sense of them with respect to one another in this space describes its unfathomable vastness in my mind, and in my imagination I course through it as I would the stelliform conduits between the veils, knowing that each point of light is a doorway into a place that some part of me in time past has called home.

*　*　*

I step out to the terrace, the greater Underworld beyond. Frozen in the air just beyond the canyon is what looks at first to be nothing more than a weathered boulder. In fact it is half of the face of a young woman carved from stone, an element of a great monument passed into the Underworld in the moments before I was returned to the library. She looks at me with a single eye carven beneath a thin rope lariat upon her brow.

Among the flotsam scattered over the dunes beneath it is a great toppled iron bell. The statue will strike it the instant I leave this place.

* * *

I go through the spatial threshold, leaving Ellianastis's study behind for the perpetual gasp and roar of the sepulchral library. Before me the chasm and its downward churn of blackglass needles, each now bearing a subdued iridescent glint to my eyes. Above and below, the infinite spiral of shadow doors.

I walk round the chasm as I had done when first I entered this place. My sense of the chronicles of memory is unaltered by this shade change in the library's skin, and it is not long before I come upon a shadow door through which I know one is to be found. Through it I pass to find my self in a barren stone reliquary in which various small artifacts are strewn in dusty heaps. Among them, a small golden sphere, its luster dulled with age.

I kneel to examine it. Etched over it are bands of script from a long-forgotten mortal language, evenly interspersed and spreading outward from an unadorned circle to what would appear a ring of islands opposite it, afire and succumbing to the sea. Between these are vertical depictions of an array of characters, archetypes of their kind: the priest, the villain, the farmer, the virgin. All cower and recoil as if beset by some inescapable scourge.

When I touch it the images are suddenly made animate, and the script flows over the surface of the sphere. And then, like the release of an ancient echo trapped within a hollow, there arises the sound of a distant voice:

> *Clouds a memory. The sky, a blanket to take warmth. A harvest of dust.*

As the last echo wanes a pale darkness descends within the reliquary and the cold walls seem to fall away, and then I am lying prone in the dimness of a great empty pyramid of stone. High above, secured at its apex, a golden orb in place of the wrathful, unforgiving sun. For near a lifetime I have seen only thin shafts of its light through the narrow slats that abound my prison, then only to empower the hexing inscribed on these dark walls. It has taken our crops, kilt the fishes, soured the health of the people, and we have perished, all returned to the sea. I have aged and will die here shaded from its authority, my own family long since dead. I was forbidden even to bear witness to their exodus, so sacred my duty to preserve our legacy.

All now ever so very still in the absence of their voices. The birth of an age of quiet. I alone remain, its final herald, the last mind to stir in the lateness of my own passing our final spells that will stretch our voices out beyond this age, beseeching the universe for eternal living memory of us beyond our departure. Yet in my sterile hermitage I have come to understand the creativity of our destruction, and I know now our only bestowal to the drift of time should be the pureness of our dismissal from this existence. And so there will be no spells or memories of us, and with my passing this world in all of its broadness shall be free at last of mind.

* * *

I am Demithyle again, returned to the grayness of light in the dusty reliquary to ponder the intimations of this . . . remembrance. Why should a reaper whose primary purpose is the defense of his realm against militant threat be in possession of the mind of a lone thaumaturgic archivist, cursed to linger beyond the eventide of his civilization? In what way is this purpose further served by my knowing his impenitent satisfaction as in an act of obliviation against a people who long ago abandoned me—him—to die in peace beneath the waves?

Perhaps in as much as the knowing of his final act of nihilism is evidence of its failure, the asking of such questions is itself a manifestation of their answer.

* * *

I pass through the shadow door again to a scattering of wendlaersth, gaunt and weary and maniacal. When I walk on they will creep up from below the ledges and go into the reliquary I have left behind me to swallow what wisdom they believe I have might have discovered therein.

    I look at the mark. A new sigil has appeared in the circle.

※ *an.* sky.

* * *

I enter into a place that I can describe only as otherworldly. Here there are no walls, only a black emptiness populated by glances of sharp light adrift like glinting motes of dust. The floor is a buoying grid of energy that accepts my footing only to carry me forth to an iridescent orb encased between mirrored half-moons, hovering freely in the space. By its encasement I take it and in turn it captures my gaze, until deep within a clouded mass of color conveys a sequence of emotive impressions that imply its language into my mind:

> *The first stir of shadow. The quiet night. The stone, still warm. A fair beginning.*

    These words come to me like an incantation, likely invoked by the mysticism of my parentage to carry these slivers of existence from the aether that they be added to the pool from which were born our nascent selves. Even as I note this, into the orb my awareness is drawn, to fall through the wash of color and into a near-complete absence of light, a vague white glow at my periphery the only expression of any substance.

    Yet all is as it must be, for this realm in its entirety is but four rudiments. An early seed of Eddath's thought of creation. Of it, we are two. He is Shine, my reflection. I am Shade, his shadow. The third of our realm is Sphere. On its surface we reside. We have for one day drifted in this void. That day has never begun. Nor shall it end. Mine is to collect. His, to send. In this way we are paired. Only at the meeting of our domains is there movement. This threshold is Clash. He is our offspring. By his vigor our realm endures. He alone gives rise to memory of it.

    All is fine.

    Perhaps the name for this realm shall be Parity.

    With this thought arrives a new offspring. A fifth rudiment that we call Confluence. A sister for Clash. To grow our realm. To perhaps bring into it Music?

But our children seek. They long to create. They covet our rule. They take from us in unequal measure to bring more rudiments into being, many more, these to then do the same. At last is begotten Chaos, who deposes us. We will drown in his thrashing. Parity diminishes, splits, renamed Devour and Deprivation. This realm a failed thought, now to consume itself.

* * *

Another ending, though this a beginning also. Another failure also. Within me is the full knowing of its innocence and disappointment.

What forces are at play to penetrate the ages thus, to wield as tools memory of the most primordial of events, before creation itself had taken hold? They are as symbols brought to life that perhaps I alone now know to have rung out in the unfolding of time.

I look at the mark. *munus*. female.

* * *

I pass into a narrow corridor that is dark but for a pattern of dancing light some distance beyond. It is very warm. As I advance the passage contracts, so that soon I am forced to crouch and finally crawl to what proves a blaze of fire in a chamber below, casting its light through the rungs of an iron grating in the floor. The grating raises easily, and I slip beneath it and drop below directly into the flames.

Though I feel its heat the fire does not catch, as if refused by the aging bibliosophic robes given me by this place. The walls of the chamber are thick brambles of iron pikes festooned with thousands of blackened skulls, some thickened with crusts of burnt flesh. In the center of the chamber is an altar over which is unrolled a scroll of iron sheeting, glowing red hot and displaying its passage:

> *Through soil travels eyeless the worm. The sake of blood, a sleeping tree. Terra Strife, denuden.*

For an epoch and more I have cut this faithshrift seraph. From its bleak eyes to its ludicrous neut. High into the blinding sublunaria to the fecal moilground of the mortal plane, and deep into the mireden and the blackoil cauldrons of my spawning, in the lowpool reek and fumes of the forges that cast infernis in its fireblood glow. I rake it with claws of rusted metal, gnaw it with teeth poisoned by the corrupted flesh of its abstaint kin whose meat I have savored.

And still the wretched manikin will not die. It fights with its gleam of blade, unflagging, one beggardlien archangel enslaved to its sterility; our blood is a monsoon upon the realms, a pestilence to amuse Nergal, or Shakpana, a whip upon the back of the upstart custodian who drowns in a superfluity of souls.

Its wings long broken, my own torn useless by its obstinance, we scour the dry rock surfaces of Hell. I entreat my brethren for aid but they are amused by our melee. Finally, I falter. Its weapon crushes through my shell to burn my heart to ash. With my last breath I take hold of its gullet and I am cast down on the blooded rock face with it still in my razor-blade grasp, my final joy the sound it gives as it chokes upon a flood of its own cursed blood.

* * *

A celestial battle. Perhaps a microcosm of their war. The smell of it familiar from my first effervescence of recollection as one among the ancient Vanguard.

I look upon the mark, curious now of what it might draw from such a record of a demonic celestial being. But it seems no more significant. *nag*. drink.

I go on.

* * *

I enter directly into the moonlit clearing of a meadow. In it I am drawn to a thick slab of broken stone standing among others of its like scattered throughout the clearing amid tufts of verdant grass. Its fragments are covered over with etchings of three disparate origins, and they hover solidly in place by indiscernible means, adjoined to the empty space where large elements of it are missing.

I scan the fragments for the incantation that will act as catalyst to draw out the memory I feel pulsating within it, as had done the others. It is not until I peer into the empty space between the fragments that I mark the script drawn in a gleam of blue upon the air.

A weighted leaf, a riverbed. Water of the mountain. From the mud, snails.

> My feet pound the dry needlebed turf in the cold dawn to a rush of screams of fury as we mass forth from the edges of forest fog to meet the invaders, our axes and hammers notched by the taking of their fathers' heads. This sovereign ground is our only treasure, and they shall not take it. They are trespassers and transgressors and we will kill them to the last man.
> We charge so thick we take cuts from our own blades but we ignore them in our battlefervor, our blooded arms and legs the only commanders of ourselves. But then we falter as if against a traitorous soil to become a fray of our own confusion, and the sounds of our cries twist from fury to frustration and surprise as we fall forth, down, pressed by the rear advance still ignorant of the trap dug deep into this sacred field in our own homeland, our vast numbers a crush upon ourselves as their treacherous spears and stones and arrows rain upon us.

* * *

Militant failure. The smothering of pain and confusion. Battlefury. These things of a kind that all reapers had thought would ever be their sustenance. In our simple communion we had not believed ourselves inhabitants of our realm but its sentinels, to be destroyed in its protection and remade by they who commanded us. It was enough for us then. For he who has become this Demithyle, it will never be again.

I look upon the mark. ⌇ *du*. foot.

* * *

Goaded by the numinous accumulation of glyphs within the mark, I follow my sense of self into ever stranger and deeper corners of the faint-infested library, taking in these visions with little respite save brief meditations on their breadth of significance to my being and purpose: The sea shall always take me. I have eaten of the flesh of my brethren. The babe cries in darkness. The bloodied heretic will not confess. They are conjured by the incantations brought by as many means as there are ways of being: The drinking of water from a clay cup. The lighting of a brazier to illuminate runes upon a wall. A pattern of light from a crystal-encrusted stone. A simple manuscript on a shelf in an abandoned manor, forever otherwise to have been overlooked. A step into darkness and a freefall, with verse carried by the sound of the wind.

Some seem to elapse within mere moments, others span greater lengths of time that like the dream upon waking are impossible exactly to determine. All are accompanied by what awareness of life or existence was kept by their originators in their meetings with Death or their otherwise ultimate endings of being. Whether this is so by way of value ascribed by my makers to an intimacy of pain and failure in the creation of a soldier, or by the overriding influence of my father in his delivering unto me the mark, I can not be certain. But all are as revelations to me, both of self and of what is possible for a self to be, and though their enrichment of the mark remains disparate and vague I find my self ever more invigorated by the reliving of them.

In time my unflagging pursuit of these memories begins to weigh upon me just the same, and I call for my hostess's airy elemental to guide me again to her sanctuary in order that I may meditate upon these many visions and perhaps assess the completeness of my task. There I discover from the terrace a greatly altered picture: the statue's half face, once frozen well above the dunes, has now made its way down along its path of infall to crack against the bell. A puff of its grit hangs in the air around the place of impact and there are globules of yellow light like flowing tears from the hollow of her sole eye. They seem to slowly scintillate and subtly to alter even as I look upon them—like the drifting of distant clouds, their movements revealed only by subsequent glances. Their light casts a bilious pallor over what carven features remain of the woman's face, which taken with the cracks that have spread over it gives the impression of its youth supplanted by agedness.

And then I note that the cracks appear to have deepened even within the last few breaths. And looking again at the shifting globules of light I realize they are in fact sparks born by the abrasion of the massive stone upon the bell's metal, now forcing their way into completion even through the arresting of time, as if no force could restrict their pursuit of catharsis.

Thus is given to me some direct measure of the time passing here relative to the Underworld at large: if by my reckoning the lifespan of a single spark is so elongated there, what expanse of time must have elapsed that would carry down a falling stone?

* * *

I look at my self. My robes have become threadbare and soiled, and upon inspection I find many tears and holes in their fabric. My flesh, dry and thin. I try to calculate the breadth of time that has elapsed for me here. Decades? But how can it be thus?

Thinking to draw from my sword a measure of reassurance and reminder of duty, I reach for Cryptmourne and am shocked to find it missing. How had I not sensed its absence? I can not recall drawing it or otherwise unfastening it from where it has long been set at my hip. I close my eyes and reach for its essence, but I feel only the volumes, the countless thousands of memories waiting to be unveiled.

I look into the sanctuary toward the library atrium, bright and unassuming by this illusory perspective. Somewhere there also is my sword. I will have no hope of collecting it if I leave now. I must find Cryptmourne.

I look at my hand. Many new glyphs are inscribed over the mark. But a great deal of it remains empty. No meaning could possibly be derived from this random acquisition of elements. My task is yet incomplete.

I look again at the nascent sparks. Ellianastis had described Death as moving between moments. Like as not he watches. Surely he will call when I am needed, before the hour is at its direst.

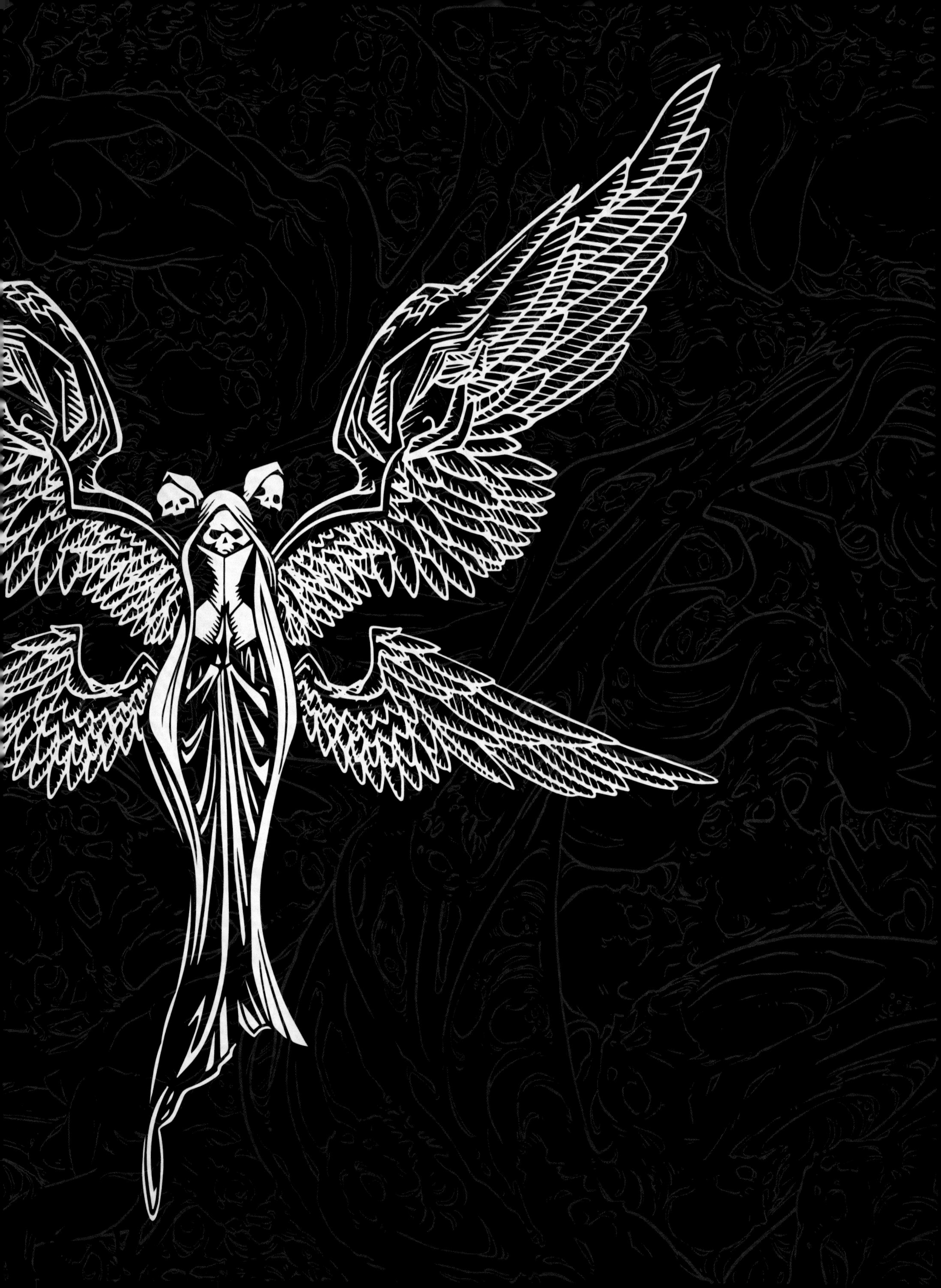

XXVIII.
HUSHHYDE

Gignoth and Melthis could feel the misery in the aether even before they had fully descended the mountainside. It blew against them on the updrafts as they leapt, a tearing at the gut of fear and loss, and a deep lamenting, as if driven over the adjacent foothills with the coldness of wind.

The rock face gave way to a more gradual slope, and they climbed over the crags until they found the narrow twist of road that wound around the foothills at the wallward outskirts of HushHyde. Both had visited more than once the dark and sprawling enclave in their explorations of the city, as much to be amid the lightness of being of the child spirits of the Underworld who dwelt there as to convene with the fostermurden in their care for the damaged damned, those wayward soulborn whose fragmented selves had left them with little agency of their own.

Here it stood before them, a baroque bouquet of gothic steeples, pagodas, minarets, and belfries standing against the mountainside opposite the Harrows. It seemed like a compact microcosm of the city, aglitter with spiritous light from its countless windows, lanterns, and lattices, alive with calls and belltolls all its own. In its center, an immense cathedral rose above the surrounding edifices. Its structure diminished by height so that at its summit it was a single wall of floating stone elements within which was housed an enormous, rounded pane of vibrantly stained glass.

Gignoth looked up at it from their sidelong approach toward the wallward entrance to the courtyards, trying to discern its present depiction. The mourners of Illverness they had encountered had uniformly referred to it as Death's Door, asserting its changeable imagery to be a reflection of the state of the Alltaker's humor. Here now it looked to depict a corpse being devoured by a massive book, the iron armatures between

the colored panes arranged so as to invoke the slatwork of a cage.
Ill humor indeed.

* * *

The air of malaise had grown steadily in strength with their approach, and when they passed through the unadorned wooden gate to the courtyard they were confronted by a powerful wave of it that caused them both to balk, and pausing for a breath they exchanged silent, grave looks before continuing forth.

In fact, Gignoth had noted Melthis's unusual reticence even before they had entered. Her acerbic, easy manner had been a fine balance to his own frank practicality. Both in their own way viewed the coming battle with the baelreivers as part of a broader era of upheaval in which they happened to exist. After this threat was defeated, no doubt some subsequent doom would come to call. They would meet it as they had the horde and all dooms to be laid before their Alltaker: with the fervor and fidelity of beings whose purpose was as unambiguous as their newness of being. In the meanwhile, they were the spiritbairn of a dark and fascinating world, and even as they anticipated the taking up of their mantle as reapers of souls in the Mortal Realm, they reveled in the Underworld's many dark oddities wherever together they found them.

As the meirs of Demithyle's absence had worn on, Gignoth was looked to as their surrogate commander. Yet Melthis's unflappable nature remained true—indeed he had come to rely on it. Now, as the black nausea arrived, she seemed as shaken as he. Both understood that they were suddenly closer to their enemy than they had ever been. The foulness seemed to carry the violent unmaking of their own selves, as if their demise at the hands of the baelreivers in the battle to come was to be delivered with such ferocity as to drive them backward from the shattermeir.

And as they made their way toward the dead garden in the courtyard at HushHyde where the afflicted lay in the shadow of the cathedral, there was something else. Something cursed, like a lingering glee for their pain, as if their souls had been stained by a vileness of spirit left by they who had bestowed upon them their wretchedness.

* * *

The garden of tombs, mausoleums, and sarcophagi had been enclosed by a blushed tarpaulin of skin stretched tight over branching stalks of bone, bent over them to form a swath of interconnected domes, which as they neared they could see were pulled beneath the ground around its perimeter. At their approach a portal opened, revealing a thick layer of wiry gray silk spun against the skin. They stepped through and it quickly resealed itself behind them, leaving only a woven gray wall.

And suddenly they felt the sickly emanations cease, as if all that they had felt of it had been as psychic poison drawn out and cast through the protective shell. What remained in the ambient gray quartzlight was a blanketing cocoon of placidity and warmth.

"By the Old Giver . . . ," said Melthis.

Set amidst the garden structures were many biers, each bearing an afflicted soulborn in some advanced state of dissolution, some barely recognizable as mortalkind. Missing limbs. A half-devoured head. Great weeping holes bored through torsos. Their wounds simmered with a putrid, incandescent violaceous ooze and appeared to deepen by the moment, like sandstone traversed by water, and to spread over them so that in places their wrappings were burned by its wasting advance.

Between them the fostermurden drifted, casting their warming glow wherever they went as they wove quiet madrigals of comforting sounds, mopping brows, delivering fresh wrappings, cutting away fleshrot. They grasped pain-wracked hands with soft, fleshy tendrils they extended from their chimeric skullforms and emoted kind assurances from their spectral overlays, each which took the form of some recuperative figure or deity drawn from the deep remembrance of the soulborn they tended.

Gignoth looked round, at a loss. None of these pitiable beings seemed cognizant enough even to be engaged, let alone interrogated. They made their way through the garden until through the open doors of a large mausoleum they marked an unattended female who seemed to be watching them curiously, her eyes as twin glimmers in the dimness within. She was tightly wrapped below the waist with thick, blackstaint calico.

Before they could step inside, however, one of the fostermurden appeared in the doorway to interpose, her many long tendrils tucked below her core. Her spectral visage projected at them a face that wore a patient kindness but also an underlying firmness, waiting expectantly to hear of their intent even as she floated.

Gignoth and Melthis bowed in unison. "Solemn Healer," said Gignoth, rising. "Forgive us the interruption of your ministrations. In your care for these souls, our spirits are yours."

She waited, hovering before them, features unchanged.

"I am the reaper Gignoth. We have come to learn what we might of this the enemy of us all, in advance of our meeting of it. We would speak with any who would speak of the baelreivers that have done this to them."

The fostermurden shifted her countenance, now offering eyes filled with pity.

"The lost bael . . . ," she began, in a voice that rose from her core like a billow of volcanic ash, even as the spectral visage remained still. "Poor, lost sprites . . . they inflict as they have been inflicted on . . ."

Naefukkin' dregs, muttered Melthis through wisp. *Fuk their sprites, if this is what they give.*

Gignoth stole a glance past the fostermurden at the afflicted female soulborn, hoping to mark her awareness of the intent he had spoken. But he saw then the strip of wrapping pulled over her eyes, and he understood they glowed not with curiosity but with the telltale violet hue of the burning fester.

"What is happening to them?" he asked.

"They are staint by a devouring blight . . . there is no remedy . . ." Her inner physicality turned then as the woman stirred. "Come and see . . ."

They followed the fostermurden to the soulborn, watching in impotent frustration as she unfurled her tendrils and worked to apply a viscous, sizzling secretion over the wounds.

Her spectral overlay turned again to engage them even as her physical self continued its work. "We can only grieve with them . . . ," she said in a wistful voice. "Help them to forget, and know they shall not be forgotten . . . we can not even take their pain . . . its root is beyond us, beyond our reach . . . we can only ease it . . . send it away as quickly as we are able . . . aid them in their falling, fading . . ."

"They fall to oblivion?"

"No." The word penetrated forthright, as if directed to pierce a cavernous depth. "We would not allow that . . ."

Gignoth waited for the fostermurden to elaborate, but she only continued to float before him, her luminous projection a graven image of patience and sympathy.

"Do you know how they escaped the wraiths?" asked Melthis.

"Through the veils . . . their own portals between places, which they kept . . . to the wallows nearer the city, some, not all . . . and sealed them in their traversing . . . but not before the lost baels had touched their beings . . . alas, not before . . ."

A hideous scream pierced the embrace of calm in the mausoleum.

The reapers felt more than heard it, like a clawing of hooks that tore at their spirits.

"What in cakk was that?"

"I do not know that we want the answer to that."

But the fostermurden seemed to understand. Already she had drifted to the aid of another of her kind who had begun to carefully wrap the shell of a soulborn who had wasted almost completely away. When it was covered the two spirits fanned their clusters of tendrils together to create a floating gurney, and they carried it from the mausoleum.

And then the Queen Mother of the Dead was standing on the threshold, tall, regal, imposing, and profoundly despondent, a thick bundle clutched in her arms. Though they had heard her voice in song in their explorations of Illverness, the reapers had not seen her since the day of their naming. But any thought of reunion was banished by the tragedy they read in her face, its lavender flesh torn, its eyes cored to scorched hollows.

She found the eyes of another fostermurden even as it moved swiftly to attend to her, and the gentle creature guided her to the now-empty bier. There she laid the remnant of yet another ravaged mortalborn, this one so wholly devastated as for his fragments of soul to lie exposed. The Queen Mother stood by as the fostermurden slathered his flesh with cooling unguent secreted from their tendrils, and as they began to wrap him tightly with thick strips of linen Gignoth found himself transfixed by the raw ethearic energy of the mortalborn's exposed soul. It writhed and glimmered in its apparent retreat deeper into what remained of his physicality. How odd, he thought, that this should be the source of that substance that sustains all of the Cosmos, over which all wars save those fought by the mortals themselves are begun. That there should be a creature made to incubate it and amplify its potentcy, and yet with no ability or even means to grasp it, nor even true awareness of its existence.

Etherea. In the very moment the spiritborn mortis were pressed into existence by means of its protean power, they were given also clear sense of its purpose and theirs. But the soulborn, it seemed, could carry only illusions inherited from a parentage no less blinded by ignorance than they. Merely by their accumulation of moments did their burden of mortality speed them ever closer to their universal doom, shucked to the last from their greater beings by their harvesting, their spilt scraps of memory collected by the denizens of the Underworld to be traded for trinkets. Yet the Alltaker had seen fit to claim these as revenant mourners in his realm. This, if nothing else, should lend gravity enough to their significance . . .

"Is their worth so hidden from thee?"

Gethsemoni continued to stare at the mortal as she spoke, her back bent and narrow, raked by claws and dappled with acid scars.

"'Tis only natural," she said. "Into thee we did plant threads of mortal lives lived, yet not so mortality. Perhaps we ourselves are the slaves of creation, and 'tis these spilt scraps of memory we trade for trinkets that shall prove the loftiest of its pillars."

The reapers shifted where they stood, drowning in the moment for want of how to commune with one so deadly and benevolent as she, to whom they had never spoken directly. Gignoth, feeling chastised, could only withdraw into his wish to ponder further. How fortunate then that his companion was Melthis.

"Got intae a bit of the maul, haven't ye, Queen Mother," said Melthis. "If we can bring ye tae the mend, we won't wait, will we Gig. Or get us at the mauler, like . . ."

Gethsemoni tilted an ear but gave no reply. Then she turned to look at them with two glistening, embryonic eyes, and they saw the sparks of sinew and flesh regrowing in the wounds that tore her face.

"There are instants . . . ," she said, "slivers of vision, so clear . . ." She turned to vaguely watch the fostermurden in their palliative ministrations of the other afflicted.

"When I look upon them, at times I must deem them our only true wonder. Their existence is a humility. 'Tis an inborn innocence, made and kept by the haplessness of their pursuit. All that they admire and achieve and suffer, locked behind a shadow curtain of uncertainty. And yet, there is light enough in their world to glimmer here. Canst thou envision purer consecration of their being?" she said. "It may be humanity is Eddath's precious gift to the Cosmos. If so, she is they. If so, they are we."

The reapers drank in the light of their Queen Mother as they listened, trying to feel what she felt. But the dramatic injuries to her flesh overrode their thoughts with dismay and shame that she should have suffered by the viciousness of the baelreivers they had been created to defy.

She turned to them now, smiling as she looked at them each in kind with eyes near fully reformed. "Trouble not thy spirits, dear reapers," she said. "This was not the time for the mustering of the reapers. We three would have rushed to confront the wraiths in any event, foolish as we are. No, this failure rests not with thee."

Despite her words, there grew within Gignoth a kernel of anger. Against baelreivers, and the Celestials that had seeded their profligate nature into the Cosmos. But against his own captain also, the presumed commander of the reapers by whose absence it seemed the mortis had failed in this first test of their conviction to honor the Vanguard whose names they bore.

* * *

There was a flash in Gethsemoni's eyes then, and her face went blank as she seemed to stare directly through them. When after a moment clarity returned she appeared deeply troubled. And then the air shimmered behind her as Ellianastis phased into view in an elaborate unfurling of what seemed multiple gowns draped from her shoulders, and the reapers looked on as both sisters went to stand beside the mortalborn. Then, as Gethsemoni leaned over his wretched form as if to whisper in his ear, Ellianastis looked toward at them, eyes gleaming hollow white with spirit fire, and wearing a crooked smile she beckoned them forth.

"Our mutual friend has found himself in something of a predicament," she said.

The reapers exchanged a look. "You speak of Demithyle?" asked Gignoth.

"Yes," said Ellianastis. "It's my fault, really. I'd thought him rather more resilient than all that. But then I hadn't guessed the Alltaker would choose to burden the poor thing with his own troubles, particularly now. He really ought to have gone out long ago, I think."

"So you know where he is?"

"Why, yes. He's in the library. My library, that is. Did no one tell you? Well, there he's been for quite some time now, by his reckoning. And if we don't manage to reach him very soon, I'm afraid he's likely to become a permanent resident, and a committed one, at that."

"Get us after him!" said Melthis.

"We cannot," said Gethsemoni. "'Tis a peril of the self he faces. And of the mind. He has made himself alone, and so from it he alone can withdraw."

"But how can that be?" asked Gignoth. "We mortis are made to be as one, to share every peril. Surely he does not wish to be alone."

"Basically," said Ellianastis, "he's swallowed up in his own head, a place which has now become so crowded he can't remember who he is, nor his reaper nature, nor much of anything, really. Rather hard to explain. But he's blocking everyone out, and we can't find him. But we think you can."

"Why in the bloaty cakk would he—"

"We will of course assist as is within our power," said Gignoth, holding up a calming hand to Melthis. "What must we do?"

"The bond between thy kind is as strong as each thy own governance of self," said Gethsemoni. "Reach for his presence. Through thee might we be allowed a tether toward his spirit's embroil."

"We have not been able to sense him, Queen Mother," said Gignoth, "though oft we have tried."

"That's because he doesn't exist in anything close to a shared moment with you," said Ellianastis. "In the time it'll take for me to finish this sentence, you see, for him, nearly a meir has elapsed."

"What?"

"As I said, it's all very difficult to explain. Suffice to say, time is of the essence." Ellianastis's form seemed momentarily to fall into flux, as if twin beings overlain, before snapping together again. "I will bridge your wisping link into the library's frame of reference," she said. "And then we shall cross our fingers, as the mortals like to say, and hope you'll be able to locate your bedeviled leader."

She looked down to the soulborn on the bier, his flesh decaying before their eyes.

"After that," she said, "everything will be down to this rather hardy fellow, here."

"Looks tae be lost tae the rot, he does," said Melthis.

"His soul perseveres," said Gethsemoni, "as is the mortal affinity. A fleeting present, the passing of which will see his existence erased by this cursed blight. Nor can we arrest this . . . befouled demise. He who was once the most trusted of my emissaries . . ." She looked at the reapers, her face now nearly whole, but for the scarred channels down her cheeks left by acid tears. "For the span of thy wisp," she said, "we will see this one's soul into the physicality of Demithyle, should thee discover him in his place of an uncounted time. There to cohabit it, until his final errand, to rouse thy captain from oblivion, is complete. A great mercy for one, salvation for the other, perhaps for us all."

She leaned over the soulborn, again as if to whisper into his ear. And in the empty space above him Ellianastis drew thin lines of etherea, burning a sigil into the air which she then coaxed down before it could fade, to settle into his brow.

Gethsemoni raised herself again. "Reach, children," she said. "Reach now for thy captain."

The reapers exchanged looks again, before both then withdrew into their minds, reaching through wisp as they had done innumerable times since Mortis Veth in search of Demithyle. Deeply they probed, receding beyond sense of the reaper corpus, seeking for the familiar color of Demithyle's aspect, until it seemed they spied blips through the aether of his spiritous entwine. And pursuing these in tandem they two felt a furtive grappling, thrown from what seemed an adipose gelatin of apathy and heedlessness—for an instant only, as if an echo of recognition falling upon them far removed from its voice of origin, entombed beyond their ken. But in that instant, through the aether of their awareness a pulse of blue-white light flitted forth, directed along that echo's path, before as quickly as it had gone it returned. And then, nothing.

"It is done."

* * *

They opened their eyes. Ellianastis was gone. Gethsemoni leaned over the soulborn again to kiss his brow a final time, the tattered ornamentation of her headdress brushing across his chest and face. Then she strode out of the mausoleum, beckoning for the reapers to follow as the fostermurden returned to refresh the mortal's bandages.

Outside they found her communing with another of the floating caretakers, who nodded sympathetically before drifting away to attend to the other afflicted set about the area. Then she turned to them, renewed kindness in her eyes.

"I thank thee again, dear reaper children," she said. "Yours has indeed become our body guardian." Stepping forward to Melthis, she said to her: "Thy voice in its throat screams out our rage and fervor." Then to Gignoth: "Thy foremost eye guides us through light and its absence."

She kissed them both and looked up at the soft gray canopy even as a portal opened for her there, and she leapt through it and was gone.

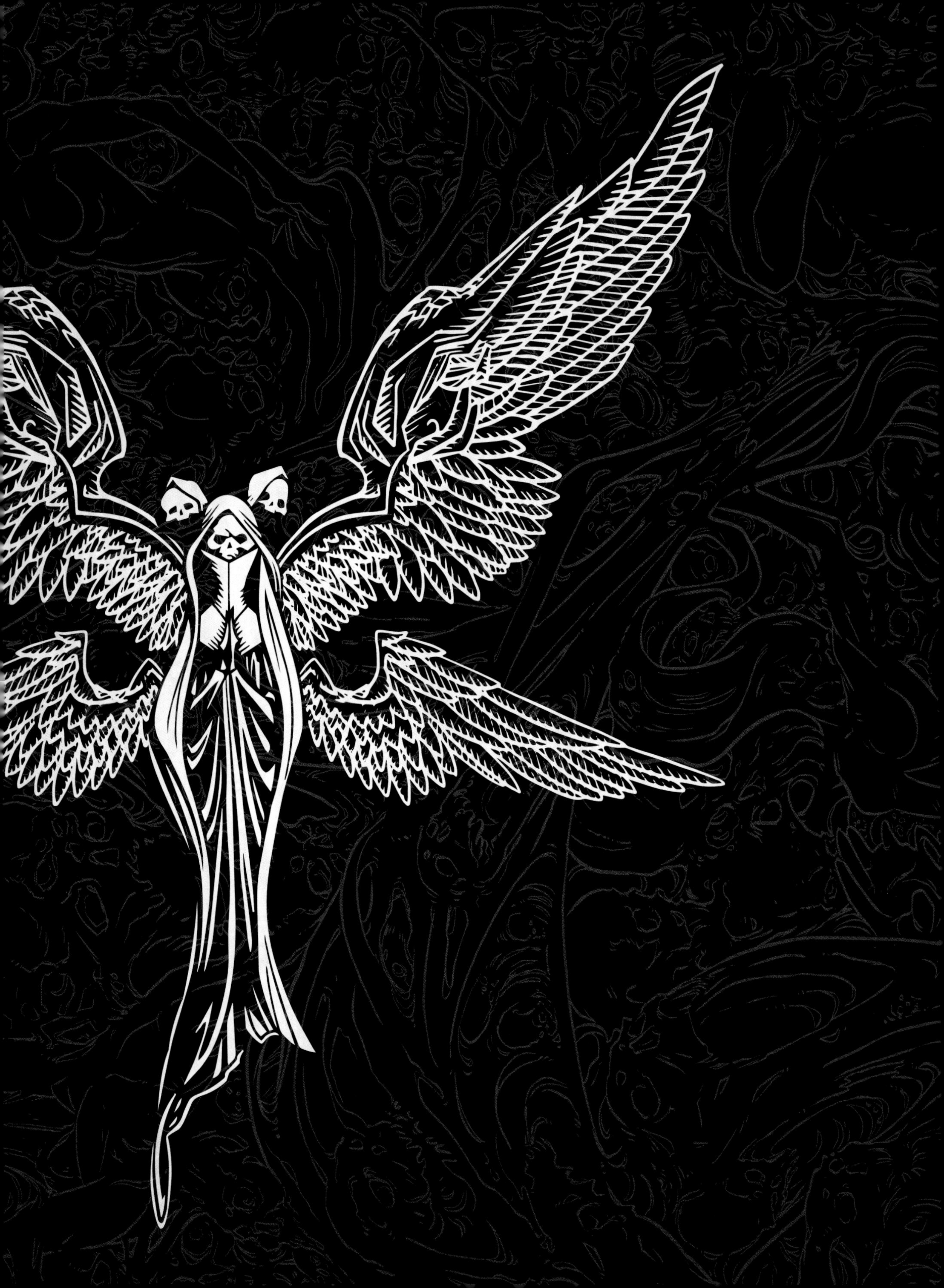

XXIX.
EGREGIN

Mine is the truth of teeth. The fear that is cut from our bellies. My heart clutched in a billow of steam. Her cries ring out like mourning birds. A long draught and my breath is stolen. The fire crawls quicker than I run. Naught but a whisper heard. The finest red mists above.

The slow blindness.

His reflection a horror.

Rot, the stench of time.

A blanketing soil.

Throat of stones. Iron given cold. Eyes insensate. Voice unknown. Speak it. Scream. Break. Take. Fall. Fall.

***

Through the realms and the veils between places went the Destroyer, spreading nothing before itself, leaving nothing in its wake.
From the ashes of the Underworld was it pursued by the Executioner, so given this name by Death, and with it the vigilance and power to unmake he who would become the Destroyer in the very instant of his succumbing to the Dreadsgrip.
Yet he failed and so in his failure was he named Herald to the Unmaking of All Things, his own doom to follow as it tore unhindered through an Ever Shrinking Cosmos. For in Destroying Death it had taken the Dirth

Forge and had drunk dry the well of Mortal Souls that was the power of all who might stand against it.

And so finding itself at last before the gates of the Celestials, it drove into their realm all of its viciousness and bloat, all of its desire for the unbeing of everything that had been created. Down fell their stars, down their Warring Heavens, down the Kingdoms of Hell and the effete children of both. Swallowed into entropy was everything they had been or would become, everywhere they had gone or would go, all they had touched or seen or dreamed. Not to be devoured—for devouring is an imbibement to sustenance of being—but to be dispelled of ever having been. To become nothing.

When the last fragment of Order had been shattered from the Cosmos the Destroyer turned next to the unraveling of Chaos, and Creation fell ever deeper into its final diminishing.

All the while tireless the Executioner pursued, many times striking into the Destroyer. But its cavitous void had swollen to a vastness of unbeing such that his blade could find naught but emptiness there. And finally when Nothing had supplanted Everything, the tiny sphere that was All of Existence rendered inert but for these final entities, the Destroyer turned at last to deliver its ravenousness upon its pursuer.

But bearing witness to the Executioner's weapon, a mighty wave-bladed flambard raised high above his helm, remembrance of its shape and luster glimmered within the vast Nothing of its being. And with this remembrance Memory itself, long ago removed from existence, returned once again as a fundament of the Cosmos.

Thus is the frailty of Nothing, that only by forgetting can it stand absolute. For the Destroyer's memory of the Sword became as a seed from which moments of its possession emerged into recollection, and therefore into being, and in that moment the Cosmos began once again to Grow.

And so the Destroyer shunned all remembrance of the Sword yet held aloft by the patient Executioner, denying the weapon's familiarity and promise of wholeness and completion in its furious staunching of Recreation, until looking upon the blade's weathered gleam all that remained was its lust for its steel to be rent as all other things had been rent.

But then from the Sword itself there came an Utterance, cast over motes of ephemeral reality lain through the nullifying dark to burrow into that which remained of the Destroyer's Mind:

We are Demithyle, wielder of Cryptmourne.
Never in possession of one shall the other be lost.

The Executioner lowered the Sword as in their midst of nothing the Destroyer was given pause.

By all that's holy, you've really gone and fucked yourself up in here, haven't you, Demithyle?

sayeth he.

And ensorceled by the dawning of understanding it could not deny, the Destroyer's eyes were once again raised to look upon the Sword.

Spoke the Executioner:

Waking up, are we? Good. Ellianastis said the sword would eventually do the trick, didn't she? Shouldn't leave such nice things lying round just wherever you like, though. Hard to say which is worse for it, your face or its dusty, lonesome ghost.

And thereupon by his invocation of the name of the Oracle, the Executioner witnessed the flood of substance into the emptiness at the Heartroot of the Destroyer, and raising once again the Sword he pierced into it and delivered into its remembrance all of the anguish and dismay he had collected in its wake, filling its void with the final moments of all entities whom it had sundered throughout the Cosmos, until at last its ravenousness was sated. And so at last was destroyed the Destroyer.

And yet this was not its ending.

For in the midst of its recoiling in agony came an explosion of reality rekindled, and in its grasping of this the mind of the entity who had become the Destroyer prevailed, and with the twin sparking of the emerald fires of his eyes he looked all around as the emptiness filled round him to become a verdant place, and music arose in his ears, unheard since long before all voices had been bled from Creation.

My, my. You should really see yourself. You look like one of these idiotic wiederlarts or whatever she called them.

The . . . wendlaersth?

Right. Windowlarps. That's you.

Who . . . ?

I am Egregin. No one you'd know. I've been sent into your head to try and dig it out of your ass. Up to now you've been too deep up it to hear a goddamn thing. Here's hoping I've finally gotten through to you.

I do not understand.

Look around. Notice anything different?

Music . . .

Ah, yes. Thought I'd add some atmosphere, something pleasant for a change. Watch a rampaging cosmic nightmare behemoth thing destroy every single other thing and you'll know what I mean. Water, a little foliage, some song. A few warmish lasses never hurt the scenery either, did they?

This is not a memory.

Well, the thing about the end times is, Demithyle, there usually aren't a whole lot of people left to remember it, are there? So, no. This is a dream, or a vision, whatever you'd like to call it. Can't do much with memory but sit in for the ride, which is how come I've been stuck in your head chasing after you for Diwia only knows how long, waiting for you to come up for air. Turns out all I had to do was weave us up an adequately terrible dream. Took a while to work out how to cram it into your memory pool, then even longer to get you to confront me, but here we are.

You are mortalkind. A soldier.

Once upon a time I was. You see me here like I was in life. A soldier surrounded by beautiful women, yes? From a place we called Aeolia. Nowhere you'd know. I met your father at the ass end of a far longer life than I deserved, after managing to avoid his attention from one losing catastrophe to another across I don't know how many battlefields. For reasons he never expressed to me, the Alltaker plucked me from the Forge to exist in his Underworld. And here we are. Two dead soldiers surrounded by beautiful women. Could be worse!

I . . . am a soldier also.

You were. If we can manage to dig you out from your own asshole, maybe you will be again. If we can't, well. I've a pretty good idea what we're all in for. We'll get to that. Either way, your sword seems happier already, so I guess that was a good place to start.

Cryptmourne. Where?

It's as much in your hand as I am in your head.

I do not understand.

Okay. That's okay, we can go slow. Your body is still in the library. If you can believe it. I figure it's been about, oh, five decades since I got here. Five decades of failure, then, of me trying to reach you. Add that to the five or so I figure you'd already spent in here and you won't be shocked by the kind of dusty, dry shit you're looking like these days. Yes. Not holding up so great, are we? You should see your face. I'd offer you a mirror, but I'm supposed to be getting you out of here, so. Better not risk you cracking up again, now that I'm finally getting somewhere. Anyway, lucky for you only about an hour has gone by outside is my guess. Enough time for the junk that was stuck floating in the air when I arrived to get halfway buried under the dusty dunes, but not enough for that empty bag to work its way across the valley there. This place is so weird.

Yes, and not long enough, I guess, for what's left of my body to decompose where it lies in the care of the bonnie fostermurden back in HushHyde.

So, as far as what's happened: Death had you digging through your memories for something. What, I don't know, never been able to it figure out. Just that he had you picking through all the ones that have something to do with him. In other words, all your memories of people dying. I guess he didn't figure you for someone who'd get thrown by that. But then, he didn't know you, did he, not as well as I do now. Any of this coming back?

The mark.

Oh, yes. Looking pretty flush by now, isn't it? Good for Death. We'll get to that. As for me, I was a humble emissary for our mutual Matron of the Flesh. She sent me to the fringes of the Underworld, where I got myself devoured by your friends the baelreivers. Some of them apparently got sent in advance of the horde to scout the city, and I got coughed back up when the sisters engaged and destroyed them. That's right. While you've been on your little jaunts, things have been happening. When Ellianastis learned you were becoming a wiederlarper in here, she and Gethsemoni sent me into your head to try and bring you back.

Why you?

Why me. Well. Gethsemoni . . . knew me. Enough, I think, to believe I might be able to reach you. Entreat your sense of duty, one soldier to another, see. I suspect it was also an act of mercy on her part, bless her. Like I said, I'm pretty much done in. Some sort of wasting infection from the baels. She figured this way at least I'd get to hang on to existence in the library a while longer, before oblivion took me forever. Can't blame them for not knowing I'd end up getting killed a thousand more times in your head. Anyway, it's been an experience. Better than nothing at all. Nobody comes back from oblivion. And it was nice to see home.

But I'm not going to last much longer, I can tell. Better get on with things. Farewell for now, fair lasses . . .

* * *

What do you see?

Fire.

Yes. Fire. A whole lot of it. That's Illverness, or it was. See all those disgusting things devouring the mourners running out from Curio Cryptus there? Those things, they used to be reapers. Your reapers.

No.

Yes. Turns out, once one of you gets swallowed up by the dreadsgrip, it doesn't take much for the rest to follow. Especially if he's the great undead hope. I'm no expert, but from what I can tell, that's pretty much what we're looking at. What you've set them up for, that is. Want to see what you've been up to in the meantime?

. . .

I'll take that as a no. Too late. Here you are, once the apparent Reaper Protector General of the Underworld. Now . . . a dirty, waify, big-eyed wurderlurtz mindlessly devouring books. Oh, what's that? It's turning into a hideous monster? And now the library is burning too? What a shame . . . there goes all of everything. Do you hear the screams? Well. Everything'll be nice and quiet once your new generation of baelreivers takes control of the Forge. They'll drink the Mortal Realm dry, starve out the Celestials, chew up what's left of the Underworld and everyone in it . . .

No . . .

That is, unless you end up—oh, there you go. Now you've gobbled up Death himself. And there go all your monster soldierkin next. And according to the lore you've forced every which way down my throat, next is unleashed the Destroyer to ravage the Cosmos. Nicely done, Ser Winderlertz.

Why show this?

Because this is the path you're on, as far as I see it. Even if I succeed in waking you up, who's to say you won't just start in all over again? And also because you've dragged me through some pretty hideous shit over the last handful of decades and it's only fair. But Gethsemoni said I had to get you out, one way or another. So. Tell me. How would you describe your time wallowing in all your memories? What would you say you got out of all that?

. . . Deaths without end.

Right. Don't get me wrong, being able to slip into all those lives like you do would be . . . seductive. I get it. Definitely some ups and downs. And good on you, trying to look yourself in the eye, see what you're made of. What am I meant to be? A warrior? A pawn? A leader? A sacrifice? But here you go through a century of deaths without end, as you say, and you figure, that's it. I'm made in my father's image. Death is what I'm about. Next thing you know, look out, Cosmos. Here comes the Destroyer.

But hey. Trust the man who's been hanging around in your head for the last half century. You're made of far more interesting stuff than all that. More to the point: I fought underneath a lot of bad people in my life. Got ordered to do a lot of . . . awful things. All I can say is, good, bad, my actions made me. My choices. Once I figured that out, I didn't have to look any further than my own hands to know what I was.

Sorry. Sorry for the dark. Stay with me. My head is . . . leaking. Something.

Listen.

I've been up to some . . . sifting of my own.

Through your memories. Your real memories.

Even before your eyes lit up, you were trying to work out . . . what you were made to be, to do. What your place in all this was supposed to be. What they intended. Listen. What does it tell you, that you can even wonder? If they'd wanted a puppet, they'd not've made an entity. And I'm here to tell you. Beyond that, there is nothing. No greater intent for the Cosmos. Just love and lust and . . . stars and whatever holds our feet to the ground. Fate is for slippery soothsayers who don't want to bother with cause and effect. Never mind living up to whatever you think their purpose for you was, Demithyle. Sure, they created you. But all you are now, you created yourself.

I created my self.

Yes. Couldn't have said it better. How I see it, anyway. I don't know, I'm . . . just a soldier. Maybe your mind got sparked up from a pool of other people's lives, but it's every choice you've made since that makes you Demithyle.

I . . . am Demithyle.

Ah, there he is. Alright. Good. Don't you every forget that again, or I will find you and kick it back into your head. You want to know . . . what you were made to be, my friend? The answer's simple: you were made to be. The sooner you get on with that, the closer you'll be to whatever truth . . . you thought you'd find in this place. So. Fuck the mark, fuck the library, and fuck the Alltaker. One cosmic entity of . . . violence and destruction is more than enough. He can bear his burdens on his own. Get yourself out of this place, give him his trophy, and . . . don't look back. Because if you do, in the end this darkness is all . . . that'll be left.

Not the end.

No?

No. I will not allow this to happen.

Good. Very good. Yes.

Thank you, Egregin. Your words have been necessary and wise.

Well. I don't know about all . . . that. I'm not even standing here. Just in your head. And not for much . . . longer at that.

Where is Cryptmourne? I wish to be returned to my sword.

It's in your hand. All you have to do is . . . wake up. Before you do, I have a . . . request. You owe me. Listen. Take all that savagery you've churned up. Over the last century of death and dying. Give it to the baelreivers. Bring back some of that Destroyer, and . . . shove it up their asses. I've . . . seen through their eyes, Demithyle. They are vicious. Beyond what you might think. It has to be . . . met in kind. And, they deserve to suffer. For what they did to me and . . . my friends. Make them pay. I'll take it as a kindness. Fuck them up.

You have my word, Egregin. From one soldier to another. The injuries they have brought upon you and yours will be returned to them many times over.

Okay. Good. Thanks, Demithyle. I'm thinking . . . I'm thinking we're about done here. Out of time, anyway. You don't want to see what they left me with. Not expecting to exist much longer. One last thing, though. A gift. Sorry. It'll mean one last swim . . . into someone else's past. But I want you to see it. To have it. It's something I've . . . kept with me. You'll see. Please. Wear it well. Maybe come and find me after, just the same. That is, if you don't . . . turn back into an idiot.

* * *

I stand alone in a room empty but for a single shadow door hovering against the wall in its absence of light. The sword is in my hand. Cryptmourne. I feel its presence even before I recognize the weight of it. When I raise it before me I hear in its voice our shared satiation as it speaks my name as by our rejoining it shuns off the dust and corrosion of neglect from guard to tip along the waves of its blade, so that the spiritlight from my eye stares back into me from deep within its newly polished steel as if to reaffirm our conviction that never again shall we be so parted.

* * *

I look at the mark on my hand. It is replete with a full circle of symbols, many of which have overwritten or combined with others to present glyphs of greater, more inscrutable depth. They seem to move and alter even as I ponder the cost of their acquisition.

I let the hand fall. My father will receive his enigma. I will not look upon it again.

* * *

I step through the shadow door to the rushing dark chasm that is the infinite library. I wish to call for the airy elemental, to command it to bring me to any door that will take me directly from this place. But there is yet a thing to recover. A gift.

Of all the rooms throughout, only one now is captured in my awareness. When I find it I step through to find my self in a long wooden shack. Its walls on both sides are lined with small beds of animal skin, and strewn about each are small trinkets. Carven beasts with wheels affixed to their feet. Dolls of straw and canvas. Small but sturdy swords of oiled wood, dented and worn.

At the end of one row there is a bed larger than the others. I am drawn to a wooden box that is set upon a small table beside it. Its sides are painted to depict mortal soldiers standing at attention. Though none bear a weapon each holds forth a large shield, as though to create a guardian wall around the perimeter of the box.

Inside is a single coin of pressed gold. It is scarred by many cuts and scratches and its face is long since faded, but its origin is marked by the Aeolic name *Boeotia*.

Its opposite side is worn nearly flat but for a short inscription carefully scratched into the gold. It reads:

I, GUARDIAN.

When I read this aloud there is a sound of ocean waves, and the room falls away as I find my self set upon a moss-covered stone on a grassy rise overlooking the shore of an unknown sea.

> The waves lap unceasingly, ignorant of us. Our craft, beached by the outflowing of the tide, lists against them as if wishing to press farther ashore. The slavers I killed far out at sea that their bodies would be claimed by its depths and give no mark of our passing, throats cut in the night while the children slept below. Here even the heavens are ignorant of us, and these winds I have made my allies. They will not betray the voices of these children, or even carry them beyond my reckoning.
>
> They run now through the sand and surf, even

as the sun falls low behind me. Soon I will bring them inland, build a fire. But there is yet time. Let them play. The stars will suffice as shelter tonight. For now I wish to listen to the water and the sound of their laughter. Perhaps come the morn I will take the youths to scout for food and water. I will need to teach them hunting. I will need to teach them many things.

No one will ever find us here. None will ever possess these creatures or count them among their wares. They who are innocents, in whose inquisitive eyes the light of all of creation resides. Whose quiet dreams must drive the fates.

No one will ever hurt them again.
This is their home now. Our home.
I am their guardian and their guide.
I will kill anything that threatens them.
I am Demithyle.

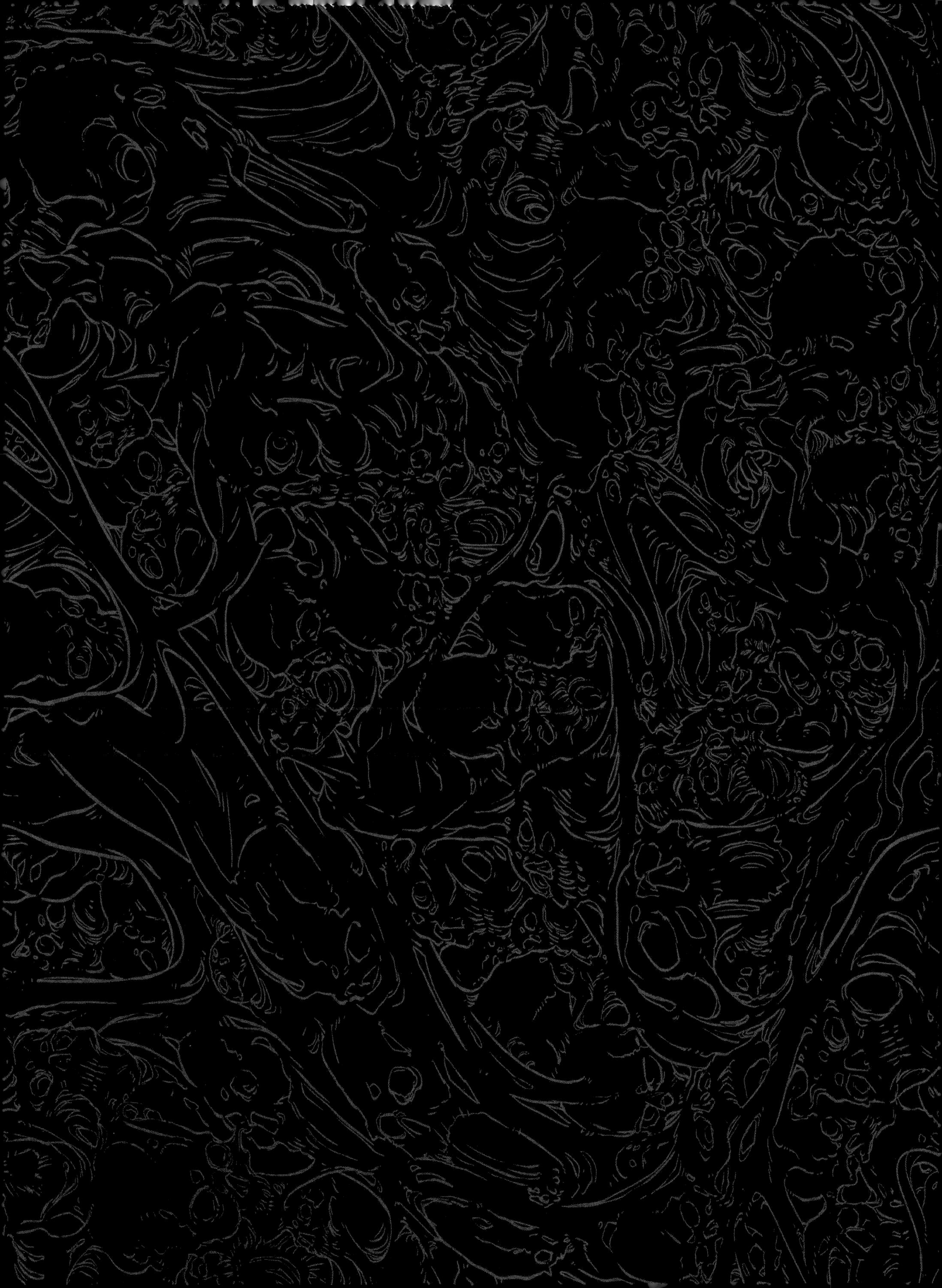

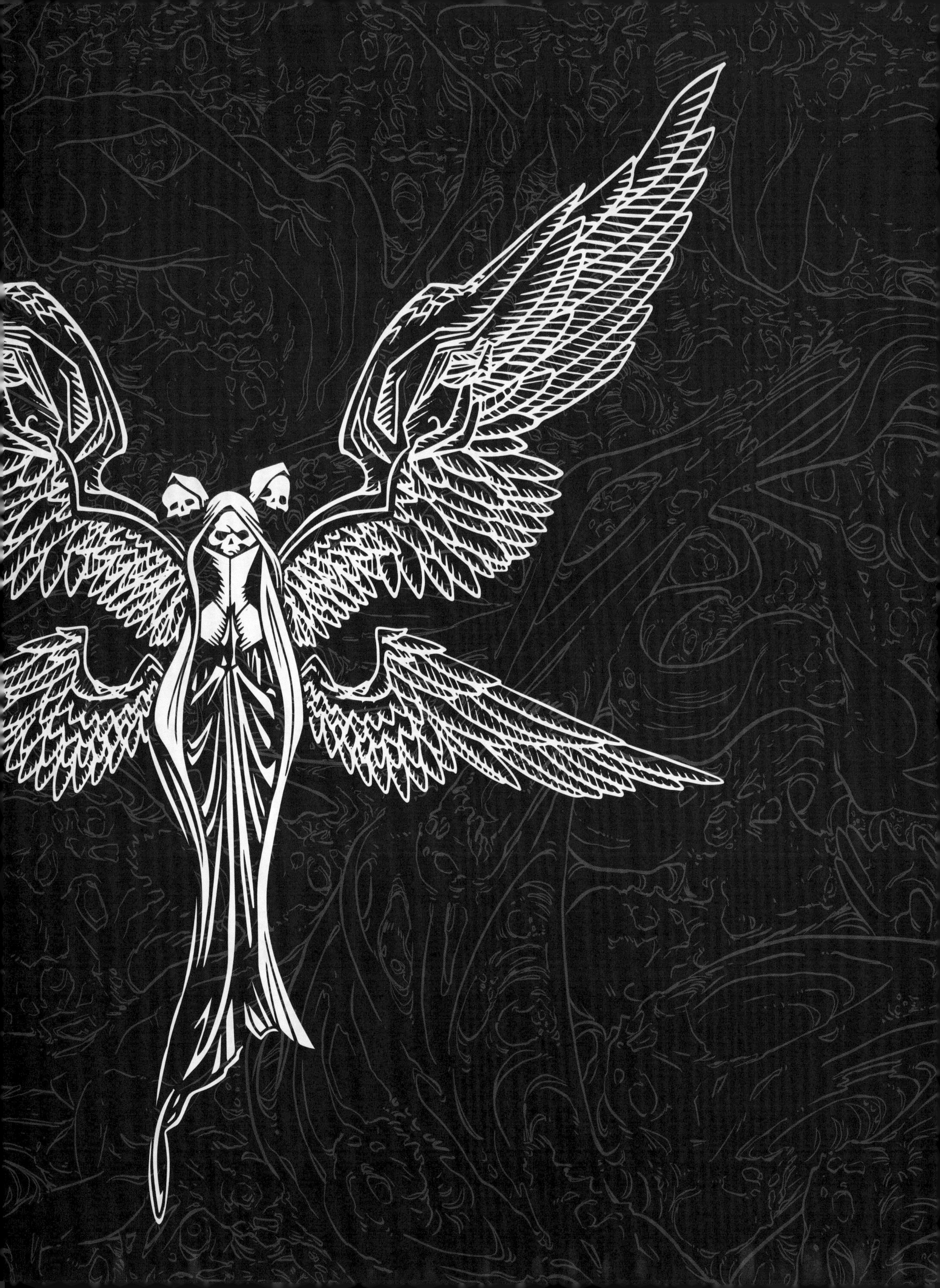

XXX.
RETURN

"Fuck me living."

Gignoth could only nod in agreement as they both stared up through the canopy, watching the hole reseal itself behind Gethsemoni's retreating figure. Fuck me living, indeed.

And then they felt him.

Steeling themselves, the two reaper cibori passed through the threshold of the enclosure and crossed the courtyards, and following the pathway out from the cathedral to the main gate they were relieved to find the waves of black nausea gradually abated. And looking down the winding, bramblestrewn inroute to HushHyde they then saw a hooded rider emerge from a wiry rotroot underpass, drafts of wind billowing his cloak over his strange six-legged steed.

He rode tall at a steady gait, his bearing contemplative and grim until seeing the reapers at the top of the hill he held aloft his three right-side arms in salute, and Melthis and Gignoth knew then that Demithyle had returned to them at last.

To their eyes he appeared oddly weathered, more as if by age than action, but even at a distance his orbits burned with an infiltrating soulfire gaze. Nearing the gate he dismounted and walked to them directly, leaving his strange mount to follow slowly behind him, its eyes glowing orange as it huffed short breaths of blue mist from its long skelliform muzzle.

Demithyle gave them a deep bow in acknowledgment of their long-delayed reunion, then pulled back his hood, revealing a craggy, naked skull.

"Gignoth. Melthis."

"Demithyle," said Gignoth.

"Our grim commandant, returned tae the fold, like," said Melthis. "Finished yer respite, have ye?"

"By the shiver of winter, yes, I hope it is so," said Demithyle. He clutched them both by the shoulder then, and gave each in turn a solemn nod. "You have my great thanks for your part in bringing me." Then he stepped back a pace, as if to assess their condition. "You both appear intact."

"As is possible," said Gignoth. "Barring today, the meirs have been uneventful."

"The rest of the knights?"

"Similarly intact, save a few minor bits. We left them watching the spectacle beyond the horizon to come here. They await us in Calvum Harrows."

The two cibori were uncertain whether—and quite how—to devise a full report on the reaper doings in the near fortmeir since his disappearance. Did he know of the Scions' encounter with the baels? Did he wish the reapers to muster? Had he even been made aware of his station as leader of their army?

But then, as if reading their impulse, Demithyle's aspect arrived through wisp, and with a holistic awareness of their corpus more complete than either had felt since Mortis Veth immediately they unveiled a swell of images to wash over him. These he probed with great thirst, yet of his own experiences they were given very little, as if his own memories lay locked behind a bramble shell of alien complexity such as to require time and diligence to unravel.

"So," said Demithyle, at last. "You are principal among the lieutenant cibori of the mortis. And I am to be your captain, to lead our defense against the horde."

"By Xiall's wisdom and decree, yes," said Gignoth, bearing out his blade in salute. "A corpus command well attained, at that, my friend."

"Aye, ye didn't see any of us in there pebbling a naefukkin behemoth," said Melthis, punctuating a salute of her own with a fist against Demithyle's shoulder.

Demithyle gave them a nod, seeming somehow troubled. "In his assessment of our corpus, it seems, Torbrenth was correct," he said, more to himself than they.

"Yes, well," said Gignoth, uncertain of his meaning. "He also was named among the cibori by Xiall. Though she has certainly brooked no restraint in exacting casual reciprocity against some impertinence he has thus far seen fit to keep to himself," he added.

"Aye, among other things, like," interjected Melthis.

"Five in all are we," said Gignoth. "He and we two, and Sithik and Thrael."

"And beneath you?"

"Stanchions of twenty or so, each. The flighted among us under Sithik's banner."

Demithyle seemed to consider that.

"Well," he said after a moment. "I have come to HushHyde in search of they two of my kin who first stood with me against the relentless machine of our first crucible, and who aided in the guidance of my return. And I have found them, in full hardiness and ferocity. That is enough, for now."

"Well, fer yer own part ye look like shriveled skattik," said Melthis. "What in phalkfuk's happened tae yer armor?"

Demithyle glanced down at himself, then looked at each of them, as if seeing the dark plates beneath their cloaks for the first time.

"It . . . ," he began. "It became necessary to part with it, long ago. So long ago, now, I had forgotten the weight of it."

"Oh aye," said Melthis, "they tried tae explain that, like. Yer what then, one of the ancients now?"

"That will take more effort to convey than a mere passing exchange through wisp might afford, I am afraid."

"Well. Good luck tae ye, Xiall's like tae part yer head from the rest of ye when she hears ye've left yer skint cracked open tae the breeze, like."

"Will you tell her?"

There was a huff behind Demithyle, and he turned as Ycnaf sidled up to stand at his shoulder. He patted her broad neck with his hand, and she bowed as the reapers did the same, both as much captured by the dread intensity of her skelliform bearing as by the potent arcane aura about her. She rose again to height and sputtered a billow of ethereaic fume, through which she gazed at the reapers with sapphire-orange, crystalline eyes set deep within her equine orbital hollows.

"She is Ycnaf, of the wyspstride realm," said Demithyle. "She expresses a sentiment of honor to be among the kin of her rootmate."

"Rootmate, eh?"

"This you will know yourselves, soon enough," said Demithyle. He looked up at the fragmented summit of HushHyde's high cathedral tower, beyond which the glow of the Dirth Forge diffused through the skymist of the darkmeir. The tower's stained glass portraiture had altered once

more, showing now a ring of prismatic shards, between which galloped an unbroken ring of crystalline steeds.

"Aye, welcome to Illverness," said Melthis.

"Indeed," said Demithyle. And then, quietly: "At long last, I have come home."

The cibori only nodded, allowing their captain the moment, feeling similarly requited even as they marveled at his weathered appearance. They saw for the first time then the tiny glyphs branded all along the charred flesh of his smallest limb—hundreds of them in a seeming spiral outward from the palm of its diminutive hand, each throbbing separately with dim blue light as if cast from luminous bones beneath.

And then with that hand Demithyle reached into his tattered cloak to retrieve what appeared to be a small golden coin, worn and scarred with age, which he stared at for an elongated beat before closing his fist over it, and turning to his cibori, he said:

"There is another here, upon whom in fact I hastened my return to call. The soulborn. He is yet extant?"

The two cibori exchanged a glance. "Aye, last we saw him," said Melthis. "Only just before you got here, like."

"Take me to him."

* * *

No sooner had the three reapers entered the mausoleum than did one of the fostermurden move to usher them from it, nudging them with an insistent clutch of tendrils, her ghostly expression polite but firm as she directed them to leave. But Demithyle began silently to commune with her, gesturing subtly toward the soulborn where he lay upon his bier until finally the spectral caretaker nodded gravely and made way.

The blight had crept upward over his torso and into the gray, leathery flesh of his throat, such that it seemed unlikely his head would remain attached for long. The remains of his torso had been wrapped to a tapered point, for he had rotted nearly half away, and already the putrid seepage had begun to burn through the bandages.

"Not like tae wake, that one," said Melthis.

Gignoth shook his head. "Let us hope he does not."

But then he did.

Stirring at the sound of their voices, his eyes slowly opened, clouded and obviously wracked with pain as they scanned the reapers who stood over him. The fostermurden leaned her spectral aspect forward and parted her lips as if to blow a long breath upon him, and there came a gentle mist from within her ferine skullform that wafted out to settle over his tormented form. And in that moment a measure of his pain seemed to subside, and with a final nod to Demithyle the fostermurden turned and drifted away to attend to others of the afflicted.

Demithyle leaned further over the soulborn, who looked up at him with markedly clearer eyes.

"So," he said, his voice phased and distant. "You made it out. Good for you. Good for you."

"Egregin, my friend."

Egregin looked past him at the cibori, who stood by, rendered speechless by the strangeness of the event unfolding before them.

Straightening, Demithyle stepped aside to give him a clearer view of them. "These are my comrades," he said.

"I know. I was in . . . your head. Remember? For so strange a . . . time. So long a time."

"I remember," said Demithyle.

"And here. I am. After all." He looked at Demithyle. "It pleases me," he said. "To look upon you. To speak . . . to you. Here. With my own voice. You should be . . . proud. Even lost, you kept . . . one hand. Ready. To take mine. To grasp . . . your sword. To reach out, for your . . . fellows. Good for you. I thought that, then. Good for you."

He turned his half-dissolved face away then, and stared at the ceiling of the mausoleum.

"You have my gratitude, Egregin," said Demithyle. "Now and always."

Egregin twisted then, as if against a sudden spasm of pain. But he looked again to Demithyle and smiled. "No," he said. "You were always going. To make it."

"Please. I am sorry, my friend," said Demithyle, placing a hand on Egregin's thin shoulder. "The Underworld must ask still more of you."

He closed his eyes. "I know. What you would . . . ask."

"You were taken by the blightwraiths," said Demithyle, "brought into their blight. You know them as they are now, as do none other yet extant and aware, even the Three. What can you tell us of their minds?"

A panic leapt into Egregin's face, and though he quickly swallowed it there remained in him a mark of distance and renewed pain, and when he opened his eyes again it was to look upon the two reaper cibori.

"Do you know," he said to them, "I heard everything. The Queen Mother . . . said. About us . . . the great worth . . . of mortals. I am grateful. To her, to them. They gave me more . . . time. A final . . . purpose. It was . . . interesting."

He paused a long while, twitching against still more spasms of pain. Yet he did not break gaze from the cibori.

"But listen to me," he continued. "I lived . . . among mortals. For more . . . than a lifetime. I witnessed them. Inflict every sort . . . of pain. Upon themselves. Suffering, at every . . . scale. Bound only . . . by imagination. I ask. How much is worth. The memory. Of the rape. Of a child? The slaughter. Of her village? Of forcing her. To murder . . . her parents? We are creators. Oh yes. Of countless . . . devices. To stay Death. For as long, as . . . possible. Not for love of life. For amusement of . . . torture. Screams. Blood to stain . . . the sea. Enough, to fill . . . the Heavens . . . and Hells . . . alike. Let me tell you, reapers. If . . . the Mortal Realm. Is supposed to be. The pillar . . . of creation. Then, my . . . friends. Creation . . . is fucked."

* * *

There was a silence then. Egregin's gaze lingered on Melthis and Gignoth, perhaps reading that they did not understand his words. No reaper save Demithyle had ever witnessed so macabre and heartless an image as these that this soulborn lamented. To the cibori, it seemed a cruelty to ask this being to visit again the experience that had so ravaged him. But their commander had been strangely withholding of his thoughts, and whether he felt this, they could not discern.

"There is always more, Egregin," said Demithyle. He held up the golden coin the cibori had seen earlier and showed it to him. "That is what you told me, remember?" he said, gently pressing the coin into the mortal's blight-ridden hand. "I was there on the far shore. I saw what you did for them. We are not the only protectors, my friend. There are always more."

Egregin smiled then as he coughed through the flapping remnants of his throat.

"Gleaming diamonds . . . in the rough . . . we are, eh?"

"Please, Egregin," said Demithyle. "What of the horde? We must know."

But the soulborn turned away.

"It was . . . a horror," he said. "No being. Could . . . describe it. I am sorry, Demithyle."

Demithyle stood, frustrated, at a loss.

"Maybe it's better not tae have such poison cakk swimming in our heads, like," said Melthis.

But then the reaper commander cocked his head as if to stow a thought, and in that moment Ycnaf sputtered into being before them in a misty cloud of etherea. The two locked eyes for a time, and then Demithyle leaned in again over the wretched, tormented soulborn.

"Then let us take it from you," he said, softly.

Egregin turned back to meet his eyes.

"Your spirit and mine are yet intertwined," Demithyle said. "Ycnaf can use our root to draw out from you the memory of this experience, if you wish. We will take it into ourselves, and you will be free of it. Will you allow us to enter your mind, as you did mine, my old friend?"

Egregin let out a papery, whistling laugh.

"You don't. Need to ask. Me twice," he said, wincing against the pain of the act. "Do it."

* * *

They felt their anger the wound the betrayal it burned within them fed them drove the fang the memory of the father and the mother and the brother and the sister and the self the sick and foul rejected self . . .

They read the hunger they were the hunger the world entire a violet crystal composition of ethearic ghosts each a fume of fear they drank the craving of it the glee of overtaking they who fled and fell who could not break free the glee of their unmaking lost erased the taking from creation one more who should have never been . . .

One by chaos driven one they were the lightning conjured by infinities of dust to capture sightless vapors far beyond the reach of mind of reason their lust to feed there was no meeting no defense against the frantic whim and when they massed the art of it the shaping of the breath of it the curl of ssskin they flayed to lay against their own an organ givennn then be taken and thennn given and then taken and then given and then takennn . . .

* * *

The reapers released their hold on one another, all but collapsing to the ground. Ycnaf shied away, and following a wordless look at a wobbly

Demithyle she departed to wait for them beyond the threshold of the mausoleum.

"Priss-tamped mother of necrofuk," said Melthis, as all three reapers staggered back from the bier, trying to shake their heads free of the lingering trauma.

"You didn't say anything about actually becoming a wraith," said Gignoth.

"I did not anticipate that," said Demithyle.

"Well, whatever we might've got out of that, I'm crakked if I know."

Returning to the bier, they looked upon the unconscious soulborn whose tortured spirit they had just imbibed. The smoldering violaceous blight had traveled well into his head; one eye and much of his face had been devoured by it. It was clear that his existence would come to an end any moment.

As they looked upon this destruction wrought on his form, it seemed the perfect summation of the fury, lust, and sadism of the baelreivers they had experienced. But even as they recoiled from these things that had been brought into their minds, there was something else, a yearning hollowness that was incongruent with all that they had previously known of their enemy, like a profound unvoiced despair over their fates.

They stared for what seemed a long while, as if waiting for a spell to be broken, until finally Demithyle spoke.

"This was a great boon," he said.

The cibori looked at their commander with surprise, at a loss for his meaning. But he only continued to stare down at the bier.

"We have been given an intimacy of their minds," he said. "We know that there are among them individuals who retain a semblance of mind to direct the others. Probably the one hundred who by the corruption of their names created the others. We know that though they behave reactively as a swarm, these must control the overall shape of the horde. It is likely that the destruction of these would sow disarray among the whole, at least temporarily, and that they would therefore be shielded against targeted attack by the movements of the main body of baels surrounding them."

Demithyle stepped forward to lean over the bier.

"Greater than this," he said, laying a hand on Egregin's shoulder, "we know their desire. We know their hunger. We know that whatever mind they possess, even the greater of them can not deny their thirst for etherea. We have felt the ravenousness of their being, we have seen it eclipse the reach of their diluted minds. It is this knowing above all that we will bring against them."

The cibori kept their silence, moved by the solemnity and portent of the moment as they contemplated the insight of their commander. And then Egregin stirred, as if he too had felt the weight of it. They looked at him and saw that though he was yet in great pain his eyes conveyed a greater peace than they had seen in him. He stared through them, and slowly he presented the withered hand that held the scarred, golden coin that Demithyle had returned to him.

"Carry it," he said. "Be . . . victorious. Then find . . . a place for it. For all . . . of them."

He looked at Melthis and Gignoth then, meeting their eyes directly each in turn, before doing the same with Demithyle.

"May your own . . . totems . . . wear . . . none . . . . . . of . . . . . . your . . . . regrets . . ."

Demithyle accepted the coin and looking down at what remained of Egregin he gave him a final, soldierly nod.

"Thank you for finding me," he said.

All pain fled from Egregin's face. His grayness of form folded into itself like the drying of a leaf and, as if in a final cleansing of the blight that had destroyed him, he diminished to dust that blew gently away from the bier.

The fostermurden returned then, her spectral maiden presenting them with a compassionate visage. Then it cast its gaze upward, as if to the sky.

"Look for him in the darkmeir . . . ," she said. "Shreds of him will reconvene in light, then to travel skyward, ever still to give . . . as with all things here . . . ever to add to the myriad mysteries of our realm . . . if you knew him well, you will find him there . . ."

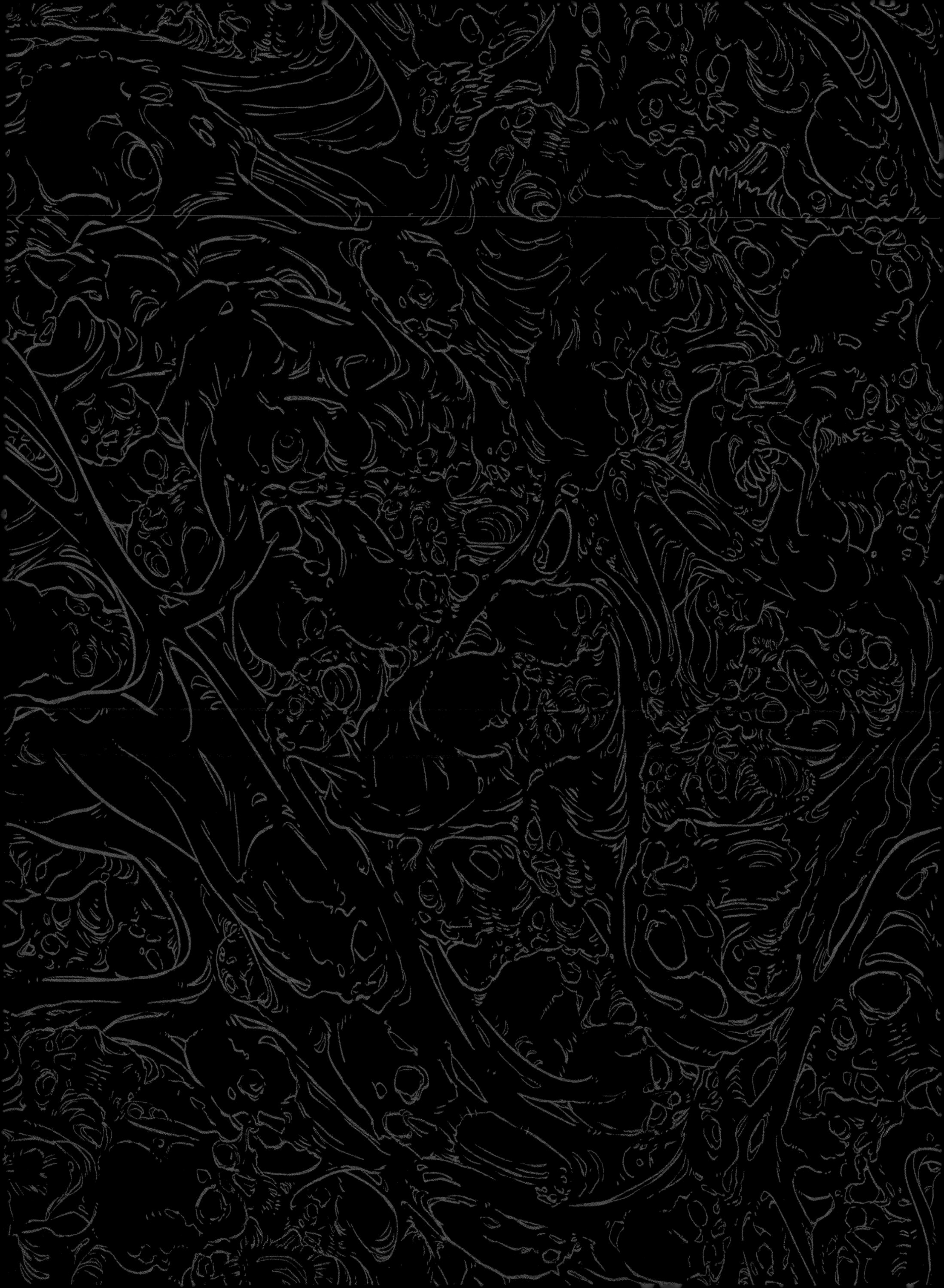

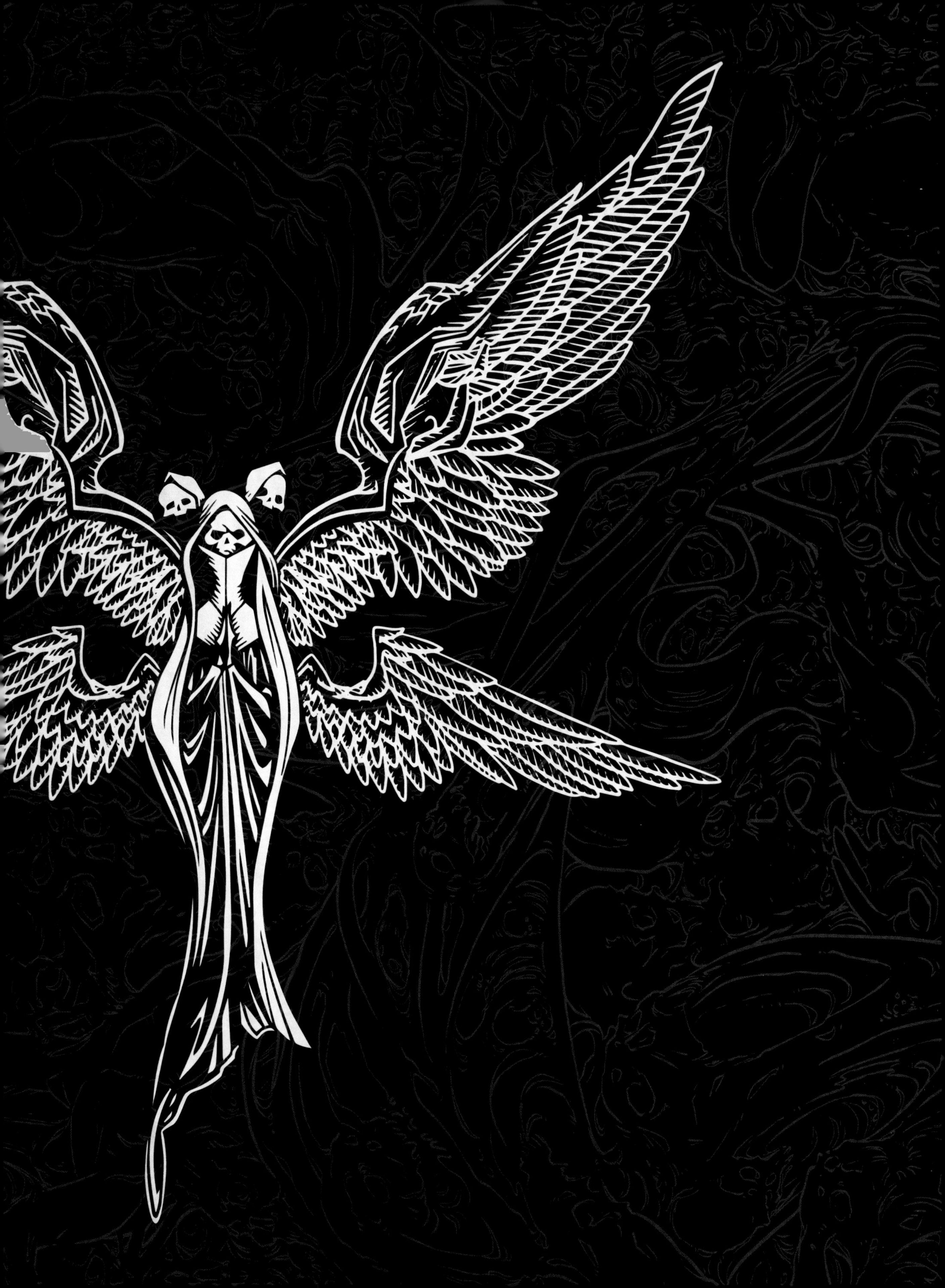

XXXI.
XIALL

Shall I describe it for you, Xiall? Our callow Vanguard made once again one hundred in this the very chamber of their awakening. Their thousand thousand slivers of soul aswirl bodiless about this twisted menhir, new-emblazoned by their inviolable names. Thereupon to witness the conjoining of their minds, fierce, restless, soaked heavy by what richness of being they had gathered into themselves: glories, boredoms, follies, enlightenments; all that they wished to share drunk from their communal cup as they lay rapt by oneness purer than any we had designed them to enjoy. 'Twas a recommuning dearly to be envied, my daughter.

I am certain it was enrapturing indeed, Alltaker. Where is Demithyle? He was to await my arrival here when they had finished all of that.

Interesting. I should have thought you would bear witness to their reunion.

Where, Alltaker?

I sent him away.

Why?

Two centuries of existence in the library has rendered Demithyle's physicality rather the worse for wear. He has been taken by the shroudreive to the flesh mines at Cryptus Akhor. Why do you sneer?

I have better things to do than chase him into Gethsemoni's brothel.

'Tis our paucity of time that finds him there. The shroudreive would have him lain out for ritual inscription. The mists of the fleshbaths will suffice.

If he does not find himself unsoldiered by carnality.

The enfleshing will of course be measured for utility, Xiall. I am certain its invigorating effects will be trivial.

I see their biers are reset. Gethsemoni, no doubt. Why the reapers should wish to convene in this sterile atrium I can not imagine.

'Twas Demithyle's wish. To see them as he had first laid eyes on them, now that he is at last returned to them.

Sentiment.

Logic delivers us to finite shores, Xiall.

The baels do not suffer sentiment, Alltaker. Nor do they tarry. The horde advances even now, no more than two meirs' ride from the gate. We must discuss final preparations.

It is in hand. Demithyle intends to draw them to the Blackmeir Tower. He is certain they will be unable to resist the essence of their fallen, should we gather it forth from the city. We will await its accumulation by our defenses until its potency there would eclipse even that of the Forge.

He is certain of this, is he?

He and two of his cibori have borne witness to their minds. They know them as do none other yet extant.

So I have heard. And quite how did he manage such a feat of vision?

Does it matter, Xiall? He is every bit the captain we had hoped would arise among them, and more. Through the whole of his journeys he hath kept his duty as if the heart of him. And by them he is become as formidable of sight and mind as of sword. 'Tis a boon, for our warrior progeny and for us all, my daughter.

We are lucky to have him back at all. Or did you imagine sending him on a bottomless plunge into own head would be without risk?

We exist in an era in which there are risks to every action, Xiall. The mark was a powerful discovery, and well timed. No less, Demithyle's revelation of the Vanguard's missive on the very mournmeir of his birth. 'Twas necessary to learn the implications of both, beyond mere intimation of some unknown thing hidden in the Mortal Realm, where I dare not tread lightly.

Perhaps the risks were greater than you describe, Alltaker. Setting aside the perils of that faint-infested dungeon, why commit the one commander of all our defensive forces? I question your timing.

He is able to move into the past to relive the memories he carries. To pass at will through time and space. Can you do this? Even Ellianastis can not, nor can the shroudreive determine even how 'tis possible. Imparting to him the mark meant he would bring it with him into whatever spectral reflection was captured by the library by each memory of the Mortal Realm he inhabited. There also would be echoes of those arcane forces that first drew me to the discovery of the mark, and awakened by its presence might be given to further unraveling this mystery that has plagued me for many aeons. 'Twas an opportunity I could not ignore. Even so, I have admitted this as an error in judgment. I did not know my own destructive influence would be so imprinted upon the mark, nor the effect of this on Demithyle's hold upon his self. Indeed, I conveyed as much to him in his return of it to me. Certainly he was as glad to be rid of it as he was eager to depart his father's proximity. A valuable lesson that I assure you was as well learned as earned.

That does not alter the reality that, but for forces beyond even your ken, all would have been lost.

Fair to say. No less, your own secret machinations.

What?

We are fortunate the wyspstrides know no malice, Xiall, else Demithyle might yet be awander through the labyrinth.

Ah. Told you, then, did it?

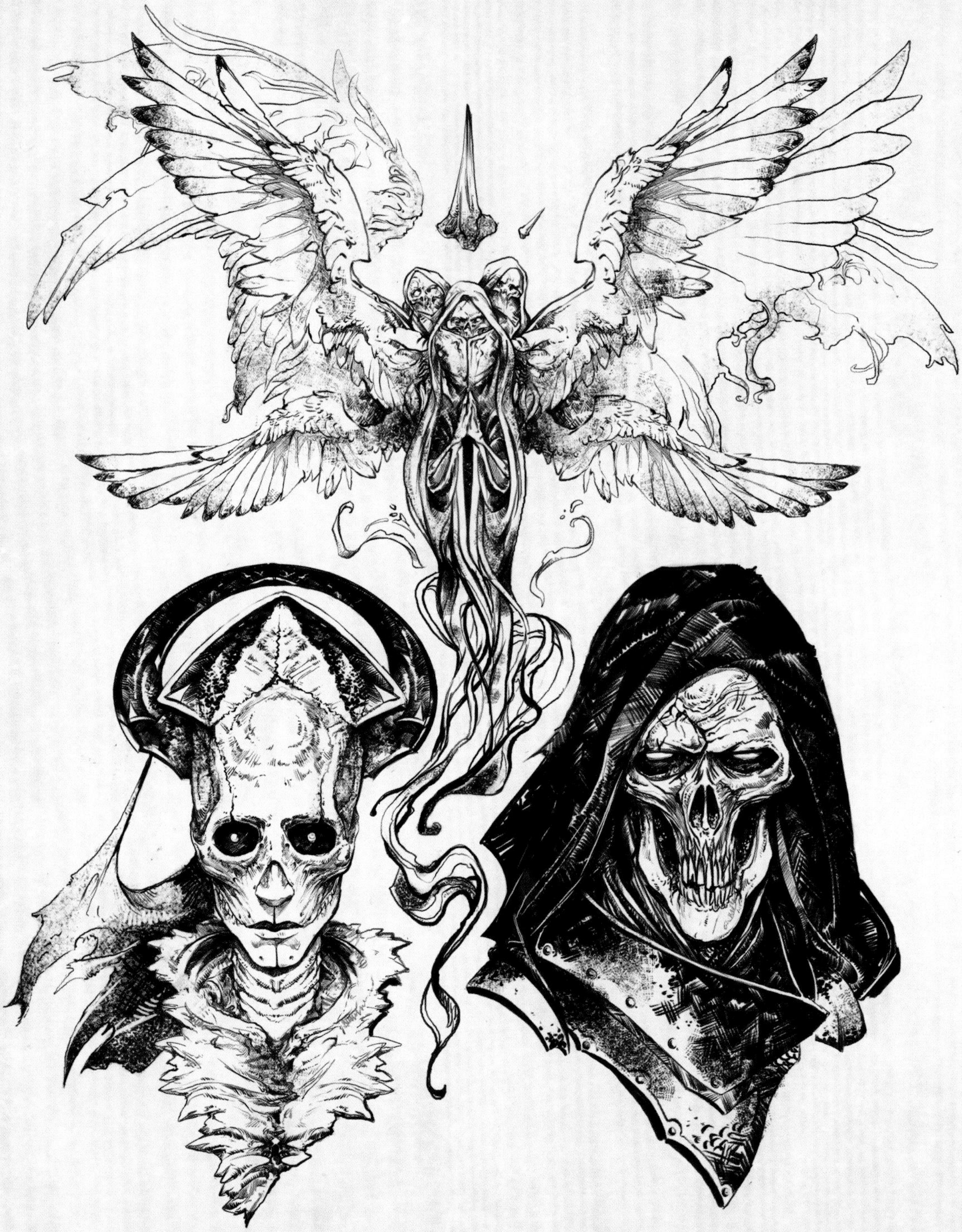

I am undecided which is the greater disappointment: that you left the creature imprisoned, or that you did so in order to enact the separation of Demithyle from his fellows. That you as well did nothing knowing also of the creature Simmel's wanton acts of malice in that place is still further discomfiting.

If I had said anything it would have given me away. I too saw opportunity, Alltaker. Entering and navigating the labyrinth came at no small cost. I could not have freed the wyspstride even had I wished it. It was all I could do to get it to agree to find and bring Demithyle back. Nor was the cost demanded by my sister's veilknife to deliver him there a pittance. For several meirs did I lay soporose at Voxxingard, with only my guardians to attend to Tsingvath. And I am very sorry if she is so spliced between the veils that she did not learn herself of the gatekeeper's treachery. In any case, the wyspstride is welcome enough to take its vengeance against the it, if it has not already done so.

Ellianastis is dealing with Simmel. And your actions have in the end delivered to us an unexpected bounty: Demithyle's companion, whom he hath given the name Ycnaf, was but herald to the greater arrival of her kind, at long last, into the Underworld.

Oh?

Indeed. Made possible unknowingly by the guile of she our Great Osteomancer, an alliance is struck.

"You see? Everything was always going to turn out for the best."

"There is no such entity as 'always,' Xiall. I should think you would have come into this wisdom by now. Much taken for granted will begin to change should we prevail against the bael reivers, perhaps foremost the labyrinth. Yet my concern lies with your interest in separating Demithyle from the rest of the reapers. To do so in the very moment of their victory in Mortis Veth . . . 'Twould seem a strange cruelty, and I would hear your logic for it."

"We knew that a commander would arise in Mortis Veth, Alltaker. I only made certain that commander's education would continue appropriate to that of a leader of a desperately outnumbered army. A commander who must not look upon his soldiers as his fellows to share in their glory but as rugged instruments, the employment of which not a thought can be spared for fondness or sentiment or anything that arises from the intimate knowing of their beings *you so admired here. You have your purview, Father, grandiose and fairly fretted. Mine is to prepare our Vanguard to confront the greatest threat the Underworld has yet known. Demithyle is a stronger leader than we could have hoped for, potent of will and instinct and presence. But it is very likely he will have to sacrifice every one of his fellows before the battle is decided. We made them beings to revel in their collective oneness in the hope of solidifying their unity to match that of the swarming masses of the horde. But I alone understood that this would prove their greatest weakness: for not only will Demithyle have to watch his fellows suffer and be destroyed each in turn; he will have to feel the destruction of their beings as if they were his own. He will know the moment of the ending of their existences with greater intimacy of awareness than any commander has ever been cursed to possess. As he directs them in battle he must do so beneath the pall of their unmaking, while the rending of their spirits and the corruption of all they have come to be unfolds within him. Take heed, Alltaker: that they have organized themselves as a focal corpus with Demithyle as both its crown and heartroot should fill all of us with dread. For each loss will be as a spear driven into its bosom. Should he be overwhelmed by pain, grief, or empathy, he will fail. Should he doubt by his fear for their entity, he will fail. Should he hesitate to act in any way, or recoil against the expenditure of their beings for advantage against his enemy, he will fail. We will fail, and all will fall.*

* * *

The Alltaker listened to her words and then vanished without comment. Whether he had heard them, Xiall could not know. Had she expected any among the Court to understand her reasonings she would have involved them in the first place. She was satisfied enough to be left now to her task, though the image of the flesh mines brought with it a heavy sigh.

The nearest portal that could take her to the flesh mines would be found in the forgeworks below the main halls of the Calvum Harrows, accessible, she knew, by way of a dormant lava tube connected to this atrium's catacomb. First, however, she would indulge the curiosity she had masked from the Alltaker. Approaching the menhir in the center of the chamber, she traced her bonewhite fingertips over its beveled spiral as it slowly spun. And marking the fine glow that gently pulsed through the glyphs inscribed over its gleaming black surface, she saw also her own warped visage reflected, carven and severe.

* * *

Finding in the catacomb the mouth of the darkened shaft, Xiall followed its steep descent, picking her way forward with her staff until its darkness ebbed against a rising underglow of deep maroon, and abruptly it widened to a massive cavern. At its heights was a crowning circle of toothy fissures from which thin firefalls were drawn down by the intermittent release of mechanical sluices, directed by means of a descending network of chutes and abutments to pour continuously into the glowing forgeworks in the cavern's center below. Beyond this lay the portal, here a viscous curtain of lava drooping down over a gap in the far wall.

 She leapt down the short rocky slope to the honeycomb of thin, intersecting stone pathways chiseled out by the excavation of ores, the tracest veins of which glinted blue and green deep into the shadows below. Over these she walked, careful to give wide berth to the hearth, a snarling monstrosity of iron draconiforms set around a white-hot pool of magma. Each shared an adjoining eye with its neighbor, furious by the fires within, staring outward as if overseeing the work of Ruse's hulking automatons, which tossed sulphurous stones through their open maws to the release of great rolling belches of flame.

 Even at this distance the heat set her outer layers of cartilaginous shell to ruffle, and she passed through great bouts of steam rising up from the chasms that flanked the path. Here and there also she was obliged to step over cooling piles of slag splashed out by the alchemical metallurgy of the automatons. Yet to Xiall, this was a place both hypnotic and meditative, and she diverted here often in her traversing of the city to feel the fireglow and listen to the music of the tireless cadre of farriers.

 She watched them now as with great steelbone claws they grasped white-hot lumps of arcane metal, and placing these upon misshapen anvils they raised again and again their massive hammers to smash away impurities, scorching the air with lucent streaks that curled away to vaporize. With ever finer strikes they folded and worked the amorphous metalforms until they quenched their curious shapes in deep troughs of black miasma, drenching the cavern with metallic screams. Drawn into the open air again, the forms ignited in prismatic blooms of fire, which the smiths held aloft to burn out as if by way of consecration. And all shadow was chased from the cavern as they knelt before thick honing wheels of glittering stone and touching the metal to it sent up blinding fans of sparks that spilt into the surrounding chasms, standing only when the weapon's edge had been so refined as to cut between filaments of connected thought.

* * *

There then was Ruse, the ancient weaponsmaven for whom Calvum Harrows was created. Surrounded by a nest of armaments, she hunched like a myopic tinker over some artifact of interest, her scarabesque form wrapped in a dizzying complexity of leather strapping to accommodate her kit and instrumentation. Oblivious to Xiall's passing, she peered intently through a veil of rusted iron so near to the hearth it glowed red from the heat.

Xiall knew better than to disturb her. It had taken the scion an enormous amount of time and subtlety even to gain her audience, though certainly the maven had been only too happy to deliver one of her treasures to find its use. Xiall smiled, noting the spiritous halo surrounding some of the armaments. Though she knew of spirits who wished to exist in such a way, she suspected more than one bound thus waited to be released, having incurred their matron's wrath by disturbing her meticulous examinations.

Interesting that Ruse should devote herself so unflinchingly to the arming of armies that do not yet exist, thought Xiall. Ten times the reaper force could not use even a fraction of the weapons made here by the darkmeir, to say nothing of the rivers of them that floated throughout the halls above. Though he had never spoken of it, Xiall knew that the Alltaker had long ago tasked her thus in preparation for open rebellion against the Celestials—a distant shattermeir that seemed never to draw closer.

Yet Ruse did not flag in her duty. Hers was a stratagem that did not calculate for defeat, nor ever did she doubt her design in the broken clockwork of the Cosmos. If anything were to be envied in this Underworld, it was this.

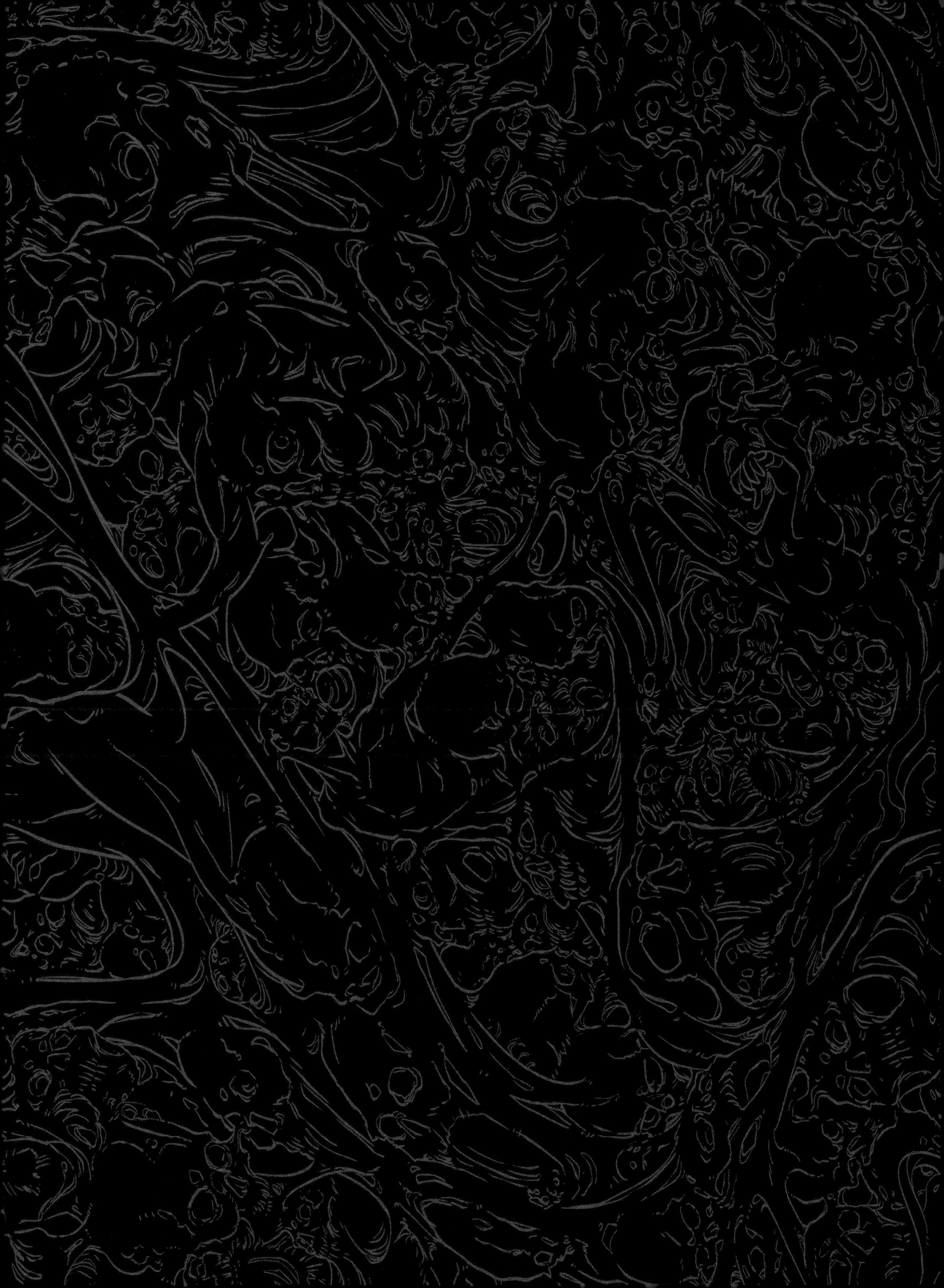

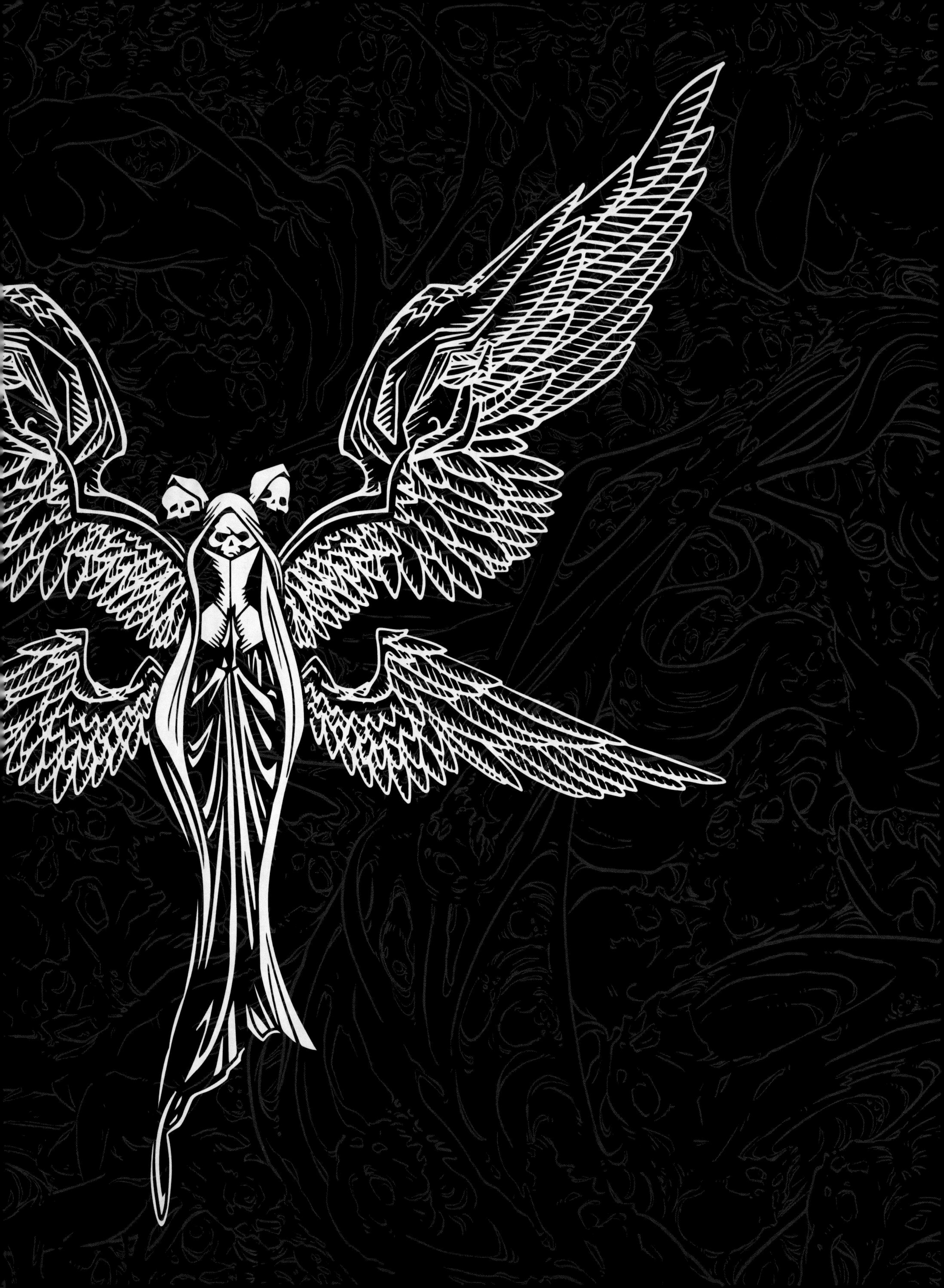

XXXII.
COMMUNION

Xiall found the lava curtain sizzling over a branching pathway in an otherwise dark alcove of the cavern, and unmaking her staff to so much bonedust she stepped into its flow. It burned away her form, releasing her spirit to soar through the intradimensional scoria toward the portal at the ferrowood grove on the opposite side of the Dirth Forge. Even before she had fully reconstituted she could hear the chiming of the wind through the grove and the rippling naiadic voices from the stillwater brook in which she found herself emergent. Rising, she shed the water's filmy plasma from her newly hardened form, and then growing up her staff from its riverbones she climbed out.

It had been long since she had heard the music of the grove. Certainly before Akhor had shat the flesh mine into it. Entering, she found that a flaky mucous residue was all that remained of the undergrowth, and many of the trees had become little more than thin skeletons of rusted iron. Still others appeared to have been stripped hollow of their ferrous veins; one released a puff of orange powder as she passed, and she found it alive with thousands of tiny ironmites billowing out from its cracks and crevices.

The mine lay in a clearing, capped above ground with a compound of bulbous, fleshy eggs shining red like polished leather by the light of the midmeir. Surrounding it was a herd of elaborately antlered spiritborn stags, silently nosing at the ground and one another with their hollow muzzles. Taking notice of her arrival, they raised their skulls and stared, their quiet spiritfires smoldering in animalian orbitals, and then turning away, one by one they retreated into the grove, their mottled flesh bouncing over their skeletons.

One remained, and it continued its stare with an altogether different fire; ethearic blue bespeckled with orange, and colder than the void, and she saw that it was not a stag at all, but Demithyle's wyspstride.

She gave it a curt nod. It looked much larger than she recalled. "And so, here you are," she said, walking toward it. "My thanks for your assistance. How fortunate that I found you in that place."

The wyspstride did not acknowledge her in any way. Nor did it break from her its gaze.

"It all worked out exactly as I described to you, yes? I understand your kindred have even come to help us against the baelreivers."

Still it stared, its only movement the fume of strange etherea from its crystalline eyes.

"Demithyle is inside, no doubt," said Xiall, watching it for reaction as she spoke his name. "How vigilant of you to stand by in wait of him." She sidled over to an elongated protrusion from the main mass of the compound. "I assume the entrance is to be found here, yes?"

The creature turned its spiny head to watch her but made no indication of answer, or even acknowledgment of her queries. Xiall could not bring to mind a precedent to such disdain.

"I imagine it is possible you are displeased," she said. "This however is of no interest to me."

She turned her attention deliberately to the fleshy starburst of blisters that had begun to grow over the wall as if by her proximity to it, trying to ignore the presence of this creature and the waves of power that seemed to roll outward from it. When she stepped closer, the blisters grew and broke as the wall thinned and rotted away, revealing a wide, circular vestibule glowing faintly pink within. With a final look at the wyspstride she went in, sighing heavily as the wall quickly regrew behind her.

* * *

The vestibule connected via a short hall to a wider antechamber with three apparent branching arteries of egress. Its floor was as supple as had been the exterior walls, so that walking upon it Xiall was given the sensation of being perpetually on the verge of slipping down a wet hill. A soft, pink glow passed through a drapery of veiny membranes that drooped from a pentagonal framework of fibrous yellow tendons that formed the shape of the interior canopy. The air was surprisingly crisp and floral.

Looking between the three passageways, she stabbed at the soft floor with the tailspike of her staff, leaving behind a bony thorn. "Well?" she shouted, her voice muted by the thick walls.

A lump began to grow in the fleshy floor in the place where she had pierced it, and enveloping the thorn it swelled upward like a blood-engorged fungus. When it had matched her in height a tumorous protrusion emerged from it and produced a pox of glistening nodules, roughly collected to express a face.

"Ss?" it queried, gasping through a small crease between the nodules that formed its mouth.

"You are joking," said Xiall.

"Ss?"

She sighed. "Demithyle," she said.

"Ss. Drgthl."

She waited, but nothing happened.

"Well? Take me to him."

"Ss. Frrgbl."

The tumorous attendant led her into the leftmost passageway, borrowing the skin of the floor as it rolled its mass beneath it. A narrow, fleshy tube mottled throughout with vaguely luminescent bruising, the passageway folded and twisted with maddening freqeuency, steadily narrowing as they advanced, giving Xiall the impression she was being squeezed through the guts of some corpulent behemoth.

At the end of the passageway was a door of hardened resin that flaked away at their approach, and she followed the attendant out onto a thick mezzanine of yellow callus, where she was presented with what at first seemed the interior of an immense insect hive. In the ensuing meirs since it had been dropped here by Cryptus Akhor, the mine had oozed itself as deep into the ground as her own emergent citadel was high. Its walls were composed of perhaps hundreds of fleshy pockets, most of which were obscured by an opaque film. Its thin canopy, flapping just overhead, was a patchwork of translucent cells rippling with fluid.

Thick placental tubes wafted down its center, wracked by shadowy figures within as they writhed downward. Most tubes were connected variously to the subsequent levels by thin platforms that reached outward from all around their circumferences, giving the overall impression of great hollow avian bones. Xiall followed as the fleshy attendant advanced rightward beneath the surface of the mezzanine, leaving a trail of waxy scurf to waft down over the edge as it rolled toward the nearest of these.

A row of cells was aligned along the wall. Each cast a faint glow through a thin film stretched over its doorway. The sounds and shadows that reached Xiall as she passed them proclaimed a cavalcade of mourners engaged in unimaginably bizarre varieties of intimacy: a muscular goliath immersed in some sort of aggressive, damaging bout with itself; a pair gently cooing as one steadily absorbed the other; a wriggling cortege of individuals passing between adjacent cells. One of the cells lay open, though for what reason of immodesty Xiall could not begin to imagine. In it were two mourners thick with borrowed flesh, strapped back-to-back to iron chairs. They touched only by the naked soles of their feet, which were pressed together beneath them. As she passed, they twisted their heads completely around and stared deeply into one another's eyes.

Xiall found that she was moved by the sight. In her private accounting of places of value in the Underworld she had long chosen to deny the existence of these flesh dens laid by her sister's roving citadel—as much in avoidance of their lascivious nature as by the fact that they existed in a given location only for as long as the mines were fruitful. Once dry they shriveled up faster than an insect's carcass. She had assumed Gethsemoni had sought only to claim accretions of sunken etherea found hidden throughout the substrata in order to convert it to her own purposes and that what mourners found their way here did so foremost to emulate the hedonism of the mortal world. But the naked exchange of spiritous being between these two was more . . . intriguing than lascivious. Perhaps it was not hedonism that drove the mourners, she thought, but connectedness, catharsis. The worship of a shared present.

It all seemed so disorderly. Distracting. And yet. It would be a dishonesty to deny it as also stirring.

* * *

The attendant led her from the mezzanine out to a narrowing strut connected to one of the flapping tubes, then made way as if for her to enter. She looked over the edge of the platform—far below, the white pools of fleshmilk steamed, and from this angle she marked several wriggling stairways leading upward to the first of the mezzanines, some of which bore newly enfleshed mourners no doubt in search of an open cell.

She looked at the flapping chute, and following its course down with her eyes saw that in fact no other platforms intersected with it; it appeared to lead directly to the bottom.

She looked at the attendant.

"Demithyle is down there?" she asked, pointing down.

"Ss."

"All the way at the bottom?"

"Ss."

"Why in the . . ." Sighing for what seemed the twelfth time since arriving in this place, she looked down and stepped over the edge.

* * *

The levels raced by her periphery as she dropped through the mine, and looking down she beckoned jointed bonespires to tear up through the shining leathery floor to receive her. They caught her feet with a cushioned downward lurch, grasping round her legs and lowering her slowly as they retracted.

Her feet touched the bottom and the spires uncoiled and disappeared, the supple, reddish skin already healing itself as she stepped away. Xiall was again surprised to find the air here woody and sweet, evocative of seer's sage and lily. Hanging from the underside of the first mezzanine were lanterns of filigreed resin, and vaporous eidolons drifted within the soft red glow of each, moaning quiet melodies so that together they environed the room with light and somber choirsong. Everywhere trails of smoke drew up from blackened incense lamps and candles melting over thousands of skulls set in piles all around the perimeter. The floor was pocked with several gurgling fleshbaths, each lipped with thousands of blunted teeth and slightly recessed within a centerward slope of the floor. Seemingly unperturbed by the arrival of one of the preeminent courtiers of their realm, the mourners continued to splash their way into and out of the baths, their thickened forms dripping with milky elixir reabsorbed by the fleshy floor even as they staggered off to be carried away by the groping stairways.

There was no sign of Demithyle. Then she spied movement of light and shadow playing over the rounded wall of an adjoining artery of egress, and making her way between the baths she passed through its curtain. She was met instantly with the new scent of burning olibanum, and even as the thin curtain resealed behind her she heard the familiar busy mechanical shiks and slices coming from deeper within.

There he was, splayed out upon a grated shelf over a luminous vat of fleshmilk, nearly completely flayed. Three of Gethsemoni's scuttling shroudreive clacked and clicked around him, sparks of etherea flying from their instruments as they scraped at his skeleton, restrung ligaments, scooped away viscera, squeezed black sludge into body cavities, worried over his joints. They paid her presence no mind as they busily cut away what remained of his decrepit flesh, peeling off his gray musculature in slimy strips and dropping these to dissolve in the vat below him.

"She of dry and white," said Demithyle.

Xiall stabbed her staff into the fleshy floor and walked to the edge of the vat beneath his feet and looked up—the rounded walls of the small chamber extended unmarred far above to the surface light, like a deep, tuberous smokeshaft.

"That would depend on my mood," she said, looking back down at him. She walked round the vat to his side, obliging a shroudreive to skirt away elsewhere. Demithyle continued to stare ahead. Finding his greatsword stabbed into a cluster of thick translucent vesicles bubbled up from the floor, she took it by its hilt with both hands and pulled it free. "I presume that is the name given me by your wyspstride," she said, holding the sword up, watching the slime burn away from the blade. "It was rather less than enthusiastic at our reunion."

Demithyle said nothing. She gave the sword an awkward one-handed swing, then lowered it to look at the leather-wrapped hilt. Where even other reapers might have struggled to heft it, Xiall paid little mind to its weight. Yet it seemed woefully imbalanced in her grip. She suspected this more a feature of the aspect she sensed present within it than of any flaw in its construction. Another loyalty collected.

"An unusual presentation," she said, holding it out over him to look down the worn and wavy blade. "I am told it altered itself for you?"

"Yes," said Demithyle. He looked at her. "I have not spoken of it."

"No?"

She stepped back to level the sword at his head. Feeling it nearly leap from her hand at the act, however, she quickly aimed it away. She looked for a hint of satisfaction in Demithyle's eyes. Finding none, she smiled.

"Ruse, of course," she said. "She retains intimate memory of all relics she acquires, particularly those of such unique significance. Tell me, were the other knights so opportune in their pairing of arms?"

Demithyle watched her a moment as the shroudreive worried over him, as if seeking out her purpose.

"The reaper Ilbaerth possesses a blade that finds her hand at the thought," he said, after a moment. "And Sithik of the cibori is joined to a pike that has at one time been shaded by blood of the Celestials."

A shroudreive peeled away a large swath of decrepit flesh from Demithyle's leg, straight down to an oddly elongated toe. There was a cathartic hiss as it dropped into the vat below.

"How apt," she said. She threw the sword to stab deep into the vesicle cluster again. "I come to collect you. When you are finished with this pampering, you are to accompany me to my citadel outside the city, where you will find yourself armored once again. Unless you wish to ride to war wearing only your pretty new skin?"

"I mourn the loss of the vestments given unto my making, Lady," said Demithyle.

"Indeed?"

"Yes. As nothing given might award a reaper greater value than the honor of riding to war in defense of our home, neither would its commander act to weaken our forces."

Xiall squinted at him as if searching for hints of irony. How curiously melancholy this one's voice, she thought. Before now, she realized, she had heard him speak only by way of Ellianastis's shapeshifting foolishness. Even in Mortis Veth he had kept his own thoughts, nor had she been moved to probe them. She was struck now by their sobriety, their absence of guile. Yet they fell heavily upon the air, as if each were formed with quiet regret.

"Our home, indeed," she said with a nod. "So it is. It is well that you should also see it thus, for your armor is ours."

"I would not have parted with it but for the direst of need, Lady."

She stepped closer, looking over the flayed creature who lay before her. She touched the bones that crossed the hollowness of his chest, tracing thin, white fingers over their arcane scrimshaw even as she noted the absence behind them of anything so burdensome as a heart. *The Alltaker spoke truth. We have done well with this one.*

Demithyle looked up at her with the green spark of his eyes. She drew her hand away and stepped back. The three shroudreive backed away then also, and even as Xiall marked his form now completely removed of flesh the shelf upon which he lay diminished and crackled away, and buoyed by unseen forces his body tilted forward to stand hovering over the luminous vat, legs dangling, his emaciated left swordarm held as if to accept alms, his rightward arms fanned out like a skeletal wing. All of him carved down to ligature and bone, he kept his gaze upon her with no hint of modesty at his nakedness, at once vulnerable, fateful, dangerous, and beautiful. To Xiall, in the meeting of his stoicism with this consummate undeath, he seemed an expression of profound artistic asymmetry.

There was a mewling cry as one of the shroudreive peeled down a wide, fleshy leaf from a bulbous sac near the vat, revealing within a muculent, pulsating knot of viscera. Beads of blood emerged over the inner skin of the leaf, and forming a single drop it trickled to fall to the surface of the white liquid. The entire vat began to churn and bubble, coughing out little clouds of steam that rose up to curl around Demithyle's form, which had already taken on a grayish, glistening film.

Xiall scanned the room to find that the three shroudreive had departed. She looked at Demithyle, floating within the thickening fume, examining his limbs as the chamber slowly filled with a cloying, gray fog of fleshmist. Then a thin, almost imperceptible *shik* was heard as a narrow needle of bone sprang from the floor to pierce the fleshsac. It twitched against the point but fell still as it was pierced again by a hundred more, and as the needles retracted rivulets of blood streamed from it into the vat. The blood spun a dark spiral within the basin, and Demithyle met her gaze just before he was obscured by the eruption of thick white spouts of steam that grew in a cloud so thick she saw only white, and she reached outward as if to steady herself as she was taken from her feet by the sudden dense liquidity of the air. But catching sight of her own enfleshed hands she held them before her, and she touched her face with a soft finger and felt the odd suppleness and warmth of it.

Through the white she searched for the spirit glow of Demithyle's eyes, and she found them floating above even as she was ascended by the mists. Reaching blindly she found his outstretched hand, and at their touch she felt between them the traveling of warmth and exchange, as if in equal measure clarity and surrender. And when he pulled her to him she knew by the earnestness of his strange new visage and the depth of his opalescent eyes that he felt it also.

She turned away, releasing him at the shock of it, and as distance began to reassert itself between their respective ascents she looked back again to mark his peculiar bulk, knowing her own must be yet odder. He a bizarre, six-limbed mortal approximation, smooth skinned and overmuscled, like a simplistic manifestation of some romanticized demigod; she a new facsimile of her sister Gethsemoni in all her vanity of pulchritude, more naked by this draping of her ossein physicality than without it.

Separately they rose as the expulsion of enfleshing vapor continued unabated, and Xiall allowed herself to drift alone in the weightless, white obscurity, the better, she thought, to regain vantage of logic and reason. But then somehow his hand found hers again, and she pulled him in and grappled him with the entirety of herself, intent on taking all that she wanted from him as she had always done. But as she felt her softness of form grasped by the thick rigidity of his arms, by the strength of his hands, the probing interest of his fingers, his face, his lips, what welled up within her was the awakening of something akin to abandon, an airy trust in the finality of the power of this being and his ability to supplant her own, and for the first time in the long unbroken span of her existence she gave over her will to be conveyed by the strength of another.

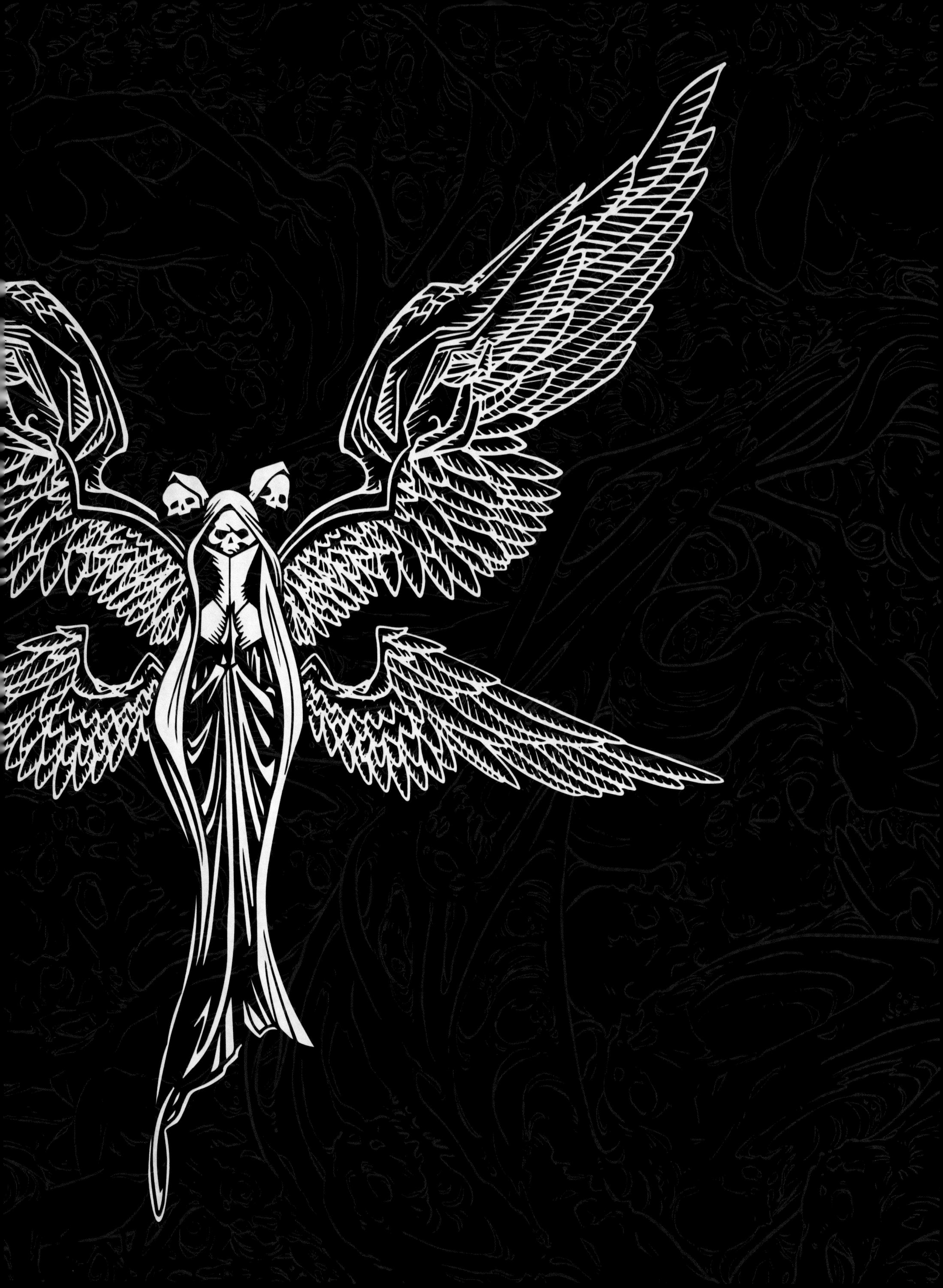

XXXIII.
VOXXINGARD

Demithyle looked at his hands. Their flesh now deflated, cold and gray, returned to the tightly wrapped tools of a soldier. These were not the hands to share warmth. To find the rhythmic pulse. To know the constellation of touch of another's form.

Yet this they had done. And the memory of it was his own to keep.

He let himself fall into it. When in the blindness of their mutual ascent they had spun together weightless, and in their culmination burst through the glimmering canopy in a white tempest of vaporous flesh. When they had grappled through the discordant expanse of the grove, his chest weighty and thick, heaving mighty breath into her fire.

This chest that had been wracked from within by the pounding of a heart he knew he was not intended to possess.

And the sight of her through corporeal eyes had rippled with electric ferocity he knew they were not created to behold.

Here now they lay, two mummified physicalities becalmed in a nest of shattered gravestones in a forgotten burialground far outside the grove, wrapped together in the waning meir of their passion, the dawn of his calling yet beyond the darkmeir. Not even in his long vivisepulture in the past had such a thing ever been made real for him. What clearer testimony could be presented a reaper for its calculated evanescence than to be created absent this want for completion by another? And therefore what greater evidence of transcendence than the discovery of this contentedness?

He looked at her hand, lying rarefied upon his chest, and for the first time he knew with the fullness of his being that it did not matter to what purpose he was created. He existed in this moment as a conjoined entity, two children of the same Underworld, a reaper and his Demigoddess of Bone, and in that moment, for the first time, it was enough.

* * *

Xiall stirred next to him. She reached her willowy hand for the smallest of his where it lay against his breast and turned it over. Its burns were gone, cleansed by the renewal of his skin. Yet remnants of the Alltaker's mark remained.

She drew her thumb over the vague shapes of its glyphs.

"Do you resent it?"

"No," he said. He worked the hand over her thumb, now dry as bone. "It was a gift."

"One of many."

"Yes."

"Many truths you have learned by way of it."

"Perhaps."

"You do not wish to speak of it?"

Demithyle looked at her. How different now her black eyes from those with which she had gazed at him so recently.

"I think that is so," he said. "Much . . . time was spent in examination of things long past, and the vaguely possible. Perhaps I fear the present atrophies by neglect."

"And yet you have come to know many battles."

"Many deaths by way of battle," he said.

"There is no greater teacher than failure," said Xiall. "Mortis Veth should have taught you this, above all."

"Yes," he said. "And it is true that the reapers are made better for the sharing of these examinations."

"The Alltaker was quite taken by his witnessing of that."

"Indeed?"

"I believe he described it as 'a recommuning dearly to be envied.'"

Demithyle could think of no appropriate way to respond.

"Perhaps you might paint a clearer picture," said Xiall.

"You wish to know of the sharing of the reapers' minds?"

"I am not accustomed such spiritous exchange," she said. "I begin to see my complement in you, perhaps. But you are . . . unique. To swim naked among the minds of so many is a thing alien to me."

Demithyle considered.

"It is the realization of great injury only by its mending," he said after a moment. "A quickening of mind and sight beyond the self."

He looked at her, wondering whether she read his dissatisfaction with the abstractness of the answer, whether she shared it. How does one express the process of being made whole? But there was only patient interest in her eyes as she waited for him to continue, and so he thought upon it again.

"The library," he said, "was a place of contradiction. I was not alone. Yet I was alone. Time passed. Yet it did not. I sought ever more fervently to uncover what pillars of my self I could discover there, that I learn all that was mine to learn. Yet by this did I eclipse what I had made of my self by doing. I was no longer Demithyle, he that had chosen that honorable name and lived by it. I was to become the immortal intimacy of a thousand wants, unified by nothing save the twin realities of hunger and its absence. I was many and yet no one. By the intervention of another did I emerge with sanity intact, yet even as I stepped away from that place it felt as if much of my self were left behind, unknown. It was only by the rejoining with the reapers that the surety of my own significance was returned to me: a hundred minds to grasp all that I had seen and been, our greater organism to dilute the poisons of doubt and malaise that we become immune to its destructive influence. From many but no one, to one among many."

"You can feel them still?"

"Yes. Always by our wisping, do we know we are never truly alone. Though I am at the heartroot of our force, it is they who are the heart of me."

"The heart of you."

"To the extent that I possess one," he said.

"And would you readily lay down this newfound self, which you have dug so deeply to uncover?"

The truth of this Demithyle knew more clearly than that of any other thing.

"I have sworn it," he said. "I would again."

"And those of your comrades?" said Xiall. "Would you so lay down theirs as well, before even your own?"

"If by their sacrifice we are brought closer to victory, yes. They would not have it otherwise."

"And what of your wyspstride companion?"

Demithyle looked at her.

"The wyspstrides keep their own fate," he said. "They are beholden only to their herd. It would not be within my purview to demand their sacrifice."

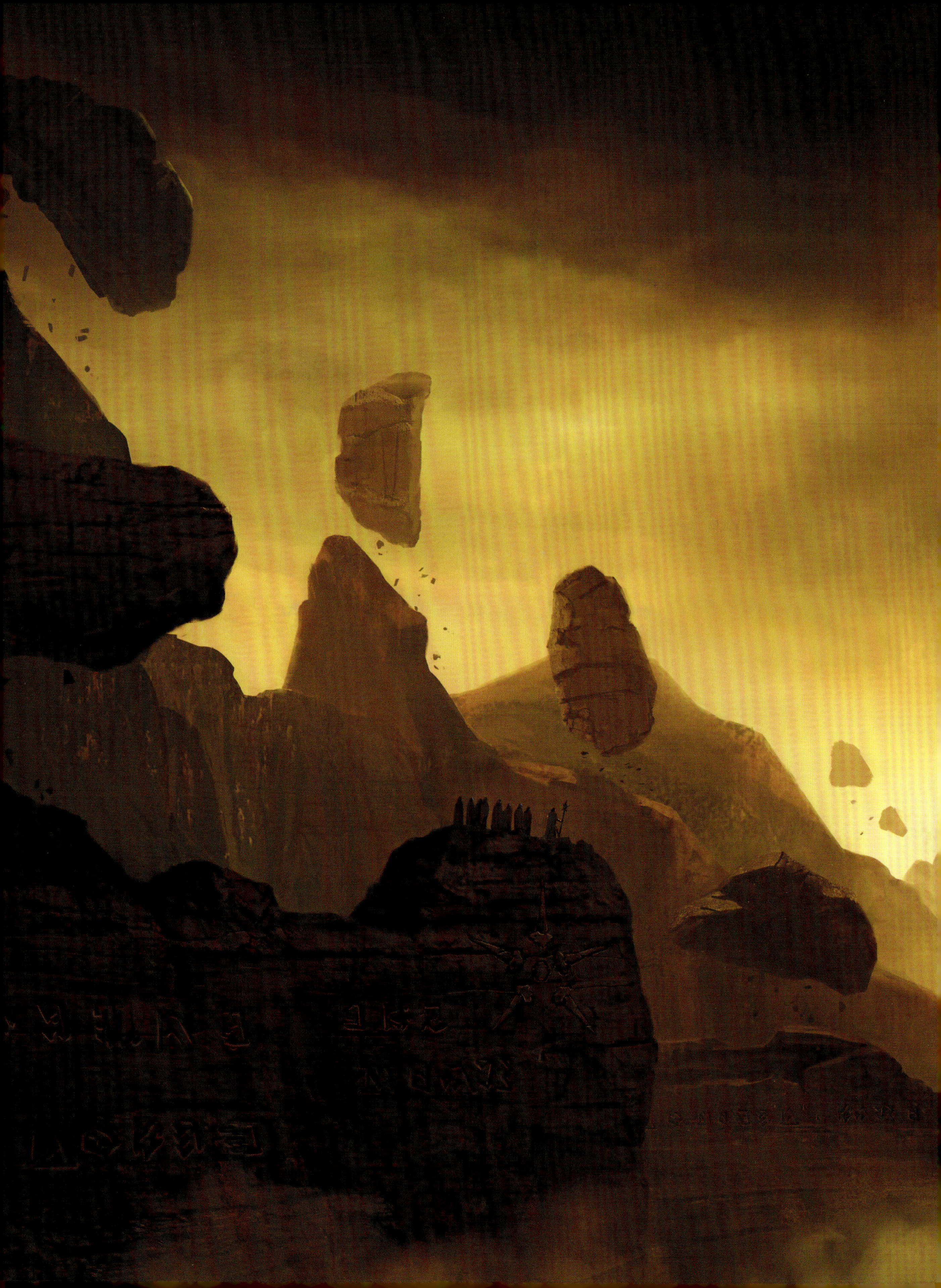

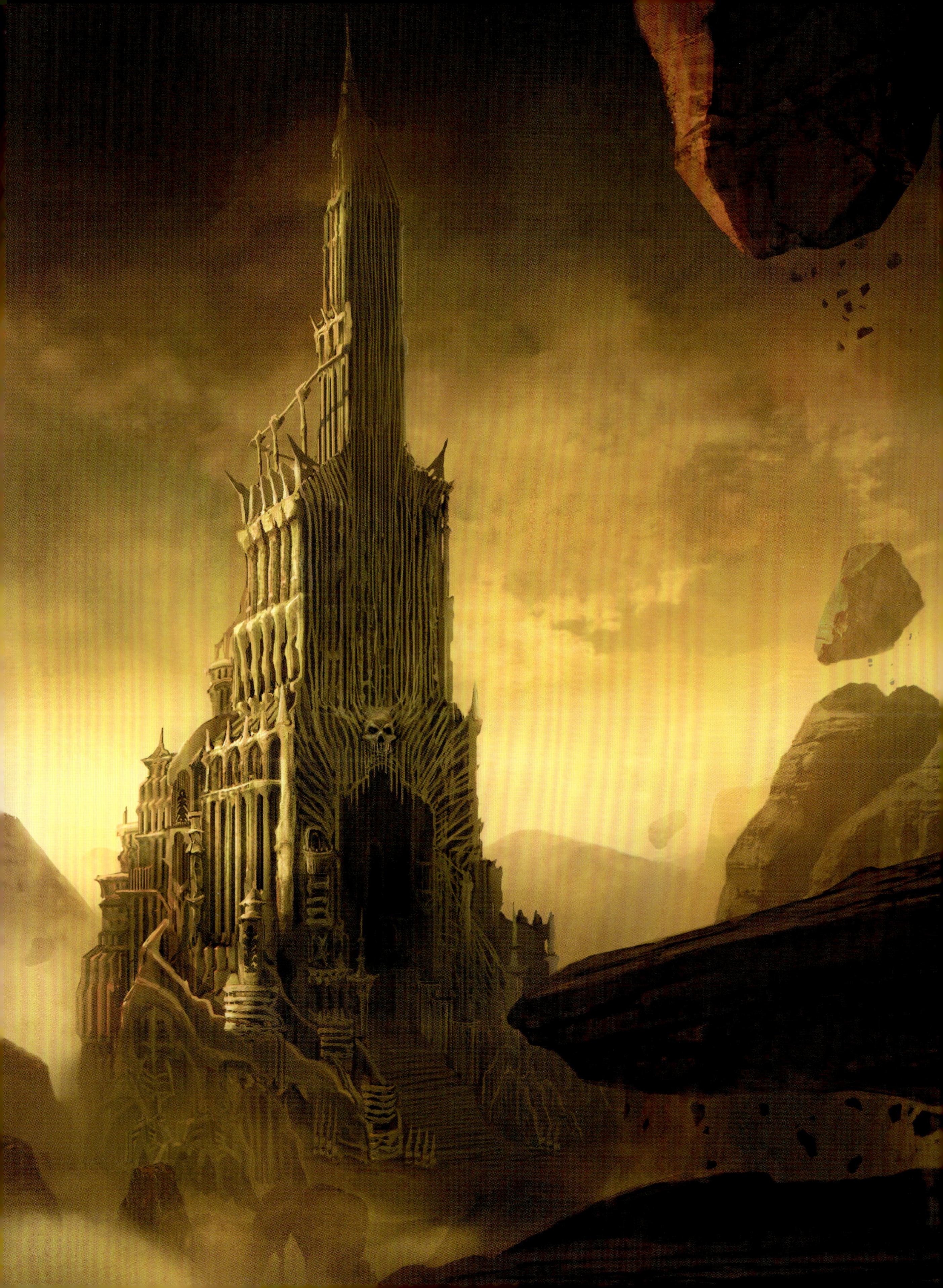

He had not intended to speak so evasively. Xiall regarded him a moment, then leaned away to reach for her staff.

"It is time to go," she said.

* * *

Bone grappled them, pulled them down through the stone and into the ground. For a time all was in darkness as they were taken through the archaeological strata that were the unseen foundations of the Underworld. And then they lurched suddenly forward and Xiall cast forth a light from the mouth of her staff, displaying the great groping arms of bone that preceded their advance, spitting in from all directions to pull and press aside the compacted elements of infall, bracing the tunnel even as they themselves were carried swiftly forth.

Demithyle could mark no direction, though he knew they had passed beneath the walls of the city. In mutual silence they progressed, slapping through hollow pockets of debris and structural chambers that had not seen light for aeons until finally they broke into the moody midmeir of the Underworld.

"Welcome to Voxxingard," said Xiall. "Or what shall in the shattermeir become it."

They stood upon a rocky ledge overlooking what seemed a vast construction effort, the soundscape dominated by the clattering drone of hundreds of bony workers below. Demithyle saw then that they were in fact uncovering the ruins of an ancient temple, scouring away the land with tool and claw and carving out what promised to be a broad canyon surrounding it.

Drawing up a bone scaffolding Xiall laid a long, bridging pathway before them, high over the busy canyon toward the towering structure. She strode out upon it, but as Demithyle moved to follow, he paused, looking back toward the city.

"My sword," he said. He had given no thought to it since before their emergence from the mine.

Xiall pointed at his hip. "You mean that sword?"

Demithyle pulled aside his soiled robes. There was Cryptmourne, secured by its familiar weathered leather strap. He touched the hilt, pleased as much by its fidelity as the equanimity its presence delivered to him.

"Come," said Xiall.

Shaking loose grit from his robes, he followed her along the bridge, its elements falling away to disappear into the ground behind them as they advanced toward the broken edifice.

"I have only begun to uncover it," she said, tipping her staff toward the ruins as they walked. "It stands over one of but a few intersections of the ethearic ley lines that act as energy root for this realm. In time I will have cleared out the surrounding canyon. I will remake this a fortress citadel, the seat of the Faction of Bone."

"What is a 'faction of bone'?"

"A lodestar for logic and order in this realm," she said. "One which I intend many to follow, to the betterment of our realm."

Demithyle looked at the half-buried citadel. It looked as if all of its exposed facades had been patiently clawed away, leaving the entire edifice rippling with deep striations.

"I have come to believe in the great discordancy of the Underworld," he said. "Why would one wish to impose greater order upon it?"

"Better you should ask why its necessity has for so long gone unrecognized," said Xiall. "Whether by fate or design, factions are beginning to arise in the Underworld. Bone, Flesh, Spirit. The Cosmos makes way for many perspectives, and we, the foremost scions of its destructor apparent, are powerful actors for each our own. It was inevitable that we would begin to organize ourselves and our realm according to our respective leanings and interpretations. The various players throughout the Underworld will be drawn to one or another of each, and so much the better shall we all be for our orderliness. What do you think all of this squabbling over you has been about, Demithyle? My sisters thought they could charm you with spiritual tours and respites of the flesh. But I understand you better than they can know. Soon enough you will see. The ribald truth of things has never been hidden from you."

"I do not understand."

"You shall, in time."

Demithyle hesitated. The rhythmic clacking and creaking of the work in the canyon below followed them unabated as they continued over the bonebridge toward the citadel.

"It would seem . . . divisive, Lady," he said, choosing his words with care.

Xiall stopped, planting her staff into the bony planks as she turned to face him.

"Only for they who would refuse to understand it," she said. "It is the evolution of paradigms to greater organization, and it can not be denied. I have watched you, reaper. You are a being of consummate conviction. You think as deeply as you feel, yet you do not hesitate to act. Your every action is in turn measured for effect. You espouse the tenets I would prescribe for any faction under my leadership. Indeed, you inspire them. You will see. Once you have aligned yourself, your eyes will be all the clearer for the focus of it."

"Yet one needs wonder who shall reap greatest gains from such orderliness in the shattermeir," said Demithyle.

"Enough," said Xiall, whirling again toward the citadel. "The factions arise. There is nothing you can do about it. Your actions have led you to congruency with my own. If you survive the horde, you will find here a home within a home. If you do not, then perhaps your greatest feat of leadership shall be that of example."

She strode forth, and Demithyle followed, nudged ahead by the disintegration of the bridge behind him. Demithyle saw the logic behind such an initiative—as well, perhaps, as its inevitability. But it chafed against the image he had come to construct of his home. Yet he held his tongue as they continued along the bridge, thinking it best to let the matter drop. He looked rightward toward the city. The thin sapphire beam of the Dirth Forge speared up into the celestial tumult behind its great rearward wall, imposing even at the distance, the sigils of its banners only just discernible.

* * *

The last remnants of the bonebridge fell away as they reached the outskirts of a modest stone courtyard, and she led him past a cracked, scoured gate through the ruins of an ancient vestibule, then into what had once been a main hall, now missing a large section of its ceiling, along with the uppermost reaches of an adjoining tower, and so it was open to the sky. The air was frigid and speckled with crystals of ice, and a thin frost glinted over every surface save neatly piled stacks of bone set along the walls. The floor in the center of the hall was recessed from the surrounding architecture by a descent of three concentric rings, within which stood a copse of stunted, fractured trees, white and clearly ossein.

"Like so many things," said Xiall, picking through a nearby heap of bones, "this entire place was pulled into the Underworld from some unnamed realm of some untold age past. And in this case, certainly long after it had been abandoned—even chambers preserved by its burial here were found damaged, and there are many signs of battle throughout. It was a temple, I believe. I have named it Voxxingard, for the throat of they who built it, carried through the aeons for my reckoning. There was once much music here."

Drawing from the heap a broken mandible, she tossed it to the circle, into the midst of the tree forms. To Demithyle's surprise, the stone accepted it as would viscous liquid, and it quickly sank below the surface. A bony thorn then sprouted there, and from this another, and then both swelled, cracking aside neighboring shells as it grew to a misshapen tree.

"You'll find the ground fertile here," said Xiall as she walked into the circle. Touching its barkless shell, she leaned in to examine the new growth more closely.

"Ah," she said, straightening again. "This one was a seraph."

Stepping back she held a hand toward it, then wrenched as if to wrest free a cord of empty space. An alabaster lump tore away as the tree exploded in a cloud of bonedust, its limbs cracking over the stone, leaving behind only a stumpy husk of bone. The lump then cracked and bloomed in an emergence of what could be described only as a skeletal mimic of an angelform, as if only the vaguest remembrance of itself could be drawn from the seeding bone.

"These bones were collected from inside this citadel," she said, nodding at the pile from which she had taken the mandible. "I never tire of the surprise. As often as not it turns out a Celestial. Their war is truly inescapable."

She spoke a command in the creaking speech of dry bone, and the creature retreated into the darkened recesses of the broken tower.

"Come," she said. "There is someone I would like you to meet."

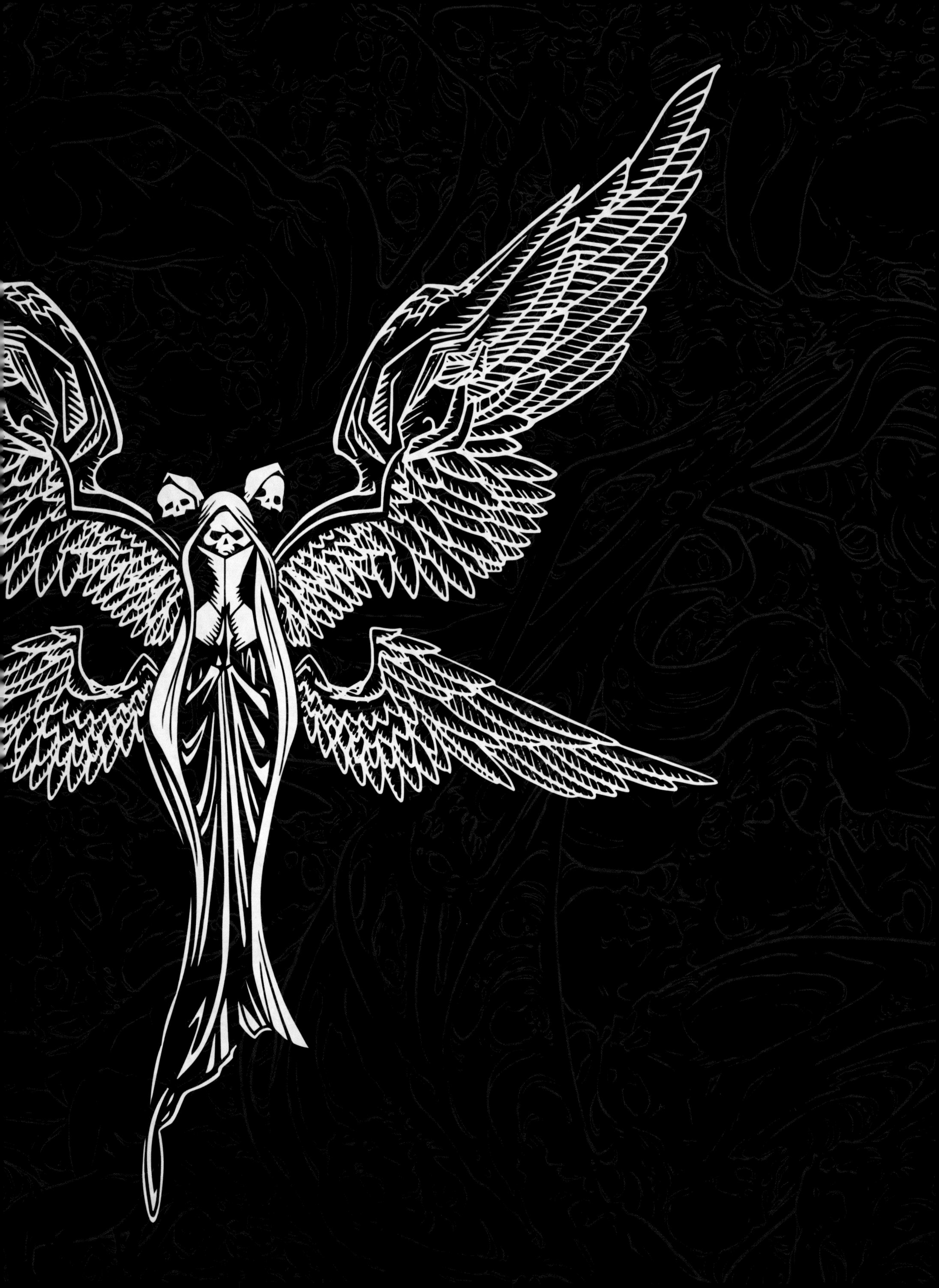

XXXIV.
A FINAL LESSON

He followed her from the hall through a lamplit corridor and into a high-ceilinged chancel, the city-facing wall of which was torn mostly away as if destroyed by an interior explosion. There in its recesses was a doorway to a darkened stair, and climbing its gradual wind they found themselves released into the broken shell of the uppermost level of a roofless watchtower.

In the center of its circular floor was what seemed to Demithyle a broad stone column broken halfway up to where the ceiling had once lain and subsequently carved to the effigy of a stoic entity embedded against it by a webbing of thick tendrils. It stared outward toward the city with huge, shadowed eyes apparently locked in deep contemplation.

"Hello, brother," said Xiall. "We have a visitor."

It was then that Demithyle saw that the figure was not of stone but of dry bone, at rest beneath a thick layer of gray ice. His form seemed to have sprouted ossein roots where it was secured against the pillar, splitting into its stone, likely encrypting him there long before the ice had set.

"What did you do to him?" asked Demithyle.

"Nothing was done to him," said Xiall. She brushed flecks of ice from his shoulders and stony face. "He can get up and leave any time he wants. He is Tsingvath."

"How long has he been this way?"

"I can no longer remember. I do not even know the last time I saw him move. He sits there, mourn to darkness, meir upon meir, staring at nothing, thinking, grappling, fighting."

"Fighting?"

"Many are the conflicts in this plane, seen and unseen. When we discovered this place we knew it a fulcrum point, a place where we might touch the latticework of psychic energies that permeate the Underworld. Tsingvath grapples with its astral fabric even as he ponders the end of his task, seizing it for our purposes, shielding us from the ingress of usurpers."

"Your purposes?"

"Our purposes, Demithyle," she said, shaking her head. She pointed cityward with her staff. "Mark the structures in the wallows that surround the walls. When the attack comes, it is likely the Alltaker will pull heavily on the power of the Forge. Like so many refugees, the wallows and all of the surrounding area will be drawn inward by its pull. Do you understand?"

He did.

"Good." She looked at him. "We all of us follow the auspices of our Father, Demithyle. Do not mistake factional organization for dissolution of unity. Our vision may be divided threefold, but neither my sisters or I would hesitate to sacrifice ourselves for one another. As for my brother," she said, nodding to Tsingvath, "one day he will wake to find that all has changed in the Underworld, and I would have it be a place in which he would wish to remain awake. But he is not the one I have brought you to meet."

* * *

They went out onto the battlement that extended from the watchtower, and Demithyle followed her into another tower and down through another winding stair, this one aglow by sickly yellow light from the eyes of thousands of mortal skulls embedded in the curving walls. It flattened out to a narrow torchlit corridor that they followed to the ruins of a modest, circular observatory. It was surrounded by buttress pillars that climbed upward to claw broken into the empty air high above, once sharpened by the relentless scouring of ice crystals on the wind, now sheltered beneath a dome of blackmirror glass. Segmented between them, the walls were decorated with reliefs depicting armored, undead warriors standing in formation with tall, dead trees, each connected by their branches to varied stellar constellations of mortal skulls.

Centered in the room was a large, pentagonal dais of polished white marble, over which a small, blackened fragment of metal hovered at shoulder height. Stepping upon the plinth Xiall took it into her hand, and instantly there appeared standing at the points of the dais five sentinels crowned in five-pointed warbonnets of scarred red bone—the very same changeling creatures that had whisked the reapers from the Calvum Harrows.

Ignoring them, Xiall left the dais and gave Demithyle the fragment.

"Morghistus," she said. "He from whom you derive the potency of your guardianship spirit. It is all that remains of him."

Demithyle held up the fragment. Curved, blackened as if by fire, its surface was smooth but for trace elements of decorative embellishment.

"What happened to him?" asked Demithyle.

"He was unmade preventing the destruction of the realm."

"What threatened it?"

"The Alltaker himself."

Demithyle stirred.

"Our father was betrayed, long ago," said Xiall. "An entity of his own making known as Raevells the Wanton sought to unleash the destructor within him, a thing he had long struggled to subdue. It was this very struggle that itself was all of our salvation: as each of we his scions were one by one made manifest by his explorations of being, so was created Morghistus, the Guardian of Living Armor, by Death's striving against his own destructive nature. And in the end it was Morghistus who stood between the Alltaker and his usurper."

Xiall nodded, seeing Demithyle's forlorn gaze.

"Yes," she said. "You know this struggle well. You have seen the destructor within your own self."

"I have been it," said Demithyle.

"And you have defeated it."

"No," said Demithyle. "It was another."

Xiall regarded him, as if weighing in his eyes the measure of his own self worth. She walked to him, and taking the clenched fist that gripped the fragment at his side, she raised it between them and caressed its fingers open.

"This is the last fragment of our greatest defender," she said. "It is a lodestone, kept here to collect into itself all aspects, dreams, and emanations of thought that would exalt the guardian spirit."

"For what purpose?"

She stepped aside. "Throw it onto the dais," she said.

He looked at her, then at the dais. He threw it as she bade, and even as it passed between two of the red sentinels they all suddenly leapt up and backward to occupy narrow niches set into the walls above. The fragment stuck into the whitestone dais as if the marble were wet sand, and as had the angelic jawbone in the main hall below it quickly sank down into the stone. Pinpricks of sapphire-blue light found their way to the surface, then a brilliant ethearic projection whirled up and spun over it, glimmering in chaos before settling, coalescing to the vaguest spiritform of an armored figure even as thin, bony twigs grew up into it, interlacing like probing, jointed roots throughout its shape, then swelling through the form they fused to encapsulate it within the shape of an immense white tree. Demithyle then saw glistening everywhere upon it a filmy oil that quickly blackened as if by exposure to the air, finally coagulating over it to a depthless black skin.

Demithyle stared, for he knew it as an image that had lingered unseen in the far reaches of his mind, like a memory he could not recall. Now solidified before him, the great blackened tree conjured some deeper knowing within him.

"It is familiar to you, then," said Xiall. "Good. Very good."

"A dream," said Demithyle, unable to look away from the tree. "I am a mortal child. I stand before a tree with bark of charred flesh, holding my mother's sword in my hands. A great beast has awakened. It came up from the ground and destroyed my village. I ran away, through the forest, trying to reach the river. But it gave chase. I can hear it smashing through the trees. I know that if I do not reach the spirit within the tree, all other villages will be destroyed also."

"And then?"

"I cut away the bark to reveal a trunk of bone. I cut into it again and again as the beast nears until a clear sap seeps from the wound. I touch it, and bring it to my lips. It tastes electric, like steel. I lean forward to drink it."

"And?"

"I do not know," said Demithyle. "There is no more."

"Then perhaps the time has come to find more," she said.

Demithyle looked at her, but she only waited, the sentinels watching impassively above. Looking back at the tree, he drew Cryptmourne and stepped upon the dais. He brought up his sword and touched its point to the surface of the tree as if to feel its hardness. And then with a quick lunge he buried the sword tip into it, sending a pulse of force through the blade that cracked the heartwood beneath the blackness of its skin.

As he pulled the sword free large pieces of the tree fell away with it, revealing within a blackened cuirass, tethered to the hollow of the tree by a tangle of rooty filaments. He stepped closer to look upon it. It bore an ornate filigree of lily vines surrounding a penitent figure, cloaked and cowled with four wings splayed, hands pressed together beneath its three skulls as if entreating mercy. Twin dragons clawed at the skirts of its cloak, from which spindly, demonic legs reached to grasp in their talons a pair of winged, cherubic heads.

Joining him on the dais, Xiall drew her fingers over the filigree and then down the seam where the back of the cuirass met the breastplate.

"Morghistus himself conjured the image upon the plate," she said. "It was meant as a symbol of the Alltaker's vision of ultimate unity between the three realms—Mortal, Celestial, Underworld. Perhaps it shall now also serve as reminder of the unity between the Factions."

He looked at her.

"It is a rare general who can occupy both the head and heart of an army," she said. "This armor will shield you from things to which your knights are likely to succumb. And you will see them fall, everywhere around you. You will know their unmaking even as you deliver them to it. Are you prepared for this?"

"I have no illusions," said Demithyle. "Every reaper would eagerly trade existence for surer victory. I will do my duty as their commander, as you have made me."

"As you have made your self," she said. "And victory achieved, what then? The Alltaker has designs for you and for us all. Would you lend your loyalty to the clarity and symmetry of Bone, that we together might see these designs manifest?"

"Loyalty is the act by which the covenant is made absolute," said Demithyle. "Without the act, the pledge is nothing more than empty words."

"Words that fall conspicuously short of an oath of commitment," she said. "You stand before the sphere toward which you have driven yourself since the very day of your creation. What say you, reaper?"

"If the Underworld must be divided into factions, then so be it," he said. "I would be honored to take my place here, insofar as a balance of power is sustained among them."

And then Xiall gave a sound reminiscent of the slow crushing of a skeleton, which Demithyle realized was a laugh.

"Balance is a fool slipping over bottles while trying to catch his hat," she said. "A frantic doom of perpetual correction to achieve that which symmetry possesses as a rule."

Stepping clear of the dais, she took up her staff.

"But this you will also come to learn," she said. She pointed her staff at the tree behind him. "Take your armor, then, Demithyle, our loyal Reaper General."

No sooner did he turn to look upon it again than was he by a swift blow to the back sent crashing through the center of the tree and into the breastplate, which flew off into the corner of the room as he smashed through and slammed into the far wall, the tree collapsing in pieces between them. He stood up just in time to see Xiall bring the head of her staff before her pursed lips and blow at him a cone of dust. When it reached him it ignited in a white fire that instantly incinerated his cloak and set his head alight, burning away his last clinging scraps of thickened flesh.

Xiall followed up with a series of agile blows, and he parried each in turn as he positioned himself away from the wall so as not to be pinned against it.

"Now that looks more like the phallus of a reaper," she said.

She concentrated her attacks along the central line of his body: he raised a leg against a sweep of her staff and letting it fall planted it to bring the other into her foot against before it her forward kick could gain momentum, knocking her off balance only long enough for him to shuck away the smoldering remnants of his cloak. Anticipating a punch to the throat after a blinding flash from her hand he pivoted, only to catch the butt of her staff between his arms before it could stab into his naked chest. He refrained from delivering a blow of his own, all the while losing ground, Cryptmourne yearning at his hip to be drawn.

"You fight like a nanny," she said.

Another attack, this one a pirouette and a sweeping downward arc of her staff aimed at his neck. Demithyle met it with a raised hand, pierced through the palm by its leading point.

"Root, sacral, plexus, throat, eye," she said. "How aggressively you defend them, even to the sacrifice of your hand. In what grave shall you be discovered when they have gone?"

"You forget the heart," said Demithyle. He drew the hand swiftly back so that she would be forced to step into his reach or let go, and watched her instead leap inverted over his head, flashing him an knowing look at the apex of her arc before tearing the staff free from his grip as she landed lightly behind him, her feet guided down by a pair of waiting skeletal hands.

There she held, waiting for him to come.

"The heart is a connection," he said. "Is it not this above all that sets us apart from the baelreivers, that which we were made to keep? From it we draw great strength, fervor, dedication. It was only by way of it that

I was not lost. The heart of us, the heart of me. It is the root of our power and mine."

Xiall sighed then, and Demithyle was given pause. But she then launched a flurry of strikes along his center line again, exactly as she had done before, and Demithyle was easily able to anticipate and parry. Yet somehow his programmed defense left a hole, and she struck a blow to his head that staggered him, and even as he grabbed her staff in a tight defensive lock he felt himself pierced through the back, pinned in place by a pylon of bone sprung up from the ground.

Releasing her staff, he looked down to see a hand of bone at the end of the pylon, cracked and yellowed, sticking out of his chest, palm held up as if waiting to accept alms spilt from his mouth.

Xiall stepped back. "Do you see anything in that hand?" she asked, nodding at the gaping hole in his chest. "No? Look closely now."

She stepped forward and pushed her hand into his chest as the bone pylon slid out of him, holding him up by the rib bones she grasped within.

"As I suspected," she said. "You do not have a heart. You do not have a family. You do not have a companion. Your reapers were made dead. The only sentiment you must bring to battle is fealty to the designs of your makers. This the armor of Morghistus will shield, and nothing more, for he came to know that which you shall only too soon: there is nothing else to protect."

THE DREAD MARCH OF ILLVERNESS

horns, resounding, shrill
a sky tainted, sickly, bruised
snapping bolts of magenta lightning
the unrelenting gale
the psychic fear
come the plague storm of the baels

the reapers stand
readied for war
their dreadful ferocity
among them, Death
his pride a realm its own
the scytheblade of his Elder's Clutch he draws across their brows

My children, my awakened reapers
Be now my Mortis Knights
Grim and stalwart
Now thyselves
Fire and fervor
Many and one
For 'tis time to go to our war

a shimmer through their ranks
crystalline eyes ablaze
one hundred wysps
their otherworldly power
the ardor of their reapers
one by one to root
their bearings to align
frightful warrior steeds

The Dread March of Illverness

their commander observes
wordless
upon his wysp, the first
his filial piety
his simple precept
venerable beyond his time
in flowing cloak and full black armor
his Cuirass of Morghistus
sword at his side, ancient, without equal
agleam by the light of the Forge

his soldiers mount
he takes their head
soundlessly they march
their banners bent on poles of carven bone
tearing against the wind
the Vadlum Gates are open

Illverness perceives
its parishes, niches, ethearic streams
its shadows
the hollows of uncounted skulls
come the shades and apparitions
come the specters, ghasts, grotesques

the gossamer flute of Ellianastis
its quality embroidered by the ear

thus ariseth the Dread March of Illverness
its rhythm coiled to hooves and stone
to metal and bone
carried by the city's mourn
memory, dream, regret
its ebb and flow

a swaying shadow
a floating citadel
the procession caressed by its tentacle underreaches
Akhor
sanctuary to Gethsemoni
upon her parapet
watching
as so many mothers
her loves, her loves
to war
her song falls upon them like a last embrace

> *Dear treasures, go*
> *Children, into the sunder, go*
> *A blight to break, the penitent stake*
> *It seeks us, oh, it seeks us*
> *Shifting through our bleak-eyed spires*
> *Ascatter in our figment pyres*
> *It seeks us, and now the time is come*
> *Thou wilt not flail*
> *To power, poison, lust, betrayal*
> *Our Underworld to fall to rusted swale*
> *Take with thee boon of thy mother's voice*
> *Take with thee the promise she sang*
> *For thy sword, thy fang*
> *Thy strength of bone*
> *And spirit honed*
> *Thy flesh underneath her blessing shone*
> *Against the wrath and curse of our forgotten brood*
> *Our shame, our tainted name*

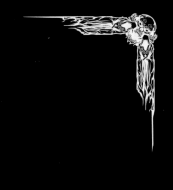

Waver not
At frigid peak
At shatterreek
At gate and tower
At bath of moan
Thou to stand, to soar, to fight
Thine image burned in fever night
Thy battle cries of gallows' height
Beneath their blight of shrieking breath
Of Death
A pale unbroken shibboleth
Prevail
And worry not
'Tis not thine own
But thy mother's
Thy strength of bone
And spirit honed
Thy flesh underneath her blessing shone

Death listens
the song of his Scions
of his realm
the feet of his wyspstride allies, darkly majestic
who carry his reapers, his needful hands
to act where he dare not

the gate
the city shudders
shuts its massive doors
forever or till victory

he steps between places
Daer Gholl, its court
its swaying undead retinue
costumed in mourning
embracing in silence
the echoes of the battle hymn lingering through the High Hall

he passes as smoke and shadow
into the dark recesses

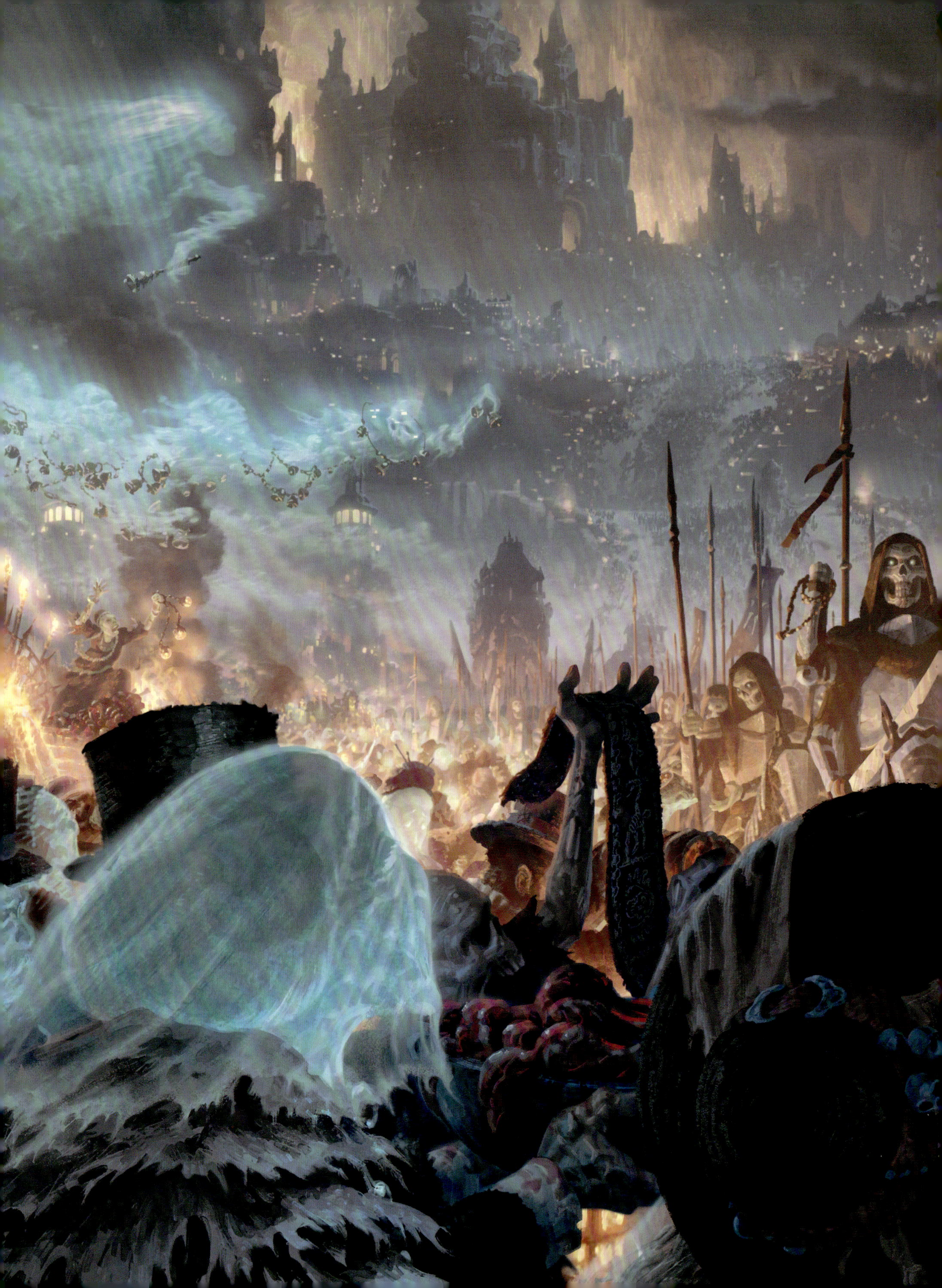

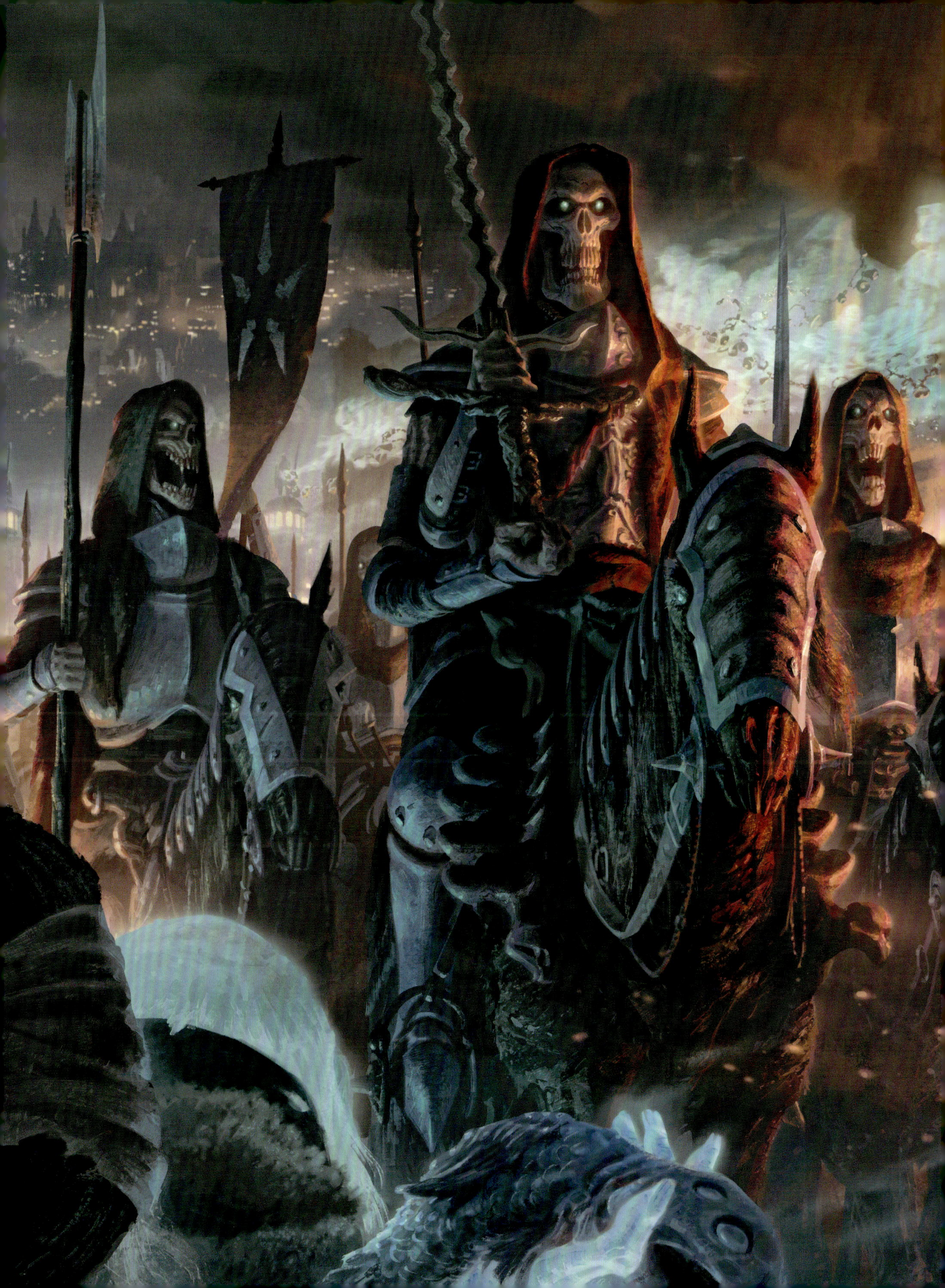

down
down
past the low catacombs
down
as if backward through time
through the layered outgrowths from that first place
a stone hovel
colorless, jejune
once the realm entire
his sanctuary

groping tendrils of ethearic light spilt from the Well of Souls
its keeper returns
they curl around him
they draw him to it
to coarse corporeality

awash now in its shallow pool
he sheds his raiment, his scythe
his ossein mask
his face, which none would see
necrotic, cadaverous
his eyes the biting simmer of mortal souls
fuming, unrestrained by its enchantments
as alone and naked as that primordial time

another he dons
primordial, recondite
long ago fashioned to lost purpose resurrected
an augment
upheaval to his soulfire fume
from his face, a wellspring
eyes to course in searing waves

his hand
writ upon it the mark
engorged with consequence
the trials of his General
From its intricacy, a sigil cut
his ichor cast black to the pool

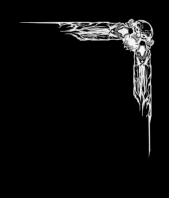

Awake, souls
Misspent by thy Sister Realms
Thy lives remembered anew
From the aether I thee remake
Claim thy selves again
Together to stare into our blight
Remember thine anger
Awake

the Forge answers
its sorrowful howl abates
groweth up a corpse
restful
wrapped round a twisted spire of blackiron bone
bent through yellowgray clutches of skulls
nested beneath it, two more
embracing, entwined
still more, to the broadening of the corpsespire
stirring, awakening in their rise

another sigil cut
another, his ichor cast
five corpsespires to enclose him
to rise

he feels the march above
far above
the sapphire-blue ripple at his feet
he touches his palm
he seeks for conduit
a thinness of the shell of the Mortal Realm

rising, summoning his Elder's Clutch
he brings it down
a crack to shake the foundations of the Underworld
a spindle of ethearic fire
a fount
as blood from arterial wounds
cracks across the well
beneath his feet

all around him an eruption
a violent current
his masks, his artifacts
his sundry of grim relics
arcane talismans
trifles from the Mortal Realm, inseparable of memory
whipping wildly about his sanctum
to crash against the walls
shedding their wafts of raw power
held aloft by boundless tumult
his helm screams into him
a buffer against destructive paroxysm
still he struggles for anchor
he alone untethered in the Cosmos

outward the blackstones
to smash through the walls of his sanctum even as they break
outward
through the greater emptiness
upward
through the strata
to the city walls
grow there, grow
conduit for his power
that of his scions
aegis for the city

in the maelstrom
a single memento
he grasps it in his pain
a spearhead of bone shards
girded with rings of rusted iron
Yes.
this will do
when the time comes
when his General calls for him
when Demithyle calls out for his father
he will come

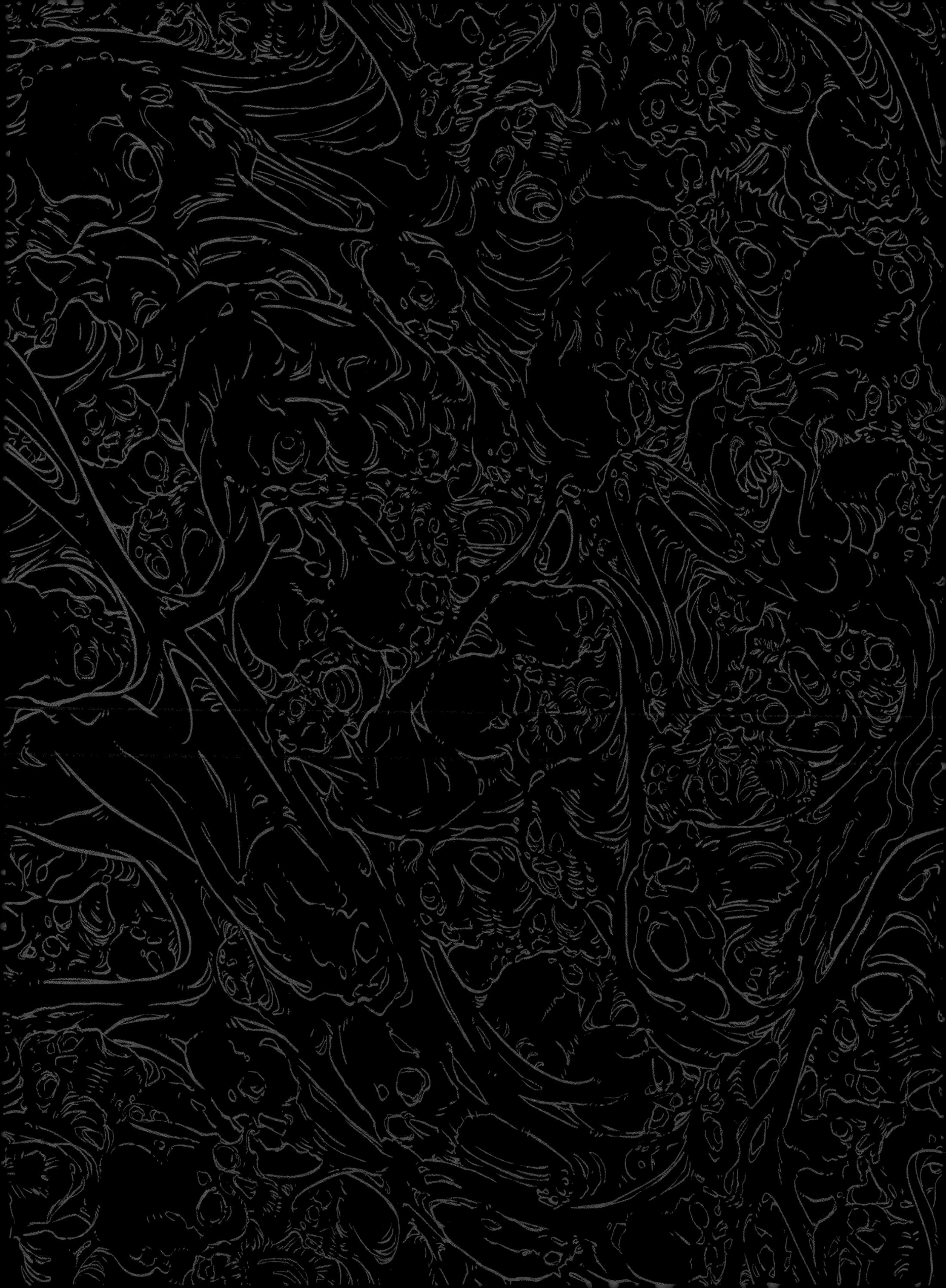

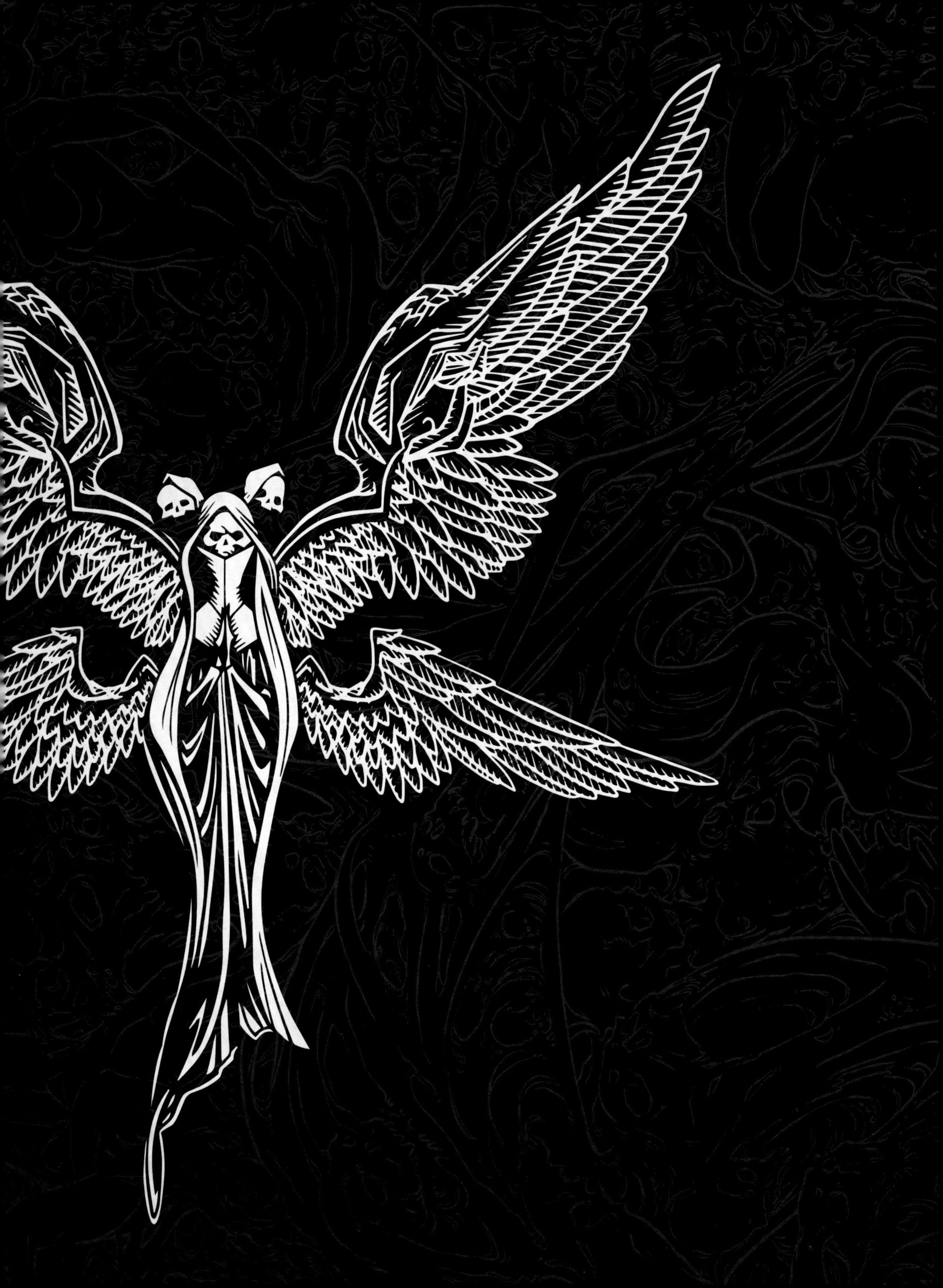

XXXV.
SIEGE

Death spread his arms outward within the brilliance of the maelstrom that contained him, coaxing upward the writhing corpsespires from his sanctuary even as he entreated their accumulation by way of the reclamation of souls. Upward through the strata of his realm they grew as if five great grasping fingers reaching toward the city, until piercing the surface just outside the walls of Illverness they rose up through the crumbling ground, two to flank the Vadlum Gates at the fore and one centered opposite, beyond its darkened rearward postern, and two ascending where the left and rightmost parapets jutted from the battlements.

As the spires clawed up above the reach of the city walls the ethearic light of the forge was cast over the corpses entwined around them, and as if by recollection of its forlorn wail the reclaimed souls within them were awakened to stir their newfound conduit of being, eyes flashing bluewhite as in their seeking awareness they drove their soullight between themselves to flood all throughout their agitated midst, down through the skullclusters knotted along the length of the spires, deep beyond the catacombs and into Death's maelstrom. Caught by the violent whirl, its potency was amplified manyfold as bearing the pain of it Death sent their essence upward again to drive the spires still higher, so that when finally their ascent ceased aligned to the jagged pinnacles high atop Daer Gholl, they were everywhere enlivened within fluctuating sheaths of soulfire in rival to the brilliance of the forge.

Bathed in this light Death's three scions then rose, wild-haired, cloaks whipping in the violent gale, held imperially aloft each by their own expressions of power, and each looked outward beyond the gate to witness the march of their army, far out into the graven expanse of otherworldly monuments that was the wallows even as the land was drawn behind them to crowd inward around the city by the growing intensity of the Forge. On toward the distant Blackmeir Tower they rode, each upon their mystical steeds, the realm beyond them now fully overtaken by the violetblack cloud of the horde.

The horns blared again, and purple lightning streaked across the shrouded sky as denizens all across the city climbed over the knotted skullforms and corpses of the spires, some in oblivious curiosity, others to find vantage there in defense of their home. From within his maelstrom Death inhabited all the city he had created, and from its belltowers and gables he watched with the affection of a father as his trinity of scions turned to embrace in their final rumination.

And then as one they looked outward toward the horde with eyes filled with the same soulfire that broiled his flesh, as his voice reached them from deep below:

So is arrived the meirdrem of our entity. As our enemy is all that I once was, all that I am resideth in you. May what we together have become be our Vanguard.

* * *

The second and third of the Scions of Illverness swept themselves out in flashes of bonegleam and spiritfire to take up their places of guardianship; Xiall weaving her bulwarks of bone out from the rearward spire, Ellianastis filling the air leftward with uncountable shimmering apparitions.

Gethsemoni lingered a moment more, her eyes gleaming bluewhite as she approached the withering barrier of the Forge's upward flow. She grasped into it, ignoring the agony of it as she cast her own spiritous reach to find the tormented aspect of Death that was held there, and finding it she conveyed her sympathy for his pain and fortune as in that instant both entities expressed what they could of all that which they had together loved and envisioned for their realm.

Then with the tearing away of her flesh by the stream she could feel him no longer, and she turned toward the corpsespire that loomed susurrant and agitated high over the right flank battlements of the city, the rise and fall of its ashen tethers of power crackling against her flesh by the renewal of her disintegrated limb.

* * *

Death braced against the tumult, against the searing pain of his maelstrom restrained. He cast himself into the breadth of his massive Vadlum Gates, deepening their aura of menace. From within its many depths he seethed his own anticipation to the bristling of the towering spires.

A dark, spiritous fog had begun to descend around the city walls, unperturbed by the force of the gales. Death could no longer sense the Blackmeir Tower or the army that marched to their places there. He felt as his own the dawning dread and exhilaration of Illverness in this long-awaited confrontation. His General had devised an intricate defense for the city, buffered in no small measure by the myriad vistas he had traversed. There was now reason, greater than could ever once have been hoped, to imagine they might prevail.

Yet there was part of the Alltaker that longed for intimate reunion with his aberrant offspring, they who even now whispered at him through the aether, *betrayer, betrayer, betrayer*. If the reapers should be overwhelmed, if the spires should fall spent and with them the scions, the Destroyer alone would remain to stand against them.

Should that moment arise, my fell creations, I am yours.

* * *

There was a pale hush as the violent winds that assailed the city abruptly ceased, and the vast panorama of the Underworld disappeared behind the still thickening murk. And then from everywhere there came a great collective shriek like the unrooting of a thousand souls, and with a rush of wind a swarm of ten thousand eyes burned violet everywhere throughout the fog before they poured forth from all sides in a black fume of claw and fang and wretched snarl. They massed around the city just beyond reach of the spires, and then long scathing tentacles of abominates drove inward from their horde, loping and flying low over the inner wallows with their twisted remnant limbs and wings of raw sinew. They snarled and screamed and spit black acid mucus and violet fire as they slammed themselves into the city walls, clawing over one another to scale them even as the fliers attacked above.

* * *

The scions met them with cries of their own fury, pulling on the power of the spires to lash the horde wherever it massed with macabre bolts of bone, spirit, and flesh interwoven, annihilating their twisted physicalities by the score, leaving only violet smears of blighted etherea and blackoil sludge as clouds of their wretched limbs exploded out to rain down upon the surrounding terrain.

* * *

At the pinnacle of her spire Ellianastis hovered, carried by a wind of her own as she swept her apparitions outward as extensions of her spiritous self, driving them against the wraiths in enervating howls even as she sent forth blankets of white fire to cleanse their bones of plagueridden flesh, their charred remains rattling in disarray over the walls. What plague and violet fire and black acid viscera they vomited against her was blown back by the gales of her ghostly acolytes coursing through the city within the ethearic rivers of Daer Gholl.

* * *

Xiall vaulted through her razorbone latticeworks along the city's jagged postern, singing out her disdain for the enemy as she cut them down with long sweeps of her staff, slicing through whatever baels attempted to smash or fly their way through the bulwark above the wall. She drove up new stalks of piercing bone to meet her feet wherever she leapt, shedding plates of carapace shell where their caustic ichor splashed over her as she maneuvered between black streamers of their venom. Following a cloud of wraiths that tried to ball their shrieking mass against her waves of boneslivers she screamed into it through her scepter, burning through its roil a hole of dust and cinder, and into this she sent her boneshiv drones to tear away their wings and throw them shrieking down upon the barbed wallspikes that pulsed up from the wall to skewer them.

* * *

And no sooner were these dragged down torn and wriggling than were their abominate forms obliterated by thunderous hammerstrikes from the goliath flesh revenants of Gethsemoni, sent out to skirt the battlements, the dark queen having flung herself out beyond the wall into the horde as it advanced against her spire. She plunged into their frenzy, grasping into their midst to crush their skulls and rip them away as she laddered herself up through their ruin, screaming out her wrath, her lust for their reckoning smoldering black the flesh around her eyes. She snapped them down with long reaches of entrail and sinew cast from her wounds, flaying them with electric nerve clusters that exploded outward from her core as in her wake she spilled down a bilious, flesh-devouring froth that mired them in swathes of putrid flesh and bone to slap in steaming lumps in the shadow of the city wall.

* * *

From deep within his sanctuary Death reached up his influence through the corpsespires, and by his sense of the city's presence he grasped the soul energy and sent it to course throughout the towering complex of the Vadlum Gates, and from the phantom sentinels within its turrets, embrasures, and parapets a continuous hail of vitiating lances thumped into the shrieking, undulating mass of the horde, withering macabre gaps through its collective physicality as the skewered baels immediately shriveled and wasted away. Wherever groups of attackers were carved away from the mass he bade the city's forward defenses to drive them by slash and shadowy flare between the towering forward spires, whereupon they were instantly reduced to so much aged dust in bright flashes of white light by the nullifying threshold he wove between them.

All the while the mounting fury of the maelstrom tore against his form, the pain of it threatening every moment to unravel him even as the voices of his exiled children cast their hatred into his ears. They screamed relentlessly for his submission, sneering at the strenuousness of his defense, as if viciously amused by its futility. He tried to reach out to them; he could feel the semblance of their being among the density of the enemy. But all but a sliver of them had been diluted amongst the horde that they had created from the entities of his Underworld they had sundered in their exile, creatures he had brought to this place for renewal and sanctuary or that he had created in wonderment, now corrupted and destroyed.

* * *

Death grasped more tightly within the forgeflow, restraining the growing maelstrom of soulfire to a compact vortex of power. Everywhere around the city the disparate remnants of the wallows crushed together in a craggy spider web of deep chasms and ancient architecture as they were drawn inward by the pull of the vortex.

Through this the baelreivers now twisted and flew and bounded, their violence seemingly unabated by the great volumes of their number unmade. Their destruction released far more etherea than could be drunk by the remainder. Though they heaved it back along the tentacle ranks of their assault it had begun to accumulate in thick, diseased bands of mottled violet that wrapped around the spires, and soon the city grew dark beneath the growing pall of wraithstaint etherea, mingling with smoke from dozens of fires as it roiled against the constant, concussive peals arising throughout its density.

Still the baels hurled themselves against the defenders. The scions fought them wave after wave, never allowing them to cross over the walls, tethered always to their tormented sire by the ashen tendrils of the spires. Death felt their exhaustion to match his own, and he felt the spires threadbare by the steady shedding of their skin of soulborn corpses, their reclamation of etherea spent. He reached through the cloud of tumult, out to the black void of the tower, seeking, seeking. But by its intensity the ancient mask that kept him extant within his maelstrom began to crack, and though the knowing of his realm was always and absolute, the pain that drove into him tore against his mind and he was all but groundless, adrift, and finally it was Demithyle who found him.

It is time, Father. Send to me this affliction. It is the business of the mortis now.

Death released his hold on the maelstrom. The city was seared brilliant emerald blue as the last elements of his physicality were shredded away.

And in that moment, in some quiet plane of his imagination he stood before his firstborn in exile, the remnants of they who had become unnamed, and he looked upon them with his naked eyes as he had never done in the earliest time, when sent from their home by the father who shunned the part of him they were created to supplant they were bequeathed an existence of fear and self-hatred by the eyes of all in the mortal realm who beheld their advent.

The words he then spoke he knew would never reach them:

Forgive me. Forgive me. I am so sorry.

* * *

Death released his hold on the maelstrom. It flew out from the spires in great arms of etherea that whirled around the city, swirling with the curtain of diseased etherea in a broadening tempest of such force the masses of the horde were taken up to reel and crash within its churn of corpses and battle debris, their shafts of purple lightning cracking throughout the dense spirals of etherea, the menace of their shrieks receding from a city becalmed.

Steadily outward it swept, until circling through the scattering of derelict structures in the outward wallows it met with the spindleshaped silhouette of the Blackmeir Tower which stood tall in gateward parallel to the Forge, whereupon a jagged dazzle of white light coursed downward from the tower's darkened conical heights as if escaping along the edges of the thousand black-clouded mirrors that were intricately coiled against it, now stirring as eddies of etherea twisted and narrowed from the tempest into their depthless glass.

And by this the tempest was drawn to wrap in counter rotation round the tower, condensing around it as rapidly as the force of Death's maelstrom had driven it from the city even as released from its grip swaths of the baelreiver horde dropped round the broad skirting of ironworks at its roots, screeching and bloated by the ethearic glut, railing their abominate forms against the conflicting forces that gripped them.

But before they could untangle themselves the last of the ethearic tempest was swallowed into the blackglass pinnacle high above, and for an instant all light and sound vanished with a shudder. Then down through the dark spindle of mirrors a ripple of light pulsed, reaching the base of the tower with a deafening shockwave that threw outward the snarl of blightwraiths, scattering them in every direction to tumble over the desolation of the outer wallows before crashing wretched and prostrate before the waiting reaper army, who in their gleams of weapon and fume and spiritous eye stared down upon the arrival of their enemy from astride their wyspmount counterparts, dark and wrathful, like warrior vagabonds of a land brought low by some eager and inevitable cataclysm.

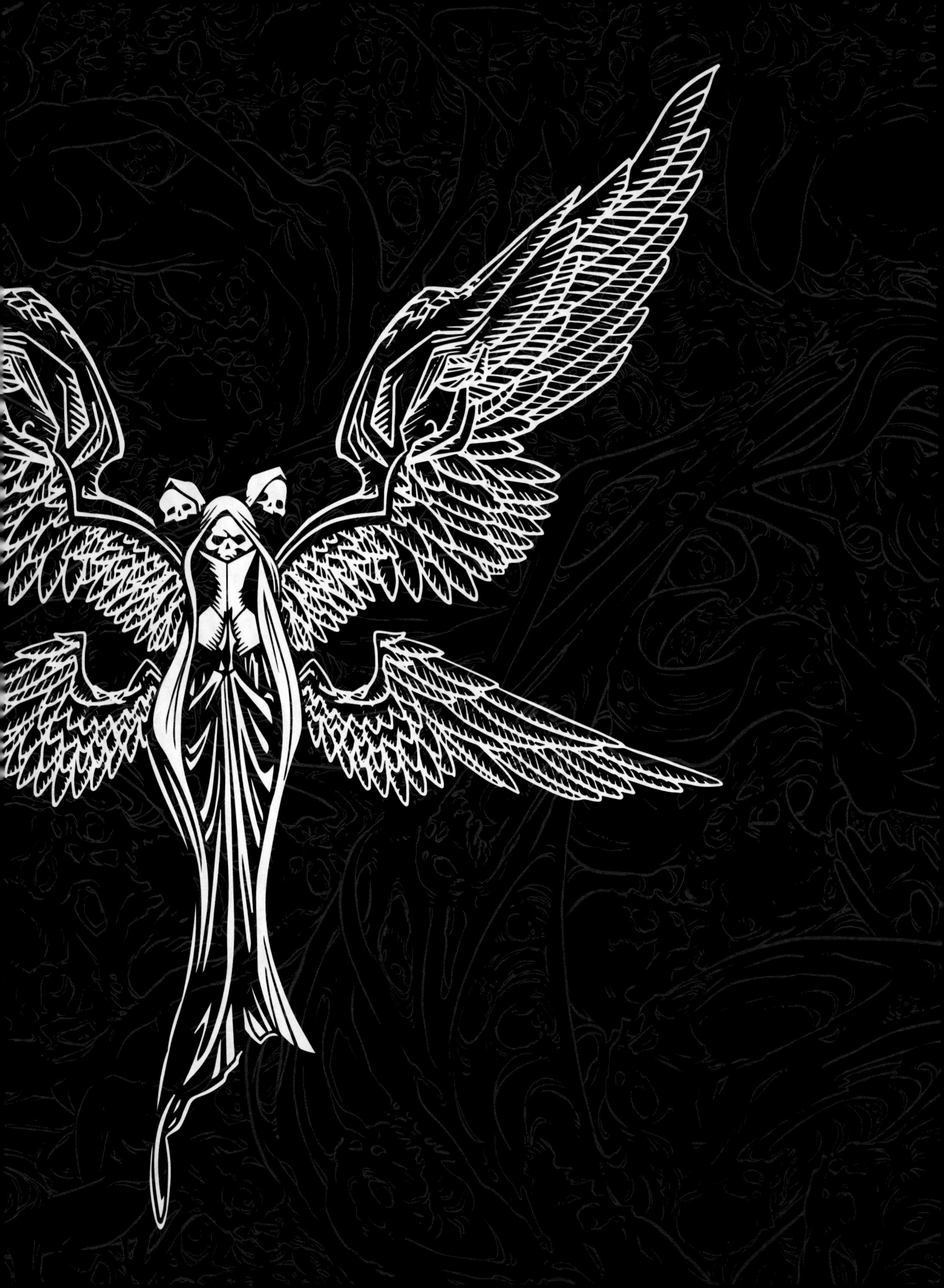

XXXVI.
A REAPING

The baels, fully halved by their destructive siege, shriek and scramble to right themselves, ignoring the knights in their midst, who only watch as from all across the outward wallows they race toward the city and its infinite fount of etherea.

Then the tower begins its bloom.

As the thousand black mirrors slowly unfurl a graystorm pall bleeds out from its pinnacle, soaking up the ambient light as the expanse of the terrain around the tower is torn from the surrounding landscape to fold steadily upward, so that even as by crooked wing and elongated appendage the baels hurtle themselves cityward over its rumbling concavity the gates and then the forge itself is obscured by the rise.

* * *

Throughout this slowly enclosing sphere the knights stand fast, each of their orientations altering according to their preordered positions to settle round its circumference horizontal to the tower's reach, the banners of their cibori aimed separately inward toward the focal point of its pinnacle.

* * *

From their place the far edge of the tear, Demithyle and Ycnaf move between the rise of shifting crags created by the closing aperture of strata, the expanse of the celestial sky steadily eclipsed beneath them as the scrambling masses of the baels hurtle over the opposite concavity toward it until by finality of its closure the strata is driven as a mountain up through their path, swelling into their frenzy, their masses thrown into disarray around it as reaper and rider rise above them upon its peak, his black cloak whipping amid the streamers of her ethearic mist until the filigree of his armor catches a dark glimmer and he looks up through the epicenter of the battlesphere to witness the pinnacle of the Blackmeir Tower aimed down an arrowshot above their heads, the glinting spiral of its breadth unfurled widening in opposite symmetry to the mountain into the darkness and dust of the opposing hemisphere.

* * *

Casting his gaze across the circumference, Demithyle marks the halo of banners of his cibori around it, and then looking down the settling slope of the mountainside before him allows himself a sense of satisfaction as huge fragments of churned up stone tumble down into the froth of his enemy.

He reaches outward through the aether, casting his awareness through the fullness of their reaper corpus, before wisping a single word:
Attack.

* * *

As if from the enraged throat of the Underworld there comes a single penetrating cry, and then from all around the battlesphere a hundred hollow voices answer as the streaming banners of the Mortis Knights descend on the fragmented churn of the horde, calling out their cries for war come at last, each their own deities of war by the immortal sublimity of their dreadful culmination, so that amidst the thunder of their wyspstride mounts their spiritflame eyes are brought ablaze to wreath their skulls in arcing trails of ethearic flame.

Split in three by the mountain's rise the stymied baels recoil in confusion and fear, scattering, clawing over themselves among the crumbling hillocks of ancient architecture all around it to escape the withering hail of skull and sapphire flare sent into their midst from the charging army even as it spirals downward against them, so that wherever the wraiths make to leap outward to take flight they are brought down again. And then, sickle, sword, and ax aimed over the cometous muzzlefumes of their mounts, the knights smash into them in a great crunch of metal and bone, their gleam of weapon and armor flashing through the smoke and cinder, quickly blackened by the sludge and sinew spilt.

And from destroyed forms of the baels their polluted etherea

A Reaping

swirls up, and taken into their spiritmander the knights cycle it between their ranks, burning into the air those lotus patterns of the cibori beneath whose banner they ride. And grasping it each in turn they shape its power to open the ground beneath their hapless enemies, and they throw out cutting swaths of boneshard, and wither them beneath membranous entrapments, and conjure vengeful emanations of their own spirit bodies, whispers of black ash that roar through the masses leaving only an oily fume of charred skeletal grotesques to dissolve in their wake as the wyspstrides dart and evade, skating between moments, carrying the mortis body beyond the reach of the baelreivers' tooth and claw and acid black viscera, their vision of fluctuating termini a perpetual denial of every violet crack of lightning. Then the air shakes with their pummeling breath as, observing from above, Demithyle compels open the focal corpus, and as the dust clears five paths are revealed, splaying outward from the hillocks through the chaos of the horde.

With crush of hoof and wilting cough the otherworldly mounts break from the ruptured masses. They leap up and outward again over the fractured terrain as the wraith and abominate horde pursues, snarling, spitting, shrieking, the spirits of the unnamed that drive them shining pale and diluted within their tumult.

Then like the spreading of his fingers Demithyle splinters from the trailing banners riders readied with pike and ethearic lance, and he bends them back toward the tail of their adjacent line. And casting to their eyes his sight of the unnamed, he throws the riders through the horde's charging midst, so that all around the sphere the trailing baelreivers are at once transected by downward-slanted lines of reapers, and in their blindness to their enemy's insight half of the unnamed are destroyed instantly, and suddenly bereft of the organizing influence of their sires the horde's pursuit buckles and curls in on itself. In that moment each of the cibori cries out their command, and every wyspstride halts simultaneously against the terrain to turn their knights about, and with renewed fury in their voices the reapers once again charge down into the chaos.

Yet as Demithyle had feared the shivering aspects of the unnamed endure to flee back from the fray, and he watches them as taking up the remnants of their fallen they sculpt anew their twisted physicalities.

And then with voices drenched in the carnality of the dreadsgrip that long ago took their hearts, they scream their fury and malice into the aether, seeking among the usurpers of their names the one who should read them even so diluted amongst their twisted progeny.

. . . it knowsss the names it takesssss the names of usssss alone names of oursssss alone alone it seeesssss usssss spitsss upon uss from the salllow shit and fungusssss in itsss skulll its ssspying eyessss obscenitiesss then come to ussss become uss find the song of uss we sssing beyond the aether beyond the veilsss beyond eternityyy . . .

From the summit of the mountain Demithyle brings up Cryptmourne to flash in the murk, and he draws it down across the palm of his inward hand, through the remnant of his father's mark, the Stain of Death yet described by the blood they shared. Holding it out, he casts his essence through it, and through the realm of true spirit that exists between the folds of every other realm an emanation of his soulfire burns.

Witness, abominations, he calls. *Taste the essentia of the Alltaker among you. Sip the bitter beer of your own violate selves, for here your betrayer is come.*

A long howl reaches out from the depths of the spirit realm, bearing the voices of the unnamed, yet strangely cloying, devoid of anger, forlorn and thick with sadness.

And then, down among the debris-strewn hillocks at the base of the mountain, Demithyle locks eyes with one of the unnamed, its remade form boiling with black mucilage, at once ominous and wretched within its violet fume of etherea. It stares at him across the distance with its luminous purple eyes plainly wracked by agony and filled with such naked hatred for him that he is for a moment held in its gaze unmoving, the fluidity of his thoughts broken by the sheer force of its desire for his destruction.

Then its form is overtaken by a scathing flurry of its abominates pouring over the hillocks around it to bound up the mountain slope, pressing before themselves waves of their anger and hunger and pain. Demithyle sets Cryptmourne at his hip and leans forward upon Ycnaf as amidst her sputter of ethearic breath she leaps down from the summit to meet them, and within their billowing comet he raises himself to spread wide his four arms, fingers poised as if in this sanguinity of his becoming to pluck the interlacing fibers of the existence he had through time and toil woven for himself, each its own vibration in the brilliant spectrum of color now washing over him: the Vanguard of his name, his specters of mortal memory, the voices of Illverness, the burden and remorse of Death his father, the whimsy of Ellianastis, the warning of Xiall, her touch and the guardianship of Morghistus, whose legacy quickens all of reaperkind and whose armor shields his barren chest where hangs the coin of Egregin, the Old Soldier, in place of a mortal heart.

And rooted beneath him, to him, Ycnaf his other, her many voices entwined with his in the eternal echoes of their silent battle cry.

Ycnaf's six hooves touch the ground again close enough to the loping abominates for the foulness of their essence boiling in their throats to be seen, and carried upon her gait Demithyle brings a single arm down before him and a cadre of Sithik's winged Mortis Knights swoop across his path, tearing the baels from the mountain in a blur of weapons and fiery cataclysm. Ycnaf bounds forward over the ruins and he brings down another arm, then another, conducting twice more his knights to smash clear the way in his descent toward the unnamed at the mountain's root, whose fractured spirit wavers always in his sight.

It hisses its cloud of purple bile, bringing up a final bulwark of its creatures around, and leaping the final length Ycnaf crushes against them; Cryptmourne in his grip Demithyle flies from her back through their snarl of broken claw and fang, gathering their smog of etherea even as he sinks the sword's point into the belly of the unnamed, by each of the blade's cutting waves burning its form from within before with his shoulder he shatters through a calcified shell. He catches the ground amidst a hail of its char and cinders, and pivoting to peer up the mountain slope he leaps to be taken up by Ycnaf again, who brays out her challenge at the deluge of wraiths swarming down over it.

Amidst the ubiquitous shriek and clash of war there is a sudden sweeping enervation of light, and high overhead beyond the summit of the mountain the inverted tower pinnacle pulses its dark glimmer and a wave of swallowing blackness sweeps along the full length of the tower spiral to the far surface, and then the fire and etheraic flash of a hundred skirmishes is reflected from all throughout the battlesphere as its jagged mirror leaves swell out in their final unfurling.

Everywhere in the growing gloom the shadows elongate and deepen, as if cast by unseen light beaming from the tower pinnacle. And in their charging, into one of these shadows steed and rider pass.

To fall weightless, timeless through the deep veins of darkness between realms.

Then to find the etheraic twilight of the battlesphere rippling from the hellpools at the Tower's root and to pass through their own parceled reflections captured by its mirrors, emerging once again from the depth of their own shadows cast upon the mountain, crushing upward into their enemy's bulk to explode them down the mountainside, only to pass once again beyond reach.

Thus do steed and rider assail the wraiths in their ascent, parting and rejoining through crag and chasm, shadow and smoke, evading bite and lash to destroy their enemy unawares. With the long reach of his sword Demithyle cuts the wraiths down and blasts them to clouds of bone iota, and with the grasp of his hands he tears them from the air to break their spines and dash them across the stone. Ycnaf's hooves spark wild over the debris as she breathes her incinerating whispers to blow pockets of erasure through their blinking advance, so that their course up the mountainside is marked by scorched and broken remnants left in the midst of her dissipating incandescence. And from everywhere there arrives a chorus of furious shrieking as by this consummation of the Tower every shadow is made an ally to the Swordarm of the Underworld, again and again to find the throats of the defilers.

Nearing the mountain peak Ycnaf begins to pick up speed, and with a flourish of the fingers of his smallest inward hand Demithyle quenches the soulfire still burning from it and grips himself against his companion's flanks before with a leap she bursts through the last grabbling slurry of wraiths there, scattering them outward in their soaring up from it, forward into the grayfade eye of the battlesphere.

There they pass between the dark prismatic streaks of ethearic mist from those wyspstrides rooted to Sithik's stanchion in their shifting between battles, and looking back over his shoulder Demithyle spies the snarling fury of the wraiths they'd left behind, cut down and driven back down against the mountain by the bonepikes and scythes of Sithik's winged reapers.

Past the pinnacle of the Tower they descend to circle along its spiraling clusters of blackmirror leaves, each glimmering at its edges with light restrained from the carousel cracks of violet lightning trailing after them from the wraiths. And then the cavalier battlecries of Sithik's stanchion call after them before pieces of their pursuers rain upon the planeless nullifying blackglass of the tower and a cascade of reaper knights join their descent, displacing like reflections over a shattered mirror as they blink in and out of the leaves. Through the descending layers of black smoke and violet flash they weave their ropes of etherea, whittling down the separated mass even as it gives chase, drawn by the aspect of their betrayer. And over the shriek and cannonade arrives Sithik's chortling verse behind them:

> *The diregoat baels thought to beguile*
> *and bite the phalk of Demithyle*

and found instead their tongues in shit
and now they crave the taste of it!

Then Sithik's knights spread wide their bony, membranous wings to catch the air, and casting down their cumulative plexus it wraps round their descending commander and his steed in a glowing capillary stint before broadening to slice through the remaining frenzy of pursuing wraiths even as they are carried upward again amidst the crooning of their cibori. And Demithyle spies out beyond the widening of the tower's root a bleak-spirited tangle of abominates massing in the darkness in ambush against the howling advance of Melthis and her stanchion as they cut round the outer circumference of the sphere.

Demithyle draws Cryptmourne and aims it toward their mass, and as he speaks a silent word to Ycnaf and her eyes flash sunfire orange she weaves them outward through the conflicting gales until vaulting against a passing wraith to send it tumbling away she slams into their midst, withering a crater of abominates unmade by the expression of their arrival even as Melthis's stanchion thunders by.

Immediately they are set upon by the baels, and Demithyle spies, shining pale beyond their disease of yellow and purple and black, the muted spirit of the unnamed even as its form is overtaken by the abominates mustered against them. Beheld in its freezing violet gaze, rider and steed advance through vomit and fire, striking forth along the arc of the terrain, parrying claw and barbed appendage, separating raking limbs and snarling heads, and returning their tainted etherea to them in hollowing swaths of ashen bone and fuming flesh that press away the shadowsmoke to unveil the unnamed a swordstrike away.

Raising Cryptmourne, its own hunger matched only by that of its mark, Demithyle lunges, only to be thrown back by a second unnamed unseen at his flank, the vehemence of its attack knocking him from his feet and sending his sword to clatter away even as a third races against him. The darkness parts in a flash of ethearic mist as Ycnaf catches its assault in mid-leap and both fly up above toward the tower's tilt. Without thought Demithyle brings out a shielding waver against his assailant's streamers of acid blackoil, returning it with a torrent of his own as grasping the bael's fanged maw he tears it open to fill its depths with a breath of embers. Blowing back its husk amid a hiss of black mist he turns to face the advance of the third even as it passes to caustic vapor, and anticipating its reforming in the darkness at his flank he holds his swordarm out and Cryptmourne is there in his grip again. He brings

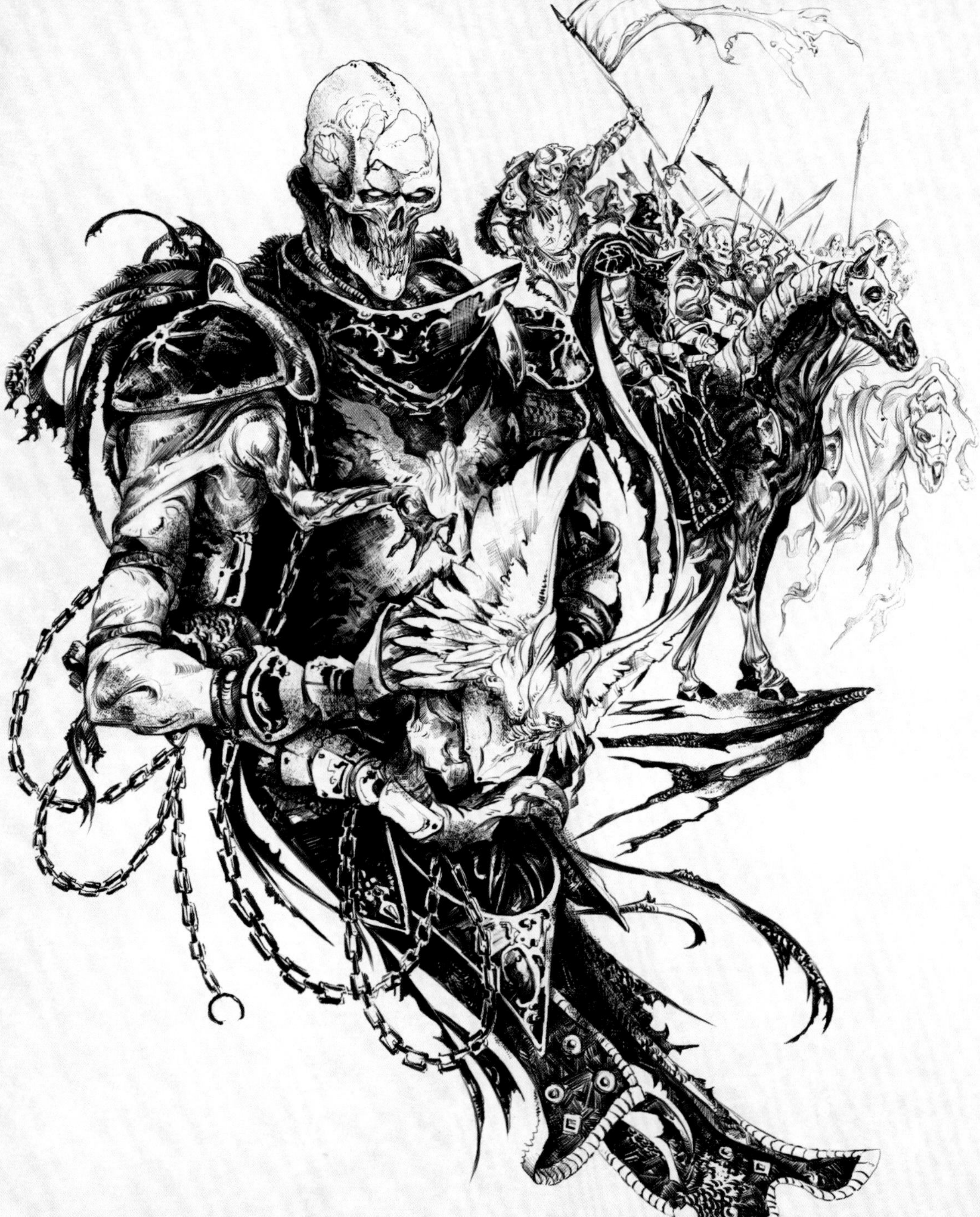

the waved edge down to crack through empty carapace, and too late Demithyle sees the pale spirit draw down into the terrain beneath him and before he can leap clear it spears itself into him, driving a wretched appendage upward from the ground beneath his cuirass.

Reeling against the pain, Demithyle finds himself sinking, dragged down through the ground by the bael's thorny grasp. And in that moment there arrives a scream of shock and pain as through wisp the knights as one feel the tearing of the reaper Cyrith, wrenched halfway into mirrorshadow to the rupture of his ghost, and the final howling of his innumerable aspects is overwhelmed by the shrieks of the drunken ravenous abominates as they drive their teeth into him.

Waves of cruel glee emanate from the unnamed as it drags him down. Through the pain Demithyle peers across the sphere as he is pulled under the surface, marking the last of Cyrith's aspect flailing into dissipating smoke as the breadth of their corpus is seized by the unmaking of others in sudden, rapid succession: Thissaelv. Shethet. Caersth. Each of them torn screaming, their names unwound and greedily reclaimed by the unnamed as their shadows are impinged in the midst of traversing the hellpools beneath the tower. Their wisping floods with the frantic dismay of the cibori throughout the battlesphere.

> *They anticipate the mirrorshadows.*
> *We must shun the tower.*
> *It is only the unnamed.*
> *Stay clear of the unnamed.*
> *How then to reclaim our kin?*
> *What becomes of their spirits?*
> *Where are their wysps?*
> *Ours do not sense them.*
> *They did not return.*
> *They did not return from shadow.*

The voices of the cibori quiet as the breadth of their army staggers, awash in a deluge of its memories of their fallen. Yet the echo of his own restraint reverberates through their ranks, as gathering their pain into himself he shapes their reaction to adapt their focal corpus, to fury their skeletal rigidity, rally unity between mind and pliant body.

Grasping the piercing appendage he pours into it the full extent of his collected etherea. An explosion of debris and viscera sends him wild across the battlesphere bowl, smashing through the frenzy of abominates somewhere near the base of the tower. His body cracks once against the terrain before his momentum is suddenly arrested, and regaining his senses he flares his sight to find himself wedged beneath a toppled fragment of wall.

Instantly he is set upon by a mob of abominates. It is all he can do to keep their clawing at bay with his sword, each thrust bringing with it pain and awareness of scraping bone. Then there is a glowing arc of blue above him and half a dozen bisected abominates collapse into view in a bilious spray of viscera, and the mammoth silhouette of Thrael steps among their remains.

"Baelreivers come for Death. Find reapers. Come to Thrael, fiends. Come and find her iron and stone. Come and find your reaping."

Glowing splashes of violet ichor penetrate the smoke and darkness as she stomps down a charging abominate with a heavily spiked sabaton and in the same motion hefts her glaive through a cluster of incoming wraiths, setting their pieces careening separately afire by the ethearic blade conjured along its length. Reaching up to skewer another from the air she stabs it down into the debris as releasing the weapon she turns to brace against the clawing pounce of two enormous loping attackers.

They slam into her, and her stance little alters. Grappling them against the breadth of her breastplate she shoves a hand into the gnarled skull of one and tears it free of its form, and bashing to splinters that of the other drops their ruins, holding out her thick arms as if to measure the absence of additional foes. Then with a mighty snort she bows out her chest and sucks their etherea in through the jagged fissures of her helm, and her eyes flash deep within it as she brings up the cracked skull to spit into it a black, fuming mass before throwing it deep into the midst of the surging horde beyond.

The ground quakes with the explosion to a chorus of stifled shrieks, and then again with the thunderous arrival of Thrael's knights, and the sounds of scraping bone and metal are pressed back. Then a mammoth hand grips the gorget around Demithyle's neck and he is dragged out from beneath the fractured wall and hauled to his feet before Thrael, her helm still dripping with the baelreivers' ichor. She grunts at the detritus of her destroyed abominates and wraiths.

"No more for Demithyle," she says.

Demithyle leans against the shattered trunk of a nearby grayiron tree. He scans the area but finds no sign of Ycnaf, nor does he feel her through the aether.

"There are always more," he says.

Thrael gives a cavernous laugh. Then her wyspstride appears from shadow at her side, twice Ycnaf's stature by their rooting. She turns to her glaive and raises a boot to crunch down the inanimate wraith still skewered by it, and pulling the width of the blade through its shell she mounts and to once again crash through the tumult.

Demithyle watches her vanish into the hills of smoke, scanning the battlescape as everywhere the gloom is broken momentarily by fire and flashes of purple lightning and the sapphire-orange streaking of the wyspstrides through rivers of polluted etherea. The blinking eyes of spiritfire as reapers everywhere pass between writhing shadows, snuffing out clustered pinpoints of violet cruelty amidst the crack and thoom of the mushrooming terrain.

He looks up into the swarming core of the battlesphere, a cloud of evisceration out from which a constant hail of detritus is drawn to fall to the ground in every direction. Away from the epicenter, the mirrored silhouttes of mountain and tower fade from peak and pinnacle into the battlehaze as if the frozen grains of a great blacksand hourglass, the direction of its flow long forgotten to the enduring ignorance of the passage of time. The latest among his collection of purgatories. Perhaps this will be the fullfillment of their purpose: the whole of reaperkind, old and new, mortis and bael locked safely away from the rest of the Underworld, forever to war within a hollow globe.

*　*　*

He reaches out through wisp.
It is time.
The sphere comes aglow throughout by the blooming of lotus patterns of spiritmandered etherea, growing more brilliant sapphire blue by the moment as it cycles through their focal corpus.

Demithyle steps into shadow as by his command every reaper across the battlesphere lets fly their spiritmander to whip round the globe unbounded, before like a striking serpent it snaps to their commander in his reemergence at the base of the tower. As fast as the blazing ropes of etherea pour into him he shapes it to braids of sapphire carrion crows winged with ethearic blades to wrap round the spiral-mirrored tower above. And below his feet a starburst shockwave of white light cracks far out through the bloom of the strata as with his marked hand he once again beckons the baels to him, and enslaved by their twin lusts for etherea and the destruction of the betrayer, the unnamed affix their hatred upon him from afar, so that when their voices reach him through the aether this time they arrive sodden with a naked intimacy of loathing for his name:

. . . the shit of the father demithhhyle the bloat of his cauldron demithhhyllle seeethe we ssseeethe with fondness for the flesssh of thy fallen kin taken by our fangsss toothsssome are their bonesss their fearrr we relisssh ssstilllll their ssscreams of horror sssweeet and ripe the flavor of it quickensss us it ssswimsss within us ssstilll demithhhyllllle come and tassste and sssee and sssmelll and feeel and feeeel and fffffeeeel and feeeeeeeelllll . . .

 From all across the battlesphere they tear their creatures away from engagement with his army to pour toward the base of the tower, the wraiths screaming through the air over the heads of the loping abominates, driven to his devouring.
 The viciousness they cast against him through the aether grows steadily in his mind until it seems their scathing voices scrape across the inner surface of his skull. Demithyle returns their stare in kind, watching through the permeating darkness as suddenly their twisted forms are dragged down through the surface by great stone limbs cracked free of sculpted postures and jointed by ethearic wire.
 By the luminous thrashing of their expiry stonecarven visages are underlit, revealing effigies of devotion and warding carved by otherworldly hands long reclaimed by time. Up from beneath the ground the animate statues shamble and lurch, everywhere stymying the charging horde as the fleeing aspects of the unnamed sweep from their shattered forms.
 And in that moment the full extent of the mounted reaper army charges from shadows around the tower threefile astride their wysps to rip through the abominates with sword and shield and militant incantation, abrading the abominates between them as they close to a boiling phalanx.
 And as the wraiths pass unflinching over the breaking assault, Demithyle calls the avian conjurations from the tower to swarm down into them, showering the knights below with their remains as the reapers displace against the stymied horde wherever it surges through its own polluted essence to assail them. He shapes his shredding avians to follow the rise of the frantic wraiths, painting knots of evisceration through the airspace everywhere throughout the battlesphere.
 As the rivers of their etherea flood into him from the spiritmander of his knights, fueling his engine of destruction, by the sublimity of his possession of it some measures he retains to well within himself, and a measure more as the burgeoning surety of their victory goes undiminished

by the dreadsgrip's call. No note or hint of it does he sense.

And in that seeming quietude it seems suddenly, should he wish it, he might in this very instant end finally the threat to the Underworld, and he looks at the mark and thinks perhaps he has all along understood the true source of his resolve. Calling into himself every iota of etherea, he would command his body of reapers to lay down their arms and be overtaken by the enemy, and taking theirs also he would keep it until, burning through his hollow chest and even the Cuirass of Morghistus, it would pour from him into the sphere, and he would close his mind to the voices of the unnamed and looking into the horde with spiriteyes unclouded wait until the nearest of them drew within reach of this diminutive arm, and his last act would be to lay this hand upon its brow as if in benediction, before compelling the tower to collapse around them, all within to be destroyed utterly, the city and all the Underworld freed at last from scourge. What better culmination than for the Vanguard to be unmade in sacrifice for the deliverance of the home they were created to protect? What better honor to their names than the cleansing of the stain of the unnamed?

traveler

Ycnaf, cracked and broken, emergent from the root of the tower. From his sense of her, sight of the missing herd is brought finally into his knowing, and image of them torn and struggling, locked deep in the tower, assailed unendingly by unseen forces from which she had only barely escaped. And looking round he understands the gambit of the unnamed, who in their shrewdness had hidden their numbers by the delaying of their remaking.

And casting these awarenesses above he sends the eyes of Sithik down into the tower to seek them. Down through its darkened fulgurite arteries the cibori soars, down, down amidst the darkening ripple of corridors to a rise of acrid blight, and there lay its pulsating heart, the boiling of plague spreading purple through its veins from the pale and withered shadows of the unnamed around it.

And in that moment all sight and mind ceases from his cibori, eyes cut suddenly from his skull, all of him taken away from Demithyle's senses. And then Ycnaf screams and through her he feels a dozen entities torn above by slivers sent to pierce the aether through time and space, no dimension of evasion, a termini unknown. They are sudden fear and then nothing. Looking up he sees them, shriveled and hollow through the smoke and murk, the wyspstrides of Sithik's stanchion caught everywhere along the expanse of the tower, their essences glimmering along a widow's web of lashing filament cast from every mirror leaf.

Away from the tower. Every knight and wyspstride, all of you. Away from the tower, now.

Weightless, his body pressed by Yncaf's meteoric force toward the sucking vortices of smoke and etherea and the sudden receding of the tower. There is a great cracking of its stem as with the tearing of the battlesphere comes a mountainous shower of razorglass, and the great collective moan of the knights buried beneath it.

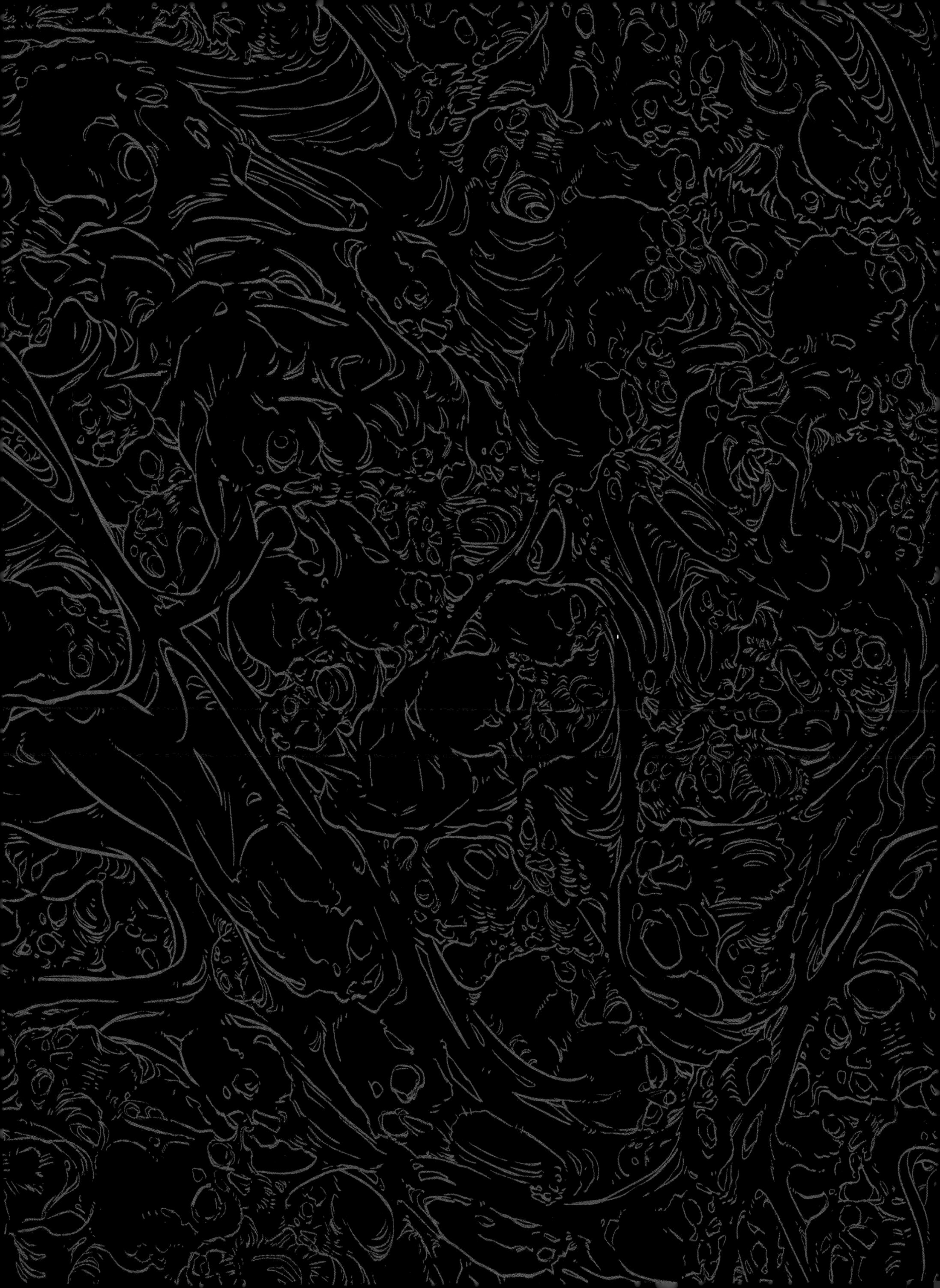

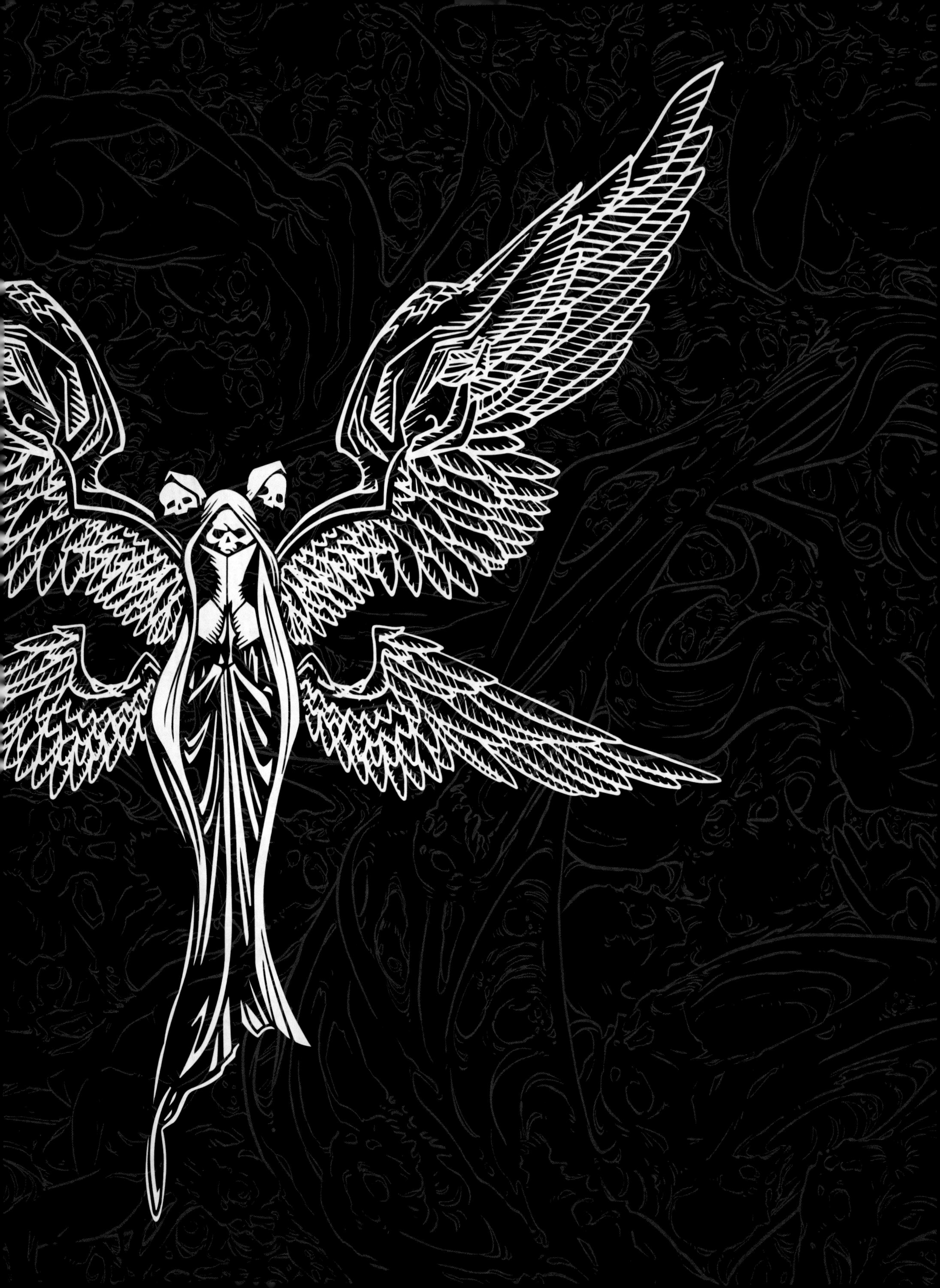

XXXVII.
A RECKONING

By the sundering of the tower the veil that had taken up the surrounding wallows into its sphere was obliterated. The fringes of the wallows parted where they had come together above the tower pinnacle to thrust down the mountain, releasing the crag now in great segments of rock and debris that smashed down into the shattered ruins of the tower, now a mound of null-black slag that still shunned the light, so that even the violent flashes of the baelreivers lightning that crossed the emergent sky went unreflected by its mass as the land began its slow, thunderous unfolding.

    The knights raced over the unfurling curvature of the terrain to converge toward its descending gateward ridge, vaulting over fissures and dashing between falling debris even as several of their number were crushed or swallowed by the devastated landscape. Reaching the outer wall of upturned strata left by the releasing of the mountain, they ascended its disparate peaks and then leapt outward to soar across the deep gorge in the wallows left by the gathering round the city of the wallows, a scattered formation of threescore wyspstrides and mortis propelling themselves forth by way of might and ethearic expression to alight across the exposed escarpment of the inner wallows.

* * *

Demithyle rolled forward as he and Ycnaf landed upon a precipice at the uppermost edge of the escarpment, each as torn and wretched as the other. Fighting for balance upon the violent shaking of the ground he stood, sword in hand, and cried out for the Mortis Knights to disperse into the crush of the inner wallows, then turned to witness the final collapse of the battlesphere.

As the last of its terrain descended in the near distance it was like a changing over of the meir, a great loam curtain momentarily blotting out all light, before the arcane explosions within were unveiled in a sequence of flickering shadows as it sank into the expansive pit of its excavation, arcs of white lightning flashing between huge fragments of monument and edifice as it spread itself outward to fill it.

Returning to Ycnaf's side Demithyle braced against the swell of dust and soot that rolled in over the gorge and blew up the escarpment, whistling through the gaps between its crowded architecture, and scanning through it he wreathed his sword with ethearic flame even as he wisped steadiness across the breadth of their corpus behind and below him. Shrouded by the swell there came snaps of violet lightning amidst intermittent, faint pulsations across the feverish sky. But no sign did he mark of the baelreivers giving chase.

And then the sickly churn of their etherea became visible aglow around the remnant of the tower, now a mound of jagged debris amidst a glittercloud of settling blackglass. He could hear their distant, frenzied shrieks as helplessly he watched their flitting about to snap at the luminous aspects of his reapers seeping up from their buried remains as they were drawn to the spiritual sanctity of the city.

He tore away his gaze. How many had he lost? A score and ten, at least.

And all of his cibori.

He had been joined to Sithik's being when he was wrenched from existence by the unnamed at the heart of the tower. Thrael he had watched vanish beneath the collapse, anatomized by the razorfall of its shattered leaves.

What of the others? Melthis, Gignoth, Torbrenth. He had felt no sense of their unmaking. Yet he could find nothing of them now. Perhaps they lay yet extent beneath the collapse, somehow beyond reach of his wisping awareness, the last of them to be rooted out and devoured in time.

They had expected losses. They knew the baels to be vicious, driven. Devious, even. Their fury would be as unrelenting as their numbers were vast. He looked across the gorge. Even so, there had been little doubt that if the baels could be contained within the sphere the collective might of reapers would prevail. And if not . . .

As anticipated, the destruction of the tower had released the gathered terrain of the battlesphere to accumulate in a broad crater around it, nested just within the full circumference of the excavation, so that the upper ridges of its ring overlooked a deep trench far below, all the way around it—except for its cityfacing arc, where the reapers had guessed the pull of the Forge would draw the terrain forth to spill toward the edge of the wallows.

And so it had. Still further compressed around the city by the pull of the Forge, the inner wallows had left behind a wide gorge into which the falling landscape had been drawn to spill, creating a long, rugged downward slope from a dip in the crater's ring toward the edge of the inner wallows, now effectively a high cliffside wall. To press their attack, the enemy would now be forced either to scale the inner slope of the crater's ring, and then negotiate the surrounding trenches below it, or pour through the choke point created by the gap. They would then have to cross a vast expanse of open ground before being forced to scale the wallows escarpment, all the while enduring attacks thrown down from the spires and from the forward knights, who even now positioned themselves all across its span.

It was a good defensive position, provided the wraiths could be managed. The scions would prevent them from flying over them. He could only hope now that there were still enough wyspstrides yet extant to protect their flanks.

He looked to Ycnaf, battlescarred and pocked with acid burns. She reciprocated from within a rise of her mists, but said nothing.

"You know what I would ask," said Demithyle.

She stared out toward the tower.

what of the herd.

"Yes," he said.

She released a contemplative curl of amber light to dissipate within her enveloping mistcloud.

de-mi-ta'il memories. a traveler to know entity, yes? to live to be. to know of entity beyond its terminus. a being, a traveler to keep always.

"Yes," said Demithyle. "That is so."

so the herd. herd to roam to be, always to know. an entity always to see the fluctuating termini. pain, yes. wonder, ire, fury, yes. to do in knowing, all finding a joy. all an ascendancy, blind to sorrow and doubt. then to choose among the termini. a choice, a final ascendancy. an entity the herd always to know. the scent of their voices, ours.

"I understand," said Demithyle. "Thank you, Ycnaf. The wyspstrides do us honor beyond measure by their sacrifice. It be not forgotten by the mortis. I will not forget it."

She beheld him in her amber gaze as he let the idiosycrasy of her mist permeate his own battered physicality.

a traveler and a traveler.

He reached beneath her broken muzzle with his diminutive innermost limb and touched the fount of her spirit essence that swirled there.

"As here as now," he said.

* * *

There was a sound of sucking air followed by a *zip* in the distance, and there atop the crater's ridge Demithyle saw an unveiling of a curtain of shadow, revealing two reapers dragging the upper husk of a third. The air was flooded with the unmistakable vociferations of Melthis.

"*NAEFUKKIN' DREGS!*" roared Melthis. "*I'll chapefuk every naefukkin' one of ye in HALVES, I will!*"

As the other restrained her from charging back into the crater Melthis instead leaned forward and unleashed a deafening scream, emitting a force from her maw that swept all the way across the crater to the snarl of baelreivers crawling over the tower ruins, one of which was staggered to tumble from its perch, losing hold upon one of the mortis it had captured, and Demithyle watched as the reaper's spiritous aspect flitted up beyond their reach to swirl toward the city in the aurora currents.

By the effort of her scream the ridge beneath Melthis and her counterpart crumbled and they fell backward from the ridge, and with a nod to Ycnaf Demithyle sent his steed forth to intercept their descent. She blinked away immediately, and reappearing at speed in a burst of blue and orange midway down the crater's outer wall she swiped beneath them, catching the two intact reapers, the remains of the third tumbling down to disappear into the trench as she streaked back upward toward the escarpment.

The reapers dropped from Ycnaf in a hail of Methis's curses, Demithyle's hopes confirmed as he saw that the other reaper was Gignoth. No sooner had Melthis regained her feet than did she make for the edge as if to leap down into the gorge, and with quick a nod to the reaper commander Gignoth hurriedly followed. Getting between the furious cibori and the edge of the escarpment, Gignoth pressed restraining hands against her shoulders.

"There is nothing more to be done, Melthis," he said. "He is gone. All of them. All of this, we knew that it would . . ."

She knocked his hands away and shoved him back hard, forcing him to grab at a piece of jutting debris to arrest his fall. And turning to Demithyle with sweltering flames in her eyes she went to him as if to whisper in his ear, and though no sound reached him from her open mouth his mind filled with the wails of their comrades, reaching out to their kindred mortis and their captain through the aether as they were devoured by the baels.

She backed away and stared at him a moment longer, then with neither word nor wisp she stormed away to disappear into the wallows crush.

Demithyle looked to Gignoth, whose gaze lingered after Melthis for a time.

"How many?" said Gignoth, finally.

"A score and sixteen."

"Eddath's eye . . . ," said Gignoth. "A third our number." He looked out to the crater. "I can still feel some of them."

"I know," said Demithyle. "What of your wyspstrides?"

"My own I released to join the others," said Gignoth. "Melthis's was destroyed from beneath her as she rode toward the tower's collapse."

"Toward the collapse," repeated Demithyle.

"A fury had taken her," he said. "She was near enough the tower to witness Thrael and the others discorporated by the mirrorshards. Whether her intent was to extricate their spirits, or to destroy herself in a foolish act of vengeance . . ." He shook his head as if angry at the thought, then looked back to the reaper commander. "A moment more and she would have succumbed," he said. "It was all I could do to reach her in time to shelter us from the fall."

Demithyle observed the spirit of his cibori as it rippled within his form, waiting for the tumult of its shifting colors to settle.

"Because of you, Gignoth, our corpus is far stronger than our enemy would have it," said Demithyle, finally. "It is well then that you succeeded. But our allotment for such temerity is spent."

Gignoth only nodded.

"Torbrenth?" said Demithyle.

Gignoth shook his head. "I have no sense of him."

"Nor I," said Demithyle. "The last I felt of him he rode at the tail end of our retreat."

Gignoth looked askance as quietly he sought among their wisp.

"All but two of his stanchion are accounted for," he said.

"Yes," said Demithyle. "Most of our fallen are the knights of Thrael and Sithik. The loss of our fliers will prove perhaps the deepest wound. Without them, the wyspstrides will have to guard our flanks on their own."

"Surely we would have felt his—"

The ground erupted beneath their feet, throwing both reapers back from boil of black fume suddenly emergent around the hulking, twisted form of a baelreiver unnamed. It locked its deep set, violet eyes with Demithyle's where he fought to regain his feet as from the pit of its emergence a shrieking cadre of its abominates sprang, and together with their master they flung themselves at the reaper commander.

But then Torbrenth was standing there before him, flanked by two of his knights, all three reapers crowned in a sapphire blue haze by the blazing spiritfire of their eyes. They brought up their hands in uniform motion as if to draw a stitch through the vision of attacking baels, which were then brought down as one as each were split across their cores. As a fount of the blightwraiths' viscera splashed to Demithyle's feet his reapers burned them down, melting their forms like sand into glass that shatters even as it is pressed down through the surface.

Drawing in the waft of the baelreivers' etherea, the three standing reapers quickly poured it down into the pit. Then, as his knights silently departed into the wallows crush, Torbrenth turned to Demithyle and him to his feet, shards of crystallized baelreiver spilling from his cloak.

"Their behavior in the sphere suggested they had read our leadership organization," said Torbrenth. "In fact their own is not dissimilar. I followed the unnamed in its pursuit of you as the tower began to fall, but lost sight of it as soon as we passed beneath the surface. But anticipating its intent, I found it here."

Demithyle nodded his thanks as he had done with Thrael not long before. He glanced at the place where he had stood oblivious a moment before, now a blackened roil of cooling magma. "And what then have we to thank for our late awareness of your continued existence?" he asked.

"Late, but no less opportune," said Gignoth, stowing his sword as he joined his comrades. He offered a welcoming hand, and gesturing into the wallows with the other, he said: "You might consider unveiling your aspect to the mortis, my secretive friend. At least for a near moment's turn. Many will be pleased by it."

Torbrenth accepted the hand of his fellow cibori, though awkwardly, before turning again to Demithyle he pointed toward the crater. "There is something in the strata," he said. "It interferes with our wisp, as well as sense etherea below, the closer we get to the Forge. I observed the phenomenon when Thrael conjured her statues. I intuited then that the unnamed would discover it as well."

Demithyle went to look out beyond the precipice for sight of the fleeing unnamed, But sure enough, neither there nor in gorge did he find hint of its unmistakeable paleness of spirit.

"They tried to break through our lines to cut off our head," said Gignoth. He looked at Demithyle. "Did you not burn away the mark?"

Demithyle nodded, unconsciously flexing the charred hand of his innermost arm. "I believe it was more personal than that," he said.

The winds around the reapers were beginning to rise. Flashes of magenta lighting flashed around the tower, where it seemed the baels had begun once again to mass.

"They will corrupt the mortis to remake themselves," said Gignoth. "Physicality and spirit the same . . ."

"That is not certain," said Demithyle. In fact he had already weighed the possibility of encountering the faces of their assimilated kin among the attacking horde, and whether it was wise to warn the knights even as they mourned their losses. At the moment, however, there were more pressing concerns. He looked at the pit again. "If the baels are able to evade our luring of them by traversing the strata beneath us, sending all of our etherea to the fore will be ineffective. We must alter our strategy. We will instead position ourselves across the escarpment wall, and hold them here."

"No," said Torbrenth, and they followed his gaze over the wallows toward the city, where the spires now came aglow momentarily by a weaving accumulation of soullight upward through their corpse-shells. Reaching the pinnacles of each, all five pulsed as one as the etherea braided downward through their structure, and for an instant all the wallows was underlit by a sweeping of ethearic luminescence beneath the surface, before as quickly as it had arrived all faded back to shadow.

They looked at Torbrenth.

"The scions have woven an ensnarement through the subsurface ley lines," he said, all but shouting over the rising gale. "Any of the blight-wraiths seeking beneath us will come upon it blindly and be destroyed."

"How will they sustain it?" asked Gignoth. "Their focus must be the defense of the city . . ."

"It is not necessary to sustain it. It is empowered by an artifact from another plane, an amulet which I reclaimed from the creature Simmel."

Demithyle watched him through the thickening, grainy haze.

"It is as Ellianstis has contrived," said Torbrenth, seemingly unperturbed by his commander's scrutiny. "I was sent by her into the labyrinth, to destroy the one who had destroyed so many there."

"Did you?"

Torbrenth hesitated. "No," he said. "I released it instead to wander, lost. Bereft of its power, its threat there is ended."

"The baels could come at any moment," said Gignoth, looking out toward the crater. "We should make ready."

"Fall into to your focal positions," said Demithyle, eyes lingering still on Torbrenth. He turned to Gignoth. "Watch your knights. They will be angered by our losses. You and Melthis must ensure they do not use the etherea they take, or the baelreivers will be drawn from their frontal assault. Dispatch interlopers with might and weapon only, and as quickly as possible! Send all essence forward to Torbrenth. No retaliation!"

And then turning back to Torbrenth, he said: "May your judgment prove as wise as it would seem."

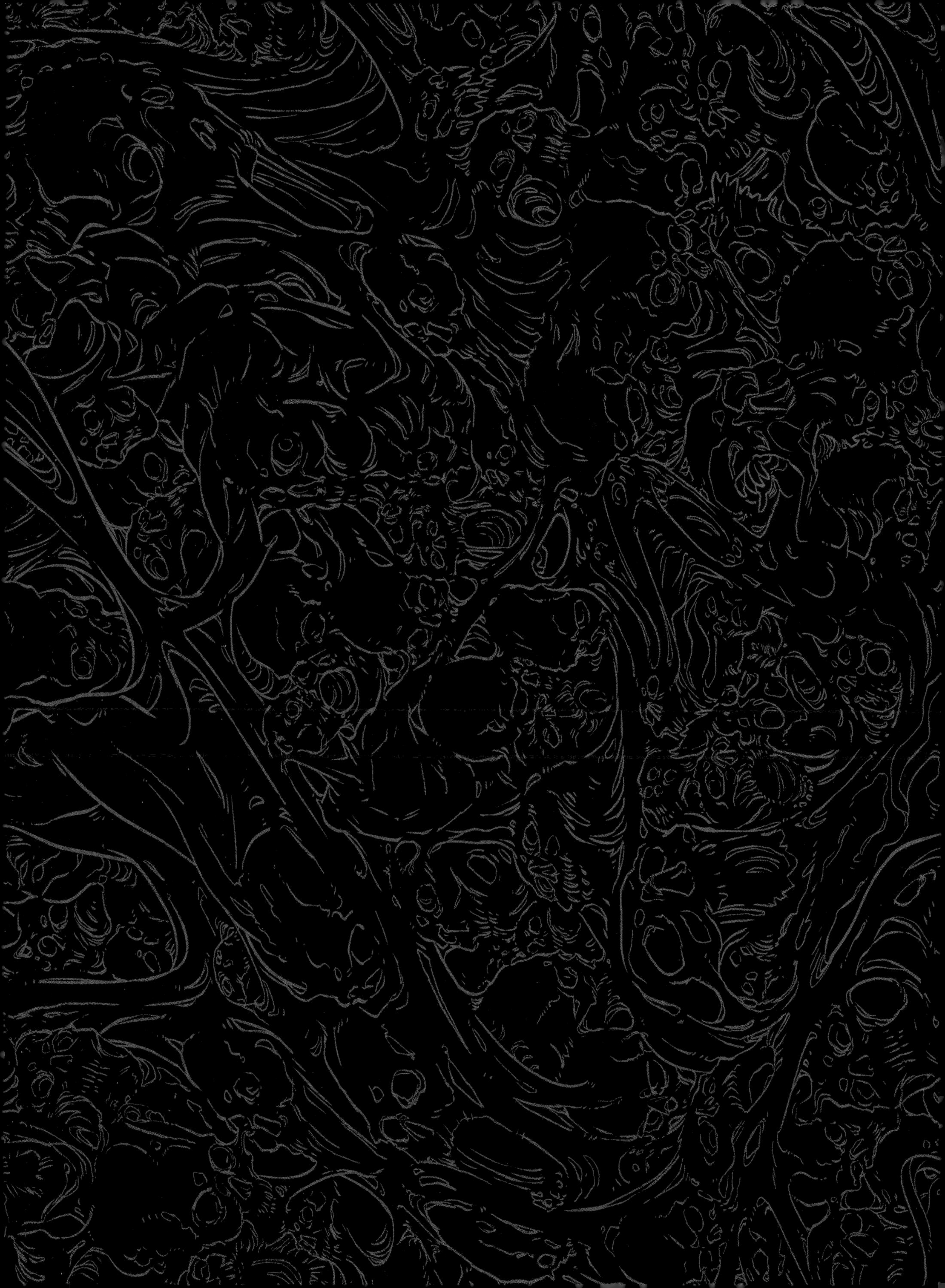

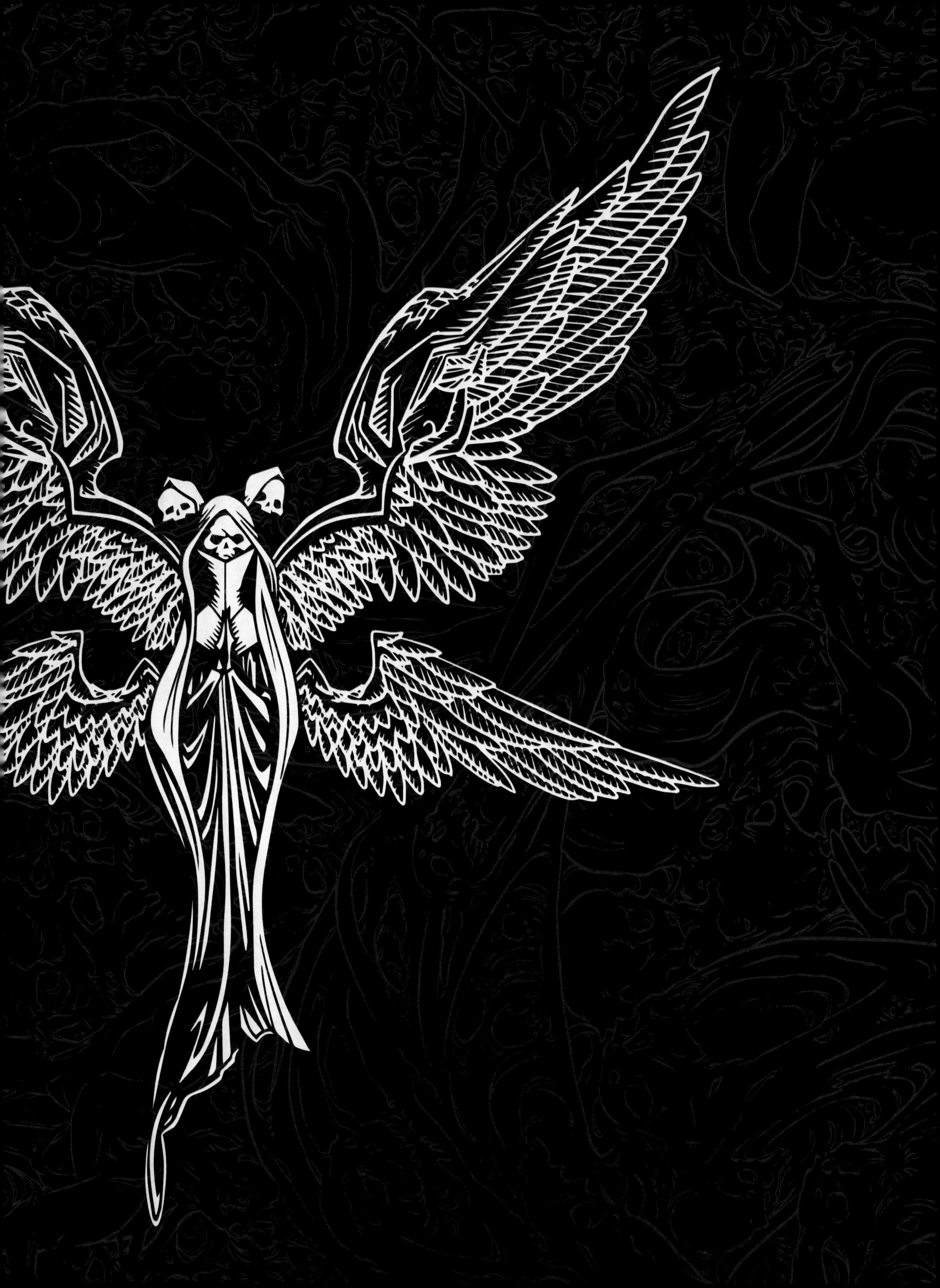

XXXVIII.
MOTHER OF THE DEAD

Ycnaf alighted atop the Vadlum Gates and Demithyle dismounted, and marking the distant turmoil of the crater he went to the forwardmost parapet to look for hint of the baelreivers' advance. Seeing nothing but flashes of their lightning through their thickening murk he grasped the stone of its turrets, and he cast his touch far down through the gate's superstructure, probing its roots through the bedrock. But he felt nothing, only the intermittent vibrations of the thunderclaps that rolled like sinister taunts out toward the city from the ruins of the tower.

He shifted his gaze to look out over the makeshift urban sprawl of the inner wallows below. With his spiritous vision he marked the luminous aspects of his knights arrayed throughout, their calls slipping up to him upon the rising gales as each of his cibori made ready their stanchions for defense in depth: Gignoth nearest, left; Melthis, forward right; Torbrenth's stanchion spread out along the front. Through wisp Demithyle guided them as sparingly they expended etherea to manipulate the crowded structures throughout to create choke and ambush points, trench lines, and pitfalls, reordering among these what knights whose wounds of physicality and spirit were not being tended by the shroudrieve and the fostermurden, respectively.

The whistling through the wallows grew more insistent, and the banners hung from the gatehouses and bartisans, eager but soberly bending from the walls only moments before had now begun to whip against them vigorously. Once again Demithyle gripped the cold stone of the parapet, but there yet remained no cadence of ferocity en masse.

Troubling. In their assault on the city, and the battle within the sphere, the baels had been content to throw their horde wildly against everything in their path. It would seem that their encounter with the knights had taught them patience. Yet another irony among many. Demithyle thought of the cold, hateful intelligence behind the eyes of the unnamed. That the winds rose steadily in the absence of their advance appeared to confirm Gignoth's fear that even now they scoured the ruins for the remains of the fallen to remake themselves. What quantity of the enemy would be replenished thus, Demithyle chose not to ponder. But he did not doubt that the unnamed would make a sport of torturing and desecrating the spirits of his kin in their corruption of them for this purpose.

In the few meirs' span since his return to the reaper fold, Demithyle had endeavored to engage individually with the mortis as often as was possible amid their preparations. As often as through their wisping bond he had allowed himself to simply swim in their collective entity, every part of his aspect open and unguarded, so that at times it seemed as though he had in fact never left the presence of the reapers with whom he had shared his first discoveries of existence, and alongside whom he had begun to explore and refine the founts of reaper might and purpose. But the moments were not few that he lamented his long absence from them. He peered into the pall, trying to mark the telltale blue glimmer of their aspects. How surreal that they should be so extinguished. Each an entity the sum of want and doing, their unique dimensions of persona refined by the elapse of time, transcendent even of the intimacy of their communing, now simply gone forever.

He could feel the simmering anger of the reaper army. Most now wished as Melthis had wished, to claim the spirits of their fallen. To revisit tenfold the devastation they had witnessed upon their enemy. To destroy.

He closed his mind to it. The commander of the Underworld's final Vanguard could ill afford to indulge in destructive imaginings. Better instead to grasp what orderliness of mind he yet possessed to disseminate among them. Perhaps to join with what temperateness might to be found elsewhere among the mortis, perhaps among the cibori. As he had done in Mortis Veth he reached out for sense of evenness and calm, and found Torbrenth.

The dispassionate other with whom he had discovered and implemented the reapers' completeness of being by way of their focal corpus. Though Demithyle had been the instrument, it was Torbrenth who had enacted the destruction of the megalith. Who had appealed to him to embrace the erroneous perception that Demithyle alone had accomplished this feat.

Certainly he would not have done so had he not been waylaid by first the labyrinth and then the library. But was it not this misperception which brought the mortis to follow him to the destruction of the orrery? Perhaps Xiall had been aware of it, perhaps not. Perhaps he had taken her appointment of him as Reaper General too much for granted. In either event, the scions, or at least Ellianastis, had clearly recognized Torbrenth uniquely capable enough to send him into that place.

What manner of arrogance had brought him to forget?

"'Tis beautiful, is it not, our realm?"

Gethsemoni's voice slipped between the waves of the gale like the tinkling of stone chimes. Demithyle turned to see her looking out over the parapet with him, seemingly unmoved by the ravaged, smoke-enshrouded expanse, gazing pleasantly through it as if taking in the full breadth of the realm as it existed in her memory. Her hair and garments were burnt almost entirely away. Much of her face had been dissolved away. No part of her was not torn of flesh.

"It is, Queen Mother," said Demithyle.

"How long ago did I gaze upon it here, just so, awash in the storm?" she asked. "I can not remember . . ."

Demithyle could only nod his acknowledgment, as humming quietly she turned to Ycnaf, who met Gethsemoni's proffered hand with the muzzle of her cracked and broken skullform.

"Thy thoughts lingereth upon one of thine own," she said.

"Among the weight of many," said Demithyle.

"The weight of many lost," she said.

"Yes," he said.

"And yet this one was not lost," she said, smiling. "Perhaps 'tis that thou hast discovered thyself less distinguished among thy kind than imagined?"

"Perhaps," said Demithyle.

Gethsemoni stroked Ycnaf's haunch as all three stared out into the tumultuous distance, the creaking of the corpsespires the only sound reaching them from the city amidst the low howl of wind.

"Brooding is a balm, is it not?" said Gethsemoni. "'Tis as a warming cloak to thee, I think."

"Upon what do I brood, Queen Mother?" said Demithyle.

"Upon whether another might better have been suited to lead thy Vanguard."

Demithyle looked at the sky above the murky crater. He thought of those meandering spirit constellations that had drifted unbroken through the auroras. It seemed a sudden comfort that they at least had escaped confrontation with the blight.

"There have been moments of late," he said, "during which I have found my thoughts returning to the labyrinth. It was a maddening place. But there was much beauty to be found there, and fascination, and peace."

Gethsemoni said nothing, only listened quietly beside him.

"These thoughts I was given to upon learning of Torbrenth's passing into the labyrinth: Only by the thinnest chance was I able to escape the labyrinth intact. By what logic another of the Vanguard of Illverness should have been imperiled in this way, I know not. Nor why he should have chosen to withhold the knowing of it from our communing. But a part of me was also . . . impassioned. Pleased that in my absence another of our kind had engaged in a journey of his own beyond the singularity of our task. Intrigued that he had borne witness to that realm of infinities. This part of me wished for nothing more than to commune with this one in quietude, to share and ponder what experiences there we had acquired."

He turned to Gethsemoni.

"This voice within me wishes for that even now, Queen Mother. At the meir of the Underworld's greatest peril, when every thought must be bent to its guardianship, I pine for at least one moment with one of the mortis that is not overshadowed by one war or another. It is this that threatens to bring me doubt. Perhaps it is this voice that seduced away my perception such that I was left insensate to the treachery of the unnamed. Had I been but deaf to the former, the obliviation of a third of my mortis army, perhaps to the doom of us all, might not be have been invited by blindness to the latter."

One eye milky and faded, she regarded him with what seemed amusement displayed over the shredded flesh of her face.

"How very mortal of you," she said.

He looked quickly away, strangely pleased by her response.

"The Alltaker choseth his champion well," she said. "Tell me, what wouldst thou do, so granted such a moment in time?"

Demithyle envisioned the inexhaustible stretch of unchanging walls only his scream of abject frustration had allowed him to escape.

"Perhaps foremost I would wish to learn what quality he possesses to have traversed the labyrinth with such apparent ease," he said.

"Many are the gifts spirit-born to reaperdom," said Gethsemoni, amused, "as thou hast thyself come to witness. Broader still, their use."

"There is also the question of undue peril invited," said Demithyle. "Why would one of my cibori be sent to so forbidding a place on the eve of invasion?"

Gethsemoni gave a dry laugh. "Woe unto they who seek to understand the fractured mind of Ellianastis," she said. "But woe also to the entity who splits her spirit so. For learning from thee the vileness of the creature Simmel, my sister in that very moment stood also before the reaper Torbrenth to beseech in wrath his willingness to aid."

"To enlist him as executioner," said Demithyle.

"And yet he choseth otherwise," said Gethsemoni. She reached down to lift his swordhand, stained black by countless baelreivers slain. "Wouldst thou have done the same in his stead, so sent?"

Demithyle looked at Ycnaf, gaunt and pocked with wounds, her ethearic mists made sallow and thin by her battle with the unnamed in the tower. He saw her trapped in the soiled crystal, imprisoned and alone in the chamber among the ruins of the entities ambushed and destroyed by the Fisher. He saw Simmel's fishy, needletoothed grin in the cove, heard the sickly sneer of its voice as it sent them into the well in the hope that the worm would devour their minds.

Gethsemoni nodded. "Thy passion is given by the flame of thine eyes," she said. "Through thee, the judgment of Ellianastis would have found surer conduit, I deem. By his actions in Mortis Veth she had thought Torbrenth bound less than thee by the contrition of the father, who even now wars against his own destructive nature beneath the catacombs of Daer Gholl. Or, perhaps 'tis that she had read thy spirits with true clarity, her bestowal of a slaying errand upon one who could not feel the bitter ire that thou keepeth yet the latest asseveration of my sister's own warring duality of spirit. It matters not. We are all of us crafted anew by the flavor of our moments, and so there can be no knowing of the entity but by the deed."

She receded from the parapet, turned toward the city. But for the enduring light of the Dirth Forge, its shadowy presence recalled for Demithyle the embattled arena of Mortis Veth. Fire and smoke, mystical and otherwise, rose from battlements blackened by ichor. Ellianastis's smoky phantoms soared between edifices little altered by their crumbling, interconnected throughout by Xiall's latticeworks of bone. Below, the shroudreive clacked and skittered through the streets, avenues, and baileys, gathering the last few remnants of the baelreivers destroyed in the initial assault.

"Look to the spires," said Gethsemoni. "What seest thou?"

Flickers of soul energy coursed intermittently throughout the height of the spires, between the threadbare intertwine of corpses all but still in their dormancy, the light of it lingering in each of their awakened eyes.

To Demithyle, the rise of the spires had seemed from afar as a crowning of the city in a great animate embrace of undead defiance. But marking the scintillating soullight here and there came a fluttering of familiarities, as if each flash of eye were an invocation of a dream long held, its essence present even where its substance had been forgotten.

"They are pillars of thy self."

He turned to her, uncertain of her meaning. He could see the ligature of her face reweaving itself beneath her shredded flesh as she took his smallest hand and held its palm upward between them.

"The emblem," she said, her voice softening. "A mark carried with thee through thy trials of remembrance. An inscription from thy father, a memento of thy fall. And in haste to be rid of it, its bounty unknown. 'Twas by your embroidery of it, reaper Demithyle, that each soul upon these spires was reclaimed from the Celestial beyond."

Demithyle looked again at the spires. Though many of the cadaverous forms had dropped from them, thousands yet remained affixed throughout their reaches.

"So many," he said, finally.

"'Tis testament to the depth of thy descent, indeed," said Gethsemoni, nodding. "Hereafter these mortal souls shall be gathered to exist as mourners in the Underworld. As Death has entreated them with this promise, they know also that 'tis by your remembering of their entities that they were delivered from their fugue of conscription and woe. That in fact their existences, proved futile in their breaking from the Mortal Realm, bore significance after all. And so is their soulfire offered first to burn for our cause."

Demithyle looked at her.

"Yes," said Gethsemoni. "Thy failure was their deliverance and also ours. For without their power we surely would have found need to take hold of the Forge in our defense of Illverness, risking the wrath of the Celestials, and worse still, the call of the dreadsgrip. Nay, we have not the fortitude of the mortis to resist it. Death and his scions are in equal measure the Underworld itself; as our lust for etherea is easily enticed, so would any of our succumbing to it be the doom of this realm and beyond."

He looked out again over the expanse. He could feel the guardian presence of Death emanating from the stone all around him. He wondered how might the Celestials regard this creation of theirs, an entity they had made solely to enact destruction, who now endeavored in earnest to sustain this home of dark magnificence and beauty that he had himself created. Where spiritborn and soulborn exist unchained unto the shattermeir, to come into what beings our agency might bring us to claim for ourselves.

He drew his sword. No, he thought. The baelreivers will never take our city. They will not destroy this home of the undead. He looked out across the murk-shrouded sky. And should I fall, another of the Mortis Knights will rise in my stead to lead the reapers to the realization of his hope for the Cosmos, bearing forth as one all that we have separately come to know and understand of it.

He felt a hand upon his skelliform face. Gethsemoni. She turned him to meet her eyes, reformed to their glinting darkness to stare into his well of being, smiling with the affection of a mother as she had done in the black and the deep of his awakening.

"Demithyle of the Mortis," she said. "Yes, I believe that Ellianastis has seen thee truest. By trial or fortuity, thou art indeed a spiritborn ensouled. 'Tis a duality to match thy twin burdens: skull crown to thy Vanguard's corpus and its heartroot also, one to wield the greater body . . ." She looked down to his chest, and dropped her hand to the deep gouges over his breastplate, the place where a mortal heart would reside. ". . . the other to imbue it with thine inexplicable soul. Yes. But for that which Xiall would have thee deny, the baels would even now lay destroyed to the last, along with thee and all of thy kindred reapers amidst the ruins of the Blackmeir Tower. Sundered not by the enemy, no, but thy warrior's prudence. One extinction bought by another, all the Underworld cleansed of blight."

There was a distant shrieking. He could feel the winds beginning to rise.

"And yet," said the Queen Mother, meeting his eyes again, "without the enigma that is the heart of thee, these souls, damned, forgotten, could not have been brought as novitiate mourners to soften the scar of our blight. The ferocity of their remembrance could not have been brought to bear in defense of our home. Alliance with the wyspstrides would be yet beyond our reach. All would be already lost, ashen, and hollow."

A subtle vibration passed through the stone structure of the parapet, followed by a muted thoom from the distance. Demithyle looked out over the wallows as a crackling distortion split through the air from the crater, washing over the wallows crush. He could see the alarm in the spirit aspects of the reapers arrayed throughout as the last of the shroudreive and fostermurden receded through the gate below.

He looked again to the parapet but Gethsemoni was gone. Ycnaf abided patiently nearby, adrift in her ruminations with the herd, seemingly unperturbed by the now forceful gales blowing in from the wallows. He looked back at the spires, the fingers of the Alltaker whose voice he could no longer hear, clawing up from the lowest depths of his realm as if to clutch his beloved city.

He looked at the Dirth Forge, watched its sapphire lightflow pulse upward through the murkshroud to pierce the darkened firmament. He thought of his spirit sojourn and the sanctuaries of the mortals he had traversed within its stream. Their emanations of home created by the last vestiges of their agency as they were taken from the mortal realm and into bondage. Certainly it could not be that he possessed a soul. He knew that he did not. He wondered what his own sanctuary might be.

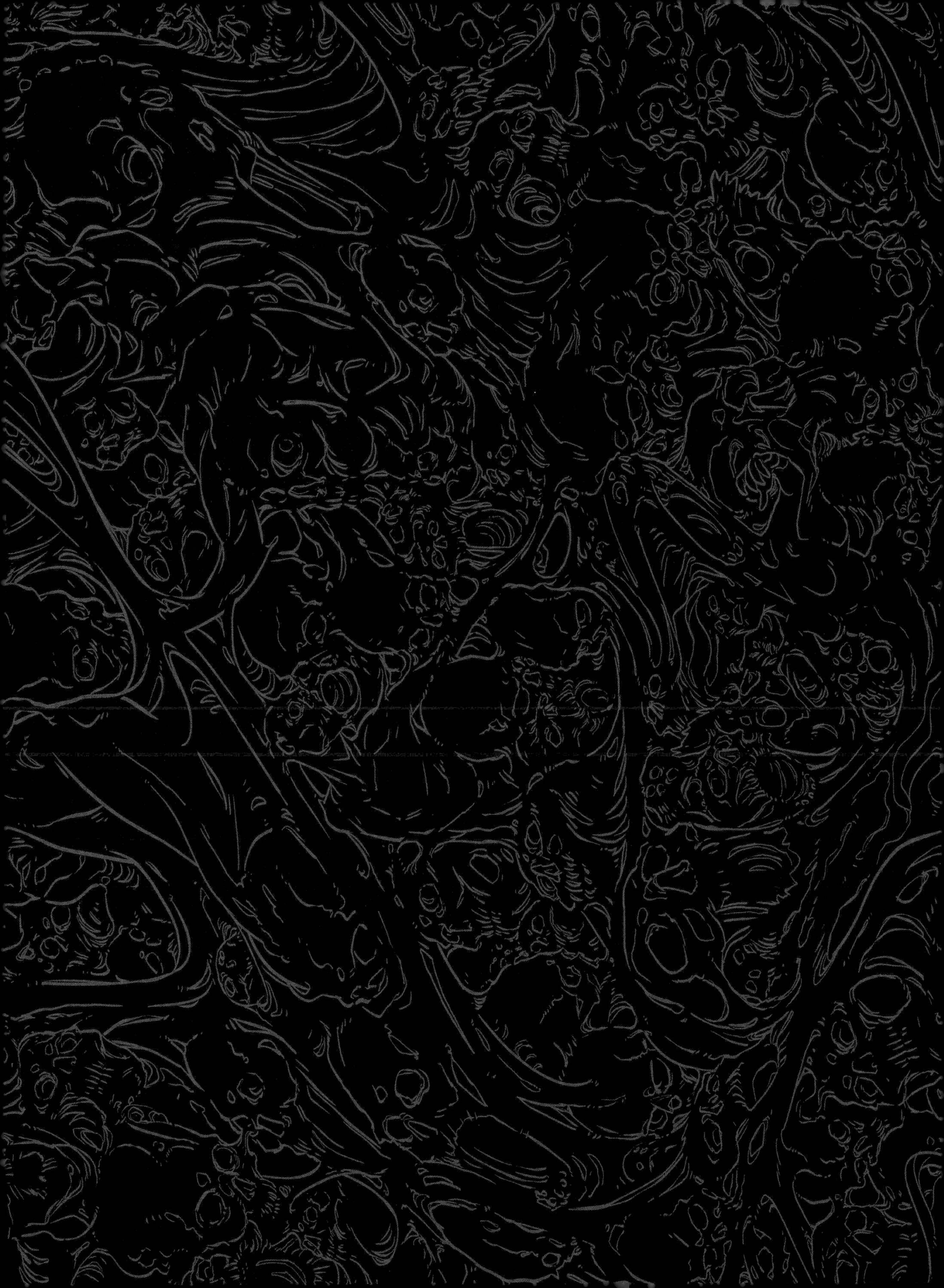

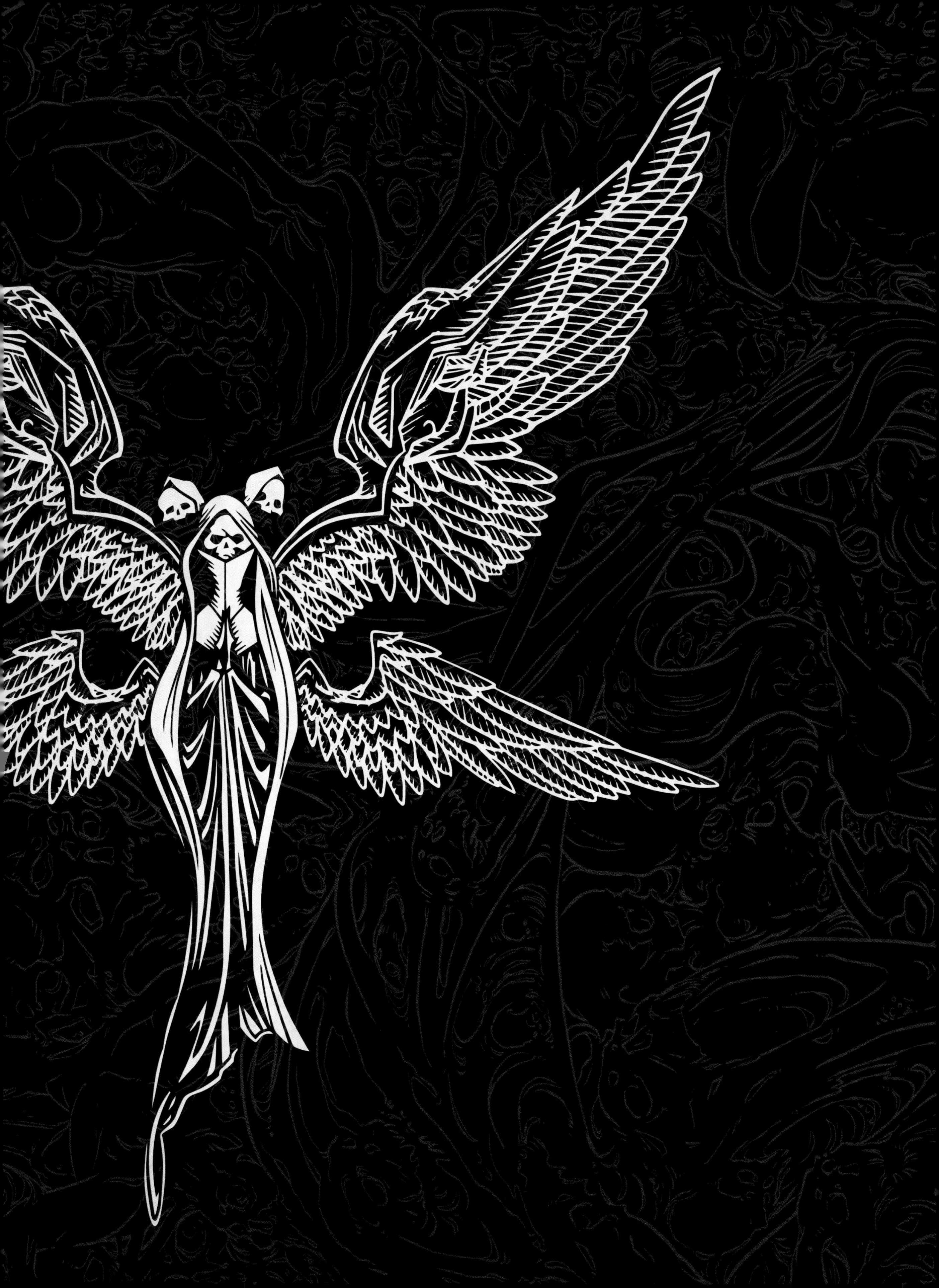

XXXIX.
TORBRENTH

The gales that had grown steadily in force since the destruction of the battlesphere now suddenly dropped to a mere breeze, the rush and howl giving way to the everpresent shrieking of the baels. The roils of their fume surrounding the ruins of the tower now began to accumulate, creating a dark pall that soon obscured even the flashes of magenta lighting. It loomed before the wallows escarpment like a dark barrow at the edge of a realm reduced, spilling over the ridges of the crater and down into the gorge.

And from this there arose a new fog of black mist, spreading outward across the gorge and darkening the sky, permeating the wallows crush. And between the jagged shriekings of the horde, a perpetual low sursurrus.

They watched as one by one the pale and loathsome spirits of the unnamed appeared within the shroud along the ridges of the crater—one hundred cruel and wicked stares smoldering in the gloom, saturated with hatred, casting out their hexes of hunger and sadism and glee.

The shrieking of the baelreivers seemed then to rise and coil as one, elevating in pitch to a shrill whine that thinned into crescendo of near silence before suddenly collapsing into a ragged, piercing roar.

A thick billow of their diseased etherea bulged through the black fume. It rolled down the crater slope swollen with a thousand violet eyes, finally giving way to an emergent mass of filthy, twisted flesh and slivered bone as the horde threw itself through the brink of the crater.

* * *

Through the surfaces beneath the reapers' feet, a deep vibration hummed as behind them the spires were brought once again alive around the city walls, the raw bluewhite light of their mortal essences skittering up from their roots and through the corpsesheaths, welling in skelliform crevices and hollows thickly entwined ribbons of flesh, bone, and spirit swept from their pinnacle heights to whip out over the wallows crush and strike down into the horde.

The ribbons shredded across the slope, burning away flesh with white-hot soulfire, ripping meat from rotted bone wherever the baels sought to press into the gorge. And by the liquid density of the horde's undulating mass the reapers saw then that it was not a siege of wraiths and abominates remade they faced but the advance of a single conglomerate organism, impossibly gargantuan and knotted throughout with grotesque conjoinings as if failed attempts at individualities of form.

Blasted again and again to dismemberment and char by the ribbons it surged through its own steaming clouds of skullform and limb, here and there growing out from its wounds black tendrils and great aggregate limbs amidst streams of its bilious ichor to grapple the forward ground. Continuously it bled forth its soiled etherea, and drawn to the pull of the forge it spilled through the strikes of the spires to flow down the slope and into the gorge, and as it came within reach of those reapers positioned across the fore they drew it to flood up over the escarpment wall.

* * *

Hovering above the ruins of a watchtower at the center of their Vanguard, Torbrenth watched the sheet of etherea rising over the edge of the wallows, calling for restfulness among his knights below as he directed them to draw and cycle it through their ranks. Shifting them subtly by the changing shape of their enemy, he gave the order to attack.

All across the front his necromancer knights threw out their spiritous fire, concentrating their attacks wherever the baelreiver advance threatened to pass between the strikes from the spires stabbing down overhead. They cast their influence down into the strata to drive pikes of bone up through the mass. They took up slabs of masonry and hurled them into its tumbling snarl. They threw out whirling ethearic trilliums and waves of disintegrating skulls, and glittering bursts of obsidian shards to explode wherever it knotted thickest, its conglomerate essence pouring down the gorge like a poison fog.

* * *

Then from Demithyle came a command: *witness the unnamed.*

Torbrenth looked across the gorge and through the black mist and acid smoke he spied the hulking silhouttes of the unnamed plunging from the ridges of the crater into the aggregate horde still flooding from within it, each of their forms absorbed immediately as their corrupted spirits swam outward through the mass amidst its violent churn.

They flowed out evenly toward their ravaged forward presence, skirting round and between the hails of fire and disinegration. The etherea that had poured from their destroyed masses then ceased its flow into the gorge as it was drawn into their clustered presence, and cordings of rotted flesh and sinew grew up from them

As the last release of the baels' essence trickled up the escarpment wall Torbrenth called for halt, and the clamor of battle returned to shrieking waves punctured by the rhythm of the spirestrikes as the knights withheld the remnant of their etherea to cycle it across their front, watching the transformation of the horde, now wriggling throughout with scores of corded physicalities into which the aspects of the unnamed now flooded themselves.

Those not obliterated by the sweeping lashes from the spires twisted round them to quickly grapple up their lengths even as they thrashed away and dissipated, swathes of ichor splashing across the escarpment as the wormlike tubes of what had been abominates and wraiths were shredded and whipped throughout the mist-laden gorge.

But with each such entanglement Torbrenth could see the unnamed pulsate within the grappling tubes, their spirits ablaze bluewhite even as they slipped from the destroyed tubes back down into the mass. And peering back over the wallows along the ephemeral extent of the lashes he saw them each momentarily sheathed with shadowy crystalline webs, shot instantaneously up along their length to pierce the spires' apices as each time swathes of their corpses were shed to tumble around the walls.

They leech the soulfire.
In order to feed their horde.
The scions can not see it.

Indeed, the ribbons continued to lash unabated into the horde even as the spires were steadily diminished, and surveying the carnage Torbrenth could see the segments of baelreiver shredded from the mass made animate everywhere throughout, scraping themselves along veiny networks of viscera grown over the gorge from the mass even as it pressed and bulged through its own devastation ever closer to the escarment.

Looking back toward the spires Torbrenth called up four of his knights to float up from the wallows with the sum of their cycled etherea, and rising in five-petaled formation with them to the heights he wove each of their grasp to extend through the aether as in unison they cut thin streaks of null space across each of the spires' apices.

From all around the city there came a slow creaking groan as all five pinnacles cracked from the spires. They crashed down amidst a rain of the corpsesheaths, leaving the striated skeletons of the spires to stand as a cold and broken crown around the city.

* * *

He destroys the aegis of Illverness.
He destroys the scions' reach.
He acts beyond our corpus.
Once more you defy the scions.
The scions do not know the horde.

Torbrenth closed himself from wisp even as Demithyle appeared astride his mount high above the Vadlum Gates, staring into him from across the wallows crush, several wyspstrides rising to flit about the darkened spires.

Torbrenth looked down into the gorge. The necessity of his act was beyond doubt. The flailing serpentine cords, having ceased their upward growth from the baelreivers's mass, dropped everywhere to be reabsorbed into the horde, now brought aglow in the murk with the stolen soulfire that pulsated through a network of veiny growths which seemed to root outward from the mass and down into the strata in advance of its relentless scouring toward the wallows. As well, unimpeded by the spires and without the reapers' ethearic attacks to draw its focus to the front, much of the shrieking bulk of the horde now began to twist out toward the left and right curvatures of the escarpment, clearly intent on surrounding the forward defense.

They would be the business of the wyspstrides. Even now, Torbrenth could hear the streaking explosions of the otherworldly steeds. Sending his knights to return to their places, he descended with them and alighting atop the ruined watchtower he cast a final look back up at his commander. He grasped the hood of his cloak, now laden with the blackoil fog, and pulled it over his head before climbing down into the wallows crush.

* * *

There in muted shadow he waited, listening back through the wallows toward the gate. But from neither the city nor the other ciboris' positions at the flanks did sounds of engagement arrive.

He could hear the distant voices of the wyspstrides raised in their own strange breed of fervor, the clipped penetrations of their strikes through the splinter bands of the blightwraiths. The rhythmic snapping through the wallows of his knights' cycling of their remaining etherea. The stone-cracking advance of the main body of the horde through the gorge. The insistent, goading sursurrus beneath the sickening totality of its screeching. The elevated fury of both to the sudden quake and rumble from all around as finally it met the base of the wallows.

* * *

Situating his awareness across the breadth of his knights, Torbrenth witnessed the roiling organism of the baelreivers throw itself upward toward them, suffusing the escarpment wall with its pulsating ligature, stabbing enormous resinous outgrowths into it to drag itself steadily upward.

He bade his knights to keep their places, to beckon the baels by their continued cycling of etherea. To hold fast, even when reaching the middle heights the horde speared its protrusions upward to drag them from the wallows to be destroyed through the eviscerating mass, his final command to them to thread back their spiritous essence as seeking with their eyes he compelled the collective weaving of his remaining knights to cavitate the face of the escarpment wherever the baels had affixed to it, wracking the wallows with shockwaves that blasted outward to tear through the scrabbling agglomerated physicalities, throwing out ichor-drenched limbs and still-snapping maws into the murk as the upward reaches of its mass flopped backward from the wall, tearing away the rest of its grasping ligature and bone to crash through the ashen well of fog at the base of the gorge.

* * *

Deeper into the mist-drenched underwarrens Torbrenth and his stanchion receded, down between broken columns and archways and half-crumbled mausoleum walls of cut stone, all which quaked by the renewal of the horde's ascent, and by the rattling calvalcades of explosions overhead, where the hooves of the wyspstrides burned white streaks through the battlesmoke pall as Demithyle directed them to slam against the knots of flighted blightwraiths and disparate swarms of raking abominates seeking in the absence of etherea at the fore to claw their way toward the gate via the wallows' heights, so that as the knights arrayed themselves for their defense in depth midway to the gate it was amidst a rain of smoldering scraps of blackened flesh and bone, and incongruent elements of armor which they recognized instantly even in the deepening darkness as belonging to their comrades that had fallen in the sphere.

* * *

  Then from his rearward flanks on either side of the gate Torbrenth heard the warscreams of Melthis and her knights amid the quiet clash of steel and bone, and a moment later the shadows and coagulating mist all throughout their line gave way to the blue tendrils of etherea spiritmandered to their fore, bringing ablaze the silhouettes of his knights as once again they cycled it between themselves.
  And there the roots of the underwarrens began to rattle as well by thumping bursts arisen from beneath strata as the baels attempting to assail the now etherea-soaked defenders from below were caught by the amulet's enchantment. Here and there structures toppled as thin protrusions of darkened, slivered crystal speared up through the surface, each with a sharp crystalline *ting*, and through the darkness and dust and debrisfall the knights could see the fading of cold eyes as the spirits of the unnamed fled from the murky forms entrapped within.
  The enemy's shrieks became an ensemble roar pressing everywhere through the pocketed ruins even as their crash and quake of the wallows ebbed and fell away by the dividing of their agglomerate body through the makeshift trenches and channels created by the crush. And then throughout the depths of shadow scatterings of cold violet eyes appeared to flit between the darkened gaps and niches, and murkstaint skelliform visages emergent razorclawed limbs that raked over the edges of the stone, the rise of their collective shrieking a force unto itself.

* * *

Torbrenth guided the fluctuation of his reaper line, directing the concentration of its ethearic violence, displacing knights and reordering them to weave varying complexities of its expression to throw back the enemy and bring down the wallows upon them, to further segment and carve down their wretched aggregations, to tear open the substrata beneath them, swallowing them mid-shriek into the amulet's entrapment, to shatter their remains and burn them within their glassforms even as they were buried by the downpour of wreckage and ruin.

※ ※ ※

The devastation brought by the knights against their enemy's assault soon carved out a broad clearing across their line, and here and there clusters of wyspstrides crashed down to wreak their havoc through it, trampling, incinerating, and otherwise crushing the disparate abominates that wriggled, smashed and vaulted into it from what was now a far wall of toppled ruins.

And yet the emergence of the baels would not abate, and though Torbrenth again and again anticipated their surging he could not keep his staggered line from shifting backward through the underwarrens—ever closer toward the clash and clang of Melthis and Gignoth, whose own knights now found themselves in recurrent melee with a steady parceling of errant baels managing to break outward from the masses to attack the flanks, and the etherea they spiritmandered to the fore now wound its way through the shadwoy ruins in an unbroken and scintillating river of blue.

All the while, the oily black mists continued to accumulate, darkening the wallows, challenging the knights' visibility and their footing as it condensed to slicken the surfaces, even as their cloaks were made heavy by its saturation. It seeped between their armor plates, invading the integrity of its leather strapping, and beneath their mail to froth over their cadaverous flesh, and cries of frustration soon arose as pauldrons and breastplates snapped away, encumbering the knights and hindering their focus, becoming cries of pain as the line began to fail.

※ ※ ※

You are spread too thin.
    Yes.
    Torbrenth threw down a snarling attacker and bearing another momentarily aloft with two other knights all three grappled separately its flesh, bone, and sliver of spirit and wrenched it to slap, clatter, and flicker into nullity. Gathering its wafts of etherea, the cibori threaded it to the others, who taking hold of it together then slid down a rubble embank-

ment, toward an emergent roiling of the shadows below.

He peeled back his mist-drenched cowl, and shaking his skull clear of moisture he scanned through the globulous murk, across the chain of chaos that had become his line. As much as he could discern it appeared as a craggy seawall repeatedly smashing away swells of burning refuse. The baels had begun to angle their attacks, wedging themselves between defensive positions and spreading them farther apart, forcing Demithyle to shorten the front line to array the knights as independently interlocked protective triumvirates. Torbrenth's stanchion stood now at the fore a besieged archipelago all but detached from the greater corpus. The sounds of fighting at the rearward flanks had risen to echo the fury of the front as more and more baels slipped through to chase back the glimmering rivulets of spiritmandered etherea. Two of his reapers had so far fallen.

He looked above, only for his sight to cloud as globules of the mist ran down his skull, welling into his orbits. Cursing, he flared the spiritfire of his eyes to burn it away. Demithyle was correct. They were about to be overrun.

Fall back to the gate.

Even as he gave the call he was hit by an impact from the side. It knocked him into a nearby wall, and crying out he grasped just under his left arm, round a thick blackened spear. And through his pain he marked across the clearing the simmering violet eyes of two of the baelreiver unnamed.

They sprang forward screaming. With a grunt he tore the spear from his chest and threw it down the throat of one even as taking its etherea he brought an obliterating fist through the core of the other, destroying it in a blast that threw him back again, this time hard against the wall to a rippled cracking of rib bones along his back.

To keep from screaming Torbrenth cast his mind into the spirit aether to join with the storm of violence that reverberated there, and he clutched at the broken edge of the wall so that the flesh of his hand tore away and his fingers clawed raw over the stone, tracing over it thin scrapes of wet bone powder.

Gasping, he slid himself down the wall, seeking through the thick curtain of mist for further hint of the enemy. But there was none, nor was there any sign of his reaper retinue. He reached through wisp to grasp for sense of his formation, only to find it everywhere in flux. Though much of his line was engaged in a systematic defensive withdrawal, many of the knights seemed stymied throughout by—what? Sudden emergences from below.

It could not be from below. He had seen to that. He had seen to it.

He looked at his hand. Flaps of torn flesh at the palm, the scoured bones of his exposed fingertips frothing with tiny grayish bubbles. So it is a devouring fog, then. He clutched the sleeve of his cloak to examine his flesh beneath it and instead tore the cloth away, the rotted fibers disintegrating between his fingers. Bringing up his arm, he found the skin mottled as if by advanced decay.

He slid himself back up against the wall, inwardly cursing the debasement of the baels that it should give rise to such corrosive breath as this. Gingerly he raised his cowl as if to recede from it. But neither could he escape the persistent whispering that had been brought with it, which seemed now only to elevate, a disconsolate, sibilant chatter that needled his focus, unsettling his control of the pain. He closed his mind to it as best he could. For all their training and preparation, the reapers had not accounted for such penetrating vexations as these. He could not decide which inflicted greater hindrance. Whether the baels were more cunning than even Demithyle had intuited, or simply fouler, was perhaps also unknowable. But should the blightwraiths prevail, Torbrenth was certain, it would be these more than any other of their abominable vehemences that will have brought them their victory.

* * *

From across the clearing, the telltale crack and shriek of the horde's push through the crush. Gritting his teeth, Torbrenth rolled his shoulder round a break in the wall, edging himself into the relative shelter of a darkened, derelict structure. There he listened a moment before making his way quietly through the darkness out onto a jagged exterior precipice, and taking care to restrict his ethearic flow he lifted himself through the mist-drenched air, out of the depths of the underwarrens and up through the crush.

Following along a slanted column he alighted in the archway of an empty belfry. Though here the mists were thinner, the dispiriting sursurruses persisted unabated. Indeed, they seemed all the more penetrating with the rise of his agony, as stumbling into the hollow bell chamber the flesh of his back was pierced by protrusions of his broken ribs. This time he could not restrain his scream, and as the swell of agony diminished he screamed once more if only to chase away the voices.

He scanned the gateward vista, where the light of the Dirth Forge flickered with the intermittent flashes of the wyspstrides, whose muted trails he could see burning through thick billows of smoke rising steadily from the wallows. He could make out their bestial warscreams inlain with the screeching of the baels, one which halted mid-rise as the hissing seemed then to elevate as if with a sinister glee, and he watched a wyspstride drop from the sky like a fading cinder swallowed by the blacktar smoke. He wondered at its voiceless pain. His own steed he had lost in the sphere. He had not allowed himself to feel it. Its final wisping cry, shut from his mind . . .

A mind replete with the knowledge of screams. So reverberant and unrelenting. Reverberant? A chamber, somewhere in the labyrinth. The remains of a temple, its roof open to some mystical projection of an alien sky, its floor half-subsumed by whatever cataclysm had delivered it into this forbidding place. There he had found the sniveling creature, in the glow of a warming fire it had made for itself. He'd caught it up, the vambraces of Demithyle's armor knocking ridiculously round its waifish legs as it twitched about. Against the ground he'd splayed it, thrashing. He'd staked it through its neck and wrists, knelt upon its ankles. Its screams as incessant as they were hideous as he passed the blade beneath the gray of its flesh, scraping through callus and wart, cutting what patterns pleased him one moment to the next. Each sheaf of skin he'd laid flat to glisten upon floor beside it, beckoned by the screams to return once more to draw the tip of his skean along the underflesh of its arms. Around the soles of its feet. Up and over the bulge of its belly. Along its jawbone and across its brow to remove its fishlike face, its tongue, its fingers, its shriveled genitalia . . . It had screamed until its throat was ruptured and could only choke its suffering out through naked cartilage, wheezes of its horror and misery and grief as its skin steamed by the heat of the fire, lit crimson-violet by the spiritflame spilling forth from his Mortis eyes . . .

The whispers ceased, and Tobrenth released a grunt as thick ropes of his fluid whipped out through the louvered windows of the belfry, a malformed appendage driven high up under his rib cage. Staring into him, the cruel eyes of the unnamed, pulsating violet in its monstrous hollows amidst a simmer of black ooze. It lifted him off his feet, watching with interest for the rupture of his spark. Grappling the cibori's limbs with its own, it drew its appendage down through his torso, opening him directly over its broadened maw, a hissing gurgle rising from deep within its core as it drank in his essence. Churning with the fading echoes of Simmel's screams, driven into his mind by way of a dark insinuating vision—that memory of torture not his own, no, inflicted upon him, surely, by an enemy far shrewder than the reapers had been given to suspect. To bring them as much to doubt as to falter. An arithmetic of malice designed to undermine the self, yes, delivered by these inescapable goading whispers. These voices of jubilant sadism which Torbrenth had lamented as unforeseen by the imprudence of a neophyte commander. Which even now chased him into the darkness. How very . . . cunning.

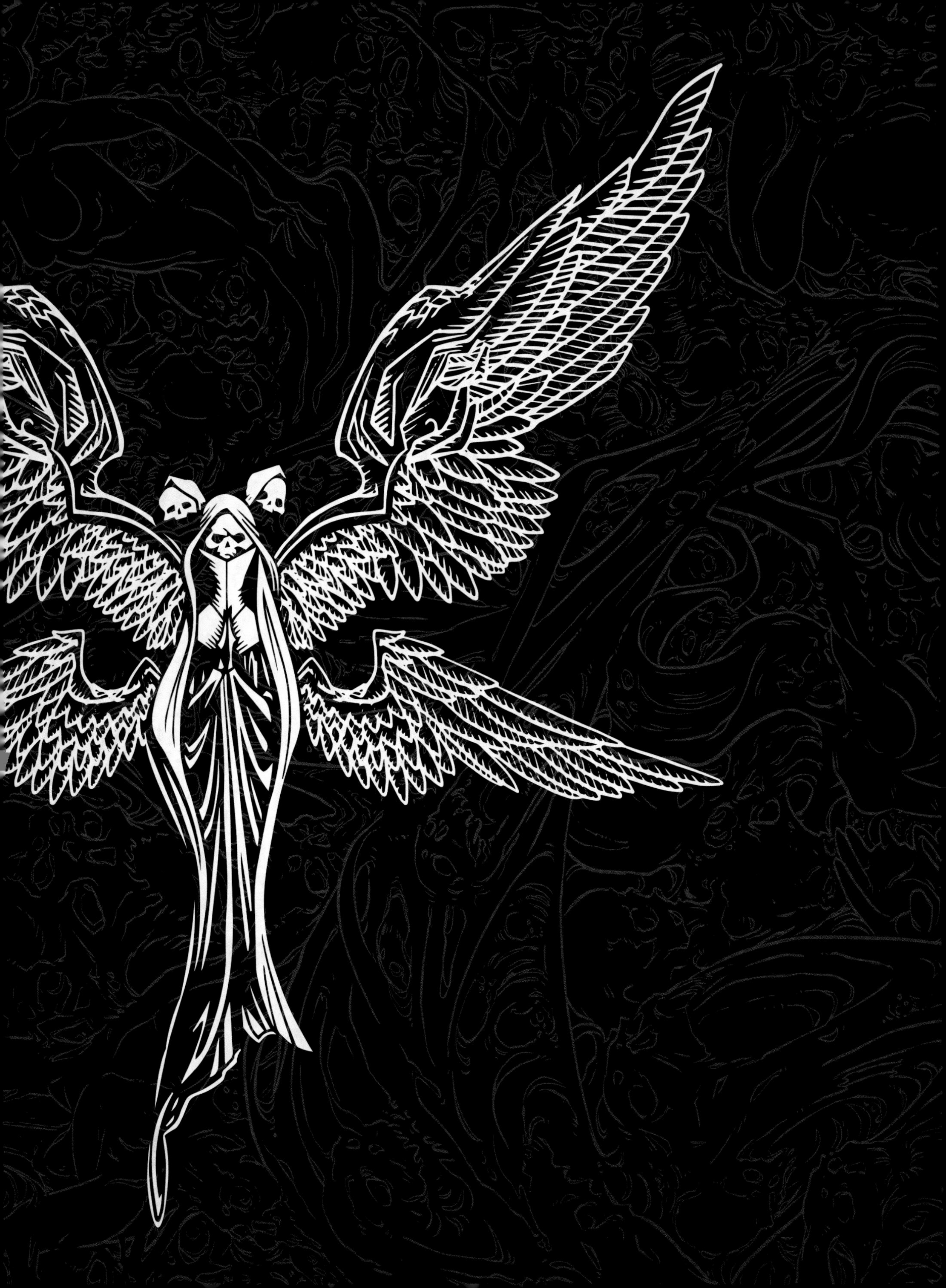

XL.
THE MAW

Melthis threw her ax across the collapsed upper floor of a building, pinning a bael against the half-ruined wall it had scaled in pursuit of her. Leaping into it she cracked through its skull with her own bone-studded brow, splashing its ichor across the stone, already glistening with the black oil fog that seemed to grow thicker by the moment. She tore free her ax and screaming out her war cry dropped down to catch another bael mid-pounce in ambush against one of her knights, who answered her cry with a scream of his own, their voices commingling in furious harmony that echoed throughout her ranks as she grappled the bael's sinuous neck to rip its head from its thrashing abominate form. Bearing it aloft, she brought her knights to scream in chorus once more, for the honor of the Vanguard and the arousal of all of its savagery, to be brought in reprisal against these fiends that had profaned the spirits of their sistren and their brethren.

✳ ✳ ✳

Then came the call for knights of the front to recede into the crush, and the etherea Melthis bade her knights to spiritmander there buckled against the disarray as it was returned to spill back throughout her place across the rightward flank.

And then, Torbrenth's pain. Reverberating through their wisp. The diminishing of his aspect, drained. Greedily, lasciviously. His final sentiment not fear but deference to the strategem of his destroyer. And then he was gone.

Demithyle's aspect permeated their corpus consciousness, his directive clear:

Melthis is now cardinal. Thread to the Maw of our Corpus. Thread to the banner of Melthis.

* * *

The Vanguard dwindles!
Another of the Mortis taken.
Devoured.
Three lost since the Tower.
Vengeance! Conflagration!
Destroy them all.
UNITY. SERENITY. HONOR THE Vanguard.
Destroy them all.

* * *

The fog, now a lingering black mist, stirred as if by a great pressure shift, as from everywhere throughout the wallows crush the horde cast their shrieks toward Melthis and her knights, returning to their positions at the right flank of the gate, flooded now shadowy violet with the befouled incandescence of the blightwraiths' etherea sent from Torbrenth's retracting center, and from Gignoth's guardian force, striking up from the shadows of the underwarrens at the opposite flank.

From among them the color of Liftholch's aspect effervesces into their wisping awareness:

We burrow like pigs in shit.
Keep to your place, Liftholch.
Keep your own, reaper.

She shut it out as a cracking billow of dust rolled toward her from a cluster of tumbling columns. One of the unnamed. A hulking mist-soaked wretch prickled with rotted limbs. It shrieked as it saw her, knocking aside the heavy stone debris as it lunged. She gripped her ax such that the arcs of its twin blades came aglow with the swelter of her anger. She cut away its raking arm and aimed a shoulder up into its midsection, cracking through its exposed ribcage and jerking it to crash onto its back. But before her blade could reach it again it righted itself and scrambled away, down through a shallow trench in the strata. The naefukkin wretch. She called out her warcry and leapt after it. It raced along the trench and then around a bend it scraped up its wall to smash between two reapers, throwing them aside to unleash against her pursuit an abominate they'd only just ensnared. She slid beneath its attack to cut through the mass of its torso and lop away its leg, and she rolled to her feet again, the unnamed now beyond reach, bounding straight toward the center.

Borrowing Demithyle's spirit sight she peered through the crush along its heading and to witness the haggard aspects of Torbrenth's knights gathering somewhere beyond, their displacing erratic, in haste, energies here and there fluctuating as they fought off pursuit.

Then between the thunderclaps from above, Demithyle's voice in her mind:

Do not allow them to break our line.

Aye, ye think?

She gulped etherea and bracing her stance bellowed into its wake, forming from its own trail of violet fume a manifestation of ephemeral blades that sailed through the bends of the trench and struck into it, obliterating its physicality to the neck, sending the rest of its ruin thrashing away.

She looked back across the fog-laden ruins of her position. Etherea swirled high and low. Her knights, finally able to make use of it, had already leveled a broad swath of the wallows in their pummeling of the encroaching baels. A storm of fire and conjurations amidst the stench of burnt tar and flesh; a match to the chaos of the wyspstrides streaking about overhead. She looked up. The sky was a canopy of black smoke, flashing red and orange as it bowed and swirled with the strikes of the wyspstrides.

Somewhere beneath it all, a rise of susurruses. As if gnawing at the mind. She raised her ax; rivulets of the mist ran across the gray steel. She wicked them away.

melthis. more.

Aye, ye auld steel. More.

aye. more.

Aye, then.

* * *

Three more of the unnamed spilled elsewhere into her line, these now adjoined to scrambling lengths of abominates, like monstrous flailing arthropods that strove immediately toward the center. Going after it from the rear, are ye. Clever cakkshites. Backing off her knights to hold against further incursion she waited for the baels to be smashed into the crush again, then drawing in a great gasp of etherea she bounded through the ruins on hastened legs to outdistance their advance as curving into their path she quickly ascended a lone stairway leading into nothing to hack down into the broad back of the foremost of the three, holding fast to its thrashing girth as Thrael had done in Mortis Veth.

Channeling etherea through her ax she drove its head deep into the ground, and was bucked from its back as a burst of crystallization crackled up over its extent. Catching a ledge above she vaulted up still higher to sink her ax into another throwing itself between middle-tiered facades, before with a jerk she hooked round its spine, dragged down its elongated form in a thick splatter of bone and viscera.

With a casual gesture she burned away its remains, then climbed a half-buried mausoleum. She turned to look back toward the crack and rumble of the third, the ruins steadily toppling toward her like a forest succumbing to an avalanche.

"Pristampt shite, yer a big one . . ."

By what fukkery it had suddenly engorged itself to such immensity she could only guess at as turning away from its advance she sprang down and fled through the crush, diving through vacant thresholds and hurdling over low stone walls, until debris thrown forward by its mass hit squarely against the back of her cuirass, sending her crashing into a broad clearing, where sliding across the dirty tiling of what was once an interior floor, she gained her feet and rose again to face the enemy.

But as its facade of skulls smashed into view its bulk was immediately hit by half a dozen jets of searing yellow acid, burning into it from the surrounding elements, steaming shreds of its mass spraying backward through the fissure it had carved through the crush as it was steadily boiled down to a husk and then to nothing.

* * *

There within the various ruined facades at the edge the clearing appeared a bedraggled clutch of Torbrenth's reapers. All were sodden with the mists, their cloaks hanging down in tatters beneath their mail.

"Gethsemoni's tits," said Melthis. "Shite if ye don't make for a weepy pack of skullits, like."

One floated down. Gaunt and corpselike, the gray flesh of his face lined with deeply soiled creases. Eireth, Torbrenth's right arm, who she'd seen rising with him over the wallows. She grasped his shoulders.

"Aye, Eireth," she said. "Ye look drug out the mung-rotten swamp, like."

"Cibori Melthis," he said, returning the gesture. He coughed. "A not entirely inaccurate observation, as military assessments are concerned." He released her and nodded to the bubbling carcass. "The loathing you inspire in the baels is impressive, Melthis, to burn hotter even than their hunger for the blue."

"Aye, it's been said," she said. "That bloaty slap of skinshite was one of the unnamed. Well done, that. Though ye might want tae watch throwing out the spark away from the front, with yer mortis Demithyle watching on high, like."

He coughed again. "A measured necessity," he said.

"Aye. How many are ye, then?"

Before he could answer, she stepped back a pace to look across the fog-shrouded crush. All of the reapers she could see appeared as Eireth: tattered of cloak, stripped to their mail.

"Where the sluvvi fuk did all yer armor get tae, eh?" she called to them. "Aye, ye think tae follow yer man Torbrenth's way, eh? Ye've minds tae follow him down the gullet, give the blighties their ravin, eh?"

They said nothing, their eyes only penetrating the mistshroud from within their various niches as unblinking pinpricks of green.

"We're mortis, dreadbaern, we are," she called out again. "All as one, aye? Not one more of us do they get tae take, ken? Not one."

She looked at Eireth again. He held her gaze a moment, before with another rattling cough he nodded toward her right arm, and she brought it up to find her bracer hanging awkwardly from her wrist, one of its leather strappings rotted through at the clasp.

"The breath of our enemy," said Eireth, passing his hand through the damp air as if to clutch it. "As you see, far fouler than a mere aura of their corruption. Even now, it thickens against us."

He gestured across the breadth of the clearing. "Demithyle sets this as a point of ambush. We stand about midway through the wallows crush, in direct line with the gates. We have held it here well enough while the others of our stanchion harrass the enemy elsewhere."

She scanned the hollow vista before her. She could only barely make out its dimensions through the mist: a meandering network of low walls surrounded by rubble, as if the footprint of a single expansive structure. Its columns had apparently been blown outward into the crush. Fractured domes leaned askance here and there within several of its sanctums.

"The remnant of a basilica," said Eireth. "It had stood unmarred until Demithyle sent into it a single wyspstride."

"Aye, that'd do it," said Melthis. She held up her bracer again, its metal covered with the grayish, oily beads of moisture.

"Insidious, yes?" said Eireth.

"That's one word fer it," said Melthis.

His voice reached her through wisp:
If only our commander had foreseen our enemy thus.
She shook off the bracer to slap into the mud.
"Ye know exactly what he's seen," she said.

* * *

The thunder above ceased, followed by semi-distant crashing through the wallows. She felt back toward her banner to an ebbing of encounters there. Nor did sounds of battle arrive from the opposite flank, the quietude there confirmed by Gignoth's impression. She could feel his probing awareness of her.

Looking above, she reached instead to Demithyle.
Aye, then, captain. Show us that naefukkin essesster, like.

* * *

She felt him take hold of their corpus, and in her mind's eye the spirit forms of the knights fluttered and shifted into alignment as Demithyle reordered his mortis army to a single interlocking arc, forming a defensive pocket up from the flanks in the underwarrens toward the basilica clearing.

Looking across the breadth of open ground before her, Melthis understood his intent, and shifting her gaze toward its central floor she parted her teeth to exude a terse entanglement of quiet hisses. And there a shaft of iron grew up between the stones from which her banner then unfurled to show its circle of five carven poniards of bone, aimed outward in silhouette from an inverted triangle of etherea, fuming at its center.

Looking skyward once again, Melthis witnessed her commander's descent from the now becalmed canopy of smoke, bent forward astride his steed in formation with the last of the remaining wyspstrides, a grim shadow amidst a hail of astral fire.

* * *

The ground shuddered, and a moment later a deep thoom rolled up from the underwarrens. All throughout the clearing Torbrenth's reapers seethed as the goading whispers of the unnamed arose like the call of an insect plague, the distant choir of shrieks arriving with the thunder and crack from the wallows ahead. Demithyle's battery of the wyspstrides began to drive the baels against his army's forward lines.

Melthis gripped her ax. She could feel its anticipation pulsating through the metal langets in its handle.

wield. wield.

Aye, auld steel, aye.

aye.

* * *

Etherea swirled down the line to flood the clearing, and with it the shrieking of the baels. Melthis leapt across their arrival at the shadowy edges of the crush, screaming her obliterating warcries, punishing them for daring to leave it. Anchored to her banner via ghostly cords of etherea, cycled with those knights she passed to jointly burst the pilfered physicalities of the unnamed. Heaved to incinerate clustered abominates with their own befouled essence. Her ax, imbued with desire to rend their ligature and entrails. To shatter their skeletons and split their skulls. To destroy them all. The sounds of battle now barely louder than the unrelenting whispers. She drowned them with her war cries and rallied the knights to do so also, the collective of their voices resonant as if from the undead throat of the Underworld.

* * *

A snarl of abominates smashed through one of the domes and immediately dragged away two knights in the midst of their cycling an ethereaic lotus there with a third, who unable to restrain its intensity alone released it to lash out across the battleground, the brunt of its force driving directly into Melthis.

It threw her backward to crack over a low wall, and for an instant all went black.

* * *

Her senses returned to pulsating pain, and a rhythmic shaking of the ground.

A knight stomping toward her. Mesithre. A survivor from Thrael's stanchion, folded into Torbrenth's. Drenched from the mists, the oily gray globules of it streaking from her rotted cloaks slapped under her mail. Her pounding steps split up the soiled tiles of the basilica floor as she slid between the downed cibori and the pounce of an enormous bael, turning to deflect its attack with thick arms braced before her.

Even without armor, Melthis had seen blocks of stone bound away from this one's stalwart aegis. But not this time. Invaded by the devouring mists, Mesithre's physicality simply came apart, exploded by the weight of the bael reiver's thrust into her, her mail emptying of bone and gore as it flapped wildly from its slivered protrusions.

* * *

Even before she had regained her feet she was upon it, ax in hand, the voice of her rage dampened by its viscera as she tore straight into its core, and then with a jerking pivot burned it from within with a hiss of molten lead forced outward through its corrupted veins.

Its steaming remains split round her, stinking metallic and of flesh corrupted, and she stepped from it, trying not to kick the pieces of Mesithre scattered over the tile as from every direction she was assailed by cries of pain, frustration, and surprise. A knight skewered and pulled into the shadows. The headless body of another dropped from somewhere above. Two collapsing nearby into a single gurgling mound of black ichor. Wherever she looked it seemed a moment too late, a stride too far to save them.

* * *

The ground quaked, and with it came the sound of wet scrapes and heavy cracking thuds. All around the clearing murky glassform began to spike up through the ruins, throwing chunks of masonry high into the air amid a staccato of clipped shrieks as bits of the baels' morbid, plague-staint physicalities were here and there pinched off by the crystalline enclosures of Torbrenth's warding ambit to slap lifeless into the mud.

They try to break through the strata!

Cursing, ignoring the stabbing complaint of her bones, Melthis ran to her banner, and locking eyes with Eireth at the edge of the clearing she tore it from the ground and hurled it toward him, screaming out even before he'd caught it for every knight to fall into the perimeter. Hastily they dashed between the jagged blooms, some which jutted in their path, catching them mid-stride, entangling them, throwing them to the ground, and the cibori smashed her way among them, cracking through the frozen outgrowths of the enemy to gather up the downed reapers and bark them forth toward the surrounding crush, the sight of it ever more obscured by the growing snarl.

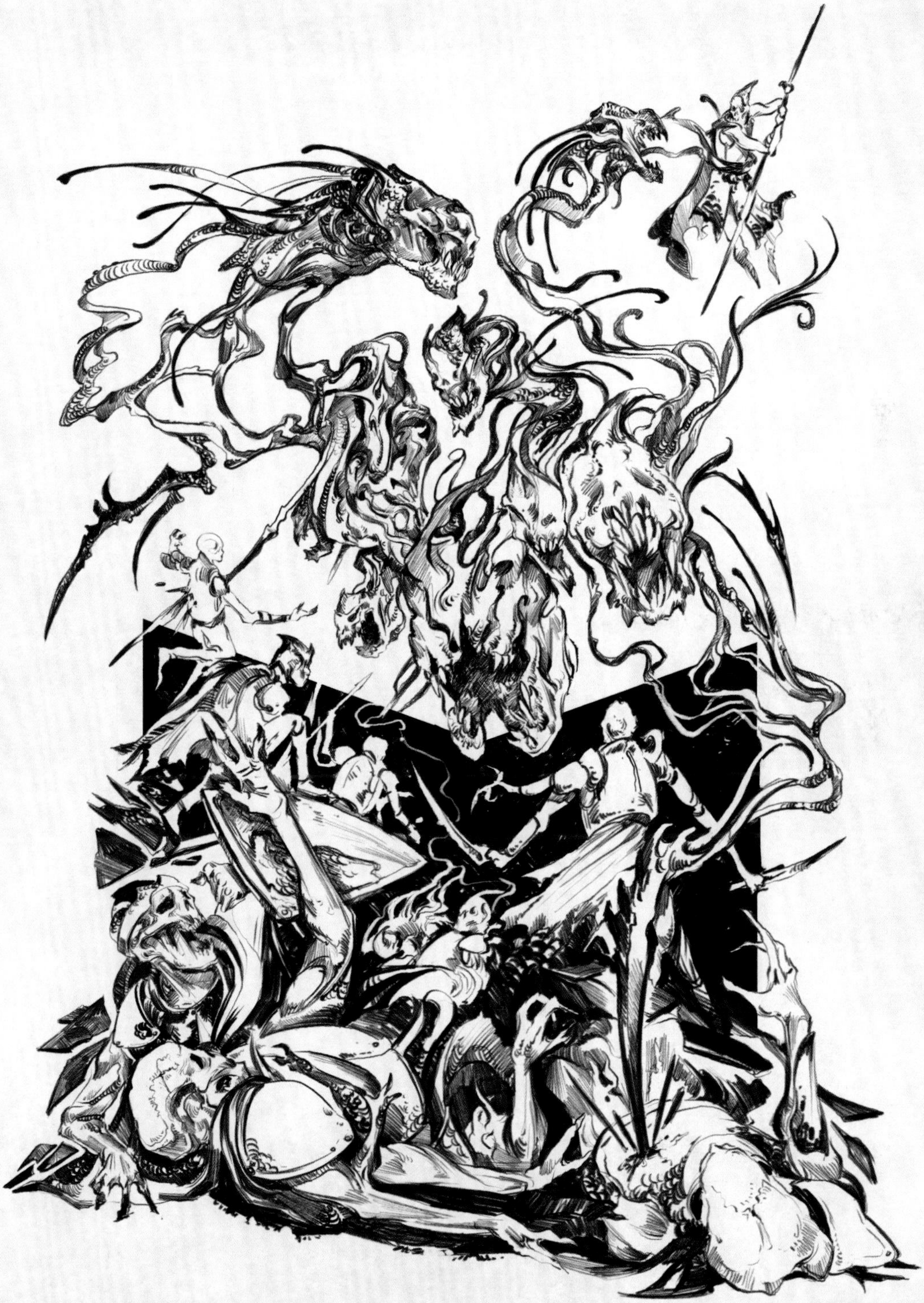

Turning to wave the last of the knights from the center, Melthis was staggered back by an outgrowth rising to surround the reaper advancing toward her as in that same instant a bael, one of the unnamed, lunged swiftly up through the center to rake open his chest, its claws slicing clean through his ringmail before the soiled crystal rose to engulf them both, the reach of the unnamed locked in the midst of its killing blow, the flicker of her brother's eyes extinguished deep within the murky glassform.

And granted Demithyle's spiritous sight, Melthis watched in horror as the befouled spirit of the unnamed escaped downward again below the strata, dragging with it the partly devoured aspect of her kin.

* * *

The choking fury of her scream of denial was lost beneath the crackling influx of ethereal. Commanding the knights to pour their spiritmander into her she opened wide her maw and breathed forth a continuous dark fire to sweep out across the battlefield, freezing the everpresent globules of mist to blackglass slivers that tore through the enemy and shattered the crystalforms, flaying knots of emergent baelreivers to bone and carapace.

Through this maelstrom she witnessed the spirits of the unnamed yet gathering just below, as if to taunt her with the spirits of her kin they had devoured, whose voices seemed to mingle with the malevolent whispers in her mind, calling upon the anguish swirling within her cavitous void to become that deepest appetite she had never before been challenged to deny, that lust for the essence of the Cosmos which would grant her the vengeance for which ceaselessly the voices of the fallen cried from beneath the ruins of the Tower.

And so staring downward she split her maw still wider to force it round a now charybdic whirl of electric glimmering blue, swallowing rivers of etherea, stealing it away even from the knights' cycling of it to sustain her onslaught, to burn away the very landscape to reach them if she must, so that the spiritflame of her eyes suffused her skelliform orbitals and acidic boils drew out over her flesh before bursting to melt it away amid tendrils of purple fume, curling round an emergence of thorny protrusions from her skeleton as in her mind the voices persisted, and with them her own screams, arriving as if an essence of memory conjured from the ruins of the battlesphere . . .

. . . *she'd screamed for them to flee . . . throwing stragglers to the fore as the tower began to fall . . . Two sent on the back of her wyspstride before she'd spied Thrael, there facing away unmoving—why unmoving?—beneath a bloom of black mirror leaves. She'd called out the other cibori's name, racing toward her over the rumbling terrain, the ground everywhere slick with reaper blood, steel-blue as a thunderstorm at sea, sizzling over blackened pieces of armor, smeared over swaths of debris, pooled in the hack-scarred ground . . . and then nearing the base of the tower she'd found herself surrounded by mortis remains, their chests blown open, sinew strung between their own broken weapons, all partway buried, as if corpses coughed from their graves . . . And there amid the shower of blackmeir shards Thrael had turned to stare at her sister cibori with purple fire in her eyes, and ripping away her massive breastplate she then leaned the blade of her glaive against her chest and dropped herself through it without unlocking her gaze, the purple fount of her etherea springing from her carcass to give rise all around her to an emergence of the wicked shades of the unnamed . . .*

"YE NAEFUKKIN CAKKSHITES!"

She hit it hard enough to break its torso half away—a bael looming over her, its razor limbs readied to strike. The wretch. The mindworming maggot. She hit it again and then again with her ax, swept as if of its own accord up into its left side, and out again through the base of its neck.

* * *

Her legs gave out and she collapsed to lie in a heap of gore not her own, her form reduced, ravaged by onset and then atrophy of the dreadsgrip. But ax in hand.

melthis.

Aye, auld steel. Aye.

* * *

She raised herself up on her elbows to look at the ruin of the creature at her feet. Its etherea trickling away from her, drawing elsewhere, the thought of it a nausea. Maybe it was one of the unnamed, maybe not. She no longer cared. She could see a remnant spirit in its shell as it stared from a face that might in fact have belonged to Thrael, gaping, choking out wheezes, as if crowing with the last of its breath its disdain for her.

* * *

And in that moment, Melthis could not help but see it for the reaper as which it had after all been made. A thing more kindred to she and they of the mortis lost to their obscenity than was the mutual Father, who it seemed had created them for nothing more than to war with themselves. As had done his own creators, Priam and Abraxiel, in their parceling the Cosmos to Heavens and Hells. All of this, an extension of the Celestial game. An echo of civil atrocity as much cherished by creation as war itself.

* * *

She raised up her leg, dropped a heel down onto its face. It broke apart it into the muck with a satisfying crunch. Exhausted, she let herself fall backward, only to be caught by an armored grasp.

Gignoth.

* * *

He dragged her into a nearby dome, and leaning her in shadow against its slanted interior rim went out again to scan the immediate area, now eerily silent, the sounds of battle arriving primarily from beyond the clearing, deep into the crush. Then returning into the relative darkness of the dome, he crouched before her.

"Aye, ye slirvsome lummox," she said, coughing. "All the way here tae grab a bit of the skint, eh?"

He looked at her through the gloom, weapon resting over his knees, the worn metallic tracery of his cuirass catching the spirit gleam of both of their eyes.

"I heard something incredible was happening," he said. "I didn't want to miss it."

"Aye, well," she said, "it's over now, isn't it. Ye might want tae think about fucking off, get ye intae some more diblivvy warmongrel shite someplace down the line, like."

Gignoth looked out again. The sounds of battle remained distant. "You made quite a hole there," he said.

"Aye," she said, coughing again. "Had tae show our rippers . . . which way tae aim their withered little phalkers, didn't I?"

"Hm," said Gignoth.

"Blighties've got tae be running out of meat by now, like."

Gignoth said nothing. His gaze lingered toward the ground at the middle of the clearing. He looked back at her. "We need to get you to the shroudreive," he said. "If for no better reason, Cibori Melthis, than that it is inappropriate for a Knight of the Mortis to present her skeleton so absent of flesh as you seem to have made yourself."

"Aye," said Melthis. "Maybe if ye give us a kiss, we'll grow some of it back fer ye."

Well he wasn't going to wait for her to ask twice.

* * *

The brief moment their spirits' entwine passed with their blue returning to the questionable sanctums of each their battered physicalities.

But even as Gignoth brought her from the dome and toward the rearward perimeter, all throughout the clearing the basilica foundations were split by rings of jagged crystal, spiking up through the strata. Scabrous pods shot up through the center of each, all of which were shucked from the quickly unfolding forms of the unnamed before Torbrenth's trap could engulf them.

And as beneath each trailing arc of crystal-encased viscera these corrupted physicalities alighted, they were immediately recognizable to the reapers as perverse reconstitutions of their fallen comrades.

Melthis laughed.
"What's funny?"
"Nothing."

* * *

From all around the perimeter the reapers descended to engage them. Their resolve little shaken by the ploy, which all had guessed the baels were certain to bring against them eventually, the newly emergent bramble garden of glassforms was quickly brought low as the knights threw, smashed, and blasted the simulacra all throughout.

But neither the cibori nor Demithyle had thought to prepare their ears for the resurrected voices of their fallen, nor the caustic, antagonistic mimicry with which the baels spat against them mechanical utterances poached from those same memories which through the intimacy of the reapers' bond with one another they had once shared.

And when they sensed also within the shells of these baelreiver unnamed the anguished spirits of their fellow mortis embroiled in perpetuated suffering, they balked, the clarity of their unity clogged by uncertainty, and the knights found themselves pressed back into frantic defense, each singularly assailed mind and body by the hateful ferocity of the enemy.

Then through their shared wisp permeated the tempered composure of Demithyle's commanding aspect:

Serenity, mortis. Kindly has the enemy returned to us the spirits of our kin. Let us thank them.

* * *

Watching from the edge of the clearing, Melthis felt among the knights a collective releasing of themselves upon hearing the words of their commander, as instead they reached toward sense of one another throughout the battlefield. Already their patterns of attack had narrowed. She brought up her ax.

"Wait," said Gignoth, raising a hand.

"Why?"

"You can barely stand, for one thing," he said.

"Aye, get tae fuk," she said. "Ye'd have us as a pair of innardlorn polts at the—"

"Just watch," he said. "In a moment, you'll see what has to be done."

The channeling of the knights' anger had now returned to them the initiative, and as one by one the simulacra were destroyed the mortis spirits entrapped were released to course a final time throughout the reapers' collective awareness, before passing into the aether.

But the unity of their corpus was incomplete—several knights, it seemed, fought separate from the others, and one especially so, howling between taunts thrown at friend and foe alike, exploiting opportunities created by the reaper formations as he pounced from one bael to the next, each time stabbing into them savagely with his three arms in unison.

"No time for sleep, morts. Hua!"

"*Shassst,*" muttered Melthis. "Liftholch. Ye want tae speak of polts . . ."

"Yes," said Gignoth. "I followed him here after he cajoled several others to break ranks with him. I lost track of him when I saw you. But it's etherea he's after; with your banner here, I knew he'd be back."

The mists had returned, thickening by the moment. Melthis tried to keep her eyes on Liftholch's haphazard movements as he leapt about through the flash and shudder, discorporating and reappearing randomly in the murk as he siphoned etherea from the knights' spiritmander, obliging them each time to adjust their postures.

"Aye, look at the chaos he gives," she said, coughing. "Shite, Gigs, if ye can't keep yer sticks in a bundle . . ."

Gignoth shook his head, eyes darkening in the haze as they followed the erratic maneuvering of his knight.

"That one cares nothing for the corpus," he said, finally. "Only etherea, and the *kerissst*. He severely wounded one of the wyspstrides at the gates. And I am near to certain that he killed one of my knights."

She looked at him. "What?" she said.

They were interrupted by a cry, as in his frenzy Liftholch leapt directly into another reaper, forcing her to parry his blades before being knocked to the ground as he kicked himself from her chest to drive an attack against another of the baels nearby.

Gignoth stared a moment more. Then, into wisp, he said to Melthis: *Stay here.*

He stepped sidelong into a swath of shadow and disappeared. Scanning ahead, Melthis found his aspect passing within the fragmented remnant of the dome, before it then began to flit between pockets of darkness surrounding the clearing, as if a phantom hunter narrowing on its prey.

* * *

In the growing fervor of his rampage Liftholch drank in more and more of the knights' ordered spiritmander, and the whirls of etherea that now followed his howls amid the clamor began to draw down dense currents of fog from the broader area, so that for a moment sight of him was alternately obscured by both the brilliant sear of condensed etherea and the thick wet shrouds of mist.

* * *

From within this a deep magenta haze emerged, and looking upon it Melthis was struck by a wave of nausea as the whispered refrain of the baels once again speared into her thoughts, amid stark recognition of this as his aura, clouded by the emergence of the dreadsgrip she had only just denied, now taking its hold of Liftholch.

Struggling to stand, wanting desperately to intervene, she tore her eyes away to find Gignoth's aspect, there among upper reaches at the far perimeter, sword readied in his silent tracking through the shrieking tumult below.

No, Gig.

Demithyle's jolt of alarm reverberated through their wisp:

What are you doing?

Gignoth froze, as if caught by the grip of an invisible force.

Stop, Gignoth.

Let me go.

Back away, cibori. Leave him to me.

No. You do not understand.

A sharp screech snapped through the aether as Gignoth severed his link to the corpus. Freed of his commander's grasp, he leapt round in a final dash, then dropped, sword aimed down toward the back of Liftholch's neck.

But Demithyle was there to parry the strike, appearing in a blink of firelight to send Gignoth hurtling into the shadowy wallows.

* * *

Taking hold of Liftholch by his wrists Demithyle forced the snarling reaper backward from the fray, his urgent voice pleading over the chaos:

"Serenity, brother! Hear our consonance of mortis voices, and remember your self! Serenity!"

But Liftholch only howled and kicked his commander away, grasping casually into the skelliform visage of a knight battling behind him to wrench him backward over a raised knee before leaning over to vomit fire down the other's throat, quickly separating his blackened skull from the rest of his body.

Melthis screamed, and just as Demithyle was there to grapple Liftholch again, the entire clearing bowed suddenly upward before collapsing down into a low bowl, as embrittled by the baels the strata below gave way, breaking apart like so many leaves of shale into a seeming depthless black chasm. From her place at the edge of the chasm Melthis could only watch as what knights did not follow Demithyle and Liftholch's wordless tumble were entangled by thick ropes of viscera whipping across it, sealing their final struggles within the murky crystalline crawl of Torbrenth's hermetical ensnarement.

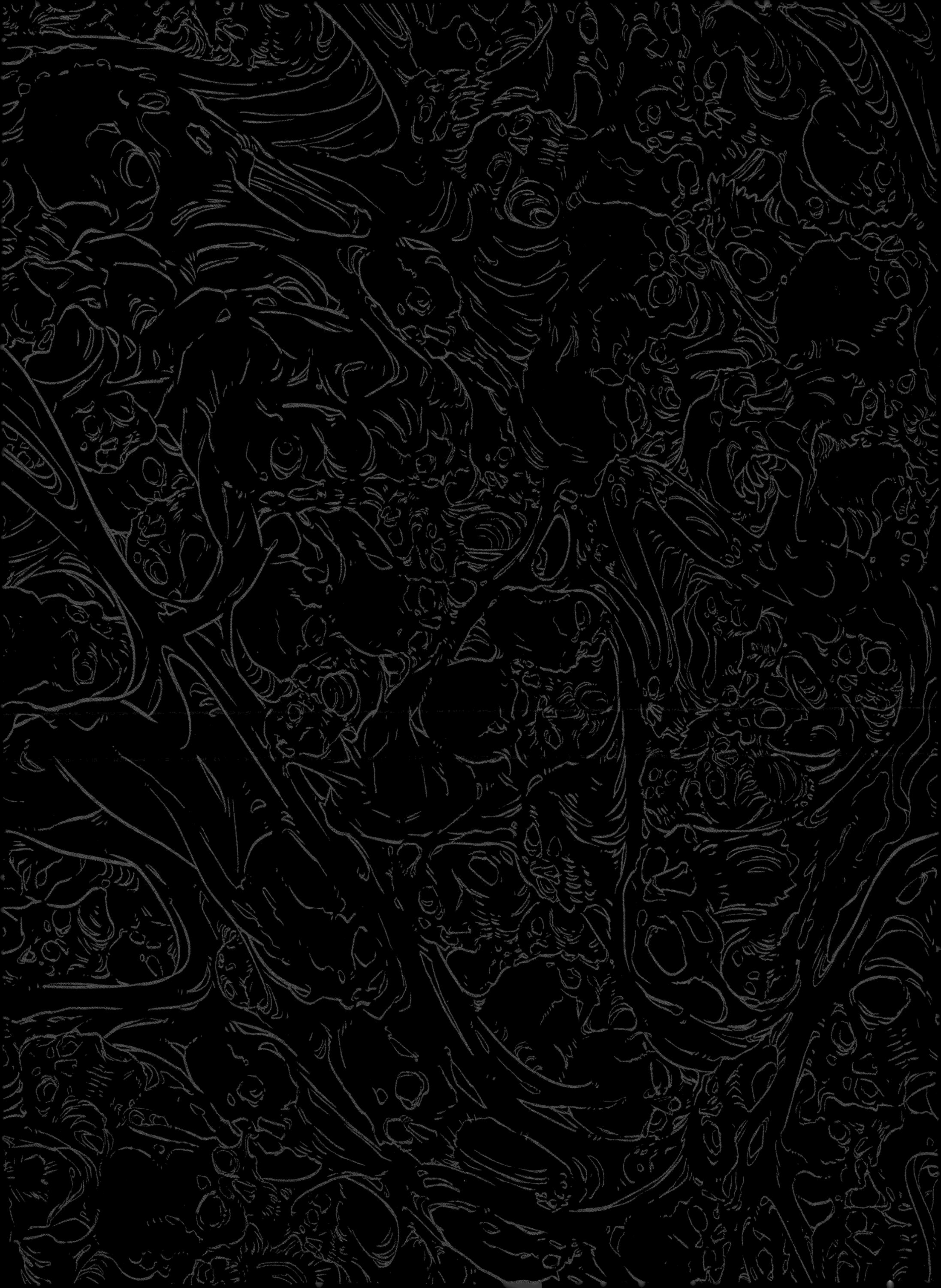

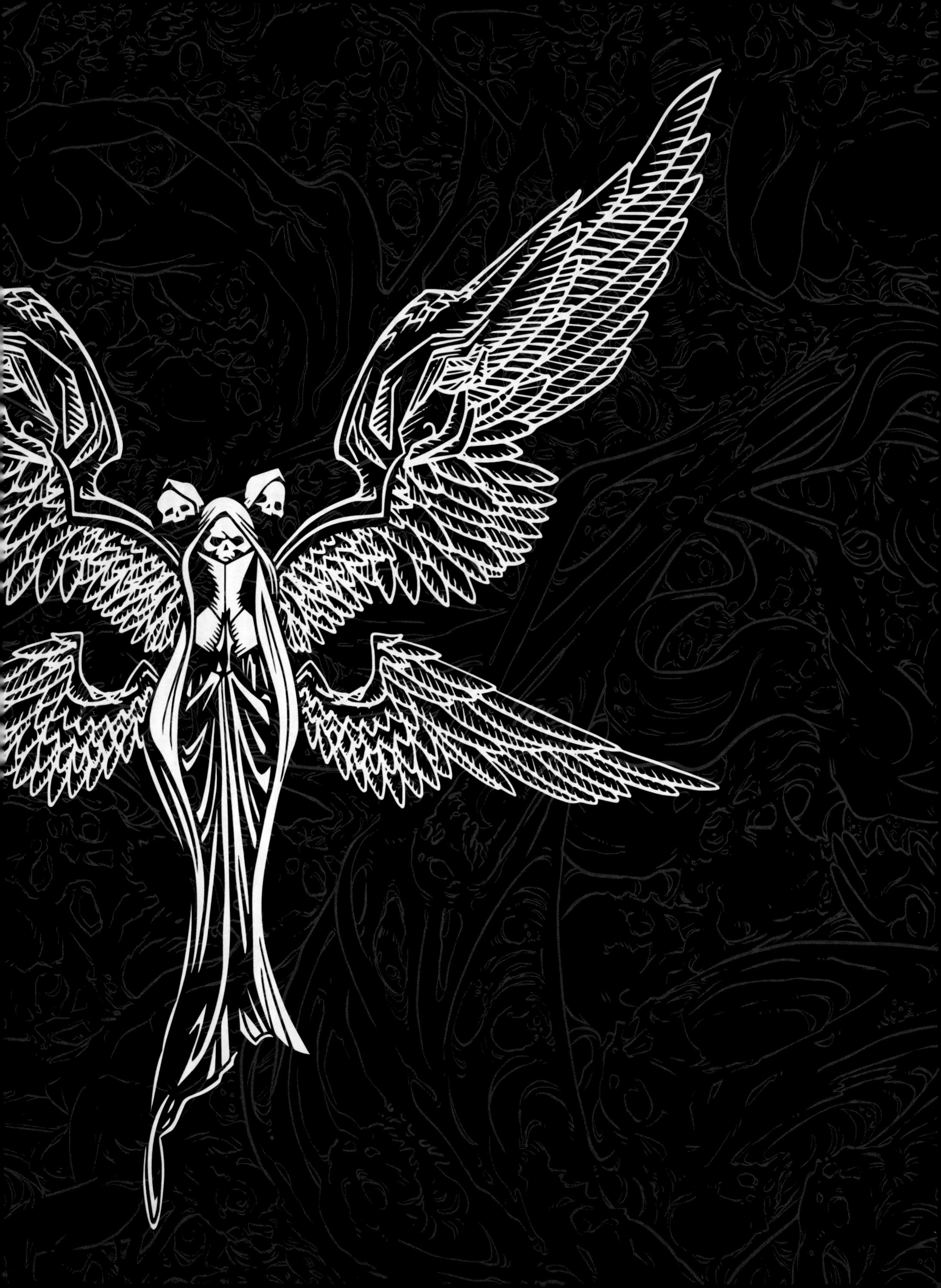

XLI.
MORTIFICATION

The black and the deep. The first thing I have known. A state of becoming and departing. Now as a crucible upturned. Beyond it, the crack and thoom of all that I must do and become. Capped within its iron weld, a failure I must first witness.

* * *

Liftholch. My awareness of his presence is fleeting, as if I am continually summoned and rejected by it. His hunger pounds to me through the aether from a dreadsgrip of ethearic lust I had come to imagine the gift of our mortis nature had given us flatly to deny.

    We lie apart on shelves of stone. With my sense of him in the darkness comes also that of another, though her presence is weak and even now diminishes. The color of her aspect I know by little more than name. And even this I can not now bring to mind. Let this be my insignia of station, if any. For I am now become a commander who has presided over the fall into corruption of one of his soldiers to the unmaking in fear and pain of another whose person he had never troubled himself to.

* * *

I mark the muted shade of his aspect below, already deep violet. He stands, hunched over, his back swollen, engorged flesh pinched round slivered outgrowths from his skeleton. I drop through the chasm to alight upon a slab beside his own. His bones pull free of his flesh as he turns to find my sound, as if from roasted meat, releasing eruptions of black pus from his body. With eyes boiling with etherea he finds me, his mouth held agape in a whispered scream, streamers of flesh flapping from teeth stained storm-blue with reaper blood. He stands tall and strips of ligature strung from them snap from the fleshy mass spread over the stone at his feet, and I see that it is the remains of the reaper I had felt, now dissolved of all but her mail, her aggrieved aspect lost within this creature of hunger that now stands before me.

*   *   *

With a bestial shriek he is upon me. I roll back to kick his center bulk against the far wall. Looking to a shelf of stone above him I bring it down, pinning him rigidly in place.

"You are Liftholch of the Mortis Knights and you will not succumb," I say. "Not to the dreadsgrip. Not to the whispers of the unnamed who speak only with its voice. Come with me now, brother. Our only victory awaits above."

He breaks the stone, connecting with my chest, and I am knocked back. He strikes quickly, snapping for my throat as taking hold of each of his arms I throw him hard against the wall again.

"You will not betray the vision of our father," I say. "I will tear the blight from your flesh before I allow it."

Instead I reach into his mind, as deep as I would dare against the assailing turbulence of his hunger.

You are a stone in the mountain's rise. Made connected as all the Cosmos shall in the shattermeir become. We two, rooted in this aeon to witness it.

I parry, yield ground, parry again.

Come to your self to witness it with me, brother. You are not alone. Even in your fear and hunger, you are not. No mortis need ever be so.

I hit him. His skull cracks. Pus glistens over the stone in the darkness. I hit him again. His polluted etherea billows from him, dissipates. *I will stamp out the poison from you. And then we will rejoin our war.* He lunges. I hit him again.

I cry into the aether: *You will not succumb!*

I offer my knowing of all that I have seen and been. What songs and entreaties I have gathered from those voices of memory through which in my wandering I have swum. An ocean of my self to fill his void. But that which was Liftholch only screeches, ignorant of all but lust for my essence. Again I am pressed back.

I draw my sword, leap away, beyond our reach of one another.

I can not destroy him.

"I can not let you succumb," I say, quietly.

He hurls himself against me, as if inviting my blade into his belly. But then there is a flash of light as in mid-leap his form is suddenly crystallized within a solid gray glassform that smacks solidly against the rubble behind me as I step aside, before sliding down it rocks once upon the slab beside me and falls still, Liftholch's twisted form frozen within, his eyes still pulsating, now as violet as those of any of the unnamed.

Lowering my sword, I turn toward the orange-sapphire glow in my periphery to find Ycnaf floating there within the wafts of her etheraic breath, her shell cracked and gouged, two legs curled uselessly against her breast.

a traveler found.

* * *

Hovering near her skullform, a circular amulet of ornate brasswork, a small gray crystalform braced in its center.

"Torbrenth's artifact," I say, as she decends with the amulet to alight before me. "He must have set it somewhere down here, as part of his rite of exude its influence through the strata. How did you find it?"

essence of fisher within.

I nod. So. Torbrenth did not destroy Simmel. But neither did he release him unpunished.

"We will deliver him to Ellianastis," I say, as echoing thooms shake gravel down from above. I look outward into the unbroken darkness as if to seek the downrushing torrent of her library. "She will determine his fate."

essence of fisher, a stain.

I look at Ycnaf. Her eyes burn deep amber in their fractured hollows.

essence of fisher, essence of betrayal. ycnaf to mourn alone, one and none other, time and time more. scent of herd, taken. ycnaf to mourn. de-mi-ta'il to know. root to ycnaf to share.

No part of Ycnaf has before conveyed her desire for vengeance against the creature Simmel. And yet as I look upon the artifact held aloft beside her, I understand that it was for the sake of my deliverance from the labyrinth alone that she did not enact it when, freed from his treachery at last, she had stood before him again.

Looking again to my companion, I offer what consent she would wish of me. With an ethearic huff she lets the amulet fall to the stone slab where she meets it with a crushing blow of her foreleg.

There is a flash and then and then everywhere over the debris there appears phantom sprats of memory, which fade and then vanish completely.

I look to that which had Liftholch, locked still within the cloudy translucence of the crystal, hanging partway over the ledge. His polluted fume extinguished. Whether he remains extant within I can not sense. Bringing out Cryptmourne I stab it into the stone to crack away the ledge beneath him, and watch as he slips into the darkness.

* * *

Ycnaf blasts us upward through glassform and rubble as seeking Gignoth's aspect I am drawn upward toward the city. We break through the surface below the rise of steps to the Vadlum Gates. What few remaining knights there are now gather their strength enclosed within a single formation before me, burning back a shrieking deluge of agglomerate baelreivers not more than an arrowshot beyond, the sapphire blaze of their ethearic potency cycling between their ranks, ordered round the banner of Melthis at the center, who stands frail and scorched beside it.

And there braced against her is Gignoth, who sensing my arrival turns to mark my approach with eyes of ice, even as the head of a knight next to him is shorn away. Hearing Melthis's subsequent cry, Gignoth hops to shift his weight to throw his attention again to the fore, and I see that one of his legs is mangled to the knee. But it is when Melthis turns to witness also my arrival, and I bear witness in turn to the strange amalgam of indifference and resolve writ upon her face, in place of the unassailable buoyance which had inhabited the spark her eyes throughout all of our designs, that the true irremediable calamity of my failure dawns.

* * *

It is all I can do to advance through the fire and black smoke, the errant spikes and splashes of acidic ichor, and the perpetual hail of flesh, bone, and metal from the horde as withering blasts sweep overhead to burn across its shrieking undulations from the Vadlum Gates behind me, toward my cibori, gathered round the banner with the last of my knights. Ycnaf alone among her kind driving against the tempest to buffer path for me to reach them. Throughout the wall of blight, the spirits of the unnamed, flooding intermingled, as if parasitic worms devouring through the meat of their organism, as presently they prod its mass to twist upward in ribbons twice again the thickness of the gate, and as they rear above in their accumulation I call out warning to the knights around the banner, who seem collectively to curse as they look overhead.

As I near, Melthis looks at Gignoth, and he shakes his head as if to deny her intent. She looks to me, the lower half of her skull gone entirely, and yet over the tumult I hear the smile in her voice as she says:

"What are they but a pack of cakkstaint phinkershites, aye, captain?"

There is a deep moan overhead, and then the horde rushes downward. With a firm push Melthis sends Gignoth out to me from their formation, waving me back as I catch him before turning back she looks up again to face the horde. And collapsing their lotus to a wavering shell of etherea above her banner she then holds out her arms as if to brace against the quaking air as she opens wide her maw and screams upward through it.

The force of her voice shatters into the horde's downrush, rupturing its mass to billows of dessicated bonesliver as a molten slag of their polluted beings scorches down over her and the others, dissolving their flesh, smelting mail to scalded bone as helplessly I witness, Gignoth heavy in my arms, until by the continuance of her song the warrior spirits of my reaper kindred are driven from their boiling physicalities to be gathered through the throat of Melthis in a final etheairc wail that explodes away the trailing mass of the surge. The fierce resonance of her voice ringing metallic over her petrified remains. Fused as one to the last of the Vanguard of Illverness. Amidst the blackened stalk of her rallying banner. Her maw drawn open still, silent and cavernous, locked in deathless exhortation of what can only be our souls.

* * *

Ycnaf takes us up into the air, beyond the reach of the recoiling baels. Gignoth heaped against her withers before me. Melthis's voice still ringing out shockwaves throughout the surrounding tumult. For a moment we are free of battle. All is quieted. Distant.

Then a snarl of acidic tendrils reaches up from below to grasp Ycnaf's hind legs and we are brought back to our war. We slam down against the broad steps, our bones and our metal and our carapace breaking, as much of our selves as we have not yet lost, scattered toward the gate.

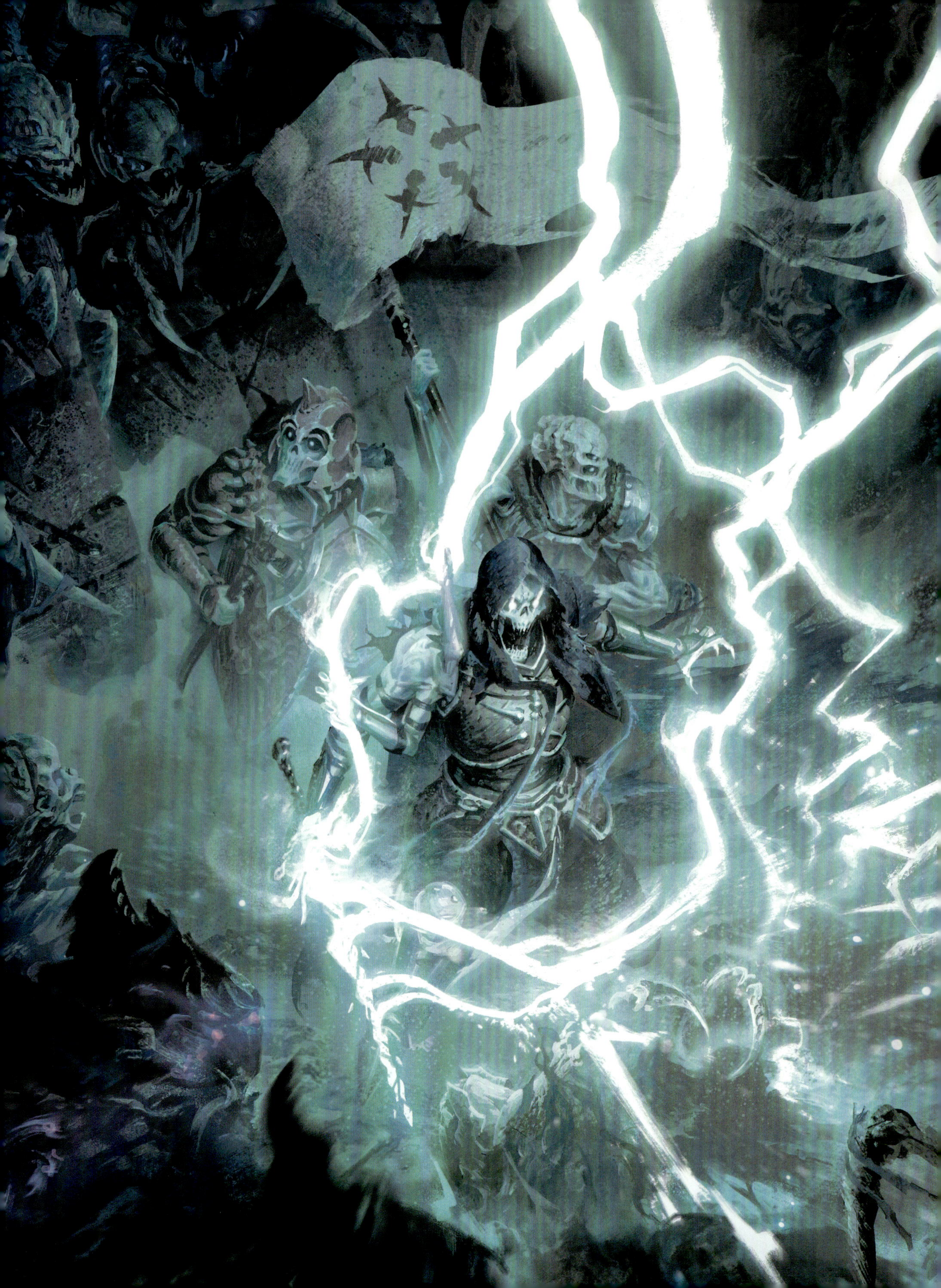

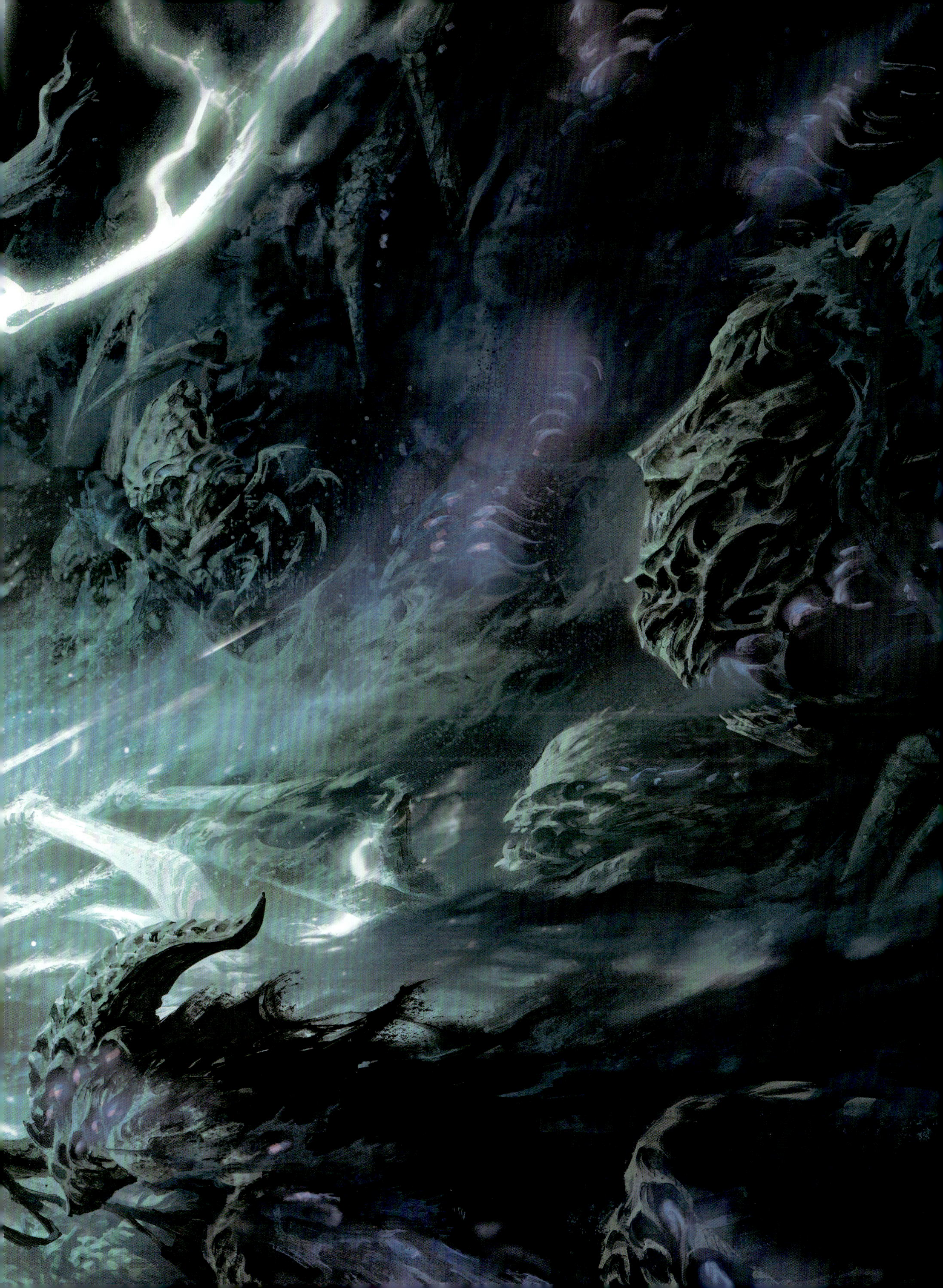

* * *

For a time I struggle to stand, and then I am standing. I have somehow dragged what is left of Gignoth to lie against the base of the gate. I do not know whether he is still extant. My sword is in my hand. My sword is always in my hand. Faithful, faithful Cryptmourne.

My sense of Ycnaf's pain forces sight to my eyes. I feel her fighting just to advance toward me. I see her through the curtain of viscera and fire that slams down all around her, keeping the baelreivers from reaching her. Gestures of my parentage, sent down from the gate and from within the city. Thank you. She hobbles forward, collapses, rises once more to drag her bulk until we are together. Her face is broken and most of her has ebbed. But we are brought together. Thank you.

* * *

There is something more.

I can feel it below us. Yearning to meet me. The Forge. Another offering? This from the city itself. The city that is my father. He offers it now. Yes. For me to take hold of. It boils up through the strata. It waits below the surface. Hidden from the baels. But I can see it. I can see its mark painted over ground. For me alone.

The strength of the scions is spent. None dared take hold of it. Only the gate presses back the baels. I look at my hand where once the mark had resided, and when I look again at the ground it is too late. The baels have encroached and I can not reach it.

With this thought Ycnaf stirs. Her head boiling with etherea, half burned away. She leans toward me and rests her skull against mine. Her mist rising round us, soft and elegant, miniscule sunflares glinting between motes of dust aswim upon the currents of our being. I can not recall what of greater beauty I might have elsewhere touched in my existence. Perhaps all of the worthy things that I have discovered have borne no greater substance into my self than these ashes that abound. But here, now, is a love that I have known.

She puffs her mist from her muzzle, and her words waft over me.
goodbye, traveler.

I cry out but she has already turned to send herself into the horde. Just over the mark she pierces their mass, and by the sundering of her a rift in the veil there its torn, and they are taken into it, shrieking, torn inward as the last of she who had been Ycnaf is devoured also.

I am down the broad steps with my sword raised, and as their remaining churn of viscera rallies above me to attack I find the mark and I stab down into it.

The fount of etherea courses through me. Exploding away my flesh. Laying bare the thaumaturgic incantations writ upon my skeleton. I howl my agony into the blight even as it wraps its profanity around me. I burn them to ash, cleansing the realm of their stain wherever it falls beneath my gaze.

* * *

Soulfire white swirls over the spiritous aegis of Morghistus. A projection of the mysticism of my armor. Peering eyes surrounded me and for a moment I take them as exalted witnesses to our victory, come at last to deliver me from my war.

* * *

And then I hear their gnawing whispers. Goading, bodiless as they force their woe upon me. Moved to sudden fury I rail against them. With this power of the forge that yet courses through my bones I will dismiss them utterly from existence. Yet they do not recoil, nor do they press closer. They only watch and whisper. Their voices aggrieved, pregnant with pain. A desperation that only deepens my anger as I seek for them to wither and lament before me with this bottomless fount power that I will bring even to the doorstep of the Celestial Cosmos if I must, the kingdoms of Heaven and Hell unmade if I must. That I will use to reform the sum of all of the pain they have inflicted, to bring it against they who have tainted their names and destroyed my kin and my companion, who spit at me even now, unperturbed even by this force that relentlessly I throw against them. I can feel the inevitability of these things. I search among their eyes, so many eyes of the unnamed, but there is no fear, only vicious glee. More. More I must take into my self now I must take these eyes force them to witness their own destruction their destruction I will destroy them

the blackening burning anger of unknowing

flung away, self

being, annoyance
sail it away
away

The whispering, sneering voices of the plagueridden and there is nothing in my hand, twisted flesh within an ooze of black and purple fume *yesssss destroy usss destroy usss yesss destroy the betrayer become usss to become destroyer of our betrayer become becomme the dessstroyer destroy our betrayer dessstroyyyyy . . .*

A weight in my hand. The bones yet ablaze by the forge's flood and yet beneath it a separate light. A coin. A totem. Weathered by mortal war and now my own. Once it bore a voice. Finer than these needling whispers. I wish them shut from my mind, and then they are gone and from within my pain I feel the presence of all that is my realm as in my own voice I call its name into through the aether:

Father.

The world of time winds down, and a specter of Death arrives to press wordlessly through the raging fountwall of my soulfire, quieted now to a glimmercurtain of sapphire blue. He looks at me a moment as if assessing his creation as like a mortal child I hold out to him my hand, and he reaches forth his own as if to lay into it a totem of his own. And with its touch upon my palm I feel the cold and wet stones of the bank of a snowmelt river, its water so clear as to be all but invisible until I plunge naked through its surface, diving down through the enveloping cold for the curiosity lying there upon its bed of clean river rocks. Up again to the empty air I swim to the sandy bank to examine my prize: a spearhead of boneshards girded with rings of rusted iron. Shivering I dress again and then admire it in the sunlight for a time before I make my way through the trees to an adjacent shore where my mother and father prepare for our journey across the greater sea. I show my father and he looks at it and then at me and asks, Do you know what this is? And I say yes even though I do not. My father smiles and shows me where the rings can come undone to release the shards of bone into a pile in my hand, and again how to remake it, and then he gives it back to me and I take it into the woods. When I do as my father has shown me the shards spill across the sand and some stand like sprigs amid the disarray. It makes me think of the animals and people described by the brightest of the stars and when I look closer I decide that I have made the shape of an aged woman weaving a blanket. And so I make a game of scattering them over and over to create many shapes until finally my mother calls for me that it is time, and gathering them up I can not find the rings so I press the shards into a hard green fruit. And then that night as the waves lap quietly against the boat and my father watches ahead, I lie against my mother and she asks me, What is that? And I show it to her and she takes it and she laughs. It looks like a little man, she says. She gives it back to me and I hold it up against the stars until I find some that are bright around the points of the shards, and I think about the shapes they made in the sand also, and I decide that this must be a way the creatures and shapes and people in the sky are decided.

* * *

Time recalls itself to the present and I look again upon the diluted spirits of the baels and their shrewdness and their cruelty seems to my eyes small and very sad. It seems a poverty of self to be pitied. Their voices pleas long ago forgotten even by themselves. To speak their names would be to destroy them utterly, for by each recitation I would bind them to the fount of my own being, to all that is the heart of me as antithesis to their dreadsgrip and thus a repudiation of their existence.

    But in so doing all that is my self would be unmade. All that I have come to learn and love dispossessed of significance by my ebb, all who have dwelt within the Cosmos that is the heart of me I have created never more to exist. Better that I should be destroyed and released to become the aether than be dissolved to oblivion. And so I relinquish the aegis of Morghistus that guards me and with its dismissal my resistance to the smother of the unnamed bleeds away. And as they fall upon me I pour the strength of soulfire I have been given not against them but into the Vadlum Gates where to the hilt I plunge my sword, and with this deliverance I cast also my knowing of their names, emblems of glyph burned into its eidolon of iron and stone that they who had first been gifted by the father the names of the Vanguard we have hallowed might forever be bounded to reside there, never to be sundered more.

    In their terror they shriek and make to flee. But the remembrance of the Underworld burns outward into them and into me, and then all is dark.

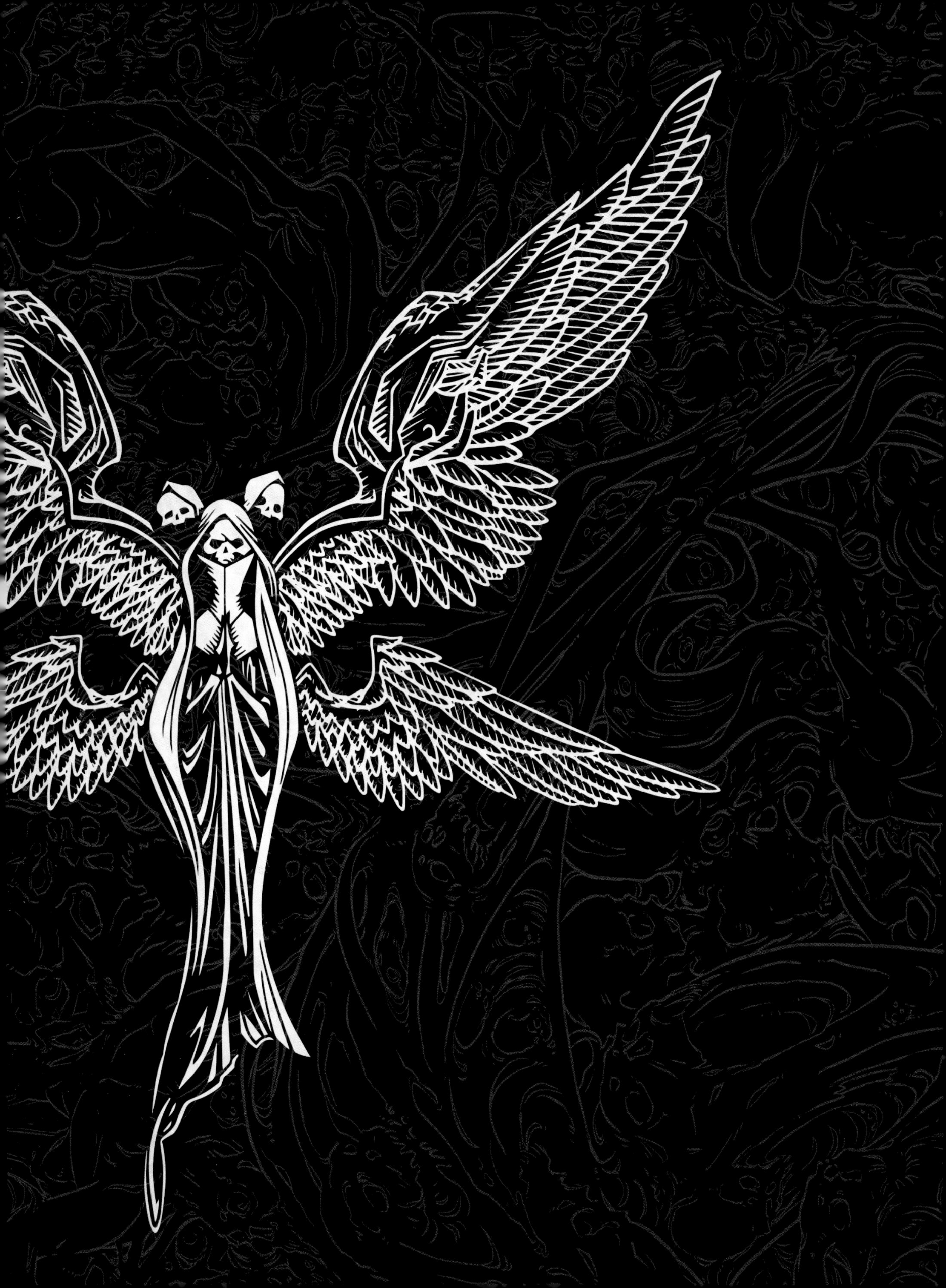

XLII.
A TREE

I open my eyes. I am lying in a mausoleum. It is dimly lit by candlefire.

I can hear the voices of the fostermurden. Their light passes over the ceiling as they drift near. I move to rise but I can not and so instead I raise my head to examine the state of my self. A shroudreive is crouched over my hip, sawing at strips of gray flesh hanging loosely there. My legs and all of my arms are gone save the smallest, its flesh once again charred, as is the rest of what remains of my body. I am without armor or cloth of any kind.

I lower my skull and it clacks against the stone slab I lay upon, filled still with the furious shrieks of the wraiths. Though I try I can not mute them and for a moment I am frozen by the thought that they have left their stain upon me and that perhaps l will never be free of them.

"All too true, in a manner of speaking," says a voice. "Which is to say, of course, that in another manner it is not at all."

I turn my head. I have never seen this entity before. His clothes are haphazard of cloth and color. His face is that of an undead fool at court, its flesh as mismatched and poorly stitched as his garb.

He eyes me curiously. "Hello," he says.

"Who . . . ?"

"The name you are groping for is Malavestros," says he. "Though there is no particular reason that you should have managed to grasp it, being that before this very moment I did not in fact exist."

"I . . . what?"

"An interesting choice."

I look at him.

"Some might say: My, my, Demithyle! By stuffing the baelreivers into our gate, you have succeeded in returning them to the fold! Indeed, 'tis fair to say, says I. You could very easily have destroyed them. Or banished them. Or turned them into chickens . . ."

"Chickens?"

"Instead you have turned them into a gate. And as I say, an interesting choice. Worth chewing on, eh?"

"Then Illverness stands secure," I say.

"Secure, hm," says Malavestros, looking away, pinching his narrow chin. "Rather a subjective term, wouldn't you say? Outside the context of blankets, that is."

I turn away, if only for reprieve of the mind, for not since my encounter with the mad undead avian in the labyrinth has it been made so addled.

"Ah, heh," he says with a toothy smile. "I can see this is going to take rather longer than we have. Why not let's cut straight through it, then, if you do not object."

He watches me for a moment with a raised brow as if waiting for an objection. Then he claws his hand over his face, tearing it off to reveal my own skull visage behind.

"Why, Malavestros," he says with what I must presume is the sound of my voice. "Whatever has happened?"

He slaps the flesh of his face back onto his skull, then turns slightly as if addressing someone else.

"Isn't it obvious?" he answers, cackling in his own voice again. "The baelreivers are gone, Demithyle! You've done it! The city is safe! Also, you were partially destroyed!"

He tears down the face again: "Fair enough! But wherever am I? And just who, pray tell, is this handsome Malavestros with whom I speak? My, truly that color suits you."

"Why, thank you, Demithyle! You are too kind. You are of course at HushHyde, where I am your host, humbly, humbly at your service. Wait a moment—did you just now speak my name?"

"So I did!" he says, occupying his former position.

He looks at me, the face slipping off his skull.

"Then in fact you know *exactly* who I am."

I am at a loss for how to respond. "Where is Gignoth?" I ask him.

"Oh, he will be round, by and by," says Malavestros, his face returned as it had been. "He is rather under the weather, I am afraid, so it may take some time."

"Under the weather?"

"You were protected from the blight by the guardianship of Morghistus. Your cibori was not."

"Melthis? The others?"

He does not answer.

"It is all rather poetic," he says after a moment.

"What?"

"Spoken like a poet!" he says. "You could have destroyed the baels, yet you did not. Please tell me why, that I may flaunt this knowledge every place I go for the next century to come. *He told it to me himself,* I will say. *Fool you who do not know it.*"

I do not know why. But I tell him a reason anyway: "They are as much a part of the Underworld as we, are they not?" I say.

"Hm. Quite literally."

He waits for me to elaborate but I do not.

"Disappointing," says he. "Though I imagine of course the Alltaker will be pleased. You must tell him yourself, if he returns."

"If?"

"He has business with the Celestials," he says. "They tend to notice when you mess with the flow of the Dirth Forge. Generally they are not a pleasant sort, and certainly they don't miss an opportunity to denigrate their custodian. Though they ought to be happy, being that the flow is all the wetter. He'll be up there genuflecting and flattering for a while, and with any luck we'll have him back intact."

"With any luck," I repeat.

"More than some of us, at any rate," he says, looking at the space where my legs used to be. "Oh!"

He suddenly slaps at the pockets of his ragged tunic.

"He left a message for you! Let me see if I can find it."

He pats himself down for what seems an elongated moment.

"Ah!" he says, slapping both hands against his face. "Heeeere we are . . ."

When he pulls his hands away he is wearing the Alltaker's mask, and in that instant I I know that it is in fact he.

"Father," I say.

He regards me.

"Xiall was right about you," he says after a moment. "As much as she was wrong."

"I do not understand," I say.

"You do not possess a heart. 'Tis the Underworld that possesses you."

"Our meeting at Voxxingard," I say, not fully understanding his meaning.

He nods. "You have brought me with you all along your way, Demithyle," he says. "Indeed, Malavestros might be thought of as a summation of that journey. He is the humility you have taught me, perhaps. And the eyes to find it further. For 'tis this that finally proved antidote and antithesis to the dreadsgrip; how, finally, I knew you would resist it."

"No, Father," I say. "I would have succumbed, if not for the intervention of your vision. I . . . wished to destroy them. For all that they had done, I would have destroyed them."

Again he regards me, his smile painted wide upon Malavestros's lips beneath the mask I have never seen my Father without.

"A memory shared is one given," he says. "And so, 'tis your own. And so, the witnessing of it is as much your propriety as that of the mortal child who long ago created it. And even freed from its grip, you bent the Forge to creative expression."

"You know it well."

"I have kept it as reminder of my obligation. 'Tis not so easy for me to walk among the mortals as you, Demithyle. Theirs is a vicious, cannibalistic realm. A place dominated by tyrants, they who would cloak their callous tribalism in a glamour of piety to a dogma itself woven to sustain them. And by predators who for want of greater calling commit themselves to lifelong indulgence of ever-baser appetites. The mortal coil exists as a treatise to the dreadsgrip; indeed, 'tis that itself.

'Twas simple enough in my spying of them to await they who though quite within their power to enact gratification would shun such easy bestowal of ruin. Who, like you, could obviate neither life or redemption, nor be blinded by anger or lust to destroy that which could be used to build to greater purpose. The mortals exist as do we, components integral to this Cosmos, such that I begin to discern that a key to its salvation might be found among them.

"But by virtue of your own odyssey I know now that 'tis in fact the mortals themselves who are this key. Your affinity with them has gifted me far greater intimacy with their hearts than I could have discovered otherwise. Their realm was made by design ignorant of its place in creation, left alone to be governed only by invented doctrines of conflicting realities and of violence ever to be met in kind. And yet, in a place where beauty created by the toil of generations might be destroyed utterly in less than a moment, beauty is made to bloom there all the same. Ever broader does it flourish, and ever more creative by the dawn. I know now the great compulsion that resides in their souls, and the striving of their hearts to match my own.

"'Tis the clouded veil of their mortality by which their true heritage as rightful kindred of the Cosmos is hidden from them, by which they are doomed ever to succeed and fail in ignorance of their place and purpose. But we shall chase away their ages of darkness with the parting of the veils. We shall await them here, the Underworld their crossroads to wander before choosing their higher path. Heaven and Hell, remade by their mutual yearnings and their pains, shall know their parity among us all. And the knowing of place and purpose amidst the clockwork shall be birthright to every mortal, each of whom need only seek communion beyond their realm to find it. This, above all else, I owe to them."

"I understand, Father."

"I know that you do. Together, my Reaper General, we shall supplant this era of destruction with one of creation for its many sakes. The three realms shall be joined as but a single tribe: the Children of Eddath. 'Tis as she intended the Cosmos be sustained. And so we have much to discuss, when I return. You have a knighthood to rebuild, and our burden of the reaping of mortal souls can not much longer be left to lesser entities. Until then, you have my undying thanks, Demithyle. May you never cease in your seeking."

"It has ever been my honor, Alltaker."

But Malavestros has already removed the mask. His own mismatched face has returned beneath it.

"Sorry, the Alltaker is not here right now," he says, grinning. "Please try again later."

He starts rifling through his pockets.

"By any chance," he says, "would you happen to have dropped something recently—small and shiny, rather the worse for wear?"

"The coin," I say. "It is lost in the underwarrens."

"Ah, what a shame," he says, holding Egregin's coin between his thin fingers. "And here I thought you'd found it!"

He holds it up to his sharp, rotted teeth as if he were spying in it their reflection.

"Oh my. I believe I have a tooth worm."

"Where did you find it?" I say, holding forth my sole remaining hand.

Malavestros drops the coin and I catch it.

"The better question is where did you leave it? And to save you some trouble, I shall answer for you: close to heart. Now if that is not an unusual place for it, I'm sure I don't know where is."

"It was . . . dear to me," I say.

"Gasp! An undead skelliform monster, holding something dear," he says. "My, my, my, my, my, my, my. Perhaps I shall rush off to inform Xiall of this sentiment."

"I would prefer that you did not," I say.

"Oh, you might be surprised by her reaction. It seems your name is rather commonly spoken throughout the rickety pockets of Illverness. I'm told there is a song in the works. Someone called Mud—or Marp? Narg?—is apparently regaling the Curio Cryptus."

"I do not doubt it," I say.

"Indeed, indeed," he says. "Well after all, where would we be if not for the reapers, and that one in particular? I believe someone has even erected a soldiers tree in their honor, upon the ruins of the tower, of course, since it wouldn't do to be anything less than melodramatic while we're at it."

"Someone?"

"Well, don't look at me," he said, touching his fingertips to his breast.

I look at the coin. All that is Egregin is contained within it. I had thought it my last connection to the Mortal Realm. I close my hand around it and hold it to my breast.

"I didn't mean to literally look away from me," he says. "You might be interested to know the tree has been quite popular of late. It seems someone arranged a pilgrimage there for any mourners who wished to pay homage to our fallen reaper protectors. It is now positively dazzling with trinkets bearing the memories of them. I only mention it because it would be a shame if your soulborn soldier's totem were to get lonely . . ."

He opens my hand as I had done with Egregin in the final moment of his existence, and taking the coin into his fist he touches it to his other, then lays open the second to show the coin now attached to a long, thin leather strapping.

"Thank you, Malavestros," I say.

"Oh, do not thank the fool," he says. "He who is just as like as not to be buying something with this coin. Would you happen to know what that might be?"

"No. Tell me, please."

"How am I to do that, when I do not know either?" he exclaims. "Wrinkled skattik, I had pinned such hopes. Ah, well. I will let you know when I find out."

He looks around.

"I believe I will take up residence here in HushHyde," he said, eyeing the fostermurden as they drift by. "The view at least is better than in oblivion. Thanks for my existence, General!"

He stands and abruptly walks away, leaving me alone with the shroudreive, who have begun to attach newly reformed legs to my torso. But then suddenly he is seated again next to my bier exactly as he had been a moment ago.

"By the way, I almost forgot," he says. "Don't loiter around here forever. Someone is waiting for you outside."

And then he is gone.

* * *

The shroudreive nudge me from the bier. I sit up, limbs now fully restored. I stand. I expect a difference, but all feels as it was. The shroudreive poke and nudge and cut away and restitch flesh where it is loose. When they are satisfied they scuttle away.

I look at Egregin's coin. How long has it been since I was with him here? I do not know. I look around the mausoleum but I do not see Gignoth. Nor do I sense his presence. Still it pleases me to know that at least one of my reapers will be with me.

I hang the coin round my neck. The moment I step outside the mausoleum, I can feel her.

"Ycnaf," I say.

It is there. A wyspstride, tall and elegant. I know that it is her, but also not her. It nods, releasing a fume of etherea with an orange flash of its eyes.

de-mi-ta'il.

I go to stand before it.

de-mi-ta'il of the world under. new and old also. many fluctuating termini. eyes to see. eyes not to see.

"You wear an aspect of Ycnaf," I say.

yes. ycnaf breath into the herd. before now and now and beyond now. always the herd. always ycnaf.

"I understand," I say.

ycnaf a traveler. voice?

"Yes," I say.

companion, mighty traveler. voice?

"Yes," I say. "She was mighty."

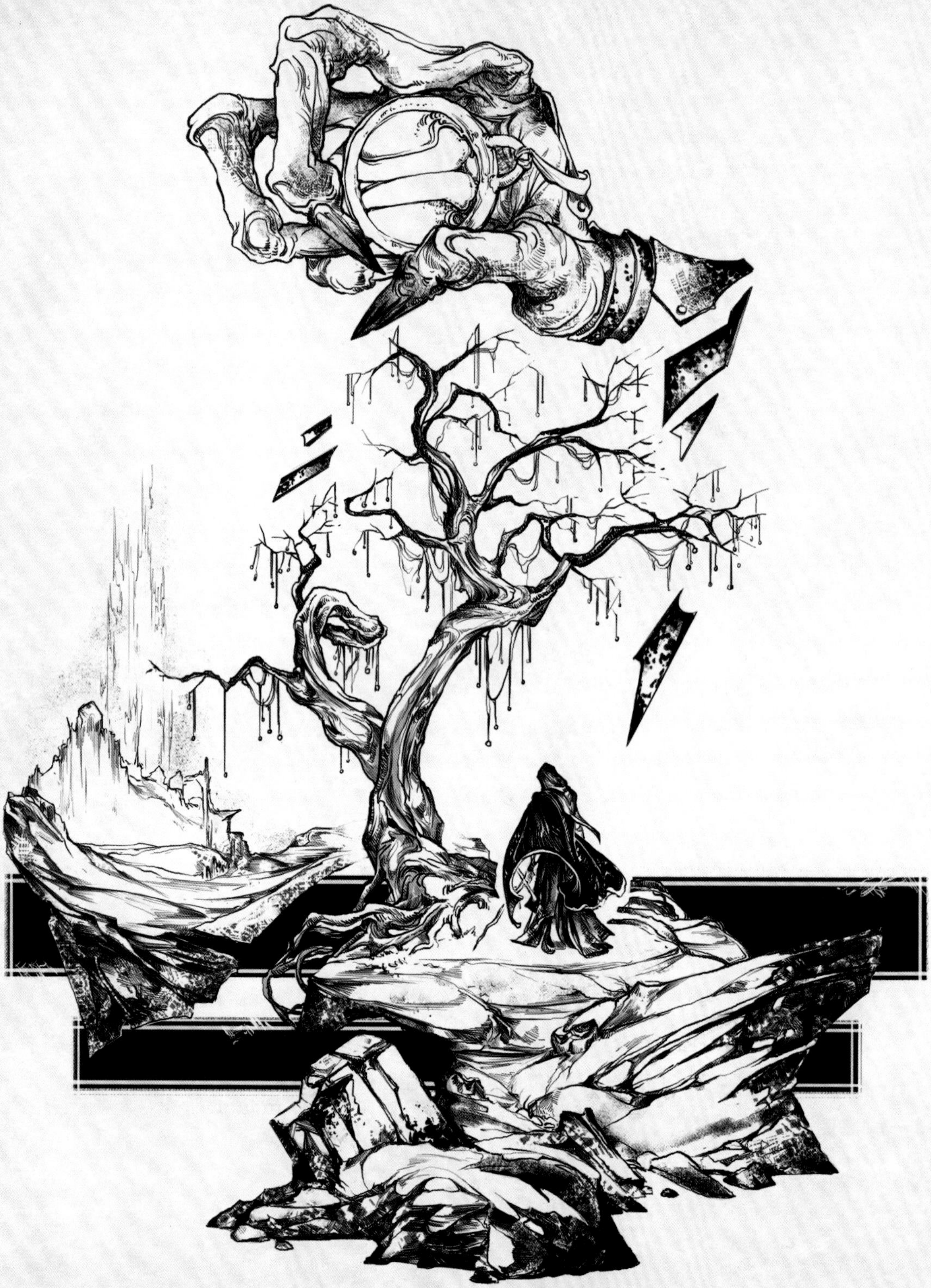

A Tree

It looks into me for a time.

ycnaf mighty traveler to root. cloud of breath to de-mi-ta'il. this one ycnaf to root from reaper.

"You wish to root with me?" I ask.

ycnaf from herd, ycnaf from de-mi-ta'il. ycnaf to be. to root to be. breath of voice to be to come. seed of termini. memory to begin.

"I understand," I say.

ycnaf and de-mi-ta'il again. as one again. yes?

"Yes," I say. "I would wish that."

It looks into me, waiting. I raise a hand and touch its muzzle, and slide my palm up to the space between its eyes. Its mist of etherea pours over me, and I feel her emerging as if from within my self even as she begins to alter her form.

traveler, a traveler.

* * *

She takes me out beyond the gate. The spirit traffic here moves through it as it had before. It is strange to see. As if no battle had occurred. It is strange to be here to see.

Melthis. She has been left as she was among the remnants of my soldiers. My kin. At first it seems an indignity. But as we slowly pass I mark the ferocity in her face, and I remember her eyes as she threw her own companion clear of the killing blow. As she turned to face it. To look upon her own demise without fear. And so she stands. And so I understand the remembering of it as its sanctity.

* * *

We walk the road into the wallows toward the mountain of shattered blackmirror just beyond the rise. Sithik and Thrael and many of the reapers who stood with them are buried within it. I try but I can not remember where Torbrenth fell. Only that he fell. The voices of the rest rang out for the last time everywhere along this path. I hear them.

The tree stands sparkling at the summit of the mountain, its silhouette like a shadow cast before the celestial sky. Its branches weep low over its broad ironwood trunk by the many totems that hang from its boughs, glinting by the light of the Dirth Forge as they sway on the muted breeze. Even at a distance I hear the metallic clinking.

I pull back my hood and take the coin from round my neck.

The fostermurden spoke of the aspect of Egregin rising to join the spiritous constellations that drift over our realm. I look above the tree, to the aurorae swirling through the sky there, eyes attuned to his memory.

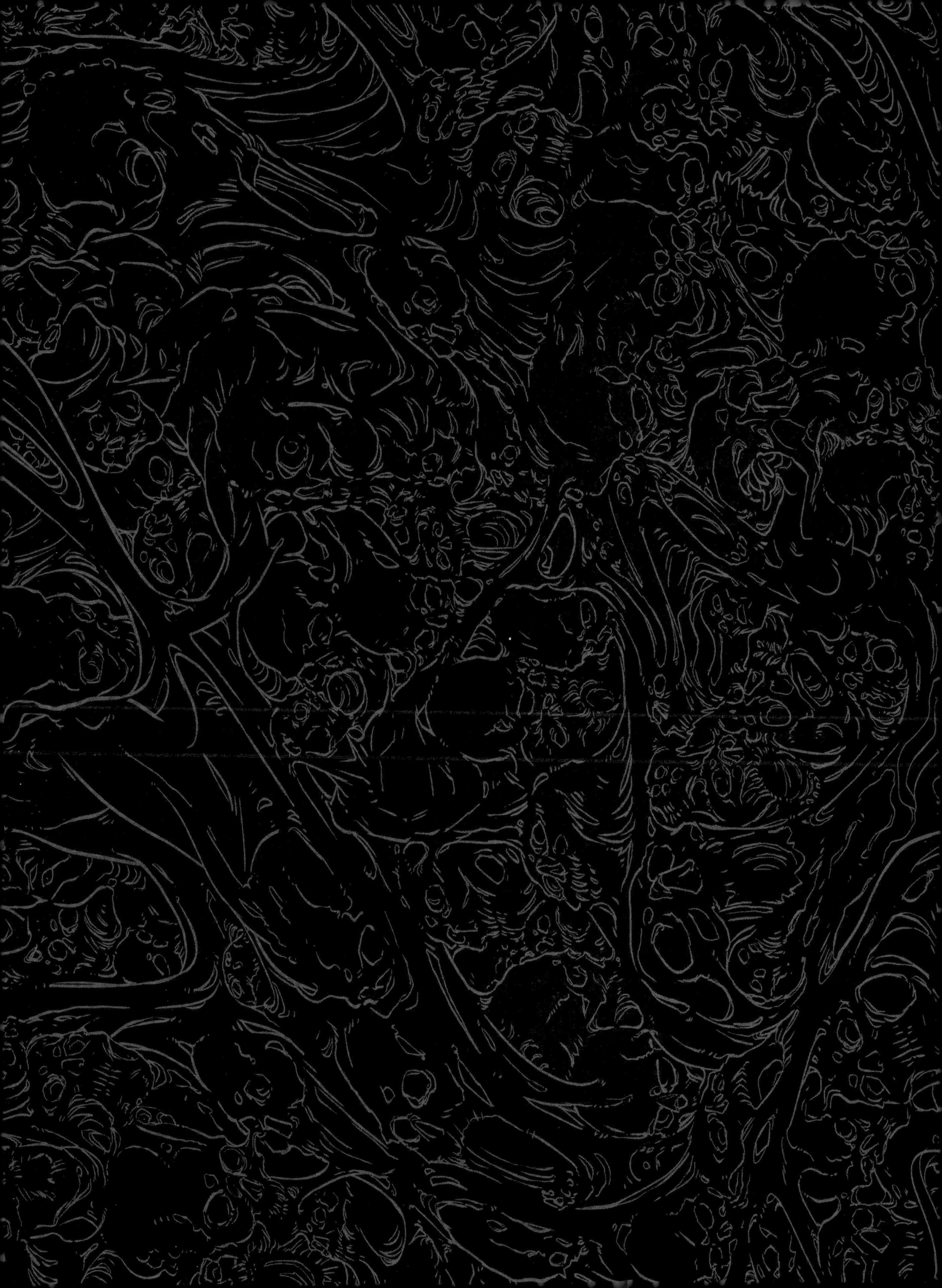

GLOSSARY

agit | an idiot
baerthik | innocent, like a baby
bloaty | lazy
broob; broobling | new guy among soldiers; pejorative
cakk; cakkshite | exclamation of frustration
catmint | cute; stirringly attractive
cavernal | an enfleshed face characterized by its resemblance to a skull
cellandr | affectionate term of accord
chapefukt | a humiliation kill; "chape" is the metal tip of a scabbard
churb-shat | a detestable thing, invoking the feces of an angel (cherub)
cibori | lieutenant rank among the Mortis Knights
clawfinger | a miser
claxed | imprisoned
crack your throat | "shut up"
crakked | made a pariah by way of insanity
crisstblack | violent cathartic reciprocity (an enemy put down hard)
diblivvy | crazy, out of one's mind
diregoat | more silly than scary, unintentionally
dooom sik | the pleasure of an ally's killing blow
dreadbaern | a new soldier; a newborn reaper
dreg | a worthless spirit; wasted undeath
elall | exclamation of delight; lit. "of the happy spirits"
essester | a well-executed display of military prowess
extant | yet in existence ("alive" for the undead)
fitcrakked | aimless or absurd
frinked | horny
fuk | fuck
grow some gussiks | grow a pair; lit. "accumulate some battlescars"
gussik | a scar
innardlorn | in the act of thinking deeply; brooding
kerissst | a particularly pleasurable, up-close kill; reaperly expression of enthusiasm and/or approval
lash | a gentle touch
liplicker | a lascivious person
meir | the span of an underworld day
meirdrem | the span of an underworld hour
meirdrem loam | formal greeting, as in, "the hour of the soil," or the moment following death when one traverses into the Underworld
mournmeir | early day in the Underworld (morning)

mung | very gross, vomit inducing
naefukkin | vulgar term of emphasis
necromank | an unknown but surely unpleasant place; also, a rotting stink
neut | neuter, gender-neutral being
niddlepeck | to defeat with relentless little attacks; wear down with time
phalker | vulgar term for penis
phalkfuk | vulgar term of emphasis
phinker | asshole, anus
pinslick | a cheat
pit | tiny
pitfukt | spiraled out of control; beyond hope of success
pitshin | a pitiable entity
polt | a coward
Priax | informal reference to Priam and Abraxiel
priss | vulgar term for vagina
prisstampt | fucked; also screwed, as in "We're totally priss-tampt"
puntrix | a whore
scaltic | abrasive or foolish meddling
shassst | expression of sudden disappointment
shattermeir | the unknown future
skattik | shit, offal, feces, etc.
skella-kess; skella-kaecth | term of endearment for an undead pet or a beast (-kess f.; -kaecth m.)
skelliform | a fleshless, bony body or head
skint | a person's naked ass
skullit | addict, junky
slirvsom | famished
slope | an exposed female buttcheek
sloshed | inebriated
sloshweave; sloshwoven | shitshow; disaster; clusterfuck; as in, "crafted by a drunken weaver"
slugg; reeksoss | shit liquor; also: disappointment, as with an unsatisfying kill
sluvvi; sluvvidess | a hottie
spritelicker | freeloader
stanchion | reaper platoon consisting of about 20 knights
swelt | a braggart
swelt and pinslick | expression of partnership or bond between cohorts, i.e. "thick as thieves" (braggart and thief)
up the forge | give up by way of suicide, i.e. "send your spirit up the forge"

ACKNOWLEDGMENTS

You should think of this book as the work of an ardent daydreamer who for a time found her spirit harmoniously intermeshed with that of the extraordinary creator Tom Gilliland. At the earliest stage of this process we two recognized in one another a kindred appreciation for meaningful, uniquely imaginative moments of epiphany, adventure, and character. Having immersed myself in the expansive lore that Tom has meticulously, lovingly woven into the Court of the Dead for the last decade, a delightful exchange of mutual inspiration and ideation followed between us which would propel my crafting of his core vision for Demithyle's origin story through an ever-evolving exhibition of impossible things. Tom's scientific devotion to intricate behind-the-scenes detail was a match to his effusive enthusiasm for my own creative drives. This confluence of support would prove invaluable as, released to run wild in this vast creative playground, I sought to explore what it might mean to be set adrift alone among the direst naked truths of the Cosmos. Thank you, Tom, truly, truly, for letting me in.

I'd like to add a special thanks to Corinna Bechko, whose great work in the development of Tom's initial concept for this book can still be felt in its bones.

Thank you to Greg Solano, whose strikingly human editorial guidance went far beyond obligation; to Rachel Roubicek, whose passion for the Court pours from every dreamy line of her beautiful illustrations; and to Ricky Lovas, whose masterfully elegant design work was finally responsible for the gorgeous presentation of this book.

To Greg Anzalone: Thank you, Greg, for taking such good care of your tribe, especially during such an immeasurably, shockingly trying time. You've shown yourself among many other fine things to be a paragon of humanistic leadership, a stalwart example to all of us.

Finally, thank you to my dears Anna and Orion, whom together have been the long-suffering heart of me.

B. van Slee

To all the Court of the Dead "Mourners" who have invested themselves into this world, I thank you. Thank you for your patience in traveling along with this project through all its revelations. It is my sincerest hope that this novel rewards your anticipation, as it tells the first full story of the Underworld's journey to rise, conquer, rule!

Dearest Beatrice: Thank you for finding your way through the architectural asylum where I had walled myself in. The world of the dead is a setting most often assigned only to wicked decay and despair, and ruled by a master that craves only destruction. Yet I envisioned an Underworld haunted by unlikely notions of nobility and valor; inhabited by a repentant creator seeking beyond all the odds to be recast in a benevolent image of his own making, and driven by a deep desire to make all things right. While I had labored long to craft the maps and schemes to build my vision, and laid the bricks and mortar that made the place what it was, and the beings in it who they are, what I could not see through the crypt door was how they might achieve their ends in greater scale. Missing in this effort was a kindred spirit who could see this world and its "mourners" similarly to myself and complete the chain of thoughts in which I was so entangled. In you existed that, and more. Onto the rickety skeleton of Demithyle I had rendered, you crafted flesh to make the tale more real and breathed spirit into its golem-like construct to give it its soul. You made it ever easier to let the bonds of control slip through my fingers into yours as you charted a path through the concepts, lore, and ideals—leaving no gravestone unexplored in coaxing an even-greater truth into the tale. Thank you beyond words for the personal presence you instilled into this work that echoes with our harmonious thoughts on every page.

It would take a stack of tombstones to draft the fullest list of those that have aided the efforts to tell the Underworld's story and I thank you "Mourners" one and all!

Corinna Bechko, Stacy Longstreet-Heath, and Landry Walker: Your contributions to the world this story inhabits and the initial exploration of what Demithyle's tale might be were invaluable to the crafting of this book.

Rachel Roubicek: You infused the story with meticulously studied and finely drawn illustrations. Each one is a testament to your care and expert knowledge of Court of the Dead lore and characters. On many a day, I ponder if you don't know this world better than I.

Fabian Schlaga: Your fantastic colors highlight the story with pitch-perfect mood. Your paintings conjure the full scope of the epic tale we sought to tell in these pages.

Vincent Proce for your tremendously iconic cover painting of Reaper General Demityhle! It's a long fun story to its creation and I thank you for it and the additional interiors!

Ricky Lovas and Anna van Slee: Without you both, neither this book nor any of Court of the Dead's other endeavors could exist.

Ricky: Your ever-patient and clever management and design of the book's layout brings it not only wondrously together but does so as though it were an artifact of the world it comes from.

Anna: Your orchestration and belief in this project is the fuel that propels it to lengths we'd not have attained without you. Even when all seems darkest you find the light to guide us forward!

To my brothers and sister at Sideshow—Greg Anzalone, Robin Selvaggi, and Mat Falls—I thank you for your patience, trust, and willingness to let me run amok with my vision.

To my family—Nita, Amber, Chance, and Noel—who have often wondered just what the hell am I working on. I love you and thank you for your enthusiasm when you see the results and your patience, love, and understanding when I shut my office door for hours at a time. You may be on the other side, but your spirit drives my efforts from over my shoulder nonetheless.

Finally, thanks to you, Dad! I treasure the mythical visions of my boyhood, and the insight of adult reality that let me witness the complex duality of a man that was both larger-than-life and very human. Your quiet lessons travel with me every day.

Additional thanks for contributions to this novel and to the world of Court of the Dead: Amilcar Fong, Jason Bischoff, Stone Perales, David Palumbo, Martin Canale, D. J., and John Godfrey.

Tom Gilliland

INSIGHT EDITIONS

PO Box 3088
San Rafael, CA 94912
www.insighteditions.com

Find us on Facebook: www.facebook.com/InsightEditions
Follow us on Twitter: @insighteditions

Copyright © 2021 Sideshow Collectibles. All rights reserved.

Published by Insight Editions, San Rafael, California, in 2021.

No part of this book may be reproduced in any form without written permission from the publisher.

Library of Congress Cataloging-in-Publication Data available.

ISBN: 978-1-68383-124-2

Insight Editions
Publisher: Raoul Goff
VP of Licensing and Partnerships: Vanessa Lopez
VP of Creative: Chrissy Kwasnik
VP of Manufacturing: Alix Nicholaeff
Senior Editor: Greg Solano
Senior Production Editor: Elaine Ou
Senior Production Manager: Greg Steffen
Senior Production Manager, Subsidiary Rights: Lina s Palma

 SIDESHOW

2630 Conejo Spectrum Street
Thousand Oaks, CA 91320
sideshow.com

ISBN: 978-1-64722-441-7

Sideshow Collectibles
Creator of Court of the Dead and Chief Creative Officer: Tom Gilliland
Chief Executive Officer: Greg Anzalone
Brand Director: Anna van Slee
Author: Beatrice van Slee
Design and Art Direction: Ricky Lovas
Black and White Illustrations: Rachel Roubicek
Color Illustrations: Fabian Schlaga
Cover and Endsheet Illustrations: Vincent Proce
Voxxingard Illustration (pg. 352): Mauricio Calle
Illverness Illustration (pg. 252): Stone Perales

To learn more about the studio's environments, the talented artists, and the unique Sideshow creative process, check out the behind-the-scenes videos at Sideshow.com

ROOTS of PEACE REPLANTED PAPER

Insight Editions, in association with Roots of Peace, will plant two trees for each tree used in the manufacturing of this book. Roots of Peace is an internationally renowned humanitarian organization dedicated to eradicating land mines worldwide and converting war-torn lands into productive farms and wildlife habitats. Roots of Peace will plant two million fruit and nut trees in Afghanistan and provide farmers there with the skills and support necessary for sustainable land use.

Manufactured in China by Insight Editions

10 9 8 7 6 5 4 3 2

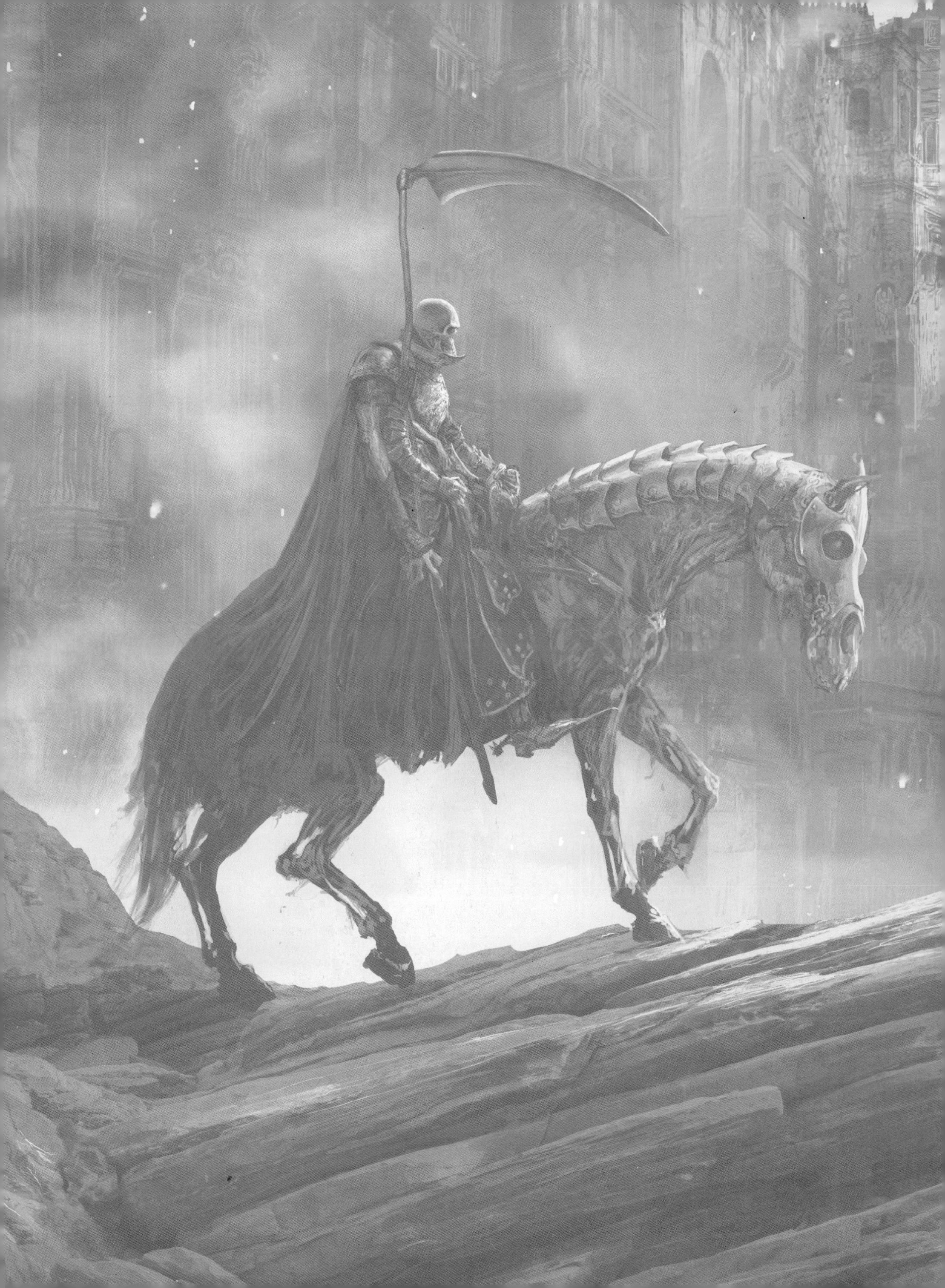